ALSO BY KRISTEN BRITAIN:

Green Rider
First Rider's Call
The High King's Tomb
Blackveil

KRISTEN BRITAIN

BLACKVEIL

DAW BOOKS, INC.
DONALD A. WOLLHEIM, FOUNDER
375 Hudson Street, New York, NY 10014

ELIZABETH R. WOLLHEIM
SHEILA E. GILBERT
PUBLISHERS
http://www.dawbooks.com

First printing, February 2012
19   20   21   22   23   24   25

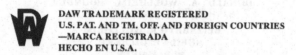

ACKNOWLEDGMENTS

My thanks for the support, feedback, and many memorable Wednesday evenings at Darthia Farm goes to the Peninsulans: Annaliese (of Greywood) Jakimides, Elizabeth Noyes, Melinda Rice (OSSC), and Cynthia Thayer.

As always, thanks to team DAW for all they do to publish terrific books, especially my editor, Betsy Wollheim.

Thank you also to my agents Anna Ghosh and Danny Baror for helping to get my books out into the world.

My thanks to Ruth Stuart and Jill Shultz for providing comments and/or suggestions on certain aspects of the story. Thank you to Leila Saad for the use of her Italian carnival mask!

Thank you to Roger Czerneda for designing the all-new www.kristenbritain.com site and entertaining me with assorted apple flingings. And of course to his wonderful significant other, Julie, for her continuing encouragement and peach muffins.

I am always grateful for the existence of Acadia National Park for providing so much inspiration and mental and physical retreat over the years. Likewise for the music of Enya, Moya Brennan, Tingstad & Rumbel, and others that is often serene backdrop to my writing.

Finally, I always mention my four-legged buddies here because they mean so much to me and are generally great writer companions. Sadly, my last feline muse, Percy, a.k.a. Silly Orange Boy, passed away during the writing of this book, which is in part dedicated to him. He will never be forgotten.

As for Gryphon? Terriers to the fore! Want cookies!

For my sister, Sheri Flanigan.

Blackveil/Argenthyne

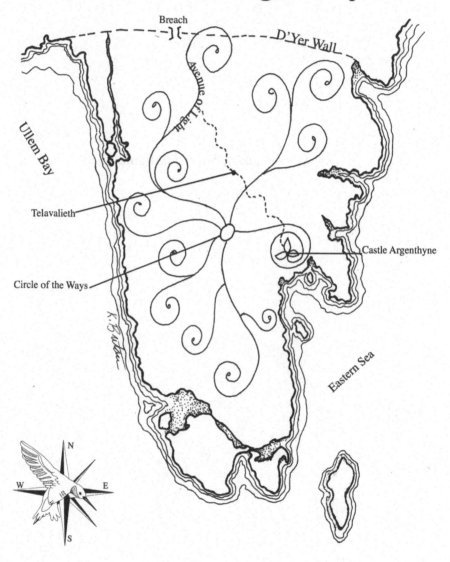

⋖ BLACKVEIL ⋗

"**R**emember, we are all prey here."

As one, Grandmother's retainers glanced down at the puddle of blood soaking into the duff of the forest floor. It was all that remained of Regin.

"Do not step outside the wards," Grandmother said, "where I cannot protect you."

As if to augment her words, a bestial cry rang out from the forest. Sarat whimpered, and the others shifted uneasily.

Grandmother said some appropriate words in memory of Regin. He'd been a good, strong porter, always helpful with camp and obedient to her every wish and devout in the ways of Second Empire. During their break, he had left them to relieve himself. By necessity, the warding Grandmother set when they were stopped for a mere break was not great in circumference. Regin had taken but a couple steps too many past its protection. They heard his scream, its sharp cutoff, and he was gone.

Blackveil Forest was dangerous. Perhaps the most dangerous place on Earth. Grandmother frequently reminded her people of the forest's treachery, but Regin proved that a moment of inattention could be one's last. A harsh lesson to them all.

It did not help anyone's flagging spirits that they were lost. Again.

Grandmother pulled her hood up against the unceasing drizzle. It was late winter, but snow never seemed to reach the ground here. It was as if the whiteness of snow was too pure, too clean, to exist within the darkness of the for-

1

est. The drizzle seeped through the canopy of crooked tree boughs and matted clumps of pine needles, and anything that dwelled here lived in perpetual dusk. At night, the blackness was total.

Blackveil was the product of conquest and defeat. Long ago, Grandmother's ancestors, led by Mornhavon the Great, sailed from the empire of Arcosia to the shores of the New Lands seeking resources and riches. Not only did they find these in abundance, but they also found resistance from the native people, who rejected the will of the empire, sparking a hundred years of war.

The first land to fall to the empire was the Eletian realm of Argenthyne, which covered the whole of a peninsula that bordered Ullem Bay to the east. Mornhavon made it his capital and renamed it Mornhavonia. At first his campaigns to quash rebellion and dominate the New Lands went well, but then supplies and reinforcements stopped coming from the empire.

Abandoned, with dwindling forces and many enemies arrayed against him, Mornhavon fell in defeat.

The Sacoridians then walled off the peninsula, trapping within the residue of darkness left behind by Mornhavon. The perversions he created with the art festered here for a millennium. The forest rotted amid etherea defiled by the use of the black arts during the war, gripping the land and spreading like a disease; ignored, neglected, and forgotten, until an Eletian coveting the residual magical power of the forest breached the D'Yer Wall three years ago.

Their journey through the forest was not only dangerous, but toilsome. They attempted to follow an ancient road of upheaved cobblestones. Sometimes it vanished into bogs or was swallowed by masses of thorny undergrowth. Patiently they sought ways around the obstructions and more than once found themselves led astray along remnants of side roads, or following paths toward traps set by wily predators.

This time an impenetrable thicket of scrubby trees, exhibiting wicked daggerlike thorns, had blocked the road and sent them off course. During trials such as these, Grandmother began to believe their situation hopeless, for she could not even consult the sun or stars for direction in this cloaked, shadowed place. She thought they'd die, forever lost in the tangled wilderness of the forest. She assumed they might yet. Their chances of survival, even if they found their way back to the road, were not good.

She was careful never to convey her doubts to the others. She could not. She must hold them together. They expressed complete faith in her, believed she would bring them through this. But if she fell apart, they'd fall apart, too, so she maintained a facade of confidence, even though it was a lie.

She gazed upon her weary retainers. There were only five of them now. Five, plus her true granddaughter, Lala, who sat upon a slimy log playing string games. Lala never issued any complaint, remained implacable as ever, trusting in her grandmother.

To find the road again, Grandmother would have to use the art, and do so before Regin's death, and fear, had a chance to grip her people. From the basket she carried over her wrist, she removed a skein of red yarn and cut a length of it with a knife that hung from her belt. Her fingers were cold and stiff, but moved nimbly to tie knots, and as she did so, she spoke words of power.

In Blackveil, she was cautious when it came to using the art. The etherea of the place was unstable, tainted, and apt to warp even the simplest spell. She'd discovered this the hard way when she tried to ignite an ordinary campfire with a touch of power to the kindling. A tree beside her exploded into flame, almost torching her skirts. Fortunately the forest was so damp the blaze did not spread to a full-scale forest fire, but after that, she did not draw upon magic except when needed for wardings and wayfinding, and even then it was reluctantly.

When she finished tying the knots, she breathed on them, and they tightened of their own volition, flexing and melding together into a single mass that transformed into a luminous red salamander perched on her palm. Her people, she knew, still only saw a snarled wad of yarn.

"Find the road," she commanded the salamander, for it was a compass.

It gazed at her with eyes of coal and lashed its serpentine tail this way and that until it settled on a direction, pointing the way with its tail. The others probably saw nothing more than a loose end of yarn lifting in an air current.

"We must carry on," Grandmother said to her people. "We must continue our journey. Regin would wish it."

Swiftly they took up their packs, one or two with tears in their eyes. They redistributed Regin's burden, setting aside personal items of his they could not use. Grandmother then turned, stepping carefully through the forest, following the direction indicated by the magic salamander's tail.

In a moment Lala was there beside her, grasping her free hand. Grandmother smiled down at her. Lala gave her the strength to carry on, as did her conviction that the empire must rise again.

After an hour or two of bushwhacking through undergrowth and wading through muddy, sluggish streams, they found the road. The salamander had led them true. They all cried out their thanks to God and Grandmother. Grandmother then released the salamander to the wind, and it vanished in a quick, brilliant spark. Only when she stood firmly upon the wet, mossy cobblestones of the road did she close her eyes and loose a sigh of relief.

Her relief turned to a cry of joy when the shifting of mist unveiled a huge, stone figure ahead of them. The statue, carved in the likeness of Mornhavon the Great, marked the joining of the Circle of the Ways. The salamander, it turned out, had led them better than true.

The roads they traversed were not built by the Arcosians, but by the Eletians of Argenthyne long before Mornhavon's arrival. When Grandmother and her little group left Sacoridia by passing through the breach in the D'Yer Wall into the forest, they followed the Avenue of Light, the main artery heading south to the center of the peninsula. There it terminated at the Circle of the Ways.

In the chronicles of Grandmother's people were maps of the peninsula and the Eletian roads. Apparently Eletians rarely built in straight lines, for the Circle was indeed a circle, and from it spun six main roads, including the Avenue of Light, that tailed off in graceful spirals where once there were major settlements. Her ancestors had not straightened the roads. Perhaps with the Long War raging, they hadn't the resources.

"Here we shall pass the night," Grandmother announced. After the day's exertions and loss, they needed rest, time to collect themselves and prepare for the next leg of their journey, which was to follow the eastern half of the Circle toward the south. They'd bypass the junction of Way of the Dawn and continue to Way of the Moon.

Yes, they would spend the night beneath the statue that to her was like a guardian. Mornhavon: strong, heroic, the heir to an empire, his gaze stern and looking outward toward the Avenue of Light, with shield and sword at hand and hair flowing back from his face. His boot crushed the bodies of his enemies, the faces of those souls contorted in agony. According to the chronicles, each junction of the Circle had such a statue to greet travelers and to remind them of who ruled here.

The pedestal had once held some other statue, something Eletian. Whatever it was, it was toppled and replaced long ago, as well it should have been.

The statue filled Grandmother with pride, never mind Mornhavon's nose, and most of the sword, had crumbled away, and the stone was darkened with moss and lichens, vines creeping up his legs.

Mornhavon may have been defeated, but that did not mean he hadn't fought valiantly, despite great adversity. No one knew why Arcosia abandoned him, and perhaps they never would, but Second Empire lived to resurrect the ideals of Mornhavon and the empire, to continue the conquest and make it succeed.

We will make things right, Grandmother promised the statue. *I shall see to it.*

Setting up camp was a well-practiced routine, though now they had to attend to Regin's duties as well. Deglin attempted to build a fire with the sodden wood collected from around them. He did carry a faggot of dry kindling, which he used sparingly. He struck steel to flint with a resolute expression on his face, for he knew Grandmother was reluctant to help after what happened last time. She did not doubt his efforts would prove successful, and she looked forward to the warmth of the resulting fire that would chase the damp chill from her bones.

Griz and Cole set up their tent shelter. The oiled canvas could not dry out and smelled of must and mildew. She thought wistfully of her small but cozy house with its kitchen garden, now probably blanketed by snow, that she had abandoned in Sacor City when the king started running down members of Second Empire. She must not dwell on the past, however. There was much to look forward to.

Min and Sarat sorted out pots and pans, and discussed what supper would be. Either a thin stew, or gruel. They, too, must be careful with their stores, for much of the vegetation in the forest was poisonous, and the creatures too dangerous to hunt.

With these reassuring and accustomed chores taking place beneath the statue, Grandmother focused on her own task, which was to set wards in a perimeter around the campsite. She removed small balls of snarled yarn from her basket: red, indigo, sky blue, and brown.

She placed them in a wide circle around their camp, murmuring a word of command as she did so. Each glowed briefly, then faded. When all were in place, she shouted, "Protect!" The forest rippled around them as though viewed through water, then stilled, all appearing normal. The eyes of wild creatures might glow yellow and green around them in the night, but nothing would pass the invisible barrier she had created. At least, nothing had thus far.

Weary beyond belief, Grandmother hobbled over to the statue and sat at its base, watching her retainers continue with their duties, not really taking any of it in or listening to their chatter. Lala sat beside her and leaned into her. Grandmother put her arm around the child. "Not an easy journey for little girls or old women, eh?" she murmured.

Lala did not answer, for she never spoke. Grandmother stroked her damp hair. "It will be worth it," she said. "This journey, even Regin's passing. He died for a just cause. We shall awaken the Sleepers as God instructed, and they will be the weapon that allows Second Empire to rise up and claim what is ours. Our legacy."

Yes, the time had come. Colonel Birch would be organizing their people on the other side of the wall, building their army, while she raised a weapon that would shatter the Eletians and terrorize all of Second Empire's enemies.

The incessant drizzle, the damp cold, the sacrifice of her people, all would be worth the fall of Eletia and Sacoridia.

◄► HOMECOMING ◄►

The house strained against the onslaught of the gale, its timbers groaning and windows rattling. The wind sheared some shingles off the roof and they whirled away, vanishing into the maelstrom of blinding snow squalls. Winter was reluctant to loosen its grip on the world this year.

The house, fortunately, was sturdily built with its coastal location in mind by one who understood the sea in all its fickle and hazardous moods. Stevic G'ladheon, the foremost merchant of Sacoridia, also possessed a fortune that ensured his house was built with the very best materials by the very best carpenters—shipwrights, mostly.

A cold draft seeped through the room where he sat reading. He shivered and turned up the flame in his oil lamp, welcoming the extra illumination and warmth it emitted. A robust fire burned on the hearth, and he wore layers of woolens and a scarf, but he still couldn't keep warm enough.

He had sensed the storm building all day, saw the leaden sky fill with heavy clouds and spit fitful flurries. He smelled the damp of the sea mixed with the bite of the cold, and he knew they were in for a real blow.

Sure enough, the storm shrieked up the coast with a banshee's fury. If he chose to part the drapes from his window and peer through the frosted glass, he'd see only a wall of white.

He could, he supposed, abandon his icy office for the kitchen, the warmest room in the house, but his sisters were in there, and the servants, too. All that female energy crammed into one room was more than he thought he could bear.

He hunkered more deeply into his armchair and glared at Brandt's *Treatise of Commerce*. It was impossibly dry, and Brandt such a self-absorbed egoist that Stevic considered throwing the volume on the fire more than once. But books were precious, and he'd as soon burn one as he would his own house. He could always set it aside, but he was far too obstinate to give up on it now. He'd read the entire thing even if it killed him.

He gazed into the golden flames on the hearth and thought of the Cloud Islands, and of how easily he could have assigned himself to this winter's trading mission there, but he'd sent Sevano instead. His old cargo master deserved the voyage to the tropics.

Stevic sighed, thinking of the glorious sunshine rippling across azure waves, waves that rolled onto fine sand beaches; of luscious, sweet fruits always in season. He missed his good friend, Olni-olo, who welcomed him into his home—really a hut on stilts situated on a tranquil cove—as one of his family, a family that consisted of five wives and dozens of children. He remembered all those children charging across the sand toward him because they knew he brought candy, and there were the hugs and the laughter. All beneath the tropical sun.

Aaaah, the sunshine . . .

Someone pounded on the front door, jarring Stevic from his reverie of balmy island days. *What fool is out in this storm?* he wondered, and he rose from his chair and left his office for the entry hall to find out. His butler, the ever efficient Artos, swept by him and yanked the door open.

Snow rushed inward with a bitter gust and a figure of white, like a frost wraith of myth, emerged from the tempest and stepped across the threshold. Stevic helped Artos heave the heavy door closed against the wind.

Whew, he thought when that was accomplished. He turned to their visitor who set a pair of saddlebags on the floor and commenced brushing snow off him- or herself. Quite a lot of snow, actually, but it did not take long for Stevic to discern Rider green beneath.

"*Karigan?*"

The figure turned to him and tossed back her hood. "Father!" She started toward him, pausing only to slip out of her snowy, dripping greatcoat and hand it to Artos. Even as Stevic held her in his arms, he couldn't believe she was there.

"What are you—" he began, but just then all four of his sisters spilled into the hall, their voices raised in astonishment, happiness, and consternation, and asking a flurry of questions Karigan had no hope of answering. Just as suddenly as she had come into his arms, she was gone, embracing her aunts and kissing their cheeks.

"Artos!" Stace snapped. "For heavens' sake, man, don't just stand there gawping. Go tell Elaine to ready a bath for Karigan. She's an icicle!"

Artos obeyed immediately.

"What on Earth were you doing out in this storm, girl?" Gretta demanded.

"I thought I could outride it." Karigan's reply was met by *tsk*ing from all her aunts.

"You're as daft as your father," Tory said.

"Now wait a—" Stevic began.

"I shall have Cook stuff a goose," Brini announced, and she bustled back toward the kitchen.

Stevic watched helplessly as Stace, Gretta, and Tory commandeered Karigan and urged her toward the stairs.

"You need dry clothes, girl," Gretta said.

"And slippers," Tory added.

Stevic scratched his head in bemusement as his daughter and sisters disappeared up the stairs. "Breyan's gold," he muttered.

He stood there alone in the hall for some moments, still overcome by the unexpected appearance of his daughter. Only puddles of melted snow and the saddlebags remained as evidence that Karigan had really come through the door. He thought to pinch himself to make sure it was not some dream. She'd felt real enough in his arms . . . Usually she sent word ahead if she planned a visit. Either advance word had not arrived for some reason, or she was here on business.

It was hard enough to know what his daughter was up to all the way in Sacor City, and she hardly ever wrote, and when she did, it was often a reassurance that all was well and that the king kept her busy.

He did not doubt her duties were demanding, but vague reassurances about all being well only served to rouse his suspicions.

He decided to make himself useful and grabbed Karigan's saddlebags. He carried them upstairs and left them outside her bedchamber. From within came the voices of his sisters rising and falling in good-natured scolding. Stevic smiled. His sisters were a force to be reckoned with, and it was no surprise that under their supervision Karigan had grown up to be the spirited and rather hardheaded young woman she was.

Stevic headed back downstairs to his office. He'd pass the time there until Karigan sought him out, as she always did, as soon as she was able to escape her aunts.

Stevic tried to engross himself in the *Treatise of Commerce* while he awaited Karigan, but he repeatedly set it aside to pace, the wind howling without. He was anxious to see her and discover what, precisely, brought her home.

And, as he often did, he wondered why she had to be a Green Rider when a relatively safe and prosperous life as a merchant was ready and waiting for her here at home with her clan. She'd explained the calling to him, the magical compulsion that made her a Green Rider, but it only further appalled Stevic to know his daughter was snared in some spell that forced her to serve the king. Well, maybe *force* was not the right word, but one could not trust magic. He'd thought all remnants vanquished long ago and was content in that belief, but oh, no, there was just enough to take his daughter away from him.

He hated worrying about her, that she might fall prey to brigands along the road, or tumble from her horse, or foolishly freeze to death in a blizzard. He ground his teeth, then paused his pacing to gaze upon the portrait of his wife behind his desk. Kariny was gone so many years now. The light was dim in his office, but even so, she looked out from the canvas luminous and breathtaking, almost as if she were about to step through the gilded frame and be there with him alive and laughing, chiding him for worrying so much.

To a casual viewer, her countenance appeared as serious as that of any portrait subject, but he saw the hidden smile, the glint of humor in blue eyes. Eyes the artist captured so well. She'd been amused when he commissioned the portrait, and during the sitting, she teased him it was too much of an indulgence to hire such an artist of renown to paint a wife as "unworthy" as she.

Never unworthy, he thought.

She died within a year of the portrait's completion, and Stevic was grateful he'd commissioned it. Otherwise, he feared losing the details of her features in his memory. Whenever he wished, he had but to look at the painting and Kariny came back to life for him in some small measure, the living, breathing woman, her touch and mannerisms, her chiming laugh, the feel of her hair flowing between his fingers.

And there was his daughter, who so strongly resembled her mother. Karigan was now about the age her mother had been when this portrait was painted. So young.

Stevic would never see Kariny grow old. He knew she would have done so with grace, her beauty only refining, not fading, as the years passed. Instead, she was stopped in time, captured forever in youthful potential.

He shook his head. In a sense, he too, was stopped in time. Stopped in time when Kariny, along with their unborn child, died from fever. It made him determined that their first child would go on to live the long, fruitful life denied Kariny. But now that Karigan had grown up, it was impossible to protect her. It did not help that she worked in the king's service, in a profession that was dangerous.

Stevic tore his gaze from the portrait of his wife, and his restlessness led him out into the main hall. He was met with the aroma of roasting goose. His stomach rumbled and he decided to brave the kitchen. There he discovered not only his sisters, but Karigan, gossiping over tarts and tea. Cook stood at the hearth turning a goose on its spit. As one they looked up at his entrance.

Why hadn't Karigan come to see him first? He found himself a little hurt that she had not.

"It's about time you decided to join us, Stevic," Stace said.

"I was awaiting Karigan."

"What? And you expected us to allow her into that ice
shed you call an office with her hair still wet? She'd catch her
death of cold. She's been drying her hair in here, where it's
warm."

Stevic glanced at Karigan, bundled in civilian clothes and
woolens, and saw that her hair was indeed still damp. And he
let out a sigh of relief. He'd had a fleeting notion that maybe
she was avoiding him for some reason, but that was prepos-
terous. What cause had she? Still, he wondered why no one
bothered to at least inform him she was done with her bath.
"Well, I didn't know I was invited."

"Oh, for heavens' sake," Brini said. "As if this weren't
your house."

"Sometimes I'm not so sure."

Brini made a sound of disgust and fetched him a teacup,
but did not pour for him. He half-smiled and pulled a chair
up to the table. All his sisters were older than he, Stace being
the eldest; all unmarried and showing little inclination for it.
And why should they when he supported them in relative
luxury?

When they came to Corsa to live under his roof, their
backward island ways had vanished in due time, but not their
pragmatism; nor did they stand on ceremony with their little
brother. Often, just as when they were children, it was four
against one when some argument came up. At least they no
longer sat on him to force him to submit to their wishes.

Henpecked though he might feel from time to time, he was
grateful for how they stepped in when Kariny died. Karigan
had been so little, and he so lost. They provided that maternal core for Karigan, took over when his own grief made him
incapable of minding his affairs. They raised Karigan while
he traveled on merchanting ventures. While he traveled to
escape the pain.

Yes, he owed his sisters much. He grabbed the teapot and
filled his cup.

"Karigan is too thin," Gretta said. "I do not think much of that Rider captain if she cannot keep her people properly fed. Now don't you roll your eyes at me, young lady."

Stevic assessed his daughter and he did not think she looked as starved as Gretta suggested. Karigan's hair hung long and loose, and had acquired a funny cowlick, but essentially, she looked unchanged. The same, but now that he thought about it, different. Something in her eyes. He could not put a finger on it and frowned.

"So, what brings you home?" Stevic asked Karigan. "If we'd known you were coming, we could've readied your room."

"Sorry," Karigan replied. "I'm actually here with messages."

Business, then, Stevic thought in disappointment.

Karigan smiled. "Though I may not be able to leave for a couple days with this weather."

As if to accentuate her words, the house shuddered with another blast of wind. Stevic sent a prayer to the heavens that the storm would not abate too soon, stranding Karigan for an extra day or two. Not that he had any faith in the gods, but it couldn't hurt to ask, could it? He missed her!

"Have you been well?" he asked.

"Yep," she replied, and she reached behind herself for the message satchel hanging over the back of her chair.

"How are things?" he pressed. "They aren't working you too hard, are they?"

"Weapons training is not fun," she replied with a grimace, "but otherwise things slow down in the winter. I've been helping to train new Riders."

The chair creaked as Stevic sat back and folded his arms. It wasn't a very satisfactory answer to his thinking—he wanted details. What might she be holding back?

She did have a knack for finding trouble. He'd heard all about that swordfight she got into with some brigand at the Sacor City War Museum. The story was all over the merchants guild, and of course he'd received a detailed letter of the event from his Rhovan colleague, Bernardo Coyle, who, as a result, did not consider Karigan a proper match for his son. Stevic had crushed the letter and cast it into the fire, thinking Karigan deserved far better than some ignorant Rhovan for a husband anyway.

In contrast to what he heard from his fellow merchants about the museum incident, he found Karigan's own accounting rather lacking. All she ever said about it was that the outing with Bernardo's son hadn't gone well. Nothing about any brigand, nothing about a swordfight.

"You are scowling," Brini told him. "Careful, or your face will freeze that way."

"I am *not* scowling."

"Hah."

By now Karigan had undone the flap of the message satchel and drawn out a letter sealed with the familiar gold imprint of the winged horse. She passed it across the table to him. He assumed it was the usual request from Captain Mapstone for supplies. Almost three years ago, Stevic pledged to outfit the Riders if Captain Mapstone helped find Karigan, who, at the time, had gone missing from school. She had managed to get mixed up in Rider affairs and had played a part in preventing a coup attempt against King Zachary. When Karigan had turned up alive after all her adventures, the captain had made sure Stevic followed through on his pledge.

He cracked open the seal and found Captain Mapstone's neat, precise writing within. *Dear Clan Chief G'ladheon,* she began. He wished she'd be more informal with him by now, but he supposed familiarity was inappropriate in official correspondence.

The letter was, as he thought, a request for additional supplies, but the quantities she asked for took him aback. *Over the last year,* she wrote, *our complement of Riders has grown significantly, to which Karigan can attest. We've been grateful for your generous donations of supplies in the past, but the king and I understand this sudden increase in demand may pose a difficulty for you. Therefore the king proposes to compensate you at tax collection time with relief on your annual burden, or to provide a direct payment.*

Then, to his delight, she chose to address him personally and in his mind's eye, he imagined her leaning closer and lowering her voice as if to take him into her confidence, but his pleasure proved short-lived as he read on: *Stevic, the king is preparing for future conflict. Opposing forces are on the move—old enemies of the realm. I cannot say more about it here, but I wish to impress upon you the deep need for these supplies. We look forward to the earliest delivery as weather and your schedule permit.*

Stevic rubbed his chin and read the last line of the letter to the sound of Cook chopping parsnips at the sideboard: *Whatever may come, you can be sure my Riders will be in the thick of it. Their readiness to face all enemies depends on you furnishing the supplies they need.*

He glanced up at Karigan, who was laughing at something Gretta said.

Captain Mapstone's Riders—*his daughter*—would be in the middle of this conflict, this threat, facing these enemies the king was preparing for.

Despite the warmth of the kitchen, his insides turned as cold as the storm that raged outside.

⋘ MESSAGES ⋙

Karigan watched as her father folded the letter from Captain Mapstone, running his fingers over the crease again and again, his expression grave. It seemed more lines were scribed into his forehead and around the edges of his mouth than she remembered; that more gray swept from his temples.

She didn't know what the captain wrote in that letter, besides the request for more supplies. Obviously something that disturbed him, and she wondered what it could possibly be, but protocol required she not ask—not even her father. It was up to the recipient to decide whether or not to speak of a message's contents.

It had been quite a while since Karigan last visited home. Except for her father looking a little older, the rest seemed unchanged, including her aunts. Well, maybe Aunt Tory had grayed a little more, too, but everything in the kitchen was in its place, pots and pans hanging where they'd always hung, the same old farm table of amber wood beneath her hands, Cook at the sideboard. Nothing in her bedchamber had been touched either, her old clothes were still hanging in the wardrobe, a couple years removed from the latest fashions. If anything, the house seemed just a little smaller, as if it had shrunk the tiniest bit. Or she had grown.

Maybe I'm just used to the castle, she thought. Her father's house was large; the castle was rather larger.

It was comforting to be in the familiar confines of the home she grew up in, to be among people she knew and loved; a completely different world from the fast pace of Sacor City and the castle, where she was surrounded by so many strangers.

At the same time, she felt uneasy being home, even on official business, for there were other matters she needed to address with her father. Matters of a personal nature. He'd kept secrets from her, and not good ones.

She twisted her teacup in her hands, gazing at specks of tea leaves swirling in its depths. Her aunts chattered on beside her, and she only half-listened. She managed to put off coming home for months, thanks to winter storms that kept everyone cooped up in the castle, but suddenly Captain Mapstone needed the one message conveyed, and it was time, she said, that Karigan's father receive the others, as well, and who better to bear them than his own daughter?

Her father cleared his throat and Karigan looked up. "You mentioned there were *messages,*" he said. "More than one?"

"Oh!" she replied, and grimaced. She withdrew from her satchel the lesser of the two that remained, and passed it to him. "From Lord Coutre."

"Lord Coutre?" he asked, raising his eyebrows in surprise. Her aunts ceased their chattering. He took the letter and broke the seal. He read rapidly, and exclaimed, "Order of the Cormorant? You've been granted lands in Coutre Province?" He read on, then gazed at her, his eyes wide and full of questions.

Aunt Stace snatched the letter right out of his hands and read it for herself. When she finished, she was the mirror image of her brother. Aunt Brini grabbed the letter next, and the others, including Cook, clustered around her to read over her shoulder.

"You rescued Lady Estora from abductors?" Stevic asked faintly.

"I, er, *helped,*" Karigan replied, her cheeks flooding with warmth. The other reason she didn't want to come home was having to explain her deeds without causing them all to faint. Just remembering the dangers she faced was enough to make *her* shudder.

When her father and aunts recovered, they demanded details. Karigan kept her responses vague: "I was on a message errand to Mirwellton—right place at the right time." And, "No, Lady Estora was not harmed." She emphasized the role others played in the rescue and left herself out of much of the story.

She told them how the traitorous group, Second Empire, used the abduction as a ruse to distract the king and his Weapons so its members could infiltrate the castle for "information." She did not bring up the book of Theanduris Silverwood, and in fact managed to avoid referring to any supernatural or magical elements of the story altogether, knowing her father's dim view of such things.

Nor did she speak of her adventures in the royal tombs beneath the castle. The realm of the tombs, while not precisely a secret, was not something casually discussed.

Her explanations appeared to satisfy them: evil plot, abduction, infiltration—all thwarted, and Karigan helped! She was afraid, however, her third message would only provoke more questions, and with a sigh she withdrew it from her satchel. It bore the royal seal of the firebrand and crescent moon. Her father stared in disbelief.

"More? The king's seal?"

Karigan nodded, waiting in a sort of dread while he read it.

When he finished, he looked at her with a stunned expression, and passed the letter to Aunt Stace without a word. Her aunts and Cook gasped as they read, and gazed at Karigan as if seeing her anew.

Her father then laughed. It was a mirthful laugh that filled the kitchen with warmth. It wasn't exactly the reaction Karigan was expecting.

"I don't think it's funny," Aunt Tory said, with a sniff. "It's a great honor to Karigan and our clan."

Stevic G'ladheon continued to laugh, wiping tears from his eyes, and Karigan could only shake her head in disbelief.

"Great honor, yes," he said. "I've always been so proud of my daughter, no matter what odd course in life she chose. But never in all my existence would I ever imagine a G'ladheon being knighted. Not only that, but it's an honor not conferred upon *anyone* for hundreds of years." Karigan's father was not overly fond of the aristocracy, and she had recognized the irony of the honor the moment she received it. Not that knighthood exactly raised her to the aristocracy, but still . . .

"My daughter, Rider Sir Karigan G'ladheon!" He grinned. Then sobering, he said, "Karigan, I understand the Coutre award, but this is above and beyond. What aren't you telling us? Did you save the entire kingdom again?"

Karigan squirmed in her chair. "Well, Lady Estora *is* the king's betrothed . . ." When she saw this wasn't going to mollify him, she added, "I helped stop the Second Empire thugs in the castle. The king was very pleased."

Her father sat back in his chair. Wind gusted down the chimney, scattering ashes on the hearth and causing the fire to flare. The juices of the roasting goose hissed.

"That's it? You're not going to tell us how? Is it a secret?"

She almost said, *Well, after I helped rescue Lady Estora, the death god's steed came to me and led me through the "white world," where we bypassed time and distance to reach the castle. I was then made an honorary Weapon and got to wear black, so I'd be permitted to enter the tombs without being forced to become a caretaker and live out my life dusting the dead. I chased the thugs through the royal tombs while pretending to be a ghost. I fought them and rescued a magical book that may or may not help us repair the breach in the D'Yer Wall. If it does, then we're all saved!*

I then took a nap in the future sarcophagus of our future queen because I was very tired and bleeding all over the place—oh, did I mention almost having my hand chopped off earlier? But that's a whole different story! Anyway, I dreamed about the dead rising. That's what I remember, and is it surprising considering where I was? When I woke up, the magic book gave us quite an eyeful.

And *that,* she reflected, was not the half of it. However, rather than reveal her true thoughts, she asked, almost pleading, "Can't you just be happy for me?"

"I am, I am!" he replied. "I just worry, and you never say much about your work."

"She's got another land grant with the knighting," Aunt Brini broke in, as she scoured the king's letter. "Anywhere in the realm."

Karigan saw the light flicker in her father's eyes, the slight smile, as if he calculated to what advantage he could use her land grants for the clan business. It was a wonder he wasn't rubbing his hands together. The diversion, however, proved short-lived.

"Will you not tell us how you inspired such notice from the king?" he asked.

If only her father knew how loaded a question that was, and how much she wanted to pound her head on the table. "There's not much to say about it." The lie rang hollow even to herself.

"I don't believe it for a minute," her father said. "You are keeping things from us."

Karigan squirmed in her chair. Why couldn't he leave off? He certainly kept his own share of secrets, so how dare he demand that she reveal her own?

"Like how you never bothered to tell me you crewed a pirate ship?" she blurted.

Ominous silence followed.

Oops, she thought. She hadn't meant to broach the subject so abruptly, but there it was now, right out in the open. No preamble, no gentle prodding, no hiding.

Cook hastened to the cutting board and her parsnips, and her aunts scattered, making themselves busy elsewhere in the kitchen, but all within earshot even as they pretended not to be listening.

"I planned to tell you about that," her father said after a few moments.

"When?"

"Well, I . . . Soon. I wanted to wait till you were old enough."

"How old? Like when I'm eighty?"

"No, of course not. I— How did you find out?" He glanced at his sisters in accusation, and they filled the kitchen with loud denials, waving spoons and knives in emphasis.

Before someone got hurt by an errant utensil, Karigan said, "You don't realize how close this information came to damaging the clan. The king knows."

That quieted everyone down.

"What? How?"

"The Mirwells dug it up, a crew list for a known pirate ship, the *Gold Hunter.* Timas—Lord Mirwell—sent it to the king."

"But *why?* Why would he?"

"I'm not sure," Karigan said. "Except Timas Mirwell hates me. He has since school, and he probably decided to get back at me by trying to disgrace the clan." He'd given her the message to deliver to the king. She, of course, had no idea of what she carried at the time. It was only after the knighting ceremony that she learned of it from one of the king's advisors.

"Damnation," her father muttered. "*Aristocrats.* Aristocrats and their games of intrigue."

"We're fortunate the king thinks highly enough of your service to the realm that he's dropping the matter," Karigan said. "But if Mirwell, or someone else, decides to make public accusations, it could be embarrassing. I destroyed the crew list, but it could still look bad even without the proof."

"I see." He shook his head. "I'm sorry you learned about it this way. I should have told you."

"I wish you had," Karigan murmured.

"At least you know now," he said.

"Yes, but none of the details."

"It was a long time ago."

"Then you should have no trouble telling me all about it now."

He raised an eyebrow. "I see knighthood has done little to gentle your tenacious curiosity."

"Father."

"Tell me, in court do they address you as *Sir* Karigan? Shouldn't it be Madam Karigan, or some such? Maybe Madam Sir Karigan?"

"Father." She might be tenacious in her curiosity, but he was exasperating. "This is *serious.*"

"Yes, yes, of course it is. Very well. I suppose there is no avoiding it." He paused, turning more reflective, his hands loosely clasped on the tabletop. "As I said, the *Gold Hunter* was long ago, and I was an ignorant young boy fresh off the island when Captain Ifior's men snatched me from a tavern and forced me into service."

"A press gang," Karigan murmured, a little mollified her father had been taken against his will.

"I didn't fight it, I will admit."

"What? Why not?"

"I saw it as an opportunity."

"Opportunity? A *pirate* ship?" Ignorant boy, indeed.

"Now, now," her father said. "The *Gold Hunter* wasn't a pirate to begin with, but a privateer with letters of marque to seize ships violating the blockade of the Under Kingdoms."

"How'd it become a pirate?"

"The embargo was lifted," he replied, "and Captain Ifior decided to keep taking ships. It was profitable."

"No doubt." Karigan's head throbbed, and she rubbed her temples. She was weary from her long journey through the storm, and it was no easy thing hearing from her father's own mouth he'd been crew on a pirate ship. All she knew of pirates was that they were unruly, bloodthirsty cutthroats, and she did not want to believe he was of that ilk, no matter how far distant in his past it may have been.

"Kari—"

"So you stayed on even after the captain turned to piracy," she said.

"Yes. Captain Ifior had a good head for business, and I learned much from him."

"Like how to steal? And kill?" Karigan winced as soon as the words left her mouth. She hadn't meant to speak so brashly, but she needed to know. Needed to know who her father really was.

He did not answer, but sat there absolutely still, his expression stony and white-edged. Karigan held her breath, bracing herself for the storm that was certain to come, but he abruptly stood and left the kitchen without a word.

His silence, Karigan thought, was more terrible than any mere eruption of anger could be.

One by one her aunts turned to face her. Cook studiously ignored the scene, keeping busy at the sideboard. Well, she'd done it this time—turned a reunion with her family into a disaster.

"What?" she demanded of her silent and forbidding aunts. "I have a right to know."

Aunt Stace's mouth turned to a grim line before she spoke. "Your father talks little of the past, even to us, but we do know he was caught in circumstances not of his devising."

Karigan could relate to that, but surely her father had more choice than she ever did with the Rider call. "He could have run away when their ship made port."

"True," Aunt Brini said, "but he had his reasons for staying. You see, Captain Ifior was more a father to him than our own was. His mentor and guide."

"Who taught him to kill and steal."

"Oh, child, you can't know—"

"I am *not* a child," Karigan said. No, not after all she'd experienced in her own life since becoming a Green Rider, but they'd never understand, even if she told them every detail of her exploits. No matter what she did with her life, they'd always see her as their little niece, not mature enough to deal with more adult matters, like her father's past.

"I suppose you are not," said Aunt Stace, "but you are acting like one."

Karigan's mouth dropped open.

"Only a child would utter whatever came to her mind without thinking first. I should have thought you learned better in the king's service."

Karigan sat there stunned that her aunts would take her father's side in this. It wasn't her fault he'd been a pirate.

She pushed her chair back and stood. She grabbed her message satchel and left the kitchen, heading for the stairs. She took the steps two at a time, and when she reached her bedchamber, she slammed the door shut behind her.

If her aunts couldn't handle her asking about the pirate ship, just wait till she brought up the brothel.

 ABOUT THE
GOLD HUNTER

Karigan couldn't sleep. She tossed and turned beneath her pile of blankets, listening to the wind slam into her window. She'd risen a time or two to stoke the fire, but the cold drove her back beneath the covers, despite the woolens she wore over her nightgown and her heavy stockings.

It wasn't so much the storm that kept her awake, but thoughts of her father and how the evening ended so badly before it had even begun. She chose to close herself in her room, with Elaine bringing up her supper. Her aunts did not even stop by to wish her a good night.

They're mad at me, she thought, even though it wasn't her fault her father had served on that pirate ship. And still, as justified as she felt in her own judgments, she was assailed by a sense of guilt, as if she were the one in the wrong simply because she needed to know the truth of the matter.

Her aunts were right on one point, she admitted after some reflection: her tendency to open her mouth without thinking. She could have approached the whole mess in a more circumspect manner that would have alleviated some of the hurt feelings. But her father had pushed her just a little too hard about her own life, and she had pushed right back.

The thing was, she loved her father—loved him powerfully and had always admired him as the dashing, strong, and successful man he was; the man who loved her mother so much he never remarried. She wanted to be like him when she grew up, planned to follow in his footsteps. Until the Rider call changed everything. Still, she'd considered him a paradigm of what a father and merchant ought to be without question. Until she heard about the pirate ship. Until the brothel.

She gathered from Elaine he hadn't attended supper, either, and ate alone in his office. Karigan sighed. They were too much alike for their own good.

Finally, when she couldn't take the twisting and turning anymore, she braced herself against the cold, threw off her blankets, and dressed by the fire.

Karigan trudged through drifts that were as high as her thighs, from the house toward the stable, her lantern providing a meager glow against the night, large snowflakes beating against it like moths. The wind sucked her breath away.

When she reached the stable and stepped inside, she found stillness, and her restless mind calmed a notch. The glow of her lantern enlarged, providing golden warmth, and she released a breath she did not know she'd been holding.

Her father's horses occupied almost every stall; sleek hacks he rode for business and pleasure: his favorite, a fine-limbed white stallion named Southern Star; matching pairs of handsome carriage horses; and several drays who hauled cargo-laden wagons during the trading season. Standing among them was one that did not quite fit in, an ungainly chestnut messenger horse. All were blanketed and bedded with fresh straw and snoozed in contentment, some snoring, hooves shuffling, all apparently oblivious to the storm raging outside.

And why shouldn't they be when the stable was as sturdily built as the main house? There was nary a draft in the place.

Often Karigan sought out the company of her horse, Condor, when troubled. Somehow being in his presence calmed her, soothed whatever agitated her. She moved down the central aisle, leaving clumps of snow behind her, until she came to his stall.

Sensing her approach, the gelding poked his head over the stall door and gazed at her with sleepy eyes, his whicker of greeting half-hearted.

"Woke you up, did I?" she asked, stroking his nose.

He whiffled her hand, his breath smelling of sweet grain.

Karigan chuckled and hung the lantern on a bracket beside his stall. She pulled a freshly baked oat muffin from her pocket. She'd found a pile of them on the sideboard where Cook left them overnight to cool. Condor grew decidedly more alert.

Now she laughed and fed him half. It vanished almost instantly and he nudged her for more.

"Greedy beast," she said and gave him the rest.

She checked his water bucket—it was full and hadn't frozen over. His blanket was straight and secure across his back. When she rode in, he'd been one tired horse after pushing through all those snow drifts. Ice had clung to his muzzle, making him look a hoary old man. The stablemaster had helped rub him down, wound his legs with quilted wrappings, and prepared him a warm bran mash. When Karigan left him, she had no fear he was in any discomfort and knew he was as happy and snug as a horse could be.

She yawned, patted his neck, and sat on a nearby pile of hay bales. She found a discarded horse blanket and pulled it over herself, and before she knew it, with the soothing sounds of slumbering horses all around her, she, too, fell asleep.

"Karigan?"

She'd been dreaming. Something about sunny, gold-green grasslands, where wild horses roamed . . .

"Karigan?"

Her eyes fluttered open and she lifted her head with a grimace. She had a crick in her neck from sleeping at an odd angle, and lantern light glared into her eyes. Her own, hanging by Condor's stall, had sputtered out.

"Father?" she said. "What are you doing here?"

"That's what I meant to ask you."

"I couldn't sleep," she replied.

"Me either, so I decided to check on things. When I stepped out, I saw your tracks in the snow and followed them here." He hung his lantern on a bracket and sat next to her on a hay bale. The light reached Condor's eyes as he gazed at them.

"I'm sorry—" both father and daughter began at the same time.

When Karigan opened her mouth to speak again, her father forestalled her with a gesture. "I admit I should have told you about the *Gold Hunter* long ago," he said. "I never wanted this ill feeling to arise between us, but it has, and all because of my silence. If I tell you more about it now, will you hear me out?"

Karigan nodded, vowing to keep quiet and not interrupt him this time with accusations.

"Good, good. Perhaps you will come to understand, then, why I chose to remain with the *Gold Hunter* even after she became a pirate. I will warn you now, however, that there will always be some details I will never speak of. Even your mother did not know everything. Just as I expect you've secrets you will never tell me."

Karigan scowled, but he was right, and so she held her tongue.

"Ready?" he asked.

She nodded emphatically, more ready than he could ever imagine.

He inclined his head in formal acknowledgment. "Very well, then," and he inhaled deeply to begin.

"The captain of the *Gold Hunter,*" he said in a voice that took on the tone and cadence of a storyteller, "was not an evil man, but deeply motivated by profit. And so, yes, when the embargo was lifted from the Under Kingdoms, he continued to seize ships. He was as good a naval tactician as he was a businessman, and the *Gold Hunter,* well, she was a beauty in her day, with swift, trim lines. In barely a puff of wind she'd skim the water, overtaking any other vessel in sight, especially those heavily laden with cargo."

His hands moved to illustrate the ship's size and dimensions as he spoke. Karigan did not doubt he envisioned the *Gold Hunter* before him, felt the wind in his hair and the sea spray against his face; saw dolphins leaping the waves that curled from the prow.

"We took merchant vessels plump with cargos of every description," he continued. "Casks of Rhovan wine, bundles of tobacco leaves, metal ore, spices, ceramics . . . anything you can imagine. Even a ship full of goats."

Karigan almost questioned him about how many sailors had to die when the pirates "took" a vessel and its goods, but she managed to remain still and just listen. She glanced at Condor, and his unblinking gaze steadied her.

"The *Gold Hunter* was fitted with an iron ram," her father said, "and crewed by hands who were well-armed and skilled fighters. Few vessels outran us, and because of the reputation we attained for fighting fierce battles, Captain Ifior convinced most merchantmen to yield before combat even began. He was fair with defeated crews, especially those who surrendered, and they were free to go as they willed once we made landfall. Some chose to remain with the *Gold Hunter*.

"I myself was a mere cabin boy, and I will not claim life on board was easy or pleasant. It was hard work and the captain stern. He had no patience for slackers and he was quick to flog any sailor he deemed wasn't moving fast enough." He rubbed his shoulder, grimacing with some memory. "Likewise, since I was the smallest on crew, others saw fit to kick me around for no particular offense except I was there."

Karigan found it difficult to imagine her father as a boy, for he'd always seemed so tall and indomitable to her, not one to be pushed around. Those boyhood experiences must have forged him into the man she knew. They certainly did not break him, nor did they turn him into some monster that gave back the same as he got. It was amazing, really, and she, who had a gentle, loving upbringing, could only admire him for it.

"But as difficult as life could be on the *Gold Hunter*," he said, "it was no worse than I experienced fishing with my father. Easier in many ways. More lucrative, too, and so I stayed." He paused, loosing a breath that was barely perceptible to her, like a light slackening of the wind in the sails, a release. She glanced at him and saw he was far away, far off on the sea, perhaps, watching gannets plunge from the sky into the waves after fish, and the sun lowering beyond the horizon of the world, not sitting anchored in a stable in the middle of a snowstorm. She wondered at the memories she forced him to dredge up, wondered what parts he recalled but chose not to tell her.

"The most important reason I stayed," he said, "was because of what I learned—not just the writing, reading, and figuring, but what I observed when I accompanied the captain to market. Remember those goats I mentioned? Not worth a great amount here in Sacoridia, or other ports on the continent, but on Mallollan Island? A different story."

Mallollan, Karigan knew, was part of the Cloud Island archipelago, where her father maintained ties to this day.

"There were no native livestock animals there," he continued. "They did have some scrawny cows and hogs acquired in direct trade, but most had to be brought over on the long and dangerous passage from Pikelea, where the customshouse was based and all the international and *legal* commerce occurred. Which meant the purchasing of goods was more expensive and heavily taxed, and the returns more modest.

"Captain Ifior, however, stayed away from the main island, thus avoiding paying duty and evading any officials seeking his arrest for piracy. Instead, he sailed directly to Mallollan, where he was welcomed by people with little access to trade goods, but who were eager to obtain them.

"I watched him barter with the chiefs of various villages on the island. The captain had been right—they wanted those goats. Not only for milk and meat, but because owning them would elevate their status across the whole archipelago. What the captain received in return were goods plentiful to the islanders, but in demand elsewhere: sugarcane, pearls, nutmeg, cinnamon . . ."

Those items were still in high demand in Sacoridia and elsewhere, and brought princely sums, creating huge fortunes for several merchant clans. Karigan's father still traded with the islands, and even pioneered the shipping of ice harvested from Sacoridian ponds and lakes to the tropics, yet it was textiles that had brought him his greatest wealth. She shifted beneath the horse blanket, realizing she'd never heard precisely why and how textiles, and not those other things, had become the core of her father's business. There was much, she supposed, she had taken for granted.

"You see," her father said, "it was the captain's genius for knowing the markets I wished to emulate, and from then on, I worked hard; became the best cabin boy he'd ever known, and soon he entrusted me to keep his ledgers. He even showed me how to save and invest my share of a prize. Best of all, he continued to take me to market where I watched and learned."

He then sighed, his gaze cast downward. "The end came when merchantmen, aware of the *Gold Hunter*'s reputation, started hiring protection when traveling the routes Captain Ifior prowled. Our prey, with its extra protection, turned bold, more aggressive, and our battles more pitched. In what would become our final voyage, the captain was slain in a clash with a Tallitrean ship, and he wasn't the only one we lost. The fighting was vicious, and the *Gold Hunter* was badly damaged." He shook his head. "We limped into port, all scorched and nearly dismasted. If it weren't for Sevano, we wouldn't have made it home at all."

"Sevano?"

Her father smiled. "He was first mate and took command when the captain died."

"I knew he'd sailed with you, but not on—not on—"

"You didn't picture him a pirate, eh? No more than me, I suppose."

She pushed a stray lock of hair out of her face. The cargo master was like a part of the family, and was the first to show her how to defend herself from anyone who might do her harm. He was proficient with weapons, but she hadn't thought it unusual for a cargo master. He must have learned those skills as a mariner.

"Where Captain Ifior was a father to me," he said, "Sevano was an elder brother. When fights broke out over whatever cargo remained in the hold, he managed to claim some of it for me, me being the scrawny boy I was back then. No one wanted the bolts of beautiful cloth we'd taken off a Durnesian merchant, especially when there were other goods of more obvious value, so they were mine, and I took them to market. I guess I had an eye for quality, and with my training, I got a very good price."

When Karigan's father fell silent, she could only gape. This was the origin of Clan G'ladheon's wealth and prestige? Stolen bolts of cloth? This was her father's first step toward becoming the premier textile merchant of Sacoridia?

If he hadn't taken that step, where would she be now? Probably back on Black Island, a fishwife, and constantly pregnant, living in a modest cot already full of squalling children.

Would she have heard the Rider call?

She didn't know.

It was odd how a single decision, or a chance meeting, could change the course of not only one life, but that of others. If her father had not run away from Black Island, had not learned all he had from Captain Ifior, her vision of herself as a fishwife would likely be all too true. Instead, because of her father's choices, she'd grown up privileged, very comfortable, and well-educated. In light of all that, it was difficult for her to stay angry at him for being a cabin boy on the *Gold Hunter*. She still didn't approve of piracy, but she couldn't blame him.

Condor shook his head, ears and mane flopping. He gave her a sleepy look, then turned inward, toward the depths of his stall.

"There is shame in being involved with piracy," her father said in a quiet voice. "It is wrong, and I see it now with maturity, especially now that I wear the cloak of a merchant. Ironically, I deplore those who would attack my caravans, or ships I've invested in. They are criminals, as I once was a criminal.

"A part of me wonders if I would have achieved success without all I learned from my association with the *Gold Hunter*. I think I probably would have—I am a persistent sort, and determined to succeed. But it would have taken longer, and the success might be less." He smiled. "I was motivated to achieve because I knew a beautiful girl waited for me back on the island. I would not take her as my wife until I'd proven myself a man—shown that I could support her, and support her well. She deserved no less. I vowed she would not be a poor fisherman's wife. The *Gold Hunter* allowed me to bring her to Corsa and marry her all that much sooner. I cannot say what would have happened if I'd chosen some other path, but your mother and I, we had dreams . . .

"In any case," he said more brusquely, "piracy is not an admirable thing. And . . . and I was ashamed of what you would think. Seeing disappointment in your eyes when you confronted me earlier—that was the hardest thing I've faced in a long while."

"If only you had told me sooner."

"I believed you were too young to understand the implications." He paused. "I know now you are not, but I fear I can't help but still see you as my little girl in her party dress and ribbons, with scraped elbows."

Karigan thought as much.

"You're frowning," he said. "Be careful or your face will freeze that way."

She only screwed up her face more.

"Well, if that is all, perhaps we should retire to our beds. I didn't work so hard for so many years for my daughter to be sleeping in the stable." He rose and watched her.

The wind had quieted. Karigan wondered if it was a lull in the storm, or if it was actually dying out. "There's one more thing," she said.

Her father stood there, just waiting.

Before she lost her nerve, she said, "When I passed through Rivertown last fall, I met a friend of yours—Silva Early. In fact, I stayed at her . . . her establishment, the Golden Rudder."

The blood drained from Stevic G'ladheon's face.

⇜ MOONSTONE ⇝

Several horses, including Condor, peered from their stalls, watching father and daughter like spectators at a tournament. The silence was excruciating.

Finally her father spoke. "What were you doing at the Golden Rudder?"

"My Rider-in-training, Fergal, almost drowned in the river during our crossing." That was definitely the short version of the story. "Cetchum brought me to the Golden Rudder after. I didn't know what kind of place it was. Not at first."

"Cetchum," her father murmured. The ferry master would, of course, be well known to him. Cetchum's wife was a maid at the brothel, so he'd seen it only as natural to take Karigan there.

"I was surprised to learn from Silva," Karigan continued, her voice trembling, "that my father was a favored patron." Incensed and betrayed was more like it.

He placed his hands on his hips and turned away, gazing into the dark. When he faced her again, he replied, "I said there were things I'd never explain, and certainly not to my daughter."

"What about Mother?" Karigan demanded. "Did she know?"

"This has nothing to do with her."

It has everything to do with her! Karigan wanted to scream.

But her father simply walked away. Walked away and out of the stable, and out into the snow.

What had she expected?

She expected a lot, actually, especially of her father. Expected him to honor her mother, to be truthful and upright. Not a . . . a *patron* of brothels. Not a pirate. It felt like he'd lived a whole secret life without her. If he kept those secrets, what else might he be hiding?

Her father had become a stranger to her.

With a sigh, she tossed off the horse blanket and shivered in the cold. With one last pat on Condor's neck, she grabbed both lanterns and left the stable. To her surprise, the pitch black of night was lightening to dusky gray, and the wind had died almost to a whisper. Fat flurries descended in lazy swirls from the sky, nothing like the earlier squalls.

She used the trail her father had broken between the stable and house, thinking they needed to talk things out, not avoid one another. So when she entered the house, she lit a lamp and looked for him in the kitchen and his office; went from room to room, finding only darkness and silence. Upstairs, she heard snoring from behind the doors of her aunts. She halted at her father's door, which stood ajar. No light shone from within, and she heard nothing.

Hesitantly she pushed the door open and peered inside, thrusting the lamp before her. The blankets on his bed were rumpled, but he was not in it. Where could he be?

She stepped inside, letting the lamplight fill the room. Her father's bedchamber was spare and neat, just as she always remembered. There were a couple paintings of maritime scenes hanging on the wall, and a ship model was displayed on the mantel. It was *not* the *Gold Hunter,* but the river cog *Venture,* the first vessel he'd built as the primary investor.

A few faint embers glowed on the hearth, and Karigan threw some kindling on them and fanned the fire back to life. Once she had a satisfactory blaze going, she glanced around the room again.

Had it always been this spare? Was it like this when her mother was alive? She found she could not remember.

Her gaze fell upon the chest pushed against the far wall, beneath the window. Her mother's dowry chest. There had been, in fact, no dowry, for Kariny's father had not approved of Stevic G'ladheon as a husband, and so the couple ran off sometime after his voyages on the *Gold Hunter.*

Her father commissioned the chest so her mother would at least have a sense of coming into the marriage with the goods a bride needed to begin housekeeping. Karigan remembered the chest as filled with fine linens. She had not looked in it since she was a child.

Now she took tentative steps toward it, setting her lamp on a bedside table. She knelt beside the chest and passed her hand over the mahogany, running her fingers over carvings of seashells and ships. To either side of the latch stood a man and woman with hands joined, seabirds circling overhead, and clouds billowing in the sky, a sunburst rayed behind them.

The latch was not locked and Karigan lifted the lid, inhaling the strong scent of cedar.

She found inside not only the expected linens, but other unexpected items, as well. There was a large conch shell as one would find on the beaches in the Cloud Islands. Karigan had some, too, that her father brought back from his voyages, and they were displayed on the mantel in her bedchamber. This one, however, was enormous. She took it out and carefully set it aside.

Beneath it was an infant's gown, crisp and white, with a blue and yellow needlework design around the hem. Begun, but not finished.

"Oh, gods," Karigan murmured. This had not been one of hers, but one her mother made for her forthcoming child, the babe that had never been born.

As she continued to explore the contents of her mother's chest, she found dresses, some let out to accommodate pregnancy. Beneath them, she found an elegant gown of ivory silk. She could almost feel her mother's presence there with her, and she crushed the dress to her as though hugging her mother. They'd had so little time together.

Karigan sat on her father's bed, trying to imagine her mother wearing the dress, meeting her father at the altar of Aeryc, reciting their devotions before the moon priest and witnesses.

She sighed and pressed her face into the silk, perhaps trying to feel some essence of her mother in it, but only inhaling the scent of cedar clinging to a garment left long in storage.

She curled upon the bed with the gown, and finally, exhausted, she dropped into sleep.

Karigan awoke to daylight filling the room. For a moment she forgot where she was and sat up shaking her head. She pushed aside her blanket. No, it was her mother's gown. Then it came back to her—she was in her father's room. She rubbed sleep from her eyes.

"Well," Aunt Stace said in an acerbic tone from beside the fireplace, startling Karigan. She held a poker, and was hale and quite wide awake. "Good morning to you. It is the tenth hour of the day."

"Doesn't feel like it," Karigan mumbled.

"I imagine not. It seems both you and your father kept late hours."

"Where is he?" Karigan asked, wondering why he'd not evicted her from his room.

"Out and about on his snowshoes. He came in briefly at eight hour for tea and a muffin, then headed straight back out." Aunt Stace shook her head in bemusement. "Said he was out checking the grounds and roads."

Karigan raised her eyebrows in incredulity. *"Why?"*

Aunt Stace rolled her eyes. "If I knew that one, Kari girl, I'd tell you. You know how he gets when he's some notion in his head—whatever it is."

Karigan nodded. She did know. Nothing would stop him no matter what obstacles lay in his path—not even a snowstorm. She glanced at the window as if to catch a glimpse of him tramping around on his snowshoes, but saw only frost coating the glass.

Probably checking if the roads are passable so he can be rid of me.

Aunt Stace set the poker aside and came to Karigan, smoothing her skirts as she sat on the bed. "What brought this on?" she asked quietly, touching the gown. "Something your father said?"

"No. I ... I don't know. But Mother—I miss her. I hardly remember her." Then, out of nowhere, tears came and Aunt Stace wrapped her arms around her, holding her close. She smelled of soap and cinnamon.

"I know, dear, I know." Aunt Stace rubbed her back. "You do realize she loved you very much, don't you?"

Karigan sniffed and nodded.

"Good. That's the most important thing."

"I remember she liked to sing to me."

"Yes, she did, and she sang sweetly."

"One thing I didn't inherit from her," Karigan said, and she laughed.

"But you've her eyes, her hair, and many of her lovely attributes," Aunt Stace said. "Never forget she lives on in you."

Karigan almost started sobbing again, but swallowed it back, and wiped her nose with her sleeve.

"I think," Aunt Stace said, "a hearty breakfast would make you feel much better."

Karigan nodded. She *was* hungry.

"Good. Then let me help you fold this." Aunt Stace smoothed a sleeve of the gown. "Your mother was so beautiful in this. Absolutely radiant. Your father on the other hand ..." Aunt Stace chuckled, and it grew into a hearty laugh.

Karigan's aunts had told the story of her father's wedding enough times that all one of them had to do was say the word *wedding* and they'd all break out in helpless laughter. Except her father who would usually groan and leave the room.

"He—he turned white as the belly of a rayfish when he saw Kariny." All of Aunt Stace jiggled. "He was so nervous!"

It *was* amusing, Karigan thought, to imagine her father sprawled in the moon priest's arms while the lord-mayor of Corsa and all the elite of the merchants guild looked on. She couldn't help but join in with Aunt Stace's laughter.

When they'd mostly recovered, they lifted the gown to fold it, and something solid tumbled from it and plopped onto the bed.

"What in the heavens ... ?" Aunt Stace scooped up the object.

"What is it?" Karigan asked as she finished folding the gown and placed it carefully in the chest.

"A crystal of some sort." Aunt Stace opened her hand to reveal a clear, rounded crystal that glinted brightly as the light hit it. She rolled it atop her palm and it seemed to collect all the daylight and firelight in the room and recast it in rainbow hues that shimmered on the walls and ceiling. "Pretty thing."

"*Muna'riel*," Karigan murmured, shocked to stillness.

"Say again?" Something odd lit in Aunt Stace's eyes.

"Muna'riel." Karigan knew exactly what it was for she had once possessed one, but what in the name of all the gods was an Eletian moonstone doing here among the folds of her mother's wedding gown?

"Moona-ree-all," Aunt Stace muttered, scratching her head. "Now that jogs something from a ways back . . ."

"What?" Karigan asked.

"I'm thinking." Aunt Stace glanced down as if searching her memory. "Moona-ree-all. It was something your mother said . . ."

"Mother?" Karigan trembled, resisting the urge to shake her aunt to jog her memory.

"Aaah, that's it," Aunt Stace said, as if to herself. "We'd wondered what she was talking about, but put it down to the fever."

"What? What do you mean?"

"It was near the end," Aunt Stace said, and she sat on the bed again, patting the mattress to indicate Karigan should do likewise.

A moonstone, Karigan thought as she sat. *My mother had a moonstone.*

"Your mother was so very ill," Aunt Stace continued. "In and out of delirium. She sang in words we did not know, pointed out dead relatives in the room no one else could see. *She sings to me,* she kept saying. *Who?* we'd ask, but she'd only answer, *Like when I was pregnant with Kari. She sings to me.*" Aunt Stace shrugged. "We didn't know who she meant, but then she pointed out her grandmama and grandpapa, long dead of course. Maybe it was her grandmama that did the singing?"

Karigan shuddered, wondering if she weren't the only one in her bloodline with a talent for seeing the dead.

"Then quite suddenly," Aunt Stace said, "she grabbed Stevic's wrist—made us all jump. Makes me shiver to remember. Stevic leaned down close to her to hear what she said."

"And what did she say?" Karigan asked, almost whispering.

Aunt Stace's eyebrows drew together. "*Give Kari the moona-ree-all.* That's just what she said. *Give Kari the moona-ree-all.* She kept saying it till she dropped Stevic's wrist in exhaustion. She went peacefully after that, simply faded in her sleep, almost . . . almost smiling."

Karigan had heard a little about her mother's final moments, how she died peacefully surrounded by those she loved. Never did she hear about her mother seeing dead family members, or about her request that Karigan receive the moonstone.

"I guess this is yours," Aunt Stace said, holding the crystal to the light, entranced by its beauty. "It is yours, come to you after all these years. At the time, we had no notion of what your mother was talking about, nor were we aware of the crystal's existence, so we could not give it to you as she requested, and we thought . . . We thought it best not to tell you about her last words, because we could only guess it was the fever that made her speak so, and we did not want an account of her confused state to sadden you."

More secrets, Karigan thought, but she was not angry. Just stunned. Stunned and perplexed.

"Here you go, dear." With some reluctance, Aunt Stace rolled the moonstone onto Karigan's outstretched hand.

The moment it hit her palm it illuminated with such brilliance they both had to shield their eyes.

"My heavens!" Aunt Stace exclaimed. "How did it do that?"

"It's Eletian," Karigan replied. "A muna'riel is a moonstone—it contains a moonbeam."

"Eletian magic?" Aunt Stace asked in a hushed voice.

Karigan nodded, and the moonstone's radiance faded to a soft, silvery glow. It sent warmth through her palm and up her arm. She had not been sure if it would light up for her, but it had, just like the very first moonstone she touched. That one had belonged, originally, to a pair of eccentric, elderly sisters who lived in the heart of the Green Cloak Forest. It was one magical artifact among many others their father, Professor Berry, had collected over his lifetime. The Berry sisters had been so impressed it lit up for Karigan when it never had for them that they had given it to her.

She was never clear why the magic worked for her and not others, but a while after she had acquired the moonstone, she had met an Eletian named Somial who had told her the moonstone's favor meant she was "Laurelyn-touched," a friend of the Elt Wood. Exactly what that meant, she could not say, especially when some Eletians treated her more like an enemy.

Laurelyn the Moondreamer was a fabled Eletian queen of old, queen of the legendary, lost realm of Argenthyne. Fabled until Karigan learned both Laurelyn and her realm had truly existed. Argenthyne had been conquered by Mornhavon the Black and transformed into Kanmorhan Vane, the Blackveil Forest. Laurelyn's fate was unknown, even to the Eletians.

At the moment, however, she was more overcome by the idea that this moonstone had been her mother's. How? Why? And Kariny had wanted her to have it, which only prompted more questions.

When she glanced up, her aunt had that look in her eyes again. "It is strange," she said. "Strange your mother should possess such a thing. Eletian, for heavens' sakes! And yet ... And yet, it is in a way not strange to me."

Karigan waited, not daring to interrupt.

"Your mother, as sensible a woman as she was, also had another side to her. A bit dreamy. Came down the maternal line, no doubt." Without explaining the last, Aunt Stace continued, "That's where all the songs and stories came from, from that dreamy part of her nature. How she loved to tell you those stories and sing to you!"

It occurred to Karigan, with a prickling on the back of her neck, that her mother most often sang of Laurelyn the Moondreamer and Argenthyne.

"Then there were the times," Aunt Stace said, "when she'd

ride out at night. To sing to the stars, she told us. Stevic often
joined her, and they were like two youths caught up in love
for the first time, rather than married folk with responsibilities and a child to attend to."

"I don't remember," Karigan said.

"There is much a child will not remember, especially
when it's something that happened after her bedtime! And,
actually, they went out like that well before you were born.
Two young lovers. It would not surprise me in the least if you
were conceived during one of their jaunts."

Out in the woods? Her parents? Among the trees, ferns,
and wild creatures? Karigan's cheeks warmed. Knowing her
parents were her parents was one thing, but thinking about
the act that made them her parents was quite another. She
rubbed her eyes with the heels of her hands as if to banish
the image now planted in her mind, of her parents joined
together on the mossy floor of some forest glade with the
moonlight beaming down on them . . .

Aunt Stace smiled in amusement, seeming to know exactly where Karigan's thoughts ventured, but then she so-
bered and resumed her story. "Even when Stevic was away,
Kariny rode out into the night alone. Sevano used to have
fits over her safety, but she refused his escort and always returned unharmed and happy. She especially loved full moons.
It makes me wonder . . ."

"If she was having an affair?" Karigan demanded, her
mind still stuck in that moonlit clearing.

"No," Aunt Stace replied thoughtfully. "It was not in her,
I think. She loved your father wholly, was devoted to him.
But I wonder if, in her wanderings, she met Elt out there."
She gestured vaguely to indicate the countryside. "Ever since
the trouble at the D'Yer Wall, you do hear about more sight-
ings of the Elt. Even near Corsa. But maybe they've always
been out there and just didn't show themselves. Maybe they
befriended your mother and that's how she came to possess
the crystal."

It was as good an explanation as any, Karigan thought.
Eletians did wander, and had, as her aunt suggested, always
been "out there," even though for most Sacoridians, they in-

habited only legends. They'd become more apparent after the D'Yer Wall was breached, no longer characters in fairy tales and songs, but very alive, and very real.

She tightened her fingers around the moonstone and rays of light thrust out like blades between them. Her mother wanted it to come to her. Her mother had called it by the Eletian name, *muna'riel.*

And Karigan had thought her father kept secrets.

At Aunt Stace's encouragement, Karigan went downstairs to have some breakfast. Food did much to restore her spirits. While she ate, Aunt Stace insisted she show the moonstone to her other aunts. The moment it left her hands and passed into theirs, its light extinguished and it became nothing more than an exquisite lump of crystal.

She did not know what to make of it. Why, she wondered yet again, did moonstones light up for her when they would not for others?

Laurelyn-touched, Somial had said.

It filled her with a sense of something larger going on, something beyond her own ken. She felt caught in a story not of her own making, powerless to direct her own destiny. She shuddered. She did not like it when outside forces intervened in her life, like the Rider call.

"Ugh," she said. Maybe she was reading too much into it, but so much had happened in her life in recent years that the feeling wasn't easy to dismiss.

After breakfast, she wandered from the kitchen into the main hall, fiddling with the moonstone in her pocket, and soon found herself standing in the doorway of her father's office. Since she had no ready answers for the mysteries surrounding the moonstone, and little else to do with her idle time, she decided to at least try to distract herself by looking through the family collection of books.

Her father was still out and about and so she had no compunction about entering his domain. She strode in and over to the shelves, and as her gaze slipped across the spines of numerous leatherbound volumes, she was conscious of the portrait of her mother behind her father's desk. She almost felt a sensation of being watched, of someone peering over her shoulder. Maybe it was having handled her mother's gown earlier and talking about her that made her feel so present. Karigan tried to shake off the feeling, but couldn't quite, so she focused her attention as best she could on the books.

The G'ladheon library held numerous old ledgers and her father's copy of *Wagner's Navigation*. Karigan used to love leafing through it to look at the charts bound within, with their vibrant colors and drawings of fantastical sea creatures. There were also some histories and books on commerce on the shelves, and another favorite, Amry's *Book of Leviathans*, which contained intricate prints of all the porpoises and whales that inhabited the deeps. It was a venerable guidebook found on many a whaling ship.

There were few novels, but Karigan's gaze was drawn to her favorite, *The Journeys of Gilan Wylloland*. She pulled it off the shelf; the leather cover was dyed a deep green, and the pages were edged with gold.

She sat with the book in her father's armchair, flipping through pages worn by her own numerous readings. The book told of the unlikely exploits of Gilan and his sidekick, Blaine, as they traveled around the imaginary land of Arondel slaying dragons, rescuing princes and princesses, running off outlaws, and the like.

It occurred to Karigan that Gilan and Blaine did not seem to have any family or home, or any reliable way of supporting themselves, except for the occasional award of gold from a grateful prince or a treasure found in a goblin cave. They escaped every adventure more or less unscathed, more than ready for the next.

There appeared to be few lasting consequences for their actions, even for the blithe killing of villains. And while women continually swooned into Gilan's arms, poor Blaine was permitted no such romantic attention. The author, however, made sure Blaine was devoted to Gilan and admired him with the whole of her heart, no matter he was, Karigan reflected, a self-absorbed boor.

Funny how her perspective on the book had changed with her own experiences. If she were to write a sequel, she'd have Blaine smarten up, leave Gilan to his own folly, and work for a more noble purpose than simply gadding about the countryside in hopes of encountering adventure. No, she'd have Blaine offer her sword to the good prince who ruled his lands with a fair hand. Blaine's adventures would have more purpose, be more realistic.

Maybe she should make Blaine a royal messenger? Karigan laughed at herself.

She removed the moonstone from her pocket to better view an illustration of the mighty, impossibly muscled and handsome Gilan clasping a sword in one hand and the bloody head of a monster in the other while Blaine gazed upon him with typical adoration.

The light dazzled, brightened the office as it never had been before. Objects leaped into brilliant relief, and the colors of the illustration jumped off the page. The gold edging sparkled.

On impulse, Karigan craned her neck around to gaze at her mother's portrait. It was almost as though her mother came to life, the flesh so warm and real looking, her hair shining and eyes alight. There was more of a smile to her lips than Karigan remembered. She glanced away with a shiver and stared into the silvery white luminescence of the moonstone, the book forgotten on her lap.

She could almost hear her mother singing to her, singing to her of Laurelyn:

> *The Moonman loved Laurelyn, brightest spirit*
> *beneath the stars, and he built her a castle*
> *of silver moonbeams tall,*
> *in sylvan Argenthyne, sweet Silvermind . . .*

Karigan couldn't help but glance once more at her mother's portrait, remembering the warmth of her mother's arms around her as she sang of Laurelyn.

That, combined with the discovery of the moonstone, was, she thought, a remarkable coincidence. Too remarkable.

Did her mother meet with Eletians in the woods as Aunt Stace suggested? How else would she have received the moonstone? The Berry sisters said an Eletian gave their father the one they possessed. If that was the case, then perhaps it was not so extraordinary that her mother had acquired one.

And yet, it was.

As beautiful and as useful as a light source moonstones were, they were powerful when unleashed. The one given her by the Berry sisters had ultimately become a weapon when she fought Shawdell the Eletian, who had breached the D'Yer Wall. She had wielded its light like a blade, sharper and stronger than any earthly steel. When the wounded Shawdell fled, all that remained of the moonstone were crystal fragments on the palm of her hand.

She could not imagine the Eletians giving away moonstones to just anyone. What was their purpose in giving one to her mother? So that it would eventually come to Karigan, as Professor Berry's had?

She closed her fingers around the moonstone, the sensation of being part of some greater plot washing over her once again. Her aunts were pleased the mystery of Kariny's final words was resolved, but for Karigan, there was no resolution, just more questions.

Secrets, she thought. *Too many secrets.*

She was jarred from her thoughts by the sound of the front door opening and closing, and feet stomping in the entry hall.

"Stevic?" Aunt Stace called from somewhere deep within the house, followed by footsteps as she strode down the corridor.

"Snow's stopped," he answered. "The clouds look like they're breaking up."

"Good, good," Aunt Stace said. "Then maybe you'll take a few minutes to visit with your daughter. It isn't often she's home."

Karigan pocketed her moonstone and crept to the doorway of the office. She peered into the entry hall and saw her father heavily cloaked and holding a pair of snowshoes. Snow crumbled off his boots and shoulders. Aunt Stace faced him with her arms crossed.

"I will," he said. "But I still need to—"

"You need to talk to your daughter. About certain things."

"Certain things? What things?" Then Stevic G'ladheon's features clouded over. *She told you about the brothel?*"

Aunt Stace's eyebrows shot up. "*Brothel?* What brothel?"

Silence filled the hall as brother and sister regarded one another.

Aunt Stace shook herself and Karigan could tell she was just bursting with questions, but instead said, "You need to talk to Karigan about her family. Kariny's family."

"Why? What for?" Stevic's manner was guarded.

"She's a right to know," Aunt Stace replied, "about what was said back on the island concerning the Grays. How some of the women of that line—"

"No."

"Stevic—"

"No. I will not talk about those lies. None of it was true, and I will have no such talk in my house."

"But you—"

"It's bad enough my daughter is cursed and that damn Rider call has taken her from me."

His words stunned Karigan. Cursed? He believed her *cursed?* She tightened her grip on the moonstone in her pocket.

"But Kariny—"

"Do not speak of her—do not even bring up her name—not when you discuss magic. She was untouched by the taint. She was *perfect.*"

Karigan swallowed hard, feeling as if the floor beneath her feet were falling away. She knew her father's views on magic, an antipathy borne of fear. It was not uncommon among Sacoridians whose ancestors suffered so under the depredations of Mornhavon the Black.

Yet the vehemence in his voice, the hate—it took her aback. He saw her as cursed, as tainted by evil. A small cry escaped her lips.

Her father and aunt both looked toward the doorway where she stood.

"Karigan?" Aunt Stace said.

Her father blanched.

Karigan barely registered the tears on her cheeks.

"Karigan," her father said. "I didn't mean to say—"

But then she removed her hand from her pocket, the moonstone on her palm. It lit the entry hall in a brilliant silver-white hue, illuminating her father's flesh with a deathly pallor.

The snowshoes crashed to the floor.

"No," he whispered.

Before Karigan or Aunt Stace could say another word, he flung the front door open and bolted out into the wintry landscape.

Karigan sank to her knees, the moonstone clenched in her fist. In two strides Aunt Stace was there, holding her.

⊰ ISLAND LORE ⊱

Karigan's aunts had always been of the opinion that applying food to a problem usually solved it. They placed before her a bowl of goose and leek soup from the kettle simmering over the fire, as well as peach preserves, tarts, and muffins.

Aunt Tory uncorked a bottle of pear brandy. Tea, she declared, just wasn't efficacious enough to succor the distress caused by her brother, and after splashing a dram into a goblet for Karigan, she poured herself a cup near to overflowing. Then she took a long, hard draught of the stuff, ending with a satisfied sigh. She refilled her cup while her sisters looked on in astonishment and severe disapproval.

For Karigan's part, she sat at the kitchen table with head in hands, the fire warming her back. She had no appetite whatsoever and sat mute while Aunt Stace recounted her confrontation with their brother.

"We should sit on him," Aunt Tory said.

"I'm not sure that would help Karigan," Aunt Stace replied.

"She could sit on him, too. The more of us, the better."

Aunt Gretta snickered, a mischievous glint in her eyes.

"He believes I'm cursed," Karigan said plaintively.

"Do not take it to heart, Kari girl," Aunt Stace said. "He's just angry the Rider magic took you away from him. He fears for your well-being, for he knows your work can be dangerous."

When Karigan finally succumbed to the Rider call, she had to explain to them why she had to leave to be a king's messenger, why she must go to Sacor City. She had to explain why she could not be a proper merchant's daughter, working with her father and marrying to produce heirs that would carry on the line and clan. Her announcement predictably upset her family, especially her father.

"I know he doesn't like magic," Karigan said, "but I've never seen him like that."

"It was very much part of our upbringing to regard magic as evil," Aunt Stace replied. "Our father was strict on the matter and every rest day we had to listen to the moon priest rail against the evil of the old days. He preached that if it were ever born upon the Earth again, it ought to be destroyed, along with anyone with the ability to use it."

Green Riders kept silent about even their minor abilities because of this sort of irrational fear and intolerance. What would her fellow citizens think if they learned magic users served the king? How could they trust the king or his messengers?

"Our father," Aunt Stace continued, "was particularly fervent in his beliefs and used a switch liberally if any one of us even uttered the word *magic*. All we knew was that it was vile and corrupt."

"And of course," Aunt Brini said, her gaze focused on her needlework, "Stevic was smitten with Kariny Gray."

"What does she have to do with it?" Karigan demanded, turning to Aunt Stace. "You were telling father to talk to me about her."

"Yes, so I was. And since he's seen fit to run off into the snow again, I daresay we'll do the telling for him." Her sisters murmured in assent.

"Your mother's line," Aunt Brini said, "has always been known on the island to be a trifle . . ." And here she whispered, *"fey."*

"Uncanny," Aunt Tory added.

"Just a touch," Aunt Stace emphasized. "You see, there was not so much written history on Black Island, but quite a lot of spoken lore that has been passed down through the generations and discussed as if something that happened a century ago happened only yesterday. Your thrice-great grandmother, for instance, is said to have had conversations with fishermen who never returned from the sea."

"Their spirits," Aunt Tory interjected, features animated, "would come to shore on foggy nights, it is said, smelling of brine and moaning like the wind, seaweed dragging at their feet!"

"Tory!" Aunt Stace snapped, and her sister subsided. She turned back to Karigan with an annoyed expression. "You see how these stories get embellished?"

After Karigan's own experiences with the spirits of the dead, she could not discount Aunt Tory's description, but she simply nodded.

"There were others in your mother's line," Aunt Stace said, "who were held to be uncommonly *knowing.*"

"Uncommonly knowing?"

All four aunts nodded.

"Knew things beyond normal ken," Aunt Gretta explained. "About the weather, the fishing, and peoples' lives. The future."

"Your mother," Aunt Brini said, glancing up from her needlework, "laughed when she heard such talk, and said they were just stories. She was a very practical woman with her feet planted squarely on the ground, except for her penchant for riding out at night as Stace already told you. Of course, we all have some odd habits, like Gretta who must make her bed at least three times before she is satisfied."

"I do not!"

"Hah! You do, too! I've counted."

"Well, you only eat one thing on your plate at a time," Aunt Gretta said.

Aunt Brini sniffed and punched her needle through cloth. "It's a texture thing."

Aunt Stace rolled her eyes. "Your mother's family," she told Karigan, "was mostly well-regarded on the island, for not all held as harsh a view toward magic as our father did. There were a few, certainly, who might smile to your grandmother Gray's face, then make the sign of the crescent moon when she looked away, and some whispered of witches in the family and other rubbish. But on the whole? They were considered law-abiding, productive members of the village who followed the traditional ways. They even endured the rantings of the moon priest on rest days."

"Why didn't anyone ever tell me this?" Karigan asked. Magic in her mother's line? The brandy was beginning to look good.

"You never asked," Aunt Stace replied. "And no doubt our own antipathy for our past on the island made us reluctant to discuss it. But getting back to your father, he was so smitten by Kariny, he'd defend her and her family's honor if he heard someone make a remark about their more uncanny side. This usually led to fights."

"Black eyes and bloody noses," Aunt Brini intoned, nodding.

"Not to mention an additional beating from our father," Aunt Stace said, "who believed all the lore about the Grays and did not approve of Stevic's interest in the youngest girl. If he spoke her name, or even glanced her way, out came the switch."

"Which of course," Aunt Gretta said, "did not stop Stevic one jot. One evening our father spotted Stevic carrying some burden for Kariny from the village mercantile. The whipping he received—it was ferocious. That's when he left the island."

"He promised to come back for Kariny," Aunt Tory said, "as soon as he found work, made his way in the world. We had no hope of ever seeing him again, but his love for Kariny made him true. He came back and sailed away with her. We soon followed."

"Kariny never doubted him," Aunt Gretta mused, and the others murmured in agreement.

And that brings us back to *you*," Aunt Stace said. "Taking into consideration your own touch of magic, it is our belief that the lore about Kariny's bloodline wasn't just stories as she claimed. That uncanny touch has come down to you."

Karigan had already arrived at the same conclusion. It only made sense. How else could she explain the Rider call and her minor ability with magic? Where else would it have come from?

She wondered how powerful her ancestors were, but she

was sure her aunts would have told her if they knew; if there was anything of note from the island lore. Perhaps, just like Karigan, their abilities were minor, remained buried just below the surface, dormant until awakened. Karigan's own surfaced because of the Rider call. The Green Rider brooch she wore, a winged horse, augmented her ability to fade from sight, seemingly to vanish.

She brushed her fingers over her brooch, the gold smooth and cool. Her aunts probably saw some other piece of jewelry, or maybe nothing at all, for a spell of concealment had been placed on the brooches long ago allowing only Riders to perceive them properly.

"Your father," Aunt Stace said, "loves you. Loves you deeply. He was not thinking when he spoke out earlier."

Despite her aunt's reassurance, her father's words still hurt. Karigan's hand went to the moonstone in her pocket. She believed her father was very much in denial about her mother. *Perfect,* he had called her. Pure from the taint of magic.

Karigan shook her head, thinking she should just pack up her scant belongings and begin the journey back to Sacor City. Coming home had been a mistake, though she wasn't sure how she could have gotten out of an errand assigned her directly by the captain. All she had done was stir up turmoil. The brothel and her father's pirate past no longer seemed to matter.

Then she remembered she couldn't leave without her father's reply to the captain's message. That meant having to face him, but at least it would be as a king's messenger, not as his daughter.

Just as Karigan resolved to leave as soon as she could, the kitchen door opened and her father entered, cold air drafting around him. "I have hitched up the sleigh," he told her. "Grab a coat. We are going into town."

⋞ ARROWDALE ⋟

Karigan outfitted herself in an old wool coat, wrapped the scarf that Aunt Brini insisted she wear around her neck, and pulled on heavy mittens. In the sleigh was a thick, coarse blanket she and her father could throw over their laps, and sea-rounded cobbles that had been heated at the hearth to keep their feet warm.

Her father took up reins and coach whip, clucked to the pair of drays, Roy and Birdy, and the sleigh lurched forward. The sun had broken clear of clouds and clumps of snow dropped from fir boughs along the drive as they glided along.

The air felt lighter, not so bitter, and the chatter of birds reminded Karigan the worst of winter was done and spring was on the way.

"Why are we going to town?" Karigan asked.

"You shall see."

Karigan settled beneath the blanket, slightly annoyed. She said no more, however, figuring her father would reveal his purpose in his own time, and no sooner, even if she pestered him. So she kept her peace as the horses paced steady on through drifts, their brasses and harnesses jingling in a cheerful rhythm.

The G'ladheon estate sat in the country just outside of Corsa, and once they joined the main road, they picked up speed, for the road wardens had already knocked down drifts and compacted the snow. Such maintenance was spotty throughout the realm, but Corsa was prosperous, and the city masters paid attention not only to the harbor, but to the roads as well, knowing that while a great deal of trade happened along the waterfront, goods must also be transported to and from the harbor overland. Proper road upkeep, they asserted, could only promote the city's continued prosperity and its reputation as the foremost merchant port in the lands.

Soon the woods thinned, opening up to field and pasture, the snow smooth across the landscape like thickened cream and undisturbed save for the meandering tracks of hare and fox. Houses appeared with more frequency as they approached Corsa. Karigan could sense the ocean, too, feel the moist draft of it upon the air. And still her father did not speak. He just sat there, subtly guiding the horses, his gaze fixed on the road.

In Corsa proper, the streets were lined with homes and shops, folk sweeping and shoveling snow off front doorsteps. Children played in the street throwing snowballs at one another, and a few shoppers struggled along on uncertain footing.

Her father halted the sleigh before a poulterer's shop with plucked chickens, geese, and turkeys displayed in the window.

"I'll be back momentarily," he said. He hopped out of the sleigh and entered the shop, returning minutes later with a large, dressed turkey, and deposited it in the back of the sleigh.

He left her again for other shops, returning with a huge wheel of cheese, a sack of flour, a jug of molasses, a tub of butter, and other foodstuffs to amply fill any larder. Karigan could only watch in astonishment as the back of the sleigh was filled up. She did not think Cook's pantry had been so barren.

"What is . . . ?" she started to ask, when finally he sat beside her again and collected the reins.

"You'll see," he said.

He guided the sleigh onto Garden Street. It wasn't a particularly gardenlike neighborhood, even when it wasn't winter. Still, it was a solid street of middle- to lower-class merchants and tradesmen. Their houses stood tightly together, smoke issuing from chimneys.

Her father brought the drays to a halt in front of a tall narrow house sided with cedar shakes, just like all the others.

"This is Garden House," he said, startling her. "We shall go in for a brief visit—it's time I brought you here, because as my heir, you will one day become its steward."

What was he talking about? Before she could ask questions, however, he said, "Look and listen, and you shall see."

He spread blankets across the backs of the horses, then removed a basket from the sleigh, leaving the rest of his purchases in the rear. He strode toward the house and Karigan could do nothing but follow.

Her father bounded up the front steps and knocked on the door. Within moments it was opened by a matronly woman with steel gray hair. At once she smiled.

"Master G'ladheon!" she exclaimed.

"Greetings, Lona," he said. "How are you?"

"Never better," the woman replied, "and now even better than better to see you. Come in, come in out of the cold!"

Karigan followed her father into the dim entry hall and was conscious of others peering from doorways and around corners.

Her father handed the basket over to Lona. "Fresh baked oat muffins," he said.

She lifted the cloth that covered them. "Ooh! They look delicious!"

"There is more out in the sleigh," her father said.

"Oh, Master G'ladheon, you shouldn't have!"

He grinned. "Of course I should have."

"Jed! Clare!" A boy and girl came running down the stairs at Lona's shout. "Master G'ladheon has brought us some things. Please unload the back of his sleigh for him."

Without taking the time to put on coats, the youngsters dashed out the door.

"You must have tea with us," Lona said, her gaze falling curiously on Karigan.

"I'm afraid we must decline. Another time perhaps. But, I wish to introduce my daughter, Karigan. One day she'll be watching over Garden House."

Lona gave Karigan a solemn curtsy. "I am pleased to meet you, mistress."

"Me, too," Karigan said, much bemused.

"We are grateful for all your father and Mistress Silva have done for us," Lona said.

Karigan glanced sharply at her father at the naming of the Golden Rudder's madam. Garden House, however, did not have the air or appearance of a brothel. She didn't know what to make of it.

"Have we any new residents?" her father asked.

Lona nodded and glanced down the hall. "Vera, dear, please come meet Master G'ladheon. Don't be shy; he is most kind."

A figure emerged from the shadows of a doorway and limped toward them. When more light fell upon her, Karigan's heart skipped a beat. Much of her face was a mass of burn scars. Karigan was immediately reminded of her friend Mara, whose own face was badly scarred when Rider barracks burned down. Karigan judged the young woman to be her own age. She did not approach closely.

"Vera," Lona said, "this is Master G'ladheon, our patron, and his daughter, Karigan."

Vera curtsied, but did not speak.

"Hello, Vera," Karigan's father said with a nod. "I want you to know you are most welcome here. Welcome to stay as long as you need. And safe."

"Thank you," Vera said in a tentative voice, and she receded back into the shadows.

Lona drew closer to Karigan and her father, and said in a low, confiding voice, "Vera's husband hurt her. Threw lamp oil on her and burned her for no reason other than his dinner was a little late." As Lona spoke, Karigan could hear the fury behind her words. "He did that, and other things. One of Mistress Silva's people brought her to us from Rivertown. It was best, we thought, she be hidden some distance away from her husband."

Karigan glanced at her father and saw his brows knitted together in anger. "You did right," he said.

Just then, Jed and Clare returned, arms loaded with some of the foodstuffs Karigan's father had purchased.

"Master G'ladheon, it's too much!" Lona said.

"There's more out there," Jed said, with wide eyes.

Karigan's father just grinned.

Lona decided Karigan must meet the rest of Garden House's residents, and one by one, they filed by to curtsy and bow to Karigan and her father. Mostly they were young women, some with children, a babe or two of suckling age among them.

Her father greeted each of them by name, and received a kiss or smile in return, none so reticent as Vera had been. Meanwhile, Jed and Clare brought in the rest of the goods from the sleigh.

There was much oohing and aahing over the size of the turkey, which seemed to dwarf Jed, and once again Lona asked that they stay for tea or supper, and once again, Karigan's father declined.

They made their good-byes and walked in silence back to the sleigh while the residents of Garden House watched and waved from the front step and windows.

As Karigan's father removed the blankets from the backs of the drays, she demanded, "What was that all about? Who were those people?"

"They are those who've come on bad times; some profoundly hurt and mistreated by those who are supposed to love and protect them. Garden House provides them refuge, when they cannot find it elsewhere.

"It was Silva's idea, actually, and she founded the first in Rivertown. It's called River House. She seeks out the abused, those with no place to go, and offers them a place for as long as they need. One in her profession has occasion to find such persons." He set the blankets in the back of the sleigh and they both climbed up onto the bench. It was cold right through the seat of Karigan's trousers.

"But why . . . ?" she began.

He clucked Roy and Birdy on. "Let us just say Silva was once in a position similar to those she aids today. She was inspired to help others because of a stranger who once helped her."

"You?"

He smiled enigmatically. "Silva and I go back a long way."

Karigan was glad he and Silva helped those in need, truly she was, but she found it difficult to reconcile the Golden Rudder and Garden House as being part of the same equation.

"Silva runs a brothel," she said.

"Yes, she does," her father replied. "It's what she knows. And, she is very good to those in her employ. She does not force them into labor or to stay as others do."

Karigan remembered Trudy, one of the prostitutes at the Golden Rudder, speaking well of Silva. But it was still a *brothel*, a business that traded in flesh. It was a demeaning profession, and just plain wrong.

Her father drove the sled down the main street of Corsa, past shops where one could purchase exotic teas and spices and other goods from afar, and by landmarks Karigan knew well from her childhood: the counting- and customshouses, the stately residence of the lord-mayor, and the offices of important merchants, including her father's. She picked out its bold, granite facade as they drove by.

A branching street was inhabited by the guild houses of the merchants, coopers, and longshoremen, among others. Another street held housing for dockworkers and shipwrights. All appeared quiet, and would remain so until the spring trading season picked up.

They paused on the brink of a hill before the street descended straight down into Corsa Harbor, to take in the view. The harbor bristled with masts, some vessels tied up to wharves, others anchored offshore or moored to buoys. The snow concealed the usual squalor of the waterfront, made it appear more quaint. Traps and nets, pilings and barrels, all the ephemera of a busy waterfront, were bumps beneath the covering of snow.

Gulls lined up on the wharves and waves thudded against wooden hulls. A way off, Karigan could make out a raft of eider ducks adrift, undismayed by the swells the storm had created. It was nearing sundown and the edges of billowing clouds were tinted orange, while small islands across the harbor, with their crowns of spiky spruce and fir, fell into silhouette.

A crumbling keep of the Second Age stood jagged on the headland of a larger island at the entrance to the harbor, maintaining a ghostly vigil over all who passed. Mordivelleo L'Petrie, a clan chief of old, had built the keep. He'd known the harbor's importance and stoutly defended it from those who'd contest him for it, namely pirates and invaders from foreign lands. After repelling a particularly ferocious assault from the Under Kingdoms, he was formally invested as the prince of the region that included the harbor, today's L'Petrie Province.

Karigan's gaze swept along the crescent contour of the shoreline, and there, near where the Grandgent River emptied into the ocean, were the warships of Sacoridia's navy, and the yards that serviced them. It was a testament to Corsa's importance as a port that the navy's largest fleet berthed in its harbor, guarding it, the realm, and the all-important river from any enemies. Mordivelleo L'Petrie, she thought, would be pleased.

"I was going to show you Garden House when you finished service with the king," her father said presently, the sunset casting an orange glow on his face as he gazed out to sea. "But it seemed appropriate to take you there today. I hope you consider it a worthy endeavor, something to keep going when the time for you to inherit comes along. Many of our residents have moved on and done well for themselves." After a long pause, he added, "I don't suppose I've redeemed myself in your eyes at all."

"Is that why you brought me to Garden House?" Karigan asked.

"I did not wish for you to judge my relationship with Silva based purely on your knowledge of the brothel."

"What *is* your relationship with Silva?"

"We are friends of long standing."

"And you're a client of her brothel."

Her father did not answer, but snapped the reins over the haunches of the drays and guided them away from the harbor.

*   *   *

They left the town behind, the sleigh gliding into the deepening dark. With the setting sun, the air chilled perceptibly and Karigan burrowed beneath the blanket. The cobbles at her feet had gone cold long ago.

She would receive no real answers about the brothel from her father. He had told her there were things he'd never discuss with her. And, she supposed, she did not want to know the specifics. What she really wanted was for none of this to have happened in the first place. She wished she had never heard of the Golden Rudder; she wished he'd deny his connection to it and say that it was all just a huge misunderstanding.

But he did not, and it was not. She could wish all she wanted, but it wouldn't change a thing.

And yet, she reflected, because of his association with the brothel and its madam, he was doing good works such as supporting Garden House, his efforts no doubt saving the lives of those like Vera. Karigan may have had a privileged upbringing, but she wasn't so naive that she didn't recognize the need for such places.

As she thought about it, she realized she'd only known a single, narrow facet of her father. Now she had discovered he was just as complicated and complex as any other person.

So absorbed in her thoughts had she been, that when the sleigh hit a bump, she was surprised to discover her father was not taking the main road home, but rather a narrow lane bordered by forest.

"Where are we?" she asked.

"Arrowdale Road," her father said.

Karigan's disorientation faded immediately. Arrowdale was a meandering old track that was the "long way" home. She used to go riding on it sometimes, but to her it had always seemed so forsaken, a little spooky. There were only a few, long abandoned homesteads along it, taken over by the march of the forest. History held that some battle of the Long War had taken place in the folds of the land, hence the name Arrowdale.

"Your mother and I used to ride out this way at night

sometimes," her father said unexpectedly. "The stars were always lovely, and no one bothered us out here."

Karigan glanced up, and between the bordering tips of evergreens, the stars were bright. The Hunter was making his seasonal trek to the west, and the Sword of Sevelon was in the half-raised position, slowly rotating upward from its winter's rest.

They entered a clearing and the full expanse of the heavens opened overhead. Her father halted Roy and Birdy to gaze at the stars and Karigan imagined her parents young and in love coming to this spot.

"Now that you know I am quite imperfect," he said, "can you accept that I misspoke earlier? I can't say I like magic, or the fact it puts you in harm's way, but I would never view my daughter as cursed."

"You never told me about mother's bloodline," Karigan said.

"Stories. Stories told by superstitious islanders." He paused, then said, "Tell me, where did you find the muna'riel?"

"You knew of it then?"

She perceived, more than saw, him nodding.

"I found it in mother's chest among her things."

"How did it . . . ? I had it locked in my sea chest, down in the study." He shuddered beside her. "Magic. I guess it wanted to be found."

It was, Karigan thought, a perceptive statement from one with an aversion to magic. "You didn't give it to me as mother wanted."

Silence followed her words, then he said, "I desired to protect you from the magic. Or, at least not encourage it. I even let your aunts believe your mother was speaking nonsense in the end."

Karigan wished she could see his features better in the dark, but she imagined his expression downcast to match his voice.

"I see I was wrong," he continued. "Magic found you anyway. Do you have the muna'riel with you? May I see it?"

Karigan dug beneath her coat and into her pocket to retrieve the moonstone. She held it aloft on her mittened hand, the shock of light making the horses snort and bob their heads. The brilliance of the stone chased shadows deep into the woods, and the snow in the clearing intensified the silver-white light almost to blinding.

Karigan's father shielded his eyes until the light ebbed to a more gentle glow. The snow on the trees that ringed them glittered as if strewn with diamonds.

"I forgot how bright it was," he murmured. "I can't remember when your mother first showed it to me. After we were married, of course, but before you were even conceived, I think. She never explained how she had acquired it, but she said it was Eletian. When I pressed her about it, she'd only laugh and find ways to distract me."

"She knew how you felt about magic," Karigan said.

"Yes, I suppose she did. And I suppose I chose not to see it in her, even though the muna'riel would light only for her and not me."

"I wish I could help you understand," Karigan said, "that it's not the magic itself that is evil or good, but the user who makes it so."

But he did not reply. He sat there, his eyelids drooping and head nodding until his chin rested on his chest. He breathed deeply as though asleep.

"Father?" Karigan asked. She nudged him, but he did not stir. She jabbed him harder, and still no response. He seemed only to sleep, but . . .

She glanced at the horses, and they stood with heads lowered as if also slumbering.

A light blossomed in the center of the clearing. A silvery, fluid flame that flickered and grew into a column the height of a person.

"Five hells," she murmured.

The light of Karigan's moonstone spread toward the flame, surrounding it as if to embrace it.

Finally, a voice said, *you have come.*

⋖ MOON DREAMS ⋗

Transfixed, Karigan stepped off the sleigh, her feet sinking deeply into the snow. A figure rippled within the column of flame.

"What are you?" she whispered.

The figure did not answer, but its radiance grew, spread outward, and though Karigan backed away, it overtook her until there was only the light. Everything else, her father, the sleigh and horses, and the surrounding forest, vanished into shadow. She could not say for sure she was still in the clearing, or even in Sacoridia for that matter, though the snow still glared with its reflected light.

I am weakening, said the figure in the flame; a woman's voice, distant, strained. *Under siege ... for so long ...*

"Who ... who are you?"

Losing hold ...

"Of what?" Karigan demanded. What was this? What was going on?

The grove. The figure shimmered, cried out in pain, and Karigan discerned darkness staining the fringes of the light, black branches scratching against radiance.

You must come. The voice held a desperate tenor. *You cross thresholds.*

Cross thresholds ... The words kindled some memory buried deep in Karigan's mind and came to her like the shreds of a dream: the spirit of a Green Rider, a quiver of arrows strapped to his back, the royal tombs. *When we fade,* he said, *we are standing on a threshold.* Something about passing through the layers of the world.

She grasped at the shreds of the memory, but it dissipated

until she could not recall even the ghost and was left with only an impression of something missing. Karigan rubbed her temple. Her head felt strange, full of cobwebs. "Where is it I must come?"

The figure extended her hand of quicksilver from the flame, and a globe, much like a snowglobe, hovered above her palm. Karigan stepped closer to see it better, squinting against the intensity of the figure's radiance. The globe was a blotch of blackness in the light and as she neared it, she discerned in it the scene of a dark forest of decay and murk.

Karigan recoiled. "Blackveil?"

You must help the Sleepers, the figure said, her voice increasing in urgency. *If awakened by the enemy, they shall be a deadly weapon.* She cried again in pain and the light wavered. *I am losing hold!*

"Sleepers? What . . . ?"

The dark on the edges of light began to close around them like a claw. *Keep the muna'riel close, daughter of Kariny. It is your key.*

The figure and her flame sputtered like a dying candle.

"Wait!" Karigan cried. "The key to what?"

You will recall our encounter only when you are given the feather of the winter owl.

The figure dimmed and waned, writhed as though in the throes of some agony.

"Please!" Karigan cried. "You must tell me more!"

I . . . I cannot hold on, I— The figure screamed and her flame extinguished.

The world was cast into a midnight void and Karigan staggered back, her muna'riel dimming as if in sympathy. The globe that contained the scene of Blackveil hovered in the air for a moment before rupturing and, for a single instant, transported Karigan to the forest, its rotten tree limbs arcing over her, clawing for her, the mud of the forest floor sucking at her feet, the wild screech of some creature seeking blood piercing the thick, wet air. Then the vision was gone and the shattered pieces of the globe cascaded into the snow like crystals of ice.

There was a sigh upon the wind and an anguished whisper that came to Karigan from far, far away: *Argenthyne*.

Then silence.

Karigan stood there in the deep snow of the clearing, the muna'riel glowing on the palm of her hand. Before she had a chance to grasp the apparition and her words about Sleepers, thresholds, keys, and Blackveil, or even the reference to her mother, the filament of memory was drawn from her so it was as if none of it had ever happened.

"We are nearly home."

Karigan started at her father's voice. The sleigh was in motion, the brasses and silver of the harnesses jingling. The drays stepped at a good pace, knowing they were headed for the barn.

"What happened?" Karigan asked, looking about herself, but discerning little in the dark.

"All my talk put you to sleep, I guess."

Karigan tried to remember back, but it was all so foggy. They'd stopped in a clearing. "We were talking about the moonstone." She patted her pocket and felt the bulge of it there.

"Yes, and I was trying to apologize."

They rounded a bend and ahead were the lights of the G'ladheon manor house. Her father halted the drays once more and turned to her.

"No matter what," he said, "you are my daughter and I love you. I am trying to be at peace with the magic. Just know I am proud of you, and of the accolades you've received. I'm glad the king recognizes your worth—he is a good man, and our land is fortunate to have one such as he as our sovereign."

He paused, perhaps gathering his thoughts, and rubbed his chin. "I just hope you can one day forgive me for the secrets I have kept, but also understand why I cannot apologize for the choices I've made in my life."

Karigan felt depleted of anger. It was clear he had never

stopped loving her mother, and if he did not exactly like magic, he was at least trying to accept that it was a part of her life. She did not like the secrets, but acknowledged all those she kept herself.

She could not pick and choose the parts of her father she liked and disliked. His dealings with the brothel and piracy were part of the same package as the successful merchant and loving husband and father. All of it made him who he was.

That's what love was about, right? Accepting the bad along with the good and without condition?

"You and your mother were always the most important things in my life," he said. "I lost her, and I do not want to lose you."

"I know," Karigan said.

They hugged, and being in her father's arms once again made her life as a Green Rider, and all the battles and dangers she'd endured, seem very far off. She was once again a daughter, finding safety and comfort in her father's embrace.

A couple days later, Karigan stood at the cairn of stones that covered her mother's grave. Her father had seen Kariny buried in the old way, the way of the islands, with her head oriented toward the dawn. Karigan's aunts said he'd erected the cairn himself in his grief, day after day bearing rocks and thrusting them onto the pile. Some were enormous and she wondered how he had managed it. According to her aunts, he would accept no assistance, and by the look in their eyes when they recounted the story, she could tell how difficult it had been for them to witness his pain.

Karigan remembered little of it. Only that her mother wasn't there, and people dressed in somber colors had spoken in hushed tones around her, and that all the windows and mirrors had been draped, leaving the house in a perpetual state of darkness.

The cairn was coated in ice. In the intervening day since the storm, the sun had shone bright and warm enough to melt snow, which refroze during the night, forming a glaze of ice that cascaded over the rocks like a waterfall trapped in time.

Beside the cairn was a monolith of granite, as if heaved

up from the earth itself. Her mother's name was carved on it, along with the inscription: *Of the island born, to the starlit heavens embraced.* The sign of the crescent moon topped the inscription, and the face of the rock was carved with a looping design that reminded Karigan of fishermen's knots. It represented continuity, no beginning, no end.

Karigan held the moonstone in her hand, its light muted by sunshine, but its inner glow still brilliant. She'd searched the house top to bottom to see if she could find further clues of her mother interacting with Eletians, but she found nothing. She guessed everyone had secrets, even her mother, who took hers to the grave.

She thought to leave the moonstone on the cairn as a sort of offering, but something inside her fought the notion. Her mother had meant for her to have it, after all, and she did not want to go against Kariny's wishes. She returned it to her pocket.

Finally she kissed her fingertips, touched them to one of the icy boulders of the cairn, and departed along the wooded path that led back to the house.

She arrived just as the stablemaster led a groomed and tacked Condor out onto the drive. The gelding bobbed his head upon seeing her, eager to be off.

"He's a fine fellow," the stablemaster said as she approached. "I'll miss him." Condor gave him a nudge, almost knocking him over. Karigan smiled.

Her father, resplendent in a long beaver fur coat, and her aunts emerged from the house to bid her farewell. She hugged them one by one.

"Are you sure you have to leave already?" Aunt Stace asked.

"I think I've drawn out my stay as long as I can," Karigan replied. "I must return to duty."

"Well, don't forget us here," Aunt Brini said.

"I won't. Of course I won't."

Aunt Gretta dabbed her eyes with a handkerchief. "You must write us every day."

"Er, I'll try." Karigan grimaced. She was not known as the most diligent of letter writers.

"Oh, stop sniveling, Gretta," said Aunt Tory. She took Karigan's hand. "Now, dear, there is a fine young man down Bellmere way, of good stock, whom we think—"

"No!" Karigan pulled away from her aunt. "No matchmaking!" She remembered all too vividly the fiasco of her father's last attempt.

"If you turn down every male we dangle in front of you, you'll end up like us—alone and without husbands."

"I never thought it so bad," Aunt Brini said.

"I should think not," Karigan's father grumbled. "With me to support you, you want for nothing."

This pronouncement was followed by sisterly remonstration. Aunt Gretta flicked her handkerchief at her brother.

"See what I must endure?" he asked Karigan. "They are forever uniting against me." This incurred yet more sounds of disdain. He grinned and handed Karigan a purse.

"What's this?" she asked, knowing precisely what it was by its weight.

"A little currency to help you get by."

"But—"

"Yes, I know. You earn pay for your work, and room and board, but such a pittance does not help you purchase the occasional trinket."

"But—"

"And, you never know, but your aunts might find the right young man for you and you'll need something special to wear. With your new title, I imagine there will be dozens of suitors tripping over themselves for your favor."

Her aunts nodded eagerly at this and Karigan scowled, but she knew it was of little use to try and return the purse. She'd use some of the currency to bring her friends treats from Master Gruntler's Sugary, but most she'd leave at Garden House. Yes, she liked that idea very much.

"And here is my message for Captain Mapstone," he said, drawing the letter from beneath his coat.

Karigan slipped it into her message satchel and embraced him one last time.

"Take care of yourself," he said. "Stay out of trouble."

"You, too," she replied in earnest. She was both sad and

relieved to be leaving her father and aunts. She would miss them, but not all the complicated expectations and emotions that came with family.

She mounted Condor, and as they set off, she overheard Aunt Stace say, "Now Stevic, what is this business about a brothel?"

There was silence, then a quick exchange of words.

Uh oh, Karigan thought. Her father was in for it now.

Before she lost sight of the house at the bend in the drive, she turned to wave one last time, but no one saw her. Her aunts were clustered around her father, apparently deep in heated discussion, arms gesticulating wildly.

Karigan could not help but smile.

She rode on, unaware of a winter owl, in its snowy plumage, perched high up in a tree, watching her as she passed below.

 A HOWLING IN
THE WOODS

"**H**ah! Three knights—I win!" Laren Map-stone, captain of His Majesty's Messenger Service, the Green Riders, slapped her cards down on the rough-hewn table and grinned in triumph.

The man across from her, older, weatherworn, his hair faded to a creamy white, gazed mournfully at his queen and pair of ships.

"No need to gloat," he said.

A pile of chestnuts sat in the middle of the table and Laren drew them all toward herself. A few rolled off onto the dirt floor. "Mine! All mine!"

"I guess that's it, then," the man said. "I'm all out."

"You are?" When Laren looked, she saw he hadn't a single chestnut left.

"You'd have thought I'd learned not to gamble with you years ago."

"What do you say we roast the loot then?" Laren asked.

Elgin Foxsmith, retired Chief Rider of the Green Riders—the first Laren ever served under—collected the chestnuts and dumped them into a pan and placed them before the hearth. He threw another log on the fire and limped back to his seat at the table.

Two horses and a donkey watched the proceedings in the dim, one-room cabin through a window cut into the wall of the adjoining stable. One horse was Laren's gelding, Blue-bird, and the other, Elgin's mare, Killdeer. Killdeer was getting on in years, her sweet face looking grayer than ever, and Laren worried how Elgin would cope when the time came for her to pass on. He lived a solitary life out here in the woods, claiming he'd had enough of all kinds of people during his stint in the messenger service to last a lifetime.

She worried about him all alone out here, especially with the harsh winter they'd had, so she made a point of visiting him as often as she could, bringing him news, preserves, books, blankets—anything she thought he might need. He was nearly self-sufficient, keeping a garden, a milk cow, sheep, and some chickens. Hunting and fishing rounded out his larder.

And while reclusive, he wasn't entirely a hermit. He made periodic trips to the village to acquire goods, like fodder and grain. Still, he wasn't getting any younger, and Laren did not know how much longer he could handle this rugged life on his own.

A *bang-clatter* in the stable made Laren jump.

"Bucket!" Elgin shouted. "Enough!"

Bucket was the donkey, and Killdeer's companion. He had a habit of banging his food bucket around, hence his name. He was, Elgin claimed, not much good for anything, but Killdeer liked him so he remained. Laren knew that without Bucket, the garden would not be tilled, wood would not be hauled in, and items couldn't be carted in from the village.

"So, Laren said, "have you considered my offer?" This time, she came not only to check on Elgin's welfare, but to present him with a proposition.

Elgin grumbled something, then passed his hands through his hair. "Don't think I can go back there, Red. Besides, my brooch abandoned me a long time ago."

"Unless I'm mistaken, your knowledge and experience have not."

"All those people crammed into one place," he muttered. "And who would look after the girls? I can't just leave them."

Elgin referred to his chickens and the cow. "I don't know," Laren said, "but there are ways, it seems to me. And if you don't like the work or being back at the castle, you could leave anytime."

"And what about your current Chief Rider, eh? Can't she handle the job?"

"Mara is a wonderful Chief Rider."

"See? You don't need me. Besides, I wouldn't want to step on her toes."

"You wouldn't. Our numbers have more than doubled over the last year. Mara has only just recovered from terrible wounds, and while the winter has kept our senior Riders close to home and helping with training, spring is nearing and soon Zachary will have them off on errands."

The cabin shuddered in a gust of wind as if to counter her words.

"Heh, hard to think of the prince a man full-grown, and getting married, too," Elgin said.

"King," Laren reminded him. *"King* Zachary."

"Er, right. Just a lad when I last saw him." Elgin had served Zachary's grandmother, Queen Isen. He sighed. "Look, I appreciate you thinking of me, Red, but too much time has passed. I don't know how things work up there at the castle anymore. I'd be no better than a green Greenie myself. Besides, I've no mind to be scraping and bowing to all the gentry. All those people! I'm my own man here."

Laren folded her hands on the table before her. They were roughened and calloused, and nicked with scars. They looked old to her. Just as old as she sometimes felt, especially when she got up in the morning all aching and stiff. She could appreciate Elgin's desire to stick to his life out here in the cabin—no need to adapt to the expectations of others, which, she thought, was all she'd ever done. She couldn't remember a time when there weren't orders to follow, or to issue. Her life was not her own, yet she did not resent it, for the messenger service gave her purpose.

Elgin was well beyond her in years, but she was now older than he was when he retired. In fact, most Riders left the messenger service within four or five years, if they were not killed doing their duty first. But the calling still clung to her as strongly as it had when she first came to the service some twenty years or more ago. It appeared there was work for her yet to do, so long as she was not cut down in the process.

"There is another reason I request that you come to assist in the training of the new Riders," she said. "The king is preparing—quietly, mind you—for conflict. He does not know when or how, but he wishes to be prepared."

"Conflict? Is this about the Blackveil business?"

Laren nodded. She had regularly apprised him of all that had come to pass during each of her visits, and especially the involvement of the Green Riders. "Mornhavon the Black will return sooner or later, and we're already contending with Second Empire. We've word they're consolidating their forces." Green Riders had died trying to bring back the information.

Elgin scratched a bristly cheek, deep in thought. Presently he said, "I am an old man. What am I against all that?"

"We're not asking you to solve the world's problems," Laren replied. "Just to help us so we can take care of it. Maybe you don't remember how young some Riders can be. Our newest boy just turned twelve. Your experience will help give them what they need to survive—prepare them for the storm to come."

He turned away and she wondered if she said the wrong thing, hit too close to his heart. The cabin dimmed even more and creaked in the wind. Sparkling snow blew through cracks in the chinking and beneath the door. The horses and Bucket watched with ears perked, as if expecting some momentous proclamation.

But Elgin remained silent.

"I'd better get going," Laren said, rising from her bench. "I want to reach the city before it gets dark. The clouds were building like it might snow again."

Elgin nodded. "Best take your chestnuts with you. Should be ready by now."

Shortly after, roasted chestnuts warmed Laren's coat pockets as she sat astride Bluebird. It was already snowing and it looked like it could really pick up.

"Be careful," Elgin said from his doorway. Snow mounded the path to either side of him, and a thick layer overhung his roof. "I've lost some sheep to critters. Been thinking about getting a dog."

Laren thought a dog a sensible idea. "You be careful, too, Chief. And if you decide to give us a hand, know that you'll have the gratitude of your king. And me."

He made a dismissive gesture and went back inside. Laren reined Bluebird down the path away from the cabin.

"I think he's interested," she confided to her horse. "At least he didn't tell me to go to the five hells."

Bluebird snorted and Laren slapped his neck.

The snow fell heavily, dropping through the woods in curtains. It damped down the world, blanketing it all in an eerie hush, except for the creak of a tree limb or the thud of Bluebird's hooves.

Laren was glad the path from Elgin's cabin was wide enough for his cart, for it made the way obvious in the snow, when a narrower track would have been obscured, the terrain and sameness of the trees disorienting. She supposed if she got lost, Bluebird would know the way home, but it was, nevertheless, reassuring to have a clear path to follow.

She rode on, warm in her fur-lined greatcoat, confident in spite of the weather and the fading daylight. The rhythm of Bluebird's steady pace and the mesmerizing flurries floating down down down, allowed her to lose herself in an array of mundane thoughts. What was the next day's schedule? Meetings. There were always meetings, and piles of paperwork, and checking on the progress of the new Riders. Many did not have even a rudimentary education, so in addition to learning court etiquette, how to handle a sword, and ride, they must also be taught writing, reading, figuring, and geography. The long winter had been a bonus, keeping her senior Riders available to assist.

A howl raked the serenity of the forest. Bluebird sidestepped nervously. Caught unaware as she was, Laren kept her seat by sheer instinct. No sooner did she steady Bluebird when the howl came again.

Wolves? she wondered.

More cries followed, some closer, some farther away, and the hair on the nape of her neck stood.

Ordinarily she wouldn't be too concerned about the wild creatures, as they tended to shy from people, but with such a severe winter, she imagined they were desperate for a meal. Bluebird was definitely a prey animal, and if the howling creatures were starving, they would overcome their natural fear of her.

She urged Bluebird forward into a trot, peering into the graying forest, and the cries came again, louder, closer, all around her. If she pushed Bluebird into a gallop, wouldn't it just incite pursuit?

When the cries filled the forest again, they didn't sound quite right. Not exactly like wolves or coyotes. There was an almost human quality to them.

Groundmites.

"Bloody hell," Laren muttered, and from the corner of her eye she caught the movement of a manlike figure lumbering among the trees. Manlike, but not human.

Then she saw another and another . . .

She drew her saber and jabbed her heels into Bluebird's sides. If winter had been rough on other creatures, it was certainly hard on groundmites. Starvation must have driven them this far into Sacoridia.

Bluebird kicked up snow as he lunged forward. Laren crouched low over his neck, the hilt of her saber gripped firmly in her gloved hand.

The groundmites, no longer attempting to conceal themselves, rushed her and Bluebird, waving clubs and primitive hatchets, their cries chilling. As Bluebird charged by them, Laren saw only a blur of their furred and snarling faces. The groundmites flung themselves out of the forest into the path trying to block her way. She cut one down, then another, blood spraying across snow.

Enough of the creatures scrambled into the path that they obstructed it; others charged in from the sides. Laren spun Bluebird on his haunches only to find the groundmites had cut her off from behind as well. They had effectively tightened the noose around her.

Her only chance was to fight through and make for Elgin's cabin, and there they might make a stand.

She hacked off a clawed hand that reached for Bluebird's bridle and blocked a descending hatchet. She drove her saber into the groundmite's neck.

These groundmites were cloaked in rags and hides, pitiful, really. None appeared to be wearing armor, which improved her chances.

Bluebird kicked one from behind and she heard a wet sound like a melon being smashed. A club hammered her left thigh and she swept her sword over Bluebird's neck to slash the groundmite's face. It mewled in pain and fell away.

Bluebird plunged at their attackers, kicked and bit them, trying to break free even as he received blows all over. It only enraged him more and he bellowed a challenge before striking down another groundmite with his front hooves.

Laren was tiring, and she knew Bluebird was, too. If they did not break free soon, they'd be in deep trouble.

None of the groundmites seemed to be armed with a sharp blade, and just as she was thanking the gods for it, a short sword swept at her from out of nowhere, catching her coat. Chestnuts poured from her slashed pocket.

She parried a second blow, then hacked into the skull of another groundmite that clubbed at Bluebird's face. Her saber stuck in bone, and in that moment, the short sword flashed toward her.

She saw the inevitable. She would fall, and so would Bluebird.

⋙ ARROWS ⋘

As the short sword drove toward Laren, everything slowed. It had happened to her before in battle, this stretching of time, allowing her to absorb minute details. She saw the twitch of the groundmite's catlike ears, its yellow fangs, and its gaunt form beneath its rags and patchy fur. Yes, it was definitely suffering from starvation.

She saw the blade, rusted and dirty and notched. She discerned individual snowflakes drifting down between her and the groundmite.

Even as time stretched, however, she could not free her own sword to block the thrust.

What a pity, she thought, for there was so much left to do, so much left unresolved. She would not be around to support Zachary as his kingship was tested to its utmost. She would not be there for her Riders when so many of them were young and untried.

And what about Melry, on the cusp of womanhood? A difficult age. Laren had adopted her when she was found abandoned as a baby in the Rider stables. Now Laren was abandoning her.

As the sword's point closed in, hoofbeats that were not Bluebird's pounded the ground.

"*Red!*" Elgin cried.

Just before the sword impaled Laren, just at the last, possible moment, Bluebird reared.

The sword missed. It missed and stabbed into her saddle, through leather, into the wooden frame.

Before Bluebird reached the apex of his rear, arrows

whispered by her, skimmed so close she felt the trailing air. White arrows slicing through the flurries on a resolute and deadly course.

They were not meant for her.

They were aimed as if to anticipate her movements and Bluebird's, so perfectly coordinated she wondered if the archers moved through time differently. If everything slowed for them, too.

The arrows thudded into the groundmites and they fell away. By the time Bluebird's front hooves touched ground again, none remained standing. Groundmites lay piled around her, bristling with white arrows.

Bluebird's sides heaved and he blew puffs of steam from his nostrils. Elgin sat astride Killdeer some paces ahead of her. Even at this distance she saw how wide his eyes were.

Taking a breath—had she breathed at all during the attack?—she turned her gaze toward the source of the arrows. There, all in white against the backdrop of snow, stood three Eletians, each holding a longbow.

Elgin was the first to move, trotting up on Killdeer and glancing sidelong at the Eletians.

"Red! You all right?"

"I . . . I think so," Laren replied, stunned just to be alive. Westrion was not ready to deliver her to the heavens this day after all. She nudged Bluebird forward, and once she was clear of the corpses of groundmites and the trampled, crimson snow, she dismounted, staggering when she touched ground. Already the exertion was catching up with her, and she'd be feeling it for days. Her thigh throbbed where she'd been clubbed.

Not as young as I used to be, she thought, as she often did. She wiped the blood off her saber in the snow and sheathed it.

Elgin dismounted and led Killdeer over to her. The mare did not look the least bit winded, despite what must have been a hard ride from the cabin.

Elgin looked Laren over as if to make sure she was all right for himself. "I heard that howling," he said, "and knew you were in for it. Killdeer was practically busting the wall down to get out."

Laren noted he'd ridden out bareback, hadn't even taken the time to saddle the mare. He wore his old Rider-issued saber, the sheath and belt well oiled. She guessed the blade was in just as fine shape and honed to a razor's edge.

"Who are your friends?" he whispered.

Laren glanced at the Eletians. Two were picking among the dead groundmites, retrieving arrows. A third approached, striding effortlessly through—on?—the snow.

Laren recognized her flaxen hair, drawn back in braids and adorned with white feathers. Graelalea was her name. She was sister to Jametari, prince of the Eletians.

"Greetings, Captain," she said, coming to a halt before Laren and Elgin. "This is an auspicious meeting."

Laren swallowed back a surge of hysterical laughter. The words were said as if it were some everyday occurrence, like they'd bumped into one another on market day.

"Auspicious," Laren said, "seems an inadequate description. The groundmites—you arrived just in time."

"We heard them, knew they were on the hunt. Our paths, you see, run near this place."

Laren was too dazed "to see," but she nodded. "I thank you. You saved my life."

"It is well," Graelalea said. "And now we may proceed to your king."

"What?"

"Our meeting is auspicious for we travel to speak with your king. Our paths have crossed, therefore we shall travel together."

Laren closed her mouth when she realized it was hanging open. Elgin's expression registered awe tinged with wariness.

Eletians were like that—enchanting, unearthly, the embodiment of *magic*. It was difficult to know the Eletian mind, for they'd been absent from the world for so long, their ways were alien. And they were dangerous. Laren had no doubt about it. She had only to look at the pile of dead groundmites behind her.

"My horse," she said, "is tired. He needs rest and care."

Graelalea made a graceful gesture indicating Laren should look at her horse. When she did, she saw the other two Eletians caressing Bluebird's muscles and applying salve to cuts.

Graelalea herself set aside her longbow and stepped up to Bluebird. She spoke softly to him in Eletian and ran her hand down his nose, over his eyes, behind his ears. His eyelids drooped and his breathing softened. He lowered his head so that it rested in her hands. Killdeer appeared to watch and listen with interest, her ears pricked up and her gaze alert.

"He is well enough to continue," Graelalea said in the common tongue. "We shall travel lightly." Then, observing Killdeer's interest, she turned to the mare and petted her. Killdeer curved her neck and loosed a deep sigh at the attention.

Laren and Elgin exchanged wide-eyed looks.

"She is an old soul," Graelalea said of Killdeer, "but with a young heart. She will be your good companion for years more."

An amazing transformation rippled across Elgin's face. The hard lines softened and Laren thought her old chief was going to weep. But he did not. Almost more astonishingly, he bowed to the Eletian.

"Thank you," he said. "I have never heard finer words."

There was a hint of a smile on Graelalea's face. They all stood there as the snow fell down around them in dizzying swirls and the forest darkened.

"I'll ... I'll take care of the corpses in the morning," Elgin said, as if needing to break the silence. "Whatever the scavengers leave, anyway."

Graelalea nodded and turned to Laren. "Captain? Are you ready?"

"I ... I guess so."

"If you mount and ride, we will travel more swiftly."

While they were on foot? But Laren did not question the Eletian. She put her foot in the stirrup and mounted Bluebird, grimacing at sore muscles making themselves felt.

"Sip some of this," Graelalea said, and she passed Laren a flask.

Laren took a cautious sip, and then another. She'd tasted its like before when the Eletians last visited Sacor City. It was cool on the tongue, but heartening, and as the liquid passed down her throat it warmed her body. She thought of summer meadows and the golden sunrise on dew-laden grasses. It removed her from winter and loosened aching muscles and joints, restored strength and energy.

A small amount slaked her thirst and she took one more sip before giving the flask back.

"It's wonderful," she said.

"A summer cordial of Eletia," Graelalea replied.

They bade Elgin farewell and simply walked into the woods. Graelalea led, with Bluebird following, and the other two Eletians ranging alongside or behind. Laren wondered if she were being led into some trap, as Karigan had once been trapped—caught up in spells and a web of dreams. But she did not think so. What reason had they? Just to be sure, she used her special ability and perceived from them no guile, only the truth. Truth and peace. Satisfied, she gave in to trust.

As night deepened, Graelalea produced a moonstone. Its light was not glaring to the eye, but produced a soft radiance that captured each snowflake that fell around them, flashing like silver glitter. Even with the light, however, Laren could not discern the path Graelalea followed, though the Eletian strode ahead without hesitation, entirely certain of her way.

It was almost a passage through a dream with no sense of time or place. Her whole world existed within the glow cast by the moonstone—the snow, her horse beneath her, the gray boles of trees they passed by, and Graelalea leading them. Laren felt buoyant, as light and insubstantial as the snowflakes that landed on her hair and eyelashes.

The Eletians glided through the forest so unhindered that Laren thought this must be one of the ancient paths they used long ago to travel into the land now known as Sacoridia. Graelalea's brother, the prince, had spoken of them. He said the land recalled them.

Did the trees bend out of their way and the terrain mold itself to make their footing smooth? Laren almost laughed at the notion, but it *was* uncanny how she did not have to duck beneath branches and Bluebird did not stumble over uneven ground. There was not a single snag to circumvent their progress or a fallen log to step over.

A time passed and they stepped out of the woods. The illumination of the moonstone spread around them revealing a snow-covered field. Laren, disoriented by the change, took a few moments to recognize where they were.

Graelalea suddenly extinguished the moonstone, and when Laren's eyes adjusted to the absence of its glow, she picked out the flickering of lights in the distance. The gates of Sacor City were not far.

"Let us continue," Graelalea said. "We shall speak to your king soon."

So mesmerized by the journey had Laren become, that she had forgotten its purpose. She shook herself as if to awaken from a long sleep.

"What is it you wish to speak to him about?"

"Kanmorhan Vane," Graelalea replied.

Blackveil. This time the shudder was involuntary.

⟪ AN INVITATION ⟫

Once Laren entered the city gates with the Eletians, she sent a guard up the Winding Way to inform the king of their arrival. When they reached the castle, they were ushered into a meeting chamber, which was warmed by blazing hearths at either end; the table was set with an array of refreshments.

Zachary sat at the head of the table in a smaller version of his throne, Lady Estora to his right. Since autumn, he'd included her in his meetings and audiences, and she took to her role as queen-intended naturally, remaining serene and dignified, but unafraid to speak up when she felt it necessary. Laren thought she'd probably learned well from her mother, the lady of Coutre Province.

Zachary maintained an air of respect toward her. It was difficult for Laren to ascertain how well they were getting along on a personal level, for he would not confide in her on this matter, but she hoped it was quite well for the sake of their mutual happiness. In a state marriage, however, personal compatibility certainly was not a requirement.

Absent from the chamber, Laren was pleased to note, was Lord Richmont Spane, Estora's cousin and self-appointed counselor. Laren tired of him constantly whispering into Estora's ear like a spider perched on her shoulder. And there was that smug smile of his, as if he were on a level with the king himself.

With Estora to be queen, Clan Coutre was in ascendance, and Spane was in a greater position of influence than ever. While his maneuvering for power irritated Laren, it was not unexpected; for what other reason did the aristocracy exist if not to seek greater authority and position over others?

To Zachary's left sat the Eletians, with Graelalea sitting between her two companions. Laren remembered Telagioth from the Eletians' previous visit—how could she forget his clear, cerulean blue eyes? The other Eletian was introduced as Lhean, his hair pale gold like the cool winter sun. The Eletians outshone everyone else in the room, including Estora, who was considered the great beauty of the land. Laren had to drag her gaze from them.

The king's other two primary advisors—Colin Dovekey and Castellan Sperren—also joined them. Footmen moved unobtrusively from person to person with ewers of wine and filed seamlessly out of the chamber when they finished. Only one of the king's Weapons stayed with them, silent and statuelike, his black uniform allowing him to fade into the shadows of the corner he stood in.

The Eletians remained stoic while Laren spoke of their encounter in the woods and the demise of the band of groundmites.

When she finished, Zachary put his hand to his temple and bowed to the Eletians. "I owe you a debt of gratitude," he said, "for I'd be lost without the captain." There was a tremor in his voice and Laren warmed with affection for him.

"We are pleased to have been of aid," Graelalea said. "Our meeting, however, was not entirely chance. We were on our way here to speak to you, at the behest of my brother, Ari-matiel Jametari."

"I see," Zachary said, "and what did he—"

At that moment, the chamber door opened and Lord Spane burst in. "Many pardons for being late," he said, giving Zachary a perfunctory bow. "I just heard we have guests."

Laren bridled her annoyance at the intrusion.

"I am Lord Richmont Spane," he announced to the Eletians. "Counselor to Lady Estora. I look after the interests of Coutre Province."

Graelalea nodded in return.

An awkward few moments passed as an extra chair was brought in and Spane insinuated himself at Estora's right hand, forcing Colin to move over. If Spane was the least bit impressed by the Eletians, he did not show it, and if Zachary was at all perturbed by the interruption, he hid it well.

When everyone was settled, Zachary started again. "What did your brother wish for you to speak to me about?"

"My brother," Graelalea replied, "wishes to inform you of his intention to go ahead with sending an expedition into Kanmorhan Vane."

Already Spane was leaning toward Estora to whisper something to her.

"I thought it likely he would," Zachary said softly. "He seemed determined to proceed when we spoke in the fall."

Graelalea did not respond. Laren remembered how she protested to her brother when he mentioned the idea to Zachary. It would be, she said, a fatal mission into a land that was a sad corpse of what it once was. The expedition would be led, Jametari said, by his sister. When Laren looked upon Graelalea now, she saw no fear in her. Only calm.

"When will you go?" Zachary asked.

"When day balances with night," Graelalea said, "and no sooner. The equinox. We dare not enter the forest while night still dominates."

"I don't understand," Spane said, his voice abrasive against the somber mood. "Why would anyone go into that evil place?"

Laren supposed it was a fair question, since he was not present to hear Jametari's reasoning, and Zachary had not discussed it with anyone beyond his immediate advisors.

"Blackveil was once Argenthyne," Graelalea said, "and it is our prince's desire that we see what may remain of it that is good."

"Argenthyne!" Spane said in incredulity. "Why that's a child's tale ..." He trailed off when Graelalea leveled her gaze at him. Maybe, as he looked into her eyes, eyes that had witnessed the passage of centuries, he recognized whom and what he addressed. He blinked rapidly and looked away.

"Argenthyne is no legend," Graelalea said. This time no one countered her words. "My brother," she continued, turning her steady gaze on Zachary, "expresses his hope you will not impede our passage through the breach in the wall to reach the forest."

Laren suspected the Eletians would not be deterred one way or the other, and that Jametari was simply conferring a courtesy by giving Zachary notice of their intentions.

Zachary stroked his mustache. "Is there anything else your brother wishes to express?"

Graelalea did not appear put off by his lack of affirmation. "Yes," she said. "If you wish to make this a joint expedition, that you choose worthy individuals, and meet the *tiendan* at the breach no later than the equinox. On our part, our number shall be small—six of us—so that we may travel lightly and swiftly."

"It's insane," Spane said. "Sire, surely you won't even consider anything of the sort."

Zachary ignored him, his countenance unchanged. Laren, however, knew his thoughts. When Prince Jametari first told them of his desire to send an expedition into Blackveil, Zachary later confided to her that the Eletians would not go without Sacoridians along. Whoever went was not likely to return, yet she understood why he must send his own people. He needed to know what lay on the other side of the wall, too, to learn what they faced should they be unable to repair the breach.

She also knew he wanted to keep an eye on the Eletians.

And now Zachary would not have to force the issue. The Sacoridians had been invited.

"I thank you for bearing Prince Jametari's message to us," Zachary said. "I will consider his words."

Graelalea nodded as though she expected no more.

"Have you accommodation for the night?" Zachary inquired. "We would be honored to house you."

Lhean made what looked like a warding gesture, sharp enough to catch everyone's attention.

"You have something to say, Lhean?" Graelalea asked.

"Is this place not a . . . What is the word these people use? For a house of the dead?"

"Mausoleum," Telagioth supplied.

"Yes," Lhean said. "Mausoleum. They sleep upon their dead. I feel it, and I should not like to pass a night here."

Colin looked mortified and Spane seemed about to burst out in indignation. Estora laid a gentle hand on his wrist to quiet him. No reaction came from the elderly Sperren, who dozed in his chair. Zachary looked—amused?

"Lhean," Graelalea said. "We are guests, and we do not speak so in the house of our host."

Lhean did not look shamed by the rebuke. He raised his chin, proud and haughty.

"You must forgive my cousin," Graelalea said. "He is young and this is his first time venturing among your kind."

"Young" was a deceptive concept in Eletian terms. Lhean could be hundreds of years old. And yet there was a quality about him that suggested his youth—a guilessness in his eyes. They lacked the deep knowledge and timelessness Laren had observed in other Eletians, as she saw in both Graelalea's and Telagioth's eyes.

"He only speaks truth," Zachary said.

"Your Highness—" Colin began.

"Yes, Colin, we do not speak carelessly of the tombs, but there is no reason to deny what our guests already know exists." Zachary smiled. "Though I never quite thought of the castle as a mausoleum. Now that he mentions it, however . . ."

"We thank you, Firebrand," Graelalea said, "for your offer of accommodations, but we shall begin our journey home."

"Truly?" Zachary asked, sounding genuinely disappointed. "May we offer anything else? Provisions?"

A solemn expression fell across Graelalea's face. "There is. My brother has a request. He wishes I return with something he found very precious here. A treasure, if you will."

A hush of expectancy descended on the chamber as all waited to hear the request. What treasure could he want? Laren inventoried in her mind all the precious trappings of the castle she could think of—jewels, weapons, art—and she saw that the others must be doing the same. What did the Sacoridians possess that would be good enough for the Eletian prince?

"My brother," Graelalea said, "requires many pounds of dark chocolate fudge and Dragon Droppings. We must visit the Master of Chocolate. Would his shop be open at this hour?"

*   *   *

Laren saw to it the Eletians got their chocolate. She sent Fergal, who was eager for even the most mundane of errands, ahead to alert Master Gruntler to open his shop for special customers. Then she assigned Mara to accompany them to Master Gruntler's, thence to the city gates.

By the time everything was arranged and Laren reported back to Zachary, the others had already dispersed. She found him in his private parlor pouring himself brandy. Two of his Hillander terriers sprawled before the fire and barely blinked at her entrance. Zachary poured her a glass, too, which she accepted gratefully. She sank into an overstuffed chair by the hearth, thinking it had turned out to be a very long day.

Zachary dropped into a chair opposite her. "Now tell me the truth. You are uninjured from your battle with the groundmites?"

"I'm fine," she said. She'd have a massive bruise on her thigh from being clubbed, and she ached, but that was nothing compared to what could have been had the Eletians not rescued her. And, she thought, the cordial Graelalea had given her seemed to have warded off at least some of the pain.

Zachary nodded in satisfaction. "So after you left, I listened to Colin and Sperren explain why I should not trust the Eletians or join in on a foolhardy expedition to Blackveil, and that I should forbid the Eletians passage across our lands to reach the wall. They fear such a venture would only mean certain death for those on the expedition, and that it might stir up things in the forest that might better be left sleeping."

"What did Lady Estora say?"

"Lord Spane concurred with Colin and Sperren, but the lady spoke up on her own behalf and said she'd support whatever decision I made. Her pronouncement seemed to irritate Spane." His eyes danced as he sipped his brandy. "Tell me, what do you think?"

"I agree with the others. An expedition into Blackveil will most likely fail. But I sense the profound truth in the Eletians' desire to investigate the forest."

"There can be deception in truth."

Laren smiled. "Spoken like a true king."

"I fear it is so," he replied. "All this politicking makes me cynical. I have found all too often there is truth, and then there is *truth.*"

"Like the castle being a mausoleum?" Laren spoke lightly, but Zachary's response was sober.

"To Eletians it is truth, for even the living who inhabit the castle are mortal, and therefore more or less dead. Our act of living is also the process of dying."

Laren set her brandy aside with a clatter. "Then we should all just go to bed and leave the wall untended, and let come what may."

Now Zachary grinned. "I said that's how *they* regard us. I for one believe I have a few good years left in me, and I don't think I should like to live an eternal life as the Eletians do. Some might desire it, but not me."

"Never to grow old in appearance? Never to suffer the weakening of the body as it ages?" Laren shrugged. "I guess the Eletians don't know what they are missing."

"Perhaps not," Zachary said, and they laughed. When they subsided, he continued, "You say there is profound truth in their desire to see what lies beyond the D'Yer Wall. I wonder what the deeper truth is. What it is they specifically seek."

"Specifically?"

"Yes. Argenthyne was important to their people. Graela-lea called it the jewel of Avrath on Earth, remember?"

"Now that you mention it, I remember something about it. What is Avrath?"

"From what I can fathom, it is a high spiritual place for the Eletians, as the heavens are to us. Something is calling the Eletians back, drawing them out of isolation no matter the cost."

"If so," Laren said, "why would Jametari bother to invite us along?"

Zachary shrugged. "To serve as bait? Witnesses? Or maybe it is his way of indicating his interest in the old alliance, and we're being tested to see if we are worthy. Whatever the case, it is an invitation I cannot ignore."

⋞⊳ BLACKVEIL ⊲⋟

The shallow cave Grandmother and her people sheltered in was a dismal, dark place, but it was better than being caught in the forest and getting sucked into some mire. Torrents of rain had poured through the forest canopy for three days now, best as she could figure.

They'd found the cave in a hillside that rose up beside Way of the Moon. It was mainly natural in origin, but refined by hand with stone tools they found scattered about. Someone had widened the entrance and leveled the floor, and there were signs the walls had been chipped at. Grandmother did not see it as the work of Eletians, for it was far too crude, and they did not seem to her to be cave-dwelling creatures.

They'd had to scare out a colony of roosting bats, oversized things displeased at being roused from their winter's torpor. Their eviction had been accompanied by much screaming and covering of heads by Min and Sarat, which only stirred the bats up more. Even Grandmother found herself shuddering and ducking at the leathery flap of wings so close to her head.

Afterward, Lala found herself a dead bat on the cave floor to examine. She poked it with a stick and turned it over. Grandmother took a closer look herself, amazed at its sharp claws and fangs. The bats she was accustomed to back home were diminutive, maybe the size of her forefinger at the most, and harmless. These were the length of her forearm. Grandmother and her people were lucky they hadn't been bitten or scratched.

When Griz saw what Lala was about, he grabbed her stick

without apology and used it to pitch the dead bat outside. Then he and Cole set about rigging one of their tents over the cave entry as much to keep the rain out as to prevent the bats from returning, while Deglin worked to light a fire. Meanwhile, Min and Sarat cleared the floor of guano. Deglin declared some of it would work as fuel.

A crack in the ceiling drafted smoke out from their campfire, and it was the warmest and driest Grandmother had felt since they passed into the forest. From time to time, she caught sight of large, multi-legged insects scuttling at the edge of the firelight, but as long as she stayed near the fire, they kept clear of her. Every so often Min would scream, and Cole would come to her and crunch the offending insect beneath his boot.

After laying out their gear to dry, Min and Sarat brewed tea and started to make the usual thin stew. The rain provided them with plenty of water, though it left a distinct, dank aftertaste on the tongue.

Lala occupied herself by searching out insects to stomp on, and Grandmother gazed into the fire, wondering when the rain would let up so they could continue their journey. She wondered if the Watchers sat out there in the rain waiting for them to emerge from the cave. She'd felt their gaze ever since they started along Way of the Moon. She and her people were being stalked.

She did not mention the Watchers to the others, not wishing to alarm them until there was a specific threat. The regard of the Watchers went beyond the general awareness the forest had of their passage; the Watchers were intentional in their regard. Intelligent.

Perhaps the Watchers were trying to figure out how strong Grandmother and her people were; how much of a defense they'd put up if attacked. Maybe they were just curious.

What Grandmother did know was that she wasn't going to take any chances, and so she doubled her wardings at each of their campsites, including the entrance to this cave.

As she stared into the fire, she also wondered what was happening on the other side of the wall. How was Colonel Birch faring? How went the muster and training of Second

Empire's forces? She had a way of seeing what he was up to, but the forest made the use of the art unreliable. Well, she had to try sometime, and their circumstances might not be as good later on.

Long ago she'd collected fingernail clippings from the colonel just for the purpose of seeing through his eyes. She pried one out of a tiny pouch she kept in her yarn basket. It was a fine crescent specimen, perhaps from the thumb. Birch kept his fingernails remarkably immaculate, but she supposed that was the difference between an officer expected to serve in court and a common soldier.

She knotted a length of sky blue yarn around the fingernail—knots of seeing. Sky blue was good, she found, for seeing over a distance, like looking through the clear sky itself.

"Show me," she commanded as she tied the last knot. She flung it into the fire. The fire flared. The yarn writhed as the flames consumed it.

At first she thought the spell would resist her, but then a window opened in the fire and she held her breath. Snow. Snow framed by the flames of their campfire. Squalls battered rows of tents and were so dense she could not see far.

Three figures struggled into view and halted before her/Birch. One of them had his hands bound behind his back and his face was bruised and bloody. He wore green. One of the king's accursed Green Riders.

"What do you want done with the spy?" one of the men holding him asked.

"He is a messenger," Birch said, his voice disembodied. Of course it would be, since Grandmother watched through his eyes. "Therefore we shall send the king a message."

"I understand." A knife flashed out and the man sank it into the Rider's back.

The Rider's eyes went wide. Snowflakes caught in his hair as it was tousled by the wind. Beneath the blood caked on his face, Grandmother saw he was young.

But never innocent. No, she knew better. From the beginning the Green Riders opposed the empire, acting as scouts, messengers, and warriors for their king. And yes, as spies, using their miniscule but insidious abilities with the art to commit evil upon the forces of the empire, and now Second Empire.

She felt no surge of compassion, not even when Birch's man twisted the knife in the Rider's back. The young man's mouth opened in a silent cry as he fell to his knees, sinking into the snow. Some mother just lost a son. So had the mothers of the empire lost sons, many sons, to the heathen Sacoridians.

No, she felt no compassion when he collapsed into the snow, crimson flowing from his mouth. An enemy of Second Empire was dead and she could only rejoice.

"Prepare the message," Birch said. "Those Greenie horses are clever—this one'll go right to the king."

There was laughter, then all Grandmother could see was snow, snowflakes swirling this way and that. The vision extinguished and she was left in darkness. Dark except for the one candle Cole lit on the other side of the cave. He brought it over to Grandmother and they all stared at the dead campfire. The cave smelled of damp soot.

Sarat reached for the ladle in the stewpot, but could not pull it out. "What have you done, Grandmother?" she chided. "The stew is frozen solid."

"Oh, dear," Grandmother replied. Once again the instability of the forest's etherea had twisted her spell. "I'm sorry, child. We'll have to start the fire again and thaw it out."

As Cole used his candle to light fresh kindling, Grandmother reflected that next time she'd wait until after supper to work a spell. But what she'd just witnessed was more satisfying than any meal.

⊰ BIRCH'S MESSAGE ⊱

Karigan sighed in relief as Condor plodded up the last rise of the Winding Way and the castle gates at last came into view. The fickle weather, changing from snow to sleet to rain, only to freeze again, had challenged them almost every day of their return journey.

Ironically, on this, their last day of travel, the weather turned bright and warm, slush melting into puddles on the cobbled streets, and many of Sacor City's denizens were out and about to absorb the sunshine so long denied them.

At the gates proper, she found the way blocked by a donkey cart. Chickens in cages piled on the cart cackled and squawked, and a milk cow, tied to the back end, serenely chewed her cud. The cart's master sat astride an old mare and was deep into an argument with the guards.

Karigan could not hear exactly what the argument was about, except that the guards did not wish to grant the man passage. Here she was, so close to her destination, only to be delayed yet again. At least she carried no urgent message, and so she resigned herself to waiting. The sunshine pouring down on her shoulders was not unpleasant, and her eyelids drooped.

Snatches of conversation at the gates came to her: "I will *not* leave my girls behind!" and "You just go tell the captain I'm here."

The flicker of a cooling shadow glided over Karigan. Idly she gazed up and saw a vulture circling slow and low. Another fluttering of black wings caught her eye as ravens alighted on the arch that spanned the gates. She wondered what attracted them. She glanced skyward again, and a second vulture looped on drafts high above the first.

That can't be good.

The man ahead was still bickering with the guards, but Condor, who'd been drowsing, raised his head with nose pointed to the air.

"What is it?" Karigan asked him.

From behind came shouts and a scream. Karigan swiveled in her saddle to see what was the matter. Pedestrians pointed at a horse and rider cantering up the street. The horse's strides were exhausted, and the rider's position stiff and lopsided, jerking against the motion of the gait instead of flowing with it. Ravens swooped at and fluttered around him.

Karigan squinted against the glare of sunshine on the wet street. The horse was bound for the gates, and as it neared, her horror grew by the second.

She recognized the star on the horse's nose—it was Petrel, belonging to Osric M'Grew, a fellow Green Rider. Indeed, the figure mounted on Petrel wore Rider green, though it was hard to tell, for the uniform was so saturated with dried blood. The sun flashed on his winged horse brooch.

"Osric . . ." she whispered.

He was clearly dead, his head tilted at a bad angle and his jaw flapping to the rhythm of Petrel's strides. His eyes were missing, pecked out by the black flock that plunged and fluttered around him. He was secured to a wooden frame and propped in the saddle to sit erect, much like a mounted scarecrow.

Petrel herself was almost gone, stumbling as she approached the gates, her ribs protruding, and her nostrils dripping blood. Her once gleaming coat was now ragged and dull, and crossed with striations from the attack of some predator probably attracted by the scent of the corpse upon her back. The only sounds in the silence were Petrel's harsh huffing and the sharp cries of the ravens.

Karigan could not move, could not look away, as Petrel passed by her. Osric's lips were black and peeled back from his teeth. His ears and nose were nearly pecked away. Beneath the encrusted blood, she saw a thatch of blond hair she recognized.

Yes, Osric.

The man at the gates and the guards parted to let Petrel through. Karigan retched on the sickly sweet stench of rot that followed Osric, and Condor half-reared, the whites of his eyes showing.

"*Gods,*" Karigan said. She mastered Condor and kicked him past the donkey cart, through the gates and over the bridge to the castle grounds. Condor ran hard after Petrel, and tears glided across Karigan's cheeks. She knew exactly where Petrel was headed.

In this, the final stretch of Petrel's terrible journey with her beloved Rider dead upon her back, she put on an unearthly burst of speed, giving the last of her being to end it. Condor pounded after her; followed until they reached the small stone building that was officers quarters.

Petrel came to a trembling halt, and Karigan reined Condor to a walk. The door to officers quarters flung open, and Captain Mapstone stepped out.

Having completed her mission, Petrel's legs buckled beneath her and she collapsed hard upon the earth, the corpse of Osric M'Grew going down stiff and lifeless with her.

A couple hours later, Karigan sat in the common room of the Rider wing, still not sure who Elgin Foxsmith was, except that it was the name of the fellow with the donkey cart at the castle gates. He'd followed after her on his own horse to officers quarters, arriving only moments after Petrel fell dead.

The captain, pale as bone, had ordered Karigan to inform the king, and as she reined Condor away from the awful scene to obey, the fellow dismounted and went to the captain, speaking softly to her, placing his hand on her shoulder.

As it turned out, word of Osric's return reached the king and others ahead of Karigan and they were already rushing from the castle when she arrived. After that, she did the only thing she could do: she saw to Condor's needs, then came to the common room to sit and wait. Wait for what, she did not know.

At some point, Elgin Foxsmith had come by in search of Mara, offering to take charge of the newer, younger Riders. He promised to keep them busy. Out of the way and away from senior Riders in mourning.

"I'll explain it to the young ones," he assured Mara.

Relieved of that concern, Mara went to the captain, and Elgin Foxsmith marched the young Riders out to the weapons practice field for calisthenics.

Karigan felt drained. She'd seen a lot of death during her time as a Rider, everything from the freshly killed to the ancient corpses down in the tombs, but never had she seen such a thing as Osric propped like that.

And the gaping sockets where his eyes should be . . .

Beside her, Yates was passed out with his head on the table, a goblet tipped over by his half-curled hand, and the sour stench of wine heavy in the air. Garth sat in an armchair in front of the hearth quietly drunk, his eyes glassy.

Karigan did not drink. She could not even hold a cup for all the shaking. She had not changed out of her uniform—hadn't even removed her boots or greatcoat.

The risks were known to each of them. Every time one of them set out on an errand for the king, there was the real possibility they might not return.

This was different, though. None expected to come back the way Osric had.

What color had his eyes been? Karigan found she could not remember.

Presently Mara returned. She stood in the doorway and glanced about as if dazed, then strode to the table and sat on a chair next to Karigan.

"I didn't have a chance to say it before," she said, "but I'm glad you're back. Your visit with your family went well?"

Karigan nodded. Maybe later, when some time had passed, she'd give Mara the details. At the moment, all of that seemed far away and unimportant.

"Mara, what happened to Osric? Where was he?"

Mara rubbed her eyes as if to wash away some image. "He was keeping watch on Birch's movements. Evidently he was caught."

Birch. Second Empire. They'd already lost Constance and Harry in the darkest months of winter. They'd been watching Birch, too.

"King Zachary thinks Birch is mocking us," Mara continued. "That's why he sent Osric back the way he did. Our Riders are good, but Birch is saying he's better, and he knows the king is spying on him." She clenched her hands into fists. "Osric is being prepared for the trip home to his mother in D'Ivary. I already sent Tegan to take her the news."

"And Petrel?"

"She'll be buried in the pasture."

Karigan nodded. No Rider horse went to the knacker. Still, she thought it sad horse and Rider would not be laid to rest together, but she knew how impractical that would be. She did not doubt the pair were together in the afterlife anyway, galloping among the stars.

"Who is Elgin Foxsmith?" she asked.

Mara actually smiled, though it was a tired smile. "My predecessor, or one of them. He was chief when our captain was a mere Rider. She asked him to come help with the new Riders a couple weeks ago, but we'd given up on him. Then there he was today. His timing, frankly, couldn't have been better."

When there was no more to be said, Karigan helped Mara put Yates to bed. Garth was too big and heavy to move, so they left him in his armchair staring into the fire.

Finally Karigan went to her own chamber. The door was cracked open, and when she stepped inside, she found the blanket on her bed covered with clumps of white cat hair as usual, and the purveyor of that hair lying on her pillow with his legs in the air. Ghost Kitty, who was in fact not at all a ghost, but one of the felines whose duty it was to patrol the tombs for rodents, barely acknowledged her entrance with a twitch of his tail.

"Well look who's made himself at home," Karigan said.

She set aside her saddlebags, removed the message satchel from her shoulder, and at last took off her greatcoat. She sat on her bed and stroked Ghost Kitty's cheek, and was rewarded with a resounding purr.

She'd have nightmares tonight, but at least she wouldn't be alone.

❧ OF CIRCLES AND FORM ❧

The Riders held a memorial circle for Osric, a practice conducted by Riders centuries ago, then forgotten, only to be rediscovered and revived thanks to Karigan, who had witnessed such a ceremony when she was pulled into the ancient past by wild magic.

Dakrias Brown, the castle's chief administrator, gave over his records room for the purpose. The newer Riders stood in wonder as they gazed up at stained glass windows lit from behind with lanterns, bringing to life in rippling colors the exploits of the First Rider at the end of the Long War. At one time the records room had served as the castle library and the domed glass panels had originally been open to the sunlight, but they were eventually closed in to allow for the castle's expansion. Some thought the blocking of the windows was actually King Agates Sealender's expression of antipathy for his own Green Riders.

Captain Mapstone led the memorial circle, speaking of Osric and his deeds, and her own fond memories of him. Then she said, "I remember Osric." And everyone responded, *"Osric."* After that, around the circle they went, each Rider speaking the name of some comrade who had fallen in the line of duty.

Karigan fancied spirits hovered in the shadows, in and among the tall shelving that housed hundreds of years of dusty administrative records; that they looked down upon the assembly of Riders to offer their own respects. She couldn't be sure they were really there, of course, but it seemed to her that presences other than the Riders filled the room.

Not to mention the records room had a reputation for being haunted . . .

The following day, the Riders bore Osric's coffin, draped in black, from the castle's chapel through the maze of corridors, the sound of their boots on stone counterpoint to the music of some noble's party spilling out of the conservatory.

The castle housed many different worlds: that of the monarch, of course, and all those who were close to him, the servants and administrative staff who helped run both castle and country; military personnel; various and sundry nobles; and finally, visitors of all kinds, from lowly commoners seeking an audience with the king to diplomats from other realms. Sometimes the various worlds intersected, but class and status often ensured they did not. As a result, there could be dozens of concurrent, but unrelated and uncoordinated, activities taking place among the different worlds.

While the kitchen staff embarked on a major inventory of pantries and cellars, a noble might be hosting a party when, in another part of the castle, the king's messengers mourned the passing of one of their own.

Intellectually, Karigan knew all this, but it still left a bitter taste in her mouth as they approached the conservatory. A drunk aristocrat slumped against the corridor wall raised his cup to the passing Riders with a foolish grin on his face.

They do not care, Karigan thought.

Through the entryway of the conservatory she glimpsed dancing and glittering jewels as the musicians picked up the tempo. They did not care that some lowly, common messenger had been killed. After all, it was their privilege to have others die to keep them safe. And they wouldn't even pause in their frivolity to show respect with silence.

Others in the corridors did, the more common folk. They stepped aside and bowed their heads as the somber Riders made their way past. Soldiers stood at attention and saluted. Humble servants reached out to touch the banner that draped the coffin. These people, Karigan thought, were the ones who understood the sacrifice.

At the bottom of the steps of the main castle entrance,

the coffin was placed on a cart, and Osric was sent home to his mother with an escort of Green Riders, their banners rippling and snapping in the strong breeze as they rode away.

In the days that followed, winter crumbled apart, and the sun shone more intensely and for longer each day. Snowmelt gushed from weep holes and drainage spouts on the castle walls as loud and vigorous as mountain freshets. Ice on pathways turned to slush. True spring was still a way off and the air still held the bite of the north wind, but an end was in sight.

Karigan had spoken only briefly to Captain Mapstone after her return from Corsa, to hand over the message from her father. Osric's grisly arrival was still all too fresh at the time, and the captain's expression grim and pale. Quickly she scanned the message, raising an eyebrow and pursing her lips. Was it Karigan's imagination, or did the captain's expression warm and lighten just a bit? It was like a passing brightness between the clouds, however, and all too soon, she shuttered herself once more and excused Karigan with a curt, "Dismissed."

From then on, except for the memorial circle and farewell to Osric, the Riders saw little of their captain. She was, Mara said, closeted with the king and his advisors in meetings.

"No doubt talking about Birch and Second Empire," Mara said as she and Karigan helped Hep the stablehand feed the horses one afternoon. "And probably the Eletians, too."

"Eletians? What about the Eletians?"

"That's right," Mara said, "you weren't here. I guess with Osric and all, the Eletians weren't the major gossip anymore. Three came to see the king."

Karigan almost dropped her grain scoop. "*Eletians were here?* What did they want?"

"Apparently they wished to resupply all of Eletia with chocolate," Mara said, separating flakes of hay to throw into another stall.

"*What?*"

Mara nodded sagely. "Took Master Gruntler days to get in enough sugar and cocoa to reopen his shop after the Eletians went through his stock. If you were craving Dragon Droppings, forget it."

Horses who had not yet been fed made demanding whinnies, circled in their stalls, and kicked the walls. Perhaps the noisiest of the lot was Elgin's donkey, Bucket, who, true to form, knocked his bucket around.

"Eletians came to Sacor City to buy chocolate? And that's it?"

Mara struggled to keep a straight face, but could not. She laughed, leaving Karigan completely confounded.

"Mara!"

"All right, all right. They weren't here just for the chocolate. According to the captain, the Eletians are going on an expedition into Blackveil."

Karigan just stood there, stopped by she did not know what. The noise of the horses, Mara's presence, the stable itself, all faded away. Her hand went to the moonstone in her pocket. Something niggled at her, but there was only a blankness in her mind. Was there something she should remember?

The tickle of a white feather across memory . . .

"Karigan?"

Karigan shook her head. "Eletians," she said.

Mara gave her an odd look. "Yes, Eletians."

"And the king and his advisors are debating this expedition?"

"I guess, but what they are specifically discussing the captain hasn't revealed. Not yet, anyway." Mara shrugged. "If the Eletians want to get themselves killed by going into that place, it's their business, if you ask me."

Karigan resumed scooping grain into buckets in silence. Once again, the Eletians had come to Sacor City. What couldn't she remember? She sighed. If it was important, it would come back to her.

Karigan discovered, to her dismay, no one had been attending to Rider accounts in her absence. Ordinarily the duty fell to the Chief Rider, but because of Karigan's merchant background, the captain passed the duty on to her.

As she looked over the ledgers missing rows and rows of entries, she realized she had no one to blame but herself. She'd neglected to assign anyone the task while she was away—she'd been too wrapped up in worrying about the coming confrontation with her father.

"Idiot," she berated herself over and over.

Now she paid for that neglect, frantically running back and forth between the quartermaster's office and the administrative wing of the castle, seeking any record of transactions, and she plagued Mara and Connly to rack their brains for expenses.

One late night she filled the long table of the Rider common room with ledgers, crumpled receipts, and notes scrawled with half-remembered transactions. When she thought she'd go blind from all the figures, she laid her head on the table and placed an open ledger over her face to block the lamplight. She started to drift off, but was awakened by footsteps.

She sat up, knocking some papers to the floor. She blinked blearily to find Fergal standing before her.

"You're working late," he said. "It's about midnight."

"What are you doing up?" she demanded.

"I've tomorrow off, so I was down at the Cock and Hen."

The Cock and Hen served the best bitter ale in the city, but was located in a seedy neighborhood. She bit her tongue to prevent herself from taking Fergal to task for venturing there on his own. His days as her trainee were over, but it wasn't easy for her to slip from her role as mentor. To her mind he was still so young and inexperienced.

Young he may be, but he was now a full-fledged Rider responsible for his own conduct.

Fergal took a long, hard look at the mess on the table. "Glad that's not my job."

"Someone's got to keep the books," she said with a sigh.

"Just so long as I get paid," Fergal said, and he left the common room whistling a tune.

"Paid?" Karigan said in honest horror. "*Paid?* Oh, gods, the payroll. I *forgot* the payroll." And she gently thumped her forehead on the table.

If the Rider accounts mess wasn't bad enough, there was weapons training with Arms Master Drent.

It was not every Green Rider who trained with Master

Drent. In fact, currently there was only one other, and Beryl Spencer was so often away on secret missions for the king that Karigan might as well be the only one. Drent complained to no end that he'd yet to see a Green Rider attain swordmastery as their duties interrupted training far too much. Or the Rider simply got killed in the course of duty.

Drent trained only the best of the best swordmasters and swordmaster initiates. Among those he trained were the Weapons, the black-clad warriors who guarded royalty both living and dead. All Weapons were swordmasters, but not all swordmasters were Weapons. Drent's most special pupil was the king, who was an accomplished swordmaster, though obviously the king could not become a Weapon since he could not guard himself.

Swordmasters sponsored and trained initiates, who achieved swordmastery if they passed a series of tests. From there, a swordmaster could seek service with a noble lord or go to the academy to train as a Weapon. The ways of the Weapons were secretive, and from what little Karigan could glean, the academy was located on a barren island miles off Hillander Province, where Weapons lived and trained in austere circumstances. When their training was complete they were tested one last time to determine their fitness. Drent was among those who had final say in which trainees were inducted into the elite order.

Karigan did not ask to become a swordmaster initiate, nor had she ever desired to train with Drent, but it appeared to be her fate, supported by both her captain and king. They seemed to think she had some talent with a sword. Drent was determined to prove them wrong.

She'd been training with Drent before she was officially named a swordmaster initiate, but so far there was little difference in her current training from the hammerings she received before, except for the gradual introduction of new moves and more emphasis on form. A swordmaster did not just fight for survival, but made an art of it. Being a swordmaster was more than mere fighting: it was grace, it was stealth and power, it was precision.

Karigan did not feel like any of those things, when once

again, her practice partner, Flogger, whacked her across the buttocks with the flat of his wooden practice sword and sent her stumbling from the muddy practice ring. Stepping out of the ring was an automatic kill point, and she'd lost count of how many times she had been "killed" during the day's session.

She glowered, rubbing her numb behind, while Flogger grinned at her. He'd had it in for her for months now, after she embarrassed him a time or two in the fall. Now, however, she was prohibited from employing the techniques she used before, which some would call tricks. Swordmaster initiate training, she was informed by Drent, was about the art of the sword, not tricks.

"What are you waiting for Greenie?"

Drent had crept up from behind so silently his voice made her jump. She hastened back into the small practice ring, her boots sucking in the mud.

"I want to see the whole sequence from the beginning, without pause," Drent said, his voice one of menacing delight. He smiled, and with his thick features, it was a gruesome thing. "The Greenie will do the forms, and Flogger will counter."

Karigan's heart sank. She'd be stuck to the prescribed sequence, while Flogger could vary his technique as he wished in an effort to throw her off. Others paused their bouts to watch, as they often did. Karigan's humiliation made for good sport.

They tapped swords and Flogger came at her with a simple thrust. The first form was called Aspen Leaf, in which Karigan traced the shape of an aspen leaf through the air with speed and force, meeting Flogger's sword with a solid clank and pushing it aside; followed by crosswise slashes that represented the veins of the leaf, again swiftly met by Flogger.

Clack! Clack! Clack!

In a real fight with real swords, Aspen Leaf could slice up an opponent in a dozen different ways.

Karigan flowed into Crayman's Circle and Snake Gliding, and Flogger, who knew the routine, turned her thrusts away and parried her slashes. They developed a rhythm so that the sequence became a dance, but she had to remain alert because she could become lost in it, oblivious to all else, only to have her opponent seize the opportunity to pull an unexpected move that caught her off guard.

So far Flogger remained steady on the rhythm, not pulling any of his usual stunts, his form impeccable. For some reason he was drawing out the sequence instead of securing a rapid victory.

Must be showing off for Drent, she thought. But even when Drent watched, Flogger usually tried to defeat her as quickly as possible. Perhaps there was someone else among the onlookers he wanted to impress.

And then it came, a swipe at her legs that opposed the rhythm they'd established.

Because Karigan, as a smaller, less muscular opponent, had little hope of defeating Flogger with sheer force, she'd been trained to use an adversary's own power against him, and here she did so, hopping out of the way and sweeping her blade behind his and slamming it out of his hands. The wooden practice sword flew into the crowd while Flogger looked after it in disbelief. There was some scattered clapping among the onlookers.

"Well, well," Drent said, and it was all he said before moving on to another pair of trainees.

Sweat streamed down Karigan's face, and she was splattered and soaked to the skin with mud and bruised to the bone as usual, but she could not help but feel triumphant.

Her triumph lasted only as long as it took Flogger to retrieve his practice sword, a scowl on his face.

They tapped swords to begin again.

"That's the last time you'll embarrass me in front of the king, Greenie," Flogger said.

"King?"

"Didn't see him, eh?"

No, she hadn't. She glanced across the practice field searching for him, but most of the audience had already dispersed.

THWACK!

"Ow!" Karigan cried, grasping her forearm as her practice sword tumbled to the ground. Jolts of pain shot between her wrist and elbow. "That wasn't fair!"

"Not fair? We tapped swords. You weren't paying attention."

As much as she hated to admit it, Flogger was right, but it was hard not to be distracted by thoughts of King Zachary. Had he enjoyed watching her bout? How she moved? She had not seen him since her return.

She cleared her throat and shook her hand out when she realized she was just standing there smiling foolishly, but it was more than exertion that left a blush on her cheeks.

OF SHADOWS AND ETIQUETTE

"**T**here was a brand on his chest," Laren said, trying to keep the tremor from her voice. The shadows of her quarters closed in on her as she remembered, and she shuddered.

"Brand?" Elgin asked. He helped her slip into her greatcoat.

Laren closed her eyes and only saw Osric's decaying, abused body before her on the slab of the death surgeons. They did what they could to clean him up, and she'd seen much worse, but it was still no simple thing to view the corpse of one her Riders cut down in his prime, his body defiled. Elgin placed his hand on her shoulder, and she knew he understood.

"It was a crude brand," Laren said, "but distinct—a lion mauling a skull."

Elgin scrunched his eyebrows together. "I thought Second Empire used a dead tree as their symbol."

Laren fastened the buttons of her coat. "They do, but the historians think this brand is very close to a symbol used by Mornhavon the Black's elite regiment, the Lions. Birch is not only mocking us, but informing us he's raising a superior force, harkening back to the days of the Long War."

She opened the door and squinted in the wash of sunlight that pushed the shadows to the far corners of her quarters.

"The death surgeons think," she continued, "Osric was branded after death."

"Thank the gods for small mercies," Elgin muttered.

"There was no mercy when those murderers turned the blade in his back," Laren replied. "Cowards. Knifing him

110

from behind like that. Birch may think he's clever sending us his message, but he's also shown us he lacks honor."

"Villains often do," Elgin said.

Sunshine poured down on Laren when she stepped from her doorway onto the thawing earth. The air was chill, and smelled fresh and clean, of new beginnings. It was her cue to shake off darkness. She could not afford to traverse the shadows for too long when there was work to be done and so many Riders, living, breathing Riders, depended on her leadership.

Unfortunately, leadership tended to translate to "eligible for endless meetings," and here she was on her way to yet another, albeit important, one. Zachary was bent on sending Sacoridians with the Eletians into Blackveil, and it was time to decide what and who would comprise their contingent.

"So tell me," Laren said as she started down the path, careful to avoid puddles and icy patches, "how it goes for you. Are you settling in?" Often, it was only in moments like this, between meetings, that she was able to catch up on the doings of her Riders.

"I am very comfortable in the Rider wing," Elgin said. "And my girls and Bucket are content as well, though Hep has a thing or two to say about the racket Bucket makes at feeding time."

Laren grinned. "And what do you make of my new Riders?"

"Eager to learn and do," Elgin said. "Just as they always are."

She nodded, then paused at the sound of shouting from the vicinity of the practice field. She pivoted and saw there was a goodly collection of onlookers crowded together, no doubt watching a bout. It was not unusual, but then she recalled this was the time Karigan was scheduled for swordmaster initiate training. On a hunch she started toward the practice field, the opposite direction in which she'd been heading.

"Where are you going?" Elgin said. "What about your meeting?"

"It doesn't start till eleven hour. I have a little time to spare."

Elgin followed her across the soggy grounds to the practice field. There was still plenty of snow piled up in shady spots in the lee of the castle and beneath trees, but the practice field was a churned up mire, the small rings used for swordplay particularly mucky.

She smiled when she reached the edge of the crowd, for it was Karigan's swift and lithe form against the strength of a huge fellow. They clashed through a sequence of moves that was far beyond Laren's own training, and though Karigan's opponent's arms and chest bulged with muscles, it did not diminish his own speed or precision.

They were locked in a dance, the clack of wooden swords beating out across the practice field in an almost musical rhythm, their movements fluid but also spare. As much as the big fellow had the advantage in size and strength, Karigan learned to counter that advantage and use it against him.

"She does well," Elgin murmured.

"Yes," Laren said, with more than a little pride. "She always has."

She had known from the very beginning, the way a farmer can sense how a season's crops will bear out, that Karigan would prove to be one of her more exceptional Riders. It might have had something to do with her grand entrance into the king's throne room that day some three years ago, borne by the Wild Ride and the spirits of Riders past.

But there was more to it. Despite being touched by the supernatural, Karigan was, in most ways, a very ordinary young woman, at times self-conscious and awkward. She might be good at some things, like her sword technique, but she was not good at everything. Drent still forbade her to handle throwing knives.

No matter what strange adventures came Karigan's way, her unassuming nature grounded her, allowed her to accomplish what she must. And when she received praise for her accomplishments? It was not false modesty but genuine surprise she expressed that anyone should notice.

And there was that strong will of hers. Laren thought back to the letter she'd received from Stevic G'ladheon and there was no need to guess from where, or rather from whom,

Karigan had acquired her strong will. As for her modesty? That must have come from her mother's side.

Laren smiled thinking of the invitation Stevic had enclosed with his return message. He insisted she come to Corsa to inspect firsthand the materials and goods with which he intended to supply the Riders. He wished, he said, to ensure they were to her satisfaction. She had to admit it was tempting—she hadn't taken leave in years, but there was so much to oversee here. So much to do.

Drent, she saw, watched the bout unmoving, his beefy arms folded across his chest. He might complain about having to train Karigan, but he certainly wouldn't bother with her if he didn't think she had potential.

Then she caught sight of another watching from the far fringes. Few others seemed to notice his presence, for their attention was focused on the bout, and he was cloaked and hooded. But Laren knew him too well to miss him. So Zachary had come to observe as well. Did he know that it would be Karigan specifically training at this time?

Stupid question, she thought. Of course he did.

She returned her gaze to Karigan locked in her dance, her expression one of deep concentration. She'd be unaware of the onlookers. Mud splashed around her feet and sweat sprayed from her face. Her braid whipped across her back.

She might be unaware of those who watched, but with a quick glance to Zachary, Laren knew of one who was far from oblivious. He followed the bout with all the ardor of an expert swordsman, a proud parent, or a fiercely protective guardian.

Or a lover.

She sighed. She'd seen that look before, the change in his demeanor whenever Karigan was near. Felt his intensity. Others might not perceive it, but she and Zachary were very close—she had known him since he was a child and had been like an older sister to him as he grew up. Consequently she was able to recognize his feelings for what they were, and soon figured out the object of his desire was one of her very own Riders.

She'd thought maybe his love for Karigan would fade over time. She'd sent Karigan away on errands to keep them apart, hoping he'd turn his attention to Lady Estora, perhaps even forget Karigan, but from the way he now studied her every move, it appeared Laren's efforts had fallen short.

It was not malicious intent that caused Laren to thwart any blossoming romantic bond between the two. On the contrary, she wished only for Zachary's happiness, but as a king, his happiness was secondary to the needs of his realm, and his realm needed him to marry Lady Estora for the stability and continuity it would bring his reign, not to mention how it would reinforce the loyalty of the eastern provinces.

Should Zachary discard Lady Estora in favor of a commoner, the breach of the betrothal contract could wreak untold turmoil, even civil war, the last thing they needed with Second Empire building up its forces. It was vital Sacoridia remain strong and united.

There was the possible threat to Karigan, too, that concerned Laren. So much was riding on the betrothal for some factions that they'd do anything to see it through. *Anything*. If Karigan was identified as a distraction that kept Zachary from fulfilling his duty to Lady Estora ... ? No, Laren couldn't allow it.

Elgin touched her sleeve. "Look!"

Laren tore her gaze from Zachary. In the practice ring, Karigan's opponent moved against the rhythm they'd established. He cut his sword at Karigan's knees.

Almost faster than Laren's eyes could perceive, Karigan hopped back and smashed his sword out of his hand.

"Hah!" Laren exclaimed, clapping.

Drent looked surprised, then pleased. "Well, well," he said, and he left to work with another pair of trainees.

Karigan herself appeared bemused, and her opponent plainly shocked, as he gazed at his empty hand.

Zachary was already striding away, his cloak billowing behind him, a Weapon following at his heels.

"I think, perhaps, it was time I proceeded to my meeting," Laren said. Just as she finished speaking, the bell down in the city began to peal out eleven hour. She hastened away from the practice field with Elgin hurrying beside her. "Was there something else?" she asked him.

"I've been meaning to talk to you about the training of the young ones—"

"I think Mara and Ty would be your best help."

"Ty is who I wanted to talk about."

Laren halted. "Ty? What about him?"

"Too much etiquette."

"Too much . . . ?" Laren almost laughed, but Elgin's expression was serious.

"Not enough combat and riding," he said.

The last strike of eleven hour faded away. She was late. "Chief, please address this with Mara. I've got to go!"

"But—"

"I'm sorry!" She hurried toward the steps of the main castle entrance, hoping he would talk to Mara. Ty was a natural in many ways when it came to training new Riders, but she also trusted Elgin's experience and wisdom to know when something could be improved.

Etiquette, eh? It did have its place, but she'd rather her Riders be capable of defending themselves in a fight. Osric was very capable, but it did not help him in the end. Still, she wanted her Riders to have every chance possible.

As she entered the castle, she wished she could forget etiquette and call upon her combat skills in some of these meetings she had to sit through, but unfortunately, etiquette and her wits were the only weapons she was permitted.

⤜ A CONFRONTATION ⤛

"**I** volunteer myself," Laren declared, unable to cool the heat in her voice.

Her pronouncement was met with shocked silence.

"Absolutely not," Zachary said seconds later, and the others at the table murmured in agreement.

"I will not command my Riders to do something I'm not willing to undertake myself. I will go in their stead. Do you not think me capable?"

Zachary looked taken aback. "Captain, I should think Blackveil would tremble to its very foundations just to imagine you crossing its borders, but I dare not risk you."

Laren thought the heat of her anger must fairly radiate throughout the meeting chamber. "Are my Riders so much less important that you dare risk *them* in this manner?"

"Do you think I don't know what it means to send them into Blackveil?" Zachary retorted. "They are *my* people, too, Captain, and it is no easy thing for me. I believe, however, you and your experience best serve your Riders *here.*"

"I must agree," General Harborough said from across the table. He was a blocky, thick-necked man, and he needed to shift the whole of his body in his chair to look at her. "It is the lot of commanders to send their troops into battle."

Laren knew they were both right, but why did half the company going into Blackveil have to consist of her Riders and not others? The company would only number six individuals to match the six Eletians going in, but still, three Riders meant half the contingent.

Of course, more than anyone else she knew why. Green

Riders were most suited for this kind of mission, with their ability to work independently, and their experience as scouts. No doubt their special abilities would prove helpful in dealing with the forest. But with one of her Riders freshly dead and her grief still raw, it was a hard thing to choose others to head toward so uncertain a fate.

Lord Spane cleared his throat. "Perhaps the captain does not feel her Riders are up to the task."

Snake! Laren thought. From the mouth of one who had never faced an ounce of danger himself, and who would not think twice about squandering the lives of those who served him.

But it was Lady Estora who reproached him. "Richmont, you speak out of turn. The Green Riders are capable beyond your imaginings."

If anyone should know, it was Lady Estora, and Laren bowed her head in thanks to her. The lady nodded gravely in return. Lord Spane's mouth narrowed to a thin line but he made no retort.

"Let those who go be volunteers," Colin said.

"They will *all* volunteer," Laren replied.

"Then you must use your discretion."

This was not particularly helpful advice from the man who oversaw the Weapons, whose motto was *Death is honor!* In any case, she'd known it would come down to her to decide who to send on what could very well be a suicide mission. She sighed, knowing who at least one of those Riders would be.

Old Castellan Sperren shook himself as if waking from a nap. "What of the wall, sire?" he asked. "You've got that book about its construction. Shouldn't we forego this expedition and use the book to fix the breach?"

Everyone looked to the king.

"It is not so simple," Zachary replied.

"Has the translation not yet been completed, then?"

"It is done." Zachary pressed his hands flat against the tabletop and rose. Everyone stood with him, but he gestured that they should remain seated. He opened the chamber door, gave some quiet instructions to someone outside. He remained standing, but in silence, his hands clasped behind his back.

It was not long before a page returned bearing a manuscript tied with a leather thong. The boy placed it on the table and left.

"You see before you," Zachary said, "the translation of the book of Theanduris Silverwood, his account of the creation of the D'Yer Wall."

A swell of excited murmuring arose from the king's advisors. Zachary raised his hands to quiet them.

"It is the only true account we know of that survives," he said. "Ever since the wall was breached, we have bemoaned the loss of secrets, the loss of craft. Even the D'Yers could find little about the wall's making in their own archives. Lord Fiori of Selium was unable to find anything useful, either. Much knowledge of the arcane was purged following the Long War, for anything, and anyone, associated with magic was despised and deemed evil. So while written records failed to survive the ages, spoken histories failed as well."

"How did this one book survive?" Colin asked.

"Here and there oddments of our magical heritage can be found," Zachary replied. "But the Silverwood book? It is hard to know its history, except that if you were to look at the actual volume, you would find its pages blank, and it would have appeared as nothing more than an unused journal. But despite appearances, the book does contain copious writing, and it speaks not only of magical things, but is itself an object of magic. There is only one place, for instance, where it can be seen for what it truly is and be read."

He did not mention that the only place the book could be read was in the light of the high king's tomb. The tomb of the *current* high king, who was Zachary. Down below, in the halls of the dead, a sarcophagus already awaited him.

"And so in this one place, our translator strove with the words of Theanduris Silverwood to draw the story out of the book. As a thing of magic, the words were often volatile, and our translator found himself in the care of menders more than once."

Poor Agemon, Laren thought. Agemon was the chief caretaker of the tombs and fluent in many archaic tongues, including Old Sacoridian. Since the tombs were forbidden to all but royalty, Weapons, and caretakers, the duty of translation fell to Agemon.

"I don't understand," Lord Spane said. "How could words injure someone?"

"It is not easy to explain," Zachary said, "except that there are spells woven into combinations of words or letters, or in the ink, or even in the way a letter is written. Just reading a sentence can create an unpleasant reaction. And not all words are read, precisely. They are presented in a very . . . visceral manner.

"A great mage of Theanduris Silverwood's caliber might have read the book without harm, but it still would have taken a while to decode the spells. Our translator did this at great personal risk in service to his king and country. The copy he made for us—" Zachary tapped the manuscript "—retains nothing of the magic from the original, and so is safe to be read. It is ordinary paper and ink."

It was just as well, Laren thought, that if the original was so dangerous it could not be read anywhere but in a forbidden place like the tombs.

"It is impossible to know what became of the book," Zachary continued, "after Theanduris Silverwood died, except that it eventually made its way into the private library of a collector of arcane objects, a Professor Berry. He himself is long dead, and his estate obscure, located somewhere in the depths of the Green Cloak Forest. It was from his library that Second Empire found the book and stole it. They brought it here in hopes of translating it themselves."

"Please, sire," Colin said, "do not keep us in suspense any longer. Have you read the translation? What does it say?"

Zachary smiled. "Yes, I have read it. More than once. More than twice. I learned much about the construction of the D'Yer Wall."

Laren felt the excitement building in the chamber, her own hope surging.

"I have learned from my reading," Zachary said, "that it

was perhaps a good thing that all other records of the wall were purged so such a feat could not be duplicated."

Excitement turned to confusion.

Zachary placed his hand on the manuscript. "Not only were the words written in the book volatile to readers, but as mere language, they describe a bloody time in our history. The book corroborates what Riders Alton D'Yer and Dale Littlepage have been able to find out about the wall's construction. Thousands upon thousands of magic users were sacrificed to the wall. Each granite block, every mortar mixture, was fed the blood of people, and their souls sealed in the wall to remain guardians of it for as long as it stood."

This revelation was met with silence, and Laren could tell the others didn't quite grasp the enormity of it, except maybe Lady Estora, who paled. Laren had been privy to Alton's and Dale's reports, but nevertheless shuddered to hear that the book confirmed all those sacrifices took place.

"It required the destruction of so many lives," Zachary said, "during a time when the realm's population of magic users was already hit hard by war and plague and persecution. In fact, for those opposed to the existence of magic, the building of the wall served the dual purpose of protecting the lands while ridding the world of even more magic users.

"If we wished to reconstruct the breach using the same methods, we'd have to sacrifice those with magical ability and bind their blood and souls to granite and mortar. We'd also need a great mage of Theanduris Silverwood's power to do the binding."

Most at the table were aghast, but Lord Spane shot to his feet. "We must find a great mage then! Surely one with that power survives somewhere in the lands."

"Sit, Richmont," Lady Estora said in a soft voice, and she pulled at his sleeve.

He gazed about the chamber in confusion, but at last he complied and sank into his chair.

"It may be there is a great mage somewhere out there the likes of which we've not seen in three ages," Zachary said. "And it may be there are enough individuals in our population with remnant magical ability in their blood to accomplish the task, but I am doubtful. Even if there were, I would not sanction the slaughter of my own citizens, or any others, for this purpose. I can only imagine what forces were at work when King Jonaeus decided he must take this course. His was a young kingdom almost destroyed by war, with factions attempting to wrest power from him and one another." He shook his head. "Dark times. I cannot help but think that all records, except this one, were destroyed to prevent another wall from being built."

"So it is worthless," Lord Spane said.

"Perhaps, perhaps not." Zachary slipped back into his chair. "It contains a measure of music."

"Music?" Spane said in disbelief. "What does that have to do with it?"

"Just as words have power, so may music. The souls who remain as guardians within the wall sing a song to maintain the binding. This music, too, may have some application in maintaining the wall. Theanduris Silverwood, however, did not explain its purpose."

"Music," Spane muttered. "Words and spells. It seems we are being pushed backward in time to our primitive past."

"Primitive?" Zachary mused. "It is our history for good or bad. In any case, I have sent Lord Fiori a copy of the musical notation to see what he makes of it. In the meantime, a second copy of the Silverwood book will go to Alton D'Yer down at the wall. He may see something in it I do not."

"Our only hope is a bit of song?" General Harborough said in incredulity. "To maintain the wall? *Maybe?*"

"Maintenance is important," Zachary replied. "The wall has deteriorated since the initial breach. Alton D'Yer has managed to halt much of it, but if those affected parts can be strengthened further, it is all to the good.

"We must not forget," he added, "that had the book remained in the hands of Second Empire, they would have learned what they needed to destroy the wall. It was a Green Rider, as you may recall, who rescued it." This last was directed at Spane. "Alton D'Yer will be instructed to burn his copy once he has read it. This one," and he thumped the manuscript, "will be hidden away, and no others shall read it."

*   *   *

It was not uncommon for Laren to linger behind after a
meeting to speak with Zachary, in much the same way her
Riders tried to catch up with her between meetings.

"May I have a few words?" she asked.

The others conversed among themselves and collected
their papers and coats. Zachary hesitated, then gestured they
should go into an adjoining chamber. It was set up with a few
chairs for smaller conferences, but they did not sit.

"What is it?" Zachary asked. "You are not going to plead
with me to allow you on the expedition, are you? That was
well done, but I've already expressed my feelings on the
matter."

"Yes, you have," Laren replied.

"Then what?"

She took a deep breath. It was now or never, and she
would likely incur his anger, but it had to be done. She should
have addressed this long ago.

"I saw you out on the practice field before our meeting.
You were observing a bout."

"Yes?" His expression was guarded.

"You were watching Karigan."

"Do I not have the right to observe the training of those
who serve me?"

"Certainly, but it is Karigan I'm specifically concerned
about since you hold her, I believe, in a good deal of esteem."

Zachary said nothing. In that forbidding silence was an
implicit warning that she not cross the line regarding his "esteem" for Karigan.

Laren cleared her throat, "She will be, of course, one of
the Riders I choose to send into Blackveil."

"*No!*"

"No?" she asked, unsurprised by his flash of anger.

He turned his back to her as if to collect himself. When
finally he faced her again, his demeanor was neutral, but
Laren knew him too well not to perceive how rigid his posture had become.

"No," he said with deceptive mildness. "Has she not done
enough for us?"

"It is precisely because of what Karigan has done, what she's been through, that I must choose her. She's been in Blackveil before, though she recalls little of the experience, and she has faced some of its denizens in battle. She's also dealt with Eletians more than anyone else, and has faced the supernatural. Despite all the dangerous situations she has found herself in, she has somehow managed to survive time after time. Shall I go on? Do you need more reasons?"

"I do not wish to send her."

Zachary was very rarely an obstinate man. Usually he would hear reason, but this was not one of those times, showing just how deep his feelings for Karigan went. Laren could only try to convince him of the wisdom of her choice.

"She is the one Rider with the best chance of returning from Blackveil alive." She paused, realizing how tense she was, how tightly she clenched her hands at her sides. Zachary moved to the cold hearth and gazed up at the painting of a hunting scene above the mantel, but she doubted he really saw it.

"I know how you feel about Karigan," Laren said.

Zachary glanced sharply at her, but she did not quail from him.

"I know that it isn't just 'high esteem' you feel for her. You love her and that is the reason you do not wish her to go into Blackveil."

He faced her dead on, and she could feel the storm emanate from him.

"I believe it is my duty to bring this up," Laren hastily continued, "as Karigan's captain and as your advisor, but mainly as your friend. I realize feelings are difficult to tame, especially when they move in a direction contrary to duty, but you must not allow your heart to cloud your judgment. Our country needs your strong marriage to Lady Estora. I can't tell you not to love Karigan, but you must let her go. *Let her go.*"

"I think I have heard enough, Captain." And that was all he said. He strode out of the room, through the larger meeting chamber, and out into the corridor. She cringed when he slammed the door behind him.

She'd expected his fury, but it didn't make it any easier to be on the receiving end of it. If it was any consolation, his vehemence indicated to her he knew she was right. Perhaps, with time, he'd come around and allow what was only sensible, that Karigan should be one of the Riders to enter Blackveil.

She'd needed to confront the issue of his feelings for Karigan before someone with ill intentions caught wind of it. The political repercussions, the danger to Karigan ... It had to be done, and as his friend and confidant, she was the best one to broach the touchy subject.

She could live with his wrath if it meant she'd averted larger problems. After all, it wouldn't be the first time.

Richmont Spane fussed with his papers and his coat as all the others filed out of the meeting room. He watched as Captain Mapstone and the king stepped into the adjoining chamber to have a few words. He'd another appointment to attend, but he was extremely curious and one never knew when a bit of eavesdropping might provide some useful intelligence.

With another glance to make sure the rest had departed, he crept to the doorway of the adjoining room. The door was ajar, so it was easy to hear the king and the captain speaking, though it was the captain who did most of the talking.

"Certainly," the captain said, "but it is Karigan I'm specifically concerned about since you hold her, I believe, in a good deal of esteem."

Richmont grew still, listening with great interest to the exchange that followed. When finally the king said, "I think I have heard enough, Captain," Richmont scuttled from the chamber and into the corridor just in time. He watched as the king emerged and slammed the door shut behind him. There was a wild look in his eyes as he stormed off, his Weapon peeling away from his post at the door and following briskly.

Richmont rubbed his chin. From the king's behavior, he deemed the captain had been right on the mark: the king was in love, in love with a Green Rider.

Richmont struck off in the opposite direction, thinking the captain was also correct to believe that love could cloud the king's judgment in terms of the betrothal, and that would be a disaster for the alliance with Clan Coutre, for the country, and most important, for Richmont's own ambitions. The Green Rider was a threat.

If this particular Rider was indeed going to Blackveil, it was quite possible she wouldn't survive, and that would solve any potential problem.

It was also possible she'd return alive and well. He'd have to ensure the odds were in his favor. He smiled and hastened his step so he could set his plan into motion at once. This was, after all, what Lord Coutre wished him to do, wasn't it? To make certain the marriage moved forward unhindered. He would do his duty to clan and country and eliminate any threats to that marriage.

❧ THEIR MYSTERIOUS WAYS ❧

Karigan limped away from the practice field, tired and soaked through from mud and sweat. Flogger had made her pay for the kill point she got on him earlier. At least she hadn't disgraced herself in front of the king.

It occurred to her King Zachary hadn't stopped by the practice field to observe her at all, that it was just coincidence he came by when she was there for her session. Maybe he paused there long enough only to spare her a quick glance, if even that much. She had not seen him at all, so she did not know.

She slicked loose hair back from her forehead. Did she really want him to see her looking like this anyway? Painfully, she just wanted him to see *her,* but even after her experiences in the tombs, even after her knighting, he had not called upon her to attend him.

All for the best, she decided, but such reasoning did not assuage her feelings, only made her more miserable.

So absorbed in her thoughts was she that she nearly walked into someone. Someone well-dressed and *clean*.

"Sorry, my lord," she mumbled, and stepped aside to go around him.

But he moved into her path, blocking her. She looked up, startled.

"Well, well," he said. "If it isn't the vanishing *lady*."

It took a moment for Karigan to recognize the man, for he was attired in a fine frock coat and breeches, with a spotless silk shirt and cravat. He wore his raven hair tied back, and his light gray eyes glinted with amusement. The last time she'd seen Lord Amberhill, he'd been in a much more travel-worn and ragged condition.

"If I did not know better," he continued, "one would think you were trying to dance with me."

"Hardly," she muttered, annoyed by his mocking tone. "I didn't even see you."

"I suppose I shouldn't be surprised you can't see through all that mud."

Karigan blushed, even more acutely aware of how she must look.

Lord Amberhill placed his hand on his hip, pushing his frock coat aside as if to display the tightness of his breeches.

Karigan's blush intensified. "Excuse me," she said. When she started to walk away, he pivoted and stood once more in her path.

"What? No friendly words for one who saw you through a bad night in the Teligmar Hills?"

"I'd forgotten," Karigan replied, though it was untrue.

Amberhill placed his hand over his heart. "I am wounded you should forget. After all, without me, your hand would no longer be attached to your wrist."

It was not a memory Karigan was fond of recalling, her hand on the chopping block, Immerez standing over her with hatchet at the ready to take from her what she had once taken from him. Yes, Amberhill rescued her, but she'd already thanked him for it. Perhaps he expected her to fawn at his feet and tell him how wonderful he was. He may be accustomed to that from other women, but he wasn't going to get it from her.

"Good day, my lord," she said with finality. This time she feinted right, then left to evade him, and hurried away.

"What?" he called after her. "Are you going to just vanish again? You are the vanishing lady, aren't you?"

Karigan gritted her teeth and kept walking without a backward glance. If only she could vanish in plain daylight! She strode for a servants entrance, ignoring the complaints of sore muscles. It wouldn't do to travel the public sections of the castle looking like this.

She sighed, amazed to think that King Zachary and Lord

Amberhill were related. They couldn't have been more different.

When she reached the Rider wing, desiring nothing more than a hot bath, she found at her door a pile of papers. More work. She began to wonder if she'd been called to the messenger service just to keep its ledgers balanced.

Someone moving about down at the other end of the corridor caught her attention. It was Elgin, and he was pacing. He saw her and strode over to her.

"Hello, Rider," he said. "You've some good moves on the practice field."

"You were there?"

Elgin nodded. "Your captain, too. She was most pleased."

"Really?" Karigan smiled, delighted to hear of her captain's approval.

"The look on that fellow's face when you knocked the sword from his hand!" Elgin laughed, and Karigan's own smile broadened.

"He made up for it after," she replied, thinking of the bruises she'd have to show for it all.

"You did well when it counted, what with the king watching, too."

So he *had* watched her! Pleasure flowed through her. Elgin gave her an odd look and she realized something must have shown on her face. She cleared her throat and changed the subject. "Something wrong? You were pacing."

"Oh." He scratched his head. "I'm due to take the young ones out to Gresia for arms practice, but ..."

"But?"

"Ty's still in the common room with 'em. Making 'em bow and scrape."

Karigan raised an eyebrow and felt dried mud crack. "Bow and scrape?"

Elgin grumbled something under his breath, then said, "Too much etiquette."

"Ah," Karigan replied, remembering her own sessions on the subject with Ty.

Elgin motioned for her to follow. She obliged, her bath

and paperwork temporarily forgotten. They stopped at the doorway to the common room. Ty stood at the hearth, and the new Riders faced him in rows. They'd moved the big table out of the way against the wall, along with all the chairs.

"Once again," Ty told his students. He placed his hand on his thigh, and bowed at the waist. "Thank you, my lady."

The young Riders imitated him, bowing, and saying in unison, *"Thank you, my lady."*

Karigan could not see their faces, but by their fidgeting, she could tell they'd had enough.

"My pleasure, my lord," Ty said, bowing again.

This time when he bowed, a spitwad flew through the air and caught in his hair. He appeared not to perceive it, and this time, as the Riders attempted to imitate him, there was muffled laughter.

"Attend," Ty said, straightening. The spitwad did not fall from his hair, and he remained oblivious to it. "We'll do this once more."

When he bowed again, spitwad and all, Karigan had to duck away from the door and cover her mouth to mute helpless giggles. "Rider Perfect" with a spitwad in his hair!

Elgin followed her with a rumbling sigh. "See what I mean? Too much etiquette. I need to speak with Mara about the training, but she's as hard to get a moment with as Red."

Karigan wiped tears of laughter from her eyes. "Well, etiquette is important."

"That's about what Red said, but I'd think after what happened to Osric, and what may be coming with this Second Empire, a little more emphasis on arms training wouldn't hurt. They've gotta learn to survive."

On that sobering note, Elgin paced back toward the common room, leaving Karigan to ponder the pile of paperwork in front of her door. Elgin was right, of course, but learning to placate an angry noble with proper deference had probably saved a Rider or two in the past.

She shrugged, then scooped up the papers. A letter dropped out of them, and when she retrieved it from the floor, she discovered it was from Alton. Her bath, she thought, could wait a few minutes more.

Once she was ensconced in her room and kicked off her boots, she tore the seal with a certain amount of pleasure mixed with trepidation. They'd already had one exchange of letters since the fall, he asking forgiveness for the way he treated her when last they saw one another. His mind had been poisoned against her, he explained, by Blackveil, by Mornhavon. He did not, however, offer it as an excuse, instead placing the blame on himself, saying that he'd been a fool to believe such evil deceptions. How could he ever doubt her?

The humility of his apology dissipated any confusion, any hurt his behavior had caused her. They were still friends, but ...

But.

Maybe she had read too much into his letter, but she sensed he wanted to be more than just friends. Maybe it was how ardently he expressed his desire to see her, how much he wished to make up for his poor conduct of the past. She shook her head. No, there was more behind his words, not to mention a little history.

They'd almost become "more than friends" once, but their schedules were so often in conflict that it never worked, and Karigan discovered she was actually relieved. She couldn't explain exactly why, but somehow she couldn't imagine herself and Alton that way together. It felt funny, and he was too dear to her to ruin their friendship with the complications of romance. In the end they settled for friendship, though there was always that tension between them, the hint of possibility on the horizon ...

In that light, though she was pleased to receive another letter from him, she also felt uneasy about what he might choose to express. Would he indicate a desire for being more than friends again?

Alton started the letter with the usual greetings and grumbled about the winter. He spoke of how much easier his work would be if only the king and captain would send him a small contingent of Riders, one for each tower. He and Dale had been hard-pressed to visit the towers in the bad weather, and made it only to those closest to them.

He complained about the tower mages and their penchant for partying. He mentioned names and personalities Karigan had a hard time keeping track of, except for Merdigen, whom she'd met.

He was pleased to report, however, the wall guardians seemed content. Frequently he checked them to ensure the song that bound the wall together remained strong and harmonious.

And then it came: *Perhaps the captain could assign you down here. I will suggest it. Then we could spend much more time together—it would be far better than letters to have you here with me. We could work things out between us in person. I have thought continuously of you all through the winter and really want to—* here he broke off and scribbled something out, writing instead, *see you and start over. Please come soon.*

Karigan swallowed hard. He thought *continuously* of her? And what had he scribbled out? She tried angling the paper toward the little bit of light that filtered through the arrow slit that served as her window, but he'd been too generous with the ink and she couldn't make it out. What did he really want?

What was clear was that he wanted her *there*. She had no idea if the captain would actually consider assigning her to the wall. On the one hand, Karigan would be away from the castle and King Zachary and all the wedding festivities. On the other, she would have to deal with Alton and any expectations he had of her. Maybe while he thought "continuously" of her, he'd built her up in his mind into someone she wasn't. Time and separation sometimes had that effect, instead of distancing two people.

But time and separation hadn't alleviated her feelings in regard to King Zachary, as much as she hoped it would. She didn't know why, only that just thinking about him tangled her all up inside.

Men were confusing. King Zachary, Alton, Lord Amberhill, and even her father. They were mysterious in their ways and she would never understand them.

❧ AMBERHILL ❧

She was very mysterious, Xandis Pierce Amberhill mused, as he watched Karigan G'ladheon walk away from him. Even soaked and mud-splattered, with damp locks of hair falling in her face, he did not know what to make of her. Ordinary she might appear at first, but he'd seen her exercise *power*. He'd seen her vanish for real.

He'd first encountered her at the Sacor City War Museum, he in his guise as the Raven Mask to steal a document on exhibit, and she in the guise of a lady. She'd tried to stop him, even attired in fancy dress as she was. She grabbed a sword right off a wall display and attempted to prevent him from taking the document.

He learned much later that if she'd not been in dress and corset, and had been using a sword more suitable to her size, she could have seriously challenged him. At the time he'd only been amused.

The next time he saw her, they were clear across the country in the west, in the Teligmar Hills. She had rescued Lady Estora from kidnappers, then tried to draw them away from the king's betrothed by disguising herself as the lady, only to be captured in turn. Amberhill, who'd tracked the abductors in his own bid to rescue Lady Estora, ended up rescuing Karigan G'ladheon instead. Or, at least her hand. The woman possessed enough fortitude to rescue herself.

In the wake of his adventures in the Teligmar Hills, he learned she was a royal messenger, which explained much about her courage and sense of duty. He noted the esteem with which the Weapons regarded her, and heard much later that she'd assisted them in recovering the book his cousin, the king, had been so concerned about. She'd earned herself knighthood.

And then there was the power.

She'd vanished before his eyes, yet she would not admit she possessed this ability. There was also that amazing black stallion that had been so much more than a horse he'd seen with her. Thoughts of the otherworldly stallion sent a shiver racing through him.

With slow strides he headed toward the castle deep in thought, deftly evading mud puddles and remnant clumps of snow.

As mysterious as Karigan G'ladheon was, he now possessed a puzzle of his own. He gazed at the dragon ring on his finger. The dragon's tail was wrapped around its neck. The ruby eye flickered in the sunlight with gem fire and something more that was beyond his comprehension. It would require a journey to truly understand it.

Yes, a far-off voice seemed to whisper in his mind. *A journey.*

"I plan to embark on a journey," Amberhill said. "I do not anticipate being back in time for the wedding, but I wanted to come to you with my best wishes."

Zachary stroked his beard. He had been flushed and agitated upon entering the chamber—as if he'd been in an argument or had an unpleasant encounter. Lady Estora had mentioned something about a meeting. Whatever it was, it obviously had not gone the way Zachary wanted, but as they sat there, the king settled down, calmed, and became engaged in the conversation.

Lady Estora sat beside him. She was difficult to read. Was she disappointed by Amberhill's pronouncement? She'd appeared pleased to see him when he arrived, placing a light kiss on his cheek, a pleasant scent of lavender rising from her skin.

He shifted in his chair, uncomfortable in her presence. Not because she was to be queen, and not because people proclaimed her the greatest beauty in the lands, but because he, as the Raven Mask, had engineered her abduction, only to be double-crossed by his employers, who turned out to be Second Empire. Guilt and vengeance had driven him to chase Lady Estora and her abductors all the way to the Teligmar Hills. Guilt for allowing the gentle lady to be taken into the hands of such thugs, and vengeance for the murder of his beloved manservant, Morry. He had yet to feel, however, that he'd fully righted the wrong.

So there he sat in the parlor of the royal apartments with his cousin and his cousin's intended, and an elderly chaperone pulling thread on some needlework over by the fire. Servants brought them tea and warm scones dripping with honey butter. Two Hillander terriers watched the scones with bright eyes.

"A journey," Zachary mused. "I must admit, Xandis, you've been a bit mysterious of late, and if I'm not mistaken, your fortunes appear to have improved."

"Yes, my fortunes have indeed improved, but due to a very sad turn of events. My manservant passed away. Turns out he'd put aside a good deal of currency earned while in my grandfather's employ, and made some excellent investments. Having no other family, he bequeathed it all to me."

"That's extraordinary," Lady Estora murmured.

Amberhill nodded. It wasn't every day a lord inherited from his servant. He'd come to the conclusion that in addition to Morry's regular excellent wages, he'd received bonuses from his grandfather, the first Raven Mask, following particularly successful thefts. But while Morry's wealth had been enough to begin repairs on his decaying ancestral manse and to acquire some fine brood mares to help establish the horse breeding stable he dreamed of, Amberhill's true increase in fortune came from pirate treasure. This he used sparingly so his rise to great wealth did not appear too sudden. He did not wish for people to make it a topic of common gossip, or to ask questions.

He sold exquisite pieces of jewelry and gems, as well as coins through dealers he'd worked with when he stole oddments of jewelry as the Raven Mask. These dealers were of questionable scruples, but adhered to a solemn oath of privacy as demanded by their clientele. They dealt in only the finest quality objects as well, but still raised eyebrows at some of the pieces he'd brought them. They were not only worth much for their material value, but were of great antiquity.

"I am sorry for your loss," Zachary said. "Where will you go?"

Amberhill grinned, and with a half-bow toward Lady Estora, he replied, "Why to Coutre Province to visit the lands your lady's father endowed upon me." Lands he was awarded for his part in trying to rescue Lady Estora. What would happen if Lord Coutre learned the truth of Amberhill's hand in his daughter's abduction? He'd done much to ensure that would not happen.

To tell the truth, he wasn't sure he would actually visit Coutre Province. He'd journey to the east coast, yes, but ... The pull was strong, just not specific.

Go to sea, the voice whispered. *Set sail toward the dawn.*

His new lands in Coutre were simply a convenient excuse.

Excuse or not, Lady Estora expressed her delight at his answer by mentioning sights he must not miss upon reaching the port of Midhaven, including the massive chapel of the moon there, a match to any in size in Sacor City. Her eyes took on a far away look as she described favorite haunts, her voice a song.

She sounded homesick. Zachary listened politely. Polite and reserved, sitting well back in his chair, not leaning toward the lady as if to take in her every word or absorb her essence.

Not a besotted suitor, Amberhill decided. He almost sighed, thinking it would be another of those loveless matches made only for an alliance. Love didn't matter, really, so long as the two produced heirs. It made him think, rather rudely, of his horse breeding farm.

Perhaps if Zachary put forth a little more effort toward Lady Estora? She was not difficult to look upon and was very kind and intelligent. A rare combination. Zachary should consider himself fortunate. It led Amberhill to suspect there was someone else his cousin desired. Zachary was a serious fellow, and his affections ran deeper than Amberhill's ever could . He was an upstanding man and a good, decent king, but those virtues were failing him in regard to his betrothed.

Amberhill kept his own relations with women frivolous and very temporary. He'd never fallen in love. Well, maybe for a day or two. He was fond of several ladies, and they provided him with all the warmth and pleasure he desired. Zachary should take this other woman to be his mistress and be done with it. It was a common enough practice among noble lords.

Zachary then surprised him by smiling at Lady Estora and commenting on some detail of the coast of Coutre Province. Lady Estora smiled back.

"Yes," she said, "the view of it from the sea is magnificent."

Amberhill thought he'd better attend more to the actual conversation, but the dynamics between his cousin and the lady intrigued him. It occurred to him how difficult it must be for the two to get to know one another when they were always chaperoned and often caught amid the throngs during official functions. Despite it all, and Amberhill's belief Zachary was interested in someone else, Amberhilll had to re-evaluate and conclude that there was some warmth between the two after all. They certainly were not smitten with each other, but they were at least on congenial terms. Perhaps it would evolve into more with time.

"I climbed the Seamount when I was, oh, sixteen or so," Zachary said. "I was traversing the provinces, seeing what I could see of Sacoridia. From the summit of Seamount the view of the harbor and islands was stunning. I found the blueberries growing there most delicious as well."

Lady Estora's eyes lit up and she delved into yet more reminisences about blueberries and this Seamount. The two carried on at length and Amberhill was caught in a yawn.

Lady Estora laughed. "Our poor Lord Amberhill. We're boring him with our memories."

"Not at all," he replied. "It's just that I've been at work all day arranging for the packing up of my house in the city." He'd miss his "little" rental in the noble quarter, but it made no sense to maintain it when he'd be away for an uncertain length of time doing who knew what. In the meantime, he'd directed his man-of-business to seek a suitable house for purchase. A larger, more prominent house now that he could afford it. It was all about appearances, after all.

A servant came by and Amberhill placed his empty tea-cup on a tray. Lady Estora made a sharp inhalation.

"My lady?" Amberhill asked, startled.

"Your ring," she said. "It caught in the light. May I see it more closely?"

"Of course," Amberhill replied, silently cursing the flashi-ness of the thing. Considering how he acquired the piece, and how it seemed to be attuned to certain powers, he did not want to be questioned about it. He supposed he didn't have to wear it, but he couldn't help but wear it. He did not think it safe to just leave it lying about on his dressing table, and he did not trust leaving it in his pocket. What if it fell through a hole?

Now that he'd been directly questioned about the ring, however, he could not hide it, so he held out his hand for Lady Estora and his cousin to examine.

"It is beautiful," Lady Estora said. "Beautiful and old, if I am not mistaken. Has it come to you through your family?"

"No. I acquired it from a dealer of antiquities. I could not resist it when I saw it." The lie slipped easily from his tongue.

"I can see why," Zachary said. "The craftsmanship is mas-terful, and the ruby very clear and fiery."

"Yes," Amberhill murmured, not comfortable with their scrutiny. He withdrew his hand and they sat back in their chairs.

"Many centuries ago," Lady Estora said, "in the days be-fore the Long War, there were mighty sea kings who ruled much of our coast and conquered many lands. It is said they were a brutal people in war, but generous to friends and fam-ily, and that they celebrated beauty and workmanship above all else. Their sigil was the dragon, or sea drake."

"In Hillander," Zachary said, "remnants of their villages have been found nearly washing into the sea, and the dragon sigil was found upon the few artifacts that survived—shards of pottery, metalwork, and the like."

Amberhill had heard of the sea kings before in reference to his ring, from a pair of eccentric, elderly sisters. He'd been too busy managing his affairs since then to seek further historical reference to them, so it was astonishing to learn they'd had a presence in his home province of Hillander. Perhaps because his estate was inland, and he was not much of a scholar, he wasn't surprised he knew nothing about them.

"How very interesting," he said, as if hearing about the sea kings for the first time.

"I imagine we may have the blood of their people running through us," Lady Estora said. "As for the kings themselves, it is said that during the Black Ages they boarded their ships with all their treasures and sailed east into the mist, never to return."

"Mysterious," Amberhill said, and it was. Unlike the old sisters, neither Lady Estora nor Zachary mentioned anything about actual dragons or any powers that might emanate from his ring. Then again, those sisters had been a trifle uncanny themselves.

"There are, of course, plenty of legends in Coutre about the sea kings," Estora said. "Mostly told to terrify children into good behavior. It used to give me shivers imagining those ships coming back across the sea with their dragon figureheads and pennants, and ghostly sailors manning black sails and oars."

"I wonder," Zachary mused, "what the Eletians could tell us of them. Many Eletians who live now also lived during that time. Not that you would ever receive straight answers from an Eletian." His expression was, for lack of a better description, one of gloom.

The fire in the hearth was dying down, the elderly chaperone asleep with her needlework on her lap, and the scones were mere crumbs. Even the two terriers had sprawled out, sound asleep. Amberhill guessed that an undue amount of time had elapsed.

"I must be going," Amberhill said, and Lady Estora's expression fell with disappointment. "But not without wedding gifts first. For my cousin, a colt or filly of his choosing from the first breeding season at my estate."

"Xandis—" Zachary started to protest.

Amberhill cut him off with a gesture. "It is entirely my pleasure and no hardship. Think of what fine promotion it will be for my stables to have Sacoridia's king riding one of my foals. Which brings me to Lady Estora." He smiled at her. "I've one of my stablehands bringing to Sacor City a yearling filly with a white coat, one of my Goss' first offspring. She will make a fine hunter and pleasure horse. Your old mare, as I recall, met her demise at Teligmar." That was a kind way of saying she'd been ridden to death.

Lady Estora nodded, tears brimming in her eyes, and hands clasped together. "I have missed Falan very much. Thank you."

"You are welcome, but I am not finished." He removed a velvet bag from an inside pocket of his frock coat and passed it to Lady Estora.

"What is this?" she asked.

"Look and see."

She withdrew a delicate gold chain from which hung a pendant fixed with a shining golden gem like the orb of the sun. Gold was worked around it to create the sun's curling rays. She placed one hand to her chest as though her breath were taken away. Zachary raised an eyebrow.

"A gold sapphire," Amberhill said. He'd thought it would complement her golden hair, and he was right.

"It's ... it's too much," Lady Estora said.

"Nonsense. When I saw it, I knew it must be yours." He did not tell her he first saw it in the bowels of a pirate's corpse. His jeweler had grimaced when Amberhill gave it to him to clean, but the man did a marvelous job, and fixed the clasp on the chain as well. He also asked no questions.

"Where did you find this piece?" Zachary asked. Did he sound a trifle suspicious? Or better yet, a little jealous?

Amberhill half-smiled. "Same dealer as I got my ring. He's a good eye for fine antiquities, and so do I." He wondered, as he did over many of the pieces he'd recovered, to whom the necklace originally belonged. Was she as lovely and kind as Lady Estora? Or was she wicked and cruel? As he gazed at it now in the lady's palm, it seemed to him it could have been made only for her.

"Will you put it on me?" Lady Estora asked.

"No, my lady," Amberhill replied. "That's my cousin's duty."

Caught unaware, it was a moment before Zachary stood and bowed to the lady and took the necklace to clasp around her neck.

Amberhill had chosen well. The chain sloped delicately around her neck, and the pendant dangled just above her cleavage. The facets of the sapphire sparkled and burned with flames of gold.

"Ah," he said. "You are Aeryon come to the Earth to walk among us lowly mortals." With the radiance of the gem adding to her natural glow, he could not help but think the sun goddess was truly in the parlor with them. She certainly favored Lady Estora.

"You overstate it," she said with a laugh.

"No, my lady," Zachary said with an uncertain smile, "he does not. But I knew that even before the necklace."

His pronouncement was met with silence. Lady Estora was plainly stunned to hear the words, and Zachary looked stunned to have spoken them. Amberhill privately applauded his cousin. Funny what a nice piece of jewelry could inspire.

"Now, I am afraid, I must take my leave." He stood and bowed, and kissed Lady Estora's hand. He admired the pendant close-up as his eyes roved over her breasts.

"Are you sure you must leave us—the city—so soon?" Lady Estora asked. "I am planning a ball, a masquerade ball, and we would love for you to attend."

"I hope to make my departure as soon as I may, though I will see what I can do about the masquerade. No promises, however."

There was nothing else to say, so the couple wished him a happy and prosperous voyage, and he wished them a happy and prosperous marriage. He had no idea of what lay in the east for him, he just knew he needed to go, and by the time he returned—if he returned—Zachary and Lady Estora would be well into their union together.

In the meantime, he had a late night ahead of him.

⋞ A GOOD TURN ⋟

Though the Raven Mask was "dead," Amberhill maintained his skills, roaming all quarters of the city in the dark of night, silently sinking into shadows.. He listened to rumors in the streets from those who gossiped about the betrothal of Zachary and Lady Estora, to those who expressed uneasiness about a gathering darkness in the world. He observed lovers strolling by, whispering words only lovers could whisper.

Mostly what he heard in the night was ordinary folk grumbling petty complaints about the weather, the price of grain, and one another. Still, he preferred that to his dreams of the unceasing roll of waves, the sea calling to him, calling him till he ached.

He took a deep breath as the throb built within him, and another until it eased. Cloaked and hooded in black, he stood in the shadow of a close. Few were out at this hour, mostly drunks and vagrants. Dim light filtered from the grubby windows of the Cock and Hen. Rumor had drawn him here to the lower city; rumor of a pair of unsavory characters who visited the most disreputable inns and taverns. There was a familiar ring to the details he heard about them.

As he watched and waited, the clip-clop of hooves preceded a mule cart driven up the Winding Way by a man hunched over the reins in his fists. The cart wheels creaked and wobbled as though the whole contraption was about to fall apart. The mule looked no better, underfed and swaybacked. The man reined the mule to a halt in front of the Cock and Hen. When he set the brake, he painstakingly climbed down from the cart. His limbs shook and jerked seemingly without control.

No sooner had he planted his feet on the ground than two toughs—not the two Amberhill had been awaiting, alas—appeared from around the inn's corner. Among the rumors Amberhill heard, these two figured prominently, for they sought fights unbidden and robbed the weak. They'd probably been following the old man for some time, sizing up their prey. Considering the condition of mule and cart, it wouldn't have been difficult for them to keep up.

"Hey, old man," one said, sauntering up to the cart. "What you got to give us?"

"Go away," the man said. "I've got nothing."

The second tough peered into the cart. "Not much back here," he said. "But look at this bow." He withdrew a longbow from the cart.

"Leave that be!" the old man cried.

"What else you got?" the first tough asked.

"Nothing, I tell ye! Give me my bow." He reached for it with a shaking hand, but the second tough held it just out of reach and laughed.

Amberhill saw the glint of a knife as the first one drew it from his belt.

"You got some coins, old man?" He waved the knife in the man's face.

Amberhill knew these thugs would think nothing of killing the man for no other reason than it amused them, which just would not do, so he swept out from the close, his cloak billowing behind him. He drew his rapier in a movement as natural as breathing.

"Leave," he said.

"Who's this?" one of the toughs asked, unimpressed.

"I've told you to leave, but you do not listen."

The thug opened his mouth to speak, but before any words crossed his lips, Amberhill's rapier flicked across the back of his hand and the knife clattered to the street. The thug cursed and held his bleeding hand close. Amberhill pivoted just in time to knock a knife from the other man's hand. He held the tip of the rapier to the thug's throat.

"Return the bow to its owner."

"All right, all right. Just watch it with that sword." He handed the bow to the old man.

"Now leave," Amberhill commanded. "If I catch you bothering this gentleman again, or anyone else, I shall be far less polite."

This time the two listened and ran off down the street.

The old man wiped his brow with a trembling hand. He gripped the bow so tightly with the other his knuckles turned white. Amberhill noted it was indeed a handsome bow, with graceful curves and intricate carvings decorating it.

"I . . . I don't know how to thank ye, sir," the man said. His accent was of the west.

"No need to worry about it. Those two have been asking for trouble for some time."

"Name's Miller. Galen Miller." He offered his hand and Amberhill shook it. It was a bowman's hand and he was taken aback by the strength in it, despite the man's apparent infirmity. Galen Miller then straightened; rose to his full height. He was tall and broad shouldered, but he could not control his trembling. He reminded Amberhill of an uncle of his who suffered from the shakes and declined over the years, his body deteriorating, his mind afflicted with senility, until eventually he wasted away, not at all resembling the proud, strong man he had once been.

"My pleasure to meet you," Amberhill said, not offering his name in kind. "This is not the safest of neighborhoods to linger in after dark."

"I've traveled a long way," Galen Miller said. "Aye, a long way. I am lodging at this place."

"Here?" Amberhill asked, thinking the accommodations very rough.

"It is the right place," the man replied with conviction. He raised his gaze toward the roofline. "Aye, the right place."

"If you find it not to your liking, these will help you find better." Amberhill folded three silvers into the man's hand.

Galen Miller's eyes went wide. "Sir, I couldn't! It's too much."

"It is but a trifle. A welcome for a traveler to the city."

"Th-thank ye. This . . . this means a great deal."

Amberhill nodded, wondering how to gracefully conclude the conversation so he might slip back into the shadows and resume his vigil.

"You must try the bitter ale," he said. "The inn is not the finest, but it has the best bitter ale in the city."

The man nodded. "Thank ye again." He glanced at the inn, and while his attention was diverted, Amberhill melted back into the concealment of the shadows. He watched Galen Miller turn around as though to speak to him, then scratch his head at his absence. With a quavering shrug, the old man folded into himself again before entering the Cock and Hen.

Amberhill smiled. He had not often gone out of his way to aid someone in need. He'd mostly been about helping himself, but after the debacle of Lady Estora's abduction, something had changed within him. Maybe it was that he saw how one deed could affect others for good or ill. Maybe because he witnessed how the king's Weapons and Green Riders— especially that G'ladheon woman—selflessly endangered themselves both out of duty and the desire to do the right thing. A part of him thought them mad, and another part of him thought them admirable.

He'd wronged Lady Estora, but tried to rescue her when he realized what he'd done. He helped the G'ladheon woman escape the torture of Second Empire thugs and found . . . he found he rather liked it, this helping others. He'd liked helping Galen Miller tonight.

He smoothed his hand down his shirt as though stepping beyond the bounds of his own self-interest made him nervous. He wasn't sure what he liked about it, but maybe it was the thrill of danger, like when, as the Raven Mask, he'd scaled the wall of some manse in the depths of night to enter a lady's bedchamber to steal her jewels, and perhaps other things, even while her husband slept in the next room.

Yes, there was that. The danger, the excitement.

Yet, there was more to it.

A glow of light flickered to life in the uppermost room of the Cock and Hen— perhaps the attic—and someone moved around in it. Galen Miller? Amberhill could have chosen to leave the old man to the toughs here on the street. There was a time when he probably would have. But now? He shook his head. There was the thrill of chasing the toughs off, no matter they were no challenge to him, and there was the pleasure of being the object of the old man's gratitude. Yes, he liked that.

Maybe this was also a little step in the direction of finding redemption. Amberhill could never right the wrong he'd committed against Lady Estora, and really the ripples of that wrong radiated out to her family and clan, to king and country, magnifying it a hundredfold, but he could at least take steps to redeem himself in his own eyes.

Besides, one never knew what a good deed could lead to. Maybe Galen Miller would in turn come to someone else's aid in some way. Amberhill smiled at the thought.

∞ PEARLS AND BONES ∞

A mberhill maintained his vigil into the early morning, listening as the city bells struck the hours. Patrons of the Cock and Hen came and went in varying degrees of drunkenness. He yawned, thinking he'd misheard the rumors and that maybe he'd do better to call it a night and go to bed, but just then two men staggered up the street toward the inn.

They were lumpy forms beneath the light of streetlamps, and Amberhill's nostrils flared much like his stallion's when he caught a disagreeable scent on the air. The stench of rotten fish, pickled livers, and years of unwashed grime. It was familiar. Very familiar.

The two reeled back and forth, arm in arm, as though on board a ship on a rolling sea. They sang, if it could be called such, their words slurred and their rough voices off-key. They were bound for the Cock and Hen and Amberhill wondered if even that establishment would welcome these two into its premises.

He did not have to see them up close to know he had not killed all of Captain Bonnet's pirates that fall morning in a clearing of the Green Cloak Forest. The rumors told how these two tottered from tavern to tavern each night drinking, alledgedly, gallons of rum and ale, and how they attempted to go whoring, but how no woman would have them. Seldom did pirates find their way this far inland, and the particular vileness of the duo—not to mention their ragged clothing and bare feet—left Amberhill in little doubt of who they were.

He was drawn to them like an ant to honey. He had questions . . .

He stepped from the shadows and strode into their path before they reached the inn's door. They staggered to a halt, one still singing in wretched strains until his companion jabbed him in the ribs.

"Whaaa?" the singer asked. He was short and round. The dim light from the inn glanced off the cracked lenses of his specs.

"Someone in our way," the other replied. This one was tall and skinny and carried, Amberhill noted, a cutlass on his hip.

"What does he want?" the singer asked.

"Dunno."

"I want to know," Amberhill said quietly, "if you recognize this." He held his hand before him so they could see the dragon ring. The ruby caught in a glimmer of light and turned to red fire on his finger. The two pirates stilled.

"That's Cap'n Bonnet's," tall and skinny said.

"That means . . ." short and round began. Both gazed at Amberhill. "The cap'n. Where is he? We got separated in them woods."

"Dead," Amberhill said. "Very dead. As is the crew with him."

The two pirates glanced at one another with wide eyes. Then, "You kilt them!" tall and skinny cried.

"I had little choice at the time. It was me or—"

But the pirate did not want to hear an explanation. He whipped out his cutlass.

"No," Amberhill said, "I have questions!"

The other pirate caught at his companion's arm. "Don't!"

"Git off, Yap! Lemme kill 'im!" He shook free of the other's grasp and swung his cutlass at Amberhill.

Amberhill danced away. This was ridiculous. The pirate was so drunk he could hardly walk much less engage in combat. His companion, Yap, moved out of range of the flailing cutlass and pressed his back against the wall of the inn.

"I just want to—" Amberhill began, but he needed to duck as the cutlass scythed for his neck. The momentum made the pirate spin all the way around before coming to a staggering halt. Amberhill thought he could hear the rum sloshing in the pirate's gut.

"I'll flay yer skin and wear it as a shirt," the pirate declared. "I'll..." He stumbled and wove about the street.
"I'll..." He swayed one way, then the other, as if unable to
control his feet. He swung the cutlass like a blind man and
it flew from his grip through the air and clattered onto the
street somewhere in the dark.

"Oops," the pirate said.

He started to run after it, but his toes caught on a loose
cobblestone and he tripped and fell hard, his head striking a
hitching post with a crack and snap as he went down. After
he hit the street, he did not move.

"Keeler!" Yap cried, and he raced to his companion's side.

Amberhill joined him and immediately saw that the pirate had not only gashed his head open, but had broken his
neck as well. Already the reek of decay drifted up from the
pirate's body and Amberhill grimaced. Like the other pirates
he had slain, Keeler's corpse decomposed rapidly before him,
flesh sinking into ribs, his face turning into a grinning skull.

Amberhill drew his parrying knife and cut away the pirate's shirt.

"What are ya doing?" Yap demanded, balling his fists.

"Checking for treasure," Amberhill replied.

Yap backed away. Evidently he knew to what treasure
Amberhill referred.

Amberhill turned back to the corpse, feeling like a grave
robber preparing to practice his skills. That was another
rumor he heard in the night, of menders paying fees to grave
robbers to bring fresh corpses to them so they might cut open
the bodies and learn what they could of their inner workings.
But this was no fresh corpse. He pulled out a handkerchief,
covered his nose and mouth, cut into the parchmentlike skin
of the pirate, and peeled it away from the bones.

Amid the gore within were glints of gold, and globules he
at first took to be the eggs of some creature. Some parasite?
He nudged one with the tip of his knife, then dug it out. He
held it pinched between thumb and index finger to better see
it in the lamplight.

Yap had overcome his fear or revulsion or whatever to
peer at what Amberhill had found. Amberhill wondered

briefly why the fellow did not simply run off. Curiosity? It appeared he did not perceive Amberhill as a threat, and why should he when Amberhill hadn't even drawn his rapier to defend himself against the drunken Keeler? Nor did he detect any great sense of loyalty in Yap for his dead friend.

Something rumbled in the pirate's chest. "Keeler was fond of oysters," he said.

Amberhill smiled. The globule was a pearl. There were many inside Keeler. He dropped the one into the cavity he'd created, stood, and swept off his cloak. He laid it flat on the street beside the corpse. "Help me, will you?" he asked Yap.

When the pirate saw what he was about, he helped transfer Keeler's remains onto the cloak—not that Keeler had much bulk left to him anymore. Amberhill folded the cloak to help conceal the corpse, then took up the head end. Yap, catching on, took the feet.

"Where we taking him?" Yap inquired.

"Where all bones must go."

Amberhill felt even more like a grave robber as he and Yap stole through Sacor City's deepest shadows with their burden between them. They might find concealment in the dark, but, unfortunately, little could be done about the stench. Fortunately, most citizens were abed at this hour. Just so long as they didn't run into a constable . . .

Yap kept up as best he could, his breathing harsh and his bare feet slapping the cobbles of the street behind Amberhill. His steps were sometimes clumsy, but he asked no questions, did not try to murder Amberhill, did not run off.

Fortunately, Amberhill's destination was not terribly far. It was a small, unkempt cemetery off Egg Street—one of many tiny cemeteries located throughout the city. Because space was limited, it was common practice in Sacor City to bury the dead for a time, then remove their bones to an ossuary. Some wealthy citizens had permanent graves or mausoleums, but ordinary citizens usually accepted the community ossuary as their final resting place. Some were so packed with bones that they had to be closed, and the remains therein moved elsewhere.

The gate to the cemetery off Egg Street was broken, hanging from one hinge only. Amberhill and Yap slipped in with their burden. Among the weeds were wooden markers protruding at irregular angles. They followed a worn path toward the back corner of the cemetery where the stone vault that served as the ossuary stood. It did not take much to break the lock. The door groaned inward, and the building exhaled a fetid, musty breath. It was actually preferable to the stench Amberhill had been carrying in his cloak.

"What," he asked Yap, "do you suppose is the opposite of a grave robber?"

Yap scratched his head. "A grave returner?"

Amberhill did not enter the vault, but stood in the doorway and pitched Keeler's bones inside, crumbs of flesh falling from them. As undignified as his treatment of the bones might be, it was probably better than Keeler deserved. Yap certainly made no protest.

When he finished, he brushed his hands off, then closed the door to the vault. He gathered up his cloak, carefully folding into it whatever tiny bits remained of Keeler and the treasure that had been contained in the pirate's corpse.

"What now?" Yap asked.

The moon was setting and daybreak would soon be upon them. It was time to return home.

"I have questions," Amberhill said. "Will you come with me someplace where we can talk? Voluntarily?"

A look of astonishment overtook Yap's face. "Voluntarily . . ." he murmured, as though the concept had never occurred to him. "Aye. I think I should like to."

By the time they reached the noble quarter and Amberhill's house, birds were awake and chattering in the trees. Dawn was shifting the world from night to morning dusk.

Again, Yap had followed without asking questions and seemed to absorb his surroundings with interest. Amberhill led him to the back of the house and stashed his bundled cloak beneath a shrub bordering the foundation. The groundskeeper was not due today, and it was well concealed, so it ought to be safe for the time being.

He opened a window he kept well greased for his stealthy

comings and goings and jumped up onto the sill and swung
his legs inside.

"So," Yap said from outside, "are we robbing the house, or
returning something?"

Amberhill smiled, pleased the pirate had a sense of
humor. "What was here is mostly gone, and all of it mine." He
could've entered through the front door, but old habits died
hard. He preferred no one espied his late night entrances
and exits, regardless. He supposed he could use the back entrance, but where was the fun in that?

He assisted Yap through the window, pulling on rough,
cracked hands. The rotund pirate scrabbled frantically over
the windowsill and pretty much rolled into the house, landing
on the floor with a hefty thump. Vacant as the room was of
many of its original furnishings and objects, the noise seemed
excruciatingly loud to Amberhill's ears and he hoped it did
not awaken any of his servants.

Yap clambered to his feet and glanced warily around in
the dim light of the library. The shelves were mostly empty.
There were a few chests and packing crates on the floor.

"Have a seat," Amberhill said, indicating one of the few
remaining chairs.

Yap did so tentatively at first, but then with an expression
of delight, he allowed himself to sink into the plush uphol-
stery, exhaling with contentment. Amberhill hoped the stink
of pirate would not adhere to the fabric.

He remained standing with arms folded and regarded his
guest, but could discern nothing beyond his rags, stubbled
cheeks, and straggly gray hair.

"You must be very rich, sir," Yap said.

"More so than many," Amberhill replied, "with the help
of pirate treasure." If his words had any effect on Yap, he
could not see it in the pale dawn light. "What can you tell me
about the dragon ring?"

"Is that what ya brought me here for, sir?"

"I said I had questions."

"What if I don't have answers."

"I shall send you on your way."

Yap gasped. "Ya won't kill me then? Not even for . . . not

even for . . ." He patted his chest to indicate the treasure within.

"Only if you give me cause shall I kill you."

Silence fell as Yap considered his words. "That is fair spoken. And if my answers please ya? I have no ship no more. Old Yap's nowhere to go."

Amberhill was not surprised Yap angled for some small reward. He was, after all, first and foremost a pirate.

"I am sure I can make it worth your while. *If* your information is good."

Yap took another moment to consider his words, then said, "Fair. I will tell ya what I know of the ring. It starts with the sea kings."

⇜ YAP'S STORY ⇝

The light in the library turned gray with the rising sun. Yap looked like a figure of pewter as he sat unmoving in the armchair. Would he vanish in a puff of light when full morning broke? The pirates were not entirely mundane, and whether it was the influence of some outside force that made them so, or an innate quality of the pirates themselves, Amberhill did not know. He had only to consider the treasure he'd collected from their quickly rotting carcasses as proof there was something arcane at work. He recalled Captain Bonnet mentioning a curse.

Yap, however, did not vanish, but cleared his throat. "As long as I can remember, Cap'n Bonnet was gripped by the lure of sea king treasure. He'd listen to tales in every port about the fabulous stuff the sea kings had. Funny, but none of these tale tellers could show us any proof these stories were true, or tell us who might have a piece of treasure, but that didn't stop the cap'n one bit. Oh no. Many was the time he'd pick out an island that might fit one of the stories, and he set us to digging, looking for treasure.

"Once we found something stuck in a beach. A gold torque with a dragon's head. Not worth much when you spread its value around the crew, but it was enough to excite the cap'n and off we were again chasing some other old rumor. To be sure, we still took ships and their cargoes as any decent pirate must, otherwise the cap'n woulda had a mutiny on his hands for chasing ghosts and nothing to show for it."

"How did rumor turn into treasure?"

"Why, it was a storm, sir. An autumn ripper as my old dad

153

would have called it. We were in the Northern Sea and the storm was so bad it rammed us aground on a small island there. We spent weeks making repairs and poked about the island. That's when we stumbled on the grave, sir. Well, that'd be Eardog who fell into it. He was always finding trouble, Eardog. Rigged wrong in the head if you take my meaning." Yap thumped his forehead with his finger.

Amberhill had met Eardog, so he did take Yap's meaning. "What was in the grave—besides the obvious, that is?"

"It wasn't just any grave, sir. It was a cavern, a big one, with a whole, real ship in there. The entrance hole was big enough for a man, but not big enough to push a whole ship in. Makes me think they musta took the ship apart and carried it in, in pieces, and rebuilt it. A black ship with a dragon figurehead. That's how they buried the king—in his ship with all his treasure. Aye, it was an amazing sight." Yap paused, his gaze glassy as he remembered a scene long past.

"The old king, he was laid out on a byre on deck, he being nothing but bones covered in furs and rugs. And jewels. And all around him were chests of coins and more jewels. Weapons, too, and some other rubbish we didn't care about—kettles of food and drink all long gone, or long gone bad. The treasure we loaded right quick into the hold of the *Mermaid*."

"Your ship, I take it."

"Aye, and bloated she was with our treasure when all was said and done."

"And the ring?"

"Cap'n Bonnet took it right off the king's bony finger. Saw him do it, too."

Amberhill did not think it a good omen that the ring only seemed to come off the fingers of the dead. He suppressed a shudder and gazed at his ring anew, at how the ruby caught even the dimmest shreds of dawn leaking into the library.

"We mighta gotten away clean and good," Yap said, "but for that ring."

"How's that?"

"Those islands, they were the dominion of witches I'm thinking. That's what the stories say, anyway. And the one whose island we were on? She wasn't too happy we took her treasure, and somehow she knew when the cap'n took the ring from the king. The air, it changed. Got thick. The wind keened with her voice, grief and anger in it. It was enough to skin ya. We ran back to the *Mermaid* right quick and pulled anchor. She tried to swamp us with huge waves, but Cap'n Bonnet, for all he was a bloody, murdering thief, he was a good seaman. When the storm settled, we laughed at our luck and cheered the cap'n's prowess.

"And then . . ." Yap squeezed his eyes shut and shuddered.

"Go on," Amberhill encouraged in a quiet voice.

"You won't believe it."

"There is much in what you've already said that I *could* refuse to believe."

"It's true," Yap said. "All of it."

"I'm not disputing your words. I am simply stating that your story is of a rather incredible nature." Amberhill had seen enough that was strange of late that he was not about to dismiss Yap's tale. "Tell me what happened next."

"You got drink, sir?"

Amberhill was quite sure he'd get nothing further from Yap without it, so he poured him some brandy. Likely Yap had never tasted anything so fine, unless he and his crew had stolen quality liquors off some ship and shared them out.

"None for yerself, sir?" Yap asked.

"It's a little too early for me."

Yap shrugged and threw the brandy down his throat as if it were some third-rate whiskey. Amberhill frowned, but said nothing for the drink appeared to bolster Yap's courage to go on.

"We heard her voice, a mourning song for the old king it sounded like. Then she chanted the curse."

"Who? What was the curse?"

"Why the witch, sir. Haven't ya been listening? The curse, why that was a bunch of mumbo jumbo, though some of it we could understand. Something about being stuck in mist, out of time, no land to see until the bottle is broke."

"Bottle?"

"Aye. Musta broke, cuz here I am. Why the ship ended up in a house, though, I can't say."

Then it resonated. Something Captain Bonnet had said about being "bottled up," and then later, the Berry sisters mentioning that one of their father's "things," an arcane object, had broken, leading to a pirate ship emerging in their house.

"A ship in a bottle," he murmured, and instantly he pictured one of those clever renderings craftsmen made to sell in shops. For many a sailor or shipwright it was winter's work. But for a full size vessel to be bottled? He exhaled a long, deep breath. What he knew of the world had been deeply challenged since autumn. Best not to dwell on ships in bottles. Best just to accept the impossible and move forward.

"After the witch spoke the curse," Yap continued, "the wind, it got real calm, too calm. It never picked up again. Never ever. We were dead becalmed, like the Listless Ways of the southern seas. But at least the Listless Ways will pick up now and again and ya can eventually find the trade winds. No trade winds here. We got all twitchy. Some thought mutiny. We'd soon run out of food and drink, and in time we did. It was somethin' terrible. We had all that treasure, but we were stuck someplace where the stars made no sense. By day sea smoke hung on the horizon, surrounded us like a wall. We were trapped there on that patch of sea for a long, long time. It wasn't regular, and only a curse would do that. Nope, that witch was not happy we stole from her island."

"Do you remember," Amberhill asked, "where the island was?"

"That was long ago, sir," Yap said, "and I was no navigator, just a lowly hand. All I know is that it was in the Northern Sea archipelago."

Which contained hundreds of isles.

"Do you think you'd recognize the island if you saw it again?"

"I dunno. Maybe. But . . ." The pirate shuddered. "I'd never want to see it again. Curses and bad luck."

"Hmm."

At that moment, a flicker of golden light illuminated the library. Amberhill whirled to find his manservant, Brigham, standing in the doorway with a lamp in hand. Even in his sleeping clothes and robe, the man was impeccable.

"My lord? Is all well? I heard voices." Then he sniffed and frowned with distaste, his gaze falling upon Yap. He blinked and his frown deepened.

"Good morning, Brigham," Amberhill said. "All is well."

"Then shall I rouse Mistress Landen to make breakfast for you and your . . . companion?"

Amberhill glanced at Yap, and the additional light revealed just how squalid the pirate appeared in his rags, with dirt imbedded in pores and wrinkles, and what looked like seaweed tangled in his hair. *Something* tiny scurried beneath the snarled mats. Something with little claws and antennae.

"First I should like Mister Yap to have a very thorough scouring in a hot bath. We'll burn his clothes and in the meantime he can don one of my robes."

Brigham, whom he'd known only to be efficient and unflappable, looked more than mildly horrified at the prospect of bathing Yap. Then he squared his shoulders. "Very well, my lord. As you wish. I shall heat up water for a bath."

"Good, and a basin for me, as well," Amberhill said. It would be a relief to wash the remnant gore of Keeler from his hands.

Brigham nodded, turned on his heel, and left the room, taking his light with him.

"What's that ya said about a bath, sir?" Yap asked, a note of anxiety in his voice.

"You are going to take one."

Even in the dim light, Amberhill could make out the mortified expression on Yap's face. "B-but I gave ya the story. You said it would be worth my while."

"And it will be. After your bath. I do not conduct business or eat breakfast with anyone who has not bathed in months."

"*Years,*" Yap corrected, with no small amount of pride.

"Indeed," Amberhill replied. He'd have to give Brigham a bonus when he was through with Yap. He wondered how much of the pirate would remain after the grime was scrubbed away.

In any case, he did not think his business with Yap would be concluded even after the pirate bathed and ate a hearty breakfast.

No, he did not. He had plans.

⊰ CANDLESTICKS ⊱

Amberhill rummaged through Morry's wardrobe looking for anything that might fit Yap. He'd not had the heart to go through Morry's things. Even now, it caught in his throat when he saw a familiar frock coat and remembered Morry in it, or a favorite waistcoat or shirt, and felt the texture of velvet, wool, and tweed, with a remnant of the musky scent of the old gentleman still hanging in the air.

I should give all this away to people who can use it, Amberhill thought, but every time he considered doing so, the idea hit resistance. He felt as if giving away Morry's clothing was like losing a piece of the man who had been like a father to him. It was difficult enough to think of clothing Yap in it.

So he focused on pieces that might simply fit the pirate. Trouble was, Morry had been trim throughout his life, and Yap was rather round.

He withdrew a pair of trousers that might do. A pair that might be worn at a country gentleman's hunting estate. They were looser in style than the others, though it would still be a close thing as to whether or not they fit. He found a hearty broadcloth shirt, too, and a waistcoat to match the trousers. Finally, Amberhill took out an old gray cloak that was voluminous enough to fit Yap.

As he removed the items from the wardrobe and placed them on Morry's old bed, Brigham appeared in the doorway. The sun was well up, and in the light that flowed into the room, he saw how wan his manservant appeared. He looked as though he wanted to be ill. He stood there in his

159

shirt sleeves and apron, with a scrub brush in one hand and something else in the other.

"You are done with Mister Yap's bath?" Amberhill asked.

Brigham nodded. "My lord, it was most unspeakable. The filth!" He shuddered. "I took this from his hair. Among other things." He exhibited a hermit crab, antennae twitching, on his palm— it still had some of Yap's gray hairs clinging to it. "The tub, when we finished—no! I cannot speak of it."

Brigham paled so much Amberhill feared he might faint. "Where is Mister Yap now?"

"At breakfast."

"You've done well," Amberhill said. "Take the rest of the day for yourself."

Brigham whimpered and now Amberhill thought he might cry. "Thank you, my lord." With that, Brigham turned slowly away, as though dazed, and walked down the corridor with his scrub brush and hermit crab. Amberhill hoped he wouldn't have to find another new manservant after this.

After pulling out pairs of stockings and shoes that might fit Yap, he went downstairs to the dining room. It took moments for him to realize that the man he observed sitting there sawing into a ham steak was the same man he'd brought home. Gone was Yap's straggly, matted hair. It was cropped close to his scalp, and gleamed more white than gray. Without the dirt and rags, and freshly shaved, wearing one of Amberhill's old bathing robes, he appeared more a gentleman than a pirate sitting there amid the oak paneling of the dining room.

Yap paused and said, with his mouth full, "Will ya be joining me, sir?"

"Chew and swallow before you speak, Mister Yap." Amberhill was suddenly reminded of his old nursemaid teaching him manners.

His cook, Mistress Landen, evidently had not witnessed Yap in his more odoriferous condition, and flittered and flustered to bring him fresh helpings of eggs and ham and fried potatoes. She slathered his toasted bread with butter and jam and placed it before him. She preened when he requested fresh cups of kauv, and blushed and giggled when he winked

at her. Amberhill had never seen such behavior from his matronly cook before. Just as well he gave Brigham the rest of
the day off. The man would be appalled.

Amberhill sat at the head of the table and Mistress Landen
was back with another plate filled for him.

"Eat up, my lord," she said. "You should follow Mister
Yap's example. He has a fine appetite."

Yap grinned as he chewed, and Amberhill thought he
might lose his appetite altogether.

"These here . . ." Yap paused, remembering to gulp down
his food first, and started again. "These here vittles are very
good, sir. Land flesh! How I missed it all those long years at
sea." He pushed another chunk of ham into his mouth and
chewed with vigor.

Amberhill picked at his own breakfast, amazed at Yap's
capacity for food and kauv. Time after time Mistress Landen
bustled out of the kitchen with more food and refills.

"I feel fresh as a new baby," Yap said. He passed his hand
over what remained of his hair. "Thought yer man Brigham
was gonna scrape my hide right off my bones. I wouldn't
wanna be on his bad side."

"No, indeed," Amberhill murmured, sipping his kauv.
Usually he took it with sugar and cream, but somehow he required it rather stronger this morning. "I have set aside some
clothes for you to try on."

"That is most generous, sir. This has been a most wonderful morning. Keeler wouldn't believe it."

Amberhill raised his eyebrows. Certainly Keeler would
not consider it a wonderful morning considering his bones
now rested in the Egg Street ossuary, but Yap appeared entirely undismayed by the absence of his former companion.

Once Yap filled himself to capacity, leaving both Amberhill and Mistress Landen in awe, Amberhill took him up to
Morry's room and helped him change into the clothes he'd
picked out. Before Yap pulled on the shirt, Amberhill espied
old lash marks on the pirate's back; so many that there were
more scars than unmarred flesh. Yap might be a cheerful fellow now, but it did not mean his life as a seaman had been

easy or lighthearted. Pirates could be particularly merciless in the punishments they doled out.

The clothes were close to bursting and too long in both sleeve and pant, but Yap was undismayed. "These are very fine, sir," he said. "I've worn none finer." He gazed at himself in Morry's mirror from all angles.

Amberhill rubbed his chin. He could get this ensemble, and Morry's other clothes, let out and hemmed, and have Yap measured for new pieces.

When they were downstairs in the entry hall once more, Yap whirled this way and that to see how the cloak flowed around him. Amberhill narrowed his eyes. There was more beneath the cloak than just Yap.

"Well, I'll be thanking ya for yer kindness, sir, but I 'spect you've had enough of old Yap for now. I will take my payment and leave."

"Where will you go?" Amberhill asked, playing along with Yap's intent for the moment.

Yap shrugged. "Where there be ships. I'm a seaman. I don' know nothing else, sir."

Amberhill dropped four silvers into Yap's hand, and the pirate gasped. "That . . . that is very generous, sir. I thank ya. And now, good-bye."

When Yap turned for the door, there was a metallic flash from beneath his cloak that was not the coins. Amberhill grabbed Yap's arm, spinning him around.

"Mister Yap, I have been exceedingly generous with you, as you have noted more than once. But now you insult me."

"Eh?"

"What are you concealing beneath the cloak?"

"What? Why . . . why nothing, sir!" But Yap's blush showed otherwise.

Amberhill struck viper-fast, grabbing a pair of silver candlesticks from Yap's hands.

"These are nothing?" Amberhill demanded. "Empty your pockets." When Yap just gaped at him, he said in a low threatening voice, *Empty your pockets.*"

Yap gulped, then started turning out his pockets, producing a spoon, an ornate letter opener, and a pair of Morry's gold cufflinks.

Amberhill swiped the cufflinks from him. Anger grew in him like a fever. The candlesticks and other trinkets were negligible, but the cufflinks, that was a different matter. "You do not deserve the clothes you now wear. They belonged to a good, honest man. A father he was to me. You dishonor him."

Yap backed away, visibly trembling.

Amberhill paused, breathing hard. The heat of anger turned to a sharp, cold razor. "And if you are stupid enough to steal from a master thief, then maybe I should turn you out in only the skin you were born in."

Yap's eyes went wide and were made grotesque by the cracked lenses of his specs.

Amberhill suddenly felt terribly exhausted. Exhausted and a hundred years old. Seeing Yap in Morry's old things had chafed a much too recent wound, rubbed it raw and bleeding. He licked his lips. Forced himself to calm. He straightened and passed his hand over his eyes. "You will not be stealing from me again, will you Mister Yap."

"You won' kill me, sir, will ya?" came the plaintive question.

Amberhill frowned. By all the gods, the pirate was close to weeping. He'd been broken at some point in his life. Amberhill almost pitied him. Almost, but not enough to prevent him from taking advantage of the pirate's shattered spirit.

When Amberhill failed to immediately provide an answer, Yap backed away, holding out the items he had stolen, as well as the four silvers that were his payment. "Please, sir, take 'em back. Please don' kill me. I'll leave yer things and leave ya be."

"The silvers are yours," Amberhill said. "Unlike the other items, I gave them to you. You will assure me, however, they will not be spent on liquor. I don't need men in my employ to be drunk."

"I don' . . . I don' follow, sir. You won' kill me?"

"You said you were bound to go back to sea."

"Aye, but—"

"I, too, am going to sea. On a voyage, Mister Yap. I need someone with your . . . expertise to go with me."

Yap stood a little straighter, then gazed down. Amberhill followed his gaze to his own hand, to where the dragon ring resided on his finger. Was it his imagination, or did the ruby pulse for just a moment? He thought he felt the breath of the sea against his face.

"I don' know, sir," Yap said.

"If you agree to work for me, I certainly won't kill you."

Yap blanched at the implication that if he walked out, Amberhill would indeed kill him.

"You'll be very comfortable in my employ. Regular meals and good accommodations. There will be a monthly payment, of course, so long as I am pleased with your service."

"Meals?" Yap asked, brightening.

Amberhill nodded.

"Land flesh?"

Amberhill nodded again.

"Well, sir, that is worth a thought or two."

Yap, Amberhill reflected, had no choice in the matter, whether he realized it or not. Nor did Amberhill. He could almost hear the breaking of waves, the call of the gulls.

He had no choice but to go to sea.

⊰ SUMMONED ⊱

Karigan leaned against the fence rail, Elgin beside her, watching the newest batch of green Greenies circling the riding ring on horseback at a trot under the hawklike scrutiny of their instructor, Horsemaster Riggs.

Karigan had come outside to rest her eyes after trying to untangle Rider accounts and payroll. They were an even bigger mess than she originally thought. After too many hours crouched over tiny notations, she'd grown restless. Days had passed and she hadn't received a single message errand, while Tegan had been out twice, and Garth disappeared during the night.

Maybe it was the bright sunlight and the smell of damp earth as the snow melted that made her twitchy. Birds returned from the south in chittering flocks, and the horses ran and kicked in their pastures with renewed vigor. The world was coming alive, but Karigan was stuck in the damp, dark deeps of the castle with her dim lamp and ledgers. Maybe she ought to tack up Condor and take him around the ring a time or two herself.

Some of the new Riders were clearly more acquainted with the finer points of horsemanship than others. Horsemaster Riggs did not demand perfect form. She *did* train her students to be capable riders able to sit a saddle for long hours, to keep their seat in difficult situations, even during battle, and how to pace a cross-country journey. The care of a horse and its equipment were also among her important lessons.

Currently they rode retired cavalry horses. New messenger horses would arrive later in the spring, brought by the trader whose family had supplied the Green Riders with their mounts for generations. The horses came from the wild and were very intelligent, even uncannily knowing. When they chose to be.

Pretty soon each of these new Riders would have a horse that was his or her own to ride and care for, forming a special partnership and friendship that would last as long as both lived.

"Reverse trot," Master Riggs called out.

The Riders obeyed, or attempted to obey, the command. One girl flailed her legs against the sides of her horse, who merely halted and dropped his head to graze. A boy could not stop his horse from circling. Others failed to switch diagonals as technique required for the posting trot. Master Riggs sorted them out one by one.

"They seem to be coming along," Karigan said.

"Got a ways to go," Elgin replied.

"At least it's not more etiquette training. Did you ever talk to Mara about Ty?"

Elgin made a snorting laugh.

"That would be a 'yes'?" Karigan inquired.

Elgin nodded. "I must give Mara credit for a creative solution."

"Oh?"

"Yep. Instead of confronting Ty directly, she simply sent him on an errand to Penburn. He'll be gone a good bit and I can see that these wee chicks are turned into real Riders."

Karigan had to admit it was a clever move on Mara's part. Sending Ty away would not ruffle his feathers the way correcting him on his training methods would, and he could not argue with a direct order to head out on a message errand.

"Heh, when Ty suggested she send you instead," Elgin said, "Mara told him that if he wanted his pay on time that you be left here to continue working on payroll. That sealed it."

And it explained why Karigan hadn't been sent on any errands. She sighed. The sooner she fixed the ledgers, the sooner she could be out riding.

They watched the lesson in silence for a while more. The

sun felt good on Karigan's back, and she was not inclined to return to the darkness of the castle. Master Riggs called on her students to canter. Again, some made the transition more easily than others. Some sat the gait nicely, others lurched around on their saddles.

"That Merla," Elgin said, "is coming along fine."

Karigan spotted the girl, a gawky sixteen-year-old who sat her horse competently enough, even though her elbows stuck out and her posture was slouched.

"From Adolind," Elgin said. "Her folks are tenant farmers. Real poor. No horses for them. She'd never been on one before she came here. Look at her now—a natural. See the extension on Baron? He's liking it. Now Sophina on the other hand . . ."

Karigan glanced at the young woman who rode her horse very erectly, heels down and toes up, shoulders thrown back, hands steady. Here was someone who had been taught proper equitation, but who appeared stiff and uncomfortable. It did not help she had her chin pointed up and a scowl of disdain on her face at having, Karigan assumed, to endure lessons at such a rudimentary level.

"She's a bit of a priss," Elgin said.

Karigan raised an eyebrow at his bluntness.

"Aristocratic family, I hear, and her parents none too happy she's been called. She's riding old Graft like a stick of firewood. Thinks she's too good for us and our old cav horses. No doubt her poppy provided her with all sorts of hotbloods to ride around on at home."

Karigan gave him a sidelong look. She'd had access to numerous fine horses in her father's stables herself as she grew up, and so she thought his opinion of Sophina unfair. However, she refrained from mentioning this fact to Elgin or reminding him of her own father's wealth.

"Does Graft look happy to you with Sophina riding him?" he asked.

Karigan had to admit he did not. His was a plodding sort of canter, and he chomped on his bit in discontent; it was true Sophina looked like she would be much happier in a sidesaddle on some fine hunter riding with others of her own class.

"Wait till Riggs puts them in mounted combat training," Elgin said with a wicked gleam in his eye. "Then Sophina will learn something, and I hope she does. I hope they all do because it'll mean their survival."

He was right, Karigan reflected. Riders rode in all conditions and under many circumstances. Fighting from horseback would be a whole new discipline for the young Riders to learn as it had been for her. All of her training with Arms Master Drent was fine and good. Dismounted. Wielding a sword from atop a horse required an entirely different set of skills.

"We want them to come back," Elgin murmured. "We always want that."

Elgin suddenly seemed to no longer see the Riders in front of him. Karigan thought he must be thinking of those in the past. She knew little of his history, but wondered what Riders *he* had lost. She observed him closely, saw a muscle jump in his cheek and the subtle tightening of his weathered features.

"Command is never easy." His voice was so soft Karigan thought he spoke more to himself. "Give an order, never know if they'll make it back."

Karigan thought to ask questions, to gently delve into his past, but a Green Foot runner approached at that moment with a summons from Captain Mapstone. She bade Elgin good-bye, and minutes later when she reached officers quarters, the captain opened the door and ushered her in.

The captain's chamber served both as both her living quarters and her office and was on the whole spare of personal adornment. However, books, ledgers, and other records crammed shelves, and a barrel full of maps was tucked into a corner. Her worktable was strewn with papers and a few mugs filled with the dregs of old tea. The light was dim, for like the castle itself, officers quarters were built of stone with only arrow slits allowing outside light in. The captain, Karigan knew, did not spend a great deal of time here, for she was often in the castle attending the king and sitting in on meetings.

"Have a seat, Karigan," the captain said, then proceeded

to scratch away on a paper with her pen, seemingly oblivious to her Rider's presence.

Karigan sat in a chair before the worktable, awaiting her captain's pleasure and wondering why she'd been summoned. Perhaps she'd be sent on an errand after all, though it was usually Mara who passed on those orders. Maybe the captain wanted to discuss her progress on the ledgers and payroll. Whatever it was, she did not mind the diversion.

The captain scribbled on for some moments, her expression intense. In the dim light, it appeared to Karigan that there was a little more white mixed in the captain's red hair than she remembered, a few more careworn lines along her eyes. However, when finally the captain set her pen aside and looked up at Karigan, her hazel eyes were as lively as ever.

"Deadlines," the captain said, by way of explanation, and she sprinkled sand on wet ink. She folded her hands together atop the worktable and gazed steadily at Karigan for some moments. "How goes your work with the accounts?"

Karigan described her struggles, but she wasn't sure the captain was hearing everything she said, though she made affirmative noises at the appropriate moments.

When she finished, the captain said, "We need to find someone else who can assist with accounts, and take over when you are on an errand. Mara is an excellent Chief Rider, but dealing with accounts is not one of her strengths. I'll have Elgin keep an eye out for someone who might do, and then you can train him or her up to your standards."

"That would be helpful, I guess," Karigan said. As much as she disliked taking care of Rider accounts, she feared that adding another person into the process would only muddle things up all the more.

When she noticed the captain still gazing at her with an intense look on her face, Karigan surmised the summons was not actually about Rider accounts at all.

The captain abruptly stood, rounded the table, and leaned against its edge with arms folded. Again there was the scrutiny, as if she were trying to see into Karigan's soul and make up her mind about something. Karigan shifted in her chair. She hadn't been concerned by Captain Mapstone's summons when she came to officers quarters, but now she was beginning to worry.

"I wish to discuss an errand with you," the captain said. "One that will be, for the moment, between you and me. I request that you do not speak of it to anyone else."

"Of course," Karigan said.

The captain nodded, then said, "There is no easy way to broach this other than to just say it. Karigan, I need to send you into Blackveil."

It was as though a crater opened beneath Karigan and she fell, the world rushing past her, the weight of dread speeding her on.

ON THE ROOF

Karigan blanched, but she said nothing, issued no protest, did not request Laren to reconsider. Laren did not know how anyone was supposed to react to the news that they were being sent into Blackveil Forest, but she certainly did not expect Karigan's stillness.

Laren had deemed it necessary to speak to Karigan of this now. The king's other advisors were pressuring her to officially name the Riders she'd be sending into Blackveil, and she thought if she put the mission before Karigan privately, and persuaded her that she was the best Rider for the job, Karigan might champion her inclusion herself, perhaps making Zachary less likely to object. But then, love was unpredictable and powerful and he still might overrule everyone and forbid Karigan's participation.

In the face of her Rider's quiescence, Laren could only keep talking. "As you've likely heard, the Eletians desire to cross over into Blackveil Forest."

Karigan nodded.

"The king is determined that they not go without being accompanied by Sacoridians. We do not fully trust them, and we have as much interest in seeing what is on the other side of the wall as the Eletians. The king wishes Riders to be among those who go with them. You are one of my most experienced Riders, and you have already been in Blackveil and *survived*."

"I was not myself then ..." Karigan passed her hand over her eyes.

It was an understatement, Laren knew. Karigan had been

171

possessed in turn by Mornhavon the Black and the spirit of the First Rider.

Karigan shuddered. "He was . . . he knew everything about me."

Mornhavon, she meant. Laren could not guess what it was like to have someone control your actions while you were a spectator in your own body. How much of Karigan's mind had he had access to? What an incredible violation it must have been, and it was only then Laren realized what she was asking of Karigan. Yes, Mornhavon might be gone from Blackveil for now, thanks to Karigan's own intervention, but what if he reappeared while the company of Eletians and Sacoridians were still there?

It did not matter. Karigan was still the best choice, and Laren was her commander. She could not afford to change her mind based on personal considerations. Karigan would go as ordered. It was her duty.

In case there was some hesitation on Karigan's part, she said, "I know we have asked much of you in the past and you have endured more than any Rider I can think of. If you tell me now not to send you, I will pick someone else. But frankly, I can think of no other Rider who has a better chance of returning alive from Blackveil." The implication being that any other Rider going in her place would not return, and the onus would be on Karigan.

Karigan looked down at her knees as that implication sank in. "I will go, of course."

Laren nodded. She found the manipulation distasteful, but she had only spoken the truth. "There may be answers to be found that will help us deal with Blackveil, with Mornhavon. And of course, we need to know why the Eletians are so bent on exploring Blackveil. We think they are drawn more by the desire to see what has become of Argenthyne."

Karigan continued to remain still, but upon mentioning the ancient, lost land of the Eletians, Laren saw something flicker in her eyes, that fathomless quality she'd seen before. Mysteries, a timelessness. There was a distance to her as though she already walked in that dark country. And then just as quickly it faded.

"Who else?" Karigan asked.

"What?"

"You said Riders, not Rider. Who else are you sending?"

"I've not made any final decisions as of yet." And she hadn't. It was not easy deciding which of her Riders to commit to such a dangerous mission. "Have you any suggestions?"

Karigan shook her head. "When?"

"You are to be at the wall by the equinox. The Eletians were very clear they wanted the days to be turning longer than the nights when they entered the forest."

Karigan gazed out the arrow slit. Pale light fell across her face and glinted off her hair. Her silence unsettled Laren. It would be easier if Karigan had argued, shouted, thrown her chair across the room ... anything.

"Do you have any more questions for me?" Laren asked.

Karigan shook her head and the light shimmered down her hair.

Laren's heart sank at what she believed was resignation on Karigan's part. "If you think of any questions or you just want to talk about this, do come see me."

When her ploy to elicit some response from Karigan failed, Laren excused her. After the door closed behind Karigan, Laren stood still for some moments feeling regret. She knew she would feel even more regret when she finally decided which other Riders would accompany Karigan into the forest. She must consider the experience and magical ability of each Rider and decide who would be most useful on the expedition, as well as who would be most likely to survive. She sighed, and rounded her desk to resume work, but found she could not concentrate.

Instead, she decided to seek out Zachary. They needed to talk about Karigan some more now that she had expressed acceptance of the mission. Laren set off from her quarters, thinking she would check with Cummings, Zachary's secretary, to find out his availability. She was certain this would be another difficult confrontation. Zachary had cooled toward her after their last conversation about Karigan, and she could only guess this would not improve their rapport.

*   *   *

According to Cummings, Zachary's schedule was clear for the afternoon. That meant he could be almost anywhere doing almost anything. It took Laren a long while to track him down, and when she did find him, it was in a place she hadn't been since summer. When she passed through the heavy door and stepped out onto the castle rooftop, she squinted in the glare of the sun and shivered. During the summer the roof was pleasant. Now? She did not envy the soldiers who stood watch up here every day throughout the winter. Of course, they were dressed for it and she had only her shortcoat for warmth.

A soldier greeted her and pointed the way to the king. She crossed the roof, which was a warren of guard towers and, at this time of year, warming huts. Soldiers paced the battlements and looked out on the vista of Sacoridia searching for anything that might threaten the king and his realm.

She crossed a footbridge that spanned a wide gutter, melt water rushing through it beneath a crust of ice. She found Zachary leaning against a crenel gazing southward into the city. Donal kept watch several paces away. From this height, the buildings, people, and animals of the city looked to her like a princely toy set.

She joined him, angling into the lee of a crenel to shield herself from the wind, while allowing the sun to warm her. Zachary wore a fur-lined cloak and did not appear bothered by the cold in the least.

"What do you see?" she asked him.

If he was surprised by her arrival, he did not show it. "I see a busy and prosperous city laid out before me. Earlier a formation of geese flew north overhead, while a winter owl perched among the trees." He paused, and with a faraway look in his eyes, added, "And not long ago, I saw a Green Rider ride off castle grounds. It was Karigan." He produced his spyglass as if to prove he was not mistaken.

After the enormity of what Laren had told Karigan, she was not surprised the young woman had gone for a ride. Most Riders found solace in the companionship of their horses. Many was the time when Laren herself had sought out Bluebird for much needed comfort.

Zachary had provided the opening Laren needed. She said, "Speaking of Karigan, I thought you'd want to know she has accepted the mission to go into Blackveil."

Laren thought it was perhaps more accurate to say she'd manipulated Karigan into accepting the mission, but another part of her truly believed that given a choice, Karigan would have volunteered to go anyway. She was like that, always wanting to take responsibility for the big problems. Or maybe Laren was just trying to justify her actions to herself.

There was no outburst of condemnation from Zachary. He just continued to gaze out at the city. Ever since he was a small boy, he'd been so serious and learned to rein in his emotions. He was under constant scrutiny from all quarters, and exposing his true feelings could compromise his authority, make him vulnerable to attack from his political enemies. Once in a while, as in their last conversation about Karigan, his emotions surfaced, but it was a rare occurrence.

When, she wondered, did he ever have a chance to follow his passions, to expose himself? How could he contain it all within himself? Weapons practice and the occasional hunt in the countryside no doubt helped, but surely these were not enough.

When was the last time he'd had a woman with whom to relieve his male urges? There were elegant courtesans in the city, accepted and patronized by members of the nobility, who could provide such a service. An outlet of this sort might help him in many ways, not least of which would be by diverting his thoughts from Karigan. Yes, she would certainly make some careful inquiries.

"I knew," Zachary said, "she would not refuse. It would not be like her to do so."

"Are you going to intervene?"

He did not answer for a long while. The breeze ruffled his hair and Laren tensed as she waited.

"I know the reasons why you chose her," he said finally, "and understand them. Yes, *all* the reasons. When I separate my head from my heart, I understand. My heart, however, does not want it." He rubbed his chin, his gaze toward the clouds. "Yet I am a king who must govern more with his head, and less with his heart."

Laren's shoulders sagged in relief. "I thought you would come to see the sense of it."

"Do not mistake me," he said. "I will not intervene, but it does not please me."

"Of course it does not. It does not please me to have send *any* of my Riders."

"Then I suppose," he sharply replied, "I should blame myself that Karigan is going into Blackveil. After all, it is I who made the decision that Riders should be part of the expedition."

Laren did not dare respond. There was no good answer.

"You censure me with your silence."

"No. I don't—"

"It is true," he interrupted, "that it does all come back to me. I know that as the dangers to our land increase with Birch to our north and the uncertainty of Mornhavon to our south that I will have many difficult decisions ahead that will result in the sacrifices of many, including those I hold dear."

Laren sighed. How could she have ever doubted him?

"There are times," he continued, "that I wonder how my life would have been if I were born to a fisherman or a farmer, instead of a king."

"Sacoridia would have been poorer for it," Laren replied.

"It's impossible to say. But I should have liked being a farmer. I'd have been a good one, I think."

It was not difficult for Laren to imagine him on a saltwater farm in Hillander growing crops and raising cattle. Perhaps he found the idea of it alluring because it would not only save him from the critical decisions he must make to safeguard the realm, but because it would also allow him to be with the woman of his choosing.

"You are a good king," Laren said firmly. "We need you."

"Perhaps there will be a day when Sacoridia has no need of kings and queens."

"What? That's nonsense! That's rhetoric straight from the mouths of those mad anti-monarchists that used to pass out pamphlets before the castle gates. What would we have without our monarch? Chaos, that's what."

"Not chaos, but some other way of governing ourselves. Our current system works if we have, as you say, a 'good king,' but what about those who follow me? History has shown that the throne has often represented tyranny."

Laren gazed hard at Zachary. He'd always been a deep thinker, but she'd never heard this line of radical thought from him before. He'd always been so sure of his place and the role of the monarchy. She hoped no one else heard him talking like this.

All she was certain of was that he was a fine king who put his country before himself. With serious danger threatening the land, they needed him more than ever.

⊰ PATHS ⊱

Karigan did not return to the Rider wing to work on accounts. How could she after what the captain had told her? She headed instead to the stables, barely acknowledging the others now done with their riding lesson and untacking their horses. She saddled up Condor and rode off castle grounds in a daze, unaware of the winter owl gazing at her from the limb of a towering pine, and not knowing that her king observed her from the castle roof.

Condor was full of himself, feeling the sun on his back and the change in the weather. He pranced and puffed and tossed his head. Karigan focused on holding him in as she traveled the city streets taking shortcuts, carefully wending her way through crowds, until finally they passed through the last set of gates.

She let him have his head and he sprang into a gallop down the road, kicking up slush and mud. She paid little attention to direction, just letting Condor run. When finally she pulled him up to rest, they had come well east of the city to a grouping of squat, rounded hills. On maps they were called the Scangly Mounds, but Mara simply called them the Pimples.

Some thought the mounds contained lost treasure and the tombs of forgotten kings, but all anyone found when they dug into them was dirt and rocks. They'd been made by nature, not the hands of people. All that Karigan knew was that they were good for riding and she brought Condor here now and then for exercise. The hills were barren, except for clumps of snow and coarse grass, and Karigan urged Condor up the nearest and tallest, which provided a good view of the odd terrain, but what drew her gaze lay to the west. Rising above the forest, wrapped in its granite walls, was Sacor City, the castle sitting at its pinnacle, its pale gray walls almost white in the sunshine.

It occurred to her she could just keep riding, run away from all obligations. The idea of traveling when and where she willed held a seductive quality, but if she were ever caught, the punishment for desertion would be severe. Besides, she doubted the call would allow her to abandon her duty. And things had changed. *She* had changed. There was a time when running away was her answer to everything—a way of evading responsibility or confronting difficult problems—but she had come too far, had grown up enough to realize running away was no answer. Not anymore. Not even when it meant having to enter Blackveil Forest.

She shuddered. Even on this day of sunshine, with the promise of spring not far off, a shadow touched her. She recalled little of the forest itself, but it remained a threatening presence on the edge of her awareness. And she remembered Mornhavon, the incorporeal darkness that had invaded her mind and body.

"Why me?" She had meant to shout, but it emerged as a whisper.

Maybe because she knew it had to be her. Not because the captain told her she must go to Blackveil, but because all the paths she'd been traveling were leading her there. Somewhere inside she'd known it was inevitable.

The words *destiny* and *fate* felt too weighty, and she did not like the idea of some external power directing her life. No, it was as much an internal force, like she had to see something through. Find completion. Whatever completion meant for her.

She removed her mother's moonstone from her pocket, and even in the sunshine it cast a sharp, silver glow. Her mother had passed it on to her, and this she would take into Blackveil. It would help force back the dark. As she gazed into the light, it wavered like a flame. *You must come,* she thought she heard, as some distant whisper, and she shuddered. Then she decided it was only the breath of the wind blowing among the Scangly Mounds that was making her hear things.

She tore her gaze from the moonstone and looked out upon the landscape around her thinking there was a rightness to her mission, but it did not mean she *wanted* to go or that it didn't frighten her. She'd have her mother's moonstone at least, and she was not the only one doomed to go into Blackveil, yet that created another complication: Eletians.

The prince of the Eletians, Jametari, had once explained that the tainted wild magic that had burrowed into her veins created a duality within her, a capacity for much good or great evil. The prince warned her that, as a result of this conflict, there were those among the Eletians who wished her ill because she posed a possible threat to the D'Yer Wall. Some desired to just eliminate the threat. One had tried.

The wild magic was gone from her, but she feared some Eletians still wanted her dead. In the fall, while she and Fergal had traveled west on errands, there'd been that illusionary arrow in her chest she'd received like a message after Eletians had passed their campsite in the night.

How would those Eletians who thought her a threat react to her being a member of *this* expedition?

She supposed it was just one more danger among the many she'd be facing.

Condor shifted beneath her, and she nudged him to a walk. When they reached the base of the hill, she clucked him into a canter. She rode among the Scangly Mounds, adhering to no set path, moved only by the joy of her horse running.

✥ INTRUSIONS ✥

The blood hissed as it dripped on a patch of old snow. The ring of lanterns revealed the creature's carcass bristling with arrows and weeping crimson from a multitude of sword slashes. It was a rat the size of a pony, its eyes glowing copper in the lantern light. Its jaw was lined with a row of incisors that had almost ripped off the leg of one man, but it was the claws that had taken the life of another. It was also those claws that had enabled it to climb over the repair work in the breach.

"*Damn,*" Alton D'Yer whispered.

It wasn't like they hadn't been vigilant. The breach was well guarded, and a good thing. Alton did not want to imagine the damage the creature could have wreaked if they hadn't been so watchful.

Yet, they had not been vigilant enough. Maybe they'd relaxed a little, a little too much, with Blackveil relatively quiet and the repair work done on the breach.

Hissss, came the sound of more blood sliding into the snow.

"We'll increase the guard," Alton told Captain Wallace, who was in charge of the encampment at the breach. "I'll send to my father for reinforcements. In the meantime, I'll spare as many men as you need from the tower encampment."

"Yes, my lord," Captain Wallace said. "Thank you."

As the son and heir of the lord-governor of D'Yer Province, Alton was the ranking person at the wall to whom the officers came for major decisions. Alton was also a Green Rider, whose mission was to solve the mysteries of the wall

181

and fix it. If he'd not been the son of the lord-governor, he'd be just another cog in the wheel of the encampment, which consisted of both Sacoridian soldiers and members of the D'Yer provincial militia.

Mostly Alton was able to leave the administrative tasks to the military and concentrate on his own work. Occasionally his position proved useful because it allowed him to get what he wanted and when—for the most part—but it was times like this that made his stomach clench and left him wishing he possessed no rank whatsoever.

Hissss.

"Drag this thing away from the encampment," Alton told the captain. "Burn it. But be careful of the blood."

"Yes, my lord." Captain Wallace turned and commenced issuing orders to his underlings.

Dale Littlepage, a fellow Green Rider who'd been assisting Alton at the wall since autumn, appeared at his elbow. "Gruesome," she said, looking down at the creature.

The two Riders backed off a few paces to allow the soldiers the space they needed to prepare the carcass to be dragged away.

"Leese thinks she can save the one man if his wound doesn't fester," Dale said, speaking of the encampment's chief mender. "But he'll lose his leg."

Alton sighed. Both men were Sacoridian troopers. He'd have to write a report to the king. The widow of the dead man would receive some reparations, and so would the injured man. However, the military had little use for someone with only one leg and he'd have to find another way to support his family if he had one. It would not be an easy life.

Alton glanced at the wall. Except where lanterns illuminated it, it vanished into the night, blotting out the stars. The actual stonework rose only ten feet, but magic extended it seemingly to the heavens, a bulwark that was impenetrable to the denizens of the forest and protected Sacoridia and its neighbors.

Until the breach.

Repeatedly Alton and his people had tried to repair the breach, even reopening the same quarries that had been used centuries ago to build the wall, but it was only stone. There was so much more to the wall's strength. Thousands of souls were bound to it, and their song, a song he now felt reverberate through his bones, created the magic and strength that made the D'Yer Wall what it was.

A masterwork. A thing of magic. An artifact of monstrous slaughter.

He watched as the soldiers lashed ropes around the dead rat creature. Until he could figure out how to extend the magic to the stonework of the breach, they could expect more incursions of this kind from Blackveil. The one hope he'd had, the book of Theanduris Silverwood, only confirmed that the magic used to strengthen the wall required the sacrifices of thousands of magic users.

Since Daro Cooper, a newish Rider Alton hadn't met before, delivered the translated manuscript of the book days ago, he'd pored over it time and again. Daro had also brought the news of Osric M'Grew's death at the hands of Second Empire and he'd spent time, along with Dale, in mourning. Was still in mourning.

Now his grief only hardened his determination to solve the problem of the breach.

A soldier ran toward them, his buckles and mail glimmering in lantern- and firelight.

"Sirs, our perimeter guards just caught an unauthorized person approaching the encampment."

Alton and Dale exchanged glances. First the creature and now an intruder? It was turning into a long night.

Their intruder was seated beside one of the watch fires, the soldiers who guarded her fully alert, their hands gripping sword hilts. She hardly looked dangerous, but after the incursion of the creature, he didn't blame the soldiers for their tension. And in these unsure days, one never knew in what guise danger would appear.

She rose as they approached, but it was difficult to tell much about her except that she was of a similar age to both Alton and Dale. She was plainly cloaked. If she carried any weapons, the soldiers would have confiscated them.

At first no one said anything and they gazed at one another across the fire.

"Greetings," the young woman said in a pleasant voice, finally breaking the silence.

"Who is she?" the captain demanded of his soldiers.

They all started talking at once, but no one seemed to know.

The woman's voice rose above the fray. "If someone asked me directly, I'd be more than happy to introduce myself."

"Please do so," Alton said.

She leveled her gaze at him and Alton discerned a smile. "You would be Lord Alton D'Yer," she said.

"You know me then."

She nodded. "I've heard much about you."

Now Alton frowned. "I'm afraid you have me at a disadvantage then. I do not know *you.*"

"No? I am a minstrel of Selium." She bowed with hand to temple.

Hand to temple? A minstrel who was high born?

"My name," she said, "is Estral Andovian, daughter of Aaron Fiori, the Golden Guardian." She held her hand out so they could see her ring with the sigil of the gold harp on it.

Estral Andovian—Karigan's best friend. As the Golden Guardian's daughter, she was indeed high born. And as Karigan's best friend, he did not doubt she had heard a bit about him, leading him to wonder just what she'd been told. Thinking of Karigan made him frown once more. No letter from her had arrived with the packet Daro carried from Sacor City. There were many reasons one might not have come. She could be out on a message errand, or hadn't had time to write, or, he'd just been too pushy, scared her off.

"My lady," Captain Wallace said, "you must know the wall is off limits to civilians. It's dangerous."

"I'm aware of the dangers," Estral Andovian replied. "I also know civilians are discouraged."

"Then what brings you, my lady?" Alton asked.

She gazed at him and now he saw in the firelight her eyes were a translucent green, like the hue of the sea with the moon behind the waves.

"I came as a minstrel," Estral said. "I am a journeyman, and at this stage of training, if I'm to ascend to master, I must travel, offering my services of song wherever I go."

"This is a strange destination for you to choose," Captain Wallace said.

"I do not think so. I imagine those here would appreciate a little entertainment to break up the monotony, or to take their minds off other concerns."

"True enough," Captain Wallace replied. "But the risk to yourself—"

"There are other reasons I came," Estral said. "I come as a representative of the Golden Guardian, as a witness if you will. This," and she gestured in the direction of the wall, "is where history is happening. It needs to be recorded and remembered and that is also the duty of the Golden Guardian and his minstrels."

"History, my lady?" Alton's voice was sharp. "The dangers here are very real, not a footnote in some dry old tome. People have died here. *Tonight.* I will show you this 'history.' "

He took her by the elbow and led her toward the wall where the soldiers were trying to hitch the rat creature to a horse, but the horse was having none of it, bucking and whinnying.

"The horse has good sense not to go near that carcass," Alton said.

Estral stumbled back from his grip with a little cry when she saw the creature.

"This," Alton said, "came out of Blackveil. It killed one man and savaged another. This is why I am going to insist you leave us and take your journeyman training elsewhere. This is no place for a . . . a musician, whether she is the daughter of the Golden Guardian or not."

"I . . . I am sorry about your men," Estral said.

She didn't run away, and after the initial shock, collected herself better than some of the soldiers had. Weren't most females terrified of rats? This wasn't even a normal-sized one. Outside the Green Riders, his experience with women led him to believe they were all a bit squealy. Estral actually gazed hard at the beast as if committing its appearance to memory.

"You're not going to cast her out tonight, surely," said Dale, who had tagged along.

Captain Wallace and his soldiers had also followed. "It is the dark of night. No moon."

"What?" Alton said. "I—"

"She can stay in my tent," Dale said. "There must be another cot floating around the encampment somewhere."

"But—"

"There is risk here," Dale said, "but it isn't very hospitable or safe to send her out into the woods at night either."

Alton looked at Captain Wallace for some sort of support.

"I'm in agreement with Rider Littlepage," the captain said. "I'm sure tomorrow morning will be soon enough for Lady Estral to depart."

"Yes, yes, of course." Alton combed his fingers through his hair. What kind of oaf must she think him for insisting she leave right now? He espied a glimmer in those sea green eyes and glanced away. "Tomorrow morning will be soon enough."

"Very well," Estral said. "My thanks to you, Rider Littlepage."

"Call me Dale."

"Dale it is. And none of this 'my lady' stuff from anyone, please."

Dale and Estral strode off, arms linked and chatting like old school friends.

"I will play tonight," he heard Estral say.

"Entertainment will help take our minds off tonight's troubles," Captain Wallace told Alton.

That night, Estral did sing, backing herself with a small traveling lute, her voice clear and unwavering. She sang songs that were soothing and did not bring great sorrow upon the encampment's inhabitants. She also sang songs of strength, recalling heroic deeds and great warriors of eons past.

Alton found her singing and playing was heartening and realized he'd gone far too long without hearing such quality music. He also had to admit it was intriguing to meet someone from Karigan's "other life," someone she had known well before becoming a Green Rider. What had she been like in those days? Oh, he'd gotten the hint she wasn't the best or most compliant of students while at Selium, but what details might Estral Andovian reveal if asked? What details that only a best friend could know?

It was tempting to allow Estral to remain. The gods knew they could all use the musical entertainment she would provide and the tales she could tell, but he could not allow these desires to cloud his judgment. No, Estral must leave. The wall was no place for civilians, musical or otherwise.

In the middle of her performance, Alton retrieved his horse, Night Hawk, for the ride to the secondary encampment at Tower of the Heavens. When he mounted, he could not say what ballad Estral sang, but the tone of the lute blending with her voice stirred something in him. Resonated. Not only that, but it was almost as if the voices in the wall hummed with it.

He shook the sensation off and reined Night Hawk away, the music fading behind him.

⇜ KARIGAN SAID ⇝

The next morning after a private breakfast in his tent, Alton stepped outside, stretching his back and shoulders. The weather was fine, and if it kept up, there would soon be no snow left at all. The late winter chill freshened the air and he breathed deeply. Most inhabitants of the encampment were up and about attending to their various duties which brought to Alton the sound of an ax splitting wood for cook fires and the *clink-clink-clink* of a farrier working a horse shoe over by the pickets. He caught snatches of conversation from guards on duty by the wall and heard the sloshing of a bucket being emptied somewhere behind the row of tents.

He decided the plan for this morning would be to enter Tower of the Heavens and comb once again through the book of Theanduris Silverwood. He feared missing something vital, some clue that could help him repair the wall.

On the edge of his vision he caught someone strolling toward him. He'd almost forgotten about Estral Andovian.

"Good morning," she said in her pleasant voice.

"Morning," Alton replied. When she halted before him, he noted daylight deepened the green of her eyes.

"It's very impressive," she said, gazing toward the wall. "You hear about the wall, but it really takes seeing it to get the full effect. Words just don't do it justice."

It was true. It dominated all else, soaring skyward and vanishing into the clouds as though raised from the Earth by the gods, stark, monumental, forbidding. The Tower of the Heavens shot upward like a spear shaft to infinite heights. The wall and tower, however, were not a creation of the

gods, but the handiwork of Alton's own very human ancestors. He wondered how many of them were among the sacrificed whose souls still inhabited stone. He would never know,
for those souls were no longer individuals. They had become
one, united in song to keep the wall strong.

"I chose right to come here," Estral murmured.

That may be, Alton thought, but she must shortly be on
her way. This was no tourist spot like the hot springs in her
home city of Selium. He thought back to how several of his
fellow citizens had treated the wall as just that, like a holiday
in the country, until an avian creature out of nightmare had
flown over the breach and killed one of them. An innocent. A
young lady. After that, the holiday revelers had dispersed and
the rule forbidding civilians at the wall came into existence.
Alton was relieved by the ruling, for it did not take much to
remember the tortured screams of that young woman. He
closed his eyes, hearing them now, until he felt Estral Andovian's gaze upon him. He frowned when he realized she must
have been gazing at him for some time.

"I don't recall Karigan describing you as the brooding,
silent type," she said.

Just what had Karigan told her? And what could he say in
response that didn't sound defensive? He decided the safest
course was to ignore her comment.

"I trust you had a satisfactory breakfast?" he asked instead.

"Very nice. And Dale was the perfect hostess."

"Good. Well, it was very nice to meet you, but I'm sure
you are ready to be on your way to make the best use of
daylight."

She stared blankly at him, as if surprised by the suggestion she leave, despite his adamance of the previous night.

"I'd like to stay," she said.

"That is impossible, as we discussed. You saw the danger.
This is no place for a civilian."

"But I'm not exactly a civilian."

"Are you a member of the D'Yer militia?" he asked.

"No."

"Are you a Sacoridian regular?"

"Well, no." Then she smiled. Alton was suspicious of that smile—it looked like trouble. "The Golden Guardian supports the king's forces with trained musicians who entertain, parade, and play drum and pipe during battle. So technically we are attached to the military."

She was creative, he had to give her that much. "There are no musicians assigned to either encampment. I am sorry, my lady, but I am in command here on behalf of my father and I must insist you leave."

"Very well," she said, but before Alton could be surprised by her quick acquiescence, she asked, "Have you any messages for your father?"

"My father?"

"Yes. I believe I'll go to Woodhaven to visit him. I should think he'd listen to reason and permit me to stay here. After all, I've official greetings to present to him from my own father. My father tells me that Lord D'Yer appreciates the importance of well-recorded histories."

They all did, since so much about the wall and magic in general had fallen into obscurity following the Long War, leaving them in their current fix of trying to relearn what to their ancestors was common knowledge.

"My father," Alton said, "also appreciates the dangers of this wall. It wasn't that long ago he lost his brother and nephew to it."

Estral shrugged. "All the more reason he may wish to have everything recorded for the future. I'm sure I'll be back soon." She spun on her heel and started walking away while Alton could only watch after her in astonishment. But then she paused and turned back to him. "You know, Karigan never mentioned how inflexible you were."

"Inflexible?"

Estral nodded slowly. "Yes, I'd definitely say inflexible." Without further ado, she was off again, striding away, leaving a fuming Alton behind her.

"Inflexible?" he muttered. "*I'm* not the inflexible one."

He faced the wall, arms crossed. In regard to Estral Andovian, the term *insufferable* came to mind. He'd never gotten the impression from Karigan that her friend was such a pain in the—in the rear.

He grumbled and headed for the tower. Let Estral travel to Woodhaven to see his father. If Lord D'Yer approved of Estral's presence at the wall, then *he* could be responsible for her well-being. Problem was, Alton reflected, if something happened to Estral, Karigan would not blame his father, but him. He sighed.

He paused before the tower and tried to clear his mind of Estral Andovian and whatever Karigan would think or say. It was not easy to do, but once he pressed his palm against the granite of the wall, the throb of music pulsing through it, the song of the guardians, helped him focus.

The tower possessed no door, not even any windows or arrow loops on its impassive facade, but it allowed certain persons to permeate its wall. So far those persons had been primarily Green Riders. He brushed his hand against his brooch and sank into the wall. He was absorbed through stone, the passage no more difficult than a brief submersion in water and taking no longer than half a breath. When he emerged into the chamber within, the wall he had just passed through rippled and then hardened into solid granite behind him.

The tower chamber had seen better days. Columns in the center of the chamber had fallen over and broken, and stone had crashed to the floor from above. The damage occurred when the wall guardians had been on the verge of insanity, driven there by both the breach and the influence of Alton's late cousin, Pendric. They'd lost their rhythm, the thread of song that unified the magic of the wall began to unravel, almost causing all to fall into ruin.

There was still a hole far above where snow and rain had seeped through all winter and Alton did not know how he might fix it, for no ladder reached it. Apparently there had also been an observation platform that was now a pile of rubble on the floor, but how the wallkeepers of old reached it, he had no idea for there were no stairs he could find.

Living wallkeepers had once been stationed in the towers

to keep watch on Blackveil and the wall itself, but with the passage of the ages and various wars, their duty diminished until it was entirely forgotten and the wall taken for granted. The towers, however, were not left completely uninhabited. Magical presences remained. They'd once been great mages, fully corporeal beings, but once their physical selves passed on, they continued to reside in the towers in their current ghostly manifestations.

Merdigen, the resident of Tower of the Heavens, constantly nattered at Alton about the poor state of his tower, as if Alton could fix the mess with a snap of his fingers. If only it were so easy! He'd done his best through the winter to sweep up debris and move rubble, but it would require more strength and craftsmanship than he possessed to remake columns and return the chamber to its former condition.

There was a table in the chamber that miraculously survived the destruction, and Alton did much of his work there. Books were piled on one end. Dale had promised the tower mages books if they'd work on solving the riddles of the wall, and since then, Alton's father had shipped them a large quantity of books. The mages did not seem to care what they were about, just that they were *books*.

"There you are!"

Merdigen's voice made Alton jump. As often as he entered the tower and expected Merdigen to be there, the mage always managed to surprise him with his sudden appearances. Alton turned to face him.

"It's about time," Merdigen said, tugging on his long flowing beard. It was the color of old ivory.

Alton braced himself, wondering what the mage would complain about this time.

"This is not the most convenient method to read a book."

"What's not?"

"One page at a time," Merdigen replied. "You left me on page ten of Chettley's *Theories of Light* and then never came back to turn the page."

Merdigen was right: it was not the most convenient way to read a book, or to have it be read. Merdigen was not a corporeal being, and therefore could not affect physical objects.

It was wonderful that the mages now had access to all these books, but it was not wonderful that Alton and Dale had to flip the pages for them.

"Sorry," Alton said, though he was not sorry at all. "We had a busy night." He went on to describe the incursion of the creature from Blackveil and the arrival of Estral Andovian.

"I am sorry about your soldiers," Merdigen said. "I am very sorry. We must remain ever vigilant."

"Tell me something new," Alton mumbled.

"Eh?"

"Nothing, nothing." Alton moved over to the table and started sorting through papers.

"So where is she?" Merdigen asked.

"Hmm? Who?"

"The minstrel."

"Oh, I sent her away."

"Why would you do that?"

"It's not safe here."

"A pity, though I suppose you're right to send her off." Merdigen conjured himself a chair and slumped into it. "It's been many a long year since I heard true music. Oh, Dorleon plays his reed pipe, but it does not compare to a Selium minstrel. Not at all."

Alton hardly listened as Merdigen prattled on about minstrels he once knew and the songs they sang. He supposed it was better than getting nagged about the condition of the chamber.

When finally he had sorted his papers and cleared a space for himself to work, Alton pulled up a chair and started flipping through his copy of the book of Theanduris Silverwood. He could not believe the king wanted him to destroy it when he was finished with it. He understood, but still couldn't believe it. So Alton took as much time as he could to absorb the words of the great mage who had worked the magic of the wall. Theanduris Silverwood had been pompous, and callous to all the sacrifices he insisted be made to accomplish his goals.

These people are no more than cattle, he had written of those who died. *Their sacrifice will elevate them to a new exis-*

tence, and they will serve their land more usefully as rock and mortar than as individuals.

Theanduris Silverwood saw himself as a savior, since the wall had been his grand plan, though it was the D'Yers who built it, and thousands were sacrificed to create it. The true saviors, Alton thought, were those whose blood made the wall possible. Theanduris Silverwood had not seen fit to sacrifice himself.

Alton wondered if the great mage had truly been any better than Mornhavon the Black.

"Oh, you're looking through that thing again," Merdigen said, gazing over Alton's shoulder.

"I don't want to miss anything."

"Can't miss Theanduris' overly inflated estimation of himself."

"No," Alton agreed.

"Wasn't there something the king wanted you to look at particularly?"

Alton raised his eyebrow at the pointed tone of Merdigen's question, but he reached for the king's letter and briefly scanned it. "That measure of music," he mumbled. He turned the pages of the manuscript until he came to the one that contained it.

"Do you know how to read musical notation?" Merdigen asked.

"No," Alton admitted.

"Can Dale?"

Alton shook his head.

"Can you think of anyone else who can?"

There were a few others in the encampment who played instruments, but none were formally trained. They had learned to play by ear.

"No," Alton said in growing consternation.

"Then why, my boy," Merdigen said with exaggerated patience, "did you send away the one person who *can?*"

Alton stood so fast he knocked over his chair. *"Idiot!"* he cried.

"Why there's no reason to call me—"

"Not you, *me!*"

Alton dashed from the chamber, through the wall, and out into the encampment.

"What is it, my lord?" an alarmed guard called.

"My horse! I need my horse!"

Estral Andovian could not have gotten far, but Alton was not about to waste another moment. Once he tacked up Night Hawk and mounted, he gave his horse the bare minimum of time to warm up at a walk and then galloped from the tower camp to the main encampment and down the rudimentary road that broke northward through the forest.

She'd only gotten about a mile down the road when he caught up with her.

He reined Night Hawk up in front of her to block her way. Estral's mare spooked, and while it was clear she was no expert horsewoman, she maintained her seat well.

"What—" she began.

"I need you to come back," he said. Then realizing how abrupt his behavior and words were, he said, "I mean, could you come back? Please?"

She sat there glowering at him. "I see Karigan was not exaggerating when she said you were capable of being rude."

Alton groaned. They were back to this, were they?

"In fact," Estral said, "I'd say you'd been *mean* to her."

"I apologized to her for that. She's forgiven me."

"Apologized, eh?" Estral tapped her riding crop against her boot, waiting.

"Apologized, yeah," Alton said. "I mean yes, apologies. I apologize if I came across as rude."

"Hmm."

"Or mean," he added.

She squinted at him as if assessing the sincerity of his words and character. Finally she asked, "What is it that made you change your mind?"

"It may be," he said, "that you can help us save the wall."

"Then what are we doing sitting here?"

Alton smiled. "My thought exactly."

⪻ RESONANCE ⪼

As they rode back toward the encampment, Alton explained about the book of Theanduris Silverwood, but Estral was already well aware of it. Then he remembered Karigan had gone to Selium looking for it. This Estral confirmed.

"After Karigan left," she said, "we pretty much tore apart the archives looking for the book even though we were sure it wasn't there. Word came later from the king that it had been found elsewhere." She sighed heavily. "Then we had to put the archives back in order."

Alton gathered from her expression and tone of voice it had not been the most pleasurable of experiences. As he gazed at her, he couldn't help noticing how the morning sun falling through the branches of trees dappled her hair making golden strands shine among the more subdued, sandy ones.

He cleared his throat and went on to explain how Theandris documented the making of the wall and all the sacrifices required. Estral nodded as if it only confirmed her suspicions.

"A lot of blood was shed in those days," she said, "even when the war was over. But the way in which the wall was built was kept secret, even from the first Golden Guardian, or *especially* from him." She lapsed into deep thought as their horses plodded along, eventually saying, "It's not exactly the sort of thing you want the minstrels to sing about. I imagine back then King Jonaeus found ways to keep Gerlrand—he was the first Golden Guardian—busy and out of the way. He had the school at Selium to establish and all."

"Perhaps he was in on it," Alton suggested, "but kept it quiet." When Estral glared at him, he added, "My ancestors were certainly in on it whether they wanted to be or not, and managed to keep the methods used for building the wall a secret. I do not think they wished such necromancy to be repeated, and perhaps it was the same with Gerlrand."

As quickly as it came, the anger vanished from Estral's face. "I do not think Gerlrand could keep a secret like that. It's not our way."

They rode on in silence and Alton could tell his words had disturbed her and she was now less certain.

"So how is it you think I can help save the wall?" she asked. "You're not planning to sacrifice me to it, are you?"

"I'd need more than just you for that," Alton replied.

"I don't know whether to be relieved or insulted."

Though she was smiling when she said it, Alton decided it was better not to attempt a direct response and get into deeper trouble with Karigan's friend, but he couldn't help a small smile of his own. "It's a measure of music," he said. "In the middle of Theanduris' ramblings about how clever he was, he put down a measure of music. There is no explanation as to why or what it is."

"And you think this measure of music will help the wall?"

Alton shrugged. "Who knows? Maybe Theanduris had the notion of composing some great piece of music in his own honor. But I think it's more. It is song, after all, that keeps the wall guardians unified."

Estral played with her horse's mane as she rode along, flipping it from one side to the other. "It's an interesting combination," she said. "Blood and song to make the wall strong."

"And good craftsmanship," Alton could not help adding. "In any case, I thought maybe you could look at that measure of music, see what you make of it."

It was almost all Alton could do to keep from leading them back at a gallop. He refrained because Estral appeared content to amble along at a thoughtful walk. He fell into his own ruminations, which though they started out about the wall, veered to his wondering how much he could pry out of Estral about Karigan. Oddly enough, there were some basic things he did not know about her. What, for instance, was her favorite color? It was hard to tell when all they ever wore was green. It seemed there was always something else crowding out the small details—message errands, battles, walls. Alton's own very bad behavior ...

He'd have to proceed with caution when broaching the subject of Karigan with Estral. The journeyman minstrel, he could tell, was shrewd and would protect her friend no matter how innocent his questions.

Eventually they arrived at the main encampment at the breach. Alton reined Night Hawk east to head toward the tower encampment, but someone called out to him. It was Leese, the chief mender. As she approached he noted her haggard condition, the rings beneath her eyes, the slump to her shoulders. With a sense of foreboding, he knew this was not going to be good news.

"My lord," she said, halting before them, "I thought you should know that Private Tomsen did not make it."

Tomsen. The man injured in last night's attack. Alton bowed his head.

"He lost too much blood," Leese continued. "And what was left was poisoned by the creature's bite. We worked through the night to save him but to no avail."

"You did all you could," Alton said.

The mender nodded. "I fear our skills are inadequate for the dangers the forest presents."

Before Alton could respond, Leese turned and walked slowly back into the encampment, the very picture of defeat. He gazed at Estral Andovian wondering if he'd made the right decision in bringing her back.

"Don't you dare change your mind," she told him as though able to read his thoughts. "I take on this risk myself."

Alton wondered if her father and Karigan would see it that way should something bad happen. He shook his head and nudged Night Hawk forward, Estral falling in behind.

Alton emerged from the tower with the one page of manuscript that held the music. When he handed it to Estral, she gazed hard at it for some moments.

"The script is very old-fashioned," she said, "but that's no surprise considering when Theanduris lived. The copyist seems to have made a very faithful representation of the original. And if that is the case ..." She fell into silence.

"If that is the case what?" Alton pressed.

"If that is the case, then the original measure of music was written in Gerlrand's hand. I'd recognize it anywhere." She frowned.

Alton did not think an "I told you so" would be appreciated, so he kept his mouth shut.

"Five simple notes," she murmured. Then almost inaudibly she hummed.

There was nothing extraordinary about the brief tune that Alton could perceive, but it was almost as if Estral's voice were enfolded in a current of air and carried off to the heavens.

She hummed the tune again, louder, and this time there was a slight resonance—not an audible resonance, but Alton could feel a tingling on the back of his neck. Maybe it was just the sweetness of her voice.

"Doesn't sound like much," Estral said. "I can't see how this has anything to do with the wall. Can you?"

"I don't know."

"It feels incomplete," Estral mused, "as if that last note is wanting an answer."

Answers, Alton thought. *All we ever want is answers, but all we ever have are questions.*

"If you don't mind," Estral continued, "I'd like to hold onto this and play with it. It might not do anything for the wall, but as an artifact of Gerlrand's, it's of interest."

"I'd prefer you make a copy and return this one to me."

"Of course." Estral hurried off, presumably to Dale's tent to do just that.

Alton faced the wall wondering if he should have mentioned the resonance he had felt. It had been so subtle he almost couldn't credit it. He'd keep it to himself for now and see if Estral came up with anything more as she studied the piece of music. He wanted to keep his expectations low since he'd already been disappointed time and again. He could not help but wonder, however, why Theanduris would include the music if it weren't important. The great mage had thought much of his own cleverness and Alton did not doubt he'd delight in confounding anyone who tried to solve his riddle.

Did Theanduris and Alton's ancestors have any idea that one day their great wall would be broken? Did they know the menace of Mornhavon could survive for so many centuries?

It seemed to Alton they must have known and prepared as best as they could by provisioning the wall with keepers, making sure it was patrolled. What they did not count on was the frailty of human memory, of human needs and priorities. A time had come when those other priorities overrode the importance of maintaining the wall. The keepers disappeared, the tower mages slept, and the wall was left to itself, unguarded and unmaintained.

What was needed was a permanent solution. The wall, for all its impressive craftsmanship and magic, had proved itself impermanent. It almost felt like a betrayal to Alton's ancestors to think it, but the realization was dawning on him that the wall was not the final answer. Like Karigan carrying Mornhavon into the future, the wall only bought them time. He guessed King Zachary had come to this very conclusion himself a while ago and that was why he was sending Sacoridians into Blackveil with the Eletians.

When Alton first read the king's letter informing him of the expedition, he believed lives were being needlessly thrown away. He had barely survived Blackveil himself and it had taken him a long time to recover from his experiences in the forest. However, with this new understanding, he recognized the importance of the expedition in seeking a permanent solution to the problem of Mornhavon the Black.

Even knowing this, Alton's drive to fix the wall remained undiminished. If he could fix it, keep it intact for another thousand years, maybe it would give his people the protection and time they needed to find a way of finally defeating Mornhavon forever.

Alton could only do his part.

He sighed. He supposed he need not worry about keeping busy, what with the mysteries of the wall to solve and a journeyman minstrel to keep his eye on.

STATIONERY AND GOLD INK

The same day Karigan learned she was being sent into Blackveil, she received an invitation. It had been slipped beneath her chamber door in the Rider wing and she found it after she returned from her ride among the Scangly Mounds. Her name was neatly scripted on the envelope in gold ink, and when she flipped it over she discovered two seals: the royal seal of King Zachary and the cormorant seal of Clan Coutre.

She sat on her bed gazing at the seals in trepidation. If this had something to do with the betrothal, which appeared likely, she was sure she didn't want to even look at it. Her curiosity, however, soon got the best of her and with a rattling sigh, she slipped her thumb beneath the seals and opened the envelope.

Within was a piece of fine stationery, again inked with gold. It was an invitation from both King Zachary and Lady Estora to . . . to a masquerade ball? Yes, a masquerade ball to celebrate the forthcoming end of the winter and the arrival of spring. Was this all aristocrats did? Invent reasons to hold balls and banquets and parties? Ever since the betrothal, it surely seemed to be the case.

More important, would she have to go? The very idea of it spawned even more dread within her than going into Blackveil, albeit dread of a different nature.

There was, of course, the discomfort of having to be out among so many aristocrats in one place, but worse was having to see Lady Estora and King Zachary together.

Why have I been invited?

There had been plenty of other events she'd not been invited to. Why this? Why now?

She decided to ask the captain her opinion on the matter, for this was after all, an *invitation*. The last time she attended a ball put on by the king, she'd been *ordered* to go. Her chance to address the situation with the captain came the following afternoon when finally completed the payroll. When she reached officers' quarters, the captain ushered her right in and together they went over Karigan's figures.

"I'm glad you untangled this as quickly as you did," Captain Mapstone said, settling into her chair behind her worktable. "Otherwise we'd have some anxious and unhappy Riders on our hands. I know there are a few who send their pay back home to their families. Have you, by the way, thought of anyone to back you up on the accounts when you're away?"

Karigan nodded. It had not been difficult. "Daro."

Captain Mapstone appeared pleased. "Yes, that's who I thought of as well. I understand her family runs a dry goods store in Childrey."

"Yes," Karigan replied. "She's very good at figuring and knows how to keep a ledger."

"Excellent."

They discussed Daro for a while longer and how to work some time into her schedule to train with Karigan. When the discussion ran its course and the captain looked ready to dismiss Karigan, Karigan spoke up.

"Captain," she began.

"Yes? Was there something else?" The captain looked eager to be helpful and Karigan remembered she'd been told to come to her with any questions after their conversation about Blackveil. The captain did not send her Riders into dangerous situations blithely, Karigan knew, and would do anything in her power to be supportive. Karigan had spent enough time around the castle and military to know many officers were not of that mold; they cut themselves off from the people in their command and sent them into jeopardy without a second thought as if they were not people but pieces on a game board. It only elevated her respect for her captain.

"I received this." She handed the invitation to the captain who regarded it with dismay. Why it should dismay her,

Karigan couldn't guess, but maybe it meant she wouldn't have to attend the masquerade ball.

"I heard they were planning a masque," Captain Mapstone murmured. She gazed at the envelope and Karigan's name in gold ink.

"I was wondering if it's something I have to attend."

"Have to? I think not, but you'll have to consider your position and what it represents."

"My position?"

"Yes. You are now a knight of the realm. The *only* knight of the realm. See here, it's not addressed simply to Karigan G'ladheon, or even Rider G'ladheon, but to Rider *Sir* Karigan G'ladheon. Your position, your status, is now more prominent and your absence would be notable to those who take account of such things, both friends and enemies of the king. You see, the king's highest officers and vassals are symbols of his power and authority and if one of those symbols is missing? Some may view such an absence as a weakening of the king's authority, a lack of support from one of his allies. Do you understand my meaning?"

Unfortunately, Karigan did.

"If you want to support your king, I'm afraid it's highly recommended you at least make an appearance at the ball." The captain frowned and gazed out her arrow-slit window. "I should have known this was coming, that you'd be drawn into the affairs of the court." When she returned her gaze to Karigan she looked no happier. "I would guess this is not the last such invitation you'll receive. If you decide to attend the masque, you must keep your wits about you. You are now more than a mere Rider, one whose position is of importance to the king. What you say and do will not only reflect on the king, but will be interpreted and misinterpreted by members of the court. You never know when something you say will come back to cause trouble years later. The wrong words or actions may be used against you; may be used to undermine the authority of the king and cause great harm.

"You are worthy of the honor Zachary bestowed upon you, but I wonder if he considered the consequences..."

She handed the invitation back to Karigan shaking her head. "I'm afraid with your knighthood you are entering the very thorny world of the royal court."

The captain's speech and grim expression were not at all reassuring. Karigan's sense of dread increased tenfold.

And if what the captain had said was not enough, she added, "Yours is an unusual position, Karigan. I know you will choose wisely and act accordingly."

Karigan tucked the invitation into the pocket of her short-coat wishing the captain would offer some reassurance, but she only sat behind her table still looking troubled.

Someone knocked on the door.

"Enter," Captain Mapstone called.

The door opened and a tall and rangy man in buckskin stepped inside. He was a Rider rarely seen and Karigan almost did not recognize him.

Captain Mapstone stood and rounded her table to clasp his hand. "Lynx! Welcome back."

Not all Riders were always engaged in carrying messages. Sometimes they proved useful to the king in other capacities. Lynx, for instance, used his wilderness skills to keep watch on the northern boundary, aided by his special ability to communicate with the local wildlife.

Karigan greeted him in turn and sensing it was time to go so the captain could speak with Lynx in private, she slipped outside, closing the door behind her.

She strode across castle grounds with hands in pockets against the chill. The pathways were strangely empty and she supposed people were keeping close to their hearth fires today. Winter wasn't gone yet and even in spring they were apt to get a snowstorm or two.

Karigan sighed, expelling a steamy breath as she sorted out the captain's words. She'd known that there would be some extra duties expected of her with the knighthood, but since nothing in her life had seemed to change since the knighting and everyone treated her the same, she thought maybe life would continue along normally. It appeared this was not to be so.

As for the masque, the decision to attend belonged to her alone, but as presented by the captain, it was not much of a choice. Attend and show support for her king, or by her absence dishonor him. Her absence, the captain said, would be notable.

When she was younger, she would have been thrilled by the prospect of a royal masquerade ball. According to her aunts, one or two balls had been held at the G'ladheon estate while her mother was still alive, but those would have been humbler affairs attended by business associates, minor officials, family, and friends, not a castleful of lords and ladies.

With your knighthood you are entering the very thorny world of the royal court, the captain had said.

Karigan shuddered. She would attend the masquerade ball to support her king, but she would stay for as short a time as was courteous.

As she neared the main castle entrance, she saw the prison wagon leaving the grounds. She was not close enough to see who was within the vehicle—pretty much a cage on wheels—or how many. Guards in Sacoridian black and silver strode alongside the wagon. The prisoners must have just received judgment from King Zachary and were either being transferred to the city jail or being taken to the gallows. She had not heard about any public hangings of late, but then again, she chose not to pay much attention to such things. She'd attended one public execution, that of old Lord Mirwell, and that had been one too many.

When she mounted the steps of the castle entrance, she discovered Yates there, arms crossed, watching after the prison wagon and chatting with the guards on duty at the doors.

"You missed the excitement," he told her.

"What excitement?"

"One of the prisoners went berserk," said the door guard, Mikel. "Sent Jenks to the mending wing."

"I guess the prisoner didn't like his sentence," Yates said. "He's one of Immerez's men. Took part in Lady Estora's abduction."

The naming of Immerez brought Karigan up short. Immerez, formerly of the Mirwellian militia, had been in on his old lord's scheme to overthrow King Zachary, and when that failed, he escaped justice and became an outlaw working with Second Empire. He had been behind the plot to abduct Lady Estora, but in the end she was rescued and Immerez and his men captured.

"That prisoner ought to give 'em a show down at the Hanging Square," Mikel said, and he placed an invisible noose around his neck and pretended to flail, his face contorting in a grotesque expression. His fellow door guard laughed.

Disgusted, Karigan headed inside, Yates following along.

"Was Immerez in that wagon?" she asked.

"No. The king's still holding him for whatever reason."

Karigan didn't know what more they could possibly get out of the man, but his fate was all but assured. He'd have his turn at the gallows.

"Lynx came in a little while ago," Yates said as they strode through the castle toward the Rider wing.

"I know. I just saw him. I wonder what's brought him back."

"I have my guess," Yates said.

Karigan waited, but he didn't explain. *"Well?"* she demanded.

Yates started whistling some tuneless melody.

"You're not going to tell me?"

"Nope, don't think I can."

"Can't, or won't?"

Yates smiled enigmatically. "Yes."

"You're awful! I should throttle you!"

Yates side-stepped away in mock horror almost bumping into an annoyed administrative clerk hurrying along the corridor. "Please, Sir Karigan! Please don't hurt me!" He gave her his most woebegone expression.

"Oh, you are pathetic," she told him.

"Why thank you!" He resumed his whistling.

"You don't have to be so bloody smug about it."

"About being pathetic?"

"You know what I mean!"

He only gave her that maddening smile. As they turned down the Rider wing Karigan could not help wondering what he knew that he couldn't and wouldn't tell her. And how would he know about what brought Lynx back?

It began to dawn on her what it might be, and if she were right? The last thing Yates should be was happy about it.

INVITATION AND A MULE CART

The wheels of Amberhill's carriage rumbled over the cobblestones of the Winding Way. Yap sat across from him on the verge of dozing off, a contented smile on his face and eyelids drooping. After a six course meal at the Red Coach, he ought to be content. Amberhill felt as if his own full belly would burst his trousers and waistcoat. They'd taken their meal in a private alcove where Amberhill was able to continue Yap's instruction in manners at table. Yap was a quick learner, but sometimes it was all Amberhill could do to restrain the former pirate from wolfing down everything in sight in mere seconds.

With Yap freshly shaved and his hair trimmed, and attired in brand new well-fitted clothing, he looked not only content, but dapper, like a proper gentleman, though his specs, now repaired, gave him a somewhat scholarly demeanor. No one would mistake him for a pirate, at least by appearances alone.

The two were now returning home after a shopping trip to acquire supplies useful to their forthcoming journey. With Yap's seafaring background to guide him, Amberhill purchased hardy oilskins and had shoes made that would be more suitable for being aboard ship than his fancy riding boots. He purchased woolens and even a brimmed hat to keep the sun off his face. Yap advised him to expect every type of weather once they were out to sea.

Other parcels that filled the carriage contained more new clothing for Yap, including a pair of shoes. Yap had proven strangely resistant to the idea of shoes and stockings, but he caved when Amberhill insisted.

"Sorry, sir," Yap had said at the shoemaker's shop. "Just been without for so long that barefoot is the most natural thing in the world."

He showed Amberhill the bottom of his feet which were textured like hard leather. Impressive though this might be, without shoes his appearance as a gentleman was incomplete, and that wasn't even considering the state of his toenails.

Amberhill gazed absently out his window at the traffic in the street, at all the wagons, riders, and pedestrians going about their daily business of buying and selling, building and crafting. His driver expertly guided the carriage around slower going conveyances, but their progress was still sluggish and Amberhill mourned not having his Goss to ride through the crowds. It was much easier to maneuver through the traffic on horseback than in a carriage pulled by a pair of horses, no matter how fine the pair or expert the driver. Alas, he'd sent Goss home to the Amberhill estate for breeding and the stallion would soon be having a jolly time covering mares. His offspring would, Amberhill hoped, provide some of the finest stock ever seen in Sacoridia and propel his stable to prominence.

They passed a rickety old cart pulled by a swaybacked mule and with a jolt of surprise, Amberhill recognized the driver: Galen Miller, the old man he'd saved from the thugs outside the Cock and Hen. Galen Miller guided his mule up the Winding Way at an agonizing plod, his hands trembling and twitching as he held the reins. His expression was grim and intent.

Amberhill wondered what his business was and if he'd made good use of the silvers he'd been given. But Amberhill did not call out to Galen Miller. He'd been of the shadows that night, in a different role, and he preferred not to be recognized. In his current role as a nobly born gentleman, it would be unseemly to call out and wave to someone of such obvious low station.

Galen Miller's cart fell behind and Amberhill shrugged. He had little interest in the old man's life story, but he couldn't help being curious about what had brought him to Sacor City, or being concerned about the continuing welfare of a man he'd gone out of his way to assist.

Just as well, he thought. *I've enough with which to occupy myself.*

With surprising ease he dismissed Galen Miller from his mind and busied himself by going over his various business affairs and deciding which required his personal attention prior to his departure, and which did not. Truly, there was not much he could come up with, for his man-of-business was very efficient and capable.

Presently they entered the noble quarter and the carriage picked up speed down the less crowded street that fronted many a large and extravagant manse. Yap's open-mouthed snore provided counterpoint to the sharp clip-clop of hooves.

When they arrived at Amberhill's more modest house, Brigham—who no longer paled every time he saw Yap—greeted him at the door.

"There are several parcels in the carriage that need to be brought in," Amberhill informed his manservant. "Mister Yap will assist."

"Yes, sir. Sir, while you were out, this letter came for you." Brigham handed him an envelope then stepped outside to where Yap had begun to unload the carriage.

Amberhill curiously gazed at the envelope, his name scripted in gold. The dual seals made him raise his eyebrows. When he looked inside, he saw it was an invitation to the masquerade ball Lady Estora had mentioned to him, in which she included a personal note: *I realize you must be nearly ready to embark on your journey, but I hope I may persuade you to delay your departure for a few days yet. It would make Zachary and me very happy if you could attend our ball.*

Amberhill's immediate thought was to send her his regrets, but then he reconsidered. It had been several years since his last masquerade ball and he remembered enjoying the mystery of it all, the ability to hide behind a mask and take on another role. As a man who once wore a mask regularly and moved in the shadows, a masquerade held special appeal. Who else might be in attendance? What secret trysts might occur? What undercurrents and intrigue would transpire that would not otherwise be present with unmasked guests?

He did not wish to encumber himself with people making tiresome inquiries about his journey, and he'd already taken leave of Zachary and Lady Estora. However, since he wished to remain anonymous and avoid entanglements, he could respond to Estora saying he would be coming and yet not have his presence announced to the gathering. He would not have to remove his mask.

His journey, he decided, could wait a few days. He glanced at his dragon ring and the quiet glow of the ruby. It did not protest and he smiled.

At least it was not the broil of summer, Hank Fenn thought as he leaned on his pike in the Hanging Square. He stood guard over three corpses just lowered from the gallows and laid out on the paving stones. He'd drawn old blankets over them.

Broil of summer. That's what his gramma used to call it when the air was dense with moisture, there was no wind to move it, and the sun seared everything it shone upon.

Not that it was like the old days when a criminal might hang for weeks, or was locked up in a gibbet till he rotted away to bone. Sergeant Corly, who'd been soldiering forever, said quite a stink used to fill the square back then.

But it was not yet summer, not even spring, the air was still crisp, and King Zachary did not allow criminals to hang indefinitely and so ordered them cut down after execution.

When Hank asked Sergeant Corly why, the old soldier shrugged and said, "King says it ain't civilized to keep corpses hanging about." Then he shook his head, muttering about the good old days and proper punishment for traitors.

Hank was just glad he didn't have to stand guard over stinking corpses, and if the king didn't want them hanging about, well it was all right with him. Of course he had to wait out the day to see if anyone bothered to claim the bodies. He hoped someone did, so he and Snuff didn't have to dig the graves themselves. Snuff was lazy about it and made the graves shallow. Hank wasn't inclined to work too hard himself, especially for criminals, and these men had been bad. Mirwellians who followed the traitor Immerez. They'd helped abduct Lady Estora.

A small audience had come to the hanging, but according to Sergeant Corly, executions were no longer the events they'd once been before King Zachary's time. Nowadays they were held with little fanfare or public notice. A small crowd of people still came, though, like vultures. They spat on the condemned, hurled stones and insults at them. Although Hank saw true rage on their faces, he didn't think they abused the prisoners because they had abducted Lady Estora or done some other specific criminal act. No, he thought they did it because they *could*. They could take out all their anger and frustration at the world for their problems, their poverty, on the prisoners who were the lowest of the low, who could be abused but could not fight back. Undoubtedly it made them feel stronger, more powerful, than their own wretched lives usually allowed. Hank never saw nobles or wealthy persons attend executions unless it was for one of their own.

Snuff sauntered over and nudged him. "Look," he said, pointing. "We may have one less to bury."

An old man entered the square leading a mule hitched to a ramshackle cart. He walked slowly, his shoulders hunched. When he halted before them, he drew himself up and briefly Hank was reminded of the archers up on the castle walls, for his shoulders were broad and his forearms thick with muscles. But then he started to tremble. Hank had seen those shakes before in his gramma. Some had whispered she was possessed by evil spirits and he scowled at those hateful memories. She'd just been sick was all.

"I come for my boy," the man said.

"Raised you a traitor, eh?" Snuff asked.

Hank wished Snuff wouldn't harass family members this way on the few occasions they came to collect their dead. It seemed to him they didn't deserve to be punished, too.

"This way, sir," Hank said more courteously. He brought the man over to the trio of bodies and lifted the blanket shrouding the first one. Hanging was not a gentle death and the hanged were not easy to look upon.

After a difficult moment the man shook his head. They went on to the next. Again the shake of the head. When Hank lifted the blanket of the third, the man shuddered and his eyes filled with tears. Hank's heart sank for the hanging of this fellow hadn't gone well. He'd fought them all the way to the noose, so it hadn't been set just right. The condemned man did not die quickly and they all had to watch for painful minutes as he struggled and swung at the end of the rope until finally he ran out of fight and died.

"Is this your boy?" Hank asked.

"Aye." The man nodded, his voice scarcely more than a whisper. "This is Clay."

Hank helped the man load the body of his son into the back of the cart while Snuff watched with a jaundiced look. Normally, if family came to collect a body, there was more than one to take it away and Hank and Snuff left them to it. But Hank remembered his gramma and had pity for the old man.

"My thanks," the man told Hank, brushing a shaking hand through his hair.

Hank nodded.

"Good riddance to a traitor," Snuff said loudly.

The man started, but then turned his back on them, leading the mule away. The cart with its shrouded burden clattered over the stone paving.

"Why do you do that?" Hank asked Snuff. "Why are you mean to the families? They aren't the criminals."

Snuff spat out a wad of tobacco, just missing the nearest corpse. "Those criminals got made," he said. "Someone raised them bad."

Hank watched the mule cart as it disappeared down the street. He understood what Snuff was saying, but he also could tell the look of a man who loved his son.

All thoughts of the masque were shoved to the back of Karigan's mind as plans for the expedition to Blackveil unfolded. Captain Mapstone called her, Lynx, and Yates to her quarters confirming Karigan's suspicions about which Riders would be going into Blackveil with her. Lynx, with his wilderness skills, Karigan could understand. But Yates? Dear, lighthearted, funny Yates? He was an excellent Rider, but to her mind it was almost like tossing a tasty morsel to the lions.

"Do you have to look at me like that?" he demanded.

"Like what?" she asked, conscious of Lynx and Captain Mapstone gazing at her.

"Like you think I won't survive my first step into the forest. I volunteered for this duty."

"You *volunteered?*"

"Don't act so shocked. We can't have you taking all the glory after all. I came to the captain as soon as I caught wind of the mission and offered my services."

Karigan glanced at the captain whose expression was unreadable. Karigan wanted to tell her to pick someone else, someone less . . . innocent. Well, not that Yates was *innocent* if all the rumors about his conquests with the ladies were true. But there were others, she was sure, more seasoned to the type of dangers Blackveil presented. But who? Who would *she* choose? Maybe Beryl, but Beryl was off on some mysterious errand for the king. Who else? But as she thought about it, no one came to mind that she would want to send into Blackveil and she could only conclude *all* the Riders were dear to her. They were family, even Beryl the scary spy and interrogator.

Now she understood in truth the difficult choices the captain had been confronted with and perhaps Yates' volunteering had made the decision easier.

But still . . . Yates? It just seemed wrong.

"You'll need someone to see in the dark," Yates said. "I hear Blackveil gets very dark."

His special ability was exceptional night vision and it was true it would be useful in the forest, but it would not repel the vicious denizens of the forest or prevent them from eating him.

"But . . . but it's Blackveil!" she blurted. "It's dangerous!"

"Don't worry," Yates replied. "I'll protect you."

Karigan's mouth dropped open, but she could not manage a retort. It did not help that Captain Mapstone chuckled or that even taciturn Lynx smiled.

They quickly returned to business. The captain gave them a list of instructions to help her Riders prepare for departure, which was coming up fast—next week.

When they were dismissed, Lynx headed off on business of his own leaving Karigan to confront Yates just outside officers quarters. She cuffed him on the shoulder.

"Are you mad?" she demanded. "Volunteering to go into Blackveil?"

"If so," Yates said, "then I am in good company." He sauntered off whistling, leaving her on the pathway to stew. She was torn between running after Yates and asking him to change his mind, and returning to Captain Mapstone's quarters to plead with her to reconsider. She did neither. Yates, for all his jokes and lightheartedness, was a man full grown and entitled to make his own decisions, and confronting Captain Mapstone might be construed as challenging her command.

Instead she went to the stables thinking Condor could use a good turn with a currycomb.

Over the next couple of days the trio of Riders appeared at the quartermaster's to get outfitted for their journey. Blackveil was a different kind of environment and they would be on foot, not on horseback. They were fitted with boots normally reserved for the infantry, and piled down with tents, spare woolens, stockings, and oilskin cloaks.

Lynx was additionally presented with extra bundles of arrows, spare bow strings, and the haft of an ax. Most Riders bore sabers and long knives, but Lynx preferred his stout forester's knife, longbow, and throwing ax. He checked the balance of the new haft and pronounced it acceptable.

Then it was off to a briefing with General Harborough in his office in the administrative wing of the castle, and for the first time the Riders got a look at the others who would be accompanying them. They were two soldiers from the army, large and muscular, and a third man, more slight in stature, and introduced as Gillard Ardmont, a forester of Coutre Province.

The general sat behind his oversized desk, medals on his chest gleaming in the lamplight and an attentive aide at his side taking notes.

"When we enter Blackveil," the general said, folding beefy hands on the desk before him, "our objective is largely one of observation."

"He going with us?" Yates whispered to Karigan with a mischievous glint in his eye.

"You have something to say, Rider Cardell?" General Harborough asked in a booming voice that made Yates flinch.

"N-no, sir."

"Good. Then listen up. This is no holiday jaunt you're going on."

Maybe, Karigan thought, *if Yates heard it often enough he'd reconsider his decision to volunteer.*

"The Eletians say," the general continued, "that they want to see what has become of their land since the D'Yer Wall was erected, but express nothing further of their intentions. His Highness would like to know what more they are after, if anything. Keep in mind the Eletians invited us along and they have not yet shown themselves to be our enemies." The general looked plainly skeptical on this point but continued, "I expect courtesy and diplomacy in dealing with them. Am I clear?"

"YES, SIR!" the two soldiers bellowed, almost bowling Karigan out of her chair.

This was followed by less emphatic affirmations from the Riders and the forester.

This expedition, Karigan thought, was going to be interesting.

"The king wants you to keep your eyes open to learn anything about the forest you can, especially if it's something that may help us against Mornhavon the Black when he returns. You will come back with detailed reports. You will report directly to the king upon your return. Take note of roads and ruins, the landscape and wildlife. I fear no maps of the region exist so you will be following the lead of the Eletians, an untenable situation to my mind. Therefore a vital facet of your mission is to make some maps. Rider Cardell?"

"Er, yes? Sir?"

"Your captain says you're an able cartographer. I will expect detailed renderings."

Yates looked pleased, and now Karigan knew, beyond the fact he'd volunteered to join the expedition, why Captain Mapstone agreed to let him go. And like it or not, it was true he was a good draftsman. With all the new Riders that had joined their ranks, Yates had busied himself copying extra maps for them, and even instructing the Riders on how to read them. He'd in fact been, before the Rider call, an apprentice at his father's press, which printed, among other things, maps.

"Lieutenant Grant here is also experienced at documenting and surveying. He will assist."

"Yes, sir!" Yates replied.

"That's what I like," the general said. "A good show of enthusiasm. Now perhaps Sir Karigan can provide us with some insight about what we might expect in the forest itself."

Everyone looked at Karigan and she looked back at them, surprised to be suddenly put on the spot.

"You were briefly in Blackveil, were you not?" the general asked.

"Yes, but ... but I don't recall much about it. It was ... it was a difficult situation." She was not ready to explain to the strangers in the room that she'd been possessed at the time by the spirit of the First Rider. And Mornhavon the Black, too.

By the way the soldiers gazed at her she could tell her

stumbling response did not impress them one bit. The forester's regard was different, more intense. The general's expression changed as he seemed to remember the nature of her one foray into Blackveil. Surely he'd been informed of the details. He cleared his throat.

"Then perhaps the reports from Rider D'Yer will prove more instructive," he said. All of them had probably heard rumors about the forest. Since rumors were not the most reliable source of information, the general briefed them on the little that was truly known, relying heavily on Alton's reports. He explained that some of the creatures within the forest had been magically modified by Mornhavon, changed into monstrosities more perilous than any natural creature. Even the plant life had grown dangerous with thorns that held poisons. The ground they walked upon could prove unreliable, full of quagmires and misleading paths.

"You will be using all your skills to safely navigate the forest," the general said. "I do not know precisely what attributes the Eletians will be bringing to the expedition, but I think you must assume you'll have to watch out for yourselves.

"Lieutenant Grant will command. Rider Lynx is second in command. Is that clear?"

This time Karigan was expecting the loud confirmation from the soldiers and steeled herself for it.

Afterward, the general sat quietly regarding them for several moments with a solemn expression, then said, "His Majesty is well aware of the gravity of this mission. He is deeply confident you will succeed in bringing back useful intelligence. He expresses his gratitude for your service, and he salutes your courage. May the gods look out for you on your journey. For king and country!"

The soldiers leaped to their feet. *"For king and country!"*

The general then excused all but Lieutenant Grant and Lynx. Karigan filed out into the corridor with the others. Without a word, the second soldier, Private Porter, marched off to whatever duty awaited him.

For an awkward moment, Karigan and Yates stood there outside the general's door with the forester.

"This'll be some job, eh?" Gillard Ardmont said.

Karigan and Yates had to agree it would.

"Friends call me 'Ard,' " the forester said. "Don't know whether it's short for Gillard or Ardmont, but there you are."

They laughed and shook hands, and Karigan and Yates formally introduced themselves.

"You I've heard of," he told Karigan. "I know my Lord Coutre holds you in some regard."

"He awarded her the Order of the Cormorant," Yates said with pride. Karigan felt her cheeks warm.

"Did he now. Well I look forward to traveling with you both and learning more." He touched his forehead in a sort of salute and wandered off.

"Pleasant enough fellow," Yates said, "but I'm surprised the general didn't just pick another soldier."

"I suspect Lord Coutre suggested him," Karigan replied, "to ensure our future queen's interests are looked after."

Yates stared at her.

"What?" she demanded.

"You're getting pretty good with the politics."

Karigan sighed. "I don't know if *good* is the right word." And she and Yates struck off down the corridor toward the Rider wing. She certainly didn't feel any good at politics, and she did not want anything to do with politicians, but there were going to be times when it couldn't be avoided, and after everything Captain Mapstone had told her during their conversation about the masquerade ball, it appeared it would be more difficult than ever to steer clear of the machinations of the court.

When she was in Blackveil she didn't expect she'd be worrying much about politics. No, she would have bigger problems to contend with. Politics, at least, didn't like to eat you.

With this cheery thought in mind, she and Yates arrived at the Rider wing, only to find half a dozen Weapons blocking the way like an impenetrable wall of black.

⊰ BONEWOOD ⊱

"*Whoa,*" Yates intoned beside Karigan. Karigan could well appreciate Yates' reaction. One Weapon alone was imposing enough, but a whole group of them was positively formidable. She wondered what had brought them to the Rider wing.

She did not have to wait long to find out it was herself.

Fastion, whom she used to think of as "granite face," stepped forward. "Sir Karigan, if you would accompany us please." It was not so much a request as an order.

"Why—" she began, but they swiftly closed ranks around her, neatly edging out Yates. The next thing she knew they were striding away from the Rider wing, with her at the center of their formation and Fastion leading.

"Karigan?" Yates called out from somewhere behind.

"I'll be fine," she answered, though a little uncertainly.

She knew each of the Weapons around her, or she at least knew their names, but little more. It was not easy to get close to them, to penetrate their world, though Karigan had gotten closer than most. They considered her an honorary member of their order.

Among those who surrounded her was Brienne Quinn of the tombs. What was she doing above ground? Had she been transferred? No, she wore her fur-lined cloak that helped keep her warm in the subterranean world of the tombs, indicating she'd recently come above.

"Where are we going?" Karigan asked her. "What are we doing?"

"All will be revealed shortly," Brienne replied.

Was that a fleeting smile from the Weapon? If so, Karigan was not terribly reassured.

It was hard to see around her wall of broad-shouldered escorts, but she sensed people scrambling out of the way as the formation swept through the corridors. She could well imagine herself doing the same if she were in their shoes.

Eventually they entered a large chamber and came to a halt. She'd been here before. The room was ornamented with statues of stern warriors carved from black onyx and somber black banners hanging on the walls. Tables were set in precise rows. The first time she'd been here she'd assumed it to be a meeting and dining hall of the Weapons, and seeing the place again did nothing to change her mind.

Maybe a dozen other Weapons awaited them there, and unnervingly they formed into one large circle around her.

"What—" she began.

Fastion gestured her to be silent, but in her mind she screamed in frustration, wanting to know what this was all about.

Yet another Weapon stepped between Fastion and Brienne to enter the circle. Karigan gasped in astonishment, for it was Colin Dovekey, who was not only one of the king's primary advisors, but chief of the Weapons, having come to that position after serving as a Weapon since his youth.

"Greetings, sister-at-arms," he said.

She'd been called such before by Fastion, Brienne, and some of the others, but it was somehow shocking to hear it from Colin.

"Your forthcoming journey is known to us all and we have decided we do not wish for you to enter that dark place without something of the Black Shields. Donal?"

The Weapon Donal stepped into the circle, halting beside Colin. In his hands he held a shaft of burnished black wood that looked like a country walking cane one would use for leisurely rambles along wooded paths and up scenic hills. She was surprised they would present her with so innocuous a gift, but perhaps they thought that without her horse she'd need the support of a walking cane to make it through the forest.

Colin must have perceived her underwhelmed impression for he said, "Do not be deceived by appearances."

Suddenly Donal was in motion, the cane blurring through the air in patterns faster than her eyes could follow, the shaft of wood humming. All the other Weapons remained absolutely still, but when the cane inexplicably extended to twice its length without Donal pausing his dance, and the iron tip whistled within inches of her chin, over her head, and past her ear, she wanted to scream and run.

Then Donal stopped, became totally still, the tip of the cane-turned-staff a hairsbreadth before her nose. She went cross-eyed staring at it. She closed her mouth when she realized it was hanging open.

Donal withdrew the staff and held it horizontally before him so she might examine it. "See here," he said. "It's really a clever piece of work." He touched an almost indiscernible protrusion just beneath the crook of the handle and jerked the staff. The shaft retracted to its original length. He pressed the protrusion again, thrust the cane outward, and the shaft extended into a staff once again.

"Motion, weights, and counterweights allow you to lengthen or retract it," Donal explained. "The weights make it well balanced for fighting."

He passed it to her. The wood was smooth and cool in her hands. Donal was right, it balanced well and felt strong and sturdy enough for a fight, but not too heavy to carry on a walking journey. The handle appeared to have a steel core wrapped in leather. This alone could prove a devastating weapon against an opponent. The only ornamentation was a shield carved into the shaft just below the handle, black against black, the symbol of the Weapons.

"With this staff," Colin said, "you will represent us in the forest. Since our founding, we have fought against everything that is Blackveil Forest, yet none of us will be journeying into the heart of that ancient evil. Only through you, with this staff, may we remind those dark powers we're still here and await the day of reckoning."

Karigan's mouth went dry. She was doing *what*? Representing *who*?

"Now give it a try, won't you?"

"Uh ..."

"The trigger is here," Donal said, "next to your thumb."

She pressed it and felt something release.

"Now jerk it back," Donal said.

She did so and the shaft retracted so smoothly she felt only a subtle change of balance with the moving weights and heard a snick as it locked into place.

She pressed the trigger and shook the shaft out to staff length again. She was so delighted with it she continued to play with it almost forgetting her stern audience and Colin's words of just moments ago.

"It's like magic," she said.

She perceived a stiffening in the attitude of the Weapons surrounding her. *Oops,* she thought. They were very uncomfortable with the topic of magic.

"Not magic," Donal said, "but craftsmanship. It was made by one of our own who has a knack for figuring out how things work. He studies constantly all our library and archives have to offer on the making of everything from buildings to ships, as well as smaller objects like your staff. However, it is not just the mechanism within it that makes it special, but also the wood. It is bonewood."

"Bone ... ?" Karigan almost dropped it.

"Bone*wood,*" Donal said. "Not bone."

"It is rare," Colin explained. "A member of the oak family, and very strong. It is called bonewood by us because the only place we know that it grows is in our cemetery at the Forge."

"The Forge?"

"Our academy on Breaker Island, or as the locals call it, Black Shield Island. The academy has become known as the Forge because it is where we forge Weapons out of mere warriors, if you take my meaning."

Karigan did, and it was just the grim sort of wordplay she'd expect from Weapons.

"Many among us choose to retire to the island and teach, or to be of use in other capacities, such as Geron, who made your staff. When they pass on, they are buried there. Even those of us who do not end our days at the Forge may choose to be interred there."

Karigan knew she was hearing details few outside of the Weapons were privy to.

"May I?" Colin asked, holding his hands out for the staff. Karigan did not hesitate to pass it to him. Colin ran his fingers over the shaft and gazed at it with a discerning eye. "The oaks grow straight and strong right out of the graves. Some believe that the bones of our dead are cradled in the roots, hence the name bonewood. The trees grow from strength into strength.

"No one knows where the first seedling came from or who among the earliest of Weapons brought it to the island, but legend holds the wood deflects evil intent. Dark magic."

There was an almost collective shudder that ran through the circle of Weapons.

Colin shook the staff so it snapped back into the cane. "Recently, with the breach in the D'Yer Wall, we've taken to collecting deadfall from the bonewood trees. This staff is made from a limb struck down two winters ago in a storm, and it is the first of its kind. We may have others made in due course. In the meantime, we keep a bit of bonewood close to our hearts, as our predecessors did hundreds of years ago."

Donal peeled back his leather jerkin to reveal a badge in the shape of a plain black shield pinned onto his shirt just above his heart.

"Whether or not the efficacy of the bonewood is true," Colin continued, "we honor tradition." He handed the staff back to Karigan. "Use it well, and may it protect you."

"Thank you," she said, now overwhelmed. It was as much the immensity of the Weapons revealing so much to her as the gift itself that awed her.

Colin nodded and turned as though to leave.

"There's just one problem," she said.

He paused. "Yes?"

"I've had very little training in staff fighting."

"Oh, Donal will take care of that."

~ THREE LETTERS ~

Donal immediately set about taking care of "that," much to Karigan's chagrin, and with marked enthusiasm. He instructed his fellow Weapons to move tables out of the way so he could begin work with Karigan right then in their dining hall. Someone fetched Donal's staff, and when he had it in hand he said to her, "We do not have much time before you leave. Therefore we begin now."

Several Weapons remained to watch while others, including Colin, excused themselves and returned to duty. The solemn, quiet presence of the watchers unnerved Karigan. Better the heckling she received on the practice field when at sword practice than this sepulchral attention.

Donal led her through several exercises, demonstrating with his own staff so she could get a feel for handling hers.

"The staff is a discipline unto itself," Donal said, "though you will find like the sword, true masters make an art of it using many forms and movements. Unfortunately we do not have time to make you a master, so we shall settle for competency."

That evening he showed her many defensive techniques. He played attacker, at first moving slowly so she could learn each move, then increasing his speed and power. Time after time, his staff blurred through the air and his feet glided over the flagstones, he pushed her back and back into the wall or a table. Time after time he knocked her staff out of her hands and sent it clattering to the floor.

Once when he got past her defenses and jabbed her in the stomach with the butt of his staff, she went staggering away,

225

doubled over and retching. It was a good thing, she thought in retrospect, she'd not yet had supper.

"I will not do that to you again," Donal said, "but I want you to remember what happens when you do not pay attention."

Karigan could have sworn she was paying attention, but when she could stand straight and breathe again, he showed her in detail where she'd gone wrong. It turned out she'd been paying attention to his staff when she should have been watching his hands.

She discovered, as they continued with the exercises, staff fighting could take on a rhythm very like a sword bout and some of the techniques were not so very different.

When Donal finally called it a night, he ordered her to come back the next evening at the same hour to continue training. She returned to the Rider wing at half past seven hour, hair clinging to her sweaty brow and clothes damp. She was bruised all over and three fingers on her left hand were swollen and stiff. Her new staff, she noted, was entirely unscathed. It suffered not a scratch, chip, or dent. It was evidence, she supposed of the strength of the bonewood oak.

Lured by the sounds of chatter and laughter, she bypassed her own chamber and headed down the corridor to the common room, thinking maybe she'd get some sympathy from her friends. She found the room full of Riders playing card games and tossing dice, gossiping, or just lounging in front of the fire. A couple were engaged in horseplay. Most of these were the young, new Riders. She hadn't had a chance to learn all their names yet, and it occurred to her maybe she never would with her journey to Blackveil fast approaching.

At one end of the long table in the center of the room sat Mara and Yates, as well as Elgin Foxsmith. They glanced up at her approach.

"Someone decide you were too old and frail to walk without a cane?" Yates asked, a smirk on his face.

Karigan considered giving him a good whack with it. "I have been hard at work while all of you have been loafing about here." To her disappointment, her pronouncement aroused no sympathy. She stood there pointedly waiting for someone to offer her a chair, but no one took the hint. It appeared in addition to being unsympathetic to her condition, her knighthood, as usual, failed to elicit special treatment from her friends.

She sighed and cast about for a free chair but all were full. Finally she stole one from a young Rider who briefly left his chair to retrieve a playing card that had dropped to the floor.

"Hey!" he protested. "That's mine!"

"Not anymore," Karigan said.

"But—"

"You should respect your elders," Yates said.

Karigan stuck her tongue out at him. "I'm not much older than you."

"Neither of you are very mature," Mara observed.

Karigan dragged her chair between Mara and Elgin and dropped into it with a groan of relief to be off her feet.

"Well?" Mara said when finally she was settled.

"Well what?"

"Yates said you were spirited away by a group of Weapons. What did they want?"

"They wanted to give me this." Karigan set the cane on the table with a clunk that caused the room to go still and quiet. After a moment, the chatter and motion resumed.

"*They* gave you that?" Yates asked incredulously.

"That, several bruises, and some sprained fingers, I think." With a grimace she showed them her left hand and sausage-sized fingers.

Elgin rubbed his upper lip and gazed intently at Karigan. Yates picked up the cane to inspect it.

"What in the name of the gods were they doing to you?" Mara demanded. "It's not like you're one of them—they can't be stealing one of our Riders away!"

"I am thinking," Elgin said, finally breaking his silence, "they have bestowed a great honor upon her."

"They—" Karigan began.

"Honor?" Mara's voice was aggrieved. "By breaking her hand?"

"Not—" Karigan tried to interject.

"It is obvious to me," Elgin said, "they hold her in esteem."

"But she's a Rider, not a Weapon. I should really inform Captain Mapstone of this."

"I—"

"I think Red probably knows," Elgin said, "or at least sees it."

Karigan heard an unmistakable snick as Yates' hands probed the cane.

"I wouldn't—" she began.

"If they hold you in such high esteem," Mara said, turning to her, "why are they beating you up?"

"They—"

Yates shook the cane.

"No!" Karigan cried, but too late.

The shaft extended and the handle slammed into Yates' forehead, knocking him over backward in his chair and leaving him in an unceremonious sprawl on the floor.

In the astonished silence that followed, Karigan said in a small voice, "They were teaching me staff fighting."

A clamor arose in the room, but Mara shortly had it in hand. Elgin helped the dazed Yates to his feet and took him to the mending wing to get checked out. Yates would have a bump and bruise on his forehead as a reward for his curiosity.

Mara sent one of the young Riders out for a bucket of still unmelted snow in some shady corner of castle grounds to help Karigan's swollen fingers. She sent another to the kitchens for whatever scraps were left over from supper since Karigan hadn't had hers. The boy returned with bean soup and half a loaf of bread. Everyone else Mara sent to their chambers.

When at last the common room grew silent and empty but for Mara and Karigan, Karigan was able to tell her friend all about her visit with the Weapons. Mara tried out the mechanism of the staff several times, both impressed and disturbed.

"I can't say I'm comfortable with them taking you into their world," Mara said, setting the staff aside.

"I wouldn't say they're taking me into their world." Karigan pulled her fingers from the bucket of snow and gazed at them. They were growing numb from the cold, but the swelling had decreased.

"Then what do you call this?" Mara rested her hand on the staff. "Made by Weapons with their shield on it."

"I'm not leaving the Riders if that's what you're worried about. My brooch hasn't abandoned me."

"I know, I know. I just worry about you as a Rider and a friend. You've been put into such a strange position with the knighthood. And then there's the Weapons. It just seems like they're trying to turn you into someone else."

Karigan set the bucket of melting snow out of the way and glanced at the bean soup. A layer of fat had congealed on its surface as it cooled and she pushed the bowl aside.

"I don't feel different," Karigan said. "At least inside. My outside hurts, though." When Mara did not laugh or even smile at the joke, she added, "The knighthood is just a title, and as you saw tonight, no one treats me any differently. In fact Yates seems to be working hard to keep me humble. In any case, I'm still pretty much the same old me."

"Yes and no."

"Yes and no?"

"The same but not unchanged."

"I think that's true for any of us who have been through some of the things we have," Karigan said. She watched as Mara's hand went to the burn scars on her face. The fire that leveled the old Rider barracks had changed her, and not just outwardly. How could it not?

"It's not just you as you," Mara said after some thought. "It's . . . Five hells. I just don't want to lose my friend."

Karigan was taken aback. She was surprised, surprised and touched to hear the words spoken aloud, that someone actually cared. She had come to the common room hoping for a little sympathy for her bruises and found instead something even more precious: a reaffirmation of friendship and knowledge that someone gave a damn.

Not that she ever doubted the Riders cared about her, despite the fact they often worked alone on far flung errands. She might go months without seeing Tegan or Garth, or even Mara who kept close to the castle, but there was always that sense of family, of inclusion, and the knowledge the Riders would watch her back.

Still, it made all the difference in the world just to hear it spoken aloud.

"Mara," she said, rubbing a stray tear from her cheek, "no title or gift is going to change our friendship. You won't lose mine. Ever."

"I guess I know that," Mara replied. "But Osric's death is still fresh in my mind, and now you're being sent into Blackveil."

"Lynx and Yates, too," Karigan murmured.

"I understand the reasons for the expedition, but I wish none of our people had to go."

"I know. But it's what we do. What we all do."

After that they spoke quietly for a while of Karigan's preparations, then each went to her separate chamber. Karigan lit a lamp and found Ghost Kitty nestled on her pillow. She stroked his head for a while reflecting on her day, the gift from the Weapons, and her conversation with Mara.

It was true she might not return from Blackveil; but there had been other occasions when she might not have returned from other adventures. Danger was part of the job. Knowing people cared—friends and family both—buoyed her, made it worth coming back alive.

It occurred to her that in the event she did not return, her loved ones might appreciate some final word from her. She would write letters—one to her father and aunts, and one to the Riders. She searched through the drawer of her desk for pen, ink, and paper, and using a book as a hard surface to write on, she sat on her bed and set to work, Ghost Kitty purring beside her.

Mainly she told them how much she loved and admired them. She needed them to *know* it. As she had just experienced with Mara, love and friendship was so often taken for granted that one could forget, or begin to believe otherwise.

In addition, her father would be angry, so she wanted to ensure he knew she'd gone into Blackveil willingly and believed in the mission. She could never tell him about it beforehand—he'd be an absolute wreck and she could easily imagine him coming to Sacor City to berate both Captain

Mapstone and King Zachary for sending her, something to be avoided at all costs.

When she was done, she folded the letters into envelopes and sealed them with green wax. She tucked them into the drawer and was about to put away her writing supplies when she paused and decided to write a third.

This one was to King Zachary.

She was not sure what he thought of her, or whether or not he thought of her at all anymore. He had once told her he loved her, but then agreed to the contract to marry Lady Estora, and since then she'd seen little of him. It was for the best, she knew, but it did nothing to squelch the ache she felt for something, someone, she could never have. Much of the time she could put her sense of loss to the back of her mind by keeping busy, but it never totally went away, like the undercurrent of a fast moving stream.

She felt she must put it all down in writing for him. For herself. If something should happen to her, she would know at least this one thing was not left undone; that words that should be said were not left unspoken.

She poured into the letter her dreams, her desires, and her regrets. So many regrets. She expressed how she felt for him—had felt for him for so long now—and how she wished things could have been different if only he'd not been a king or she not a commoner. She did not forgive him for suggesting that one moonlit night on the castle roof that she become his mistress, but she expressed understanding for how their births to one class or another put them in difficult positions.

She told him things in her letter she could never say now, but if she were gone, would not matter. At least he would know, and that knowledge would not affect his marriage, and hence, the stability of the kingdom. Then, before she could cross any of it out, she placed the letter into an envelope and sealed it.

The three letters would remain safely in the drawer, only to be found if she did not return from Blackveil.

⇚ LEADORA THEADLES ⇛

Over the next few evenings, only Donal met Karigan in the hall of the Weapons for staff training. She brought Mara along to prove to her friend she was not being inducted into any secret order, willingly or not. Mara, at first, gazed at the chamber with ill-concealed suspicion and interest, while Donal showed only mild surprise that someone uninvited had entered the domain of the Weapons. Maybe he did not turn Mara away because the hall wasn't actually off-limits to non-Weapons, or maybe because she was Karigan's guest. Whatever the case, Karigan was sure they received few visitors.

Donal was all business, even drawing Mara into the exercises so that Karigan had two opponents instead of one. Mara looked to be enjoying herself a little too much, sneaking in swats when Karigan was busy fending off Donal.

She learned to use the staff in both its short and extended forms to defend herself to a level Donal declared adequate. He showed her how to use the cane handle to hurt and maim an adversary.

Mara was exhilarated by the sessions, and at the end of the week, Donal presented her with a stout fighting staff of her own and made her promise to keep coming for practice while Karigan was away on her journey.

"Now look who's being sucked into the world of the Weapons," Karigan told Mara as they left for the Rider wing.

Mara, flushed and happy with the night's exertions and her new staff, could only grin.

Sprained fingers and staff training in no way curtailed Karigan's sessions with Arms Master Drent out on the practice field, or her duty to take care of Rider accounts. She showed Daro what needed to be done while she was away. Daro proved very quick on the uptake and Karigan felt sure the ledgers would not be in disorder upon her return.

There were more meetings with Captain Mapstone and General Harborough to make sure each of the expedition's participants knew exactly what was expected of them. Karigan was beginning to feel a little like baggage for she was not given any specific duty. She lacked Lynx's extensive experience in the wilderness, and Yates' skills as a cartographer. The only reason she seemed to be going was that she'd been in Blackveil once before, for whatever good that would serve them.

She was run so ragged during the course of the week that she'd not been able to spare a thought for the upcoming masquerade. In fact, she'd put it out of her mind so thoroughly she'd pretty much forgotten about it.

When finally she came to her rest day, she awoke mid-morning and lounged in an armchair before the fire in the Rider common room still in her sleeping gown and wrapped in a blanket thinking she'd be more than happy to spend her entire day this way. She was exhausted. There would be one more day of preparation for the journey, then the morning after they would depart.

"Well, someone looks like she's been out carousing all night."

Karigan looked up from the fire to find Connly and Captain Mapstone standing there and gazing at her. It had been Connly who spoke. She probably should have at least put a comb through her hair before stepping out of her room, but it had seemed like too much effort.

"No carousing," Karigan said. "I haven't had the time."

Connly nodded and smiled to indicate he'd only been joking.

"Best that you get some rest while you can," Captain Mapstone said, "since you are leaving so soon and have a big night tonight."

"Big night?" Karigan said, puzzled. Then it began to dawn on her.

Captain Mapstone raised an eyebrow. "Surely you didn't forget tonight is the masquerade ball."

"Oh, gods." Karigan groaned and sank deeper into her chair. The masquerade. She *had* forgotten. She pulled her blanket over her head. Maybe if she hid, it would all just go away.

Sometime later she still sat there before the fire unable to make herself move. *Stupid ball,* she thought. *I don't even have a mask.*

Mask? Did she even have anything to wear? A mask was the least of her problems. She flung her blanket aside and dashed into her chamber. She threw open the doors of her wardrobe and gazed at all the green hanging within. Green uniforms, some pieces of plain clothes, and one battered, ripped, and soiled blue dress. Despite all her wishing, a suitable costume did not magically appear before her.

Her plaintive wail of despair brought Mara and Tegan running to her room.

"What is it?" Mara asked.

Karigan held the dress in her arms. Her father had sent it to her in the fall to impress Braymer Coyle, but then after her disastrous encounter with the Raven Mask at the Sacor City War Museum, she'd used the dress to learn swordplay while formally attired. She'd neglected to have it fixed or cleaned.

"Masquerade ball," Karigan said. "I must attend the masquerade ball tonight and I've nothing to wear."

Mara and Tegan glanced at one another then stepped out into the corridor to confer. Karigan sank onto her bed, the crumpled dress still in her arms. Maybe she would not attend the ball after all, but the words of Captain Mapstone about supporting her king kept running through her mind and this . . . this might be her last chance to see him.

Mara and Tegan stepped back into her room.

"We have an idea," Mara said. "Get dressed. We're going into the city."

The two costume shops in the city—the only two worth patronizing anyway—were, as Tegan predicted, flat out of attire except for some mismatched oddments. Apparently everyone else attending the ball had already been to these establishments a while ago and cleaned them out.

"Now what?" Karigan asked, full of despair as she exited the second shop.

Tegan smiled. "Follow me. It's a short walk from here."

"What is?"

"The Magnificent."

"The magnificent what?"

"The Royal Magnificent Theater," Mara replied.

"You're taking me to the theater?"

"I know someone," Tegan said, leading the way, with Mara prodding Karigan from behind.

The Royal Magnificent Theater occupied almost an entire block in the artistic district of Sacor City, and rose high above the street. A sign lettered in gilt and flanked by carved masks and the royal symbol of the flaming torch announced its presence. It was frequented by all the elite citizens of the city when there was no party to attend at the castle or elsewhere. Karigan had never had the pleasure.

Plays, operas, and concerts were presented here. There were a few other theaters in the city, but they were much smaller affairs with correspondingly humble entertainment.

The great doors to the Magnificent beckoned, but to Karigan's disappointment, Tegan led them right by the entrance, around the corner of the building, and down an alley littered with crates and refuse. Karigan thought they might use a side entrance to the theater, but Tegan instead stopped at a battered door on the building across the alleyway. Blue paint flaked off as she pounded on it.

Karigan began to wonder just what sort of person this was that Tegan knew when the door creaked open and a mouse of a girl peered out at them.

"Hello, Nina," Tegan said. "Could you tell Madam Leadora I'm here to collect on a debt?"

Nina said nothing but receded into the building and closed the door soundly after her.

"Apparently not," Mara muttered.

"Oh, Nina doesn't talk much," Tegan said. "She'll be back."

"What is this debt?" Karigan asked.

"Nothing nefarious, I assure you," Tegan replied. "I did a favor for Leadora once. Introduced her to a friend who had a friend. Upshot is that she got this position with the Magnificent's theater troupe."

"What position?" Karigan asked, but before Tegan could reply, Nina returned and beckoned them inside with fingertips that flared with silver. At first startled, Karigan shortly realized the girl wore thimbles and they'd caught in the light leaking through the door.

The entry was dim and smelled musty. A corridor led back a way, its broad plank floor bare of carpeting or ornament. There were two stairways. One led up, and the other descended below street level. Nina led them up the stairs in silence, holding her skirts with one hand and using the other to balance herself against the wall as she climbed, for the stairway was narrow and lacking a handrail. The Riders followed just as cautiously.

"Huh," Tegan said. "Usually we go downstairs."

When they emerged into the space above, Karigan was immediately reminded of the sail lofts she'd been in down in Corsa Harbor, only instead of grizzled, ruddy seamen bent over lengths of sailcloth, there were several girls and young women studiously sewing bright pieces of material together.

The loft was vast and much light flowed through windows at the front of the building, softening the starkness of the rough wood floors, beams, and support columns. Bolts of cloth in dazzling hues and patterns were stacked haphazardly on shelving and strewn across tables. Lengths of material were draped over mannequins and hung from hooks on the wall. Much of it shimmered with sequins and beads and metallic threads.

There were boxes of feathers and long ruffled scarves, and a mound of mismatched shoes. Caps and hats and the papier-mâché head of a horse were piled in a corner.

The seamstresses never looked up from their stitching to see who had entered their domain, nor did they speak to one another. Their concentration was palpable. Among them paced a tall lady in a flamboyant purple gown, a measuring stick in her hand tapping on the floor with each stride. Her hair was coiffed and coiled into a perfect pile on her head, and her cheeks and lips were attractively rouged.

"Tee-gon, my dear!" the woman exclaimed when they all reached the top of the stairs, and she hastened over to them and placed her hands on Tegan's shoulders and air-kissed each cheek.

"Hello, Leadora," Tegan said, grinning.

"Tee-gon, where you been all this time, eh?"

"Oh, you know, working for the king."

Leadora clucked her tongue. "He write so many letters? You do not come to the thee-ator and it will wither your soul."

Karigan found Leadora's accent strange. She could not place it.

"My employer takes my service very seriously," Tegan said. "You know how it is."

"Yes yes yes." Leadora swiped her hand through the air dismissively. "And who are these?" she asked, glancing at Karigan and Mara. Karigan caught her quick double take when she observed the burn scars on Mara's face.

"Leadora, meet my friends Mara Brennyn and Karigan G'ladheon. Mara and Karigan, meet Madam Leadora Theadles, head seamstress for the Magnificent's theater troupe."

Leadora's gaze sharpened as it fell back on Karigan. "G'lad-hee-on? Of the cloth?"

"Er, yes," Karigan replied.

Leadora clapped her hands together. "Very good cloth. Very fine quality." Then she waggled her finger at Karigan. "But *very* expensive! Too expensive for stingy troupe manager."

"Leadora," Tegan said, "why are you up here? It's nicer, but why have you moved?"

Leadora put her hand to her hair as if to claw at it, her expression one of misery. Karigan began to wonder if the troupe's acting occurred only on stage.

"Most terrible!" Leadora cried. "It was a flood."

"What flood?"

"That terrible, terrible cellar we worked in. It leaked. The snow, the rain, the freeze, the melt. One morning I come in and our shop, it is full of water. We move into this nicer place, eh? Was shop and storage for another tenant—cabinet maker, but he move." Then Leadora scrunched her face. "He leave all his sawdust and wood chips. We must sweep and sweep." Then she sighed. "So now we are much busier. Most all our cloth and costumes wrecked by flood. Gone! Worthless, destroyed."

"Uh-oh," Tegan said.

"Yes. Is very bad. We try to make new for the next production. We must make everything from—how do you say?—from scratch. The girls work very hard now."

"So much for that idea," Tegan muttered.

"Idea? What is this?"

"Well," Tegan said, "Karigan here is in need of a costume for the king's masquerade ball tonight, and seeing as you owe me a favor, I thought you could maybe help out."

"Oh my dear Tee-gon!" Leadora started pacing about spouting a stream of incomprehensible words.

"*Where* is she from?" Mara whispered.

"I'm not actually sure," Tegan said. "But I kind of suspect she's from right here in the city."

Karigan and Mara both stared at her.

"She's a brilliant seamstress sure enough, but the rest?" Tegan shrugged.

"*Aha!*" Leadora's exclamation made them jump. She tapped her measuring stick on the floor. "I may be able to help. Then debt repaid, eh?"

"If you can supply Karigan with a proper costume," Tegan said, "yes, it is."

Leadora smiled.

⇜ MAD QUEEN ODDACIOUS ⇝

Upon their return to the castle, Tegan took charge of Karigan's preparations for the masquerade ball.

"I will not wear the wig," Karigan said.

"But it's part of the character," Tegan replied. "And I think black hair will suit you. Besides, the crown won't fit without it. At least give it a go, and maybe try being a little less grumpy about it."

"You'd be grumpy if *you* had to wear this ridiculous thing."

She gazed down at the dress with its garish red and white diamond pattern, highlighted with silvery threads. At the bottom of the skirts among the frills were sewn the images of playful cats. On her left sleeve was a great big velvet heart. Panniers made her hips jut out in a style not seen in several generations. The material was a poor quality of satin that appalled the textile merchant in her. It undoubtedly shone well enough in the stage lights and likely satisfied the troupe manager's stingy wallet, but closer inspection clearly revealed its inferiority.

She just knew that, in contrast, the nobles in attendance would be wearing nothing but the most elegant styles, their costumes constructed from only the finest materials. None of them would deign to wear so clownish a costume as this.

If the garishness of her costume was not enough, it smelled of mildew and there was some yellow staining located in an embarrassing spot on her backside. It had not, evidently, entirely escaped the flooding. Leadora supplied a train that she hoped would conceal the stain.

The costume had been created for a person much larger

than Karigan—the role was often, though not always, played by a man—so Leadora, wielding her measuring stick like a field commander, marshaled her seamstresses to alter the costume and make it fit. Karigan had feared being stuck to death by dozens of sewing needles flying about her, but she needn't have worried. The girls had known exactly what they were doing and were accustomed to working rapidly and precisely. She had not been pricked even once, and thanks to their expertise, the costume fit very well. That was something, anyway.

Tegan had found a large mirror in which Karigan could get a better view of herself than in her own little hand mirror, and set it on her desk. Karigan frowned at her reflection as Tegan lowered the wig onto her head. It was a very large horsehair affair, ludicrously tall with lots of curls. Tegan then proceeded to tuck Karigan's own brown locks beneath the wig. When that was accomplished, she placed the crown atop the wig and pinned it into place.

Some crown, Karigan thought, her mood growing darker by the moment. Little bells hung from the points of the crown like a jester's cap. The slightest movement made them jingle.

"That about does it, Your Highness," Tegan said. "When we get to the ballroom, I'll help you with the mask."

The mask lay on Karigan's desk. Since the costume's character did not wear a mask on stage, Leadora had to improvise. She found a plain black half-mask and directed Nina to glue red sequins and feathers on it.

Karigan could not help but wonder what the Weapons would make of her getup. Undoubtedly there would be more than a few on duty guarding the king and Lady Estora. They'd probably find her appearance undignified in the extreme and regret having made her an honorary member of their order. Maybe they'd ask her to return the bonewood staff.

"You must admit," Tegan said, "this costume is better than the cat or mouse. And definitely better than the horse!"

Karigan wasn't so sure. What she was sure of was that the Riders loitering outside her door would not allow her to live this down.

"You could have been the horse's back end," she suggested.

"Ha! But *I* was not invited. Now are you ready? The ball should have begun by now."

When Karigan grumbled an affirmative, Tegan helped her rise. At least her shoes fit. She'd been careful to pick a comfortable pair from the pile in Leadora's loft. She also ensured Tegan had not cinched the corset too tight so she could breathe unrestricted.

"You look very . . . um . . . audacious," Tegan said with a smile and a glint in her eye.

Karigan frowned and steeled herself to exit her chamber for the outside world where she'd have to reveal her ridiculous appearance to all and sundry.

Tegan opened the door with a flourish and announced, "Here she is, Her Highness, Queen Oddacious!"

The reaction of the assembled Riders was pretty much what Karigan expected: lots of laughter and jokes.

"Don't you mean *Mad* Queen Oddacious?" Yates called out, foremost of those crowded around her. "Where are your kitty cats?"

Karigan rapped him on the shoulder with a folded fan that came with the costume. Yates grinned unrepentantly.

Someone *meowed,* and several of the Riders joined in until there was an entire chorus of mewing.

"If you keep it up," Karigan told them, "Queen Oddacious will be mad. *Real* mad."

"Hey, where's your husband?" someone cried out in the back. Karigan realized it was Fergal. "I hear he's a real stud!"

This was followed by more uproarious laughter.

"I have become a walking pun," Karigan muttered.

"Who wears her heart on her sleeve," Tegan reminded her.

Karigan knew she should have declined the costume, but she'd been desperate. The play *Mad Queen Oddacious* was a farce about a despot queen. There was a song in the first act and Tegan knew some of the verses:

> *Mad Queen Oddacious has twenty-one cats*
> *Each named Precious and wears a hat*
> *Mad Queen Oddacious married a horse*
> *Her subjects are mice she rules by force . . .*

Then there was something about the twenty-one cats eating the mice, and a raunchy verse about the queen and her stallion husband, which Karigan suddenly realized Yates was reciting to the great amusement of all.

"He bade her mount and—"

Karigan smacked him harder with the fan.

"Ow," he said, rubbing his head.

"Come, Tegan," Karigan said. "I've had enough of these little mice."

This was met with good-natured jeers.

As she and Tegan left the Rider wing, she reflected that as much as the play was a farce, it had a more serious subtext. Tegan explained the play had been based on a real person from the distant times before Sacoridia had had a high king and the Sacor Clans were tribes spread across various territories, the clan chiefs governing their tiny realms like petty kings. According to history, they were constantly at war with one another.

One clan named a woman to be their chief, which was unusual in those days. Her rule proved hard and she nearly drove her territory into ruin by loving her treasures and horses more than her people. The people rebelled and severed her head, or worse, depending on who was telling the story. Much of the truth of the tale was lost to the darkness of time, but the play served as a cautionary tale for those with power to wield it wisely and well. In the last act of the play, Queen Oddacious' husband transforms from a horse into a handsome warrior and slays her. All the mice feed on her flesh.

Karigan rather wondered if the play were more a warning specifically to women who dared aspire to power from men who loathed the mere thought of being ruled by them. Tegan said the play had enjoyed a resurgence in popularity during the reign of Queen Isen, who had not shown the least tendency toward despotism.

It was a long walk to the ballroom and Karigan caught more than one amused look cast her way from servants and other castle personnel.

The strains of music grew as they approached the ballroom, and when they paused near the entrance, Karigan's spirits sagged as she observed ladies and gentlemen in very sophisticated attire streaming through the entrance. Just as she imagined, the gowns of the ladies were exquisite and the costumes understated. In her Mad Queen Oddacious costume, she would stand out like a dandelion among roses.

"Time for your mask," Tegan said.

"Right."

As Tegan tied the mask on, Karigan felt like she was wearing blinders; it cut off her peripheral vision.

When Tegan finished, she stepped into Karigan's view. "Remember," she said, "you are Queen Oddacious and the world is your tart."

"Oh, gods," Karigan murmured. There was another line from the song about Queen Oddacious' love of tarts, followed by other vulgar verses that rhymed with it.

"Have fun," Tegan said. "It's not everyone who gets to attend the king's masquerade. Besides, if you don't want anyone to know who you are, you don't have to remove your mask."

Then how, Karigan wondered as she approached the entrance, would anyone know that the king's knight and Green Rider was here to show her support for him if she did not reveal herself? Where was the logic in that?

With a sigh she stepped up to the door where guards checked invitations.

"Entertainment uses the servants entrance," one growled at her.

Karigan held back a sharp retort and thrust her invitation at him. He looked it over, then scrutinized her with a skeptical expression on his face.

"Er, my mistake," he said. "Enjoy your evening."

Karigan took a deep breath and stepped through the entrance into the ballroom.

❧ MASQUERADE BALL ❧

Karigan paused atop a broad stairway that led to the ballroom floor below, where couples swept around and around dancing to the music of the orchestra. Others clustered in groups conversing or hovered over tables overflowing with food and drink. Chandeliers suffused the scene in a dreamy golden light.

"My lady?"

Karigan pulled her gaze away from the ballroom to discover Neff the herald beside her, attired in his usual tabard, but wearing a simple black eye mask.

"My lady," he said, "would you care to be announced?"

"Heavens, no!" she exclaimed, and she perceived a narrowing of his eyes behind his mask.

"Rider G'ladheon—er, Sir Karigan, is that you?"

"Yes."

He smiled. "Interesting costume."

"I suppose it is," she replied.

The bells of her "crown" jingled as she descended the stairs, but were soon submerged beneath a sea of sound: the harmonious tones of the orchestra as it moved into a waltz, the rise and fall of conversation and laughter, and the swish of silk and brocade as dancers rushed by. She did not see King Zachary or Lady Estora anywhere and wondered where they might be. They were, after all, supposed to be the hosts of this event.

The ballroom's decorations suggested a sea theme. Silk banners and streamers, dyed in oceanic blues and greens, hung from the ceiling. Stirred by the motion of the dancers, they rippled and flowed like waves. A pair of barnacle-encrusted anchors had been placed at the bottom of the stairs, and ice sculptures of mermaids, whales, and fish presided over bowls of punch. Seashells, fishing nets, and dried seastars ornamented tables and walls.

Most impressive of all was the sloop, so very far from the nearest harbor, placed against a near wall with sails hoisted and held taut by lines so it appeared they were filled with the wind, the mast unimpeded by the high ceiling. Through a break in the crowd, she could see the hull was filled to the rails with ice and raw oysters and other delicacies she would investigate later.

Karigan suspected Estora's hand in planning the decorations. The ocean theme resonated of Coutre Province. Not that the king's home province of Hillander, or Karigan's own of L'Petrie, were not coastal, but their harbors were more tame, more protected. Coutre and the other eastern provinces occupied the boldest coast of all, exposed to the wide open ocean and all its fury, separated from the rest of Sacoridia by the Wingsong Mountains and the turbulent currents around the Blackveil Peninsula. The geography had tempered a proud and independent people.

Karigan was relieved to find the ball's theme had not extended to costuming in any way she could perceive. She would have hated to stand out anymore than she already did. While the dress of other guests was understated and sophisticated, masks came in a variety of shapes and colors. Some bore grotesque countenances with long curving noses, protruding chins, and demonic horns, or appeared to be inspired by animals like catamounts, bears, and wolves.

Others were beautiful works of art fashioned of gold or silver leaf, or plumed with the feathers of exotic birds. Some helmlike masks featured entire stuffed birds on them.

Of the birds represented there were an unusual number of crows—men attired in black with variations of black-beaked masks, then she realized they must not be crows at all, but *ravens*. Raven. Mask. *The* Raven Mask. They must be fantasizing about being the gentleman thief who once stalked Sacor City's finer neighborhoods stealing jewels and seducing ladies in their own bedchambers. The real Raven Mask had met his end trying to abduct Lady Estora, and Karigan thought anyone who would wear such a costume an insensitive clod lacking the wit to imagine the terror their hostess had endured at the hands of that infamous thief. At the very least, it probably wasn't the best way to curry favor with their future queen.

As she wandered the perimeter of the ballroom, she caught more than a few curious and amused glances aimed her way, and even laughter. To make matters worse, she found it difficult to judge the proper amount of clearance her oversized hip panniers required.

"Sorry," she said, after bumping a man in an antlered headdress.

"Anytime, my dear," he replied with a sardonic smile.

She moved on, cheeks burning, only to brush against a woman wearing a beautiful purple silk mask. Her apology elicited only a glare. Karigan decided that on her journey into Blackveil she would not need the bonewood staff the Weapons had given her to defend herself. No, she could just wear the panniers and take down all adversaries with a swing of her hips.

Her passage around the ballroom did not reveal a glimpse of King Zachary or Lady Estora, but among the dancers was a sight that made her want to pound her wigged head on the wall: military officers not costumed, but attired in dress uniform with simple eye masks. This was how she could have dressed, but she hadn't known and no one informed her otherwise. She tried to console herself with the fact that she didn't have to contend with the tight collar of her own dress uniform.

Entertainers circulated among the guests, juggling, tumbling, and swallowing swords. They were costumed more brightly than Karigan, but not by much. A couple of gentlemen—one in a boar mask and the other in a furred raccoon mask—stepped into her path and waited as if expecting her to produce juggling balls. She scowled and walked around them, careful to give her hips enough space, and fluttered her fan before her face. Every time she heard someone laugh, she winced, certain it was directed at her.

It was just as well she decided to remain along the fringes, near the shadows, for all the commotion, the swell of noise and swirl of color, was overwhelming. She was not interested in conversing with anyone, and certainly had no desire to dance. She had come to show support for her king, but what good was it if he wasn't even here?

Just as the dancers lined up for a new set, the horns of the heralds blared across the vast space of the room. The orchestra and conversation fell silent and all motion ceased.

Ah, she thought. *Fashionably late.*

Figures in black silently slipped into the room from other entrances, even the balconies, unnoticed by guests more focused on the ballroom's entrance. The Weapons stationed themselves unobtrusively against walls and sank into shadows. To Karigan, their presence was as much an announcement of the king's arrival as the fanfare of the heralds.

Finally, the king and his betrothed had arrived. Karigan wanted to turn away, to not be interested, but like everyone else in the ballroom, she found her attention riveted to the top of the stairs, awaiting the entrance of the royal couple.

⊰ REFLECTED ⊱

Neff the herald stepped forward on the top
landing of the stairs and bellowed, "I pres-
ent to you His Highness, King Zachary, lord
and clan chief of Hillander Province and high
king of the twelve provinces, leader of the clans of Sacor and
bearer of the firebrand, supplicant to the gods only, and his
betrothed, Lady Estora of Coutre Province, first daughter of
Lord and Lady Coutre."

As Neff went on to announce other members of the en-
tourage, including Estora's sisters, assorted cousins, and various dignitaries, Karigan's attention was drawn only to the
two foremost figures of the king and his queen-to-be standing on the landing.

Estora was stunning. She always was. She wore silks of
aqua and sea green, white ruffles flowing just beneath the
hem of her skirts like the foam of waves. Teardrop gems sewn
into her costume and woven into her hair sparkled like the
sun on the water. She held a stick mask of ocean colors to her
face, beaded so it too rippled in the light.

Someone near Karigan whispered, "She's perfect."

"Like a goddess of the sea," someone else said.

Karigan could not disagree.

The king held Lady Estora's hand as they slowly descended the stairs. The king was dressed in a deeper green,
his longcoat of rich velvet, his waistcoat silvery gray. He wore
a helm mask that was the fierce visage of a dragon, wings outstretched, its green enameled details shimmering with reptil-
ian iridescence. He presented a brooding, mysterious figure,

and even at a distance Karigan could sense his restrained power.

For a moment, she fantasized it was her hand he held, that it was she walking beside him, but when the couple reached the ballroom floor and the gathered guests bowed and curtsied to them, someone whispered behind her: "Do you smell something?"

The question was followed by loud snuffling, then a reply: "Yes. Something . . . musty."

Karigan's dream evaporated. She was no queen, just a mildewed parody of one.

The guests parted so King Zachary and Lady Estora could approach the dance floor. They came so close Karigan could have reached out and touched them. She could smell the lavender scent of Lady Estora, catch the smiles the two shared with each other and no one else.

Karigan bowed her head as they passed, just one more supplicant among the many.

When King Zachary and Lady Estora reached the center of the dance floor, he placed one hand on her waist and she placed hers on his shoulder. Their leading hands were raised with palms pressed together. He said something, and she laughed in response. With a flourish the orchestra started playing again and the two flowed into a dance, gliding around the floor as if they'd always been meant to be a pair, her delicate beauty to his strength, one piece of a puzzle to match the other.

Karigan ached to be the one in the king's arms, to be the one moving in such synchrony with him, to be holding his attention as Estora did.

I am nothing compared to her, Karigan thought, feeling ashamed of her Queen Oddacious costume and, in a rare moment of her life, actually regretted her commoner status. *He deserves Estora, not me. She is a true queen.*

As others entered the dance floor, Karigan tore her gaze away. She had to stop. She had to stop the dreams, the fantasies, the regrets. They only brought her pain. She and Zachary, *King* Zachary, were something that could never be.

Karigan resolved to push aside the pain. She would do so by giving her full attention to the food tables, though her appetite had deserted her. She turned away from the dance floor, and in her haste almost stumbled right into one of the tumblers. He was garbed in a black form-fitting costume. When she looked into his mask she caught her breath and fell back, for it was her own features that returned her gaze. The mask was a mirror, crafted of highly polished silver and formed into an oval bowl fitted over the tumbler's face. It lacked openings for eyes, mouth, and even his nose, presenting an inhuman countenance stranger than any other she had seen this night.

The mask's convex shape warped her reflection, and viewed this way, Queen Oddacious indeed appeared mad.

Disquieted, Karigan averted her gaze. "Excuse me," she murmured, but when she tried to step around the tumbler, he was again in her path and she was forced abruptly to look at her reflection.

But not the *same* reflection.

It had altered, changed, so that she was no longer Queen Oddacious, but herself unmasked, without wig or costume, her own face staring back at her.

What? What is ... She wanted to run away, escape the strangeness of it, but could not, as if some spell held her fast, and she shuddered for she was not unacquainted with the power of mirrors.

Clouds roiled in the eyes of her reflection as if she watched the sky. Then something else appeared there mirrored in her eyes, a flight of arrows, metal tips gleaming, as they sloped toward her in a deadly arc.

Her reflection in the mask did not move, did not waver.

Waited.

⋖⋗ THE LOOKING MASK ⋖⋗

Karigan's awareness of the ball fell away; the music, the chatter, became a drone in the back of her mind. The mirror mask held her captive under its spell.

But before she could see the outcome of those arrows on their deadly course, the mirror changed, darkened. It was like peering into the blackness of night, her reflection gone. Then slowly, her eyes adjusted as if she really were in the thick of night, and she began to perceive subtle changes, shapes and shading.

The texture of bark stained by rot. A burl protruded from a tree like a fist and her vision narrowed on it. The burl resembled a face, a face seeping red ocher. What was this? Where was it?

The scene expanded revealing an entire grove of similar trees, some with burls knotting their girths, some without, all afflicted with rot, gloom held captive beneath immense, spreading limbs, a mist ghosting among the trunks.

It could only be Blackveil, haunting her before she even set foot within its treacherous bounds.

The vision went up in flames.

Languid, flickering flames.

It was like gazing into a campfire, but through the blaze she saw another face. The face of an elderly woman, bags beneath her eyes, pallid cheeks gaunt, tendrils of gray hair falling over her forehead, which was beaded with sweat. Karigan knew her immediately: *Grandmother.* The leader of the former Sacor City sect of Second Empire. Like the previous vision, it was impossible to know whether this was past,

251

present, or future, but it was as if the old woman looked directly at her.

Grandmother started speaking, but Karigan heard no words. Still she could not get over the feeling that Grandmother was speaking directly to her.

A phrase came to Karigan that she'd heard more than once before: *Sometimes the mirror goes both ways.*

"No!" she cried, surprised to hear her own voice, and she flailed away from the mirror mask, the spell broken. The tumbler bounded away.

Karigan reeled and would have fallen, but she was caught by strong arms and helped upright. The sounds and light of the masquerade ball came back in a rush that surged over her like a wave. She took some deep breaths, wondering how long she'd been trapped in the spell of the mask.

As she watched the spot where the tumbler vanished into the crowd, she silently cursed. What if that had really been Grandmother trying to speak to her? Maybe if Karigan hadn't panicked she could have learned something useful from the vision, like Grandmother's location. Such information would be invaluable to the king. Maybe she should go after the tumbler and gaze into his mask again, to see if she could—

"One must not gaze lightly into the looking mask," said the gentleman who had rescued her.

So intent on the mirror and her visions was she that she'd almost forgotten the helpful gentleman. She turned to him. Like all the other nobles at the ball, he was attired in the finest of silks and velvets cut in the latest style. His mask was made of gold leaf embossed with flowing, abstract designs. A pair of light gray eyes regarded her with amusement. There was something very familiar about those eyes . . .

"Looking mask?"

"Why, yes. Are you not acquainted with the tradition?"

Karigan frowned. She knew this man, with his black hair tied back and his elegant gestures. The flash of a red ruby on his finger confirmed it: Lord Amberhill.

"No," she replied, hoping he did not recognize her in return. Oh, he'd get a great laugh if he knew it was she in the horrid Queen Oddacious costume.

"Oh, well, you'll often find a tumbler in a looking mask at a masquerade. It's little more than a parlor game these days, but our ancestors probably took them more seriously, using them in sacred ceremonies. Legend says the ancient priests could see prophetic visions in them." Lord Amberhill laughed. "They were probably so intoxicated by drink and herbs that they saw many things."

He could not have been more wrong, but Karigan was not about to discuss it with *him*.

"I wonder," Lord Amberhill said, "if my lady would care to dance?"

"*What?*"

He smiled. "It is a ball, and it is what people do. And I must admit, I am intrigued by the, shall we say, audacity of your costume. But perhaps you've another escort this evening?" He glanced about as if looking for her missing, nonexistent escort.

Dancing was the last thing Karigan felt like doing. The magic of the mask had wrung her out. She wanted nothing more than to return to her little room in the Rider wing and curl up in bed with Ghost Kitty, not dance with Lord Amberhill, who had a way of prickling her sensibilities.

"No, thank you," she said. "Excuse me."

As she started to walk off, he placed his hand firmly on her arm and leaned down to speak to her. "So are you just going to *disappear* again, my lady? Oh yes, I recognize your voice. Your eyes." His words were quiet so only Karigan could hear him.

With a flash of annoyance, she tugged her arm from him. "You're mistaken. I don't know what you're talking about."

"Oh, don't you? In the play, Queen Oddacious marries a horse. A black stallion, perhaps. You are familiar with that, aren't you? The black stallion?"

Karigan froze. Was it possible Lord Amberhill had seen Salvistar? That he'd seen the death god's steed with her that night in the Teligmar Hills when no one else had? If so, what did it mean?

"It's a play and nothing more," she replied.

"Is that so."

She could not allow him to continue his line of questioning. Whenever he saw her, he persisted in needling her about "disappearing" and she was not about to play his game. She would not reveal Rider abilities. The secret had been kept so long as a means of protecting Riders from a populace phobic of magic. She would not endanger herself or her friends that way.

She drew herself up to her full height, and in the most haughty manner she could summon, she said, "I find your inquiry most inappropriate." She spoke loud enough that anyone nearby could hear her, and indeed several looked her way. "You are a very crude man." Chin held high, she turned on her heel and strode off fluttering her fan before her face. She smiled to herself wondering if he'd be able to persuade anyone else to dance with him after that.

She crossed to the far side of the room and decided to escape the crowds and warmth of the ballroom by retreating to one of the balconies. It was cold enough outside that she doubted too many others would be there. A footman opened a door at her approach and she exited into the fresh air, sighing in relief, the babble and music fading away behind her.

The only light was that which flowed from the ballroom through the glass doors. Clouds obscured stars and moon. She stepped up to the balustrade, and shivering in the chill, wrapped her arms around herself.

Yes, still winter, no matter how close spring.

Despite the cold, she found herself comforted by the relative quiet and dark. No Lord Amberhill here. No looking mask.

And then someone cleared his throat.

Karigan jumped. She had thought herself alone.

"I did not mean to startle you."

She peered down the length of the balcony and at the far end, there stood King Zachary. He had removed his dragon mask and ran his hand through his hair.

Karigan's mouth fell open, and then she remembered to curtsy.

He smiled. "Another refugee from the festivities, I see."

Karigan realized he did not recognize her.

"Yours is the best costume I've seen tonight," he continued. "Bold and festive, and loaded with metaphors. All the
others . . . I don't know." He stroked his beard. "Dull, I guess.
So very proper. Who do I have the honor of addressing?" Before she could respond, however, he waved his hand through
the air. "No, no. Don't tell me. It would ruin the mystery, and
that's what a masquerade is supposed to be about, right?
Mystery, hidden identity, secrets."

Karigan's hand went to her mask. Her fingers found the
bow that secured it. She could not be this close to him and
not reveal herself. It had been so long since they'd had private words. In fact, any words at all. How would he receive
her? Would he be cold and distant? Pleasant and gracious?
Or, more intense, like . . . like another night three years ago
when they'd stood on this very balcony with a silver moon
shining overhead? It had been another ball, another time . . .

Her hand trembled as she pulled on the ribbon. The mask
did not fall. She tugged harder, only to realize the bow had
become a knot.

"Your Highness," she said, but just then the door at the
king's end swung open and Lady Estora rushed out onto the
balcony and his attention turned to his betrothed.

Karigan receded into shadow.

"Zachary," Estora said. "It is so cold out here. You'll catch
a chill!"

"Oh, I don't think so. The air is bracing."

"Even so, you are missed, and there is something you
should see." She took his arm and guided him toward the
door.

"Very well." He grabbed his mask and with a glance in
Karigan's direction, he paused and bowed to her, flashing her
a smile. And then he was gone.

Karigan rushed to his end of the balcony and gazed
through the door after them, her breath fogging the glass.
The pair worked their way through the crowd, hand in hand,
pausing now and then to speak with their guests.

Karigan turned away ready to tear wig and mask off and
fling them over the balcony. *Damnation!* She'd been so close.
So close to him, and the moment was lost.

In a fit of frustration, she kicked a column of the balustrade. *"Ow!"* The column was made of granite. "Ow, ow, ow!" She hopped on one foot. "Bloody stupid fool," she berated herself, perversely pleased by the pain.

After a few moments of this, she took a deep breath, straightened her shoulders, and limped into the ballroom on her smarting foot. She'd had enough of the masquerade ball, and now she would leave for the comfort of her own chamber in the Rider wing.

⋖ AMBERHILL'S MASQUE ⋗

Amberhill watched after the G'ladheon woman as she strode away from him, admiring how she swung her hips to avoid brushing her ample panniers against others as she worked her way through the throngs.

"Remarkable," he murmured to himself. He supposed he would never get to the bottom of her ability to disappear, or persuade her to admit to her association with the godlike stallion, but he enjoyed trying.

He disregarded those who glanced sidelong at him, the men who moved their ladies out of his path. Karigan G'ladheon had probably ruined his chances of finding a dance partner this evening.

That was fine. He'd find other ways to amuse himself. For instance, there was trying to identify who was behind each mask. He picked out Lady Mella with the butterfly mask almost immediately. How could he forget the delicious contours of her body, which he, as the Raven Mask, had once known so intimately? Her husband was the ancient Lord Maxim and he did not think she got much pleasure from that shrunken piece of dried fruit. No, the night he'd crept into her bedchamber her exuberance and gratitude had been most agreeable.

Others were less easy to identify. There was the young man with the lion mask dressed in red velvet. While Amberhill could not figure out who he was, it was easy to see he was nervous about something, even with his expression hidden behind the mask. He stood off by himself, not attempting to converse with anyone. He played with the cuff of his left sleeve, fidgeted, and tapped his toe, but not to the beat of the music. He kept glancing this way and that as if fearing someone or something. Likely he was hoping to use the cover of the masquerade to make off with some lovely maiden beneath the nose of her father.

Amberhill continued on to one of the food tables. He passed on the jellied sea urchin, instead helping himself to a scallop wrapped in bacon, savoring the butter and juice that slathered it. He licked his fingertips observing, with consternation, the number of guests wearing some variation of a raven mask. He supposed he ought to be flattered, but more than a few of the gentlemen bore a generous paunch, which he found repugnant. It was not at all how he viewed himself as the Raven Mask, and he could not see these fellows managing to scale walls or leap across rooftops.

He moved to the end of the table loaded with an array of sweets and pastries. As he surveyed the offerings, he overheard snippets of conversation, from the usual commentary on the weather to the price of silk. It was terribly mundane, but one conversation did pique his interest. It was between an older gent and a younger one.

"I weary of these parties," the older man said. He wore a helm mask with a stuffed seagull perched atop it. Pinned to his lapel was a cormorant brooch.

Lord Coutre, Amberhill decided. The voice sounded right. The younger man also sported a cormorant brooch, but he wore a more simple eye mask of black silk with silver-blue feathers pluming from it.

"It is your daughter who is responsible for several of them," the younger man said.

Amberhill thought the fellow likely to be Estora's cousin, Lord Spane. He was often in close company with Lord Coutre and served as Lady Estora's chaperone and representative.

Amberhill hovered over the table pretending to be caught in indecision over whether to try a piece of lemon cake or a fruit tart as he continued to eavesdrop.

"I know, I know," Lord Coutre said. "I wish we could just dispense with it all and get the two married and have done with it."

"The solstice will arrive soon."

"Not soon enough. But we must defer to the moon priests on the date since they believe it auspicious. The gods know we want it to be a prosperous marriage; prosperous with many children so Coutre maintains its influence on the throne. Think of it Richmont! One of my grandchildren will one day reign over Sacoridia."

"It will happen, my lord," Spane said.

"We must ensure nothing goes wrong and that it all happens in a way that makes Estora happy. Even if it means attending these damned parties."

"You have done everything for her," Spane reassured the older man.

"Yes, well, I want you to promise me Richmont. Promise me that you will see to it this marriage proceeds no matter what. The future of Coutre depends on it."

"Yes, my lord, on my honor. I promise nothing will interfere with the marriage. Nothing."

Amberhill caught, from the corner of his eye, Spane bowing to Lord Coutre. The man came across as a sycophant who would follow through on that promise no matter what, especially if there was some reward in it. Anyone who got between him and his goal would no doubt live to regret it.

Amberhill selected a tart filled with raspberry preserves and bit into it, reflecting that while court intrigue was entertaining to watch from the fringes, he had no desire to get caught up in it himself. Too much trouble.

He left the table thinking to make a circuit of the ballroom, but the tumbler in the looking mask bounded up to him. He grinned at his own warped reflection. "Just you, old friend, eh?"

But he gasped when his reflection misted over and vanished.

"What the bloody hell?"

The mist cleared, showing his face again, but not his present face. The mirror revealed him unmasked and his hair wild in the wind, his face unshaven. He could almost hear the cries of gulls, smell the salt of the sea, feel the sway of a ship on the waves.

No, he thought, *this is not real. I am in the ballroom.* But he could not tear himself from the vision. The masquerade ball seemed miles and miles away.

His reflected face glanced upward and a shadow fell across it. Amberhill thought he heard the beating of immense wings on the wind. He could not discern whether he should be terrified or in awe, or both. He felt the strain of muscles demanding he duck for cover.

The shadow dispersed and then nothing. Amberhill gazed at his own reflection in the present as if that's all there had been all along. He took a step back and the tumbler somersaulted away.

Did I truly see that? Or was it some fancy?

At some point he had crushed the remains of his tart in his hand, raspberry preserves oozing between his fingers like blood. Whatever he did or did not see, it left him feeling off balance. No wonder Karigan G'ladheon had been so disoriented after gazing into the looking mask. What sorts of things had she seen? She who had access to powers . . .

He glanced at his dragon ring, but it revealed nothing more than its usual ruby radiance. What had he expected? Some flare of magic? For the gold dragon to wriggle around his finger? He shuddered. Whatever the looking mask had shown him, real or not, was damned disturbing.

He could have wondered about it more, but there was an outcry from the center of the ballroom floor.

⇜ LADY ESTORA'S MASQUE ⇝

Lady Estora Coutre was thrilled by how well her efforts to create a memorable masquerade ball were being received by her guests. The comments she overheard about the event proclaimed the food unsurpassed and the decorations beyond clever. Dancers filled the dance floor without fail and it was great fun trying to figure out who was behind each mask.

Her father might grumble about all the parties, but she'd tired of the gloomy winter and the hard, unyielding walls of the castle. She was determined to bring light and festivity into her life. If she was going to be spending the rest of her days here, she might as well make the best of it.

Now if she could find Zachary, there was something she wanted to show him.

Someone touched her wrist, a woman with a swan mask. "My lady, a most excellent masque. Why, it's been years and years since there has been one to attend in all of Sacor City. Thank you for organizing it."

The compliment warmed Estora, and she almost wanted to skip like a little girl, for it had come from Lady Creen, who was usually very critical of anything that came to her attention.

Estora found Colin Dovekey at one of the tables, with his blue eye mask, filling a cup with punch.

"Have you seen Zachary?" she asked him.

"I believe he stepped out for air," Colin replied. "Would you care for some punch?" He offered her his cup.

"No, thank you." She left Colin and worked her way through the room, greeting guests as she went. She was hardly

261

surprised Zachary would step outside for air. He seemed to enjoy parties well enough, but now and then he required a respite from the crowds.

A Weapon opened a balcony door for her. She shivered when she stepped out into the cold. Zachary turned toward her. He was not wearing his mask, and she couldn't say she blamed him, for it was heavy and must be hot.

Their costumes had been inspired by legends of the sea kings. Ever since Lord Amberhill's visit and gifts, she couldn't seem to remove the stories from her mind, so she'd turned Zachary into one of the legendary kings and herself into one of the witches of the sea that beguiled unwary mariners onto the shoals of islands, capturing them body and soul.

"Zachary," she said. "It is so cold out here. You'll catch a chill!"

"Oh, I don't think so. The air is bracing."

"Even so, you are missed, and there is something you should see." She took his arm and guided him toward the door.

"Very well." He grabbed his mask as he went, and then paused. When she turned to see what was the matter, she observed him bowing to the darkness. She squinted and discerned a figure in shadow at the far end of the balcony.

"What was that about?" she asked him after they entered the ballroom.

He chuckled. "I just had an audience with Queen Oddacious."

"Queen Oddacious? Oh, yes, what a peculiar costume. She was out there?"

"Yes. Apparently a rather shy person despite the costume."

Estora would find out who it was later. It wasn't unusual for Zachary to strike up a conversation with just about anyone. He had as much respect for the lowly tradesman as those of the noble class, an admirable quality in a king. So she wasn't surprised he'd found someone to speak with out on the balcony, and she could certainly see how that costume would pique his interest, because it certainly piqued hers. Still, there he'd been out in the dark, just him and some unknown woman . . .

She nearly laughed aloud. Could it be she felt a tinge of

jealousy? She and Zachary had been spending more time together than ever, sharing afternoon tea, he bringing her to meetings and audiences, and seeking her counsel on matters of court. Of course she did not expect him to change his stance on any of his decisions, but there were times when her observations had made a difference. She was enjoying her role as she prepared to become queen, and a real friendship was blossoming between the two of them that would certainly ease the transition into marriage.

At one time Estora had been reluctant to marry, but that was before her abduction. Now she was grateful to be alive and safe. And, she had been touched by Zachary's concern for her upon her return. She didn't think it was entirely his apprehension over what her father would do if she didn't return safely, either.

She appreciated his solicitous attentions. If there was still a part of him that remained aloof, she thought that, too, would change with time. After all it would be unseemly for him to act *too* familiar with her, and because of who they were, they were under particular scrutiny from all quarters.

"What is it you wish me to see?" Zachary asked.

"Something entertaining," she replied. That was, if she could find the tumbler with the looking mask. Perhaps it was silly of her to draw him into such a trivial amusement, but when she gazed into the looking mask, she swore she saw something more than just her own reflection: just a brief flash of herself beaming down at an infant in her arms. An infant with soft golden hair. At least she thought that's what she saw. Maybe she had seen only what she wished to see. Regardless, the image had brought her much delight and she hoped Zachary would see something similar.

The looking masks she had gazed into when a girl attending masquerades back home had never produced such a vision, but she and her friends would make them up anyway. Once she had pretended she'd seen herself becoming queen. Funny that it was coming true.

"Where is he?" Estora muttered.

As if in answer to her query, the tumbler appeared out of the crowd with a backflip and landed before them.

Estora clapped her hands. "Well done!" To Zachary she said, "I've had my turn with the looking mask. Now it's yours."

Zachary half-smiled. "I haven't looked into one of these since I was a boy."

"And what did you see?"

"A boy. A boy hoping to see something great."

They exchanged grins and then he looked into the mask. Some guests collected around them to observe their king participating in so frivolous a game.

As Estora watched Zachary, she saw all signs of pleasure had fled his features. He gazed into the mirror unblinking, as though transfixed.

"He seems quite in love with himself," one of Estora's cousins jested. "Perhaps there will be no room for you at the wedding!"

There was laughter from those in hearing range, but Zachary did not join in. He did not move, and an uneasy silence followed until a few moments later the tumbler leaped away.

Zachary watched after him, looking as if he'd just awakened from a dream.

"What did you see, Your Highness?" Estora's cousin asked.

"Yes," others chimed in. "What did you see?"

Zachary smiled, but Estora could tell it was forced. "I saw," he said, "the best king Sacoridia has ever known."

"And what was his name?" someone called out.

This was greeted by more laughter, but Zachary did not answer. He returned his gaze to where they'd last seen the tumbler, his expression serious.

When the onlookers dispersed, Estora asked him, "What did you *really* see?"

She never received an answer, for a man in a red coat wearing the mask of a lion rushed toward them with a yell, a dagger bared in his hand.

Estora screamed.

✎ THE KING'S VISION ✎

Karigan wearily ascended the steps that led
out of the ballroom. On her way out, she
had paused only to sample a few of the oysters
chilling in the hull of the sloop and found them
as fresh as if she were on the docks of Corsa. How that was
managed, considering the miles between Sacor City and the
nearest shoreline, she did not know.

In any case, they had revived her spirits a little after her
disturbing experience with the looking mask, and the disappointment of not having been able to reveal herself to King
Zachary. She would not have such a chance again before
leaving for Blackveil. Perhaps never again.

When she reached the top landing, she stopped and
turned to take in one last view of the masquerade ball. It
seemed just the same as when she arrived, the dancers flowing around the ballroom floor; the music, conversation, and
laughter drifting up to her. The colors, the light, the motion.

It was a pretty picture, Karigan thought, but surreal. A
gilded dream she was not a part of. Never would be. Did not,
she decided, want to be. Riding Condor through the woods,
feeling the surge of his powerful muscles as he galloped, the
rhythm of hoofbeats, and the wind against her face—the
freedom of the ride—that was real; free of masks and all they
implied, the only dance she required.

She turned away thinking of the comfort of her own
chamber, and maybe a cup of tea, when a scream stopped her
short. She whipped around, jangling the bells of her crown.
Down below a man in red charged the king, a dagger flashing
in his hand.

It took a moment for Karigan's mind to digest what was happening. An assassin! "No!" she cried.

The scene turned into a knot of chaos. Before the man reached the king, Weapons in black converged on him, guests in colorful finery falling away. Dancers collided into one another in the confusion. Some ladies fainted. Shouts and more screaming rose above discordant music, the conductor doggedly directing his musicians as if to get through whatever calamity had befallen the ball, his musicians desperately trying to keep up with him.

The assassin struggled in the vortex of Weapons, his shouts rising above the clamor. "You killed him! My father! He died in exile. I have no land, no title, nothing!" It was followed by more Karigan could not make out.

King Zachary put a protective arm around Lady Estora and hurried her past the melee and toward the stairs. Several Weapons broke off from the main knot to accompany them. As they launched up the stairs, Karigan moved into a niche behind a marble statue of Hiroque of the Clans to clear the way.

Four Weapons, hands on the hilts of their swords, preceded King Zachary and Lady Estora. In the lead was Donal. Somehow he sensed her presence in the niche and spared her a glance and a nod. To her surprise, he did not order her to leave.

Does he recognize me? she wondered in amazement. *Even in this costume?*

King Zachary and Lady Estora followed more slowly.

"—disagreed with the exile of his father, of course," King Zachary was saying. "And apparently exile disagreed with Hedric D'Ivary. I assume from his son's accusation the old man did not survive life in the north."

"It's not your fault," Lady Estora said.

"I put him there."

"With the agreement of all the other lord-governors. That man was cruel to those border folk. Instead of offering them refuge, he allowed them to be subject to rape, murder, slavery . . . even the children."

Karigan was not sure she had ever heard such passion

from Estora, and it appeared the king had not, either, for he paused on the landing with an expression of surprise.

"You acted justly." Estora's tone of conviction brooked no argument, and none was forthcoming. She turned to take in the commotion below, just as Karigan had only moments earlier. The king also looked, and Karigan held her breath hoping to remain unnoticed.

"You never did tell me," Lady Estora said in a much quieter voice.

"Tell you what?"

"What you saw in the looking mask. What you *really* saw."

"Nothing," he replied, but even from where Karigan was standing, she could see the lines of tension on his face.

"Please do not be dishonest with me," Estora said. "It would not be a good way to commence our lives together, hiding things before we're even married. I have been very honest with you, after all."

"Very well," the king replied. "I just did not want to cause you concern." He hesitated, but Lady Estora's gaze on him was unflinching. "I saw arrows in flight. Many arrows."

"Arrows? What does—"

"I do not know what it means," he said. "Though I cannot think it bodes well. Shall we continue on? I imagine the ball is going to break up now and I'd rather not be detained by those needing to ask a hundred senseless questions."

They set off down the corridor, leaving Karigan feeling stunned and wondering if she'd paled as much as Estora had at the king's answer.

Arrows. He'd seen arrows. She had also seen arrows. What did it mean? What did it portend?

Three more Weapons filed by and a fourth paused on the landing and peered at her. It was Fastion. She stepped out from behind the statue.

"You should return to the Rider wing," he said. "It appears the ball is over."

"But . . . but the assassin!"

"He is in hand and all is well."

"But—"

"Do not worry," Fastion said. "We may be Weapons, but

we are foremost shields. We defend the king with all our skills and will die for him if necessary."

Karigan shuddered. Strangely, however, she was more shaken by what King Zachary said he'd seen in the looking mask than by the assassination attempt.

Fastion glanced over his shoulder. "Other guests are now leaving."

The guests in their masks and finery mounted the stairs, their voices shrill and laughter nervous. Fastion set off down the corridor and Karigan hurried to catch up.

"Fastion," she said. "How is it you and Donal recognized me in my costume?"

"You were the most out of place, out of your element."

That was the truth, she thought.

"We are also well acquainted with the way you move."

"Oh," she replied, taken aback.

"We would not have permitted you on the balcony with the king if we didn't recognize you," Fastion added.

"What? You—" But Fastion turned down another corridor, going his own way without another word.

Why would they have allowed even her? No, she did not want to think about it. Weapons had their ways and reasons, and she was an honorary member of their corps. That had to be it, nothing more.

She struck off for the Rider wing.

"Why's she so glum?" The chair creaked beneath Garth's weight as he sat down. "She looks like she lost her best stallion—er—friend."

Why, Karigan wondered, did it seem everyone but her had seen the play *Mad Queen Oddacious?* Currently she sat in the common room of the Rider wing, still in costume, although the mask, fan, and crowned wig were on the table in front of her. Garth, wet and muddy from the road, had only just arrived from his latest errand. Yates and Tegan had just heard her rather spare account of the masquerade ball. She'd left out certain details, like her visions in the mask and her encounter with Lord Amberhill. Maybe she'd tell Mara later if they had a moment alone.

"She didn't lose her best friend," Yates said. "She's just mad that this time she wasn't the one who got to save the king."

Karigan rolled her eyes.

"Save the king?" Garth demanded. "Something happen while I was gone? Is that why the guards harassed and challenged me all the way across castle grounds?"

Karigan was obliged to recite, once again, her account of the assassination attempt.

"Huh," Garth said. "A king is apt to make enemies. Those D'Ivarys were a bad bunch, abusing people the way they did."

"*Those* D'Ivarys," Tegan emphasized. "The current lord-governor is not of that ilk. Anyway the Weapons kept the king safe, which is their job, and his reign goes on."

Karigan wished she could be that calm about it. She knew the attack had been clumsy and the assassin didn't have a chance with all those Weapons to protect the king, but what if circumstances had been different?

And Garth was right—a king was apt to make enemies. There would be other attempts on the king's life and there was not a single thing she could do about it. If it came down to it, she would not hesitate to give her life for his, and not just because he was her sovereign and what it would mean for the country.

I am hopeless, she thought.

"Queen Oddacious looks ready to retire for the night," Yates said.

Karigan yawned and stood. "She already has."

She left the common room for her own chamber. On her bed she found Ghost Kitty waiting for her, belly up and purring. It was with much relief that minutes later she was in her nightclothes and joined him.

That was an eventful end to the evening, Amberhill thought as he stepped outside of the castle's main entrance.

The assassin hadn't even gotten close to Zachary before the Weapons were on him like a cloud of wasps. He'd seen the young man earlier and wondered about his nervousness. Now he knew.

Several carriages were picking up ladies and gentlemen as they filed out of the castle and down the stairs to the drive. The usual complement of guards at the door was doubled, and they were not permitting anyone back inside.

Amberhill shrugged and espying his own carriage pulling up, set off down the stairs, finally removing his mask when he reached the bottom. The carriage door swung open and inside Yap awaited him, looking bleary-eyed, as though he'd had a good long nap.

"Ready to go home, sir?"

Amberhill stepped up into the carriage and sat across from Yap. "It will be home no longer," he said. His ring had been quiet during the ball, but now he felt it pulling on him.

"Sir?"

"The ocean, Mister Yap. That is where we are bound."

Yap grinned. "Aye, sir!"

≈ DARK ANGEL ≈

Grandmother pulled her cloak about her shoulders, almost too weak to manage even that much by herself. Immediately Lala was by her side helping her.

"Good child," Grandmother said, patting the girl's hand. "Good, good child."

They were still in the cave, the dreary cursed cave, for Grandmother had been too ill to travel, too feeble to even move. Some days ago a welt had formed on her hand—a spider bite, she suspected—and excruciating body aches and fever followed. She dimly remembered directing Min to lance the welt and make a poultice with herbs from her pack to extract the poison. Evil dreams paraded through her mind, of being entwined in her own yarn, of it burning, burning, burning into her flesh, and of dark creatures feeding on her while she screamed; images of gore and horror that made her shiver still.

Then one day, thanks to the ministrations of her faithful people, she awoke. She simply awoke weak, hungry, and parched. So they lingered in the relative safety of the cave while she recuperated, she cursing her frailty and every moment they lost in their quest to rouse the Sleepers. If only she could stir herself to full strength.

Instead she was a feeble old woman with skin sagging from bones, unable to even place her cloak on her own shoulders.

Deglin maintained the fire just to keep her warm. He'd dared venture outside to collect more wood. He didn't go far, didn't go beyond her wards, which, thank God, did not fail while she was sick.

"Somethin' out there," he muttered to her once. "Keepin' an eye on us."

Yes, there were Watchers. She would deal with them when need be, but at the moment she was more interested in what *she* could watch. She wanted to look into the fire—perhaps God would speak to her again, provide guidance.

"Lala, child," she said, "fetch my yarn."

Lala scampered away and was back in seconds with the yarn basket. Grandmother picked through the balls of yarn with shaky hands. This would not do.

"Child," she said. "You will have to help me tie knots. I'm not yet steady." She did not like to think what kind of disaster a mistake could cause, with the etherea of this place so unstable.

Lala had learned well from watching all the time and playing her string games. Her nimble little fingers flew with each knot Grandmother named. Sometimes she'd have to prompt Lala to the form when the girl paused, her young face perplexed. "Remember the knot where the bunny goes into the hole?" Lala would then solemnly nod and finish the knot.

When Lala tied the last one, Grandmother took the snarl of red yarn and inspected it closely. Yes, her clever, dear grandchild had done very well. But now, she wondered, would it work for her since she had not done the actual tying herself? She'd tried to project her intent into the knots as Lala worked, but she wasn't sure it was enough. So she yanked some of her wiry gray hairs from her head and wove them into the snarl best as she could, impressing her intent upon it. Then she tossed it into the fire and stared and prayed.

She must have stared for a long time for she dozed off. Her awareness of her people fell away and the world turned gray, yet she was still aware of the crackle of fire. Shapeless dreams, lacking the violence of her fever dreams, came and went like dancers waltzing across a ballroom floor.

A face intruded on her dreams, formed just beyond the flames. It was a masked face. Grandmother jolted fully awake and found the face wasn't a dream at all.

"Who are you?" she demanded.

Behind the mask, haunting eyes stared back at her. Just

stared. What did it mean? Who would come to her in such a form?

"Who are you?" Sweat dripped down Grandmother's temple. The jovial red sequins and feathers of the mask mocked her.

The entity did not answer; it just stared.

In a more pleading tone, Grandmother asked, "*What* are you?"

The flames flared and the mask was replaced by a visored and winged helm of steel so bright it almost hurt to look upon it. Live symbols swarmed and wiggled across the steel, symbols the like of which she had never seen before and therefore could not interpret.

The vision pulled back revealing the armored figure mounted on a great black horse. She knew the stallion—he was the steed of the god of death the heathen Sacoridians worshipped. Black as the charcoal of her fire he was, demon spawn. He pranced and snorted, his rider armed with a lance and shield. This was not, she thought, the death god who rode the stallion, but some lesser avatar. Even so, Grandmother felt the threat of the pair, felt the hairs stand on the back of her neck.

Then the vision was gone. The fire was a normal fire, and she discerned her followers moving about the cave and chatting. The cold returned to her bones. Lala tentatively touched her arm.

"Yes," Grandmother said, her voice trembling. "I saw something. Something evil." The masked entity, who was also the demon steed's rider, was a deceiver. A spy. "An enemy sent up from hell to defeat us in God's work. A Dark Angel."

⫷ ADVICE AND BLESSINGS ⫸

The day after the masquerade, Tegan took it upon herself to return the costume of Mad Queen Oddacious to Leadora Theadles at the Magnificent. Karigan was glad to see the thing go.

On this, the eve of their departure for the wall, and thence Blackveil, the members of the expedition were given the day to use as they would to make final preparations, perhaps visit with family or spend time in prayer at the chapel of the moon.

For Karigan's part, she checked and rechecked her gear, and having no family in the city to visit or any inclination to pray, she spent time with Condor grooming him, working out tangles in his mane and tail. When she finished, she stroked his nose and whispered nonsense to him, and treated him to a handful of oats.

"Well, he's looking fine."

Karigan turned to find Elgin Foxsmith leaning on the stall door. "A little bit rangy though," she replied. "He's shedding quite a bit." She toed a clump of chestnut hair around the bedding of the stall.

"True enough. Killdeer is, too. Enough to stuff a mattress." He chuckled. "So how are you feeling about your journey?"

Karigan paused her stroking of Condor until he nudged her shoulder for more. "I don't know," she said finally. "Ready to go, I guess."

"That all?"

"Anxious. I've been kept too busy to think about it, really."

Elgin nodded. "Probably a good thing."

And probably on purpose. It would not do any good,

Karigan reflected, if the members of the expedition had too much time to worry and froze up with fear.

"You'll do just fine," Elgin said. "You know what you're getting into. That bugger, Yates, though, I'm not so sure. Maybe his practical jokes will scare off any of Blackveil's nasties."

"Uh oh," Karigan said. "Did he . . . ?"

"Short sheet my bed? Oh, yes, the rascal, and not only that. He mixed pepper in with my jar of tea leaves." He scowled.

"Oh, dear," Karigan said.

"Claims he does it to all the new Riders. The short sheeting, anyway."

"But you're not—"

"New? I'm not even a Rider at that. No, not for many a year."

Elgin had become enough of a presence around the Rider wing that Karigan forgot he possessed no brooch. He had not returned to Sacor City to answer the Rider call, but had come at Captain Mapstone's request for help.

"You'll keep an eye out for Yates, then?" Elgin asked.

"I'll do my best."

Elgin nodded. "Almost wish I was going, especially if it would spare one of you young Riders, but it's not my lot."

There was that great sadness behind his words, and Karigan wondered again what had transpired during the veteran's time as a Rider to make it so. Before she could question him, however, several of the new Riders led in horses from the day's riding lesson. Condor whickered a greeting to the newcomers, rousing other horses to neighing and carrying on. Elgin's donkey, Bucket, kicked the wall of his stall.

Elgin watched the young Riders with a keen look in his eye. "You are going into the heart of a nightmare," he said. "You, Yates, and Lynx. You've got to trust one another. Can't speak for the others going with you, but Riders are different. It is how we are, and it's what I'm trying to instill in these young ones." He paused, then gazed directly at Karigan. "It is in my experience that most folks don't have your best interests in mind, even if they're on the same side. But with Riders? That's different. You remember that."

"Yes, I will."

"Good. Now I must see these youngsters to their geography lessons."

Abruptly Elgin left her, crossing the stable floor with his limping stride. He began to chivvy the Riders to move smart or they'd be late. Karigan pressed her cheek against Condor's warm, smooth neck.

It was true, she thought. She could trust any of her fellow Riders with her life. Elgin was also right about those outside the messenger service not having her best interests in mind. Spending time at the castle and among its courtiers, she knew there were some who would smile at you one moment and slit your throat the next if they thought it would bring them some advantage. It appeared to be a game among many courtiers, one in which there was little regard for how the lives and reputations of others might suffer.

She shrugged, thinking that once she was in Blackveil the intrigues of the court would be the least of her worries.

As Elgin ushered the last of his charges out of the stables, Yates sauntered in. When he spotted Karigan, he headed right for her.

"Aren't you the somber one," he said.

"Somber?"

"My wee wittle Karwigan so sad wooking." He curled his bottom lip down and made a sorrowful face.

Karigan sighed. "I just had a conversation with Elgin."

"Oh, that'll do it."

"Be nice! He was telling me to look after you, if you must know."

"Hah! He told me the same about you."

Karigan wasn't surprised. Lynx had probably gotten a talking to, as well.

"I'm pretty sure," she said, "he's afraid you're going to put pinecones or something in the bedding of the Eletians."

"Now there's a thought," Yates murmured. Karigan could almost see the gears and shifts of his mind in motion. She wouldn't put it past him to try something so absurd.

"But for now," he said, "I'm sick of all the doom and

gloom. If Dale were here, she'd organize a party. Hey! That's not a bad idea!"

By evening it was clear Yates' idea had taken hold, for all the Riders in residence, including Captain Mapstone, attended what amounted to a barn party. He'd weaseled food from the cooks in the castle kitchen and sent Fergal and Garth to the Cock and Hen for a keg of ale. It turned out that a couple of the new Riders were not half bad on fiddle and pipe, so the center of the stable turned into a dance floor.

Even Karigan joined in, stomping her feet as she whirled from hand to hand in a country dance as old as the land. The dancing was not fancy, nor were the kitchen's leftovers or the ale, but this party exceeded the masquerade ball by miles. It was good honest fun with people who were her *friends*. There was no deception here; no one wore masks.

The horses did not appear to mind the intrusion of all their Riders in their normally sedate environs, and in fact they watched the proceedings with ears alert, some bobbing their heads and whinnying.

After one last vigorous dance, Karigan breathlessly sank into a quiet corner with the dregs of her cup of ale and watched as her friends shifted into another breakneck reel. Tegan and Garth tore up the floor with the speed of their footwork. Yates showed off by doing a backflip off a bale of hay before heading back to the keg for more ale. He would not, she thought, be very happy to get in the saddle early tomorrow morning.

Meanwhile, Fergal coaxed shy Merla into dancing with him. Others stood around the edges clapping to the beat or trying to carry on hollered conversations. In an opposite corner, Captain Mapstone stood with Elgin, laughing at some joke. Karigan could not remember the last time she had seen such joy among her friends.

She smiled. She might not bear blood kinship to any of them, but they were family nonetheless. Her family. They mourned together and they celebrated together, and as Elgin had said earlier, she could rely on them for anything.

But now she thought it time she went to bed. She didn't

want to start her journey unrested. And she wanted to avoid good-byes. So she slipped out of the stable into the cold, dark night, her smile fading. She glanced over her shoulder as she strode away, watching her friends through the doorway dancing and drinking in the glow of lantern light. She thrust her hands into her pockets and quickened her pace, turning her back on it all. Soon the music and laughter faded behind her, and she wondered if she would ever see any of them again.

On the eve of the company's departure for Blackveil, Richmont Spane stood with Gillard Ardmont, whom he'd handpicked for the expedition, just outside the suite of rooms belonging to Lord and Lady Coutre and their daughters. The forester, in his buckskin and with his weathered features, looked out of place in the refined surroundings of the aristocratic wing.

"You are a good man, Ard," Richmont said, placing his hand on the forester's thick shoulder.

Ard had been one among many servants of Clan Coutre that had accompanied Lord and Lady Coutre to Sacor City following the signing of the marriage contract with King Zachary. Lord Coutre's party had chosen the overland route from Coutre Province, which had required the services of the forester.

Richmont had helped Ard's family in the past, and in return, Ard was extremely grateful and loyal to the clan, and particularly devoted to Estora. Richmont had gotten Lord Coutre to convince King Zachary and his advisors that Ard should join the mission to represent the interests of the future queen. He'd met little resistance. It meant they did not have to choose another of their own, and Ard's forestry skills would be a welcome asset to the company.

Richmont, of course, had his own agenda for wanting Ard to join the company.

"I live to serve the clan," Ard replied.

He was a humble man, Ard, and Richmont liked that about him. Ard had no family, only his commitment to the clan. He'd been a friendly presence in Estora's girlhood, showing her the ways of gardens and woods. Estora, who was kind to those who served her, had regarded Ard as a sort of wise and rustic uncle, and when she was little she'd hold his hand as they walked garden paths and he told her the secret tales of roses, ferns, and oaks.

Ard, Richmont knew, was not only devoted to Estora, but worshipped her.

"It is a lot we are asking of you," Richmont said, "to go into that wretched place."

"The forest does not scare me, though maybe it should."

"You were always a fearless one. But do not forget your other task—to ensure that the threat to Lady Estora's marriage is eliminated. Do you still feel up to this?"

"I do. I owe you and the lady much."

"Good man, good man. Now then, the lady would like to give you her own personal blessing on the venture. Before we go in, however, I want you to know I've set aside fifty acres of my own estate that will be yours upon the successful completion of your mission."

"My lord!" Ever the humble servant, Ard bowed. Land of his own would boost his lot in life—if he survived Blackveil. "There is no need of reward. I do this for the honor of the clan."

Richmont smiled. Yes, Ard was perfect for this. "Still, it will be something for you to look forward to upon your return." It was probably best if Ard did not return so there'd be no questions about what happened to the messenger . . .

Richmont knocked on the door and a Weapon admitted them. Estora sat composed beside her parents. Her youngest sister, Cressandra, sat by the fire, engaged in needlework. She was in that delectable stage of just beginning to bloom into young womanhood. Richmont licked his lips and hastily averted his gaze. Once the bodies of females matured fully, his interest in them waned. He'd always controlled himself around Coutre's daughters. Giving in to his desires was a conflict of interest, since incurring Lord Coutre's wrath would only prove counterproductive to Richmont's ambitions.

He took pride in himself for having resisted the lure of

Coutre's daughters all these years, and found he could slake his thirst at the wells of others; girls who were not nobly born, girls whose families were generally poor and had no recourse to his attentions to their overly young daughters. Usually they were happy enough to receive payment in the end.

"Ard!" Estora said. She rose and took the forester's rough hands into hers and brought him into the room. Ard blushed, and it occurred to Richmont how oblivious Estora could be to the power *she* wielded over people just by her sheer proximity. They loved her, especially the commoners.

Ard bowed. "My lady."

Estora returned to her chair. There was some inane chatter with Lord and Lady Coutre about weather and health, and finally Estora said, "Ard, you have ever been a good servant to Clan Coutre. Your willingness to journey into the dark forest of Blackveil is beyond any call to duty."

At Estora's nod, a servant brought forth a small, ornate box. "Clan Coutre wishes to acknowledge the danger you are placing yourself in on its behalf," she continued. "You were always good to me when I was little, answering all my silly questions with patience and kindness. Because of you, I have always loved green, growing things and find solace in gardens. It hurts my heart that you are going to face the danger of Blackveil, but knowing how deeply skilled you are in the craft of forestry does comfort me a little. I believe your skills will be tested to the utmost."

"I will do my best," Ard said.

"I know, my friend. But I want to personally bless your mission, and I wish with all the speed of the gods you will return to us unharmed. We've a small token of our thanks."

She opened the box and there, perched on blue velvet, was a silver signet ring with the cormorant symbol of Clan Coutre etched into it. This was a rare and high honor they were bestowing upon him.

Overcome, the forester wilted to his knees, tears shining on his ruddy cheeks. Estora placed the ring on his finger.

"When all is dark and fraught with peril," Estora said, "Lord and Lady Coutre, and my sisters and I, hope that this ring will remind you of our high regard for your courage and honor."

"With your blessing," Ard replied, "I shall bring honor to Clan Coutre, and do all that is asked of me."

Estora placed her hand on his bowed head. "So be it."

Richmont smiled. Estora had no idea she had just given Ard her approval to commit murder. Richmont was pleased. Very pleased.

⊰⊱ DEPARTURE ⊰⊱

The next morning Karigan arose while it was still dark to prepare herself and Condor to leave. After a warm breakfast, she assembled with the other members of the expedition and their escort outside the main castle entrance. The escort comprised half a dozen soldiers of the light cavalry and, to Karigan's delight, another half dozen Green Riders who would remain at the wall to aid Alton. The small size of their company would allow them to ride swiftly and reach the wall before the equinox.

She yawned through the benediction of the moon priest, who stood on the castle steps droning on and on. She had not slept well, but at least she didn't feel as miserable as Yates looked crouched over in his saddle with a greenish tint to his face.

Condor shifted beneath her and snorted, steam pluming from his nostrils, just as anxious as she to be off, but now that the moon priest had finished, General Harborough started issuing final orders. Captain Mapstone stood next to him, hands clasped behind her back.

"I know you will conduct yourselves with the utmost professionalism," the general was saying. "And you will serve your king and country well. Captain, anything you'd like to add?"

She gazed at each of them in turn, not smiling, but not looking sad either. She appeared every inch the commander she was. "Each of you has my confidence this expedition will succeed. I want you to know how proud I am of you, and I look forward to you all returning home safely."

General Harborough grunted. He appeared ready to send them off when the great doors of the castle opened. King Zachary emerged onto the top landing and trotted down the steps, a pair of Hillander terriers running alongside him, and Fastion following behind at a respectful distance.

Leather creaked and metal jingled as the company bowed to him from their saddles. The king paused first by Lynx, and moved on to each member of the expedition to share some private word. Much to Karigan's dismay, she got all fluttery inside awaiting her turn. What would he say to her? Something personal, or just wish her well on her way?

He wore blacks and grays as somber as the moon priest's gowns, his longcoat flowing behind him as he approached her. Karigan did not feel the morning gloom or the cold or anything when he stopped at Condor's shoulder, but when he clasped her hand, the warmth of his touch shocked her. She almost missed his words.

"Do whatever you must, Karigan," he told her, his voice so quiet it would not carry, "to come back. You must come back. To me."

Before she could even open her mouth, he was on to Yates. Karigan sat there at a loss. Had she heard him right? She bit her bottom lip. It had happened too quickly, and now he had already mounted the steps and paused on the landing. "May the blessings of Aeryc and Aeryon be upon you all," he said.

General Harborough ordered them to ride out. Karigan reflexively reined Condor around, all of it a blur. However, as she rode away from the castle, she did not see the road ahead of her, but the image of the king standing straight and strong on the castle steps with his two terriers sitting on either side of him, the gleam of dawn on his amber hair, and his longcoat flapping in the wind.

She would keep that image, she knew, tucked away in her mind forever.

The sharp clip-clop of hooves on the street below awakened Galen Miller from a deep slumber. He rose from his pallet in a panic fearing an opportunity missed, and flung himself across the attic room to the window, his body ungainly from the sleep and the shaking disease that afflicted him. Could his long wait finally be over? He swung the window open and leaned out over the sill into the crisp air.

It was, he discovered, only a small military detachment riding two abreast at a smart trot down the nearly deserted street. The time was just past sunrise and the Winding Way remained darkened by the shadows of buildings, but he could discern the blue uniforms of the light cavalry and the green of messengers. There were a couple of soldiers in black and silver, and a pair of riders in what looked like forester's garb. An odd assortment to be sure, and something Galen hadn't seen before during his many hours of surveillance of the Winding Way, but certainly not what he'd been waiting for all this time.

After the company disappeared around a bend in the street, he sagged down to the floor beside the window and just sat there. The detachment was of no matter to him. He did not care what business hurried them on. No, they'd been a passing curiosity was all. He'd have to continue his vigil until what he wanted came into the view of the attic window.

He kept his longbow and quiver close by and now he reached out with a trembling hand to caress the inlay work and carvings of the bow, its graceful curves. It was truly the work of a master, both beautiful and deadly. He'd won it in a tournament when he was Clay's age, a young man still, and an archer in old Lord Mirwell's militia. He'd been the best. When he retired from duty, he used the bow for hunting and had taught Clay the ways of the woods and how to track quarry. Galen passed his hand over his eyes remembering good days spent in the woods with his son.

Clay had grown into a fine man and an expert tracker. He followed his father's path and joined the militia. Everything would have been fine, but Lord Mirwell's coup attempt failed and Clay went into hiding in the Teligmar Hills with his captain. *Captain Immerez*. Then there'd been the whole plot to abduct Lady Estora. Why had Clay gotten mixed up in all that?

The last image he had of his boy, before the undertaker nailed the lid of his coffin shut, was of Clay's swollen, blackened face, his thickened tongue jutting between his teeth, his neck ravaged by the noose. At least he'd gotten a decent burial. Thanks to the stranger who'd given Galen those silvers, Clay was put to rest with dignity in a cemetery not far away from the inn. He'd even have a marker for his grave: *Clay Miller, beloved son of Galen and Rosaline.*

There was enough coin left over from the burial, and from the sale of his old mule and cart, for Galen to keep his attic room at the Cock and Hen with its all important view of the street, as well as to purchase the bitter weed from the herbalist he chewed to calm his shakes.

Sometimes the weed, however, gave him waking nightmares of seeing his boy dangling from the noose—not the adult man, but the tow-headed boy of about ten—his legs kicking, his body swaying, his struggles answered only by the jeers of the mob assembled to see him die. In these hallucinations, Clay struggled till he moved no more, the rope creaking on the gallows from his dead weight.

Just the memory of the visions set Galen off into choking sobs. "My boy, my boy . . ." Morning bells chimed in the distance, a bright counterpoint to the shroud of darkness that perpetually lay upon him.

His only comfort was his longbow and arrows, and what he could do with them. Rightfully the bow should have been passed down to his son, but now Galen could only use it to honor him. He would maintain his vigil over the street and soon find peace.

THE MELODY OF
THE WALL

"He does seem to like looking at walls."
"You should have seen him last fall,
staring at it all day long."

Alton rolled his eyes wondering why he'd
invited Dale and Estral along on this excursion if all they
were going to do was make fun of him the whole time. Currently he faced the wall of Tower of the Earth, companion
to Tower of the Heavens and the eight others that were part
of the D'Yer Wall. He'd made contact with all the mages
who, like Merdigen, existed in the towers, except for Haurris,
who was responsible for Tower of the Earth. Even the other
mages could not reach him, and though Alton tried, he could
not gain entrance to the tower either. Merdigen said they'd
have to assume the worst about Haurris.

What would be "the worst" for a noncorporeal projection
of someone who lived a thousand years ago? Not existing
at all, he supposed. He shrugged, for such questions entered
a realm of philosophy he was in no mood to pursue at the
moment.

He pressed his hand against the wall, feeling the cold,
nubbly texture of the granite beneath his palm. The guardians of the wall sang their normal song and did not show any
resistance to him, or any alarm for whatever was wrong with
the tower, yet he could not enter. Dale had tried with similar
results.

There weren't even any cracks from the breach extending
this far, although there was no way of knowing how things
looked from the Blackveil side. All in all, there were no clues
as to what was wrong with Tower of the Earth, or what had

befallen Haurris. The only way to know was to somehow get inside.

"Hopefully he won't kick the wall," Dale said.

"He did that?" Estral asked.

"Oh, yes, and got broken toes for his trouble. Not to mention smashed knuckles from beating on it."

Alton ground his teeth.

"Karigan never spoke of him having self-destructive tendencies," Estral commented.

That's it! He whirled around. Dale and Estral sat on a blanket several paces off, looking rather languorous with legs stretched out as if they were on nothing more than a picnic. They had, in fact, broken into a loaf of nut bread and were steeping tea in a kettle over a small cookfire they'd started.

"I'm right here," he said. "You don't have to talk about me as if I'm not."

Dale stuck her tongue out at him and Estral flashed him a disarming smile.

"It's not easy to talk *to* you when you've always got your back turned to us," Dale said.

"No matter how picturesque the view," Estral added.

Alton's cheeks warmed.

"Come have a seat." Dale patted the blanket beside her. "Take a tea break."

Alton flicked a glance over his shoulder at the wall and decided it wasn't going anywhere. He joined the two women on the blanket, Dale pouring him a cup of tea and Estral carving him a slice of nut bread.

The tea warmed him up nicely, and it was a fine sunny day, if still on the cold side. Why not a picnic? Even the horses were contentedly cropping at any dormant grasses their agile lips could find, tails swishing at nonexistent flies. And here he was, being served by two attractive ladies. If not for the wall nearby, they could be in some artist's bucolic scene.

"Did you really break your toes?" Estral asked him.

"*A* toe." He'd been so angry and frustrated that the wall would not let him pass, that he could not fix it. And he'd been sick with the residue of Blackveil's poison in his veins. Sick of heart, sick of mind, he'd battered his will and his body against the granite until blood flowed.

He'd lost all sense of himself during that time, allowing his appearance to go to ruin until Dale set him straight, reminding him he was still a Green Rider and that Captain Mapstone would disapprove of his bedraggled state. He'd once taken pride in his appearance and the sharpness of his uniform, and now the old Alton, in his opinion, was coming back. No one, not even Captain Mapstone, would be able to find fault in the shine of his boots. He kept his hair combed and his face clean-shaven. He'd found himself being even more meticulous of late, since . . . since about the time Estral arrived. He choked on his nut bread and spilled scalding tea on his leg.

"Ow!"

"Here," Estral said, dabbing at his thigh with a cloth.

He jumped at her touch near . . . a sensitive area. "Uh, it's all right." He took the cloth from her and dabbed the spill himself. So much for his perfect appearance.

"So what's next?" Dale asked. "Neither of us can get into the tower. Are we just going to go back?"

"I don't know. Maybe if the two of us try at the same time? If that doesn't work, I guess I'll have to go back and ask Merdigen if he has any more suggestions."

"He didn't seem very encouraging last time you asked him."

"No," Alton admitted. Merdigen had said the situation of Tower of the Earth was beyond his experience.

"Maybe the tower is fine," Dale said. "I mean it looks fine from here. If it's doing its job of holding back the forest—"

"It could be a weak point without Haurris in contact with the others. There's just too much we don't know."

Estral scrunched her nose. "That's not very interesting song fodder: *too much we don't know.*"

"I'm afraid life here at the wall is no ballad," Alton said.

"So you've told me. But I am patient."

"Well, I say let's give it another try," Dale said, hopping to her feet. "And if it doesn't work, we'll go back."

Alton was forced to stuff the rest of his nut bread into his mouth, chewing and swallowing hastily.

"I guess I'll just practice a little while I wait," Estral said, reaching for the lute that she took everywhere with her.

Alton nodded, rose to his feet, and followed Dale. Behind him came the sound of strings being tuned. He may have protested Estral's arrival at the wall at first, but her presence had done much to raise the morale of the personnel at both encampments. She was like a library of stories and music that ranged from centuries long past to pieces she and her fellow minstrels had created. She was also teaching the few musicians among them new songs, and in the process they honed their abilities.

As for himself, he'd found excuses to often be in her company, whether she was playing music or not.

By the time he and Dale reached the tower, Estral was strumming a warm-up piece and he remembered how effortlessly her fingers swept across the strings, her eyes so distant when she played, her face placid and unguarded.

Dale faced him. "You've been blushing a lot lately. And smiling, too."

"Have not." Alton immediately frowned to remove the smile from his face, but he couldn't do anything about the blush.

"Have too," Dale said with a grin, and pressed her hand against the tower wall.

Alton cleared his throat. It galled him he'd been so transparent. Best to let it go, however. Yes. Let it go and concentrate on the task before him. He hadn't the slightest confidence that the two of them together would get inside the tower anymore than just one of them had, but it was worth a try. He placed his hand against the wall, passing his other over his Rider brooch.

Nothing.

Just the harmony of the wall guardians humming against his palm and up his arm.

Actually, now that he thought about it, they felt stronger, brighter. Almost . . . cheerful.

"Do you feel that?" he asked Dale.

"Feel what?"

Estral started singing, her voice so quiet Alton could not make out the words.

The vibration of the guardians' own song intensified.

"I felt *that*," Dale said.

"I wonder . . ." Abruptly Alton left the wall and strode back to Estral. She stopped playing and gazed up at him. "Do you think you could try something? Can you do something with this tune?" He hummed the melody of the wall guardians.

Estral started humming with him and picked out single notes on her lute.

"Yes," Alton said.

"It's a strange tune," Estral said. "Very rhythmic."

"Do you think you could keep playing it? Humming it?"

Estral cocked an eyebrow, but proceeded to pick out the tune, then filled in with full chords and hummed the melody. It was eerie. Alton had heard it often enough from the wall guardians singing in his mind, but to hear it externally with Estral's beautiful voice was very strange.

He turned to rejoin Dale at the tower, but she was gone.

TOWER OF THE EARTH

"Dale!" Alton ran at the tower, slapped palms against stone, but he could not enter. He tensed, clenched his fists, ready to throw himself at the wall, but stopped himself and stood there trembling, remembering his madness of last fall. After a moment, he realized Estral had stopped playing. He touched the wall. It did not resonate as much as before.

"Play!" he shouted at her. "Play and don't stop, no matter what!"

Surprise flitted across Estral's face, but she did not hesitate. Her music drifted to Alton and he concentrated on rhythm and harmony—hummed it in his mind, and it vibrated through him. The wall swallowed him.

When he emerged into the tower, Dale grabbed him before he could take another step. She was backed up against the wall.

"Don't move." Her voice was harsh and her face pale in the sickly green light that illuminated the tower. Her shoulder was smoking, a patch of uniform singed.

"Dale?"

"I'm all right," she replied. "Just—just don't move."

Alton glanced around the chamber seeking whatever danger had attacked her. In a glance he took in the blackened, scorched walls, the cobwebs that draped from the shadowed heights waving in the air currents like restless specters. Whatever furnishings had once existed in the tower were now jumbles of wood. In the center of the chamber, the columns that surrounded the tempes stone on its pedestal were scorched and cracked, entire chunks missing from their fluted facades. One had toppled and was nothing more than rubble. The tempes stone itself looked like a lump of coal.

And there, in the circle of columns was a skeleton in a pile of rags, a bony arm stretched out as if reaching, reaching for the tempes stone.

"Gods," Alton murmured. "It looks like there's been a war in here."

"There's something else," Dale said, her eyes darting toward the shadowed recesses above. "Something bad. In here with us."

"What?" He'd shifted his body just the slightest bit and lightning streaked through the tower from top to bottom so bright it left a white-green afterhaze in his vision.

"Duck!" Dale cried, and she hauled him to the floor just in time as the lightning forked and struck where Alton had just stood.

"Gods," he murmured.

"Told you not to move."

"I see why."

Something then caught the edge of Alton's vision, a flicker of shadow. Something in the tower's upper regions. The hair on the back of his neck stood.

More lightning exploded, this time high up, spreading like fiery lace, and he saw *it,* the shadow thing flitting through the air to the opposite wall. It was spindly, vaguely human in form. A tendril of lightning stabbed at one of its limbs and its cry was unearthly, terrible.

Dale covered her ears. "What is it?"

"I don't know." Alton stared up into the dark, but nothing moved. The shaft of the tower seemed to suck all the air upward. The silence was dense, oppressive, filled his ears. He broke out in a clammy sweat.

Moments crawled like hours. He detected a whisper of movement, like a shadow caressing his mind, subtle, close. Too close.

Lightning ripped through the chamber again just above their heads, so near Alton felt its heat. The creature hissed and scuttled away. Silence.

"We need to get out of here," Dale whispered.

Alton agreed. He hoped Estral had listened to him and continued to play her music. He called upon his special ability and wrapped an invisible shield of protection around them both. "Now!" he yelled. He grabbed Dale and heaved her through the wall, following right behind her, just as lightning blasted his footprints.

He lay on the ground panting, not able to reconcile the scent of damp earth with the darkness of the tower. Beside him Dale groaned. He rolled over and found her sitting up, gingerly reaching for her singed shoulder.

"Water!" he screamed at Estral.

The minstrel, who had listened to him and kept playing and singing no matter what, now set her lute aside, grabbed a waterskin and ran it over to him. She asked no questions, just thrust the waterskin at him. He liked that.

He crawled over to Dale. Her shoulder was an angry red.

"I'm all right," Dale said. The dazed look in her eyes suggested otherwise.

Alton poured water on the burn. Dale screamed and fell back, but did not resist. Alton kept pouring.

Dale gasped. "Don't get *all* of me wet."

"Well, hold still then!" To Estral he said, "We need to get her back."

"It stings like all five hells," Dale said, "but I'll live."

"Good," Alton replied, "but we're still going back so Leese can have a look."

Dale groaned.

"Plus," he added, "Merdigen will want to hear about the tower."

"There was something in there," Dale whispered.

"Yes. Yes, there was."

To Estral's credit, as soon as Alton said they needed to go back, she'd set about collecting their things and packing them, no small effort considering they'd brought camping supplies so they could spend the night at the wall if necessary. She then started bridling the horses and tightening girths. Dale's Plover almost dragged Estral away in an effort to reach her injured Rider. And still Estral did not question them about what happened.

By the time Alton had finished pouring out the contents of the waterskin over Dale's burn, she was shivering in the cold air. He removed his own greatcoat and gently placed it over her good shoulder and wrapped it around her in a way that would keep most of her warm but not aggravate her burn. He then helped her to mount.

"I'm all right, really," she said, but there was an edge to her voice that wasn't entirely convincing.

He lifted her waterskin from the saddle horn and thrust it into her hands, then knotted Plover's reins over the mare's neck so they would not drag. Before Dale could protest, he said, "Drink as we go. Plover knows the way."

Dale rolled her eyes, but she did not argue. Alton was glad. He wanted to get her going before shock set in. Even if it did not, the burn was obviously painful, and the sooner it was treated, the better. They had a long ride ahead of them, but he'd use all his Green Rider training to get them home faster than they'd arrived at Tower of the Earth.

It was not until they were well under way, taking a break at a walk from the ground-eating trot he'd paced them at, when Estral started asking questions.

"What happened back there?" Her eyes were large, her forehead crinkled.

"Hard to say," Alton replied.

There was an amused snort from Dale up ahead. Alton made her ride lead so he could keep an eye on her. Not that Plover would allow her Rider to fall, but he wanted to make sure. The way was easy to follow anyway, with the immensity of the wall to their immediate right.

"You just drink," he ordered her. He remembered hearing from Leese that it was important for injured people to drink water. He wasn't sure why, or even if she meant all injured people, but at the very least it gave Dale something to think about other than the pain of her burn.

"I'm getting waterlogged," she complained.

"Good. Keep it up."

Dale grumbled something he couldn't quite make out,

and probably didn't want to hear, but at least she complied
and took a swig from her waterskin.

"The beginning," Estral reminded him. "Begin with the
music."

When he explained where the melody he'd requested her
to play had come from, she gazed at him in amazement.

"The guardians resonated with your music and allowed
us to enter the tower. That begets a lot of new questions, one
being how and why they are responding like that to your
playing, and another being why they were stubborn about
letting us through in the first place."

"I don't know about the latter," Estral mused, "but as to
the former, music is powerful. It can make you laugh and
sing along, or move you to tears. It has started wars, and
brought peace. If the wall's strength is really the harmony of
the guardians' song, then it makes perfect sense to me they
should respond to my music. I am, after all, descended from
Gerlrand Fiori, and one certainly gets the impression from
the stories that there was magic in his music."

Alton just didn't know, but her explanation made as much
sense, if not more, than anything else he could think of. He
was also impressed by how casually she discussed such ideas.
He was so used to the antagonism expressed toward magic
by those other than Riders that her acceptance of it surprised
him.

"So you got into the tower," Estral said. "Then what?"

Alton removed his feet from his stirrups and rotated his
ankles to stretch his legs. He kept Night Hawk on a very long
rein, but the messenger horses appeared to understand the
need to make time, so kept to a fast walk.

"There was . . . there was lightning," Alton said. "It struck
at anything that moved. Not regular lightning, but magic."

"That's what got Dale?"

"I did not get *got!*" Dale protested. "I was grazed. If I'd
been gotten, I wouldn't be here talking to you."

Alton suppressed a chuckle, thinking she was probably
right.

"The tower was in shambles," he told Estral. "And there
was someone's skeleton on the floor. The walls were all

blackened with scorch marks. Even worse, there was something else there. A creature . . . or something." He shuddered.

"Is that what caused the lightning?"

"I don't think so because it got struck as well. It's almost as if the tower generated the lightning."

"I wonder what the creature was," Estral said, "and how it got in there."

"So do I. If some evil creature from Blackveil penetrated Tower of the Earth, what's to say the other towers aren't vulnerable as well?"

Dale suddenly halted Plover.

"What's wrong?" Alton demanded.

"My bladder is sloshing." She flung her leg over Plover's neck and slid to the ground. "I'll be right back," she said and dashed into the woods.

Estral watched thoughtfully after Dale. "She's hiding how much that burn hurts, and the riding is taking a toll."

He almost retorted that Riders often rode while injured and bore it, but her expression was one of genuine concern and he did not want to sound like an oaf, reinforcing anything Karigan had told her about him being "mean." Her approval of him had somehow grown significantly in importance, so he kept his peace and was content to sit in her company while they awaited Dale's return.

⊰ WATER MUSIC ⊱

Alton wished he could come up with something clever or witty to say while they waited, but it was as if he no longer knew how. He was out of practice. All his attention had been centered on the wall, which did not require making small talk with others. In fact, for the longest time he hadn't cared much about conversing with anyone at all, except maybe Dale and Merdigen. But now he found himself wanting to talk to Estral just to hear her voice, her ringing laugh. Her responding to him.

Karigan. He would have liked to talk to Karigan if only she'd been assigned to the wall as he'd requested, but she was not here. If only she would write him! He was so unsure of her, of how she felt toward him, or if she even thought of him at all. He had wanted to ask Estral about Karigan, but did not know how. An appropriate moment never seemed to materialize and, he realized with no small amount of surprise, he hadn't been dwelling much on her of late. He'd been ... distracted.

As if picking up on the subject of his rumination, or maybe also feeling the need to fill in the silence with conversation, Estral said, "After the excitement at the tower, I think I now have a sense of what Karigan's adventures are like."

An opening. Alton leaped on it. "Do you hear from her much?"

Estral chuckled. "Oh, you know Karigan—not the best of correspondents. Occasionally I receive a letter, but usually she's woefully terse on details. More often I get the bigger news, like the rescue of Lady Estora, secondhand."

"Secondhand?"

"Other minstrels. Sometimes Mel has a tidbit or two from your captain."

Alton had forgotten the captain's daughter, Mel, was studying at Selium.

"Yep," Estral continued, "Karigan hasn't written me a single word about her part in the rescue of Lady Estora. We did have a big old talk, though, when she came through in the fall searching for the Silverwood book."

"Did she ... did she say anything about me? Besides that I was, um, mean to her?" He grimaced when he heard himself, and felt a blush warm his cheeks.

Estral glanced away, perhaps considering how to respond. He did not think it boded well.

"That did come up," Estral said. "Your anger toward her really hurt her."

"I know."

"She understood you'd been under immense strain here at the wall, but she didn't understand why it made you angry at her. Despite that, she never stopped caring for you."

Alton felt a rush of guilt. Yes, he'd been forgiven, but he wasn't sure he could forgive himself. "How ... how much does she care? For me?"

Estral did not answer, but darted her gaze into the woods where Dale staggered out of the underbrush. In the waning late afternoon light, Dale's face looked drawn and pale. When she reached Plover, she couldn't seem to get her toe in the stirrup to mount. Alton immediately shoved all personal concerns to the back of his mind.

"Dale?" he asked. "How are you doing?"

She ignored him and tried to mount again, but Plover swerved away out of reach. Alton knew messenger horses tended to be more sensible than their Riders at times, so he slipped off Night Hawk and took Dale's arm. She was shivering and he could see the pain in her eyes. He checked the burn. It was an angry, swollen red and blistering.

"We're stopping for the night," he declared. "We've still got a long ride ahead and I think it would be better if you got some rest before we continue on."

It was a measure of the pain Dale felt that she did not protest. Alton made her sit on a rock, wrapped in his greatcoat,
while he and Estral tended the horses and set up camp.

He watched Estral from the corner of his eye as she collected firewood and dumped it in a pile before setting off
to find more. She worked efficiently, silently, and without
complaint, not at all like the citified noblewoman he had expected, but as competent as any Green Rider. His lips curled
into a smile. Then he cleared his throat and straightened his
features, remembering what Dale had said earlier about him
smiling a lot more lately.

In no time they had raised two small tents and sparked
a campfire. They installed Dale in one of the tents and now
Estral was brewing tea.

"I've some excellent willowbark tea that should help
Dale," she said. "There's an apothecary in Selium who has
only the best quality stuff, and I've been getting the willowbark from him for years. Headaches. I get them."

"Ah."

When the tea had steeped to her satisfaction, she took
a mug into the tent where Dale rested. Meanwhile, Alton
prepared a simple meal of bread, cold beef, and cheese for
each of them. They ate in silence as the sky deepened into
midnight blue above and the stars punched through with
brilliant light. The horses munched on their ration of grain
nearby and there were scurrying sounds of small animals in
the underbrush. An owl hooted in the distance.

"I want music!" Dale yelled from her tent, shattering the
tranquility.

Alton almost sputtered his tea.

"Well, then," Estral said, "I guess I have my orders." She
set aside the remains of her meal and opened her lute case,
and once again tuned up the strings.

"Any requests?" she called to Dale.

"Something good and raunchy." Her request was followed
by what Alton could only perceive as suspicious snickering.

"Good and raunchy, eh?" Estral murmured, looking
thoughtful and not at all taken aback, unlike Alton, but it occurred to him that she must get all kinds of requests depend-

ing on whatever venue she played and the type of audience present.

She launched into a song about a lumberjack trying to impress the innkeeper's daughter with the size of his pine. It contained all the vulgar wordplay he was sure Dale could wish for and by the time the tune ended, Alton's ears were burning. After the final strum, Estral smiled pleasantly at him.

"Is he blushing?" Dale asked.

"Hard to tell in the firelight," Estral replied. "But I believe he is."

"Hah!"

Alton glowered. Dale had wanted to make him blush in front of Estral. "Where did you learn *that* song?" he demanded. Surely this was not what they were teaching the young students at Selium. Surely not . . .

"Lumber camp, of course," Estral replied.

Alton could not imagine her in a camp full of such rough men. She'd be a tasty morsel to them. The stories one heard about their beastly behavior and crude ways! "Lumber camp? Are you mad? With all those rowdy, uncivilized brutes?"

Estral paused as if considering, then shook her head. "No, not me. My mother perhaps."

"Your *mother?*"

Estral laughed. "Yes, my mother. She was chief of a camp north of North. I was born there, yes in those woods, in that camp, with all those *rowdy, uncivilized brutes.* She says they were all like happy papas when I came along."

Alton scrunched his brow at the image of a group of big, grungy lumberjacks cooing at a baby. "I . . . I thought your father was—"

"Aaron Fiori? He *is* my father."

"But . . . how?"

Laughter trickled out of Dale's tent. "I think you need to explain to him about the lumberjack and the pine."

Alton scowled at the tent though Dale couldn't see him. He definitely would not travel with the two women at the same time again. "You know what I mean."

"Of course," Estral said, grinning. Alton's ears just burned hotter. "My father is a minstrel and he travels. He visited the lumber camp for a spell and my mother took a shine to him. Simple as that, and when the time came for him to continue his wandering, he left, never guessing he'd made a child."

Alton didn't know what to say. He had imagined Estral's mother to be some genteel lady strumming on a harp somewhere within Selium's walls, not a lumber camp chief who ordered around a bunch of coarse, ax-wielding woodsmen.

"Of course," Estral continued, "he figured it out about a year later when his travels led back to my mother's lumber camp and there I was. He made a point of visiting twice yearly after that."

"They never married?" Alton blurted before he could contain himself.

Estral shrugged. "Why would they? My mother was content at the camp and he was busy wandering. It has not been unusual over the generations of Fioris to produce heirs in this manner. A regular spouse would find it difficult to put up with a husband who was constantly away, and a Fiori can't not travel. Most Fioris, anyway. It's not very fair to the spouse if you think about it."

To Alton, who'd been brought up in a noble family with all its strict codes and customs, it was difficult to imagine so casual an attitude toward bastards. As much as he disliked thinking of Estral that way, wasn't that what she was? A bastard? When he looked at her now across the fire, however, he did not see a bastard, but a lovely young woman with a voice gifted by the gods. Yes, what was lineage compared to that? And if that was the way the Fioris did things, and had done it for centuries, who was he to argue? It was just startling. To his way of thinking, anyway.

"Is that why," he said more cautiously, "you go by Andovian and not Fiori? It's your mother's name?"

"Yep." She strummed a chord, then silenced the strings with the flat of her hand. "When I inherit my father's position, then I'll become the Fiori. It's as much a title as a name."

The breeze shifted and Alton waved campfire smoke out of his face. He'd never thought much about the Fioris. There'd never been any reason to. Selium minstrels and Estral's father himself had come to Woodhaven, but at the time he'd seen them as just entertainment. *Just.*

Estral started plucking a lively dance tune, this time not asking Dale for a request. It was the story of a goatherd and a milkmaid, and was not at all raunchy. Alton found himself tapping his toe and nodding his head to the beat. When she finished, muffled clapping came from Dale's tent.

"It seems our patient liked that one," Estral said.

"I think it is time our patient got some sleep so she's well enough to ride in the morning," Alton replied.

Estral nodded in understanding. "Just one more bit," she said. "Some water music to relax us all."

Her fingers picked out a series of notes that emerged like the soothing tones of a stream trickling between mossy banks, ripples curling around rocks and beneath ferns. Alton closed his eyes and let the music wash over him. He imagined following the stream to where it flowed into a lake and the music became the give and take of gentle waves. A summer lake with the sun beating down on his shoulders. He strolled along the shore and someone was with him holding his hand. He thought it would be Karigan, but he saw Estral.

A PICNIC BASKET
OF VIPERS

They arrived at the encampment the following afternoon. Alton made sure Dale went
straight to Leese. The mender pronounced the
burn bad, but not as serious as it might have
been and proceeded to make a poultice for it. She also advised that Dale spend the night with her for observation, but
Dale's protests were so vociferous that Leese gave in after
Estral promised to keep an eye on the Rider.

Alton thought he caught a muttered, "Stubborn Riders,"
from Leese before she returned to her tent.

Once Alton reached the secondary encampment, he
tended Night Hawk and then headed straight to Tower of
the Heavens to tell Merdigen about the previous day's adventures. By the time he finished, the mage was pacing.

"This is exceedingly alarming," he said. "The part about
the music is interesting and even hopeful, but the rest?" He
shook his head.

"What do you make of it?" Alton asked.

"I haven't the faintest. This is beyond my experience. You
saw no sign of Haurris?"

"No, unless that was his skeleton on the floor."

Merdigen stopped in his tracks and gazed thoughtfully
into the dark upper reaches of the tower. "No, I can't see
how. His corporeal self ought to have been burned upon a
pyre when he passed on. It's what we do, and what the keepers were instructed to do to us in the end. Unless . . . unless
his corporeal self existed long beyond the rest of us, and even
beyond the keepers. It's not likely, but it's not inconceivable
either."

Alton yawned and his stomach rumbled. It had been a long couple days.

"I need to consult with the others," Merdigen said. "And you need to get some food and rest. Do not be concerned if I am not here next time you visit."

Alton did not need much persuading to call it a day. He left the tower for the sharp air outside, amazed to find afternoon had turned into evening. He headed for the kitchen tent wondering in which tower the mages would assemble. Of course it would only be seven of them since Radiscar and Mad Leaf were cut off by the breach. There was a way for them to circumvent the breach, but it required a lengthy journey. He often wondered if it were an illusionary journey, or if magical projections truly experienced the concepts of time, distance, and danger. The mages seemed to think they could, and that's all that counted.

At the kitchen tent he filled up on a couple of bowls of stew before returning to his own tent. As he approached it, he was surprised to find the canvas walls aglow with light and soft music being played within. When he folded aside the flap, he discovered Estral sitting on one of his campaign chairs, the lute on her lap, and a lamp at low burn on his table.

"Hello," she said as he stepped in.

"Hello."

"I hope you don't mind, but Dale's tent was, er, rather busy."

"Busy?" Alton dropped into the chair across the table from her. "I thought you were supposed to be keeping watch over her."

Estral made a face. "Her friend, Captain Wallace, is, um, taking care of her."

"Captain Wallace?" Alton asked, perplexed. "Why would *he* be taking care of her?"

"Her *friend,* Captain Wallace," Estral stressed.

Alton scratched his head. "Friend?"

"More than a friend, I daresay."

"More than a . . . ? Ooh!" Alton's cheeks warmed. How dense could he be? He had not seen . . . had no idea.

"In fact," Estral said, "it was darn uncomfortable for me to stay there. Busy, like I said. Usually they go to his cabin."

Alton coughed. "I see. Wallace? Really?" How had he been so unobservant?

Estral nodded. "I didn't know where else to go. If it's a problem, I'll leave."

"N-no. Don't go out into the cold. We could . . . we could talk."

Estral plucked a series of notes on her lute. "We could. What do you want to talk about?"

"Well . . . I—" Alton fumbled about thinking hard for several moments, finally grabbing something out of the air. "The lumber camp. You! I mean, I'd like to hear more about that. When did you leave the lumber camp for Selium?"

Estral stopped playing and furrowed her brow. "When I was six. After an accident."

Alton groaned inwardly at having managed to pick what was undoubtedly a painful topic. "Karigan mentioned something about that once," he began hesitantly.

Estral appeared unsurprised. "Yes. I had wandered onto the frozen edges of the river and fell through the ice. I got real sick after, with a bad ear infection. I suppose I'm lucky I suffered no worse thanks to one of the men who saw me go in and pulled me out."

Alton recalled Karigan telling him the illness had destroyed the hearing in one of Estral's ears. So hard to believe when she was so fine a musician.

"After that," she explained, "my parents agreed it was time for me to go to Selium to live with my father. It was safer and more civilized and all that. I've been there ever since. Well, that is, until now."

"Do you miss it?" he asked. "Selium?"

"Well, I'm not much of a traveler—not at all like my father. I'm a homebody. So this has been a bit of an adjustment for me, but a fascinating one." She smiled.

That smile left Alton feeling much too warm. He glanced away. "Fascinating, eh?"

"Very. It's good to leave behind all that is comfortable

and known every so often. It opens one's mind to the wide world. You and Dale walking through walls, for instance, is one of the most amazing things I've ever seen."

Alton often took for granted how it must look to those without magical abilities. For most people, it certainly was not an everyday occurrence. To his surprise, Estral then commandeered the conversation, asking him about stone working and how, as was the tradition in his clan, he'd been schooled in stonecutting and masonry at a young age. He found himself describing how a stonecutter could sense the grain of the stone and how cutting against the grain could mean an imperfect piece, and how a blacksmith was essential to the process because someone had to keep the tools sharp.

He was flattered by her interest in what he considered the mundane details of his life. Her questions were intelligently framed and not too deeply probing. She appeared to listen to his answers with her full attention.

Suddenly he clamped his mouth shut realizing he'd been talking *a lot*. About himself. Had Karigan ever taken such an interest in him, or was all the questioning by Estral simply something minstrels were good at?

"What's wrong?" Estral asked.

"Nothing. We've— I've just been going on and on."

"It fills many gaps," Estral replied. "Karigan naturally did not tell me everything about you."

"You never did say," he began quietly, staring into the flame of the lamp, "how Karigan regards me. I'd ... I'd like to know." He *needed* to know, but now as his words hung in the air between them, a sense of mortification crept over him that he had even asked. That he'd asked *Estral* of all people. But who else was there that knew Karigan as well as she?

"I did tell you," Estral replied. "She cares very much for you."

"I was hoping. I mean ..." Now Alton was boiling in his own skin. He looked down at his hands, unable to meet Estral's gaze. "I thought maybe there was more."

"When I last saw Karigan, we talked about several things going on her life. Her father, the young Rider she was training, and other matters she told me in confidence and which, as her friend, I won't betray. In regard to you, she was confused and hurt, but it seemed to me she cared strongly about retaining your friendship."

Friendship. The word left a sour tang in his gut, but he had to remember Estral had last seen Karigan before he'd apologized. Before his letters.

An awkward silence hung between the two of them. The tent walls rustled, sending misshapen shadows rippling across the canvas. Somewhere in the distance a soldier called out the hour of the watch.

"It's late," Estral murmured. "I think I'd better leave."

"What?"

"It's getting late. I'd best find someplace to stay for the night."

"No," Alton said too sharply. "I mean, please don't leave. Where would you go?"

"I don't know. Leese's maybe."

"That's all the way to the main encampment and it's very dark out."

She raised an eyebrow.

"You stay here tonight," he said. "I've got someplace else I can go." He stood and without another word, so she could not argue, he left his tent, grateful for the cold of night bleeding away the heat burning inside him. He inhaled deeply, surprised by the tautness of his body. He scrubbed his face and strode rapidly for the tower.

Once he was inside, he found the tower chamber empty but illuminated by a soft glow. Merdigen had already left to confer with the other mages. He could be gone for days. Alton was relieved to be alone.

He busied himself by preparing a fire in the big hearth, first laying down kindling, then using flint and steel to ignite it. When a small flame crackled to life, he blew on it to enlarge it, then threw in larger sticks to build the blaze.

As he worked, he thought about Estral Andovian sitting alone in his tent. She awakened something in him that had been absent for a long while, aroused a craving for her company, her attention, her touch, and it was only growing. He hadn't wanted to leave her, but it had been too dangerous to stay. He could not trust himself. Could not trust himself now not to flee the tower, run back to his tent, and immerse himself in her presence, to quell the loneliness within that he hadn't recognized before.

Those letters he wrote to Karigan must have been in reaction to this loneliness, but her few replies had been circumspect, almost cool, which he'd found frustrating, hurtful. If she wanted to be friends and nothing more, why hadn't she been plain and just said so?

He paused, leaning against the mantel, considering, trying to imagine how he might feel in her place. He'd been volatile. Would *he* have wanted to further incense someone already burning with so much anger by telling him something he didn't want to hear? He'd put her in an impossible position. And truly, as caught up in his own fantasy as he was, he'd found it inconceivable she'd want anything less than a much deeper relationship with him.

He shook his head like a horse with a fly in its ear. Deluded by his own desires he'd built castles of moonbeams. He'd mistaken her concern for their friendship and readiness to forgive him as something more. He laughed harshly and threw another stick onto the fire. Here he was once more caught up in his own little world around which everyone else revolved. How self-centered could he be? For all he knew, there was someone else in her life now, someone he had not heard about.

As he thought about it, another man in Karigan's life made perfect sense. He'd been stupid not to see it, not to even think of it. She wanted to stay friends with him, but feared telling him the full truth would anger him. Especially because it involved another man. Who was she in love with? One of their fellow Riders? A merchant? *Who?*

He stood there stock still waiting for the eruption of his own fury, but to his surprise, it did not come as it would have in the past. It just wasn't in him now. Maybe after all this time he was finally healing from the venomous influence of Blackveil.

A tinge of jealousy did burn inside, but it was subdued. He was more saddened by the loss of what could have been between him and Karigan for he had envisioned it well and in detail. Above all else, however, he was amazed to discover he was . . . relieved? Yes, relieved and free. Karigan did not want him the way he had wanted her to want him, and maybe he no longer wanted her that way either.

The revelation set him free. And he liked it.

He had a good notion of how he would use that freedom. The sizzle and pop of the hearthfire became music, the strumming of a lute, perhaps, and in the blaze he saw her face. Not Karigan's, but Estral Andovian's. She stirred something deeper in him than Karigan ever had.

But how free was he to pursue Karigan's friend—her *best* friend?—a most sacred bond. He groaned thinking that his interference could be like opening a picnic basket of vipers.

He didn't want to turn Estral against him by seeming to wrong Karigan, yet Karigan had made her decision, unvoiced as it might be. Somehow he'd have to work around her. Karigan, after all, was not here. She was not here to be hurt, nor had she made any effort to lay claim to him. He was free to do as he wished and so was she. There should be no reason for him to feel guilty about moving on, and one couldn't help to whom one was attracted. Still, he'd have to go carefully. He'd—

"Hello."

Alton jumped, heart pounding. Standing there in the chamber with him just a few paces away was not Merdigen or any of the other tower mages, not even Dale. No, it was Estral Andovian clutching a blanket.

⇜ ESTRAL'S HARMONY ⇝

"*What?*" Alton rubbed his eyes as if confronted with a specter.

"Hello," Estral repeated. "And I thought I was the one hard of hearing." She gave him that wry smile of hers, but it was not as confident as usual. It was questioning, as if she was uncertain of her reception.

"How?" he demanded. "How did you get in here?"

"I sang to the guardians. They liked it and let me through."

She'd said it like it was the simplest thing in the world. Alton felt off-kilter and grabbed the mantel to steady himself. "You . . . you sang to the guardians? And they let you through?"

Her smile faded. "I'll leave if you want me to."

"No! No . . ." He laughed. "You were right yesterday."

"I was? About what?" Now she gazed at him with a suspicious glint in her eye.

"About music being magical. But I expect not everyone can make it magical. Not the way you can."

The smile returned to Estral's lips.

Alton smiled back. "What made you try?"

"My music helped you and Dale enter Tower of the Earth, so I thought I'd try it here on Tower of the Heavens for myself." She gazed about the tower chamber. "I must admit, I was curious."

Alton was vaguely disappointed by the answer. "You brought a blanket."

"I thought you might need it, but I see you have a fire going."

"Yes, but a blanket is most welcome. Thank you."

310

She passed it to him and backed away. "I guess I should go now."

"No, wait! I mean, you said you were curious. Wouldn't you at least like a tour of the tower? What's left of it anyway." He glanced upward where he could see the stars through the hole in the roof.

"Yes, I'd like that."

He led her around the circumference of the tower, showing her the sink that magically flowed with water when you waved your hand under a copper fish's mouth. He took her beneath the east archway that ended a short distance away at a solid rock wall. *The* wall. Around they went, stepping over rubble, he explaining how the wall almost went mad and collapsed, taking the tower and Dale and himself with it.

"They lost harmony, the guardians," he said. "They are strong when they sing as one, but when they lost harmony and rhythm everything almost came to ruin."

"Further evidence," Estral said, "of the magic of music." They exchanged smiles.

"I've saved the best for last," Alton said, taking her hand. He found it strong and limber. His own hands were bulky with muscles from stonework, huge and powerful, like a draft horse. Estral's were more like a champion racehorse or a hunter in top condition, all lean, smooth, muscle. He realized it must be from lute playing, all those hours and hours of practice and performance. He thought of those hands on him, "playing" him, and he trembled.

He tugged on her hand to cover it up. "C'mon. See what you think."

He led her to the circle of columns in the center of the chamber. There was the one that lay broken in sections across the floor and he was reminded of Tower of the Earth, the skeleton on the floor reaching.

"What's that?" Estral asked, pointing at the pedestal in the middle of the circle. On top of it the lump of tourmaline gave off a faint green glow.

Alton pushed the image of the skeleton from his mind. "It's called the tempes stone. First time I touched it, it awoke Merdigen. I think it somehow aids his ability to exist."

"I'd love to meet him," Estral said.

"You will, but he's away at the moment."

"Away? How can he . . . ?"

Alton shrugged. "He's off meeting with the other tower mages. The ones east of the breach, anyway."

"Right," Estral said.

"Now let's take a step through the columns, shall we? Be warned you may find it disconcerting."

She raised that skeptical eyebrow at him, but when they stepped through and the tower disappeared and they stood upon an impossible expanse of grasslands illuminated only by stars and moon, she loosed a squeal of surprise.

"Don't worry," he said. "If you step back through the columns you'll be back in the tower."

The tower may have vanished, but the columns, tempes stone and pedestal, and east and west arches remained visible, like the ruins of some ancient civilization. Reluctantly he released Estral's hand so she could investigate. She stepped back and forth between the columns testing the effect, then walked the circle weaving between the columns. Eventually she came to stand beside him again.

"Incredible," she said.

He could hear the awe in her voice and was pleased.

"Where is this?" she asked. "Is it real?"

"Hard to say exactly," Alton said. He'd asked Merdigen once about the reality of it, and Merdigen had shot back with his usual, "Are *you* real, boy?"

"This landscape seems to be aligned with our season and time of day, for what it's worth. I've been in Itharos' tower, and his landscape is arctic, like the great ice fields to the north. Its time of day is opposite ours, from what I can tell."

Estral shivered beside him. "It's cold enough here. The air is crisp, and though the breeze is out of the northwest, I can smell the ground thawing like spring is not far off. It's so very real." As if to augment her words, coyotes bayed in the distance.

Alton had held onto the blanket and now he placed it over both their shoulders and boldly wrapped his arm around her, pulling her close. It was very warming. She did not object and when she gazed at him, it was not with trepidation, but more assessing. She did not protest on Karigan's behalf, did not mention Karigan at all. Interesting. He was pleased.

"The stars are incredible here," he said. "No trees to block them. The Sword of Sevelon is almost in its upraised position."

But Estral did not look at the stars. Her gaze lingered on him, still assessing.

"Is . . . is something wrong?" he asked.

"No," she replied. "Nothing at all. I'm just thinking I'm glad I came here."

"And I'm glad I came to my senses and didn't let you leave."

"Like you had any say in the matter." She subtly shifted her weight so she leaned into him. Alton's heart fluttered.

He turned so they faced one another, and when he kissed her, their bodies melding into one, the music that was Estral Andovian filled him with the harmony that had been absent from his life for too long.

❧ ARRIVAL ❧

The journey to the wall, Karigan thought, would not have been bearable without her fellow Riders along. The two soldiers who were part of the expedition, Lieutenant Grant and Private Porter, kept to themselves despite friendly overtures from the Riders to sit by their fire in the evenings.

The members of the light cavalry also kept separate, sipping their brandy at the end of the day while the lowest ranked man among them tended to the camp work and saw to their comforts more as a servant than a fellow man-at-arms. Karigan, accustomed to the Rider way of things where everyone carried their own weight, thought it a strange way to instill camaraderie, but the light cavalry was composed mainly of those of noble lineage who expected not to serve, but to be served.

The forester, Ard Ardmont, did join them at the fire, laughing at their jokes, telling his own stories of hunting mishaps and of life in the woods of Coutre Province. He seemed an easygoing, genial fellow, and was a fine addition to their lively group.

At night when all had quieted and Karigan lay wrapped up in her bedroll by the fire, she gazed at the stars, too preoccupied to sleep. Naturally she worried about Blackveil and what awaited them there, and about the Eletians and how they would regard her participation in the expedition.

Yet overriding those serious concerns was her memory of King Zachary on the steps of the castle as she departed; a memory of words she wasn't quite sure she heard. *Come back. To me.* A mix of yearning and anger broiled within her.

It was not the first time, she was startled to realize, he'd spoken those words to her. She reached back through memory, well back, to the night of the coup attempt when King Zachary's brother had taken over the castle. Karigan had volunteered to spy out what was happening inside. Her fading ability made her a perfect choice for such a reconnaissance mission.

The king had protested her further involvement, wanted to protect her, but he eventually relented, knowing she was right, that she must be the one to go. Before she departed, he'd told her to come back. To him. She'd seen many things in his eyes at that moment, much that went unspoken—the words had been unnecessary—and she ran from him. Kept running from him and their dangerous feelings for one another.

It was, she discovered, hopeless to run because she'd already succumbed to the feelings. To him. A breeze cooled the tears on her cheeks; the stars blurred overhead.

Her father once said that merchandise forbidden to a potential buyer because of price often made it all the more desirable. He used this insight to his advantage in marketing goods, occasionally inflating the price of some of his wares to make them seem more attractive. More often than not, a once overlooked bolt of cloth initiated bidding wars by those who had come to covet it.

In some sense, this might apply to Karigan's situation with King Zachary, but if it had just been about desire of the forbidden, she would have tired of it long ago, forgetting about him as anything other than her sovereign. There was more to it all, something more enduring. Try as she might, she could not forget him. He came to her in her dreams. When awake, she often imagined his intimate touch on her skin. It did not help that he kept telling her to come back to him when they both knew he was committed to Lady Estora.

She rolled over on the hard ground and gazed into the embers of the fire. If she could not forget him, she could at least attempt to move on by focusing her attention elsewhere. She needed to put the king behind her once and for all, and she found herself thinking about Alton. He seemed to want to resume a relationship beyond friendship. What would happen if she opened herself up to that? She had not seen him in almost a year and maybe seeing him now would awaken dormant feelings within her.

Or, she thought as she drifted into sleep, she could just give up. What did her inner turmoil matter when so much was at stake in the world? It was hard, though, sometimes not to feel so very alone.

During the next day's leg of the journey, Garth rode beside her. She was happy to have him among the Riders. He was one of her closer friends, a big bear of a fellow whose hugs she could count on to dispel any sorrow. When the company slowed to a walk to rest the horses, Karigan gazed off into the woods only to have her attention drawn back by an *ahem* from Garth.

"Yes?"

"I was wondering," he said, "what you're thinking. I've heard maybe two words from you this entire journey."

Karigan shrugged. "I've been thinking about Blackveil is all." She would have liked nothing more than to confess all that was in her heart, but she could never say anything about the king, for her Rider friends were bound to his service, too close. She had no wish to become the source of gossip either, which was inevitable in such a tight-knit group. She had revealed herself to only one other person, her best friend, Estral. In fact, Estral had been sensitive enough to Karigan's emotions that she guessed on her own.

It had been an immense relief for Karigan to speak of it to someone, but now Estral was far away in Selium and Karigan had to carry her burden alone.

"Well, I should think you'll be happy to see Alton, finally," Garth said.

"I will be. I am." In contrast to all she held secret about the king, her relationship with Alton and its troubles were well known to her friends.

"Hmm," Garth rumbled. "Then why do you look more ready for a funeral than a reunion?"

"Because my true love is already spoken for."

"Oh?" Garth's eyes popped wide open. "Your true love? And who might that be?"

"Why you, you big lunk." She reached over and poked his meaty arm.

Garth's mouth fluttered into an uncertain smile, and when the joke set in, he let out a great guffaw that echoed into the woods. "Best not let Tegan know," he told her between laughs.

"It'll be our secret," Karigan replied. Alas, he did not know she'd only told the truth about her true love being spoken for, if not who. In any case, the joke served to deflect further questioning, and the company moved back into a trot, making any kind of deeper conversation difficult.

They made good enough progress so that by the next afternoon, Garth was sent ahead to inform the wall encampment of the company's impending arrival. The closer they came to the wall, the more apprehension gripped Karigan, as she remembered the last time she was here and imagined what was to come. The feeling only deepened as she glimpsed the wall through the leafless branches of the woods. A hush descended over the company. Most of them had not been to the wall before. They would not forget it very soon.

When finally they broke out of the woods into the main encampment, she observed her companions' faces turned upward to take in the wall's infinite ascent into the heavens and heard their murmurs of dismay at the violent appearance of the breach above the repairwork, like some chunk of flesh ripped out by a giant claw.

The encampment itself had changed since Karigan was last here, with the construction of a neat row of snug cabins, long low barracks, and fenced corrals for horses and livestock.

Soldiers, both D'Yerian and Sacoridian, lined up at attention to greet them. Next to one of the officers was a flash of green—Dale! Karigan grinned. She wanted to jump right off Condor's back and run to the friend she had not seen since last summer, but military decorum being what it was, she had to wait while Lieutenant Grant, Lynx, and Captain Garfield of the light cavalry presented themselves to the commander of the encampment. Karigan looked for Alton, but he was nowhere to be seen.

Finally, with the formalities concluded, the company dismounted and all the Green Riders converged on Dale for greetings and hugs.

"Hello, hello. Ouch! Watch my shoulder!"

When it was Karigan's turn to hug her friend, she did so gingerly.

"Your shoulder," Karigan said. "Still . . ."

When last they'd stood together before the breach, a terrible, huge avian creature had attacked the Riders and grasped Dale in one of its talons, nearly carrying her off. It had succeeded in giving her a ghastly wound, preventing her from making the journey back to Sacor City.

"No," Dale replied. "That's pretty much healed. "This is, er, something else. Long story."

Trace Burns then introduced Fergal, Sandy, Oliver, and Fern, who, being relatively recent additions to the messenger service had never met Dale.

"Green Greenies, eh?" Dale said.

"Not nearly," Fergal replied with a sniff. "I helped rescue Lady Estora."

"Ah, so you're the one," Dale replied with a grin and a wink to Karigan.

"Those of us not going over into Blackveil are here to assist Alton with the wall," Trace said.

"That's what the orders Garth carried from the captain told us," Dale replied. "Lynx, Karigan, and Yates are going into the forest and the rest of you belong to us."

"Where *is* Alton?" Karigan asked. Another glance around the encampment did not reveal his presence.

"Down by Tower of the Heavens. He's expecting you. *All* of you." Dale spoke directly to Karigan, and Karigan wondered if there was something pointed in Dale's statement, a warning of some kind? And if so, why?

Dale retrieved her horse to lead them to Alton, but Plover was so excited to see her fellow messenger horses that she wheeled and pranced and tossed her head, and made it very difficult for her Rider to mount. "Be still, you silly mare!" Dale cried in exasperation. Plover paused long enough for Dale to get her toe in the stirrup, but she was barely in the saddle when the mare continued to carry on with her high spirits, hopping and bucking and snorting. Her antics vexed Dale, but amused everyone else.

As they rode alongside the wall toward the secondary encampment, Karigan found herself nervous, pushing back a loose strand of hair and wishing she could at least scrub off some of the travel dirt before seeing Alton. She laughed at herself. He'd seen her in far worse straits before, hadn't he? She wondered how *he* was looking these days.

Ard suddenly cantered up from behind and hauled his horse to a walk alongside her. "You left without me," he said a little breathlessly. "And I'd rather not be left back there with those others. Green Riders make better company."

Karigan did not disagree.

"This is some edifice, isn't it?" he said in a low, awed voice, sweeping his arm toward the wall. "Like the gods made it."

Karigan often thought of it the same way. "But it wasn't. It was made by people like us."

"And magic," Ard muttered.

"Yes, and magic."

The secondary encampment resembled a small tent village. It appeared no cabins had yet been constructed here, which must have made for a miserable winter, more so than what Alton had described in his last letter. The encampment's inhabitants came forward to greet the Riders, mainly soldiers and some laborers. Karigan's gaze pinpointed Alton immediately as he strode forward with Garth beside him

He looked leaner, more broad shouldered than she remembered, his hair longer and wilder. It seemed to Karigan that his experiences in Blackveil and at the wall were chiseled into his face so that there was little of the softness of youth left there, making his features all the more intriguing. She couldn't help but grin at him. He smiled tentatively in return.

Then she noticed someone else with him. *"Estral?"*

✥ REUNION ✥

Alton could not remember being happier. He and Estral spent long hours into the night talking, laughing, singing, and holding each other close. He almost forgot the danger so nearby, but there was not much he could do about the wall or the towers until Merdigen returned. It surprised him he wasn't as frustrated as he normally would be. He was grateful for the respite actually, as it presented more time for him to spend with Estral.

Upon Garth's appearance at the wall and his news of the impending arrival of the company that included Karigan as a member of the Blackveil expedition, Alton had gone cold, not hearing another word Garth spoke. He spent the interval between Garth's arrival and Karigan's pacing in his tent and trying to decide what he'd say to her. *Hello, Karigan, I'm in love with your best friend,* did not seem like the best approach. Then he fell into deep thought wondering how she looked, how she'd be. She was "Sir Karigan" now, he reminded himself. How had she changed?

Fortunately Estral was absent from his agonizing. She was giving a music lesson to an off-duty guard.

"You look like you're being pecked to death by a clutch of baby ducks," Garth said, poking his head into the tent. "That anxious to see Karigan?"

"Anxious? Yes."

Misinterpreting, Garth just laughed.

And then the Riders rode into camp and Alton and Garth strode out to greet them. He immediately picked out the rarely seen Lynx, and there were Yates and Trace. The others were unknown to him. Except Karigan, who rode at the end of the line with a man in forester's garb.

Alton caught his breath. There she sat mounted on Condor, her posture that of a true horsewoman, the reins easy in her hands. Her long brown hair was drawn back into a single braid, just as he remembered she often wore it.

She grinned at him. It was like a punch to the gut and he staggered back a step. He remembered those dimples, the smile of her eyes, and a stolen kiss or two. He remembered why he'd been so drawn to her. He realized he was gawping at her.

Damnation.

"Estral?" Karigan cried, and it was followed by a squeal that made Alton's hair stand on end. Karigan jumped off Condor and the two young women ran to each other for a hug. Alton, who hadn't even noticed Estral's arrival, watched the two, feeling a little left out. Dale gazed at him with a look of amusement. He scowled at her. Garth laughed and thumped him on the back.

After some excited conversation between Karigan and Estral that was impossible to follow, Karigan came to him for a hug. They were both, he noted, a little hesitant, unsure. When he held her, she felt lighter than he recalled. She smelled of the earth and balsam fir and her horse, not at all an unpleasant combination. When they pulled apart, he asked, "How have you been?"

"Well," she replied.

Her eyes—at first he did not recognize her eyes. They were filled with night, or something he could only describe as night. Darkness, endless depth, as if there was another part of her looking out at him from some vast space that even she was not aware of, but it was gone all in a fleeting moment and her eyes were as bright as he always remembered them. He shuddered.

The next moment new Riders were being introduced to him, as well as the forester whose name he promptly forgot. They chattered gaily, Yates making rude comments about the cavalry soldiers who had accompanied them, much to the delight of the others.

Dale and Garth led them away, the laughing gaggle, off to the pickets to care for their horses. Karigan glanced over her shoulder at him as she led Condor away. Estral remained by his side.

"What are we going to do?" he asked.

"The truth is generally a good approach," Estral replied.

What *was* the truth? he wondered. He thought he knew, but seeing Karigan now? Estral reached for his hand and twined her fingers around his. When their gazes met, he was no longer confused.

At least for the moment.

Alton felt torn in too many directions. The Riders wanted food, they wanted a dry place for their gear, they regaled him with questions, wanted to explore the encampment, wanted more food, demanded a tour of Tower of the Heavens. So long away from being in the midst of other Riders, he had forgotten in all his dark, quiet time beside the wall how boisterous his comrades could be, especially the young ones. Lynx remained his cool, untalkative self, but his attitude was interested. Karigan mostly gossiped with Estral about Selium and the people they both knew at the school.

Fortunately Dale and Garth were there to help manage the questions and arrangements. It occurred to Alton that all the activity was actually an excellent diversion because it allowed him to avoid admitting his feelings for Estral to Karigan.

When they stood before Tower of the Heavens for their tour, Dale demonstrated how easy it was for the Riders to walk through the wall, with an apology to the forester, Ard, who would be unable to join them. The Riders gave it a try, first tentatively, and then with enthusiasm, passing back and forth numerous times. The nearest guard on duty watched in mortification.

Alton sighed. "Get used to it, Dixon, they're staying. Most of them, anyway."

When Alton entered the tower himself, he found the Riders peering into cabinets and flipping through the books on the table. He nearly pulled his hair out for he had arranged the books precisely, but he forced himself to calm down. Karigan, he noted, was gazing up at the hole in the roof far above.

"I'd heard the tower took quite a jolt," she told him. "But I didn't know there was so much damage."

Before Alton could respond, Dale said, "We almost got squashed!"

Karigan's eyes widened. "I see you came through it all right." When she noticed Estral had followed them into the tower, her eyes grew even larger. "Estral? How did she get in here?"

Alton smiled. "She took me by surprise the first time, too. She sings to the guardians. She says they like her."

Karigan glanced at him as if to make sure she'd heard him right. Someone yelped and they both jumped. It was Fern— she had discovered the most extraordinary feature of the tower—the grasslands in the circle of columns. The others had to experience it for themselves and there was much excited discussion and experimentation just as there had been with walking through the tower wall.

"I imagine they'll tire of it . . . eventually," Karigan said with a wry smile. "Actually, I have little memory of this place myself." She wandered away, checking the various nooks and crannies of the chamber, pausing to gaze for quite a while beneath the west archway, where Captain Mapstone had found them both half dead after their respective experiences in Blackveil almost a year ago. She drifted away from the arch and joined the other Riders near the tempes stone to view the grasslands.

Estral joined Alton and watched the Riders with amusement lighting her eyes. "It's going to be a little more lively around here, don't you think?"

"We'll see. Once I assign them to their separate towers, we may be able to keep things down to a dull roar."

That evening turned into a sort of celebration beneath the dining tent, with Estral called into service to sing and play and Riders dancing up a storm, with off-duty soldiers joining in. Alton left Dale and Garth in charge of the Riders to ensure they didn't break anything.

He sat at a table with Karigan, Lynx, and Ard. Karigan appeared deep in her own thoughts, and Lynx smoked his pipe, his eyes half-lidded as though he were in a different world altogether. Ard clapped to the beat of a rousing tavern song. Yates, Alton observed, was doing backflips, much to the delight of onlookers.

"I am beginning to think Yates was an acrobat in a former life," Karigan said.

"I'm finding it difficult to believe the captain chose him for the expedition."

"He's good at drawing maps," Karigan replied. "And he volunteered."

"Volunteered? Is he mad?"

Karigan gazed steadily at him. Besides himself, she alone knew what it was to enter Blackveil Forest. No one else who did had survived. This, he realized, was a bond they shared, a bond like no other.

"Even from here, guarded by the wall, I can feel the unrest of the forest," Lynx said unexpectedly. "Dark creatures with their dark thoughts."

Alton shuddered and Ard ceased his clapping. "Your words do little to instill confidence," the forester said.

"And so they should not," Lynx murmured.

"Well, I did not volunteer outright for this duty," Ard replied. "My Lord Spane recommended me to my Lord Coutre. I suppose it's better me going in than some younger, less experienced man with a family. Besides, I'd do anything for my lord and lady, and especially Lady Estora. Doesn't mean I'm looking forward to it." Silence followed his pronouncement and he stood abruptly. "Guess I'll see if there is any more of that pie left."

Alton watched after the forester as he made his way through the tent to where the cooks were stationed. He noticed that of anyone, Ard seemed the most interested in hanging near Karigan. Even now, from across the tent, he glanced back as though to check on her. She appeared completely unaware of his attention. Alton wasn't sure what to make of it. Maybe the forester was just looking out for her. She was the only female on the expedition and perhaps

Ard did not realize she was quite capable of looking after herself.

Alton supposed he should be pleased Ard watched after Karigan, but it bothered him. Could it be he was jealous? He almost laughed out loud at himself. He'd no right to be jealous of her anymore, and besides, he really didn't think Ard was her type. He just couldn't see it.

"No sign of the Eletians?" Karigan asked.

"Nothing."

"I suppose they still have a day before the equinox to get here."

"If they don't show, what then?"

"Oh, they'll come," Karigan said with quiet conviction. "They'll come and we'll enter Blackveil Forest. This was their idea, after all."

"What is it they're after?" Alton wondered.

"That is what our king wishes us to find out," Lynx said. "Blackveil was once their Argenthyne and they're going back to see what remains, I suppose." With this pronouncement, he rose and excused himself for the night.

That left Alton alone with Karigan. They gazed at one another in awkward silence.

"It's been a while, hasn't it?" Karigan said, smiling shyly. "We don't know where to begin."

"Well, I'd like to hear about everything that happened last fall," Alton replied. "I've gotten bits and pieces about Lady Estora and the Silverwood book, but not the entire picture. You were on a training run with one of the new ones, right? Fergal?"

"Yes, and I was none too happy about it." Karigan laughed and set to telling him about the journey and her experiences with Fergal, though true to form Alton could tell she was withholding certain details. For instance, she did not say how Fergal fell into the Grandgent from the ferry, and she was very evasive for some reason about the inn they stayed at in Rivertown. When it came to the rescue of Lady Estora, she emphasized the roles of others. She was not the type to boast or claim the credit. In fact, the less she said about herself, the more he was sure she had been integral to the rescue.

She's Sir *Karigan,* he reminded himself, an honor not conferred on anyone in two hundred years, and the only one involved in those events to have earned it. The king certainly
believed her actions had been exceptional. He half-smiled to
himself, remembering Karigan the runaway schoolgirl, but
even then she'd accomplished extraordinary deeds that led
directly to the rescue of the king from his brother's coup attempt. Alton recalled the passing darkness in her eyes he'd
perceived earlier. He hadn't seen it since, but he couldn't help
thinking there was something much more complex about her
beneath the surface than there had been before. Something
that—it sounded odd even to him—but something that separated her from the rest of the world.

"And so here I am," she said.

With some surprise he realized his thoughts had distracted
him from the summation of her story.

"Your turn," Karigan said. "Catch me up."

Alton glanced toward Estral, who was teaching the Riders a new song. Lantern light glimmered off her hair and her
smile made his heart wobble. He tore his gaze away, looked
back to Karigan, and told her of his own travails with the
wall, and he almost tripped himself up with laughter when he
realized he was withholding details from her just as she had
from him. She did not need to know, he decided, the depth of
his madness after his time in the forest. Bringing it up would
be like scratching a scab off a nearly healed wound. There
was a time, he reflected, when they would have told each
other everything. Now they acted a little like strangers. By
the time he concluded, he had said nothing of Estral except
to describe the basics of her arrival.

"I'm surprised she left Selium at all," Karigan said, "much
less came here of all places."

"We've ... we've enjoyed the music," Alton replied, not
ready to admit more.

They fell silent again and Karigan gazed at him as if she
expected more from him. He tried to come up with something, anything, but only got warm beneath the collar. Fortunately Dale rescued him by coming over and plopping herself on the bench next to Karigan.

"My, aren't we the maudlin ones," she commented. "Everyone else is having a grand old time and you two look ready to cast your lot with beggars and undertakers."

"We've been catching up," Alton said.

"Speaking of which," Dale turned to face Karigan directly, "what's this I hear about the king's masquerade ball and you being Mad Queen Oddacious? That was one of my favorite plays. 'Mad Queen Oddacious has twenty-one cats, each named Precious and wears a hat—' "

"Auuugh!" Karigan wailed putting her head in her hands. "Even here, next to the wall I can't escape it!"

"I'm afraid not," Dale said, all chipper. "Tell me *everything.*"

As Karigan told the story of the masquerade, Alton glanced covertly at Estral. The Riders sat in a semicircle around her as she told them some tale. He became lost in a reverie as he watched her until Dale let go a high-pitched, "Assassination attempt?"

Now Alton paid rapt attention while Karigan recounted the attempt on King Zachary's life. It sounded ill-conceived and inept. If the Weapons had not stopped the would-be assassin, Alton was certain the king could have done so himself blindfolded and one-handed, and yet the color drained from Karigan's face as she told the tale.

"The king could have taken down that fool with a glance if need be," Dale said dismissively. "He's as well trained as any Weapon."

"I know, I know," Karigan replied. "He's our king and I . . . I don't want him hurt is all."

Alton scrunched his eyebrows together. There was more being left unspoken in that statement.

"Well, Queen Oddacious," Dale said, "why don't we go join the singing?"

Karigan groaned and Dale laughed. Dale took her friend's hand and led her toward the others.

Alton could only breathe a sigh of relief that he'd gotten away without having to confess the truth about his affection for Estral.

❧ DARK MIRROR ❧

When the evening wound down, a few Riders excusing themselves to go to bed, Dale sat with Karigan explaining to her what had happened to her shoulder in Tower of the Earth. Alton had already told Karigan about it, but now she got Dale's version of events and it was frightening.

"So Merdigen is now consulting with the other tower mages about what to do?" Karigan asked.

Dale nodded. "We don't know what happened to Haurris or his tower, and we don't know what that creature in there is or how it got there in the first place." She shuddered.

"And whatever it is could pose a danger to the rest of the wall," Karigan murmured.

"Exactly, and there may not be a thing we can do about it. As if the breach wasn't enough to worry about."

When Estral finished playing and punctuated it with a huge yawn, the party truly broke up. She hugged Karigan on her way out and said, "It's so good to see you. I want to talk more, but now I'm about to fall asleep on my feet."

Alton was right behind her with his good nights, the last of the partiers dispersing after him, leaving Dale and Karigan alone in the tent.

"How is he?" Karigan asked. "How is he really?"

"Alton? Much better," Dale replied. "There were some rough moments, but he's come around very well."

"I'm glad," Karigan said. It was hard to discern Alton's well-being for he was quieter than she remembered, and when they talked, it was as two acquaintances, not as friends who'd been much closer. His letters had been more personal.

In fact, the Alton who had written about how anxious he was for her to join him at the wall seemed a different person than the Alton she'd seen today, almost aloof. Maybe all that time apart had turned them into strangers. If there was anything he wanted to say to her, he'd better overcome his aloofness and hurry up. She'd be departing the day after tomorrow.

And what should she say to him? That she was open to the possibilities?

"Well I'm done in," Dale said. "Think you can find your way to your tent, or do you need a guide?"

"You'd probably better help me," Karigan said. "I'll never find the right one in the dark."

And so Dale led her to the tent she was to share with Trace. Karigan hugged her friend once more.

"It is good to see you, Dale," she said. "We've missed you."

"And good to see you, too, *Sir* Karigan." Dale snorted in laughter. "Sorry, sorry," she said, still laughing. "Can't help it. Don't know which is funnier, Sir Karigan or Queen Oddacious. Good night."

Karigan watched her friend stroll away with the lantern, sputtering with laughter as she went. If Karigan had any illusions of her recently bestowed title ever eliciting respect from her fellow Riders, they were now thoroughly crushed.

She smiled and ducked into her tent.

After Karigan's late night, and with no duties assigned her, she slept well into the morning, the simple cot a luxury after all those nights on the ground. She'd have one more night on the cot and then it was into Blackveil, and she didn't even want to think about what nights sleeping in the forest would be like.

When she arose, she found Trace gone already, but the Rider had fired up the little stove making the tent toasty warm. Karigan took her time, yawning and stretching, and getting ready for the day.

Finally stepping out into the world, she found no Green Riders in sight, but discovered Yates in the dining tent spooning hot porridge into his mouth.

"Where is everyone?" she asked, sitting down beside him with her own bowl.

"Alton has them all in a meeting in the tower to talk about assignments."

"Already?"

He shrugged, and she remembered Alton had requested the help of more Riders months ago. She couldn't blame him for being anxious to get everyone working as soon as possible.

"Lynx went off into the woods to talk to the animals or something," Yates continued. "Too much civilization."

"Ard?"

"Still snoring away in his tent."

"And Estral?"

"In the tower with the others."

Karigan sighed. She hoped they weren't going to be in there all day, otherwise, how would she occupy herself?

"What are you up to today?"

"When Edna over there gets off breakfast shift, we're going to enjoy each other's company." Yates smiled and gave a little wave to one of the cooks ladling out porridge to other latecomers. She was a pretty, petite thing.

Well, Karigan thought, there was always Condor for companionship, and she would soon be missing him, but she couldn't help feeling rather desolate.

When she left the dining tent, she collected her riding gear and visited Condor, grooming him till his coat gleamed, brushing away winter coat that fell out by the handfuls. He bobbed his head and nickered in approval.

She then tacked him up and mounted, and rode through the encampment to the wall. Instead of heading west toward the breach, she reined Condor east. She put him through his paces, sometimes riding at an easy walk or lope, and then riding harder as the terrain allowed. All the while the wall remained unrelenting beside her. She could ride all the way to the Eastern Sea and the wall's cold, hard facade would not change.

As she rode, she tried to remain in the present, taking conscious note of how the woods smelled, how sunlight played on the tips of evergreens. She listened to the chatter of birds and watched squirrels pursue one another around the boles of trees, oblivious to the dangers the wall protected them from. It was hard to believe that behind just a few feet of stone a whole other world existed, like a dark mirror of the one she now rode through.

Tomorrow, the equinox would bring not just balance between day and night, but spring. While this side of the wall grew brighter, enlivened by birds returning from southern regions and green growth replacing patches of snow and ice, she wondered what spring did in Blackveil, or if seasons there were irrelevant.

Whatever the case, she wanted to imprint on her mind what she might otherwise take for granted. No matter how she tried to stay in the present, however, it was impossible to prevent the noise of thoughts and concerns from filling her mind: what to do about Alton, when would the Eletians arrive, what would it do to her father if she did not survive Blackveil.

At midday she halted to eat the cold meal provided by the encampment cooks. She leaned against the wall, peeling a hard-boiled egg and watching Condor crop at the withered greenery. What would happen to Condor if she didn't return? She expected he'd find a new Rider, just as he'd found her. It was hard imagining him partnered with someone else. It was as if he'd always been hers.

When she finished eating, there was nothing to do but turn back. As she reined Condor around, there was a fluttering above in one of the trees. A great winter owl still in its snow plumage perched on a crooked branch. It seemed to watch her without actually looking at her.

The owl nudged something deep in her mind, a hidden memory she could not grasp, and try as she would, she could not bring it to the surface. She shrugged. If it were important, it would come to her eventually.

She felt privileged to encounter such a magnificent bird on her ride, but in moments the owl itself became no more than a memory when it launched up through the branches of trees and beyond until it was out of view. Karigan let out a breath as though released from a spell.

She arrived back at the encampment just before supper.

She'd taken her time on the return, as this would probably be her last ride of any length on Condor for quite a while. He seemed to sense it as well, for when she finished untacking and grooming him, he set his head on her shoulder and she wrapped her arm around his neck. He heaved a great sigh as she stroked him.

"Dale will be keeping an eye on you for me," she told him. "So you better behave."

He flicked his tail in a halfhearted way.

There was no way to heave horses over the wall to get them into Blackveil, plus the forest was no place for an oversized prey animal, so Karigan and her fellow Sacoridians, and presumably the Eletians, would be entering the forest on foot. There was something that felt very wrong about Green Riders being separated from their horses.

She would bid Condor her final farewell in the morning when they rode to the breach. She patted him on the shoulder, gathered her gear, and walked away.

At supper, the young Riders were as boisterous as ever. Yates was presumably with his Edna, and Lynx prowling the forest. She found Garth sitting with Ard, but no sign of Dale, Alton, or Estral.

When she joined Garth and Ard with a bowl of stew, Ard said, "Grant says we're to be at the breach tomorrow before sunrise. I let Lynx know a while ago before he disappeared again. Told Yates at midday when his lass had to work another shift."

Karigan nodded and blew on a spoonful of stew.

"Where were you all day?" Ard asked.

"Just riding."

"Just riding? Where?"

"East." For some reason it irked her that he needed to know. To her, her ride with Condor was her own business. Private.

"East, huh," Ard grumbled. He did not press her for more, but his gaze lingered on her longer than she liked.

Soon Dale and Trace arrived, followed first by Alton, and then Estral. They talked and laughed through supper, and none of them seemed to care she'd been gone all day, if they'd even noticed. Alton was seated too far away from her to carry on a conversation. This wasn't the place to talk about their personal matters, anyway. Too many people around.

"Still no sign of the Eletians," Trace said. "What if they don't come?"

Ard, who appeared to be the man with the answers, replied, "Grant says we wait a few days and if they don't show, we return to Sacor City."

Karigan had stated before, and still believed, that the Eletians would come. They just wouldn't reveal themselves before they were ready.

Estral edged her way into a space on the bench between Karigan and Garth and began talking about their day.

"There were arguments about who got assigned to which tower," she said. "For some reason no one seemed particularly eager to stay at Mad Leaf's tower, so Alton had them draw lots."

"So who gets Mad Leaf?" Karigan had to admit that just the name Mad Leaf wouldn't have made her too keen on being assigned to Tower of the Trees either.

"Garth."

Karigan laughed. No wonder he sat so quiet hunkered over his food.

"I get to stay here at Tower of the Heavens when Alton and Dale visit the others."

"You'll become a regular Green Rider."

"Not very likely," Estral said. "I'll be busy working out that piece of music from the Silverwood book. We'll see how the guardians respond to it. Music is something I can do. I'll leave the Green Riding to Green Riders."

Karigan gazed anew at her friend. Estral seemed to have taken to life here at the wall, her features animated as she talked about all the work that needed to be done. Estral had loved nothing more than teaching young students at Selium, but this was something else. There was a brightness to her Karigan didn't remember seeing before.

But now Estral turned serious. "There's something I would like to talk to you about if we could get a private moment later."

Karigan nodded, wondering what it could be. Estral returned her nod with a faltering smile. Soon she was called upon to sing and play as she had been the previous night. When Karigan glanced at Alton, he was deep in conversation with Dale and Captain Wallace, going over papers of some sort. She excused herself and decided she would prepare her gear for tomorrow. She would seek out both Alton and Estral later. She would learn what was on Estral's mind, and have private words with Alton, and perhaps more if all went well.

❧ ALONE ❧

Trace had beaten her back to their tent and lay sprawled on her cot, her eyes unfocused and glassy as she stared unblinking in a sort of trance. She was communicating with Connly. They each were gifted with a special ability to mentally converse, even over long distances. Karigan learned that in the past it was useful to have Riders with such abilities assigned to different regiments in battle because it allowed generals in their various positions to communicate quickly with one another without revealing anything to the enemy.

She also learned it was the most intimate bond a pair of Riders could have, looking into each other's minds. Connly's first partner, Joy, had been slain in the course of duty and he had never completely gotten over the severing of that bond. When Trace answered the Rider call and her ability manifested, Connly resented and resisted her, but with patience and compassion, she broke down his barriers. Now they were very close, and while they might be miles and miles apart, they were probably more intimate than most couples who shared the same physical space.

Trace had said their communication involved both images and words, and Karigan wondered what it was like. A dream maybe, but not so chaotic. Did Trace see Connly as he was, probably lying on his bed like Trace and staring into nothing, or did they create for themselves a lush green field vibrant with wildflowers in which to meet?

Karigan did not know, but Trace was smiling.

Karigan unpacked and reorganized her backpack so it would rest well-balanced on her shoulders. She oiled her saber and long knife, then her boots. Her memory of Black-veil was of a wet, dank environment, and she wanted her gear made as impervious to the damp as possible.

She propped the walking cane the Weapons had given her against her pack. It would be a good companion during their journey, but of course no substitute for Condor.

She patted her pocket where she kept the moonstone, the most precious object she'd be taking with her into Blackveil—precious because it had been something of her mother's, and because it would be pure light, the light of a silver moon, in a very dark place.

Satisfied with her preparations, she left the tent and Trace, who was still in her deep communion with Connly. It must be amazing, Karigan thought, to know you'd never be alone. Trace told her that even when she and Connly were not communicating, there was always something of his warm and gentle touch in the back of her mind.

Karigan headed out first to the dining tent, but found it mostly abandoned except for a few cooks and the astonishing spectacle of Yates scrubbing pots. Edna was there beside him, of course.

Next she followed the path to Dale's tent, which the Rider shared with Estral. She found Dale and Captain Wallace just outside, giggling, leaning against one another.

Oh! Karigan thought. No one had mentioned the two were paired up.

"Uh, hello," she said. "I was looking for Estral. Is she here?"

"Nope," Dale said. "Tent's empty, but it won't be for long." The two started giggling again. "Try Alton's tent," she suggested.

Karigan hastened off, certain she was blushing, then slowed to make sure she chose the right tent. Alton's was slightly larger and set off from the others due to his rank as Lord-Governor D'Yer's heir, so it was not difficult to pick it out. As she approached it, she found the walls aglow, and it occurred to her to wonder why Dale thought Estral would be there, then she wondered, why not? They seemed to get on in a friendly manner.

But as she neared the tent, she began to hear the two in conversation, and the silhouette against the tent walls began to tell the story.

The two stood together merged, as if in an embrace.

"We have to tell her," Estral was saying. "Tonight."

"Can't you . . . can't you just tell her? You're her best friend."

"Coward. It needs to come from both of us."

"I'm not sure it's a good idea on the eve of her departure . . ."

"It's better she knows the truth," Estral said, "about how we feel about each other."

It felt as if the earth collapsed beneath Karigan's feet and the sky and woods fell in on her. Estral and Alton together? But she'd wanted . . . she had hoped . . .

"We've got to tell her now," Estral added.

"No need," Karigan blurted, and she ran, ran for the woods. She thought she heard them calling after her, but she kept on running, swatting branches out of her face, tripping on roots, the underbrush snagging her trousers. When she could no longer see the lights of the encampment, she stopped, breathing hard.

How could she not have seen it? Was she blind? She'd noticed how Alton's gaze had strayed to Estral the other night while Estral performed, but she'd thought he was just enjoying the music.

"Damnation," she muttered, and she wilted onto a rock and sat with her head in her hands.

What had she expected? Alton to come hither at her least desire? But the letters . . . It was her own fault. She'd been disturbed by how much he'd seemed to want her, but now that he was taken? And by her *best friend,* no less?

She had little right to be angry, she realized, because she had put Alton off time and again, kept him at arm's-length, told him she just wanted to be friends, but now she was stunned by the hurt of it, the betrayal. Not just Alton's betrayal, but Estral's.

She laughed. It was a hard sound. Trace had Connly, Yates had his cook, Dale had her captain, and now Alton had her friend. Who did that leave for her?

Who would care if she never returned from Blackveil? Her father and aunts would, but it wasn't the same. What of King Zachary? He'd probably be relieved. He'd be able to move freely into the life he must begin with Estora without lingering thoughts of Karigan distracting him.

Karigan wouldn't even have her horse soon.

She squeezed her eyes shut, now angry at herself for her self-pity, but she'd never felt more alone. The king could never be hers, and now Alton was out of reach. It was times like this she wished for her mother's understanding and embrace.

She did not have her mother, but she had her mother's moonstone. She removed it from her pocket and it suffused the space around her with the essence of a silver moon come to rest on Earth.

As if in answer, others blinked into bright life around her.

A glaring form of white stepped from the trees to stand before her. When Karigan's eyes adjusted to the intensity, the form resolved into that of an Eletian clad in white armor.

✑ ESTRAL AND ALTON ✑

"Grae," Karigan murmured.

"Galadheon," the Eletian responded.

She was as Karigan remembered, flaxen hair bound in looping braids, snowy white feathers woven into them. Karigan became conscious of others closing around her. She stood slowly, guardedly, all too aware she carried no weapons. There had been those among the Eletians who wanted her dead. Were they here now?

Another Eletian she recognized, Telagioth, stepped up beside Grae. "You may call her Graelalea now," he said.

"I have earned the passage," Graelalea said.

Karigan must have looked so blank that the Eletian smiled. "Even among your people your names are altered through rites, are they not? Such as when a man and woman are partnered?"

"Yes," Karigan said. However, at the moment she did not care what Grae or Graelalea called herself or why. "You've come . . . you've come to go into Blackveil tomorrow."

Graelalea nodded, and to Karigan, the prospect of that journey was now made very real.

"We saw the light of the muna'riel," Telagioth said. "We came to investigate what another Eletian might be doing here, only to find you."

"Sorry to disappoint you."

"We are not disappointed," Graelalea said, "but surprised."

"You should not have it," a new Eletian said in an accusing tone.

Karigan glanced at him. His hair was like fine strands of

339

gold, and in some way he seemed younger to her, less wise in years than other Eletians she had met.

"Lhean," Graelalea said, "the Galadheon has possessed a muna'riel before. Gifts of such are not unknown. Just rare." The Eletian's gaze fell unwaveringly on Karigan. "The first one that came into your possession was destroyed. But this one? How did you acquire a second?"

"It came to me from my mother," Karigan said. "I don't know how she got it."

Something changed in Graelalea's regard. She murmured softly, almost imperceptibly in Eletian, her hand caressing the light emitting from the moonstone. "It is a precious thing," she said. "The gift of a muna'riel to one who is not Eletian is singular. The gift of two is unheard of and signifies something greater."

"But they did not come to me from Eletians."

"Perhaps not," Graelalea said, "but that does not mean they were not meant to find you. It is not coincidence. You are Laurelyn-touched."

There was murmuring among the Eletians, and Karigan could not tell if they were agreeing or disagreeing with Graelalea. In addition to Graelalea, Telagioth, and Lhean, there were three others, the exact number King Zachary had been told would be entering Blackveil. He had picked six Sacoridians to match them.

Karigan recognized another of the Eletians. Spines jutted from the shoulder pauldrons of his armor. Last time they'd met, he'd tried to kill her. She backed up a step, ready to flee, but he did not indicate in any way that he knew her.

Eletians and their strange ways, she thought.

"However your muna'riel came to you," Graelalea said, "it will guide you well along dark paths. Alas, I fear we shall have many of those in the days ahead." She paused and cocked her head listening. "Others seek you. We shall see you in the morning."

"Wait!"

But the Eletians extinguished their moonstones and melted soundlessly into the forest. Karigan dropped her own moonstone into her pocket and darkness fell over her like a blanket.

"Karigan!" came a far off cry.

She gave her eyes a few moments to adjust and turned back toward the encampment at a much slower pace than she had left it, and found herself surprised at how far away she'd gotten. Voices rang out into the woods calling her name, the voices of her fellow Riders.

She sighed, sorry she had worried them. When she reached the edge of the encampment, she encountered Alton first, his lantern revealing lines of concern on his forehead.

"Karigan! Thank the gods. We thought you were lost."

She walked around and past him. "I wasn't lost."

"Hey," Alton said, striding up beside her, "I'm sorry you found out about Estral and me the way you did."

Karigan did not want to talk to him.

"When she came, we just sort of took to one another."

What did he want her to say? That she forgave him for leading her on and choosing her best friend instead?

"It's not like you wanted me," Alton persisted. "You never said anything, even when you did write."

Not helping, she thought. She kept walking, hoping to find her tent very soon.

"I'm not a mind reader!" The pitch of Alton's voice rose higher. "Talk to me, will you?"

She swung around to face him. "No." Then she was off again, but Alton pursued her.

"I believed you were in love with someone else," he said. "You never cared for me that much. You just wanted to be friends."

She didn't care for him that much? Like the hells. But she did not respond.

"Damn it, Karigan," Alton said. "Talk to me." He grabbed her arm.

Karigan reacted without thinking. She broke Alton's hold, seized his wrist, and hurled him to the ground. The glass of his lantern smashed, and suddenly the other Riders appeared, witnesses to it all. Garth stomped out flames licking at pine needles.

Karigan was horrified and she glanced at her hands as though they had betrayed her. It was all the training that had been drilled into her by Arms Master Drent. If someone grabbed her, she got his hands off her. It was that and nothing more.

Wasn't it?

To her shame, she realized it had felt good to lash out.

"Fight!" Yates cried with enthusiasm.

"Shut up, Yates," the others shouted in unison.

"Alton," Karigan said, "I didn't mean to. I'm . . . I'm sorry."

"No harm," he muttered. He rose, dusting off his trousers. "I asked for it. I forgot you're practically a Weapon these days." He gave her a rueful smile.

"It's not all right. I'm sorry. But I also can't talk to you right now. I just can't."

She started walking again. This time Alton did not follow.

"Can you at least tell us what those lights were in the woods?" Dale called out after her.

"Eletians," Karigan replied over her shoulder, her stride never slackening.

At last she found her tent and stepped inside. She stood there in the darkness with only a low glow from the stove playing across the wooden platform floor. Trace was gone. Karigan did not know whether to laugh, cry, or throw her cot out of the tent. No, she wouldn't throw the cot—she'd probably want it tonight.

Having made that decision, she lay on it. Thoughts of Alton, Estral, Eletians, and Blackveil whirled in her mind and she could not settle on one thing. It was going to be a restless night.

A voice from outside broke into the maelstrom. "Karigan?" It was Estral.

"I don't want to talk."

"That's fine." Unwanted and uninvited, Estral stepped into the tent. "If you don't want to talk, I'll do the talking."

Karigan did not want to admit to herself that she really did want Estral there. But she wanted Estral her friend, not Estral the lover of her former almost-lover.

Trace's cot creaked as Estral sat. "I could begin by saying it was very wrong of me to become attracted to Alton knowing your history; that as your friend I should have turned him away when he also indicated an interest in me. But I'm not going to."

Karigan groaned and rolled onto her side so that her back was to Estral.

"First of all," Estral said, "on more than one occasion you told me that you felt more comfortable to have Alton as your *friend*. Even when I saw you in the fall that was your inclination. So I did not see a terrible, shall we say, conflict of interest. At that time your thoughts were on someone else, which brings me to my second point."

Karigan wrapped her pillow around her head, sure she did not want to hear what was coming next. Estral, however, was trained to use her voice as an instrument for speaking and singing, and to project it so it penetrated the noise of a rowdy tavern crowd or filled a concert hall. Her voice clearly reached Karigan through the pillow, and probably half the encampment as well.

"If you like, I can speak this loudly so everyone can hear of matters you'd probably rather keep private."

Karigan thought about whacking Estral with the pillow, but simply released it so it no longer blocked her ears.

"Good. Back to my second point." Estral modulated her voice to a softer tone that would not carry. "When you were in Selium we discussed the person you're in love with."

Karigan groaned again.

"From the sound of it," Estral said, "your feelings have not changed. It's inescapable, that feeling, isn't it? No matter how impossible it is to have that person, you can't help but be drawn to him. Am I right?"

Karigan could only whimper.

"I likewise can't help the attraction I have for Alton. I could have, I suppose, ridden away from here, from him, if I'd known I was going to hurt my friend so. I might have even gotten over my feelings for him, but frankly, if you are an example, I don't think it would have worked very well, and I'd end up being as miserable as you."

"Ugh," Karigan said into her pillow.

"I'm not sure what that means," Estral replied, but when Karigan chose not to clarify, she continued. "I do not apologize for how I feel about Alton. I will, however, apologize for how you found out. Now I'm going to make a guess or two about how you were feeling when you arrived here."

Oh, no, Karigan thought. *Here it comes.*

"You were probably feeling bad about King Zachary's wedding coming up in a few months. I can't imagine. It must be very hard." Estral paused for a few moments. "I think maybe you had in mind that Alton could fill the void left by the king. You hadn't seen each other in a while, and maybe that old feeling you had when you first met might reawaken. There were, after all, those letters he wrote you. He told me about them, and he really had wanted something with you. But then I came into the middle of it all."

Yes, Estral had guessed it all. Hearing it all summed up like that made Karigan feel rather pathetic.

"It must be an awful betrayal," Estral said. "Karigan, I'm so very sorry. I'm sorry you can't be with the one you want. But do know your friends love you. It's not the same as that other kind of love, but you are *not* alone."

It was easy for Estral to say, Karigan thought.

Estral sighed. "Still not going to talk?"

"No. Where's Alton?"

"Out looking for Eletians."

Karigan barked a short, derisive laugh. "He'll never find them."

"Well, you know men. They enjoy the chase. Should I send him over when he returns? I think it would be a good idea."

"No."

"Do you remember in the fall when you called me a wise old mother?" Estral asked.

Karigan nodded.

"I have another piece of wisdom for you. Please, please don't go into Blackveil angry. You're . . . you're my best friend. I can't bear to have you leave angry at me."

Karigan bit her bottom lip. She so wanted to let it go, but she couldn't. She couldn't forgive so readily, so quickly. They could suffer at least one night, couldn't they?

In each others' arms, no doubt.

Estral must have found Karigan's silence answer enough for she stood and said, "I'll leave you now so you can rest for tomorrow." Her melodious voice sounded choked.

Karigan did not acknowledge her departure. She just lay there, tears dampening her pillow.

She did not know how long she lay in the dark thinking about everything and nothing when a footstep creaked on the tent platform and fresh air swirled in through the flaps. Trace must have returned. But the steps were heavier than Trace's and they paused beside her cot.

"Karigan?" It was Alton.

Oh, no, she thought. They seemed bent on torturing her.

"Guess I deserve your silence. I've been a bit of an ass, and I apologize. I led you to believe one thing, and then I go and do another."

"Yes," Karigan said. "You are an ass."

"That's settled, then," he muttered. "I know you told Estral you didn't want to see me, but I couldn't just leave things this way with you heading over the wall tomorrow morning."

It was, she thought, a little late for that.

The platform groaned as he knelt down and she felt him lean against the edge of her cot. She did not turn over to face him.

"I was right," he said. "You are in love with someone else. Don't blame Estral, but I finally wrangled from her who it is."

"She wasn't supposed to tell anyone!" Now Karigan felt doubly betrayed.

"She told me hoping it could help."

"So, are you satisfied? Did you hear what you wanted? That I'm a complete fool?"

"You are generally stubborn, and a lion when it comes to trouble—both finding it and handling it—but you are most definitely not a fool. The king is fortunate to have your loyalty. And your love." Then as an afterthought, he added, "Self-pity, however, does not become you."

Karigan whirled over on her cot. "Self pity? You're judging me? I should— I should knock you over."

Alton laughed softly. "You already did that, remember?"

Karigan crossed her arms and scowled. His words stung. Yes, she was sulking, but wasn't she entitled to a little self-pity once in a while?

He stroked her hair away from her face and his touch at once startled and thrilled her in an unexpected way, but remorse rushed in with her knowledge that Alton was lost to her. She turned her back to him again.

"Leave," she said.

"But I'd—"

"You are not making this any better."

Silence, then the easing of his weight off the cot as he stood. "Karigan," he said, his voice hoarse, "I did love you. Still do. I had wanted us to be—"

"Leave."

Again, the silence and hesitation, then footsteps as Alton left.

She had not been able to give him what he wanted when he needed it, and now the tables were turned and here she was alone on her last night before entering a nightmare.

⊰ EQUINOX ⊱

Karigan and her fellow Riders set off in the predawn dark from the tower encampment and rode toward the breach. They were all of them quiet. Even Yates was subdued, the loudest noises the hoof falls and snorts of their horses.

Karigan had slept surprisingly well after all the night's turmoil. She'd been emotionally wrung out, and perhaps sleep had provided a refuge. In sleep, she could forget.

Now she rode beside Ard at the end of the line while Alton and Estral led. She'd spoken little to them as they readied to leave. She could tell her reticence hurt them. As the group of riders neared the main encampment, the sky grayed as the sun began to creep above the horizon—not that she could see the horizon with the wall to one side and the deep woods to the other.

They found the area before the breach ablaze with lanterns and bonfires, and what must have been the entire population of the encampment collected there, a disproportionate horde facing the handful of Eletians in their unmistakable pearlescent armor. Neither side held weapons pointed at the other, but as Karigan neared, she discerned the grim faces of the Sacoridians. Even without weapons drawn, they appeared ready for conflict at the merest spark.

The Eletians and soldiers both looked up at the party's arrival, relief plain on the faces of the latter. With the Eletians, it was not so easy to tell their thoughts.

Alton halted Night Hawk and swung out of the saddle to greet the Eletians, but they strode right by him and made directly for Karigan instead.

"Ah, Galadheon," Graelalea said. "You've arrived finally."

Everyone looked at Karigan. Startled to suddenly be the center of attention, she hastily dismounted and found herself face to face with Graelalea. The two gazed at one another at length.

"It is the equinox," the Eletian finally said. "Are your people ready?"

Before Karigan could answer, a scowling Grant shoved his way in beside them. "I am Lieutenant Grant," he said, "commander of this mission."

Graelalea ignored him, did not even seem to perceive his existence. "Who are the ones that will be accompanying us?" she asked Karigan.

By now Alton and Estral had joined them as well. Karigan felt caught in a vise between the Eletians and her own people. She could practically feel Grant's glower burning into her. Even Condor poked his nose over her shoulder to view the proceedings. It felt odd to have Graelalea deferring to her when their very first meeting during the summer had been less than amicable, and Graelalea anything but deferential.

"To start with," she replied, "I should introduce Alton D'Yer who oversees the work here to mend the wall."

Graelalea finally deigned to acknowledge him with a nod. "A difficult undertaking, if not impossible, for the wall is a thing of good and evil, built with good intentions, but constructed in evil ways."

Alton bristled at her words. It was his ancestors who had built the wall and her words could be construed as an insult, but to Karigan's relief, he held his tongue.

"This is Graelalea," she said hastily. "The sister of Eletia's crown prince."

"Welcome to D'Yer Province," Alton said.

"This was once the north region of Argenthyne," Graelalea said, "before it was infringed upon by your people and the darkness from Arcosia."

Alton clamped his mouth shut as if refraining from saying something he might regret. Others among the Sacoridians grumbled and Karigan wished Graelalea would try being a little more diplomatic. Hoping to prevent an incident, she began to introduce Estral, but Graelalea turned to her of her own accord and spoke to her in flowing Eletian.

Estral cocked her head and listened intently. When Graelalea finished, Estral said, "I do not understand the words, but your meaning washed over me like music."

Graelalea appeared pleased by her response.

"This is Estral Andovian," Karigan supplied. "Daughter of the Golden Guardian of Selium."

"I know," Graelalea said. "As my words are music she understands, her presence is a song I hear. Well met, little cousin."

Estral smiled in pleasure.

It was said there was Eletian blood in the Fiori line, and Graelalea's acknowledgment only seemed to confirm it. Finally Karigan introduced the fuming Lieutenant Grant as the commander of the Sacoridian half of the expedition, not as the commander of *the* expedition. Grant appeared no happier when Graelalea offered him scant attention. When Karigan introduced Lynx, he presented Graelalea with a box.

"A gift from King Zachary," he said.

The label on the box indicated it was from Master Gruntler's Sugary, which meant it contained—

"Chocolate!" Graelalea exclaimed in delight. She showed the box to the other Eletians and they murmured in approval. "Our thanks to the king for his thoughtfulness."

By the time Karigan completed introductions, the dusk of dawn had lightened considerably.

"It is time," Graelalea said. "Daylight begins, day balances night. It is time to enter the forest."

Karigan's hand went to Condor's neck. He puffed gently into her hair. All at once she found she must say good-bye to her beloved horse and her friends. She wrapped her arms around Condor's neck, fighting tears, and handed his reins over to Dale.

"Don't you worry," Dale said. "Plover and I will keep an eye on him. We'll keep him in condition so he's ready for you when you return."

Karigan hugged her and the other Riders who were staying behind. When she came face to face with Alton and Estral, she hesitated, and then turned away.

"Karigan." Alton grabbed her arm and hauled her into an embrace. "I know you're mad," he whispered, "but I care. About you. I want you to come back safe and sound."

"Me, too," Estral said, taking her turn. "Don't take any unnecessary risks."

Karigan was torn by her anger at their betrayal and her desire to find comfort in their friendship. But she just couldn't give in, even now as she was about to enter Blackveil. Too much pride, too much hurt. If she didn't come back and they felt guilty? A small vindictive part of her thought it would serve them right. But as she turned away from them so they wouldn't see the tears gathering in her eyes, she was the one feeling guilty, alone, and, frankly, afraid.

She shrugged her pack on and with a deep breath, faced the breach. Grant was issuing final instructions.

"We stay together," he was saying. "No one wanders off."

Soldiers leaned a ladder against the repairwork of the breach, climbed up, and lowered a second ladder down the other side. Then they took up positions staring down into the forest with crossbows at the ready.

"We'll keep a daily watch for your return," Captain Wallace told them.

Grant saluted and pivoted. "I'll go over first." Without awaiting anyone to contradict him, he strode over to the breach and climbed up the ladder.

"That one will not last long," Graelalea observed.

Corporal Porter was right behind Grant. When both men had disappeared over the repairwork, Yates cried, "Woohoo!" and ran for the breach, scrambling up the ladder.

One by one Karigan watched her companions climb over the breach and disappear to the other side. The Eletians moved with grace, their armor no hindrance to them at all.

"I will see you in the shadows," Graelalea told her before ascending the ladder herself.

Karigan was the last to go. She did not lag, but she did not hurry, and when she stood atop the repairwork, she gazed one last time at the verdant world she was leaving behind, and at her friends with their anxious expressions watching from below. Estral's face was buried into Alton's shoulder and his arms were loosely wrapped around her.

Karigan turned her back on them and began her descent into the clinging gray mist of Blackveil Forest. The dawn that had begun to brighten the day on the other side of the wall no longer touched her.

✣ EQUINOX ✣

It was, by Grandmother's calculations, the morning of the spring equinox. The equinox brought change, not merely the change of season, but a perceptible alteration in the demeanor of the forest. She cocked her head, gazing into the murk of Blackveil at nothing, sensing the forest had turned its attention elsewhere. It was a subtle feeling, like a ripple on a still lake. What had caught its interest?

Something unrelated nagged at her, too, like an itch. It emanated from the north, near the wall, and she wondered what the Sacoridians were up to. The disturbance in the etherea came to her like an inaudible whisper and she could not name it.

Grandmother was concerned. Ripples could turn to storm waves, and whispers—well, whispers were insidious, dangerous.

It was Sarat's inconsolable crying that brought her back to the present. They'd found yet another pile of fresh entrails that had been dumped in their path. Min rubbed Sarat's back in an effort to calm her. The men looked on unsure and uneasy. Lala, as always, was unafraid. She squatted beside the entrails and probed them with a stick.

"It's . . . it's a curse," Sarat said between sobs. "Someone is cursing us."

Grandmother did not think so. The first pile had been left outside their cave, a great heap of innards that must have come from more than one creature. Days later they'd found another fresh pile in the center of the road they followed, Way of the Moon. This was the third they'd encountered, pink and bloody and glossy in the damp of the forest environs.

"I think," Grandmother said, "these are offerings."

"Offerings?" Cole asked in surprise.

"Yes. We have been watched since not long after we entered Way of the Moon."

Her people darted anxious looks into the forest around them and huddled a little closer together. Lala, though, remained unconcerned, winding a length of intestine around her stick.

"Thought so," Deglin said with a darkening expression. "I thought we were being followed."

"It'll be our guts on the road next!" Sarat wailed.

"I do not think we need to fear the Watchers," Grandmother replied, hoping her calm, steady voice would prevent Sarat from lapsing into outright hysterics. Her people were correct to fear the forest, but she could not allow that fear to overcome them. "I believe the offerings to be a sign of respect from those who watch. They are primitive creatures with a certain amount of intelligence, and they find power in such things. They are honoring us."

"Or warning us," Deglin rumbled.

"I think not," Grandmother said, "but it may be we have been rude, not acknowledging the gifts as we should. Even primitive creatures expect some acknowledgment in return."

She thought it over for some moments, ignoring Sarat's sobbing and the terrible damp that made her old bones ache. She still wasn't entirely recovered from the spider bite and every day they trudged along Way of the Moon was torture to her body. The men carried her pack, and Lala took up the basket of yarn to relieve her of even that minor burden. Every step confirmed Grandmother's growing conviction that she would never again walk in the world outside. Only her love of the empire and her people kept her setting one foot in front of the other, as well as her desire to please God, who commanded her to awaken the Sleepers. She would not rest until she accomplished her task.

As she gazed at the entrails at her feet, she realized they presented an opportunity, an opportunity to not only impress the Watchers, but to use the innate potency of their gift for her own purposes. Using the blood and organs of what once had been living creatures always enhanced the art. *Necromancy,* some called it, as if it were a bad thing. When cast appropriately, necromantic art proved particularly powerful.

Human remains and blood worked best, but the gift from the Watchers should serve well enough. She wondered how the infusion of the forest's etherea on these remains would affect the outcome of her spell. It could prove risky, but this whole endeavor was full of risks. What was one more? The possible benefits outweighed the danger.

"I need a good hot fire," she announced.

Her retainers glanced uncertainly at one another.

"We gonna eat that?" Griz asked, pointing at the entrails.

Grandmother smiled at his expression of distaste. "No, my son. We're going to burn it. That is why I need a hot fire. Hot and big." She then knelt down beside Lala. "Child, I would like you to help me."

Lala had picked out a carrion beetle from the pile, a nasty, large thing with pincers, and dropped it to pay close attention to her grandmother. Grandmother knew that if they did not do something with the entrails soon, larger and nastier creatures would arrive, attracted by the scent of an easy meal.

"Would you like to make the fire pretty?" Grandmother asked.

Lala nodded.

"Good. You know the knots. You will make the fire pretty to impress the Watchers."

Lala nodded again looking very serious and determined. The pair of them picked through the yarn basket for the skeins they wanted.

It was not easy building a bonfire in that wet place. Much of the dead and fallen wood they tried to collect crumbled in their hands from decay, and it harbored stinging insects. Eventually they assembled enough wood to create a good-sized mound and the men took on the unpleasant task of placing the entrails atop it.

Deglin was an adept fire maker, but the wet stuff allowed only a few pitiful smoldering flames. Grandmother needed something far more impressive and hot, so after warning the others to stand clear in case the forest warped her spell, she cast a clump of knotted yarn into the flames.

The fire surged up the mound of wood in an inferno so intense that she had to retreat several steps. The forest seemed to bend away from the blaze in dismay, and there was much scurrying and rattling of branches and underbrush as creatures fled the area. The entrails snapped and popped as they burned in the fire.

Grandmother laughed. She'd wanted a hot fire and she got one. It would certainly make an impression on the Watchers, and they would not doubt her power. She gestured to Lala to add her knots.

"Go carefully, child, do not burn yourself."

Lala approached the fire without fear and tossed her knots into it. Immediately color saturated the flames—cool blues and purples, verdant green, angry red. Shapes formed among the individual flames, people and animals. Grandmother saw a pony and she thought Lala must miss the one she had to abandon on the other side of the wall. Sparks turned to birds that flew into the canopy. A butterfly flittered over Grandmother's head.

Grandmother was in awe for it was beyond her expectations. "My dear little child," she murmured. "You are a true artist." She hugged Lala and received a rare smile in return. When she called Lala a "true artist," she did not mean one who was a master of aesthetics, though that element was certainly present in her granddaughter's creations, but rather one who was gifted with the ability to shape etherea. Grandmother would have to carefully watch over the girl's development.

Now, however, she must take advantage of the fire herself. She needed to check on Birch. She cast one of his fingernail clippings, wrapped in knotted yarn, into the flames. A vision blossomed in the roiling blaze of a small settlement in a clearing of the forest—not Blackveil, but the living green forest of the north. The rank smoke of the bonfire was replaced by the more pleasant scent of smoke that issued from chimneys. Birds awakened to the new spring chattered and called in the trees. Through Birch's eyes, she peered from the concealment of the woods at the quiet settlement. A man chopped wood, while another harnessed a pair of oxen for the day's work. A young girl helped a woman scrub laundry in a washbasin.

Birch's gaze swept away from the settlement to his side and behind him. Other men, with weapons drawn, waited, hidden just as he was. The etherea allowed Grandmother to delve deeper into Birch's mind and she learned that this was a training mission for his soldiers, that they were to take no prisoners. The point was to teach them not to pity the enemy, without regard for age or gender.

The settlement was located on Sacoridia's northern boundary and was therefore largely unprotected and certainly no threat to Second Empire. Birch, however, wanted his soldiers to taste blood, to become initiated in the kill of battle before they had to face stronger, more seasoned opponents.

It was a good strategy, she thought, so long as it did not bring the wrath of King Zachary upon them prematurely, but she sensed Birch's confidence that he and his soldiers would slip away into hiding long before the king even learned of the attack.

Birch gestured to his soldiers and they moved forward, ghosting between the trees, over patches of snow that clung to forest shadows, and they surged into the clearing with blades ready to strike down the unsuspecting settlers.

The battle cry of the soldiers was greeted by the screams and shouts of the enemy. The man chopping wood was the first to die, and a torch was set to his cottage. Grandmother observed the action as Birch did. He held back, allowing his subordinate officers to lead the attack. Some soldiers did to the women and girls as soldiers had always done while their menfolk were forced to watch. Birch did not stop them. When they finished, the women and men were slaughtered.

Grandmother watched dispassionately. Ravaging the enemy's women was a way to further defeat those who would take up arms, and she sensed from Birch that he planned to somehow make this obvious by leaving a "message" for the king.

When she saw that the settlers had been slain to the smallest child and all their buildings set afire, she felt comfortable that Birch had everything well in hand. She decided to leave him and gaze elsewhere. She tossed another length of yarn into the fire, and the image of the settlement burned away from her vision.

A new vision did not come to her. She saw only the dance of fire, but she heard a thread of music, beautiful music, just above the roar of flames.

What's this? she wondered.

She closed her eyes and the music flowed through her, joyful, serene, led by a crystalline voice. A haunting chorus echoed the singer, accompanied by the distant rhythm of hammers on stone, a sound of endurance and strength ...

It was, she realized, the whisper she'd sensed in the etherea at the wall. Grandmother snapped her eyes open before she could be sucked in any farther. "No," she murmured.

Min touched her arm. "Grandmother? What is it? Are you well?"

Grandmother took Min's hand, welcoming that human touch, the support.

"I am well," she said, "but things at the wall trouble me."

The wall was strengthening. Someone's voice, a voice that could cultivate the art, shape etherea, was leading the wall guardians in song. Who could it be? Who still walked the Earth that could do such a thing?

The who did not matter. The result did. If the Sacoridians repaired the wall before the Sleepers were awakened and the forest arose, then all her efforts and hopes for Second Empire would fail. She would fail God Himself.

She'd made a critical mistake. She should not have entered the forest without the book of Theanduris Silverwood in her hands. Was it possible her people had failed to acquire it and the Sacoridians were now using it to mend the wall? She could not tell by observing through Birch's eyes—he was busy with his own mission.

She should have waited for the book, but God had clearly told her to awaken the Sleepers. Perhaps He had His own plan, but if He did, it was not obvious to her.

Grandmother sighed and clung to Min. Her body shook with the effort she'd already expended seeking visions. To her surprise, the fire had burned down considerably, but Lala's art still colored the flames.

"I must rest now," Grandmother told the others.

As Min helped her to a blanket spread on the ground, she realized what was done was done. If the Sacoridians had obtained the Silverwood book and someone gifted with the art was singing the wall to strength, then there was only one thing she could do to prevent the mending of the wall: destroy the singer.

She eased down onto the blanket with Min's assistance, already planning on how she might accomplish the task.

✦ AMBERHILL'S VOYAGE BEGINS ✦

It was a fine morning, this first day of spring, with an offshore breeze stroking the waters of Corsa Harbor and the sun glancing off the waves. The tide was in and Captain Irvine oversaw the loading of cargo into the bowels of his vessel, *Ullem Queen*, bound for Coutre Province. Amberhill watched as some of his own possessions were loaded, but Yap supervised more closely, chivvying the porters not to drop anything.

Amberhill stood on the wharf, striking an aristocratic pose and wearing a mask of boredom amid the noise and confusion of four vessels loading and unloading at once. He did not deign to step out of the way for bustling longshoremen, sailors, merchants, fishermen, or anyone. They all had to go around *him*.

As he watched he absorbed details—cormorants bobbing alongside ships at anchor, harried porters bearing everything from squawking chickens to bales of tobacco to the various vessels tied to the wharf or tossing items down to sailors waiting in longboats below. A sailor without an ounce of horse sense tried to pull a balky stallion across a gangway to one of the ships. The stallion bellowed his dismay and with a toss of his head unbalanced the sailor at the other end of his lead rope who fell off the gangway and splashed into the harbor waters.

Coins exchanged hands, and purses were lifted by grubby waifs from oblivious passengers milling on the wharf. He caught a young pickpocket by the wrist as the boy reached for his own purse. The waif gazed up at him with large, frightened eyes. Amberhill gave him a curt shake of his head, then he released the boy, who scampered off in search of easier pickings.

Overstuffed merchant carts jammed the wharf, bearing crates and sacks and barrels and hogsheads of goods. Amberhill was less fascinated by the cargoes than by the merchants themselves. Most were finely dressed, soft-looking, and did not lower themselves to assist with transferring cargo to or from ships, but rather left the dirty work to subordinates and made notations in ledgers. All except one.

That merchant tossed aside his well-tailored longcoat and rolled up his sleeves to help unload a schooner to fill a wagon with spices, sugarcane, and what appeared to be exotic fruits. The sailors on board the ship were tanned. Amberhill guessed that this vessel had been trading in the Cloud Islands.

The merchant himself was not tanned, so likely had not gone on the venture himself, but it did not stop him from taking a heavy hogshead and hoisting it up to another man atop the wagon. This was no soft merchant, but he was no common laborer either, for he exuded an aura of command as he ordered his people about and joked with them. They deferred to him in all ways and showed him no insolence. And there was something more about the man, something . . . familiar.

Amberhill caught the bulky shoulder of a passing long-shoreman. "Who is that man?" he asked, pointing out the merchant.

"Not from around here, eh? That'd be Stevic G'ladheon, biggest merchant around."

Amberhill let the longshoreman go and grinned, thinking this an opportunity he could not pass up. He of course had been well aware of who Karigan G'ladheon's successful father was. Those who dealt in the business world of the realm could not help but know of him. What made him even more noteworthy to Amberhill's mind was that Stevic G'ladheon was a self-made man. Very admirable.

Amberhill casually strolled down the wharf, carving effortlessly through the throngs. As he approached, he observed

Stevic G'ladheon was square of shoulder and contained the energy of a young man, but a slight silvering at his temples revealed his age.

Amberhill wondered how he should introduce himself, and was lost momentarily in an imagined conversation: *"How do you know my daughter?"* the merchant asked, and Amberhill was so tickled by all the possible clever responses that he almost laughed aloud. He was not under the impression, however, that Stevic G'ladheon was the sort of man to be trifled with.

He readied himself to greet the merchant, but a ship's bell clanged and Yap was at his elbow.

"Sorry, sir," Yap said, "but Cap'n Irvine is ready to get underway and says ya must board, or he's leaving without ya."

"Wait a moment, I want to—"

"Passenger Amberhill!"

Amberhill glanced over his shoulder, the mate glowering over the heads of the crowd at him. Then he returned his gaze to Stevic G'ladheon, who looked right back at him.

"You Amberhill?" the merchant asked.

Amberhill, startled, nodded.

"Then you'd better get yourself on that ship. Captain Irvine maintains a rigorous schedule, especially with the tide turning, and he won't wait for lingerers."

"Um—" Amberhill began. A glance back at the ship revealed the crew readying to haul in the gangway.

"Sir?" Yap said urgently, tugging at his sleeve.

Amberhill wanted to say something, anything, to Stevic G'ladheon, but he'd vanished—just like his daughter was wont to do. Then he spotted the merchant aboard the vessel he'd been helping to unload, talking to a customs official.

Of all the damnable things! Amberhill thought. To be denied the opportunity to initiate a conversation with one of Sacoridia's most respected merchants and the father of an enigma. Amberhill wondered how much he knew of his daughter's powers or about mystical black stallions, but the bell clanged more insistently.

Ah, well, he thought. *Opportunity missed.*

He pivoted and hastened across the wharf to the *Ullem Queen*. The gangway had been retracted and the ship was separating from the wharf. He and Yap leaped the gap to the ship. Amberhill managed easily, but poor Yap less so. He dangled from the railing, feet scrabbling against the hull. Crew grabbed his arms and hauled him on deck. The captain scowled at them both from his position up by the wheel.

Amberhill put Stevic G'ladheon and everything else about his former life to the back of his mind as he took in the harbor and ocean beyond. He was answering a calling, a calling to sail the ocean, to seek mysteries beyond the horizon, and there was no way of knowing if he'd ever return.

By the second day of the voyage, Amberhill just wanted to return to dry land. No, he reflected, he just wanted to die. He hung limply over the rail, arms swinging with the motion of the ship. He did best with his eyes closed. Yap had urged him to watch the horizon, but it did not help. Nor did the candied ginger, hard biscuits, or tea Yap brought him. All of that and more ended up in the sea, leaving behind a vile taste in his mouth. There should not be anything left in his stomach, but the wooziness threatened a fresh surge over the rail.

Amberhill was born and raised an inlander, but he'd boarded *Ullem Queen* confidently and enjoyed the breeze and scenery of Corsa Harbor. He'd sighted a pod of harbor porpoise, and gulls wheeling at the sterns of fishing boats, looking for offal and castoffs. He admired the lines of a naval vessel slicing through harbor waters like a rapier and guessed at what was stored in the kettle-bottomed hulls of merchant ships. The *Ullem Queen* specialized in tobacco from the Under Kingdoms. Normally he found the fragrance of the leaf pleasant, but in his current state, just the mere thought of certain scents sent him reeling to the rail.

Yes, he'd been fine till they passed beneath the shadowy remains of a keep perched on an island headland overlooking the entrance to the harbor. Once out of the protected harbor and on the open bay, the swells grew and almost in an

instant Amberhill went from composed aristocratic gentleman to a retching, sickly commoner. He'd supposed himself
immune to seasickness. After all, he was Lord Amberhill and
had been the Raven Mask, scaler of high walls and master
thief. The gods were showing him what they thought of that,
by literally bringing him to his knees.

The only thing that appeared to help was following Yap's
advice to stay on deck in the fresh air, away from the fragrant
cargo and the stench of other ill passengers.

Amberhill moaned. He'd asked Yap if the sickness would
soon pass. All Yap could tell him was that for some it did.
For others? Some never acclimated. Amberhill feared he was
among the latter.

As for Yap himself, he was right at home among the crew
and had, Amberhill noticed, taken to padding about the
decks in his bare feet. His remedies had not worked, but he
kept checking on his employer.

Amberhill cracked open crusty, salt-rimmed eyes and
the turmoil of waves almost sent him into a vortex of nau-
sea again, but he noticed how the ruby of his dragon ring
shone in the sunlight, brighter than he'd ever seen it before.
Each facet had its own hue of red—the richness of velvet, the
gleam of deep wine, the brightness of fresh blood.

As he gazed at the ruby, everything came into sharp focus
in his mind. There was no longer the roiling drop and heave
of the ocean, but a solid deck beneath him and a steady horizon. His stomach ceased its torment. His mind began to work
with the motion of the waves, or at least that was the way he
thought of it.

Some strength began to flow into flaccid limbs. He rose
unsteadily at first but then gained confidence, as if he'd always instinctively known how to maintain his footing on
board a ship.

"Sir? Are ya all right?" Yap asked, practically leaping
across the deck to him.

Amberhill grinned. "Much better. In fact, I'm actually
hungry."

"Very good, sir. I'll see what cook has on."

Yap padded off, and Amberhill clasped his hands behind

his back, and took in the clear sky and blue-green water anew. The world was looking like a much better place now. Something about his ring had righted him, given him his sea legs—and his sea stomach.

He felt freshly born and like he could conquer the world. He liked the idea, and smiled.

 ❧ EQUINOX ❧

Laren struggled to keep up with Zachary, as did his secretary, Cummings, and his other aides. He stormed from one meeting to the next. During the meetings themselves he was curt, decisive, and restless, cutting them short when he'd had enough. Then they were off again, leaving behind flabbergasted officials, ambassadors, and courtiers.

Laren found the truncated sessions refreshing, but she wasn't sure it was doing much for diplomacy.

As Zachary swept down corridors on his way to his next appointment, Laren practically had to run to keep up with his long strides. Even Colin was looking a little pink in the cheeks and his expression was one of consternation at his liege's mood. Sperren would not have had a chance. The old man was in the mending wing with a broken hip, having fallen upon rising from bed this morning. Ben, she knew, was tending the elderly castellan with his special ability. In the meantime, Colin had taken on Sperren's duties.

"Don't you think you should talk to him?" Colin asked, striding beside her. "Do you suppose he's upset about Sperren?"

"I expect it's more than that," Laren replied. In fact, she had a good idea of what had gotten into him. "I'll see what I can do."

Colin looked relieved.

Laren worked her way forward through the various aides and courtiers hastening after Zachary to reach his side. She touched his sleeve and said, "Can I have a word with you?"

He came to such an abrupt halt that all who followed had to skid to a stop. Laren found herself several paces beyond him.

His expression was set, dangerous, ready for anger. "Well?"

"Privately, Your Highness," she said.

"Very well." He flung open the nearest door, much to the shock of the copyists at work within, and he ordered them out. They scrambled to obey him. Laren followed him into the chamber and he closed the door with a not-so-subtle slam. The chamber was thick with the scent of paper, ink still wet on the unfinished documents the copyists abandoned on their desks.

"Well?" he demanded.

Laren crossed her arms and directed a level gaze at him, which was not easy since he was tall and maintained a regal bearing. She saw very little of the young boy she had once known in him. The physical weight of the silver fillet he wore on his brow wasn't heavy, but the responsibility it represented was great. It was borne by a man of strength. The power of his body was a given—she'd seen him at work with Arms Master Drent, she'd watched him subdue the most unruly of stallions. One just had to watch him moving down a corridor to know his strength.

The power of his intellect, coupled with his compassion, was what made him a good king. He wasn't just a warrior king ready to ride into battle, he was a thoughtful king who put his people first.

It was this last that etched the lines into his forehead. She'd seen it with Queen Isen, how all the cares and responsibility of leading the realm wore on one.

"I know what day it is," Laren said.

"And?"

"If you wish to talk about it, I am here. Otherwise, if you'll forgive my being so blunt, your behavior is running your aides ragged and making everyone wonder what is causing their king's unpredictable mood. It is worrisome to them that there might be something happening they're unaware of."

"Are you saying that I'm behaving erratically?"

"That would describe it, yes." She smiled to take the sting out of her words. She would never have been able to speak so plainly to any other king, but their close relationship allowed it.

He did not explode, but rather relaxed. "I am not sure there is anything more to be said that has not been spoken of before. Today is the equinox, the day our people are to venture into Blackveil by my command."

"The day *Karigan* is to enter Blackveil," Laren said.

"Yes." His gaze grew distant. "If I'd had the chance, if my position permitted, I would have pleaded with her not to accept the mission because of the danger, and because I couldn't bear the thought of . . ."

"Of losing her?"

He nodded.

"I believe Karigan will come out of Blackveil just fine. I think it's the forest itself that may not survive the encounter."

Zachary actually smiled. "Yes, I doubt the forest will be the same after her visit." Behind the smile, however, were the lines of worry she'd grown all too familiar with. "So you'd like me to gentle my pace, eh? Behave less . . . erratically?"

"It would be helpful all around."

"I'm sorry, Laren, but I have this burning need to move, to keep busy."

"Then perhaps you should consider a diversion."

"A diversion," he murmured. "What did you have in mind? I do not wish to pull Drent from his teaching schedule."

"I, uh, have something else in mind." She took a deep breath, summoning the courage to make her suggestion. The idea had seemed to make sense when she first thought of it, but now she wasn't so sure. Zachary was not frivolous in his affections, but it was not as if he hadn't engaged in casual liaisons before.

"Well?" Zachary asked.

She cleared her throat. "It would be a way to engage your mind and body." She hesitated. Wouldn't Colin be the better one to address this? Another man? But she had started, and Zachary expected her to finish. There was no escape. She took a deep breath and the rest rushed out. "I've managed to procure a list of acceptable courtesans who—"

"Courtesans?" The storm once again clouded his features, and then evaporated. "Oh, Laren, I thought you understood."

"What I understand is that you are a full-blooded man with needs. I thought perhaps such a diversion would help you forget—"

"Karigan?" He paused in front of a desk to study the document atop it. "We have discussed your concerns and I'm well aware of my duty to the realm. But to suggest that a courtesan would help me forget? All the courtesans in the world and their wiles could not alter what is in my heart, and partaking of their offerings would only dishonor my regard for her. For Karigan."

"I'm sorry," Laren replied. "I do not think I've underestimated your feelings, but you still have needs."

"Everyone has needs, Laren, even you. Do you have a list of courtesans for yourself? Or, should I procure one for you? I understand there are some acceptable practitioners of the male gender."

"What?"

"Exactly." He flashed her a smile of triumph. "I do appreciate your concern for my well-being in the matter, and I think your suggestion of a diversion is a good one, just not the type you proposed." He moved rapidly across the chamber, documents fluttering off desks in his wake. He flung open the door and called, "Cummings! Cancel the rest of my appointments this afternoon."

It was only a couple hours later that Laren, on her way to Rider stables, observed Zachary riding out on a large, dappled stallion, one of his favorites. The horse was heavily muscled and a handful, but Zachary rode effortlessly, a born horseman. She was pleased to see Lady Estora riding beside him on a fine-limbed bay hunter, and there was Lord-Governor Coutre, as well, and a few other courtiers. Weapons followed on their sleek black horses, along with members of the guard, the royal falconers, and servants. A king rarely ventured anywhere without a crowd, but she imagined that once they reached open ground out in the countryside, he would put that stallion through its paces and he would be free in his own thoughts, free to think of whom and what he wanted without interruption or any expectations placed upon him.

"Captain?"

Laren turned to discover Ben Simeon approaching. He had changed out of his mender's smock into his Rider garb.

"Hello, Ben, do you have a riding lesson this afternoon?" Not that he ever managed to actually get on a horse. Horsemaster Riggs was mystified as to how to overcome his fear.

"Yes," he said glumly. He looked tired, a little pallid in the cheeks.

Guessing the cause, she asked, "How is the castellan?"

Ben brightened. "Resting comfortably. I believe I knitted the entire break back together. The rest of the healing is up to him, but he now has the hip of a twenty year old."

"Good heavens!" Of any Rider ability, Laren thought as they walked together toward Rider stables, the most miraculous was that of true healing. Ben had been trained as a mender before hearing the Rider call, and she could only believe that his prior training aided his magical ability, just as his magical ability enhanced his prior training.

Naturally Ben was in great demand in the mending wing and Master Destarion was no doubt pleased Ben hadn't taken to horses. Laren feared Ben was allowing himself to be overworked. Using one's ability had its costs—she felt those costs in her joints every day. With Ben she thought it could be even more devastating. From his haggard appearance, she deduced he was giving too much of himself, of his essence, to heal others. She'd have to make a point of speaking with Destarion later, and in the meantime wish that another true healer could be found among the ranks of her new Riders.

When Galen Miller chewed the herbalist's weed, its juices stung the sores that had erupted in his mouth. He needed more and more to subdue his shakes, but it often sent him into feverish sweats and blurred his perceptions of reality.

Some mornings he awoke to visions of the king standing over him dressed all in black, just like the wax figure of him at the Sacor City War Museum. He'd studied the figure so he'd know the real king when he saw him.

In his vision, however, the king towered over him and a noose hung still and solid beside him, its looped shadow stark against the far wall.

Raised you a traitor, eh? came the crass words that issued from the king's mouth, but didn't seem to belong to him.

"N-no," Galen would sputter. "A good lad. Clay was a good lad."

The king would float there, Galen writhing in terror on his pallet until sense came back to him. He needed to cut back on the weed, use just enough to keep his hand steady.

From the notches he made on a rafter of his attic room, he figured out it was the equinox. He was beginning to wonder if all his plans were for naught, that his boy would never be avenged. Even with the extra coins the stranger had given him all those weeks ago, he was not sure he'd have enough currency to keep his room at the inn until the king deigned to leave his castle.

Galen reached for his tankard with a trembling hand and slurped down the stale water, oblivious to the runnels dribbling down his chest. When he finished, he set the tankard beside his precious sheaf of the herb and a small vial he'd also obtained from the herbalist for a handsome sum. It contained the closure to all his waiting.

Two days ago, on inspiration, he'd spared a little of the precious fluid for the barbed heads of the two arrows he kept at the ready by the window. One tiny drop each. The herbalist claimed the poison would remain efficacious for weeks. He did not want any question of his quarry's survival. It would take only one arrow, the second was just in case. Yes, his boy would be avenged.

He rose from his pallet and crossed over to the window, sitting on the ledge and leaning against the casement. He gazed out into the street, continuing the vigil he'd carried on for so many weeks.

He awoke from a doze when he heard the hooves of several horses clopping down the street. When the riders came into view, Galen's pulse quickened.

His wait was over.

\rightsquigarrow EQUINOX \rightsquigarrow

Zachary was not, in Estora's opinion, an impulsive man. If he was, he wouldn't have lasted long as a king. His brother, Amilton, had been the complete opposite, giving in to his every urge. It cost him the throne. King Amigast had passed over him in favor of Zachary. Amilton's impulses then led him to plot against his brother, which resulted in his being exiled and, ultimately, killed.

Estora appreciated Zachary's thoughtful demeanor, though he was, perhaps, a little too driven to work, so she was surprised and delighted when he canceled all his afternoon appointments and invited her for an outing. Of course, it wasn't just her, but several courtiers, her father, and Richmont. And then of course, there were the Weapons, the falconers, and several servants. Guards cleared the street before them. Estora waved to the people who watched and cheered as the king and his companions rode by.

Estora did not know what inspired Zachary's sudden desire to leave work behind for an afternoon of recreation for he rarely spoke intimately to her about his feelings, an inclination she hoped would change once they married. For the time being she was content to ride beside him and assume it was just the promise of spring calling him from his dark, stone walls. She'd certainly had enough of winter's cold austerity herself.

She gave her future husband a sidelong glance as he sat astride his stallion. Presently he was far off in his own thoughts and where they might lead she could not guess. The wind rippled through his hair and there was the hint of a smile all too quickly gone.

He must have sensed her gaze for he turned to look at her. "What is it, my lady?"

"I was wondering where your thoughts were traveling."

"Far beyond the horizon," he said. "Too many places to recount." He fell silent again, back to brooding.

They entered a poorer section of the lower city. Well-wishers still stopped along the street to wave, but they were fewer, shabbier. Others skulked in doorways or shadowed closes glowering at the king's party as it passed. The Weapons were always alert, but Estora sensed just the slightest change in their posture.

"Hey, where's *my* falcon, King?" some man in stained clothes called out. Zachary shook his head when the guards started to move toward the man. Another king would have had him jailed and beaten for insolence. An old woman spat in the path of the king's party. She was merely escorted out of the street by the guards.

"The lower city should be swept clean of this filth," Richmont muttered.

"What would you have done with them?" Zachary asked. His tone was deceptively mild.

"Force them out of the city. Force them to work."

"Most of them did not ask for poverty," Zachary said, as though to himself. Estora, who rode right next to him heard, but she did not think anyone else had, certainly not Richmont who was muttering and complaining to her father. Richmont, whom she'd never been fond of, had gotten only more boorish since the betrothal. He had already declared his intent to stay in her service after the wedding. She would have to talk to her father about finding him something else to do.

The Winding Way curved past an inn with a disreputable air about it. The stench of old ale flowed to her all the way out into the street. Her father was pushing his horse up next to hers and appeared intent to speak to her, but something whined through the air and cut him off, and suddenly he was not there. His horse was, but he was not.

"Father?"

Cries shattered the air and everyone around her whirled into motion.

"Father?" she cried, turning in her saddle, but she could not see him. The Weapons were reigning their mounts around to surround her and Zachary.

Zachary slammed his horse into hers and the force almost knocked her from the saddle.

"What is—"

Even as the Weapons surged toward Zachary, he stood in his stirrups, blocking her. She couldn't see what was happening. But she heard that whine again, and this time, the thud of impact.

Galen's body shuddered when he loosed the first arrow, and he swore when it flew off course into some old courtier who had the bad luck to be in the wrong place at the wrong time. He had only moments before the Weapons threw themselves in front of his intended target, but as if he were still the great archer in his prime under the pressure of battle, he'd already nocked the second arrow. He must hold steady this time. He must not miss.

Faster than the Weapons could move, he drew the bowstring with an inhalation and marked his prey. Unbelievably the king rose in his stirrups to shield the lady beside him, rising above those who would protect him, as if to present a target Galen could not miss. He exhaled, loosed the arrow.

He watched it soar on its deadly path, his hopes, his vengeance, all riding on the air currents that stroked the shaft and fletching, the fletching he'd plucked from a goose himself and painstakingly glued to the shaft. He watched the arrow singing its way to the very end, its impact home. His tremors had not betrayed him, his aim proved true.

It had all come full circle, all his planning and waiting. He could rest now. Joyful and exhausted, with success and vengeance his, he could now join his wife and son in the heavens. He sank to the attic floor and whispered a short prayer, then drew the vial of poison to his lips.

CONSEQUENCES

Laren watched the scene with some amusement. The rest of the Riders had finished
their lesson and were now cooling their mounts
at a walk around the outdoor arena. Ben,
meanwhile, hadn't even gotten in the saddle, as usual. He
faced Robin, and Robin was doing his scary horse act by staring right back and flicking his tail, more like a cat than a
horse.

Elgin leaned against the fence beside her. "Don't know
what we're going to do with that one."

"Ben or Robin?" she asked.

Elgin grunted a laugh. "Either one of them. Ben's got
himself worked up before he ever gets out here for training,
and that Robin, he's too smart for his own good."

"He is that," Laren agreed, "but no one else has had this
degree of trouble with him."

"I'll warrant none of your other Riders were ever afraid
of horses." Elgin stroked his chin. "Have you tried a pony
with Ben?"

"A pony? They can be pretty mean-tempered."

"I know," Elgin replied. "They're clever little beasts, but
Ben probably doesn't know that, and if it's the size of horses
that might be bothering him, then a pony might be the answer. An old, sleepy pony might be less cantankerous."

"Hmm." If size were the issue, it was worth considering.

Off in the center of the arena, Horsemaster Riggs followed their gazes and shrugged.

"Riggs has tried everything else," Elgin said. "She's at her
wit's end."

"Then we'll find a pony. A nice, shaggy little mountain pony, sturdy enough to carry a man, and elderly enough not to care." Laren turned her gaze to the other Riders sitting with relaxed postures upon their horses as they cooled. "Everyone else looks as though they're coming along fine."

"That they are. Riggs says she's going to raise the jumps next lesson."

"Excellent." Laren was pleased, for it meant this batch of Riders was nearly ready for training runs. Several had gone on short-range errands with senior Riders already, but now longer runs were possible. The sooner this group was fully trained up, the sooner she'd have more people out and about the realm. It had been difficult to give up several of them to go to the wall, not to mention the three entering Blackveil. It had required some contortions in scheduling.

Among the group was a girl of the lower aristocracy, Sophina. Laren picked her out from her classmates. She was less relaxed than the others and wore a perpetual pout on her face. Mara said the girl had airs and actively sought ways to make everyone else miserable. She was not the first aristocrat called to the messenger service, nor would she be the last. Alton, as the heir to D'Yer Province, was of far higher standing than Sophina, but he'd never ever shown any resentment at being called. Sophina would adapt in time, learning that her status would have little bearing on her life as a Rider.

Laren smiled. It was the various temperaments of her Riders that made them such an interesting group. One's strengths filled in for another's weaknesses. They became stronger as a whole. She was, as ever, proud of them. Even her greenest of Greenies who had yet to prove themselves.

"So you have the afternoon off," Elgin said. "What will you do with it?"

"Off? I would say that my day of meetings with the king were canceled, but I've reports awaiting me back at my quarters, not to mention a pony to acquire."

"I think I could handle the pony for you," Elgin said. "I know a—"

A scream cut through the afternoon peace like a scythe. Laren's heart thudded as she looked for its source.

Elgin pointed. "Sophina!"

The girl rocked in her saddle and wailed, clutching her chest. Her horse spooked, and she toppled off its back to the ground.

"Five hells!" Laren ducked between the fence rails into the arena with Elgin right behind her. They charged across the dirt to where Sophina lay. Horsemaster Riggs and Ben closed with them. Laren knelt beside the girl who writhed on the ground, still clutching at her chest. Tears ran down her cheeks.

"Sophina?" Laren asked gently. "What's wrong?"

"The king!" the girl cried. "The king!" And she fell unconscious.

Ben placed his hand on her forehead. "I can take care of her."

"No." Laren stood, blood surging through her like a swarm of bees. "Chief! You deal with Sophina. She's come into her ability." Elgin nodded, gathered the girl into his arms, and carried her away.

"But I can—" Ben started to protest.

Laren pointed at Merla, who was still seated atop her lesson horse. "You go to Connly or Mara, whomever you find first, and tell them there's been an incident with the king. They'll know what to do."

There was a collective gasp among the Riders who had grouped around them.

"*Move!*" Laren bellowed.

Merla did not hesitate. She did not stop to open the arena gate. Instead she dug her heels into the flanks of her horse, galloped straight for the gate, and sailed over it. It was probably three times as high as anything Riggs had taught them to jump, but Merla and her horse landed smoothly on the other side and galloped off.

Laren pointed at Carson, older than many of the other new Riders. "Go to Master Destarion. Tell him to grab his kit and hurry down the Winding Way." Without another word, Carson reined his horse around and headed for the gate. This time others had opened it so he didn't have to jump it.

Next she picked out Kayd, a boy whose father was a laborer on the castle grounds and knew the castle layout well and how things worked within. "You will seek out Colin Dovekey and tell him there is an emergency. He is acting castellan and should be meeting with the kitchen staff about now."

Kayd nodded and he and his horse pounded from the arena just as the others had.

Laren turned to Riggs. "You'll take care of the rest of them?"

Riggs clapped her hands to gain the attention of her students and started shouting orders at them.

That left Ben, who did not seem to know which way to turn. "You are with me," Laren said. "Robin! Come!"

The horse obeyed immediately and trotted right up to her.

Ben shrank away, but Laren caught his sleeve. "Something bad has happened to the king," she said. "Sophina, it appears, is a seer. She saw something happen to the king. There is no time to lose." She placed her toe into the stirrup and mounted. "Now get up behind me."

When Ben dithered, she leaned down and stared hard at him. "Sophina passed out before she could tell us exactly what she saw, but if she had such a strong reaction to the vision, it can't be good. Do you understand? The king has come to great harm and if he's not dead yet, he may be soon unless you help him. Understand?"

Ben's face paled. He nodded.

"Then *mount*."

This time he did not hesitate and she pulled him up behind her. He circled his arms around her waist, clutching her for dear life.

"Loosen up," she gasped. He complied and she clicked Robin into a gallop out of the arena and across castle grounds.

She rode bent for all five hells down the Winding Way using cut-throughs all the Riders knew, and she stampeded through front gardens pushing Robin mercilessly with two adults on his back, but he was game, fearless, even, his strides unflagging. A true messenger horse. She was sure her Bluebird would forgive her the necessity of grabbing the nearest mount available.

As they careened around a cartload of bleating sheep, she imagined all kinds of scenarios—that Zachary was dead, or maybe he'd just fallen off that high-strung stallion of his and bumped his head. Maybe Sophina had actually seen something that had yet to happen and Laren would arrive in time to stop it. But somehow she knew better.

She could not give in to worry. She must keep her wits about her, for if the worst had happened to Zachary, there would be consequences for the entire realm. She loved Zachary, the little boy he had been and the man he had become, but the consequences for the country were bigger than even his life.

The ride took forever, pedestrians screaming and running to get out of her way, dropping sacks of onions beneath Robin's hooves and snatching children from danger. Zachary's party could not have had time to leave the city yet, could it? She tried to calculate the time in her head, but there were too many thoughts ramming into each other.

Robin skidded and almost lost his footing around a curve slick with melting ice. Laren was so numb with worry that she could no longer feel Ben clamped to her, but she could hear his whimpers and prayers.

Pray for Zachary, she thought. *Pray for Zachary.*

Near the second city gates, more people on foot and on horseback dashed to the sides of the street—not to get out of Laren's way, but to escape something else coming toward her.

A wagon burst free of the crowd with two cart horses running full out and a Weapon gripping reins and lashing a whip. Four other mounted Weapons thundered alongside.

"Fastion!" Laren cried, but it was clear he was not going to stop for her. The wagon surged past her and she had to wheel Robin on his haunches to catch up with it. Ben emitted a muted scream and started asking every god in the pantheon for deliverance. Laren did not think Goltera, goddess of fertile swine, would be of much help, but it couldn't hurt.

The mounted Weapons permitted her into their formation. She pushed poor Robin alongside the wagon and glanced in the back. There, stretched out on his side with an arrow in his gut was Lord Coutre, gasping for breath and his eyes wide open.

Beside him was Zachary, an identical arrow in his chest. His eyes were closed, his body moved limply with every bump of the wagon. Donal sat between the men, paying no attention to Lord Coutre, but pressing a blood-soaked cloth around Zachary's arrow wound. It was impossible to know if Zachary lived.

"Arrows are still in," Ben murmured in her ear. "Good."

Laren had almost forgotten about Ben, so focused on Zachary was she, but she didn't now. She jammed her heels into Robin's sides to press even more speed out of him.

"Fastion!" she cried. "Mender! I've got Ben. Mender!"

Fastion did not appear to hear over the clatter of cart wheels and hooves, but one of the mounted Weapons understood and reached from her mount for the reins of the cart horses. Fastion whipped his gaze around, ready to draw his sword.

"Mender!" Laren screamed. "I've got Ben!"

This time he heard and pulled the horses up. Laren hauled Robin into a sliding halt beside the wagon. The escorting Weapons arranged themselves around it looking menacing.

"Hurry," Fastion said.

Shaking, Ben dismounted, his face white as bone, and clambered into the wagon.

"The king," Donal told him. "Never mind Lord Coutre. The king needs your full attention."

Before Ben could settle entirely, Fastion flicked the reins and snapped the whip. Ben fell back, but Donal helped him up.

"Destarion should be up ahead," Laren shouted at Fastion.

She dropped back into place beside the wagon, asking Robin to keep up the grueling pace, to please keep up. Though Ben glanced a couple times over his shoulder at Lord Coutre, he worked on Zachary as Donal had ordered. The truth was, though Coutre was a lord-governor and the future queen's father, his life was not as important as Zachary's. Zachary, she knew, would not view it in the same way, but in the scheme of the realm, the truth was the truth.

Laren could not see all that Ben did, with Donal assisting him, but one moment the arrow was there, then it was out, tossed into the bed of the wagon and Ben had his hands around the wound as blood bubbled up around his fingers. He closed his eyes and a bluish glow spread out from his hands. It was peaceful, like a clear summer sky and Laren felt herself calm a notch. The bleeding slowly ebbed, but Laren saw no change in Zachary.

The blue glow sputtered out and Ben gazed at his bloody hands, blinking stupidly.

"Ben!" Laren cried. "Ben!"

He slumped and was caught by Donal who shook and tried to revive him to no avail.

Damnation. Ben must have expended too much of his energies healing Sperren, giving an old, old man the hip of a twenty year old.

Oh, Ben, she thought. How could they have known this would happen to the king? Had he been able to heal Zachary before passing out, or was their king already gone from them?

The ride back to the castle grounds was a nightmare. Donal made no indication whether or not Zachary lived, and Ben did not regain consciousness. All she could do was consider the next step for the realm and her Green Riders if Zachary was dead. If he'd named an heir to the throne, such a document would be locked away in a box of secrets guarded by the Weapons, and called the Royal Trust. If Zachary had a child, the heir would be obvious, but he hadn't even gotten as far as marrying Estora.

Even if an heir was named within the Trust, they'd have to wait until there was an assembly of all the lord-governors to open the box and reveal the name. As soon as word got out about Zachary, the lord-governors would be upon them like vultures, for they were princes of the realm, next in line for the throne if there was no direct descendent. Even if one of them was legitimately named, the others would contest it, fight over it. She prayed it would not come to civil war. They could not afford it with Second Empire building up its forces and the D'Yer Wall breached.

She could well imagine the enemy taking advantage of Sacoridia in its sudden weakness and turmoil. It wasn't as if they could keep Zachary's wounding a secret, for the Winding Way was the busiest street in all of Sacoridia, and the story of great harm befalling the king would travel the length and breadth of the lands in no time at all.

Who had loosed those arrows in the first place? How had this assassination attempt proved so successful?

Laren pushed back the rising tide of tears. All the dire consequences for the realm she could think of did not diminish the loss of one who was so dear to her.

⌁ SCHEMES ⌁

They were met by a phalanx of Weapons that roiled down the street in a wrathful tide of black, carrying along Master Destarion and an assistant with them. When Destarion reached the wagon, he ordered Donal out so he and his assistant could have room to work. Ben still lay unconscious in the bed of the wagon and Destarion shook his head.

He put his ear to Zachary's chest and peeled back his eyelids. He barked orders at his assistant who tore into his kit.

"Move!" he bellowed at Fastion, and they were off again.

A little hope surged in Laren. If Destarion was so urgent, could it mean there was still some life left in Zachary?

By the time they reached the castle, Robin was exhausted, but Laren's Riders were there to take him from her and care for him.

"The king?" Connly asked.

"I don't know."

Menders bearing stretchers rushed out of the castle. Zachary was carried away, and then Ben. A blanket was laid over Lord Coutre in the wagon. Lady Coutre and Estora's sisters ran out the castle door wailing. Laren paused on the top landing, gazing back toward the gates of the castle wall. The rest of the king's party should be coming up behind them—she hadn't even given a thought to their safety. Was Lady Estora all right?

She would know in time, but for now her thoughts centered on Zachary.

He was taken to his apartments and she and several others waited in the main parlor as menders traveled back and forth to his bedchamber. Colin and General Harborough stood off by themselves, heads bowed in intense discussion. Weapons turned the walls black with their presence.

While they waited, word arrived that Lady Estora and the rest of the party had returned unharmed. That was some good news, at least. Soon other reports came in that it had been a single assassin, apparently with his own warped agenda, who, after loosing his arrows into Zachary and Lord Coutre, took his own life with a draught of poison.

"Coward," General Harborough said when he heard. "Coward of the worst sort." The parlor had become crowded with persons who thought themselves important enough to hear the verdict on Zachary firsthand. Weapons kept them away from the private sections of the apartments. Aides came and went.

Connly reported to her that Ben was still unconscious and ensconced in the mending wing.

"It is the opinion of the other menders he'd spent too much of himself fixing Sperren's hip," Connly said. "Trying to mend the king put him over the edge."

Laren nodded. "Just what I thought."

"They will keep watch on him," he assured her.

Speculation and rumor about an heir drifted through the crowd, the repercussions of the king dying, all the things Laren had thought but could not voice herself. It hurt to hear them speak of Zachary as if he were already gone, a piece of history discarded. Perhaps he was, and she feared they would never have so fine a king again.

The hours passed and servants brought wine and food to those who had congregated. A death watch it was, though some conversed and laughed in the corners as though attending a party. Others, like Laren, paced with worry clenching their guts.

The door to Zachary's private quarters cracked open. One of Destarion's assistants poked his head out and spoke to Fastion. Fastion nodded curtly, then made his way through the crowd to where Laren stood.

"Captain, would you come with me?"

Laren trembled. Were they taking her to see Zachary? Would it be as witness to his life, or his death? Colin was pulled in as well and they were led down a long corridor to Zachary's dressing room. Destarion emerged from the bedchamber and closed the door quietly behind him, his expression grim and exhausted.

"I have ordered the death surgeons to ready the preparation room," Colin said. "Have you a verdict for us?"

"A verdict, no," Destarion said. "The next couple of days will be critical. He's held on this long because of his own strength and Ben Simeon's application of his true healing ability. It's a messy wound—the arrowhead was barbed. It did damage internally, but Ben's work repaired a pierced lung and began healing the tissue around it."

"Then there's a chance he'll make it?" Laren asked, hope surging.

Destarion remained grave. "The wound is still very serious. It appears the arrowhead was tainted with poison, no doubt the same the assassin used to kill himself. Whether or not my menders can fashion an antidote remains to be seen."

"I've sent some Weapons to question the herbalist who sold it," Colin said. "If there is an antidote, it will be found."

"I have concocted a draught that may help counteract the poison," Destarion said, "but it's already in his blood. It's up to him to fight it."

Exhausted by it all, Laren sagged into the nearest chair. He still lived, he still had a chance, and that was something.

"What of Ben Simeon?" Colin asked. "Can he do no more to help?"

"It depends on when he recovers," Destarion replied. "My menders tell me the lad poured a great deal of himself into Sperren's healing this morning, and now the king. More than we've seen him do before. Even when he wakes up, it may take yet more time for his ability to recover."

Colin turned his gaze on Laren. "Do you have any idea of how long?"

Laren shook her head. "We haven't had a true healer in my lifetime until Ben, and I've no documentation on this sort of thing. Any records have not survived the years."

She hadn't meant to sound so bitter, but it was because the realm was phobic of magic that its existence had to remain hidden, the history of the Riders had been suppressed, and now that loss of knowledge endangered the king's chances for survival.

"May I . . . may I see Zachary?" Laren asked.

Destarion nodded. "Be brief. He is not awake, but I often think the presence and words of friends can sometimes reach the unconscious mind and be of great comfort."

He led Laren and Colin through the door and into Zachary's chamber. She was struck by the light. She'd expected darkness, a somber aspect to the room, but Destarion had left the heavy drapes open to the balcony outside, and afternoon sunlight fell softly into the room and across the still figure lying on the bed.

Laren strode to the bedside and sank into the chair there vacated by one of Destarion's menders. Colin remained at the foot of the bed with Destarion. There was another Weapon on guard in a dim corner.

Blankets were drawn up to Zachary's chest where bandages bulged. The freshness of herbs in the poultice over the wound, and others steeping in a bowl of water on the bedside table, spread aromatically through the room.

Zachary's expression was placid and unfettered by the concerns of his life and his kingdom, and she saw the young boy she remembered. A young boy at play with his dogs, or chasing around with other castle children. She saw the studious young man who spent hours in the library poring over books. The strength was in his face, too, of the man, the warrior king. As Destarion said, he would need all that strength to survive the damage done by the arrow, and perhaps more.

She took his limp hand in her own and it was warm. Too warm? "I am here, Moonling," she said, calling on the nickname she used for him when he was little and tagging after her around castle grounds. "I'm here, and so is Colin. We'll take care of everything."

She rambled on in a similar vein, trying to keep her voice calm and light, reassuring. She half heard Destarion and Colin whispering together, but she did not let it distract her, not even when the two stepped out.

"You've got to hold on," Laren said more firmly.

The king's eyes fluttered open and she gasped.

"Laren." Her name barely made it past his lips, as though he hadn't the breath left in his body.

"Yes, I'm here," she replied, leaning closer.

He swallowed and rested so he could summon the energy to speak. "I did not . . . I did not want her to go."

"I know." Laren did not need to ask who.

"Tell her . . ." He drifted off leaving the rest unsaid and his eyes closed. He exhaled a long rattling breath as he settled back into unconsciousness.

Laren squeezed his hand knowing how he'd finish the sentence. "I'll tell her." If he lived, she would tell Karigan nothing. If he died, she wouldn't hesitate to tell Karigan everything, because then those feelings would do no harm to the realm. This wasn't even taking into account whether or not Karigan survived Blackveil.

Laren sighed. Too much death on her mind.

The door opened and Lady Estora appeared still wearing her riding habit, but with a black shawl drawn over her shoulders as a sign of mourning for her father. There was a querulous voice in the anteroom and Estora quickly shut the door to mute it. Laren stood and strode over to her, observing that Estora looked numb, not yet overcome by grief. None of it had sunk in for her yet.

"My father's body is but cooled and my cousin wants me married now," Lady Estora said, "while my intended still has a breath in him and is king."

Of course Spane would. Laren ground her teeth, but instead of speaking her opinion, she took the woman's hands into her own.

"My lady, I am so very sorry. What a terrible day you have had."

"It was quite wonderful until . . . until . . ."

Laren thought Estora might crumble then, but the young woman stiffened, maintaining her composure.

"I have come to see Zachary."

"Of course." Laren led Estora to his side and helped her settle into the chair. "He awoke briefly and spoke." She tried to sound hopeful.

"What did he say?"

Laren bit her lip. "Not a lot. My name. Nonsense, really. Destarion suggests speaking to him even if it appears he does not hear you."

She then withdrew, leaving Estora with her head bowed. When Laren stepped into the anteroom, she found Colin and Spane in heated discussion.

"I want her married immediately," Spane loudly demanded. "Lord Coutre would want it."

Laren strode right up to him and jabbed her finger at his chest. "You will take your argument elsewhere. This is not the time or place."

Spane's mouth gaped, then he said indignantly, "This is absolutely the time, and I will not be ordered about by some common messenger. Estora must marry before that man in there dies."

"He's not even conscious," Colin replied.

"It matters not. I've a moon priest waiting outside and I—"

"*Enough.*" The command in Laren's voice was unmistakable and both Colin and Spane stared at her. "That man in there needs peace to heal. You will shut up or I will escort you out of here myself."

"You will not speak to me in this manner. I do not take orders from you. It's rather the other way around."

Laren smiled. "*I* only take orders from the king. You are not *he.*"

Before he could open his mouth, she grabbed his wrist, wrenched it behind his back, and pushed him toward the door to the corridor.

"Get her off me!" Spane cried.

No one moved to aid him. The Weapons seemed to look on in approval, and Fastion opened the door to the corridor and said, much to Laren's relief, "I'll take it from here."

Laren closed the door behind them, but could still hear Spane spitting venom all the way. Her actions had not been politic and now she had acquired a powerful enemy, but it was well worth it if she brought Zachary some peace and quiet. It had certainly brought *her* satisfaction.

Colin touched her arm. "Wish I'd done that myself."

"He had it coming," Laren replied. "The man is a snake." She fantasized about putting her fist in his face.

"Snake or not, he represents the interests of Clan Coutre."

"More like his own interests," Laren muttered.

"Regardless, he was Lord Coutre's confidant and aide, and Lady Estora's chaperone. He has represented the clan here for several years and he is not without influence."

"He should not disturb Zachary."

"I do not dispute that, of course, but all our emotions are rather raw at the moment." Colin paused, as if gauging whether or not he should continue. Finally he said, "Lord Spane does have a point."

"What?"

"We don't know if Zachary named an heir in the Royal Trust, and if he did, we don't know who. We *do* know Lady Estora."

"Zachary is sensible and he's a scholar of history. I'm sure he named someone and it's a good choice."

"I'd expect nothing less of him," Colin said. "But it will still lead to bickering and infighting, which we can ill afford right now."

"I know," Laren replied. "But do you think the lord-governors will accept a deathbed marriage any more favorably than someone Zachary picked himself? Do you think they will readily accede power to an untried woman?"

"Untried? She's been trained to rule all her life and would be the next lady-governor of Coutre if not for the betrothal. She was born to lead, and Zachary's been very good about including her in all that concerns the realm. We'd make it a thoroughly legitimate marriage. At least that which is in our power. I'm sure we can find persons willing to testify they witnessed the, um . . ."

"The consummation," Laren snapped. "Are you listening to yourself? Zachary can't even speak for himself in the matter. It's . . . it's deceptive."

"Treasonous?"

"You said it, not me." Laren was beginning to feel light-headed from all the implications.

"It is an emergency," Colin said. "You know as well as I Birch is planning to make a move. Second Empire is out there collecting its forces. Who knows what will happen with Blackveil? We need a transition sooner rather than later, and we both know Lady Estora has Sacoridia's best interests at heart."

"Good gods," Laren said weakly. She stumbled to the nearest chair and Colin followed her. "Zachary can't even speak for himself in this."

"No, but who better to speak for him than us? Certainly not Lord Mirwell or Lord D'Ivary or Lord Wayman or any of the others. They will speak only in their own interests. Not for Zachary, not for the realm." Colin leaned over her. "Harborough is in favor, and he has the army to back him."

"You've been discussing this with others?"

"Yes. As soon as we heard the news, even before Lord Spane came to us."

"This . . . this is like a coup," Laren whispered.

Colin's expression was intense. She'd always seen him as professional and loyal, not as a schemer. The whole world had gone topsy-turvy.

"It's a wedding," he said. "One Zachary contracted for and intended to carry out. We're just moving up the date. If he survives, all the better. We can have another wedding for the benefit of all those who could not attend the first."

"I can't agree to this," Laren said. "Don't you think you should consult with Sperren first?"

"As you know he is presently indisposed, but I think over time I have come to understand his mind. I believe he'd be in favor."

"You do know my Riders will have to go to the lord-governors with the news of the king. I could certainly reveal your plan in the message they receive."

"That would only incite turmoil."

"Yes, but Colin, you know the nature of my special ability. I can judge the honesty of others, but the ability puts a burden on me and how I use the truth or falsehoods." She paused, thinking how she manipulated the truth to keep Zachary and Karigan apart. She closed her eyes and took a deep breath before continuing. "I cannot draw my Riders into such a deception. They survive because message recipients trust that the Riders are doing honest duty, not partaking of some political trickery. I will not involve my Riders in your scheme. They will bear only the truth."

"Would you consider delaying them?"

"No. That is another form of deception. Zachary would want the lord-governors notified as soon as possible. My Riders go out tonight."

Colin straightened, looking thoughtful, and suddenly he was once again the level-headed advisor she had worked with since he took over from his predecessor, Devon Wainwright. "You have made your position clear, Captain. You have given me much to think on." He drifted away to speak quietly with Destarion.

"Thank the gods." Laren was wrung out from the day's events. As if the life-threatening injury to Zachary was not enough, all the conspiracies had infected even one of the steadiest men she knew. He might be right about an early wedding alleviating some of the turmoil that awaited the announcement of the king's heir, but a deathbed wedding? It wouldn't help much.

Please don't let it be his deathbed, she thought. Tonight, after she sent her Riders out, she'd light a candle down in the castle's chapel of the moon. She had not done that in what, years?

"Captain?"

She looked up, and there was Destarion with a teacup in his hands. "Any change?"

"Not yet. Lady Estora still sits with him. I brewed some tea—thought we could all use some. It's been a trying day and I fear a long night ahead of us."

"Thank you," she said, accepting the cup and taking a sip.

Destarion smiled and made a small bow before stepping away.

Tea really was just the thing. The warmth of it soothed her. She wrapped her fingers around the cup and tried to relax as the menders came and went from Zachary's bedchamber.

She gazed about Zachary's dressing room. It was really a

well-appointed drawing room, with dark wood paneling and furniture upholstered in pliant leather. Paintings of ships on the sea hung on the walls, along with portraits of Zachary's beloved terriers. It was all very much *him* and she wondered what touches Estora would have brought to it, what life children could bring to the monarch's wing. She had little doubt Zachary would have made a wonderful father. The loss of what was, and what could be, threatened to drown her.

He was not dead yet, and damn it all to the five hells, he'd better not die and leave her here on her own, not after all they'd been through together. She finished the tea, thinking it was time she prepared the message that must go to the lord-governors before someone else concocted another scheme. She stood and the room spun.

"What . . . " She staggered trying to find balance. Her teacup smashed on the floor, and suddenly she noticed that no one else held one. Hadn't Destarion said he'd brewed everyone a cup?

The room tilted and she began to fall. The strong arms of Weapons caught her.

"Not feeling well, Captain?" Colin asked, suddenly standing before her.

"Dizzy," she mumbled. "Tired." Rather beyond tired. She was slipping away . . .

"It's been a hard day for us all," Colin said. "I'm sorry about this."

"*We're* sorry." It was Destarion standing next to Colin.

Her brain was muddled, but not that muddled and she fought against losing consciousness. "The tea! What have you . . ."

"Rest, Captain," Destarion said. "You'll feel better soon."

A vast darkness sucked the light from her eyes. Everything dimmed until there was nothing. Nothing at all.

IN THE BEST INTEREST OF THE REALM

Estora did not know how long she sat beside Zachary's bed, but the daylight that had poured so readily into his chamber earlier was now diminished. He did not awaken, did not speak.

Her desire to stay with and comfort her mother in the wake of her father's death had warred with her own need to be with Zachary, but her mother had urged her to go to her betrothed. And so here she was, where her heart told her she must be.

Here in the relative peace of Zachary's bedchamber was she able to grieve in solitude for her father. The mender said the wound had been so severe that they could not have saved him even if they'd been immediately upon the scene. She suspected the Rider-mender, Ben, could have saved him with his magic, but Zachary came first. That was the way of things.

With some surprise she realized with her father gone she was now the lady-governor of Coutre Province. If Zachary recovered and they married, the title would pass to her sister next in line, and Estora would become queen as planned. If Zachary did not survive, she would remain the lady-governor and return to Coutre to lead the province in its affairs.

She did not wish to return to Coutre. It was a revelation, but she'd become very fond of Zachary, his compassion, his courtesy, his strength. She'd also enjoyed learning about the challenges of running the realm, of trying to solve land disputes between farmers or ensuring troops were properly provisioned on the northern boundary. Day in and day out she witnessed Zachary dealing with cunning political minds.

He was as sharp, or sharper, than they, and she admired his intellect, loved how the problems stimulated her own mind. She especially enjoyed when they worked out the problems together, often discussing and analyzing them over tea after an exhausting day of meetings and audiences.

She supposed she could take on the same challenges in Coutre, but he, Zachary, would not be there. It would not be the same.

She gazed at him now wondering how anyone would want to harm him. He was a just king, a good man. He had endangered himself today to ensure she was not hurt by the assassin. He'd shielded her with his own body. If he hadn't, might he be safe now?

The Weapons intimated their initial investigation led them to believe both arrows had been intended for Zachary. Whether he shielded her or not, he likely would have been hit. Her father's death was an accident.

In the waning light, beads of sweat glistened on Zachary's brow where his silver fillet usually rested. He mumbled unintelligibly. Estora reached over and touched his cheek with the back of her hand. He was hot. She rose from her chair and hastened to the anteroom. There she found Master Destarion huddled in intense, hushed conversation with Colin, General Harborough, and her cousin. She wondered briefly where Captain Mapstone was.

"Master Destarion?"

The huddle broke apart and they all turned to her.

"Yes, my lady?"

"I believe he has a fever."

Destarion hurried into the bedchamber with his assistants on his heels. Estora intended to follow, but Colin called to her.

"My lady," he said, "may we have a word?"

"Yes, I suppose so."

Colin extended a hand to her and guided her to the nearest chair. "This has been a most difficult day, and as acting castellan, I wish to convey the realm's deepest condolences on the passing of your father. He was a good lord-governor and much loved by the people of Coutre, and I know all the eastern provinces looked to him for guidance."

Estora nodded, accepting his words for what they were.

"I've asked the royal death surgeons to care for your father's remains in accordance with your and your mother's wishes."

"Thank you." Having the royal death surgeons attend her father was a great honor. Their services were usually reserved for only the immediate members of the royal family, but now and then special personages were designated for their attention. Had Colin not offered their services, she and her mother would have had to contact a suitable undertaker in the noble quarter, which would have been very trying in the midst of their grief.

"We are most appreciative, Counselor Dovekey," Richmont told Colin. "Lord Coutre was a great man. Like a father to me."

Colin bowed. Then to Estora he said, "This has been doubly difficult for you, for now your betrothed lies injured within as well, and we do not know how it will go for him."

Estora began to wonder what Colin was leading up to, for she had never heard so many words from him at one time. She glanced at Richmont, his expression was eager, and she grew very suspicious. General Harborough stood off some paces watching the proceedings.

"You may as well come out with it," Estora said. "The lot of you obviously have something you wish to say."

Colin and Richmont exchanged glances, and then Colin explained. He told her how it was unclear whether or not Zachary had designated an heir, and they would only find out when the lord-governors all assembled and opened the Royal Trust, which contained certain state secrets and Zachary's will. Colin described the upheaval that could erupt between the lord-governors, especially if an heir was not named.

"It could be the Clan Wars all over again," Richmont interjected. "As when King Agates Sealender failed to name an heir before his death."

"It is why your betrothal to Zachary was so welcome,"

Colin said. "With a king paired with a queen, there is stability in governance knowing that children will be born to carry on the line unbroken. Unfortunately that stability is now at great risk, especially if there were to be infighting among lord-governors contesting the realm's leadership. There are enemies that would like to see Sacoridia weakened by it. The Hillanders brought unity to the provinces after the Clan Wars. It would be a disaster for it to dissolve."

Estora had no difficulty in surmising where all this was leading. "You wish to move the wedding up before . . . before Zachary dies."

"Yes, that is so. We would ensure its legitimacy, that it is indisputable you are our queen. Then, after the proper period of mourning, you may choose a husband of noble blood to join you in your rule."

"If Zachary lives," Estora said quietly, "I am not sure he'd be very pleased."

"We take the responsibility entirely upon ourselves though we may forfeit our freedom or our lives for it," Colin replied. "He will not blame you. I think in time he'd recognize we moved in the best interest of the realm."

"When do you propose to do this thing?"

"Immediately," Richmont said.

"*Immediately?*"

"The gravity of his wound dictates it," Colin said. "Destarion recommends sooner rather than later."

Estora's brain reeled. "Where is Captain Mapstone? I should like to hear her thoughts on this."

Colin shifted his stance, looked uneasy. "She took ill rather suddenly while you were in with Zachary. She's in the mending wing. I think she was . . . overcome."

Estora raised an eyebrow. Overcome? There was not anything that would easily overcome that Rider captain, nothing that would keep her away from Zachary in his need. Illness? Perhaps, but Estora was not so naive that she didn't know times such as these, with a monarch failing, were very perilous for all who surrounded him. She would see to the captain's welfare later.

"I should like to speak to my mother then."

"I will send for her," Richmont said. "She is aware of our proposal and seemed to approve."

Estora sighed. They had it all planned out.

As good as their word, they brought Lady Coutre to her, now a widow garbed in black, and left the two alone in Zachary's dressing room to speak in private. Estora's mother looked pale and severe in her mourning clothes, but stately with her shoulders held erect. Estora's parents had never met prior to their wedding day. Their coupling had been prearranged, a matter of alliances within the province. Despite being strangers to one another in the beginning, a deep fondness had developed between them. Estora recalled how her formidable mother never backed down from her father when he was in one of his blustery moods, and how she complemented his reign with her grace as the lady of Coutre Province.

"It is what I've prepared you for since you were a child," Lady Coutre said. "How to be a good wife to a nobleman of power."

"But the circumstances!"

Lady Coutre took Estora's hands, and suddenly she looked frail, scared, alone. "My dear, dear child, when we enter a marriage, we never know what will happen the next day. This morning when your father awoke from bed, he was robust, as healthy as I have ever seen him with a shine in his eyes and ready to challenge the world. By the afternoon, he was dead. Cold, so very cold.

"Tomorrow, Zachary may be gone, or he may not be. His fate is up to the gods, but it is clear to me he needs you more than ever to watch over him, and to watch over his realm. Who better to advocate on his behalf than the woman with whom he agreed to spend the rest of his life?"

They embraced and cried together, and Estora came to a decision.

The ceremony took place in Zachary's dimly lit bedchamber, the groom restless in some fevered dream beneath his sheets while an assistant mender applied cold, wet cloths to his forehead. The bride still wore her riding habit and mourning shawl. Someone had found dried flowers for her to hold since the ground was still much too cold for plant growth.

The castle's moon priest and a pair of his acolytes performed the ceremony, and it was witnessed by Lady Coutre, Estora's sisters, Richmont, Colin, General Harborough, Master Destarion, and the lord-mayor of Sacor City, who was accompanied by a law speaker. Four Weapons stood in the corners, both guardians and witnesses. Zachary's chamber was spacious, but it didn't feel so with such a crowd in it. Estora felt the absence of her father keenly and fought back tears. He should have been here.

The priest droned on about fidelity and companionship, love of the gods, love of family, and fertility. He tinkled a series of delicate silver bells each representing one of the seven virtues. They were supposed to exorcise past sins so the couple could enter marriage unencumbered and unbesmirched by the past. Estora was instructed to take Zachary's hand. It was hot and sweaty. Heavy.

"Do you pledge to the gods your love and fealty for Zachary our king?" the priest asked her.

"Yes."

A like question was asked of Zachary about her, but since he could not answer, Colin spoke for him.

"The rings," the priest said.

Colin produced the rings, both gold, both filigreed with an interlocking crescent moon design. Estora and Zachary had been measured for the rings months ago. She had not known their crafting was complete.

The priest sang over the rings, then asked Colin to slip Estora's on. He did, trembling as if he were the groom himself. Then Estora worked Zachary's ring onto his swollen finger.

"Zachary and Estora, you are wed. May the blessings of Aeryc and Aeryon be upon you now and forever."

Estora bent and kissed Zachary's unresponsive lips to seal the spiritual contract. There was no clapping, no jokes, no well-wishes called out to the bride and groom. One final rite would remain unfulfilled this night, the tradition of the bride coming to her husband's bed for the first time, the rite of consummation.

Those present paraded from the chamber like mourners to sign the legal contract of marriage awaiting them in the anteroom, proclaiming them witnesses to the event. Only Estora's mother and sisters paused to hug and kiss her. They also bent to kiss Zachary who was now son and brother to them by law.

When they were gone, Estora slumped into the chair beside Zachary and said, "I should like to hear what you'd have to say about the wedding being moved up by three months. I pray that I shall."

He did not respond. She took his hand again, the one with the ring, and pressed it to her face. "Please don't die," she whispered. "I'm not ready to do this on my own. Please don't die."

She'd already lost her first love, F'ryan Coblebay, to arrows. She was not sure she could endure another such loss again.

➳ THE LIGHTED PATH ➳

When Karigan's boots touched the ground on the Blackveil side of the wall, she felt as though she faced another wall, but this one of shifting mists that wafted between her companions, graying some of them out while exposing the others. Tree limbs reached out of the vapor, crooked, amorphous, adrift.

She was also met with a wall of silence. Her companions did not speak. The Eletians stood so still they could have been ancient statues of lost Argenthyne. Lynx bowed his head and covered his ears as if the quiet hurt them. The others peered into the forest, trying to see beyond the mist, their hands on the hilts of their swords.

"They smell of fear." Graelalea had come silently to stand beside Karigan.

"What about me?" Karigan asked. "Do I smell of fear, too?"

Graelalea did not respond, but Karigan could guess. As for the Eletians, their features remained stoic. Did they feel fear being in Blackveil? Despair? Outrage at what had become of their ancient land?

When Karigan glanced once more at Graelalea, she was startled to find a pair of tears gliding down the Eletian's cheeks. Karigan watched them plummet to the forest floor and splatter among the choked weeds and muck.

Sorrow, Karigan thought. *That is what they feel.*

Graelalea strode over to Lynx. She lifted his hands away from his ears and spoke quietly to him.

"I hear everything and nothing," he responded. "As though the world howls."

Graelalea said something more and Lynx nodded.

"I shall try it." He closed his eyes for several moments and his expression and posture relaxed. When his eyes flickered open, he said, "Yes, that worked. It's barely a murmur now."

"We must begin," Graelalea announced, and that was all it took for the company of twelve to fall in line. Grant abdicated the role of leader without, notably, a word of complaint, and Graelalea strode to the head of the line as if there'd never been any question.

They set off, keeping the wall beside them as they headed east. There was a road Karigan remembered—more from Alton's reports than her own experiences—that they must be traveling toward, an old Eletian road that intersected with the wall. They walked on in silence, Karigan in the middle of the line behind Yates and ahead of Ard. Yates glanced back at her with a grin, but it didn't look quite so jaunty now.

Karigan shifted the unfamiliar weight of her pack on her shoulders and grimaced at the stiffness of her infantry boots. She really should have tried to break them in more before now. She hoped they did not break *her* in first. Otherwise the walking cane the Weapons had given her would be needed for more than the occasional support. At the moment it remained strapped to her pack.

Thinking about her personal discomforts helped divert her from worrying about the greater threat of the forest, but not entirely. Sometimes she thought she caught the jostle of a branch that had nothing to do with wind, for there wasn't even a breeze. She heard the occasional *scurry-scurry* in the underbrush. In any other forest she'd have dismissed it as squirrels. Here? She hated to guess.

She felt the watchfulness of the forest, as if it had stopped everything to observe them. It was not the regard of a single unifying presence like Mornhavon, but on some level the forest was *aware*. It did not attack them, but reared up over them like a giant wave, hovering, waiting, inevitable. She wondered if the Eletians gave it pause, if their presence set it back. If it decided otherwise, what would happen if it stopped watching and came crashing down on them as all waves must?

They walked on, the mist revealing little about the time

of day, but making tendrils of hair cling to Karigan's face and leaving her clammy and chilled. She focused on the rise and fall of Yates' feet ahead. Ard's raspy breaths followed behind.

Karigan had no sense of how much time had passed when they halted. All she knew was that her shoulders ached and one of her heels was being rubbed raw by the boots. The damp air was acrid on her tongue.

They clustered around Graelalea. "We begin on what is called in the common tongue Avenue of Light."

Karigan glanced around but at first espied nothing that resembled a road, for the area around them was thick with undergrowth. However, when she looked harder, she discerned where the growth was a little less thick, the lines too regular to be natural. Her foot wobbled on a loose stone which was, on closer scrutiny, a sea-rounded cobble, one among many, the paving stones of a road.

"Not much light here no matter what it's called," Ard muttered.

No one disagreed.

"If we were to continue on this course along the wall," Graelalea said, "we would come to the Tower of the Heavens. But we shall take the road."

It was a pity, Karigan thought, they couldn't have all just entered the forest through the tower, but the soldiers and Ard, being neither Green Riders nor Eletians, would not have been able to pass through the walls.

They paused where they stood for several minutes while Yates made notations in a journal and Grant and Porter produced devices to take measurements of the road and its juxtaposition to the wall. When they finished, the company turned away from the wall and followed Graelalea down the road deeper into the forest. Karigan felt her last chance to run to safety slipping away.

It did not take long before Karigan decided to make use of her bonewood cane. She had no wish to twist an ankle on a loose cobblestone rolling underfoot. That they were slippery with slimy moss did not help. The stones clicked and clacked as the company made its way, and there were outbursts of swearing when someone tripped or slid. Rotting logs that had fallen across the road complicated matters, and they had to jump over gullies where the roadbed had been washed away. None of the Eletians made a sound.

In fact, Telagioth's sudden, silent presence beside Karigan took her aback. He said nothing but gazed hard at the bonewood. She stared back at him, at his cerulean eyes and effortless strides, but he did not speak. She could not contain herself.

"What is it?" she asked.

"Your walking stick," he replied. "It has an unusual quality about it."

"Would you care to take a closer look?" Karigan thrust it toward him in what she thought was an unthreatening manner but he skittered away.

"No, no," he said, raising his hands. "I am sure it will serve you well."

Karigan thought it a curious reaction. Maybe there was something to the Weapons' assertion about the bonewood after all, but she was hoping she would not have to be fending off Eletians in addition to whatever endangered her in the forest.

Despite Telagioth's caution, he still walked with her, so she asked, "What do the Eletians call the road? If Avenue of Light is its name in the common tongue, what is its Eletian name?"

"*Celes As'riel*. Avenue of Light is not a perfect translation. A better translation might be Star-lighted Path. Or just the Lighted Path."

"Celes As'riel," Karigan echoed. She liked how it rolled off her tongue, but it had sounded more musical coming from Telagioth.

"This road was made broader than any other in Argenthyne to accommodate travelers from the north, and perhaps that is why it is called 'avenue' in the common."

"I like the Eletian name better."

Telagioth smiled. He then spoke entirely in fluid Eletian, ending in a flourish with, *"Vien a lumeni Celes As'riel!"*

At his words light ignited along the edge of the road from behind tangled vegetation. Swords rang from sheaths and Grant and Porter charged toward it with shouts.

Roused by the commotion, Karigan extended her cane to staff length and took a defensive stance. Yates and Ard bared their swords. The Eletians simply looked on in amusement, especially when Grant's sword rang against what sounded like stone.

"Damn! I notched my blade!" He came back hacking away at vegetation.

The rest of them crowded to the side of the road and peered through brush only to come face-to-face with a statue. Carved of stone, one of her arms had broken off and weathering had scrubbed away much of her features, but her graceful lines remained beneath snaking vines and clinging black moss. She held in her remaining hand a large, cracked orb fogged by age and dirt through which light glowed.

"What is that thing?" Grant demanded.

"It is what you would call in your city a lamppost," Graelalea replied. "We call it *lumeni.*"

"But . . . but how did it light up?"

"Telagioth used the words of lighting. Such a command may have lit the lumeni for quite a distance, alerting, I fear, any and all to our presence."

Telagioth bowed his head. "Forgive me. I did not know after all this time the lumeni would light."

"No need to ask forgiveness," Graelalea replied. "The action was, perhaps, imprudent, but it is a joy to know Eletians have not been forgotten in this land. And why shouldn't Eletians walk proudly in their own realm instead of in secrecy?"

"Because the current residents are hungry," Lynx said, hand to his forehead. "And now they know exactly where we are."

⇒ HUMMINGBIRDS ⇐

"Imprudent?" Grant demanded of the Eletians. "You've let everything in the forest know we're here and it's just *imprudent?*"

"Your shouting," Graelalea replied, "will only serve to attract further attention."

"Oh, so you lower yourself to speak to me now?"

Karigan couldn't help but smile seeing someone else bridling at Graelalea's haughty ways. She turned away from the discussion, gazing down the road into the forest. She spotted the glow of another of the lumeni many yards away, on the opposite side of the road, its light ghostly in the mist.

Yates joined her. "Barely into this thing and they're already trying to start a war."

Behind them, the discussion had grown sharper, louder, with Lhean joining in with exhortations in Eletian, his derisive tone unmistakable.

"I hope not," Karigan replied. "We need each other to get through this."

"Look," Yates said, pointing.

Karigan heard it before she saw it, a buzzing sound like a bee. It was not a bee, however, but a hummingbird flitting in front of them, its rapid wing movements creating the drone. In the light of the lumeni, its green feathers shimmered with iridescence, a ruby patch at its throat. It looked just like the hummingbirds back home.

"I wonder if it's lost," she said. If creatures from Blackveil strayed into their world through the breach, then surely the reverse occurred as well.

"Look, another," Yates said.

A second darted at the first and chased it away. Karigan wondered what it was being territorial about since there were no flowers in sight. A nest or a mate, maybe?

As the hummingbirds zipped around the group, a third appeared and hovered in front of Yates' face.

"They're like little jewels," he said, mesmerized.

A blur of pearlescent motion, an Eletian moving faster than the eye could follow, swept his sword before them neatly slicing the bird in two in the air. The halves dropped to the ground. Karigan and Yates gazed in shock at what remained of the hummingbird, its blood trickling between the cobblestones.

"Five hells!" Yates exclaimed. "What did you do that for? It was a hummingbird!"

"You cannot trust anything here," the Eletian said. It was Spiney, the lumeni sparking a silvery glint in his eyes.

"But—" Yates began.

A droning grew in the forest around them, grew in a crescendo into a deafening roar that throbbed through Karigan's body. The limbs of trees vibrated with it, causing the collected rainwater to shower down on them.

"What is it?" Grant demanded.

"Prepare yourselves!" Graelalea cried.

A shimmering cloud of hummingbirds emerged from the woods and hovered around the company, their wings working furiously, the noise of it overwhelming. They skimmed overhead and darted between them. There were hundreds—no, thousands of them.

Ard screamed. Karigan whirled to see that a hummingbird had impaled his shoulder with its long beak, wings fluttering to drive deeper. Its throat pulsed as it drank, the ruby patch on its throat deepening to a dark crimson.

Graelalea swiftly yanked the bird out of Ard's shoulder and smashed it onto the road where it remained limp and unmoving, blood streaming from its beak.

"It is not nectar they seek," she said.

The hummingbirds attacked. Beaks pinged on Eletian armor and pinned Sacoridian flesh, yielding cries of pain. Swords flashed through the air and birds were cut down simply because there were so many of them. Otherwise they were too quick, their movements too erratic, to be fought off. Only the Eletians seemed able to cleave them out of the air with intention.

Karigan batted them away with her staff, but her efforts lagged in comparison to the sheer speed in which the birds maneuvered around her. She kept them off her, at least, and she was grateful her pack protected her back though it slowed her own movements.

Yates screamed. A hummingbird stabbed his thigh. She followed Graelalea's example and grabbed it out, its body nothing in her hand. It flicked a long thread of forked tongue at her and she smashed it onto the paving stones of the road.

She ducked just in time as another hummingbird soared for her eye. One jammed its beak into the leather of her boot. She kicked it off. Another scored the back of her hand, leaving a trail of blood.

Private Porter called out as he wobbled precariously on a loose cobble, his arms flailing. The cloud of hummingbirds paused as one, hovering, wings beating, waiting. Porter crashed to the ground, and before he could even attempt to rise, the hummingbird cloud swarmed him, a moving mass of green and silver and crimson blanketing him. He flailed and thrashed but could not dislodge the birds.

"Quickly!" Graelalea cried.

Several of the company fell to their knees beside Porter grabbing handfuls of feathers and beaks from his convulsing body, while Karigan and the others tried to bat away airborne birds around them. Porter's screams rang through the forest and curdled Karigan's blood to her toes.

Soon the screams weakened, and then stopped entirely. The swarm of birds lifted away, slow and ungainly with engorged bellies, and flew back into the woods. Karigan turned away from Porter's gruesome remains.

"The life is gone from him," Graelalea announced. "He should be put to rest in whatever manner your customs dictate."

"What of those birds?" Ard demanded. He bled from numerous wounds. "What if they come back?"

"They shall not return. Not for the time being, for they are sated."

Porter's cloak was laid over his body, and a cairn of loose cobblestones pulled from the roadbed was raised over him. Meanwhile, the Eletians, who escaped the ordeal largely unscathed, tended the wounds of the Sacoridians with their evaleoren salve. Karigan's mind eased as the Eletian woman Hana spread the fragrant salve into the wound on her hand. Compared to her companions, Karigan had fared well.

Once the wounds were treated and the cairn finished, Grant stabbed Porter's sword into the earth near where his right hand would be and mumbled a few halting words asking the gods to receive the good private into the heavens. When he finished, the Sacoridians made the sign of the crescent moon while the Eletians looked on as curious bystanders.

While Grant took time to sort through Porter's belongings, discarding most things but keeping tools essential to the mission, Karigan gazed away from the grave and down the road. She had hardly known Porter, but did not doubt he was a good, brave man. Otherwise he would not have been chosen for the expedition. His fate could have just as easily been hers or Yates'—any of theirs. It still could be.

She picked dainty iridescent feathers from her clothes. *Hummingbirds,* she thought with a shake of her head. She'd expected confrontations with one of the other horrid creatures that dwelled in the forest, but hummingbirds? She would never regard them in the same light again, even on her own side of the wall.

When wings flashed in the branches above, she thought that despite Graelalea's reassurance, the birds had come back for another attack.

⋘ OWL ⋙

The wings that brushed the air, however, were large and white, nothing at all like a tiny hummingbird. When the winter owl settled on a limb and tucked its wings to its sides, it looked like a clump of snow until it swiveled its head to gaze at its surroundings. Karigan realized she was squinting at the owl. The white of its plumage was so stark in the gloom of the forest that it hurt her eyes.

The others came beside her to look at it as well.

"Where are your arrows?" Grant demanded of the Eletians. "We should kill it."

"No." Graelalea replied. "It is not a forest denizen, and of no danger to us."

"How do you know? Those other birds looked harmless enough until . . ." His sharp gesture took in Porter's cairn and the hummingbird corpses littering the road.

"I know this owl is not of this forest, and that is enough."

"She's right," Lynx murmured. His eyes were closed in concentration. "It's from the other side of the wall. Besides, it would not retain its snowy plumage in this forest."

"I saw one yesterday," Karigan said, "when I went out for a ride. What would it be doing here? Is it lost?"

"Lost? I do not think so," Graelalea replied. "It is not here by accident. Such owls are revered in Eletia." She stroked one of the white feathers braided into her hair. A light shone in her eyes. "We call the winter owl *enmorial,* memory."

The owl preened, looking entirely at home in the dark woods. It paid them little heed, as if they were beneath its notice.

"Why memory?" Karigan asked.

"Memory is what it keeps."

Karigan sighed. It was a typical Eletian response.

The owl spread its wings and launched from its limb, circling around their heads and winding down in a glide until it alighted on Graelalea's outstretched wrist, its talons doing her no harm because of her armor. She and the owl gazed at one another for a long moment, before it lifted once more into the air. They watched it vanish above the trees and into the mist, a lone white feather twirling down back to Earth as the only proof it had been real.

Graelalea caught the feather before it could touch the ground and smiled. "Memory," she said, and she tucked the feather into one of her braids.

They left behind Porter's grave and trudged on along the road, the damp air thickening into a pervasive drizzle that *drip-drip-dripped* through the trees of the forest and onto their hoods. The gloom and the loss of Porter dragged down Karigan's spirits. She could not help wondering who would be next. Who would be the next one for whom the rest built a cairn.

Only the occasional lumeni broke the spell of darkness, welcome beacons along their path. Few lumeni still held globes in their stone hands, but those that retained even a shard cast at least a little light, and that light seemed to brighten as the Eletians passed near them.

As they approached another of the lumeni, liquid light splashed across the mossy cobbles before them, and Ard sourly muttered, "Magic."

Karigan thought the light beautiful and was glad something like the lumeni could endure in the forest for so many centuries, and she tried to imagine a different time, a different forest, when Eletians ruled this land, traveling this road freely and without fear.

"Magic?" Telagioth asked. "They collected light of sun and moon and stars. The lumeni would have been brilliant in the time before the Cataclysm."

"He means the Long War," Karigan said in response to Ard's perplexed expression.

"Oh," Ard replied. "Well, magic is magic, and you can see what good has come of it." He swept his arm to take in the whole of the forest.

"An outside influence," Telagioth said. "This land existed in light and harmony for many millennia before the coming of Arcosians. If you could see Eletia, you would understand."

"Eletia is nothing compared to what Argenthyne once was." This from Spiney, who came forward to join their conversation. He spoke as if he knew, as if he'd once tread Argenthyne's ways during the lighter times before Mornhavon.

"I suppose I'd like to at least see your Eletia, then," Ard said.

"You would not find your way in," Spiney replied. "No mortal has been permitted beneath Eletia's canopy for centuries, though some have tried." He gazed at Karigan, a glint in his eye. "The last mortal to travel within Eletia was a Green Rider. It is still spoken of in the Alluvium." With that pronouncement, he dropped back to walk in the rear with Hana.

Before Karigan could ask Telagioth *who,* he also left them and strode to the front to walk with Graelalea. Much Green Rider history had been forgotten over the years and so she liked it when she could find out more about the messengers who had come before her. Perhaps she could ask Telagioth more later.

They continued on until the gloom grew into impenetrable dark. Graelalea chose to camp on the road beside a headless lumeni, its light aiding them as they pitched tents and built a fire. The tent of the Eletians was a dark, mottled gray, and it blended so well with the environs that Karigan thought she'd fall over it if she didn't know exactly where it was. It also seemed too small a tent for six people.

"How they all going to fit in that?" Ard asked.

"Don't know how they do it," Yates replied, "but when they camped outside Sacor City last summer, their tents held a lot more than you'd think possible. That's what I heard anyway."

Graelalea told the company not to stray far, probably an unnecessary warning with the forbidding forest all around them. Everyone stuck close to the light of the campfire and lumeni as they ate their rations and prepared for the night.

Karigan was assigned first watch with the Eletian Solan. When everyone else turned in, Solan stood unmoving on the very fringe of light, gazing into the night in the direction from which they'd come. Karigan sat with her back to the dwindling campfire, her staff across her lap, and gazed in the opposite direction, down the road they had yet to travel.

Now that the company had come to such stillness, the sounds of the forest grew louder, the clacking of bare tree limbs and the patter of water spilled from branches, the wild screeches of creatures near and far. During her time as a Rider she had spent many a night alone in the wilderness, but the sounds of those nights had been more subdued, held less of an edge to them. Those nights had not been so black.

Being on watch was almost laughable, because she could not see anything beyond their light. Would something come upon them before she could warn the others? Another cloud of hummingbirds, or something even worse? She squeezed her fingers around the smooth wood of her staff. All of her old worries and problems now seemed far off. She did not dwell on Alton and Estral, and not even on King Zachary.

When she was younger and read *The Adventures of Gilan Wylloland*, she'd dreamed of a hero like Gilan coming to her rescue, sweeping her away on his magnificent war horse.

Stupid, she thought with a bitter edge. *Little girl dreams.*

How many times had she fought her own way out of trouble? No one was going to rescue her. Certainly not King Zachary, and not just because she was currently out of reach. Even when she was within his reach, she was, so to speak, out of reach.

She had only herself to rely on and as pretty as the little girl dreams were, it was time to dispose of them. Perhaps it was the forest that inspired such bleak thoughts that dampened hope. She did not care. After Porter's random and bizarre death, those old dreams lacked the weight they once held. Maybe if she left the forest alive she'd care again, but for the time being, survival was the priority. No hero to sweep her away from danger. Just herself.

She sighed. For all the darkness of her thoughts, it left her feeling somehow at peace to acknowledge what was true and what was not.

Footsteps announced the arrival of Lieutenant Grant wrapped in his cloak, his face shadowed by his hood.

"You can go to sleep, Rider. I'll take the rest of your watch."

"Sir?"

"It's all right. I can't sleep. The damned dripping—it's driving me mad. Go along now, you're excused."

"Thank you, sir."

Karigan stood and retreated to the tent she shared with Yates.

Dripping? she wondered as she ducked through the tent flaps. Yes, there were the ever-present drops on canvas, but it didn't bother her. Now Yates' snoring? That was something else.

Not to mention the occasional bloodcurdling scream of some creature meeting its end deep in the forest.

They survived the night. Those on watch reported creatures scuffling and snuffling through the woods, but nothing had come too close. Dawn arrived as another soggy, gray day and camp was swiftly packed up.

Karigan didn't think any of the Sacoridians had slept well, except maybe Yates, who snored his way through the night. Between his snoring and the rocks rammed into her back, Karigan certainly hadn't. As for the others, pouches sagged beneath Lynx's eyes, and she wondered if the voices of the forest had infiltrated his dreams. Ard looked surly and threw his gear around as if he'd like to break something. A haggard Grant kept scratching his arm and muttering to himself about the dripping.

Once everyone was ready, they set off down the road, their mood subdued, no one engaging in chatter. Nothing threatened them as they walked along, though Karigan felt as if their every movement was observed by malevolent eyes.

They paused only for a meal at midday, and when they finished, Graelalea announced, "Here we shall depart the road."

"What?" Grant demanded. "What do you mean we depart the road?"

"You don't expect us to bushwhack through this forest, do you?" Ard added.

The idea of leaving the road dismayed Karigan, too, but she withheld her protest, waiting to hear Graelalea's explanation.

"There were once paths, not just roads, that Eletians used

to travel this land. If you knew our roads, you would realize they are not ... efficient. Think of your main thoroughfare in Sacor City. Is it the most direct route to the castle?"

"No," Grant admitted. "There are shortcuts."

"Though our roads were not made to slow an invading army as your Winding Way was, the result is the same. So I seek to shorten our journey by another path."

"I see. And what will this path lead us to?"

"The heart of Argenthyne."

Her pronouncement was met by silence.

"On the path," she continued, "it is even more imperative we do not stray. The forest shall attempt to mislead us, I think, but it may be the land is not entirely opposed to Eletians."

They were not consoling words.

Karigan saw no path leading from the road, but without further explanation or hesitation, Graelalea stepped into the woods, followed swiftly by the other Eletians.

"Wait!" Grant cried. "We need to survey this for the map."

"We have paused here long enough," Graelalea replied.

"Our mission is to map and—"

"That is *your* mission. Eletians need no maps. You may stay and strike out on your own if you wish, or you may come with us."

The Sacoridians waited for Grant's decision while he stood on the road cursing the Eletians, the gods, and the dripping water. Meanwhile the Eletians disappeared deeper and deeper into the woods. Finally he plunged in after them, much to Karigan's relief, and no doubt to that of the others. She was pretty sure they did not stand a chance in the forest without the Eletians.

They thrashed through brush and branches, tripping over roots as they went, likely sounding like a pack of charging bears, until they saw the flash of white armor between the trees. When they caught up, Solan, who was last in line, cast them a smile. It was more than clear the Eletians possessed the upper hand in Blackveil. Any pretensions Grant once held about being in charge of the expedition were dashed long ago.

No words were exchanged as the Sacoridians followed.

One advantage, Karigan decided, to having others ahead was that they cleared the path, though some branches still swung back at her from Yates' passage. The trail they trod, though not easily visible beneath layers of loam and mud that sucked at their boots, was more level than the adjacent forest floor. Now and then there were hints of stonework—crumbling retaining walls and flat stones on the treadway—not entirely obscured by moss.

But here the forest felt closer, shouldering in and bearing down on them, the air stagnant, almost suffocating with wet rot. Brambles grabbed at trousers and sleeves. Yates stumbled to the ground and Karigan almost tripped over him. She helped him rise and he kicked at an arching tree root in the path.

"It tripped me on purpose," he declared, and he stepped around it, hurrying to catch up with Grant.

Karigan tapped the root with her walking cane. Was it her imagination, or did it shrink away from the touch of bonewood? Perhaps Yates had not been exaggerating. She hurried on, taking especial care to watch her footing.

Despite the chill, perspiration trickled down her face. The Eletians maintained a punishing pace, and she was grateful when they halted, until she found out why.

"Be silent," came Graelalea's order down the line.

A screech pealed out overhead. Karigan's toes curled in her boots. Eletian arrows nocked to bows tracked something overhead obscured by fog and trees. Another cry and the perception of vast wings beating the air. Water poured off branches.

It must be, Karigan thought, a flying creature, like the one that had crossed the breach last summer. An Eletian arrow sang and somewhere beyond their cloudy ceiling was impact and a screech that turned into a wail. The creature crashed through tree limbs as it fell to Earth somewhere beyond their sight.

"Good aim," Yates said.

"A large target," Solan replied. "An *anteshey*. It was hunting us."

And just like that, they were off again. Off again and not

stopping until the gloom deepened toward dusk once more. The Sacoridians staggered to a halt behind the Eletians in a slightly more flat and open space. There was stonework underfoot where not covered by black moss, and as Karigan took her bearings, she realized they were on a plateau of sorts with the far side giving way to a valley. She could only guess at its depth because of the fog. Granite steps descended into it, fading away as though leading into a different world.

Ard, who was the oldest among the Sacoridians, was bent double, still trying to catch his breath. He was very fit, but the pace had knocked the wind from them all.

"You trying to kill us?" he asked Graelalea.

"We made acceptable progress today."

"Acceptable?"

Graelalea made no reply.

Lynx spoke quietly to Ard who nodded and said, "I'm all right. Thanks."

Karigan slid her backpack to the ground and dropped down next to Yates whose legs were sprawled out before him.

"This must be one of the five hells," he said.

"Told you," Karigan replied half-heartedly, too tired to be smug.

"Don't sit around too much," Grant warned them, "or your muscles will cramp."

He was right, of course, but Karigan could not bear the thought of standing on her feet again. They hurt unto numbness, and she had no idea what the blisters were doing. She'd beg Hana for some evaleoren salve before bed.

"I'll get up if you do," Yates said.

"Right."

Neither of them moved, until clouds of biters found them and it became a feeding frenzy. They leaped up cursing and slathered on priddle cream from a tub Lynx passed them. The stuff stank, but it helped keep off the ravenous insects.

By the time Karigan and Yates finished raising their tent, someone had gotten a smoky campfire burning. Dark descended quickly, seeming to smother the fire. Without lumeni to give them light, night fell more densely than ever, until a couple of the Eletians produced their moonstones. The dark then peeled away from their campsite, and when Karigan gazed upward, she swore the trees recoiled from the light as if it burned them, the mist carrying the light like swirling smoke. Karigan did not pull out her own moonstone—she did not need to with the others alight. Idly she wondered when last a moonstone had shone in the forest.

"Ai!" cried Solan who knelt near the rim of the terrace, where the stone steps began their descent into the valley.

While the others gathered around Solan to see what the commotion was about, Yates stayed where he was.

"Tell me if it's something that'll eat us and then I'll move," he told Karigan.

She shook her head and joined the others. Solan was peeling back layers of moss from the terrace and wiping away dirt. Worms and centipedes squirmed away from the light. What Solan revealed were crystalline stars embedded into the flat terrace stone. They glittered brilliantly even beneath a film of grime. Further digging revealed a tree crowned by the phases of the moon.

"What is it?" Grant asked.

"It is a piece of time," Graelalea replied.

"You mean a time piece, like a sundial."

"More a moondial," Karigan murmured and Grant glanced sharply at her.

"I mean a piece of time," Graelalea said. "The Galadheon is somewhat correct, that the time is kept by the moon, though there is no moonlight to reach this one and it is missing its gnomon. It would have been placed here by the folk of Telavalieth whose village once lay down below."

Curiosity got the better of Yates and he managed to rouse himself enough to come over, journal in hand. He deftly copied the design, ink bleeding on the damp paper. Solan cleared more moss, but there was no more to be seen. Eventually they all broke away to attend to camp duties and eat supper.

Later, when Karigan crawled into the dark confines of her tent, she detected Yates there still scratching away in his journal.

"Do you want a light?" she asked him, thinking her own moonstone could be of use.

"Nope."

"Ah." He was using his special ability to see in the dark. Now that she thought of it, he'd be able to see everything if she changed into the big shirt she liked to sleep in.

The scritch of pen on paper paused, and as if Yates knew her thoughts exactly, he said, "No need to blush. It's not as if you have something I haven't seen many times before. Not that I don't enjoy it every time . . ."

Karigan's cheeks burned and Yates chuckled.

"You and your conquests," she muttered.

"And you are one of my greatest challenges, impervious to all my charm and good looks. You are like an ocean that cannot be crossed, a mountain that can't be climbed, a—*oof!*"

Karigan had slugged him in the shoulder. She assumed it was his shoulder. It was hard to tell in the dark. In any case, she found it immensely satisfying.

"Now move over," she ordered, "you're hogging all the space."

When he complied, she crawled into her bedroll.

"What? You aren't going to change?"

"No," she replied. "I'm on second watch, so why bother?"

"Such a disappointment," Yates said with a *tsk, tsk.* "But we will have many more nights together to—"

She kicked him, but this time it just made him laugh.

It was so strange, she thought, to hear laughter. It was as if once they entered the forest, and especially after Porter's grim death, such a thing as laughter could not exist here.

"Do you suppose," he asked after some moments, "the Eletians sleep in their armor?"

For that she had no answer—she wasn't even sure if Eletians slept, but she joined Yates in his laughter, eventually falling asleep feeling much lighter than she had since entering the forest.

≈ A PIECE OF TIME ≈

Karigan awoke with a grunt and a jerk, caught in a dream where a black tree root had snaked from the ground and grabbed her foot. She cried out.

"Karigan," Lynx whispered, reaching through the tent opening and shaking her foot.

She groaned, tatters of dream lifting from her. It must be time for her to go on watch. She unwrapped herself from her tangled bedroll, then backed out of the tent dragging her saber with her.

"It's been relatively quiet," Lynx said.

Their meager campfire, and the glow of two moonstones, accented the craggy lines of his face. Something wailed in the forest's depths.

"Like I said, *relatively* quiet." Lynx gave her a grim smile before heading for his own tent.

The moonstones belonged to Lhean and Spiney. Lhean strode around the terrace, looking out into the night, obviously on watch. Spiney stood motionless, gazing at the moondial. The light reflected from the crystalline engravings flared up around his feet like white fire.

Karigan shook off the last residue of sleep and approached Spiney. He still did not move, did not even seem to blink. A statue he was in his white armor.

When she stood beside him, the moondial looked no different than before.

"The forest does not permit the moon to shine here," Spiney said unexpectedly. "No matter the phase. Without it we cannot experience a piece of time."

"And your muna'riel is not enough."

"It contains a moonbeam, not the moon." He lowered his moonstone and placed it in a pouch on his swordbelt. Darkness draped them. As Karigan blinked to adjust to the change, the Eletian left her.

Karigan fingered her own moonstone in her pocket. She had yet to reveal it to the darkness of Blackveil, and wishing to take a closer look at the moondial herself, she did so now, wondering if her mother could have ever imagined it would be used here, in this the forest of darkest legend. Its light flooded the terrace, and once more the moondial glistened.

Her chest cramped beneath her Rider brooch. She gasped and doubled over in pain, clenching the brooch. Shafts of light beamed up from the moondial, trapping her like the bars of a cage, and the world blurred and changed around her. There was the Blackveil as she left it and the tents of her companions, but layered over it was another forest; the forest before it became Blackveil, smelling of green life, with the stars shining above.

There was smoke.

The valley bloomed with gold and orange fire, smoke pluming into the sky—or was it just the mist of Blackveil's present?

Screams of the past came to her even as some creature in the present screeched. Ghostly figures ran up the stairs onto the terrace, which appeared as pristine as if the stone had just been laid, and yet, in the doubling of her vision, it was blanketed by the taint of time and neglect.

The people ran in terror, crying, carrying children, shepherding and supporting the wounded. Eletians.

Who else would it be? This was Argenthyne. And it was Blackveil.

Hulking figures swarmed the terrace after them, their guttural war cries assaulted Karigan's ears. Arrows flew from their bows. Eletians fell. The groundmites gave chase like a pack of feral dogs driven mad by the scent of blood.

Others—not groundmites, but men—climbed up the terrace at a more leisurely pace behind them. Karigan recognized the crimson and black uniforms of the Arcosians and among them was a power. She could feel it emanate from *him* from across the ages. He was black cloaked and black hooded.

Peripherally she heard Lhean calling to her. He sounded so far away.

The one with power looked at her, *saw* her. He lowered his hood, watched her with eyes blackened by wild magic. His striking face with its strong cheekbones and chin, the curl of raven hair. *Mornhavon.*

She would know him anywhere. She had borne his consciousness in her body across time, and that power—it was like a wall slamming into her.

Others began calling for her, telling her to come back . . .

Mornhavon smiled. Reached toward her with his crimson-gloved hand.

The cramping of her brooch turned into a dagger twist. She cried, fell to her knees, and her moonstone rolled from her grasp. The light died and Karigan was absorbed into the darkness of her mind.

A tumult of voices penetrated the dark.

"What in five hells just happened?" Grant demanded.

"A piece of time," Graelalea replied.

"She nearly crossed into it," Spiney added.

Karigan kept her eyes closed. *Not again.* It was not the first time she had surpassed the ages, but she'd had wild magic running in her veins then, and now it was supposed to be gone from her. *How?* she wondered.

"How could she do such a thing?" Ard asked, echoing her thought. "It's mad."

A vision of light came to Karigan, and of lips murmuring, *You cross thresholds.* It blurred away as quickly as it had come.

"I cannot say," Graelalea replied. There was a note in her voice, barely perceived, that Karigan took to mean that Graelalea knew very well how such a thing could happen, but she was not allowed or able to say more, or simply did not wish to.

Figures, Karigan thought. There were never firm answers

where Eletians were concerned. There were no absolutes in their world. A terrible headache pounded at her temple, and she was so very cold. Just like the last time she'd traveled.

She squirmed, realizing her head was cradled in someone's lap. She squinted her eyes open and saw Yates' concerned face over hers.

"Karigan?"

"I'm fine." her voice sounded dull to herself. "Just cold."

"Stoke up the fire," Graelalea told someone, "and bring blankets." She spoke rapidly in Eletian, then knelt beside Karigan. "You were caught between the two times. If you'd crossed over, I am not sure you could have come back."

"Mornhavon was there. He reached for me."

Graelalea sat back, her eyes wide and frightened. "Then we came closer to losing you than I thought."

Karigan felt Yates go rigid. "What were you doing mucking about with Mornhavon?" His words came as a shout.

"I wasn't doing anything. It just happened."

"The piece of time is only supposed to allow one to view a moment," Graelalea murmured. "But you who have crossed through the layers of the world before should be more wary."

Karigan wanted to protest, but she was just too tired. Graelalea then pressed a cool sphere into her hand and light flickered. Her moonstone.

"You do not want to lose this," the Eletian said quietly.

Karigan was bundled in blankets and helped to the fireside. She shuddered as she looked into the flames.

"What is it?" Yates asked.

"I saw the people who lived here running for their lives from groundmites. The valley was burning."

Graelalea knelt down beside her. "Yes. It was the way many settlements ended when Mornhavon invaded Argenthyne. Here." She handed Karigan a silver flask. "A couple of sips and you should feel much better."

It was a warming cordial that flooded her veins to her very toes and fingertips, chasing away the chill brought on by the passage through vast amounts of time. After her second sip, she felt much more herself, the headache miraculously gone, though the traveling had left a dark imprint in her mind.

"Thank you," she said, returning the flask to Graelalea.

"You faded out," Yates told her. "You were a ... a ghost. And we could see faint images moving around you, like the mist taking shape. And the light your moonstone raised—I still can't see right." He rubbed his eyes.

Karigan just gazed into the fire unable to speak, overwhelmed by it all. She'd seen the destruction of Telavalieth centuries ago, and Mornhavon.

Someone stood between her and the fire. Karigan looked up. it was Spiney. He squinted down at her as if trying to see *into* her. "There are those in Eletia who believe you are dangerous," he said. "They are not mistaken." He turned abruptly on his heel and walked away.

He was not the only one giving her odd looks. From across the fire, Ard studied her while absently whittling a stick. When he realized she'd caught him watching, he averted his gaze.

"Rider," Grant said, "I'll take the rest of your watch. You should probably rest after whatever the hells that was."

With the dark rings beneath his eyes and the hollowness to his cheeks, Karigan did not think she was the one requiring rest, but she did not argue. She slipped into her tent, relieved just to escape the scrutiny of her companions.

❧ TELAVALIETH ❧

Mornhavon the Black had climbed these very stairs. Karigan had seen it. She'd been there. He'd stepped onto the terrace and reached for her. Even in the dawn of the morning after, as she gazed down at the stairway that descended into the fog of the valley, the incident was still so real, so present, she could almost feel Mornhavon's touch on her flesh. She shuddered.

With one last glance at the moondial, she followed Yates down the stairs, backtracking Mornhavon's own footsteps.

Blackveil was as dismal this day as those preceding it, but it darkened even more as they left the high ground and entered the fog of the valley. The stones that made the steps were either naturally level or hand carved, but covered with the sopping mosses and lichens that made everything so slick. Some rattled when stepped upon. A few were missing entirely, lost somewhere down the slope, forcing the company to scramble to the next solid step, their feet sending loose scree cascading into the valley.

There were several switchbacks, but the continual descent made Karigan's knees ache, so she relied on her bonewood staff to buffer the impact of each downward step she took.

Yates stumbled ahead of her.

"You all right?" she asked him.

He only grunted in response.

Karigan thought about lending him her staff when he paused a few times as if to gauge how to proceed to the next step. He'd then continue, but tentatively, clinging to trees as he went down, or leaning into boulders alongside the stairway. His hesitation caused some grumbling from those waiting behind.

As they neared the bottom, the fog created a false dusk, but Karigan perceived a change in the terrain. The stairs meandered through a field of vast boulders, which must have tumbled down the slope in some long ago time, for they were well settled and blanketed by deep moss. Ferns the size of small trees protruded between the boulders, their blotched and blackened leaflets sutured together with the strands of spiderwebs. Wiry beards of lichen draped down from the branches above, which those ahead slashed out of their path. It was as if they entered an ever more primeval world.

"Thank the gods," Yates muttered when they finally reached level ground. Karigan was relieved herself.

Graelalea did not pause to give them a rest, however. They continued along a path that was more mud and ooze than anything else, the ferns rising around them like a forest. Soon they came to a sludgy stream and followed its bank for a while. Pitcher plants grew alongside it, but not the normal sized, diminutive ones Karigan was accustomed to. These, like the ferns, were oversized vessels the size of wine casks.

One of the pitcher plants quivered. The hind legs of some mammal, like a hare, kicked over the lips of the carnivorous plant, unable to free itself. Karigan looked away, sickened.

"You know," Ard said, "it all sort of works."

"What does?" she asked.

"The forest. It is in balance with itself, the predators and the prey. Even the plants have adapted to it."

"You're saying the forest is healthy?"

"It's a twisted place for certain," Ard replied, "yet it is in balance with itself. Perhaps in time it would come to resemble more of what we're familiar with on our side of the wall."

As long as Mornhavon doesn't come back, Karigan thought.

"The balance is wrong on both sides of the wall," Spiney said from the end of the line. "All the etherea trapped here, and barely any on the other side. This is not balance."

"What d'ya want then?" Ard asked acerbically. "To knock down the wall?"

They waited for Spiney's answer. Karigan knew it was exactly what some Eletians wanted, possibly including Spiney, who had once tried to kill her for, in his opinion, interfering with the wall. The Eletian, however, did not respond.

Graelalea halted, and before them was a delicate span that crossed the stream. To Karigan's eyes the arch was almost paper thin, entirely unlike any other bridge she'd ever seen, without voissoires or keystone, without spandrel or abutment walls, just the treadway, impossible and eloquent in its simplicity. It was carpeted and draped with moss so it was impossible to see how it was made, but if it was stone, it surpassed even the legendary craft of the D'Yers.

"Telavalieth lies across the stream," Graelalea said. "Or what remains of it." Without another word, she stepped onto the bridge.

Karigan expected the bridge, fragile as it looked and subject to the ravages of centuries, to collapse, but it did not. The rest of them followed, and when Karigan reached the apex of the arch, she was glad the bridge still stood, for she would not have liked crossing through the stream. It was murky and stank of rot, and several glistening snakelike *somethings* slurped in the stagnant water. She hastened the rest of the way to the opposite bank.

"What do you suppose that was in the water?" she whispered to Yates.

"I didn't see anything," he replied with a frown.

They trudged onward and soon Karigan discerned an opening before them, a lighter shade of gray. The Eletians took off at a run. The Sacoridians hesitated for but a moment, then pursued the Eletians. When they reached a clearing they halted. It was as if something had come in and scraped the forest floor to its bedrock. Nothing grew there, not even the pervasive moss and lichens, even though the clearing did not look recent. In fact, the rock was smooth as though melted and fused. What kind of power could do that to granite?

On the edges of the clearing stood crumbling buildings wrapped in tree roots as if the very trees were intent upon crushing them little by little over the passage of years.

"Gods," Ard muttered.

Spiney fell to his knees and loosed a keening wail that rocked Karigan backward. The other Eletians bowed their heads. Everything in the woods stilled.

"What is it?" Grant demanded.

"Telavalieth had a small grove for its Sleepers," Lhean answered. "We are standing in it."

"Sleepers? What do you mean Sleepers? And what grove? What happened to it?"

"When our folk tire of the waking world, they leave it for the long sleep and become the hearts of great trees until they are ready for the world again."

Karigan remembered the Eletian prince Jametari explaining it to her. If she lived an endless life like the Eletians, she imagined she'd want a respite as well.

"Your people turn into trees?" Grant was incredulous.

"No," Lhean said with an edge of annoyance to his voice.

By now Spiney lay prone on the ground. He did not shake with tears. He made no sound.

"Lhean," Karigan said quietly, and pointed. "Is he all right?"

"Ealdaen is of Argenthyne. It may be he knew one who dwelled here."

Ealdaen. So Spiney had a name, and if he was of Argenthyne, then he must have fled before Mornhavon's invasion a millennium ago . . .

"What happened to this grove?" Ard asked.

Spiney—Ealdaen—rose to his feet and turned his searing gaze upon Ard. *"Mornhavon seak mortes."* Then he strode off.

Ard scratched his head. "What did he say?"

"'Mornhavon killed it,'" Karigan replied, surprised to hear the words coming from her own mouth.

Everyone looked sharply at her.

"I didn't know you spoke Eletian," Grant accused.

"I . . . I don't. His tone said it. And the evidence is beneath our feet."

"She is correct," Graelalea said, pointing at fused stone. "Mornhavon destroyed the grove with his power, and enough so that it would never again take root."

"That is not all he did," Lynx said quietly, gazing at the ruins in the forest.

They took their midday rest in the clearing, a few of them peering into nearby ruins. It was not easy to discern the original appearance of the structures for it was as if they'd become part of the trees themselves, absorbed by sinuous, snaking roots. Architectural details of stonework and sculpture remained, though most of it was badly damaged.

Karigan wandered toward the ruins as well, but paused to gaze back at Yates, who sat alone in the center of the clearing, staring at his knees. He'd become oddly quiet. Something was eating at him. If it kept up, she'd shake it out of him later.

A glint through the window of a nearby building caught her eye. She peered inside, but it was all shadow and stank of mildew. Curious as to what lay in the shadows, she drew out her moonstone. Instantly light filled the interior and she caught her breath, for on the opposite wall a mosaic flickered with life, a scene of a young maiden with a garland of flowers in her hair and her lover reaching for her. The backdrop was of a summer forest in all its shades of green with the azure sky above. Karigan's eyes feasted on the colors after the dullness of Blackveil.

The artist had captured a story in motion, a moment in time, the light of Karigan's moonstone rippling over the shining pieces of the mosaic making birds in emerald green and sapphire blue seem to fly; a deer in the distance looked back at her as if pausing just before bounding off into the forest. Would the maiden rebuff her lover, or would she fall into his arms for a kiss? Was their love destined or forbidden? Karigan wondered if the mosaic depicted a scene from some tale of Argenthyne, or if it portrayed the inhabitants of this . . .

Yes, a house, Karigan thought. Whatever furnishings had once existed in the room had rotted away long ago, but beneath the dirt and dust on the floor was intricate tile work. She could not discern the designs, but they seemed to weave together in a way that made her think of music.

She closed her eyes and could almost hear the music. It flowed like water, sounds of laughter, and Eletian voices.

When she opened her eyes, the moonstone still illuminated the room and she thought she saw filmy figures swirling in motes of dust in some lost dance.

But no, it was just the play of light on shadows in a place long abandoned and the whining of biters in her ears. What had happened to the occupants of this house? Had they been destroyed by Mornhavon's forces?

There was a cry and Karigan tore herself away from the window to see what was the matter. The others ran to Hana who was looking through a doorway into another building. She did not appear to be in any danger, but Karigan ran anyway, and when she peered over Ard's shoulder to see what everyone else was looking at, she reeled away rubbing her eyes.

Skulls. Skulls piled high to the ceiling.

She dared look in again. They filled the room from corner to corner, the bones matted with moss and darkened by ... soot? Striations scarred them, the gnawing of rodents. Gaping black eye sockets, empty, soulless. The people of Telavalieth.

There was no tale left for the beautiful maiden and her lover. Not here. None would know their story. They were all dead.

The Eletians huddled together and Solan sang, his voice pure, the sound of rain. The sorrow wrenched Karigan inside.

A tentative touch on her arm. She turned. It was Yates.

"What—" he began. "What is wrong here?"

"Look inside," she replied, "and you'll understand."

Yates shifted his stance, his expression uncharacteristically fearful, his gaze fixed somewhere past her shoulder.

Now alarmed, she asked, "Yates? Are you all right?"

"I can't look inside," he said, passing his hand over his eyes. "I can hardly see." He squinted. "It's gone now. My sight. I'm blind."

⋙ ROOTS ⋘

Karigan waved her hand in front of Yates' face, but he didn't even blink. She placed her hands on his cheeks and turned his head so she could look directly into his eyes, searching for any sign of injury, but she saw nothing.

"Do your eyes hurt?" she asked.

"No," he replied.

"Then how has this happened?"

"I—" He swept his hand through his hair. "I don't know. Started last night. Got worse today and now . . ." He gave a shuddering exhalation. "Karigan," he whispered, "I'm scared."

So was she. Yates stumbling blind in Blackveil decreased his chances of survival immensely, and would slow down the company.

She grabbed his hands and squeezed. "We'll figure this out, Yates. Maybe the Eletians know what—"

A clattering came from inside the building with the skulls. Karigan gazed in—they all did. A huge snakelike tentacle serpentined among the skulls, pausing here and there as if to finger the air.

"Oh, gods," Grant murmured.

It reared, sending several skulls clacking down the pile, then lunged through the doorway at them. They leaped back, Karigan tugging Yates after her.

"What is it?" he asked.

"A creature or . . ." It looked, insanely, like one of the tree roots.

Hissing grew around them, rumbling through the ruins,

tree branches quivering. More and more of the tendrils rippled to life—they *were* tree roots. They roiled out of the shadows and slithered toward them like thousands of snakes.

"We must go," Graelalea said. "Now!"

Even as they turned to flee, a root lashed out and wound around Hana. She screamed. The Eletians leaped to with swords to hack at the root, but it snatched her through the air and into the woods and out of sight in the blink of an eye. Her screams trailed behind her until they abruptly stopped.

"Hana!" Lhean cried. He surged after her, but Ealdaen and Telagioth caught him and spoke rapidly to him in Eletian.

Then to the rest, Graelalea shouted, "Follow me! Run!"

"What's going on?" Yates demanded.

Karigan grabbed his arm and hauled him out of the way as a root whipped out at them. Everyone broke into a run for the center of the clearing.

Roots swarmed the ruins, crushing walls and remnants of roofs. They exploded from the building of the skulls, the skulls pouring out through broken walls. They smashed through the house with the mosaic and Karigan thought of the maiden and her lover shattered into millions of tiny, sparkling pieces.

The roots surged across the clearing after the company, hissing against bare rock.

The companions grabbed their packs at a run, Karigan still pulling the stumbling Yates behind her, following at the end of the line as Graelalea plunged into the forest on the opposite side of the clearing. One glance back revealed writhing roots rippling across the clearing after them. The ruins, which had abided the centuries in quiescence, had been pulverized in mere moments.

"My pack," Yates said. "We need to go back for my pack."

"No," Karigan replied, sickened by the image of those roiling, fingering roots and the loss of Hana. "We can't go back."

She struggled to keep Lynx in sight, but Yates constantly tripped and fell. He could not move fast enough. Dragging him behind her and trying to keep him on his feet exhausted her. When he fell, more often than not he wrenched her down with him, and desperate to keep up with the others, she'd lunge back to her feet and help Yates to rise, and then urge him on.

The others were almost lost to her ahead.

"Lynx!" she cried. She was met with only the silence of the forest and the fading footsteps of her companions.

"Lynx!"

Then there was nothing but her own harsh breathing and the drizzle folding down on them.

Karigan yanked Yates after her and hastened through underbrush and branches in the direction she'd last seen the company, her heart pounding.

"Slow down, I—"

"We can't!" she snapped. "We're losing them." She did not say aloud that she thought they were already lost.

Yates bravely tried to keep up, but there were too many roots and rocks tripping him and he was again a force holding her back. She halted, her ragged breaths steaming the air. As she stood there and gazed at the sameness of the trees, she did not see or hear any sign of the company, and she had no idea which way they'd gone.

"Why are we stopping?" Yates asked.

She heard the fear in his voice.

"Because," she replied, turning to face him, "we are—" Something snagged her right leg, and when she looked down, she saw she'd stepped into a tangle of thorny brambles. The thorns, which were hooked and as long as her thumb, had slashed through her trousers and raked her flesh like claws. It felt like a swarm of bees stinging her leg.

"Damn," she muttered, pain pitching her voice high. She fought the urge to thrash out of the brambles knowing it would only entangle her further.

"What?" Yates demanded. "What in all the hells is going on?"

"Don't take another step," she told him. He'd stopped short, she saw with relief, of walking into the brambles. "I'm stuck in a thorn bush."

Carefully she pried away the grasping brambles from her leg, but they seemed determined to cling to her. Finally she drew her long knife and cut them away. The canes oozed a yellow ichor she hoped was not poisonous.

It seemed to take forever to free her leg, sweat streaming down her face, the pain of the stabbing thorns sending chills through her body. Finally when she was able to step clear of the bush, her leg buckled and she fell to her knee with a grunt.

"Karigan?" Yates asked. "You all right?"

"Help me up."

He extended his hand and she leveraged herself back to a standing position. The stinging pain spread through her leg again, but it held her weight. She removed the bonewood from her pack and leaned on it.

"I think we need to set up camp here," she said.

"What about the others?"

"They're gone. We got left behind and I don't know if I can locate their trail again. It's best if we stay where we are so they can come find us." She wondered if they'd even try, recalling how they had not gone after Hana. She closed her eyes and shuddered.

Whether or not the others sought them out, Karigan needed someplace to sit and remove the rest of the thorns from her leg. She could not go far like this.

She limped away from the thorn brambles, towing Yates behind her and keeping close watch for any other dangers. Of course if a flock of hummingbirds descended on them, there wouldn't be much she could do about it.

"Damn my sight," Yates said. "We're lost in Blackveil and it's all my fault."

"No," Karigan said heavily. "It's not your fault. It's the forest. It's probably affected your ability, warped it." Their Rider abilities had been considered an asset for sending them into Blackveil, but now those very abilities were working against them. Perhaps they should have known better. After all, when the wild magic of the forest had leaked into Sacoridia last summer, it had wrought havoc with their abilities. Was that why she was able to travel back in time last night?

"If I hadn't been so eager to come, we wouldn't be lost. You would be with the rest of them."

Karigan shrugged, then remembering he couldn't see her, she laid her hand on his shoulder. "We can't say what could have been. We'll make the best of this, and I'm sure the others will come looking for us." But of course she was not.

He gave a rattling sigh and slumped his shoulders.

"Oh, Yates." She wrapped her arms around him and squeezed hard. "We're Green Riders. We've been through worse."

"I don't know," he said. Then smiling slightly, he added, "Maybe you have."

Karigan lowered her pack off her shoulder and sat at the base of a tree she thought looked safe enough to begin working the thorns out of her leg. She wasn't sure she'd been through worse, either. Tears of pain welled in her eyes and she tried not to cry out so she didn't worry Yates.

Yates sat beside her. "What are we going to do about a camp?"

"Camp?" She pried out another thorn, its barbs tearing out flesh with it. She swallowed back the pain.

"Yeah, since our tent was with my pack."

She hadn't thought about it. As if to mock her, the drizzle turned into pouring rain. It at least washed away some of the blood.

"Well?" Yates asked.

"I guess we make a shelter." She knew there was no *we*. Without his sight, Yates was not going to be able to provide much help.

Karigan tentatively rose, grimacing as she placed weight on her right leg. "I'm going to go look for sticks. Stay here."

"Don't—don't leave me!" He sounded so desperate.

"I'm not going far. You'll be in my view the whole time."

Yates huddled his knees to his chest looking miserable. Karigan limped off, leaning on her bonewood cane and using it to tap sticks on the ground. Most simply crumbled apart revealing writhing insects and worms. She'd have to hack branches off trees. She returned to Yates.

"That you, Karigan?" he asked.

"Yep."

"Is there something you're not telling me? You sound different. Like you're not moving right."

Karigan picked through her pack for her hatchet. "So now you claim your hearing is that good?"

"Well, if I can't see, I can focus on my hearing."

"I got poked by thorns is all. Aha!" Hatchet now in hand she turned to their tree, gazing at it with trepidation. Might she disturb something dangerous, even deadly, by hacking into it? She shrugged. They needed sticks for their shelter, and that was that. She swung the hatchet, chopping at the lowest branches, which were bare of needles. She hoped for the best—that she wouldn't dislodge any creatures that lived among the branches, or that the tree wouldn't awaken and retaliate against them in some way.

When nothing happened and Karigan had acquired the desired limbs, she sighed in relief. Sometimes a tree was just a tree.

"If only I had some twine," she muttered.

"I've a ball of string," Yates said, "for measuring. Would that help?" Despite losing his pack in Telavalieth, he'd retained the old message satchel slung over his shoulder that held his journal and writing materials. He felt around inside it and pulled out a ball of string.

Karigan laughed. "I knew I brought you along for a reason."

"For my string and not my good looks obviously."

"Obviously."

She used the string to bind the branches into the rough frame of a lean-to, and covered it with her oilskin cloak. She placed it at the base of their tree, the tree shielding them from the worst pounding of the rain. They had to huddle close together to fit beneath the lean-to.

"I don't think I'll ever be dry again," Yates said. "I wish we had Mara here to light a fire."

"I wouldn't wish this on her," Karigan replied, "or any of the others. And if Blackveil is warping Rider abilities, I can't imagine what it would do to hers."

"Burn the forest down maybe," Yates said. "Wouldn't be such a bad thing."

Karigan wrapped one of her blankets around the both of them. It, too, was damp, but she thought it might help insulate them from the chill. They leaned together, their combined body heat helping.

She knew she needed to apply some priddle cream to her thorn punctures, something she ought to have done immediately, but getting the shelter up had seemed more important at the time. She also thought about their food supply. She'd have to share what remained in her pack with Yates, breaking it into half-rations, because there was no telling when or if the others would come for them.

The gray and damp oppressed her more than ever. She wondered how things were back in Sacor City, at the castle. Was the weather fair there? What was Mara up to? The new Riders? She closed her eyes and tried to imagine the pasture full of messenger horses, but all she saw was shadows.

She missed Condor, her little room in the Rider wing, and Ghost Kitty. And she missed . . .

She bit her lip. The king was probably going about his daily business not even thinking about them—her. He walked in the sunlit world and she ached to join him there.

"Do you think we're going to get out of this?" Yates asked.

"I don't know," Karigan replied. "I really don't know, but I hope so." If for no other reason than she could once more look upon her king.

⋙ WATCHERS ⋘

The groundmites leaped and danced around Grandmother and her retainers, fur flying. They "sang" in grunts and yips and waved spears around their heads. Some wore the skins of other animals, but most wore nothing at all, teats and male parts peeping out from beneath matted fur. Grandmother thought to cover Lala's eyes, but she couldn't do so forever. It would not be long before the girl grew curious about such things anyway. Hiding it from her would not protect her; only delay her coming of age.

Sarat clung to Grandmother's arm and whimpered. "They're going to eat us!"

"I do not believe so," Grandmother replied. "They are simply welcoming us."

After the burning of the gift of entrails, several male groundmites had stepped out of the woods, thus revealing themselves as the Watchers who had followed Grandmother's little group for so long. They had gestured for Grandmother and her people to follow them. Though they carried spears and clubs, they were not used in a threatening manner. Since they were continuing down the road in the direction Grandmother had intended to travel, she decided to accept their "invitation."

After much wearisome walking, their escorts brought them off the road to this, their village, or habitation, or whatever groundmites considered their collection of dens, really nothing more than mounds of dirt with entry holes.

The creatures carried on their dancing for quite some time. Then suddenly they stopped and a portion of the circle opened to admit a small groundmite with a humped back. She wore skins draped around her waist, her teats hanging slack to her belly. Animal bones had been knotted into her gray-striated fur. Though stooped by age, she carried herself with dignity. She gazed up at Grandmother with one rheumy eye. The other was missing.

It was clear by the way the others regarded the groundmite that she was a leader among them.

"Ugly little beast," Deglin muttered.

"They all are," Cole replied. "Smell worse than a pack of wet dogs."

"Hush," Min snapped. "You aren't smelling too good yourselves."

The old groundmite issued some unintelligible proclamation to Grandmother. When she finished, all Grandmother could think to say was, "Thank you."

All the groundmites stared silently as if expecting more. She licked her lips. "We are descendents of Arcosia," she said. "Of Mornhavon the Great's people." She pulled out the pendant of the dead tree.

The old groundmite's one eye widened in recognition. She babbled excitedly and the rest started carrying on again. They brought Grandmother gifts of bone necklaces and raw meat. It was good to know the creatures still honored the empire. Their ancestors had served Mornhavon in battle.

How, she wondered, might she get these groundmites to serve *her*?

The old groundmite patted her chest. "Gubba," she declared. "Gubba."

"What's she saying?" Deglin asked.

"I think it's what she is called," Grandmother replied. She pointed at the groundmite. "Gubba." Then she rested her hand on her chest. "Grandmother."

Gubba caught on immediately and mimicked Grandmother and pointed at her. "Grrrnmudda." Then pointed to herself. "Gubba."

Once the names were settled, Gubba pulled on Grandmother's sleeve, leading her toward one of the dirt mounds.

"Grandmother!" Sarat cried.

Grandmother glanced back. Groundmites blocked her people from following, anxiety on each of their faces, except Lala's. "Be patient," she told them. "I will come to no harm." She would not, she knew. This Gubba had welcomed them, felt that Grandmother was her equal. It did not mean Grandmother held any desire to crawl into the hole, but etiquette seemed to require it.

Gubba dropped to all fours, and despite her age, crawled agilely into the mound. Grandmother had no choice but to follow. She slowly lowered herself to her knees and crawled into the mound, dragging her yarn basket with her.

Inside, Grandmother was assaulted by the rank stench of piss and wet fur and damp dirt. Plant roots dangled through the domed, earthen ceiling, which was alive with crawlies. Gubba snatched a writhing centipede from overhead, popped it into her mouth, and mashed it with her gums. After swallowing, she peeled her lips back in a sort of smile. She was missing many teeth, but yellowed canines remained.

A clay cup filled with clotted fat made a crude lamp, the sooty smoke rancid. A woven reed mat covered the floor and Gubba gestured for Grandmother to sit. Not that Grandmother had much of a choice for the ceiling was low and the insects not far from her hair.

As her eyes adjusted to the muted light of Gubba's den, she espied gnawed bones strewn about the floor, the movements of more crawlies in the dark recesses, and a jumbled heap of . . . objects. Objects that required a second glance. They were metal, she was sure of it. Some looked like the rusted shards of swords, a pile of nails, pieces of armor, but the other bits were beyond her ken. Jointed pieces that had been made for movement, springs, and tubes—were these artifacts from Arcosia? The chronicles of her people claimed her ancestors had been uncommonly clever artificers.

Gubba raised her lamp, shifting shadows and revealing one section of wall covered with primitive paintings in soot and a red ocher substance. Dried blood? She could not say. The images were handprints, fearsome creatures, spirals, and abstract patterns, and in the midst of it all, the dead tree of Second Empire.

Certain Grandmother had taken in the tree, Gubba set the lamp down and removed a pouch from her belt, and emptied tiny bones into her clawed hand. She breathed on them, then tossed them onto the mat before her. She leaned over them as though studying their pattern.

So, Grandmother thought, *Gubba fancies herself a fortune-teller.* Grandmother did not hold stock with such cheap tricks and found herself vaguely disappointed by the display.

Gubba wiggled her fingers. The bones vibrated, then lifted from the mat to float between them. Grandmother reassessed her opinion. This was the art. Gubba had some command of etherea after all.

Gubba chittered, her gaze intently following the bones. Then with a distinct, "Oooh," she watched for a few more intense moments before allowing the bones to gently settle on the mat. She turned her eye on Grandmother, then pointed at the yarn basket.

Grandmother took it to mean Gubba desired some similar show of power. She picked through her yarn. She had no way to replenish her diminishing skeins and had taken to being very careful with what she had left. Some minor demonstration with a small knot would have to suffice. She would create a flower from flame.

She gestured if it was all right for her to borrow the lamp, and Gubba gave her a very human nod. Grandmother rapidly tied a simple knot, one of the first she had learned at her mother's knee, and dropped it into the flame.

A flower did not bloom as she expected, but the trunk of a tree sprouted from the cup and grew and grew and grew until it was immense, followed by more and more until she and Gubba sat in the illusion of a vast forest of ancient trees.

"The grove," Grandmother murmured in awe. "It must be." With the perversity that was Blackveil, the etherea had once again warped her intention, but this time with a magnificent result. Gubba's eye was wide as she took in the trees.

Then a voice thundered, "FIND THE GROVE." Gubba's den vibrated with the voice of God. Crawlies fell out of the ceiling.

Gubba shrieked and Grandmother bowed her head. "Yes, my lord," she whispered.

"FIND THE GROVE BEFORE THE OTHERS."

"The others?"

"AWAKEN THE SLEEPERS!"

The illusion faded and all was as before. Gubba reached a shaking hand over to Grandmother. "Gubba *scurrit* Grrrn-mudda. Gubba *scurrit* Grrrnmudda *ock* Sleeprrrs." She walked her fingers on the mat.

Grandmother emerged from Gubba's den elated. God had not forsaken them, and if she interpreted Gubba's gibberish correctly, the old groundmite was going to lead them to the grove of the Sleepers. Absently she plucked a twitchy insect out of her hair. Her people came to her, touching and patting her to ensure she was all right, their anxious expressions relaxing to relief.

"All is well," she told them. "Gubba is going to take us to the Sleepers, and they shall be awakened as God wills."

But doubt niggled at her. Who were these "others" who also sought the Sleepers? They must be the disturbance that she'd sensed in the forest. Then there was that music that had become an undercurrent in the etherea, like an itch she could not scratch. It could destroy everything she was working for by strengthening the wall, closing off Blackveil once again.

As if trying to survive the forest wasn't difficult enough, she now faced dangers on two additional fronts.

She hugged Lala and held her close. She would do whatever it took, sacrifice whatever she must, to accomplish her task. Second Empire depended on it.

RETURN TO TOWER
OF THE EARTH

"We should have told her right away," Estral said.

Alton sat at the table in Tower of the Heavens staring morosely at the books piled atop it. Estral stood at the other end, hands on hips. If he didn't feel bad enough about how things had gone with Karigan, he'd done the one thing he surely wished to avoid: upset Karigan's best friend. They'd been having this same discussion since the morning of the company's departure.

"I was waiting for the right moment."

"There is no right moment for that sort of thing," Estral retorted. "You—"

Dale suddenly emerged through the tower wall. She took one look at the two of them and backed right out.

"Oh, forget it," Estral said, fresh tears dampening her cheeks. "That may be the last time we ever see Karigan, and she left angry and feeling betrayed. Because of us." She turned on her heel and left the tower.

"I tried . . ." he mumbled. He supposed he ought to run after her to comfort her, but the last time he'd made an attempt she'd pushed him away. Perhaps he needed to try harder? He just didn't know the right thing to do.

"Tried what?"

Alton squawked and jumped out of his chair. *Merdigen.* It was Merdigen standing silently behind him. He placed his hand over his thudding heart.

"Can't you give a man some warning?" he demanded.

"You mean you want me to knock before entering my own domicile?"

"Yes."

"Not very likely." Merdigen conjured a chair for himself and settled down arranging his robes just so. "What did I miss while I was away? Anything new?"

Relieved to have an excuse not to run after Estral, Alton sank back into his own chair and told Merdigen all about the arrival and departure of the expedition.

"I should have dearly liked to have spoken with the Eletians," Merdigen said. "And seen Sir Karigan again. It's bad luck I missed them." He brightened upon learning Alton had sent the additional Riders on to the other towers.

"That is wonderful news," Merdigen said. "My fellow tower mages will be most delighted, and it should prove useful as well."

"And what did you and the others decide about Tower of the Earth?"

"After numerous arguments and discussions, with some breaks for ale—Booreemadhe is a very good brewer—we concluded that Tower of the Earth must be entered. By you and me. It's the only way to get answers."

"What?" Alton said. "You tried getting in there before, but couldn't."

"Very true. I took the long route that time and found too many broken bridges. But, there is one other possibility, my boy. It is not the safest approach, but it is the *only* one that remains to us."

"And what would that be?"

Merdigen looked distinctly uneasy. "You must carry the tempes stone to Tower of the Earth."

Alton, Estral, and Dale set out for Tower of the Earth the following morning, a raw, gray day hinting at the rain to come. He needed Estral because her singing would allow him to pass through the tower wall, and he needed Dale so she could provide a buffer against Estral's emotions. Also in case something untoward befell him.

Swaddled in a blanket deep in one of his saddlebags was

the tempes stone. Alton had not known the stone could be removed from its pedestal, but it lifted from the depression that cradled it with no resistance. It was heavy and smooth in his hands, rather like an oversized egg of green tourmaline. The whole time Alton held the stone and packed it, Merdigen fretted and chewed on his fingernails.

"Don't drop it! Don't drop it!" he told Alton. "If it chips or cracks—no! I can't even think it."

"Calm down," Alton said, "I'll take good care of it."

Merdigen stared at him with an intensity Alton hadn't witnessed before. "It is not just a pretty stone you've got there, boy, it's what allows me to exist. It contains my essence, who I am. My knowledge, everything."

Alton had swallowed hard, finally comprehending the significance of what he held wrapped in the blanket. "I swear to you, Merdigen, I'll see that the stone remains unharmed."

Merdigen nodded. "You do that, boy." And then resigned to his fate, he vanished, and that was the last Alton had heard from him.

Merdigen was willing to risk his very existence to see the condition of Tower of the Earth. He'd put his trust in Alton to deliver him safely, and Alton hoped it wasn't misplaced.

As if picking up on his thoughts as they plodded at a walk to rest the horses, Dale said, "Do you think Merdigen can tell he's riding in a saddlebag, or is he just asleep until he gets to the tower?"

Alton smiled. At least Dale talked to him. Estral remained silent and gloomy and he missed her melodious voice and laughter with unexpected intensity.

"You'll have to ask Merdigen yourself," he replied, "because I have no idea."

"I will never understand these tower mages," Dale said, "or what they are, exactly."

"Magical spirits," Estral said. "Like those in the wall, but manifested as individuals."

Dale and Alton gawked at her, but she rode on as if she hadn't said anything extraordinary. That she spoke at all was startling enough.

"Merdigen said something like that before," Dale commented. "But is a magical spirit a living soul?"

This time Estral appeared deep in thought and did not respond. Alton could only shrug. It sounded like a question for a moon priest. They picked up their pace to a trot. There was still a way to go yet.

It was drizzling by the time they reached the tower and they immediately tended to the horses and set up camp. Estral stowed her gear in Dale's tent and Alton sighed at the prospect of another night alone.

Afterward the three stood together beneath the deepening sky with their hoods drawn.

"Might as well get started," Alton said.

"I will not expose my lute to the rain," Estral said.

"I'm sure if you play it in the tent it won't offend the guardians any," he replied.

She only nodded, the hood obscuring her expression.

"Are you sure you don't want me to go in with you?" Dale asked. "You need someone to watch your back for that . . . that thing in there."

"It will be easier for me to shield just myself from the tower defenses. And I need you out here. In case anything goes wrong. If I'm not back out in, say, a couple hours, go to Garth in Tower of the Trees. If something happens to me, there is a chance Merdigen is fine. He may find a way to communicate with Mad Leaf, but from what he says about broken bridges, it doesn't seem likely."

They stood in dismal silence for many moments staring at the tower.

"I guess I'll go then," he said. But before he was two steps away, Estral grabbed him and hugged him.

"You will come back," she said fiercely.

He wrapped his arms around her and pressed his cheek into her hair. "I'll be back soon."

"Good. I'll play for hours if need be." She pulled away and glowered at him. "I don't need to lose you, too." And she strode toward her tent.

"Karigan will come back," he murmured.

"Karigan can take care of herself," Dale said. "You, I'm less sure of."

"Thanks."

She flashed him a smile. "Ready?"

"As ready as I'll ever be."

He walked toward the tower without looking back, the tempes stone still wrapped in its blanket and tucked in the crook of his arm. By the time he reached the wall, the familiar notes of the wall guardians' song drifted to him from Estral's lute.

He tugged on the hilt of his saber to ensure it would easily clear the scabbard if needed, took a deep breath, and entered Tower of the Earth.

\approx 'WARE THE SLEEPER \approx

As soon as Alton emerged into the tower chamber, he called upon his special ability to shield him. He was just in time as lightning forked down on him, the force knocking him to his knees. His nostrils flared at the charged air; he felt his hair rise. He remained absolutely still—more out of mortal fear than discipline—and the magic lightning dissipated. For a moment. He needed to get the tempes stone to the center of the chamber. Merdigen said it did not need to be placed on the pedestal, but it needed to be within the circle of columns.

Alton shifted his eyes, peering into the gloomy heights of the tower. He discerned no movement, no hint of the creature's presence, but he knew it was there clinging to the shadows. He knew it must be watching him.

There was no use in delaying the inevitable. The sooner he delivered the tempes stone, the sooner he could leave the tower. He checked his shield once more, then sprinted. Lightning slammed into his shield and sizzled on the stone floor all around him. Each step brought a new discharge of power trying to blast him from existence. One jolt hit him so hard it knocked the tempes stone from his hands. He fumbled with it, the blanket that was supposed to protect it hampering his grasp.

"No!" Alton cried. He saw in his mind's eye the green stone striking the floor and splintering into pieces.

As it tumbled from his fingers and plummeted, he dove after it and caught it—caught it soundly. His heart hammered in his chest and he closed his eyes briefly, taking a deep breath. He'd almost lost Merdigen!

He leaped the rest of the way between a pair of columns and fell into the center of the chamber, thudding to the floor beside the skeleton. Once again, as he stilled, the lightning ceased.

Like the other towers, passing between the columns seemed to transport him to some other place. But wherever this other place was and whatever it had once been, it was now a burned out ruin of blackened, seared ground and dark murky sky. Nothing lived here, not even a speck of grass. Nothing. It was a shadow land.

Alton moved carefully so as not to spark the tower's defenses again, making a nest of the blanket and resting the tempes stone on it. Its fiery green glow sparkled with its own inner fire, adding living light to the desolation all around. He wondered if Merdigen would know he'd almost been dropped. Alton hoped not because he'd never hear the end of it.

"Tsk, tsk," the mage said, materializing next to the pedestal and looking down on Alton. "Quite a disaster in here."

"What do you think happened?" Alton asked.

"Give me a few minutes to look around." Merdigen circled the pedestal with Haurris' sickly tempes stone upon it, and then gazed down at the skeleton. He muttered to himself and shook his head.

Alton tried to lie as still as possible, but naturally he had an itch below his left shoulder he was dying to scratch. Resisting the impulse made his eyes water. It did not help he was face-to-face with the skull. He wished Merdigen would hurry up.

"Sad, very sad," Merdigen murmured.

Alton watched out the corner of his eye as Merdigen moved beyond the columns to explore the tower chamber at large.

Where was the creature thing? he wondered. He tried to focus—to listen for stealthy movements—but he only heard Merdigen clucking to himself. All else was silence. There wasn't even a touch of a breeze in the scorched landscape he lay in. The air was stagnant, acrid.

"Are you almost done?" Alton demanded.

"These things take time," Merdigen said. He returned to the center of the chamber and gazed once again at the tempes stone, stroking his beard. "I believe the skeletal remains to be Haurris'. How he came to such an end is impossible to know. Unless . . ."

"Unless what?"

"Unless he managed to leave a trace in his tempes stone, but from the looks of it, that's not very likely. The spells about the chamber definitely have Haurris' signature, both the barrier that prevented you from entering the tower the first time, and the defensive spells. I'm beginning to think he also destroyed the bridges that prevented me from coming here in the fall."

"To what end?" Alton demanded. "Why would he want to keep us out?"

"Not just keep us out," Merdigen replied, "but to trap something within."

Alton shuddered. "Can you see it? The creature?"

"No, I cannot. If it is here, it is remaining utterly still in the shadows. Amazing that it has survived Haurris' defenses. And for how long, I wonder."

"What now?"

"I am going to take one more look around to make sure I'm not missing anything," Merdigen replied. "Then we are going to return to my tower with Haurris' tempes stone."

Alton's breath of relief raised a puff of sooty dust. He was pleased Merdigen did not insist they remain in the tower to complete his investigation of what had happened here.

Merdigen wandered away, weaving between the columns, looking up, looking down. He then returned and gazed at the skeleton.

"I would that we could collect his bones for a proper pyre," Merdigen murmured. "But I suppose they are safe enough where they are for now."

"Does that mean you are ready to go?"

"It does."

Alton checked his shields once again and rose. The lightning descended on him and he gritted his teeth. Though it did not touch him, the power of it battered him, threatening to knock him down again.

"Fascinating," Merdigen said.

It was not the word Alton would have used, but he needed to focus on what he was doing and maintain his shield. He reached for Haurris' dingy tempes stone, and at his touch a ghostly figure sputtered to life, a bent, ancient man with a long bristling beard.

" 'Ware the Sleeper," it intoned.

"Haurris!" Merdigen cried.

The figure did not acknowledge him. It flickered, and repeated, " 'Ware the Sleeper."

Alton lifted the stone from the pedestal and the figure vanished.

"I hope there's more than—" Merdigen began.

A screech shattered the still air and out of nowhere something fell from high above and collided with Alton knocking the stone out of his hands. He heard it clatter onto the floor and Merdigen's wail, but he was busy defending himself from claws slashing through his shields. Lightning ripped overhead.

The creature bowled him over and he fought to keep it at arm's length as he worked to strengthen his shields. It was hard to concentrate with that wild and savage thing— all bones and sinew—snarling and lashing at him, seemingly impervious to the lightning that struck at it.

Alton threw it off him, rolled, and staggered to his feet. Before the creature could pounce on him again, he grasped the hilt of his sword.

"No!" Merdigen cried, but too late.

Alton drew the sword. A bolt of lightning flash-blinded him and struck him off his feet. He tossed his sword away from him and lay there stunned, thinking that if not for his shielding, all that would remain of him would be a smoking pile of cinders. Then the creature was on him again, hissing and digging through his weakened shields for his neck.

They rolled on the floor. Rolled over the skeleton of Haurris, bones snapping beneath Alton's back. He heaved the creature off him once more and rose to his knees, breathing hard. His hands were covered in blood—his own, he thought. The creature crouched, ready to spring on him again. Alton could make out little of its features, except for its spidery limbs and glowing green eyes.

The creature launched at him. Alton grabbed a broken thigh bone and plunged the sharp, fractured end into the torso of the creature.

A keening filled the tower. Alton fell away covering his ears. He lay on the floor amid Haurris' bones, too stunned to move, the cry echoing in his mind.

When it faded, he saw Merdigen gazing down at the creature on the floor.

"If that had been an ordinary bone you'd used," Merdigen said, "and not that of a great mage, you might not have killed this creature."

"What? Why?" Alton asked. His voice was hoarse and he tasted blood.

"It was Eletian. Or at least it had been at one time."

The creature was nothing at all like the living, breathing Eletians he'd met. Its flesh was taut parchment spread over angular bones, the glow gone from its eyes, its hair like a snarled cobweb clouding its face.

"You may be only the second person to end the life of an Eletian since the Long War," Merdigen said. "You brought to an end an otherwise eternal life."

Alton glanced at his bloody hands. The second? Then he realized Karigan had been the first.

"Can we leave now?" Alton asked, appalled and exhausted.

"Indeed," Merdigen said. "I'll have some time to think about all this until we reach my tower. Don't forget Haurris' stone." After a pause he added, "And *don't* drop me this time."

"I did not—" But Merdigen had vanished before Alton could complete his sentence.

He ground his teeth. It wasn't fair Merdigen could just disappear when there was something he didn't want to hear. The mage had the easy end of things, too. Alton checked his shields and braced himself for the lightning that would descend on him the moment he moved.

He gathered both tempes stones and his sword, and ran for the tower wall with the lightning hammering him all the way. When finally he stumbled outside, he found himself the object of concern and attention from the two women who awaited him. Pleased by their solicitous ministrations, he thought perhaps he'd the better end of the deal after all, especially when Estral shifted her belongings to his tent.

❧ HAURRIS ❧

Once more in Tower of the Heavens, Alton carefully placed Merdigen's tempes stone back on its pedestal. Immediately the mage materialized to life beside him.

"Ah," Merdigen said. "Very good to be home, and unscathed." He strolled about, swinging his arms and stretching.

Perhaps Merdigen had returned unscathed, but Alton had been battered by his encounter with the creature in Tower of the Earth. Somehow the creature had reached through his shields and scored claw marks on his chest, and the tussle had left him banged up and bruised. Estral's care and concern had taken his mind off his hurts for a time, but now he was stiff and sore.

"Do you want me to take Haurris' stone out?" he asked.

Merdigen did not reply. He was gazing up toward the tower ceiling.

"What is it?" Alton asked.

"Do you notice anything different in here?"

Alton glanced around. Now that Merdigen mentioned it, something did seem different, but he couldn't put his finger on it. He gazed upward like Merdigen. Daylight filtered through the hole above, and then it hit him.

"That hole," he said. "Is it smaller?"

"Yes, I think so," Merdigen replied. "Not only that, but other damage appears to be mending."

It was true. The tower chamber looked tidier, as if all the minor debris and stone dust that Alton hadn't yet touched had been cleaned up. The major damage remained—the toppled column, other chunks of masonry on the floor.

"How?" Alton demanded.

"The guardians are happier," Merdigen replied. "In harmony and cadence. Who do you think put them in that state?"

"Estral," Alton murmured, his surge of joy tempered with slight jealousy that it was not his own doing. It was everything he had been working for—to fix the D'Yer Wall—and yet she succeeded where he had not. He wondered if her music had affected the damage at the breach, too. He'd have to go back and take a closer look.

"You must tell her to keep singing and playing the song of the guardians," Merdigen said, "to keep reversing the damage. It won't fix the breach itself, but it can mend what is still standing."

"What about that line of music from the book of Theanduris?"

"She must work on that too. It may be what fixes the breach."

Alton was ready to run out of the tower right then to grab Estral, hug her, and tell her.

"However," Merdigen continued, "even if the wall is made secure again, there is another problem Theanduris apparently overlooked."

Alton stilled, heart pounding. "The creature," he said.

"Yes," Merdigen replied. "Eletians are free to travel through the towers. I would conjecture this was because the Eletians were staunch allies during the Long War and they wanted to be able to travel forth into what was once Argenthyne. Or they wanted an escape route for the Sleepers should they awaken. Perhaps both. Just theories, mind you."

Alton found a chair and slumped into it. " 'Ware the Sleeper.' That's what Haurris said. That creature was an Eletian Sleeper, wasn't it? How did it get to be that way?"

"Again, theories. I can tell you Sleepers are Eletians who take a rest from their unending lives. They become part of the forest, a grove of them tended by those still wakeful. I can only guess Blackveil's influence penetrated the grove, corrupted this Sleeper of Argenthyne."

"How many?" Alton asked, his heartbeat quickening

again. "There must be more than one. How many do you suppose are still there?"

Merdigen shrugged. "Hard to say. Hundreds, thousands. The largest grove would have been at Castle Argenthyne."

"Oh, gods," Alton said, nearly overcome by the image of thousands of corrupted Sleepers descending on Tower of the Heavens. "An army of those things and they can pass through the towers . . ."

"Impossible to know if they've all been turned, or if they can even be awakened like the one in Haurris' tower. Let us see if we can get more from Haurris."

With a sense of foreboding, Alton returned to the center of the chamber and gingerly removed Haurris' tempes stone from his saddlebag and cushioning blanket. The stone had been chipped and cracked when the creature knocked it from his hands. The color of the tourmaline remained muddy, dead.

Alton nested the blanket next to the pedestal and placed the stone on it. Haurris did not appear at first, but after some anxious moments, his pale form materialized, his image distorted, fractured.

" 'Ware the Sleeper," he intoned.

"Haurris," Merdigen said standing in front of him. "Haurris, can you hear me? See me?"

"Where am I?"

"Tower of the Heavens," Merdigen replied.

"I am gone, I am gone . . ."

"Look at me, Haurris, it's me, Merdigen."

"Bridges. I destroyed bridges. I am sorry. Strengthened tower to protect . . ." Haurris did not speak directly to Merdigen, but only from the dimmest edge of awareness, a ghost.

"You did well, Haurris," Merdigen said. "The Sleeper is dead."

"Sleeper . . . Sleeper . . ."

"How did it come to your tower?"

"She asked me."

"She who?" Merdigen demanded.

"Help them. She asked me . . ."

"Haurris," Merdigen coaxed. "Who? What did she ask you?"

Haurris's figure blurred, then redefined itself. "Help them. The queen, she asked."

"Queen?" Alton interjected. "What queen?"

Merdigen gestured at him to remain silent, but Haurris turned his head to stare at Alton. His eyes were dark hollows, his cheeks sunken like a corpse's. His robes hung tattered and frayed from his shoulders. His image flickered out, and after several breathless moments of fearing they'd lost him altogether, he reappeared.

"The Queen of Argenthyne," Haurris said, his voice distant.

"Laurelyn," Merdigen whispered.

"I failed. I . . ."

Haurris vanished again, and a longer period passed before his faint image reappeared. Like a dying candle flame, it sputtered and faded.

". . . woke the Sleeper. Tried to . . . am sorry. Found me . . . tried to trap. Inside."

The flame that was Haurris died. He did not reappear and a crack resounded through the chamber. His tempes stone split in half, the tourmaline blackened.

Merdigen sighed, his shoulders sagging. "I'm sorry, too, old friend."

Alton covered the halves of Haurris' tempes stone with the blanket, then stood. "The Queen of Argenthyne? Laurelyn? How did she talk to him?"

"We shall probably never know," Merdigen replied. "Haurris was awake and corporeal longer than the rest of us, but it does not add up, for Laurelyn was lost when Mornhavon took Castle Argenthyne so very long ago."

"He seemed to think she told him to help with the Sleepers. He must have awakened the one somehow."

"But he was not able to leave the tower," Merdigen said. "None of us were, even when we were corporeal."

"You've left the tower plenty of times," Alton reminded him. "When you went looking for the mages on the other side of the breach, or to talk with Booreemadhe and the others in their towers."

"But—"

"And I took you out of your tower to go to Haurris'."

A mortified expression crept over Merdigen's face at the last. "Yes, you did, but the other times, I did not leave the tower in the conventional sense and my tempes stone remained here. I will have to think on what may have happened, but we probably will never know the how or what of it with Haurris gone. What matters most is that the influence of Blackveil has corrupted Argenthyne's Sleepers, and if they are awakened . . . well, we have seen the result."

Alton shuddered, remembering the spidery limbed creature leaping on him.

"They can pass through the towers, my tower," Merdigen continued. "And I no longer possess the magic to trap them as Haurris did."

"Karigan is in Blackveil, with Yates and Lynx and the Eletians," Alton said, thinking that if even one of those creatures was abroad in the forest, it made their expedition all the more perilous.

"Yes." Merdigen stroked his beard. "It makes me wonder . . ."

"What?"

"It makes me wonder why it was so important for the Eletians to go in there at this time. I hope *they* were not planning to awaken the Sleepers."

Alton felt the blood drain from his face, and even Merdigen looked pale.

"My boy," Merdigen said, "we must find a way to fortify the towers."

⋞ THE QUEEN'S RIDERS ⋟

"**T**he first thing I must do is see that the king is informed," Alton told Merdigen. He swung away and strode toward the wall.

"Where are you going?" Merdigen asked.

"To get Dale ready to ride out."

"Did you not tell me there was one with mind sense among the Riders you've stationed in the towers?"

Alton's cheeks warmed. In all the excitement over finding out the truth about Haurris' tower, he'd forgotten about the other Riders. *Mind sense?* He must mean Trace.

"Right. I've sent her to Tower of the Ice." He had taken two more steps toward the wall when Merdigen loudly cleared his throat.

"Now what?" Alton demanded.

"Where are you going?"

"To send Dale to Tower of the Ice to inform Trace to—"

"You are not thinking, my boy," Merdigen said. "I can contact Itharos much more quickly myself."

Alton brushed his fingers through his hair and gave Merdigen a cockeyed smile. "I keep forgetting. Trace may not have reached Tower of the Ice yet."

"Tell me exactly what you'd like your message to the king to say, and I shall relay it to Itharos, who will in turn pass it on to Trace as soon as she arrives."

Alton did, and when Merdigen vanished, he left the tower thinking that centuries ago, when the Green Riders had been at full capacity, there must have been a number of Riders who could speak mind to mind like Trace and Connly, and who enabled messages to be conveyed almost instantly. In that long-ago time Riders wouldn't have had to saddle up and rush off in a cloud of dust.

Depending on the pace Trace had set, it could be a day or two before she reached Tower of the Ice, and waiting to hear confirmation that his message was received was going to feel like years, no matter that it was being delivered at the speed of thought.

Instead of waiting around and fretting, Alton left the tower to share his and Merdigen's revelations about Haurris and the Sleeper with Dale, Estral, and Captain Wallace. Estral was more determined than ever to work out the measure of music in the Silverwood book, and he knew enough not to get in her way when she ran off to fetch her lute.

"I hope the king will send us more troops," Captain Wallace told Alton. "Especially now that we know each tower is a potential passage to these Sleepers. I haven't the manpower here to watch the breach and all ten towers."

"Nine," Alton said. "Haurris left defenses around Tower of the Earth that should keep any Sleepers out, or at least trap them."

"Do you want to rely solely on the tricks of some old, dead mage?"

"Point taken," Alton replied. "Tell me what you need, and I'll put in a request."

Alton also took time to inspect the cracks in the wall radiating from the breach to see if Estral's music really was having an effect. Since the summer he'd been taking periodic measurements and recording changes in his journal. He discovered incremental improvements—the cracks appeared to be diminishing, if only minutely. The changes were not dramatic, but were, all the same, miraculous.

When he returned to the tower encampment, he searched for Estral, eventually finding her in the dining tent. To the amusement of all, he lifted her off her feet and twirled her around and kissed her soundly.

"What was that for?" Estral asked when her feet were again on the ground. He liked that he'd made her blush.

"You are amazing," he said.

She gave him a coy smile. "You're only just noticing?"

He laughed and twirled her around again. Later on he would show her just how amazing he thought she was—without the audience. But first he wanted to check on the tower to see if Merdigen had heard back from Itharos about Trace.

When he entered Tower of the Heavens, he found not only Merdigen awaiting him, but Itharos, too. The two broke off some deep discussion when he arrived.

"I take it Trace has arrived at Tower of the Ice?" Alton asked.

Itharos bowed with a flourish of his cloak. "To my delight, she has indeed arrived, and I conveyed your most distressing message."

"And?"

The mages glanced at one another, then back at Alton.

"Trace has some news of her own," Merdigen replied. "We suggest first that you have Rider Littlepage join us, and Estral Andovian as well."

Neither Merdigen nor Itharos offered any hint of the nature of the news, but it must have been of great import if they wanted Dale and Estral present to receive it, too. Quickly he returned to the dining tent and found Estral, and together they searched for Dale, finally locating her at the pickets, running a currycomb over Karigan's Condor.

"I promised I'd look after him," she said, patting the gelding's neck.

Condor nudged Dale's shoulder to encourage her to continue, and she chuckled.

"How is he?" Alton asked. It was not a casual question. Messenger horses possessed an uncanny sense of knowing when their Riders were in trouble, and Condor, Lynx's Owl, and Yates' Phoebe had been edgy since their Riders entered the forest.

Dale settled her hand on Condor's withers. "Fretful," she replied thoughtfully. "Phoebe, too. More than they were. Owl seems much the same."

As if to punctuate her observation, Phoebe started digging her hoof at the ground. A sizeable trench had begun to develop there, evidence of her anxiety.

The three humans, in turn, fell into an uneasy silence. What, Alton wondered, and not for the first time, was going on with the company? How did the Riders fare? He was seized by another flash of regret at how poorly he and Karigan had parted. He shook himself. Whatever was happening on the other side of the wall was beyond his control, and he had problems of his own to contend with.

"Right," he said. "We are all needed at the tower."

"That sounds dire," Dale replied.

"Trace reached Tower of the Ice and has some news for us."

"Don't worry," she told the horse. "I'll be back to finish."

He swished his tail as if to say she had better be.

"What is it about?" Dale asked as they set off.

"I don't know," Alton replied. "They wouldn't say until I got you two."

All three of them picked up their pace, which carried them rapidly across the encampment and into the tower.

"This must be the esteemed Estral Andovian," Itharos said when they entered the tower chamber. "I am honored to meet you, my lady." He bowed.

"Estral, meet Itharos of Tower of the Ice," Dale said.

"It is good to see you as well, Rider Littlepage," Itharos said. "All three of you. In fact, a party would—"

"Not now," Merdigen interrupted, an irritable counterpoint to Itharos' flamboyance. "Rider Burns has received some news that you must hear."

"Well?" Alton said.

"*I'm* not going to tell you," Merdigen replied. "There is a way you can communicate with Rider Burns directly, as the wallkeepers once did. Itharos and I assume it will work anyway. It's been a while since it was last done . . ."

"There's a way to do this and you didn't tell me?" Alton demanded.

"Didn't seem necessary since you've never had anyone stationed in the other towers before."

Alton wondered fleetingly what other interesting details Merdigen had chosen not to reveal.

"You must all go to the center of the chamber and place

your hands on the tempes stone," Merdigen instructed. "Itharos and I will do the rest."

Alton wasted no time and Estral and Dale were right behind him. They placed their hands on the tempes stone. At first nothing changed in the grassy plains at the center of Tower of the Heavens. Then Merdigen and Itharos, who stood nearby, vanished. Silvery runes came to life in the air, pulsating with light, circling them.

Alton heard Estral's sharp intake of breath beside him. "Don't break contact with the stone," he told her.

"I won't."

The runes merged and shimmered until a human form materialized, Trace suspended above the ground, a corona of green light flashing around her, the green of tourmaline.

"There you are," she said, her voice sounding as if she were right there with them. "Thank the gods."

"Trace?" Alton said. "Can you hear me?"

"Yes, yes I can. I can see all three of you, too."

"Merdigen says you have something to tell us."

"I do, though it wasn't easy to get it out of Connly. I don't think he wanted to worry me—us—but when I contacted him to pass on your news about the Sleeper to Captain Mapstone and King Zachary, I could tell something was wrong."

"And?" Alton pushed.

Trace's shoulders sagged. "When I finally got him to talk, I found out . . . I found out there was another assassination attempt on King Zachary, and that this one may yet prove successful."

"No . . ." Dale murmured.

Estral's free hand found Alton's.

Trace explained how the assassin used an arrow tainted with poison and successfully impaled the king, and how Ben tried to heal him but was in turn overcome.

"The king has survived thus far," Trace said. "And each day buys more hope, but Connly does not know how much of the truth he's getting from those closest to the king."

"It isn't like the captain to hide the truth from her Riders," Dale said.

"No," Trace agreed, "it is not. Connly hasn't been able to

see her. Destarion claims she's been taken ill, and has confined her to the mending wing. He says she'll recover and not to worry."

"Who is in charge?" Alton asked, his chest tight.

"Connly is in charge of the Riders," Trace said. "He reports mainly to Colin Dovekey. As for the realm . . ." Her pause was ponderous. "As for the realm, we now have a queen."

Estral and Dale gasped.

"Lady Estora," Alton murmured.

Trace nodded, the corona of green light flaring around her head with the gesture. "*Queen* Estora."

"But how?" Dale demanded. "If the king is so injured—"

"Exactly why she's been made queen." Alton, the son and heir of a lord-governor who had grown up immersed in the politics and machinations of the provincial court, could see all too clearly what had happened. "King Zachary's condition must be truly precarious for them to go forward with something like this. A deathbed wedding."

"Someone wanted to ensure there was continuity of power," Estral added. "But what of an heir? Surely the king had someone in mind in case something like this happened."

"Even if the king had an heir," Alton said, "it would cause a disruption, not something we need right now. Just what Second Empire would want."

They all fell silent, absorbing all that Trace had told them, and what it might mean for their future. A future without King Zachary? Alton shook his head. It would be a blow to the realm, a blow to himself, for he'd admired King Zachary, who always put his people before himself. Could he already be gone, and those closest to him had not yet revealed the truth?

And Karigan. Now that he knew where her affections truly lay, he couldn't help but hurt for her. She would not know until she came back from Blackveil. If she came back. Estral squeezed his hand, and the somber look she gave him indicated her thoughts were along the same lines.

"What does Connly want us to do?" Alton asked Trace.

"To keep doing as we're doing. Our orders have not changed. Meanwhile, he's going to find out what he can

do about the captain, and take your information about the
Sleepers to the queen. He wanted me to tell you to remember we are still His Majesty's Messenger Service, but if the
king dies, we are the queen's Riders." A solemn silence followed this pronouncement.

"I'd like us to touch base daily," Alton told Trace. "More
often if necessary."

"Absolutely."

When they said their good-byes, Trace vanished and Merdigen reappeared.

"We've got to tell the others," Alton said. "Can we do it
this same way?"

Merdigen nodded. "Except, obviously, with the towers
east of the breach."

"I can ride to Garth," Dale said.

Alton nodded. "He and Fern will need to know about
Haurris and the Sleepers, as well. We need to impress upon
everyone just what Connly said, that we need to keep doing
our duty, whether we are the king's Riders, or the queen's."

⊰ THREATS ⊱

 A bell tolled through the impenetrable blackness. Its sonorous clanging scraped Laren's mind raw, and all she could think was that it was a death bell, ringing out the news. The news of ...

So trapped in the tide of the dark was she that at first she could not remember, but as she tossed beneath blankets, the horizon lightened to gray, only to falter and dim again as she dreamed of arrows, arrows impaling a little boy she loved very much.

The bell pealed out one last note that hung in the air.

"Zachary!" She sat up, blinded by light, disoriented. Where was she? This was not her bed.

Someone's hand pressed her shoulder and she sank back into her pillows. "Easy, Red."

At the sound of Elgin's voice, Laren sighed and rubbed her eyes. When they adjusted to the light, her vision was blurry and her head throbbed. "Terrible dream," she murmured. Her mouth was dry. "Terrible dream about Zachary." She floundered for a cup of water on the bedside table. Elgin saw what she was after and helped her drink. When she drained the cup, he filled it for her again from a pitcher. This time she drank more slowly.

"What happened?" she asked. "Where am I?"

"Destarion said you fell ill night before last," Elgin replied. "You're in the mending wing."

"I don't remember ..." Her head hurt too much and she was too groggy to recall the other night's events. "I heard the death bell."

466

"Death bell? Just now? Nah, that was just the midday bell."

"Then it was all a dream," she whispered in relief. "Zachary is all right."

There was a painful period of silence before Elgin spoke again. "I don't know what your dream was, and while that was not a death bell, the prince—the king is not all right, but he lives. For now."

"Oh, gods." Unbidden tears streamed down her cheeks as she pieced together shreds of memory. The mad ride down the Winding Way with Ben, the wagon charging up the street bearing Zachary impaled with an arrow and Lord Coutre dying beside him. "Tell me, tell me about him."

"Well," Elgin said, "I don't know much more than he made it through two nights."

It gave Laren hope. If Zachary made it through two nights . . . Now he just had to keep making it. He had to!

"Your Riders have been worried about *you*," Elgin said quietly.

She squinted at him, made out his blurry form sitting in a chair beside her bed. "I don't think I was sick. I don't know." She racked her brain, searching for other memories of the day. She recalled being in Zachary's quarters and talking to Colin. She remembered Lady Estora coming to see Zachary.

"Destarion said it came on rapid. He thought maybe it was the strain."

That certainly could be, she thought. However, her vision was already subtly improving and the headache lifting. Elgin was less of a blur. In fact, she could discern dark shadows beneath his eyes, a grayness to him she had not seen before.

"There is something else you'll want to know about the king," he said. "He's a married man now. We have a queen."

"*What?*" Laren sat bolt upright and the world darkened once more and she thought she might fall back into unconsciousness.

"Easy there, Red," Elgin said. "The menders wanted me to warn you to take it slow."

His voice anchored her and she blinked away the dark. "They did it," she whispered as a rush of memory hit her all at once, the heated discussion with Colin, the tea. "Those bastards. They did it."

"Er, you're not calling the king and his new queen . . ."

"No, I mean Colin and the others. His conspirators. They got Zachary married. Tell me, have my Riders gone out with the news of any of this?"

Despite her obvious disorientation and emotional behavior, Elgin remained calm, steady, her anchor. "Counselor Dovekey ordered them out late this morning with the joyous news."

Laren crushed handfuls of blanket in her fists. No doubt they downplayed Zachary's injury, as well, if that was even included in the message. Oh, yes, she had done what she could to promote the forthcoming marriage between Zachary and Estora, but she hadn't wanted it to come about in this manner. Not at all. Not through duplicity. There were those who would see through the deception no matter how well concealed, and if that happened, it would only make matters worse.

She threw her blanket off and swung her legs over the side of the bed. They'd clothed her in a sleeping gown, but she was relieved to see her uniform hanging on hooks. She jumped to her feet.

And the room slanted and the gray pervaded her vision.

"Whoa, lass!" Elgin said. "Steady now. Remember, take it slowly."

She sank back down onto the bed and glared at Elgin, her hands trembling. "They dosed me with something, Chief," she said. "They put something in my tea. They did not want me to interfere with their little plan." She thought he'd probably think her raving, delirious. He did not move or react to her words, but rubbed his chin thoughtfully as if considering her sanity.

"Huh," he said finally. "Who all is involved?"

Laren closed her eyes and sent up a small prayer of thanks to the heavens. He believed her. Colin and the others probably preferred to cast doubt on her rationality, which could only serve their own cause. If she gainsayed them, they could undermine her authority, her very sanity, so no one believed her. Her assertions would be brushed aside as the ravings of a woman grief stricken by the loss of someone she was so very close to. She'd been in such despair, they'd say, illness had weakened her mind.

But they hadn't counted on Elgin. Or her Riders. Elgin believed her. Her Riders would believe her. She'd have to move carefully so the conspirators did not work to discredit her.

"Spane," Laren said. "He started it, then Colin joined in. Destarion is the one who dosed my tea. And Colin said Harborough, with the army to back him, was in favor of it. I'm going to kill them."

"The whole army?"

"You know what I mean. The conspirators. They went against protocol, against king's law, and they didn't want me to inform the lord-governors of it."

"I see," Elgin replied, "but the king was going to marry Lady Estora anyway, and this should help secure a smooth transition of power."

"Oh, Chief, not you, too."

"I'm not saying it's right, at least in a legal sense. I'm sure Zachary will have a few things to say should the gods grant us his recovery. And it was certainly wrong of them to remove you from the process as they did. But what can you do? Gah, politics and intrigue. It's why I didn't want to come back."

Laren's shoulders sagged. "I don't think I can do much, but there is a chance before she's crowned—"

Elgin cleared his throat and looked out the window. "Too late, as of this morning."

"What? They already held her coronation?"

"Yep. Before your Riders got sent out."

"Those bastards. I *am* going to kill them. I guess the only thing left for me to do is register a formal complaint with the queen. She is now the law of the land."

"That could be dangerous," Elgin said.

"Estora has always been reasonable, but sudden power does have a way of changing people. Still, it's a risk I'm willing to take."

"I recommend you eat something first." Master Destarion appeared in the doorway bearing a tray of food and drink. "You've missed a few meals and that's adding to your weakness."

Elgin sniffed at the fine aromas rising from the tray. Laren's stomach roiled.

"I suppose the food's dosed with whatever you gave me the other night in the tea." Laren said, her voice full of venom.

"I regret the necessity of what we did," Destarion said. He set the tray on a table. Laren was tempted to upend it and throw the dishes at him, but she figured it would only be another excuse for them to dose her well and good.

"There is nothing mixed in your food or drink, except whatever spices the kitchen staff use to make it taste better," Destarion said.

She glowered at him.

"You do have the ability to check the truth of my words," he said.

She did, and she reached for where her brooch usually was, but it was not clasped to her sleeping gown. Elgin, who knew what she wanted, fetched her shortcoat, but her emotions must have been strong enough that she did not require contact with the brooch to receive her answer. *True,* her special ability told her. Destarion had not lied about the food or drink. She took her shortcoat from Elgin, and touching the brooch only reinforced the first message.

So the items on the tray were safe. The knowledge did not, however, ameliorate her anger toward Destarion. As galling as it was that she must rely on him for information on the conditions of Zachary and Ben, her concern for the two overrode her personal feelings. "How is Zachary?"

"Feverish. This will be a difficult day."

"And Ben?"

"Still unconscious."

"He over-exerted his ability," Laren said. "He could have killed himself."

"That is what we believe, but we've no experience with this sort of thing—at least in our lifetimes. I've a couple of apprentices checking back through our archives to see if there is any mention of a similar case occurring in the past."

"You will tell me if you find out anything about Ben's condition, won't you." She'd made it a statement, not a question. She was curious to know just what the mender documents said about Riders, since so little Rider history had survived the ages. It hadn't occurred to her before to search their archives. "It could help all Riders."

Destarion bowed. "Of course. Now I suggest you eat, as our queen has been asking to speak with you, and decisions have to be made."

"Decisions?" she murmured, but Destarion had already left.

"I thought he was one of the ones you were going to kill," Elgin said.

"He was. Is. After he finds out what's going on with Ben."

After Laren ate and dressed, no one forbade her to leave the mending wing. She peered in at Ben who lay peacefully in bed. He looked only to be asleep, but when she called to him and shook his shoulder, he did not awaken.

She also saw Sperren reclined in a daybed in a sunny common room, where an apprentice mender read to him.

"Captain!" he called out. "I've a new hip, is it not wonderful?"

So wonderful that Zachary was in danger of dying because of that hip, and Ben remained unconscious.

"And we've a new queen!" Sperren added. "It is a remarkable day."

Laren ground her teeth. On her way out, she said to Elgin, "I'm going to kill him, too."

"The carnage is going to be terrible."

Elgin accompanied her all the way to the royal apartments. It wasn't necessary, but she was grateful for his presence. In the course of two nights, it felt as though everyone else had turned against her.

The Weapons permitted her into the private portion of the apartments, leading her to Zachary's dressing room. There she found Colin in consultation with Zachary's secretary, Cummings. When she arrived, they stood.

"Captain," Colin said, "so good to see you up and about so soon after your illness."

"You are sticking to that story, are you? So if I make trouble it will be easier to convince everyone I've cracked?"

"I'm so sorry, Captain," Colin replied. "But it was necessary. We will face the consequences if it comes to that."

"By Zachary's hand, or mine if he is not able, you will."

Colin's expression darkened. "I hardly think it helps matters to make threats."

"I don't make threats, Colin. You know that."

"You may find yourself in a position, Captain, unable to do more."

"Who is making threats now?" she murmured.

Colin lifted his chin but did not reply. Cummings excused himself, no doubt to escape the tension in the room. Elgin remained solidly by her side.

"When Zachary recovers," Laren said, "I look forward to seeing him make you accountable."

"I pray to the gods he does recover," Colin said, "no matter what it may cost me."

His demeanor had become very humble, remorseful, and his words rang with truth, even without her consulting her ability. She would never understand the Weapon mentality of *Death is honor.* It was even more astonishing to her that this man who had dedicated himself to Zachary, Zachary's father, King Amigast, and his grandmother, Queen Isen, would betray Zachary in this manner. But then, Weapons were mysterious in their ways, and though it was never said overtly, more than being protectors of the royal family and the royal dead, their directive was to guard the kingdom more than the person who ruled the kingdom. Did they construe that directive to mean they could initiate a coup if they deemed it necessary? If Zachary did recover, they needed to have a serious talk.

"Destarion told me," Laren said, "that Lady ... *Queen* Estora asked to see me."

"Yes, Captain, but I wish to be forthright and warn you there has been a good deal of discussion about you."

"Really."

Colin nodded. "It is under consideration that you be relieved of duty, at least temporarily."

"What?" It was Elgin who bellowed out the word. Laren was not surprised.

"At this crucial time," Colin explained, "we need all of us to be in accord regarding our new queen. We are unsure of your absolute loyalty and we cannot judge your honesty in the same way your ability allows you to judge us. However, we also understand you cannot leave the service voluntarily or under coercion due to the properties of your brooch. Therefore, suspension of duty may be the preferred alternative."

"After all my years of service?"

"It pains me," Colin said. "I know how dedicated you are to Zachary and the realm. It is nothing personal, of course."

Of course not. It was political expediency. There were, Laren knew, other ways to silence her that were far less gentle than suspension. Would her continued resistance force them to resort to other measures? They were quite capable of concealing anything they did to her. There would be lies about her whereabouts. They'd inform interested parties she was not favored by the queen.

"Because I wanted to follow legal protocol you are suspending me?" she asked, her soft tone only underscoring her contempt.

"It is not for me to determine," Colin replied. "It's the queen's decision. Naturally we hope she will express confidence in you, and you will accept all that has come to pass."

"Good gods," Elgin muttered. "It's Gwyer Warhein all over."

"That was another time, a different situation," Colin retorted.

Was it really so different? Laren wondered. Gwyer Warhein, captain of the Green Riders two hundred years ago, had been vilified by his king, the paranoid Agates Sealender, for the unspeakable crime of honesty; for telling truths the king hated hearing about himself and his reign. Warhein had been a reader of honesty, just as Laren was—she wore his brooch. It had come to her, *chosen* her, from across generations of Riders. She fingered it now, the gold smooth and cool to her touch. She tilted her head as she regarded Colin.

She had worked with him long enough to know he was

no fool—far from it—and that he was well-versed in history. As much as he'd deny it, he'd see the parallels with the past—not only Laren telling truths he did not wish exposed, but how Warhein's loyal Riders had rallied to him, had gone into exile with him, despite the threat of royal reprisal. Colin and his conspirators would have deduced that Laren's Riders would do the same for her. Censuring her by any harsher means than suspension of duty would incur the wrath of her Riders, and the conspirators could not afford to lose them; they could not function without them.

Still, Laren reflected, it didn't mean the conspirators wouldn't hesitate to do what was necessary and expedient to silence her if she made too much trouble.

Despite the potential for danger to herself, she could not repress a smile, and the line between Colin's brows deepened in response.

"Gwyer Warhein is considered a hero today," she murmured as if to herself. Not only had he resisted a tyrant by telling the truth, but when old, unlamented Agates died without an heir and the realm plunged into the Clan Wars, Warhein and his Riders had helped Smidhe Hillander attain victory, bringing Zachary's line to the throne, and initiating two centuries of peace and unification. Colin would know all this, too. He could not act without considering the weight of history.

Laren squared her shoulders and straightened her back, proud as ever of her Rider heritage and the brooch she wore. "Gwyer Warhein supported Clan Hillander," she said. "And so have I. Always. And so will I continue to do."

"So be it," Colin replied. "Best not to keep the queen waiting." He led the way to the bedchamber door and opened it for her, but blocked Elgin from entering.

"It's all right," she told her old friend, and she stepped into the room to face her new queen.

⋞ DECISIONS ⋟

Sunlight flowed into the room as Laren remembered it from the last time she'd been here. Estora stood there conferring with a mender. The light turned her skin to pale marble and her mourning clothes gray. Laren blinked as though confronted with a lifelike statue. Then Estora turned to her. Gems dazzled on the fillet crown she wore. Laren had last seen it upon the brow of Queen Isen as she lay in state at her funeral.

Estora dismissed the mender and approached. Laren dropped to her knee and bowed her head.

"Rise, Captain," Estora said.

Laren did so and the two faced one another with steady gazes. Laren had to tilt her head to gaze in the eyes of the taller woman. There were shadows beneath Estora's eyes. So much she'd had to contend with—the murder of her father, the injury to her betrothed, the hasty marriage and coronation.

A low moan came from the bed. Laren licked her lips, wishing to rush to Zachary's side, but so unsure of this new Estora she did not dare move or say anything.

"He has not changed much," Estora said. "Still burning up and . . . and delirious. The menders have given him something to keep him easy. Please, please do go to see him."

Laren nodded and did just that. She found him pale, sweat runneling on his skin. His bandage was fresh and she smelled no odor of a festering wound. She brushed damp hair from his brow. His hand clenched and unclenched as though gripping a sword and he emitted a sound like a growl.

"He's been like this," Estora said, "forever. It feels like forever."

Laren glanced sidelong at the woman who was now Zachary's wife and saw genuine concern and fear. She had always liked Estora, thought her the best possible match for Zachary. Recent events did not change her assessment at all.

"He's fighting," Laren said. "It's what he does. Fight."

A sob escaped Estora's composed facade, and then another, until it was a shuddering torrent. Instinctively Laren drew the young queen into her arms, spoke soft words, soothing nonsense words as she had when Melry fell and twisted her ankle, as she had for Zachary when he was little and his brother bullied him, and then again as a young man when his grandmother died. She rubbed Estora's back and comforted her until the sobs subsided and Estora pulled away, dabbing her eyes with a handkerchief.

"I'm sorry," she said.

"Oh, my lady," Laren said, "you've been through too much in so short a time."

"But I cannot break down like this anymore."

"A crown does not make you immune to emotion," Laren said, "nor should it. It made Isen and Zachary the compassionate monarchs they were. Zachary still is."

Estora sniffed. "My mother and sisters left with my father's body today. They are taking him home to Coutre. And . . . and of course my sister must be readied to assume my father's place. I've . . . I've had no one. No one but him." She glanced at Zachary.

Laren could not imagine the terrible loneliness. "I am at your service," Laren said, "if you wish it, Your Highness." It felt strange to address anyone other than Zachary so.

"I appreciate that," Estora said, her tears now well gone, and her tone different. "But I heard you did not support my marriage."

Laren's spirits sank. So here it was. "I supported your marriage as contracted. However, when situations such as this arise, there are protocols in place, established two hundred years ago, that we are supposed to follow, no matter how much sense an alternative makes. It does not mean I'm not willing to swear my fealty to you now, as my queen." Laren went to her knee again.

Estora tilted her chin up, shadows shifting across her face like a veil. "I am not certain," she said from above.

Elgin stood a few paces in front of Colin Dovekey glaring at him with arms folded. He remembered the man from when he was just another Weapon guarding Queen Isen. Colin was a bit grayer now, but still solid and fit.

The counselor remained seated and did not pay any attention to Elgin. Instead he looked over some papers, rustling them back and forth.

Elgin did not know exactly what game was afoot, but he knew that where it concerned the royals, the stakes were high, a real life game of Intrigue. Red had gotten snared in it and he didn't like it, not at all. They hadn't listened to her. They hadn't liked what she said, so they knocked her out and now threatened to relieve her of duty. They could do far worse if they chose to, he knew, if she pushed them too hard.

Colin set his papers aside and looked up at Elgin, his expression neutral as if seeing him for the first time.

"Elgin Foxsmith, isn't it?" he asked. "Former Chief Rider?"

"That's right."

"It's been many years, but I recognize you. Had some action in the battles with the Darrow Raiders, didn't you?"

"Most Green Riders did back then," Elgin said, his tone darkening. "Including Laren Mapstone. But you wouldn't have seen any kind of action, would you, safe and sound here in the castle."

"My duty was to guard Queen Isen. She resided here." Colin's tone was not at all defensive. He folded his hands together atop his lap. "I want you to know I have nothing but the utmost respect for Captain Mapstone. She's been the king's most trusted friend and advisor for many years. And my friend as well."

Elgin snorted. "So that's how you treat your friends, eh? Then I pity your enemies."

"I realize it appears harsh, but this is an extraordinary and precarious time. Right now the queen must have at her side only those she can trust the most."

"Laren Mapstone is the most honorable person I know," Elgin said.

"I do not dispute her honor. It is, however, what has put her in her current position."

"Taken that way, it means you are admitting you are not honorable."

There was a slight downturn of the edges of Colin's mouth, but he did not show any anger. "Whatever the outcome, what we have done is in the best interests of the realm, and in Laren's, believe it or not."

"You just don't know her, do you? No matter you call her a friend, you don't know her. You Weapons, you have no idea about anything. If the king wakes up, I warrant there'll be a reckoning. He loves her, he does. Laren."

Colin's eyes grew unfocussed as he gazed across the room. "I imagine there will be a reckoning," he said as if to himself. "I imagine there will be."

Elgin had expected at least some anger from the man, and even wished it, but he sensed sadness instead. These Weapons, they were unnatural, it seemed to him. Almost inhuman and secretive in their ways.

The door to the bedchamber opened and Laren and Lady Estora—now Queen Estora—stepped out. Colin rose and bowed. Elgin followed suit. He'd never been so close to the king's betrothed. She was striking from a distance. Close up her beauty practically hurt his eyes. Humbled by her presence, Elgin could only gaze at the floor.

"Counselor Dovekey," the queen said, "I wish to relieve Laren Mapstone of duty immediately. Lieutenant Connly will assume her responsibilities at once."

"No," Elgin whispered.

"Yes, Your Highness."

"And confine her to quarters," the queen added.

"No!" Elgin wailed. He started toward her, but suddenly

a pair of swords wielded by the black-gloved hands of Weapons were pointed at his chest.

"Chief," Laren said, "peace, my friend. You cannot help the Riders if you are imprisoned. I'll be fine. Don't worry. Tell the Riders not to worry."

He watched in astonishment as another pair of Weapons took her arms and led her from the room. The queen receded into the bedchamber.

Elgin pointed an accusing finger at Colin. "I won't forget this, Weapon. None of the Riders will. Even if the king dies. Especially if the king dies."

TALES OF THE SEA KINGS

Estora sank into the chair beside Zachary's bed.

"I hope you understand," she said.

He lay peacefully, unresponsive as always to her words and presence.

Her decision about Captain Mapstone today was one of several she'd already had to make since the coronation. The ceremony had been a quick, muted affair, attended by any dignitary on castle grounds who could be found. Her mother and sisters remained long enough to witness the ceremony and then departed with the corpse of her father.

In a way, the coronation had been like her wedding, only she was not marrying just one man, but a realm. She was given not a ring, but a crown. Her fingers went to the fillet on her head. It didn't fit exactly right, and Colin said it would be no problem for it to be adjusted by the royal jeweler.

She knew more decisions awaited her attention, some where life and death lay in the balance, others less important. For now she delegated those that she could. Cummings, she was certain, was quite capable of organizing the coronation dinner on her behalf. The rest, Colin was holding in reserve for her for now, giving her time to adjust to her new role and the shock of her father's sudden death.

"You have no idea," she whispered to Zachary.

She took the cloth soaking in the bowl of cool water, wrung it out, and gently dabbed the sweat on his face. All at once his eyes fluttered open and he grabbed her wrist. She stifled a cry. Even ill as he was, his grip was crushingly strong.

"I would have begged her not to go," he said, eyes fever

bright. Then he released her wrist, mumbled something more and fell back into his troubled sleep.

"Zachary?" she called. "Zachary?" But he did not respond.

She sat back wondering if he spoke out of memory or dream, or if he had incorporated something of her conversation with Captain Mapstone into his subconscious.

Her wrist still bore the pressure marks of his grip. She flexed her hand and reached for the book on his bedside table. Sometimes she spoke to him as Master Destarion recommended, telling him of all that had come to pass, and of her sorrow, and of her hopes that they would embark on a very bright future together when he got well, ruling the realm in concert and in peace, and raising children who were healthy and happy. They were all the things any new bride would wish for, although few brides had to worry about ruling anything beyond their own households.

Estora had felt awkward speaking to him while menders were in attendance, so she'd taken to reading to Zachary instead, and even when they were alone, as now, she found she enjoyed the reading as an escape from all the turmoil around her. She hoped her voice touched Zachary somewhere inside and comforted him. Master Fogg, the castle librarian, had located for her at her request a volume titled *Tales of the Sea Kings*.

She'd already read to him the tale of Marin the Gardener, who, it was said, was an enchantress who lived in the Northern Sea archipelago and rejoiced in the growth of natural things. Her garden was an entire island: its woods, meadow, and shore, and all the creatures that inhabited it with her.

Most of the tales of the sea kings centered around the Northern Sea and its islands, and the next one she opened up to was a favorite among seamen, that of Yolandhe, the seductress who guided King Akarion to her shore and kept him there. When the enchantment lifted, Akarion remained with her out of love, but Yolandhe was immortal, and Akarion mortal. The tale always ended on a bittersweet note.

Despite Yolandhe's trickery, Estora always sympathized with her loneliness. Though, if she wished to apply logic to the tales, there were apparently enchantresses on just about every island and sailors constantly landing onshore to become ensnared in one spell or another.

"This is the tale of Yolandhe and King Akarion," Estora read to Zachary, "and how the king claimed Yolandhe's love for himself." Many versions of the tale carried a heavy moral message about how Akarion tamed Yolandhe's wicked ways. It would be interesting to see if this interpretation fell into the same trap.

It did not, but focused on Yolandhe's seduction of the king and the nearly constant lovemaking that ensued for years after.

"Don't they ever stop to sleep or eat?" Estora asked, growing warmer with each word to the point she had to fan herself with the book. "Who wrote this?" When she checked, the author was listed as "Anonymous."

She thanked the gods no one heard or saw her reading it, that even the Weapons granted her privacy by posting themselves outside when she was with Zachary. He remained quiet and unconscious. Roused as she was by the story of Yolandhe and Akarion, she ached for him to awaken, to draw her into his arms, to make love to her.

Had Zachary not lain injured the night of their wedding, they'd have already joined in the rite of consummation, an event of ancient origins attended by witnesses to ensure the new royal couple commenced the task of creating heirs. Her marriage was already legally bound, but there were those who adhered to the old ways and would not recognize it until the rite took place, and those couples that refused lost title and were shunned. Sometimes tradition held more sway than law.

She hoped, given the circumstances, the need for the rite would be overlooked and that she and Zachary could join naturally without an audience watching on, but with her cousin Richmont constantly mentioning the rite, it seemed unlikely. He just wanted to ensure, she knew, that her place as queen was unquestionably secured among all influential parties, including the traditionalists, which of course guaranteed his own place in the royal court.

She shuddered at the thought of having to perform the

act before people known and unknown to her. She resumed her reading, pushing the rite of consummation to the back of her mind, enjoying the escape as much as hoping her voice reached Zachary through his illness and reassured him he was not alone.

Later in Zachary's dressing room, which was rapidly becoming Estora's place of business, Cummings helped her to go through the volumes of well wishes and condolences that continued to flow into the castle. He told her they would hold off on a coronation dinner until several lord-governors could be in attendance. It would be, of course, a sticky situation. The lord-governors could very well challenge the manner of her marriage and hasty coronation, but she hoped Colin's handling of the whole situation forestalled such conflict. It had certainly made the confinement of Captain Mapstone all the more imperative.

The messages Colin sent out with the Green Riders told of Zachary's desire to move up the wedding out of his regard for his betrothed, and because an "accident while riding" made him reconsider the gravity of a smooth transition should any serious harm come to him. The rumors rife in the city and beyond had already muddled the details of the incident so much that the lord-governors would have an impossible time rooting out the truth. Meanwhile, Colin and his aides had begun to circulate additional rumors with a modified version of what had happened on Sacor City's streets that afternoon. The king's high-strung stallion had spooked. The king fell and was injured. He was under the care of the castle's finest menders and in good enough form to marry.

Word was that there would be official celebrations when the king was up and about and the lord-governors in attendance, but there were already accounts of the city's populace celebrating in the streets, and the joy would only spread as word moved across the country.

The lord-governors still might challenge the marriage and coronation, but the mood of the realm would be against them like the surge of an incoming storm tide.

A knock came upon the door and Estora nodded for

Cummings to answer it. There were murmurings with whoever sought entrance, but she did not glance up from her papers until Cummings stepped aside and three persons approached: Colin, General Harborough, and Lieutenant Connly of the Green Riders. They bowed to her.

"What is it?" she asked, praying it was not a crisis so early in her queenhood, as if the attack on her betrothed and death of her father were not enough.

"A crisis, I fear," Colin replied, supplying the answer she least wanted to hear. "In fact two."

Estora closed her eyes and the papers shook in her hand. *No.* She must not appear weak. She took a deep breath and steadied herself.

"Tell me," she said.

"News of both came from Green Riders," Colin said. "Lieutenant?"

The Rider nodded, and Estora wondered if he felt as lost without his captain as she felt without the king.

"Your Highness," he said. "The news comes from both the south and the north." He told her first of word he'd received from the wall, an unbelievable story of an Eletian Sleeper—with an explanation of what Sleepers were—trapped in one of the towers, and how it was possible that more Sleepers turned by the darkness of Blackveil could pass through the towers into Sacoridia.

"Rider D'Yer and Captain Wallace have requested more troops at the wall to guard the towers," Connly finished.

General Harborough opened his mouth to speak, but Colin gestured for him to wait. "Let Lieutenant Connly tell the tale of the north first," he said.

The general folded his meaty arms and waited with ill-concealed impatience.

"I've received reports," Connly said, "from Riders who've been trying to track Birch and his Second Empire renegades on the northern boundary. There've been incidents." His eyes were cast downward. "The Riders have come across small settlements that have been destroyed, the people murdered to the last babe and elder. They've found evidence that the people suffered extreme torture, no mercy, before being executed."

Estora sat back, horrified. "Birch—he's attacking our boundary?"

"Dodgy bastard," Harborough grumbled. When he realized what he'd said and to whom, he cleared his throat. "My apologies, Your Highness, for my coarse words. I'm used to speaking with the king."

To another man, she thought. "Never mind that. You were saying?"

"Yes, Your Highness. The boundary folk who settled in the wilderness up there. They're self-sufficient people, but certainly not prepared for military style raids like the ones Birch has been conducting. The reports are that the attacks and subsequent torture, rapes, and executions were methodical. Isn't that correct, Rider?"

"Yes, sir," Connly replied.

"Birch must be training his renegades for true battle, hardening them, by hitting weak targets first. He'd also know that despite the fact these settlers aren't technically in Sacoridia, that his actions would infuriate the king. The evidence Lieutenant Connly here mentioned that Birch left behind was definitely meant to provoke. Birch is thumbing his nose at us."

Estora licked her lips, fought her own fear at the realization that she was responsible for deciding how the realm would respond, that she was responsible for the lives of the boundary folk and the soldiers who would eventually engage with Birch.

She knew the general probably wanted to delve immediately into discussion of what the response should be, but first she asked Connly, "What of those people, the settlers not yet attacked?"

"Word has gotten around," he replied, "and most are seeking refuge this side of the border as they did during the groundmite raids."

Estora remembered. Some provinces, like Adolind, had been welcoming to the refugees, while others, like D'Ivary, had not. D'Ivary had, in fact, abused the refugees. As a result, D'Ivary had, by the king's decree and agreement among the other lord-governors, a new lord-governor.

She turned to Colin. "Ensure there are no problems with the lord-governors accepting refugees into their provinces. The king, as well as I, would wish for their safety. If problems arise, remind them of D'Ivary."

Colin bowed. "Yes, my lady."

"Rider, have you any more to report?"

"No, Your Highness."

"Then you may be excused with my thanks."

He bowed and hastily departed, with a quick glance at the doors that led to Zachary's bedchamber. He must be desperate to know about his king's condition, and what was going to happen to his captain. If things were different, Captain Mapstone would be here advising Estora. And if the captain were not able to be here, Estora would have asked the lieutenant to stay. But things were what they were. Connly had been briefed on the captain's suspension, and about his added responsibilities. To him it must appear a very threatening situation and she had no misapprehension about where his loyalties lay—with the king and his captain. He was unsure of her, not ready to trust, despite the past relationship she'd had with the Riders. Gradually she would try to bring him into her confidence, win his trust, but there were more pressing problems to attend to at the moment.

And she must act decisively.

"We need to hit back at Birch," General Harborough said, "and hit hard. I can assemble a force to march north and—"

"What about the towers?" she asked.

"They are not an immediate threat."

"How do you know?"

Harborough looked a little flustered, glancing at Colin for support. Colin remained neutral, did not speak. It was clear the general expected her to acquiesce to whatever he suggested. She was, after all, an untried woman with no warcraft behind her.

"We do not know," the general finally admitted. "But you heard the Rider. That Sleeper could have been in the tower for years, and there may be no others. No others that will awaken, or do whatever it is they do. Let Lord D'Yer handle it. Birch is actually attacking us. He's the bigger threat."

"If I may interject," Colin said, "Lord D'Yer has rotated his troops at the wall now for three years with only minimal support from the royal army. They are stretched thin. It seems to me more of our regulars could be assigned duty at the wall. It is a border that has been long neglected, and you see what neglect has wrought at the breach."

Lines of barely contained anger furrowed across Harborough's broad forehead. "The D'Yers were supposed to be responsible for that wall. I don't like the idea of splitting our forces on two fronts like that. We take out Birch and his renegades, then we can worry about the wall."

Colin and Harborough went back and forth, each emphasizing his point. Estora wished ever more fervently Zachary would wake up, recover. How was she to know what she should do? Zachary would know. Karigan would, too, she was sure. Karigan was the one who, after rescuing Estora from abductors, figured out how to further distract the brigands from hunting her and allow her to escape. It had been a dangerous plan, but clever. Karigan had made herself a decoy by dressing up as Estora and led the brigands away in a chase.

It gave Estora a thought.

"Gentlemen," she said, interrupting what was fast escalating into an argument. The two looked at her as if they'd forgotten she was even there. "Birch attacks with stealth, does he not?"

"Yes," Harborough began, "but—"

"And our scouts and spies have had difficulty finding and tracking his movements."

"That's correct."

"Then I do not understand how you plan to engage him."

Harborough's expression crumbled, his cheeks taking on a more ruddy glow. "We'll step up our scouting and define a field of battle."

"But he isn't using traditional battlefield tactics," Colin said. "He's attacking unprepared civilians."

Harborough's chest puffed up and he looked ready to bellow at Colin. The general was definitely not a man who liked to be told he was wrong.

"Gentlemen," Estora said firmly, "I must agree with Colin.

I think the situation calls for another approach. The Mountain Unit keeps a base to the north, does it not?"

Harborough nodded. "But it's more an outpost, too small to—"

Estora silenced him with a look. She then told them her idea and they both gawked at her, stunned.

When she finished, Harborough rubbed his chin and looked thoughtful. "I'll have to talk with my officers and strategists," he said, "but I must admit, it's a very compelling idea. It will, however, still require additional soldiers."

"Of course," she said, "but surely one unit could be spared to go to the wall, at least temporarily, even while we address the situation in the north. When the lord-governors assemble, it seems to me it would be a good time to suggest they take a more active role at the wall. The brunt of the problem has fallen on D'Yer, and yet it's not just a D'Yerian problem. It's a Sacoridian problem. Perhaps I can convince them to provide fresh provincial troops to help guard the wall."

Both men looked pleased by her solution, and after Harborough left, Colin said, "If I may be so bold, Your Highness, you did very well with such difficult problems. I am not sure Zachary could have done better."

After Colin left, Estora stood unsteadily and entered Zachary's chamber, and sat at his bedside. She ought to have felt elated, or at least relieved, but instead she put her face in her hands and wept, her unconscious husband her only witness.

"You must wake up," she whispered to him. "I am not strong enough for this. I cannot bear it alone."

⋙ DAYS OF GRAY ⋘

Karigan stirred and opened her eyes to gray, Yates' head still resting on her shoulder. They'd both fallen asleep with their backs against the tree. They ought to have organized a watch between the two of them. Not that Yates could actually *watch*, but he could at least listen for trouble.

Fortunately it was not raining as hard as it had been. She yawned, then detected movement from the corner of her eye. She looked, but saw nothing. Then there was movement again in her peripheral vision, this time in the opposite direction. She twisted around, but whatever it was was gone. She put her hand to the hilt of her sword and tried to stand, but the stinging pain ripped through her leg and she gasped. When she looked down she found it crawling with insects burrowing and biting into the wounds.

She screamed and slapped at her leg.

Yates started to wakefulness beside her. "What? What is it?"

Karigan kept pummeling her leg, regardless of the howling pain, until she realized there were no insects. None at all. Illusion? All she'd managed to do was start the wounds oozing again through their makeshift bandages.

"Karigan? What's happening?" Yates reached for her, clamped his hands around her arm.

"N-nothing. I thought . . . I thought I saw something is all."

"Are you sure it's nothing?"

"I'm sure. Bad dream, or the forest is playing tricks on me."

Yates did not seem to know what to say, so they sat in

489

silence for some time, the wet forest *drip-drip-dripping* all around them. Finally he cleared his throat, looking uncomfortable. "Uh, I've got a very full bladder. Think you can help me, er, find a place?"

Karigan did not want to stand. "I will tell you where to go."

"Promise you won't make me walk into a tree? Or fall down a hole?"

"No promises," she said in a weak attempt at humor. "You'll have to trust me."

"There is no one I trust more," Yates said very quietly.

A hollow place inside Karigan ached at his words. He trusted her, he trusted her to help him get through this, to get out of this forest. If she were seeing illusions, how could she trust herself? How could she take care of him when she was falling apart?

She took a deep breath. First things first. She directed him away, step by step, telling him when to lift his feet over a tree root or when to skirt a boulder. When he was some yards away, she gazed in the other direction to give him privacy while he took care of his needs. She'd have to take care of her own soon, but she just did not want to move her leg. She kept glancing at it to ensure there were no insects on it, real or imaginary.

When Yates finished, she guided him back. He remained standing. "I assume it's morning."

"It's gray out," Karigan replied, "so night is gone."

"You still think we should stay here?"

"Yes, in case the others come looking for us."

He nodded.

And so began a day of waiting, the mist wafting around as if it were a living mass that coiled between the trees and encircled them. Karigan and Yates ate their half-rations. Yates kept standing and sitting and standing, and looked like he wanted to wander off, but one jolting trip over a downed branch convinced him not to wander far. The monotony of gray throughout the day overwhelmed Karigan with the desire to nap and she had to shake herself awake more than once. The pain of her leg was tiring, and she feared whatever ichor the thorns contained had poisoned her. How bad? There was no way of telling.

At least nothing had come to make a meal of them. Yet. And there'd been no sign of the illusory insects feeding on her leg. She swatted her neck and corrected herself: real insects were indeed making a meal of them one nibble at a time. She was astonished that the biters of Blackveil seemed no worse than those on the other side of the wall. Perhaps biters were already plague enough that the tainted magic of the place did not affect them.

"They're not coming back for us, are they," Yates said for perhaps the hundredth time. He stood facing away from her, as if he could force his eyes to see again.

"Don't know," Karigan replied. "They certainly won't find us if we're stumbling around the forest."

"Waiting around isn't like you," he said.

She supposed it wasn't, but a lethargy had settled over her, and waiting in this instance seemed the sensible course. She laughed.

"What's so funny?"

"I was just thinking that I'd made a sensible decision to wait, and then I wondered since when had I started making sensible decisions?"

As the bleak day passed, Karigan fell into a restless sleep filled with dark shapes and a sense of loathing. A rustling awoke her. Yates was sitting beside her and appeared to be half asleep himself. He hadn't made the noise—it was farther off. She glanced around and caught movement, maybe a shadow, leaping between trees, and almost as soon as she saw it, it was gone.

"What was that?" she murmured, feeling muzzy-headed.

"What was what?" Yates asked.

"Thought I saw something."

"Forest playing tricks on you again?"

"Maybe," Karigan replied.

Some moments passed, then Yates jerked his head up. "Now I think I'm *hearing* things."

"What?"

"Horses."

Karigan was about to tell him he *was* hearing things until she heard them herself, the sound of snorting and several hooves muted on the forest floor. Then she saw them a way off through the woods, six or eight dark gray horse forms ambling between the trees, pulling at sparse vegetation from branches as they went, moving with the mist, never straying from it, almost wearing it as a cloak.

"You're not hearing things," Karigan whispered to Yates.

The horses paused, lifting noses to the air, no doubt scenting Karigan and Yates. Karigan narrowed her eyes, wondering how prey animals like horses had survived Blackveil. Then she discerned that perhaps they were not simple horses. Their eyes gleamed amber-red through the mist, and their underbellies and the bottoms of their necks were armored with scales that rippled in the weak light. In fact their movements differed from ordinary horses; they seemed more flexible, their necks more sinuous. One shook its head and she realized even the manes were not ordinary, but bristle-stiff. She shuddered, both fascinated and appalled.

The band continued along, fading away with the mist, vanishing utterly. She described them to Yates.

"Just like everything else in this place," he grumbled. "Not normal. Definitely not normal."

"They must be descended from the horses the Arcosians left behind," Karigan surmised. "Somehow they adapted to the forest." Or else Mornhavon had altered them as he had other creatures, she thought, but did not add.

The mist horses did not reappear and the interminable day began to fail.

"Maybe my moonstone will help the others find us," Karigan said, and she was sorry she hadn't thought of it the previous night.

By the time it was full dark, it had started to pour again. The light of Karigan's moonstone flared out from beneath their simple shelter, turning the rain into threads of silver fire.

Karigan awoke again to a sense of movement. They'd made it through another night even though, once more, both of them had failed to keep watch. Yates snored softly beside her. It was gray again and Karigan began to wonder if it was really the vapor of the forest, or if like Yates, she was losing her eyesight.

And her mind.

Movement. A black figure floated among the trees. She thought of the mist horses, but the form was human in shape. Had they been finally found by the rest of their companions? "Lynx?" Her voice emerged as a raspy whisper. Despite the wet of the forest, her throat was dry. "Lieutenant Grant?"

No one answered.

Using the bonewood, Karigan struggled to her feet, ignoring the pain striating her leg. When finally she stood, the figure ran off in graceful bounds, fleet of foot and soundless, and then vanished. Karigan tried to run after it, but her leg betrayed her and she fell with a cry.

Yates was up instantly, crawling toward her, his hands feeling the way. When he reached her, he patted her arm, touched her face.

"What happened? Are you all right?"

"I'm passable," she lied. "Thought I saw something—or someone—again, but it's gone. I think I'm going mad."

"Please don't," Yates said with a feeble smile. "We've enough problems."

He had, Karigan thought, no idea.

They returned to their shelter and the day passed much the same as the previous one, though Karigan felt less well and gave Yates her half of the morning ration. She did not feel up to eating, and with a sickly languor weighing her down was more inclined toward sleeping.

"You are very quiet," Yates said.

"Sorry. Not much to say."

"I wish you'd tell a story or something to help pass the time."

She thought about the legends of Laurelyn and Castle Argenthyne because of where they were, and because her mother always sang and told her stories of Laurelyn to soothe her when she was little. She did not, however, even possess the energy to tell a story.

The lethargy settled in, took on a dreamlike quality. She saw the figure again. It tumbled and leaped through the trees like an acrobat. She tried to stir, tried to speak to Yates, but could not seem to do either. Yates just sat there, gazing unseeing into the forest.

The figure somersaulted right up to her and came to rest on bent knee. His face and head were encased in a looking mask just like the tumbler that had been at the king's masquerade, but the mirror of this mask was tarnished and corroded. She could barely see her reflection in it.

The tumbler then rose and backed away, and with a flourish pointed to others stepping out from behind trees, ladies and gentlemen in ragged finery, faded longcoats and yellowed lace. They wore masks of grotesque horned demons and ferocious creatures with gaping, toothy maws, the eyeholes empty sockets. They leered at her.

Discordant music wafted through the woods and the ladies and gentlemen danced, their movements jerky, dead. A mockery of the king's masquerade ball.

This is not real, she thought. Just the bent, craggy trees with their crazy limbs seeming to drift in the fog. Just her own madness making her see things.

She still could not move or speak, but this time when the tumbler knelt before her, she gazed at her wan reflection in his mask behind the tarnish—until it changed. A vision took hold. Blood splashed the looking mask like crimson rain on a window, then smeared away revealing a face. Not her own, but one she knew well. The king's. She swallowed hard. His face was pallid, lifeless, the stained mask making it look diseased. The vision pulled back. He lay in bed and people in black surrounded him like mourners. And it was gone. The looking mask returned to its dull countenance.

"No!" Karigan cried. "Tell me!"

The tumbler leaped away.

"Karigan?" Yates said anxiously.

The dancers twirled away into the mist, and with each blink, the tumbler became more distant. Karigan staggered painfully to her feet with the aid of the bonewood and attempted to pursue him.

"Karigan?" This time Yates' voice was sharper, alarmed.

She kept going, bent on seeing more in the looking mask. Tears of pain and grief washed across her cheeks. What was this vision of the king? What had become of him?

But the tumbler was gone. She searched the shadows, breathing hard, her body shaking with exertion and pain.

Several pairs of green glinting eyes stared back at her. The shadows came to life. Large, bristling shadows.

Oh, gods, she thought.

"Karigan?" Yates called, his voice quavering with fear.

She glanced back, saw more pairs of eyes, dark forms snuffling near him. A pack of Blackveil's creatures had scented them out, two helpless people, one blind and the other injured—easy prey.

But they were *not* helpless. Karigan shook the bonewood to staff length. "Yates," she called, "draw your sword and knife!"

With another glance she saw he already had. She shifted her grip on her staff and stood ready to defend herself.

⋘ SHADOW BEASTS ⋙

The creatures circled around Karigan, wove in and out of the trees. They watched her with unblinking green eyes. Had these been her dancers? She could not see them fully, for their dusky hides blended in with the forest, but she caught glimpses of barrel-chested torsos and limber hindquarters. Gray, slavering tongues hung from bear-trap jaws. She thought them wolflike, but nothing was certain in Blackveil.

They slunk around her, snuffling and snarling, sometimes closer, sometimes farther away, always out of range of her staff. She swung it at a couple that came closest and they leaped away growling. It was clear they did not like the bonewood.

How long, she wondered, would it keep them away?

With a glance back at Yates, she saw the creatures creep close, retreating halfheartedly when Yates swept his sword through the air. His face was taut with concentration as if he listened for the slightest pad of foot or exhalation.

Karigan backed toward him. They must stand together. The beasts moved with her, and beyond, dancers swirled in the vapor, green glowing through the eyeholes of wolf masks.

She shook her head. Not dancers, just more beasts, the play of dark and mist. Carefully she inched back toward Yates, the shadows watching her intently, eagerly.

"Must hold it together," she murmured to herself, but a battle raged in her mind and she was no longer sure of what was real.

"Yates," she said, "I'm coming back."

He did not reply, but she saw from the corner of her eye the gleam of his saber as he swept it at a fleet shadow.

When finally she reached him, they stood back to back, the beasts swarming around them.

"Are they real?" Karigan wondered aloud.

Yates snorted. "I felt one breathe on my neck."

Karigan trembled with the effort to just stand. She'd eaten and drunk too little over the last couple days, and the lethargy pressed down on her shoulders like a mountain of granite. She'd no hope of fighting the creatures.

Dancers, dancers careened around them; the flow of dresses, the spiraling motion, the seesawing music.

She pressed her eyes shut and gripped her staff hard, recovering just in time to rap the skull of a beast that came close to tearing off Yates' leg. It receded with a thunderous growl.

Another charged them, but swerved away from Karigan's staff. The beasts pressed hard to one side of them, but less so to the other. Karigan wondered why. When she glanced over her shoulder, there stood the tumbler. He beckoned her. Or maybe it was Lynx.

"Lynx!" Karigan cried.

"Lynx? Is it him?" Yates asked, his voice swelling with hope.

"Yes, yes it is him." Lynx was cloaked in the forest's gloom, but it was *him*.

"Hold onto my belt," Karigan said. "We're going to him."

Yates sheathed his long knife, but held onto his saber, and with Karigan's guidance, clenched the back of her swordbelt. Leaving behind their lean-to shelter and supplies, Karigan started toward the beckoning Lynx, the shadow beasts parting before her, and rejoining the pack behind. They followed, a seething, stalking mass.

"Lynx!" Karigan cried again. He was not any closer, and she speeded her steps causing Yates to stumble behind her.

"Are we almost there?" he asked. "Are the others with him?"

"Alone," Karigan replied, pressing on. Why didn't Lynx come to their aid? Where were the others?

She jabbed her staff at a beast that edged around beside them. She totally missed it, but the creature returned whining back to the pack. Ahead, Lynx appeared ever farther away. He turned, striding into the distance.

"Lynx!"

Karigan strained against Yates' weight. They were going to lose Lynx, just like before.

"Karigan," said Yates, "I can't—"

"Pick up your feet, just trust me!"

She hastened her pace and Yates did his best to keep up. She ignored the pain of her leg, defied the wall of fatigue, and the shadow beasts rolled and crested like a wave pushing them ahead.

The distance between them and Lynx widened more and more.

"No, no, no," Karigan muttered. "Not again!"

She sprinted. Yates lost hold of her belt, and freed of his weight, she flew forward, flew forward until she was caught in midair by ... nothing.

She tried to shake her head, but could not move it, as if it was glued to the air. Her whole body was stuck.

"Karigan?" Yates. He was not far behind.

No, she wasn't stuck in the air. A net with sticky, mist-fine filaments held her. More precisely, a *web*. Strung between trees, it went for great length through the forest.

"No," she moaned.

She tried to pry her limbs free, but could not. It was not the first time she'd been so caught and a powerful dread descended on her. She panicked for a time, struggling, trying to kick her legs free, Yates calling to her. She was quickly overcome by exhaustion and hung there like a discarded marionette, realizing that panic would not help free her. She searched for Lynx, but when she found him in the distance, his form evaporated. She'd been lured into a trap by illusion or a hallucination. They'd been herded by the shadow beasts. Down the length of the net were other prey, wound in web packets, some still quivering with life. The beasts sniffed at one, tore into it, while being careful not to get entangled themselves. She winced at the squealing that came from the trapped creature. The beasts cleverly stole prey from another predator, even drove the prey into the web for an easy meal.

"Are you all right?" she asked Yates.

"They're all around me," he said, his voice desperate. "Can you help me?"

"No, Yates, I can't." Beasts snuffled at her leg. She felt hot breaths against her trousers.

Yates grunted and a beast yiped. "Think I got one!"

Tears welled in Karigan's eyes. A broad muzzle pushed into her wounded leg, nipping flesh, but another beast brushed against her and leaped on the first followed by vigorous snarling and flying fur. They bumped into the back of Karigan's legs as they fought over her, their next meal.

She could give in, give in to the lethargy that was quickly overtaking her once again. She thought of the funereal vision she'd seen in the looking mask of the mourners surrounding the king in his bed. He was gone. What did the rest matter?

Yates called to her, his voice barely registering amid her despair. "I think they're leaving!"

"What?" She tried to look around, listen, but could not detect the presence of the shadow beasts. Why would they leave? As quickly as she'd fallen into her despair, her hopes began to rise once again, until she heard an immense *something* crashing through the woods.

The shadow beasts had left them alone because something worse was on its way.

CREATURES OF KANMORHAN VANE

The creature whose web Karigan was trapped in hurtled through the woods, smashing trees aside with enormous claws as if they were nothing, the metallic gleam of its carapace a nightmare memory of the other time she'd been caught in such a web and fought the same kind of creature. Fought and survived, but not without help. She did not think that Soft Feather, the great gray eagle, would fly in to help her this time.

She cried out in despair when she saw there wasn't just one creature, but two, each like a giant crab, each scuttling forward on jointed legs, black orbs on the ends of mobile eyestalks and antennae feeling out the terrain. Tails with dagger-sized stingers arched over their backs.

So this was really it, Karigan thought. The end.

"What's happening?" Yates demanded. "Tell me!"

"It's been . . ." Karigan began, and she meant to finish with: *an honor to be your friend.* And then she was going to tell him to leave, to find his way as best he could, to go somewhere he could wait for the others to locate him. But something—someone—else caught her eye even as the crab creatures trundled closer, a flash of movement, a man.

This time it was Ard who appeared to her. She was sure of it. No mistaking him for Lynx or Grant, and certainly not the Eletians. He watched them from behind a tree.

He was no more than illusion, she concluded, just like the masked tumbler, just like Lynx. She'd lost her grip on what was real.

The Ard figure peered at the scene very carefully, and

500

with a final glance toward the creatures, he backed away and ran into the woods. Karigan watched him go with regret.

Perhaps the creatures were illusion, too, but no such luck, for Yates kept demanding for her to tell him what she saw. It was clear he could hear the monsters well enough. They'd halted several yards away from the web, swiveling to face each other. One was clearly larger and raised its claws and tail high as though to impress the other with its size. The other sidestepped away as if wanting to flee, but the bigger creature moved with it, blocking it. The smaller then jabbed its claws at the larger, and the larger caught and held them in its own pincers.

Their movement became a sort of dance, the pair circling around and around, holding claws.

If the creatures kept busy, Karigan thought she might still have a chance. The urgency of the situation cleared her mind of illusion and fear. Resolve surged within her.

"Yates," she called, "do you still have your sword?"

"Yes."

"Carry it pointed ahead, toward my voice."

"Why? What—"

"I am caught in a web. You hear that noise? The web belongs to one of those creatures making all the noise, and the last time I was caught in a web like this, I was supposed to be food for that creature's offspring." So far, with her limited range of vision, Karigan had not observed any eggs.

"*Oh,*" Yates said, the lilt in his voice telling her he remembered her story about the creature of Kanmorhan Vane. He remained silent after and Karigan feared he'd frozen.

"Yates! You all right? We haven't time...!"

"Yeah. I think I'm sometimes glad I can't see."

Karigan kept talking, guiding him slowly toward her, trying to sound calm while panic reared up inside her once again, and the two enormous creatures continued their dance on the other side of the web. They appeared transfixed with one another, their tails arced high, stingers leaking poison, poised for battle. How long would they remain preoccupied? She hoped, when they knocked over another tree, that they would not knock one down on her and Yates.

Finally she felt the pressure of Yates' sword against the small of her back.

"Stop!" she cried.

"Whew. Didn't want to run you through."

"I need you to cut me out of the web," she said, and continued to give him painstaking instructions, guiding his sword with her words.

He nearly cut off her hand, but he turned the blade just in time, slashing through the sticky, strong filaments of the web. When her arm was free, she was able to draw her long knife and cut herself out the rest of the way. She backed away from the web, pulling sticky strands off her face and hair and body. The broken filaments of the web floated after her, reaching for her.

"Can we go now?" Yates asked.

"Definitely." Karigan collected her staff and glanced back at the creatures. And did a double take. Their dance had concluded, and now the larger was clambering onto the back of the smaller, which had lowered its tail submissively to the side, its stinger planted in the earth.

A choked, half-hysterical laugh crept out of Karigan's throat.

"What is it?" Yates asked.

"They weren't fighting after all," was all she said.

"*Oh.*"

She had no idea how long the mating of the creatures would take, so she hurriedly placed Yates' hand on her shoulder and started leading him away as fast as her painful leg allowed. She did not have a plan or direction in mind, just to get as far away from the creatures and the web as she could.

"By the way," she said as she limped along, "if I say I'm seeing something, you make sure I'm really seeing it."

"Like Lynx earlier?"

"Yeah."

"How do I do that?"

"I don't know. Pinch me, kick me. Question me. Do whatever it takes."

Yates sighed. "Life with you is not dull."

Karigan lost track of what direction they were headed in.

For all she knew they were wandering in circles, but she kept stumbling on until night swooped down on them like the dark wings of one of Blackveil's giant avians. When Karigan found a seemingly safe place beneath a leaning pine—any place away from the web and those creatures seeming to be safe—she collapsed on the spot. Her leg was screaming and oozing, and all she cared about was getting off it. Immediately the languor descended on her once again. Yates slid down beside her.

"We lost our stuff," he said.

"I know."

"What about a shelter?"

"I'll make one." But she could not imagine rising again. All her remaining strength bled from her and her mind felt gray, as gray as the fog of Blackveil. With the pain and exhaustion, she just wanted to rest.

"We don't have any food," Yates said.

Why must he state the obvious? "Eat some dirt," she mumbled.

"You want me to eat *dirt?*"

"Thought I saw Ard."

"Just now?"

"Earlier. When I was stuck in the web."

"One of your illusions?"

"Uh-huh. If he saw us, he'd have brought the others to help us."

"I hope," Yates said, "this problem you're having is a temporary thing."

"Me, too," she replied, leaning against his shoulder. She wished it were all temporary. Their chances of survival were dismal at best. They were without food or a reliable source of water. Alton had somehow survived for days in Blackveil under similar conditions, but he'd found the wall and Tower of the Heavens. Karigan and Yates were far away from the wall. For all Karigan knew, they'd passed into one hell or another, and the chances of finding their way out were growing less likely, especially with Yates blind and her own sight unreliable.

At the moment, she didn't care. She just needed a little

rest. She'd rest then somehow make them a shelter. Before she fell asleep, she had the presence of mind to remove her moonstone from her pocket, its brightness raising her spirits for a moment, but even that light could not hold back the darkness of deep exhaustion, and she dropped off even as the rains came once again.

❖ THE ELETIANS' TASK ❖

Darkness seeped into Karigan's dreams, though she could not swear it was all dreams. She became aware of her head tucked against Yates' chest, his arms wrapped around her, and his hand keeping hers clasped around the moonstone. Dozens of green eyes shone beyond the edge of the light. The shadow beasts had found them again. They nudged their noses at the light, but whined and backed into the dark as if it burned them.

"Keep the light shining," Yates whispered to her.

Karigan did not awaken again until her world shifted. Yates moved and laughed, and there were other voices and enough light that she thought Blackveil must have been a dream and she was back in Sacor City in the full sun of summer. The green eyes of shadow beasts were gone, replaced by the shimmering faces of Eletians.

"They aren't real," she told Yates. She curled into a ball at the base of the tree, wondering vaguely how it could be that Yates was now talking to her hallucinations, unless he was a hallucination himself. Maybe nothing was real, just all in her head, and if that was the case, then the vision she'd seen of the king on his deathbed was similarly false. She smiled to herself and slipped away.

Someone tipped her head forward and pressed a bottle to her lips. She drank eagerly thinking it was just water, but it tasted of the cordial of the Eletians, of spring rain and ripening fruits. It was taken from her after just a few swallows.

Were her hallucinations now taking over her other senses? Could one slake her thirst?

The clouds in her mind parted with the drinking of the cordial, and when she peeled open her eyes, she found Graelalea kneeling beside her.

"Are you real?" Karigan asked.

The Eletian tilted her head as if considering, the light of her moonstone flaring around her pearlescent armor and pale hair like a halo. On closer inspection, the armor was mud-splashed and beaded with rain, wet feathers and flaxen hair plastered against her head.

Karigan heard the patter of rain, but did not feel it. She was in a tent. She sighed in relief.

"You *are* real," she said to Graelalea.

The Eletian smiled. "Yes. You were elusive, but we have found you. You should have remained in one place when we lost you."

"But I . . ."

"I know. The poison of the thorns in your blood played tricks in your mind. We shall do our best to draw it out, but Hana was the one with the healing touch among us, and she is gone."

"How did you find us?"

"Excellent tracking skills, and your Lynx felt the hunger of the beasts, felt their drive to hunt and that they had caught the scent of something unusual. He presumed it was you and Yates that excited them, and he was able to follow their desire."

Karigan didn't want to imagine what it must have felt like for Lynx to touch the minds of those creatures.

"What about Yates? Can you help him?"

"Help him see again?" Graelalea asked. "That is something beyond our power. Perhaps with time, on the other side of the wall, he would regain his vision."

"Have you told him?"

"We have not hidden the truth from him. We shall help him navigate the forest. It is remarkable the two of you survived on your own."

Karigan thought she detected respect in the Eletian's

voice. If so, it meant the two of them had come a long way in their relationship since the first time they met, when it seemed Graelalea held only contempt for Karigan.

"For now you must rest," Graelalea said.

"What ... what about my leg?" Karigan realized it did not hurt presently. In fact, she did not feel it much at all. She wiggled her toes to make sure it was still attached.

"The cordial will help with the pain," Graelalea replied, "and for the poison, Lynx suggested leeches. They are, after all, abundant here. We examined them closely and determined they are untainted by the forest. We have attached some to your wounds. Would you care to see?"

"No!" Karigan recoiled out of reflex at the thought of the leeches, mouths attached to her flesh and sucking her blood till they became bloated. Leeches were commonly used to treat a number of maladies, but Karigan had just about had it with creatures wanting to suck her blood or eat her.

"We did consider hummingbirds," Graelalea said.

By the time Karigan realized the Eletian had made a joke, she was gone and the tent darkened. The energizing effects of the cordial faded and heaviness descended on Karigan. For the first time in a long while, she felt safe, as safe as she could be in Blackveil Forest. Someone else could be responsible for Yates, and someone else could keep watch over camp.

She tried not to think about the leeches feeding on her blood, and allowed the dark and heaviness to help her sink into sleep.

She was awakened sometime during the night by voices raised in anger, dreams of white feathers falling like snow and a silver key shining on her palm slipping away from waking memory. It took her a moment to remember where she was. All was not dark for moonstone and firelight glowed through the canvas of her tent. Silhouetted shadows slashed across the tent wall with curt gestures.

"We have seen enough!" It was Grant, and he was the loudest. "There is no reason to go any farther."

"You may return as you like." Graelalea, her voice cool. "We are certainly not forcing you to continue on with us."

Grant laughed. It sounded half-hysterical. "You say that even knowing we'd never find our way back on our own and that we would be much less safe without you."

"You have been given the option," Graelalea replied. "I can give you no more than that for we must proceed with our journey. We are not turning back. Not yet."

"So you'd just abandon us?" Grant demanded.

Graelalea must have deemed the question unworthy of answer because she provided none. One of the silhouettes began to drift away.

"What is it, then, that you're after?" This from Ard. "What in the hells is so important that you must keep going on? What are we really here for? What do you seek?"

Graelalea's silhouette paused, the dance of flame enlarging and diminishing her shadow by turns. "You are here because your king wished it. I know little of his motives, but you are here by his choice. I, and my tiendan, we are here because our crown prince wishes it."

"That is not much of an answer," Ard grumbled. "*Why* does your crown prince want you here? I think after what we've been through, you owe it to us to tell us what people are dying for."

At first Graelalea did not respond and Karigan thought perhaps she would not because she chose not to, but much to Karigan's surprise, she said, "We have come back for those who were left behind."

"Those who were . . ." Ard sputtered.

Karigan imagined her Sacoridian companions looking as stunned and curious as she felt.

"Who?" Lynx asked in his low rumbling voice. "Who was left behind?"

Karigan felt the tension, the suspense, right through the canvas walls around her.

"Our Sleepers," Graelalea said.

"Your tree people?" Ard blurted.

"There is a chance," Graelalea replied in a calm voice, "that if the grove at Castle Argenthyne still stands, we may be able to awaken the Sleepers and rescue them; bring them back to Eletia."

"And if this grove is gone like the one in Telavalieth?"

"We believe it had more of a chance of surviving than the others. There are . . . were powers at work at the castle."

"You fools," Grant said. "You see what this forest is, what it does. The answer is before you. Look what happened to Porter with those hummingbirds. Monstrous things killed one of your own, too, that Hana. That's what the forest does to anything that lives here. And as for your castle and its powers? Look what happened to Yates' magic. It turned on him."

"You do not understand." A new voice had entered the fray: Ealdaen.

"Don't I?" Karigan imagined spittle flying from Grant's mouth, like a rabid dog ready to attack. "But of course, you are the ancient, wise ones, aren't you, lording it over us like we're worms. I'm telling you that it's time to turn back. Whatever your castle was, it's rubble now. And your Sleepers? Their grove probably rotted to the earth long ago."

Silence reigned when Grant's outburst ended. Silhouettes dispersed until there was only the one she identified as Grant.

"What?" he shouted. "Can't handle the truth?"

Ard murmured to him.

"Leave me alone," Grant said. "If they can't face me, what're they gonna do when they reach their precious grove and find it gone?"

Karigan sighed. Grant's tone had sounded irrational to her, but he'd made some good points. At least they finally knew exactly what the Eletians wanted in Blackveil: to rescue their people who had been peacefully Sleeping at the time of Mornhavon's invasion.

She could not help but agree with Grant that the wisest course was to retreat from the forest, but nothing, she knew, would sway the Eletians from their task. She only hoped they were prepared for the worst when they reached Castle Argenthyne, whatever the worst might entail.

 LYNX'S COUP ⋙

Karigan did not reawaken until sometime in the gray of morning when she perceived someone in the tent with her. She opened crusty eyes to discover Graelalea kneeling beside her and peering beneath the blanket at her leg.

"The leeches appear sated," Graelalea said. "They have detached from your leg."

The leeches! Karigan had forgotten about them, and thought it just fine she had. She rotated her foot and shifted her leg, grimacing as pain burned through her flesh.

Graelalea gazed sideways at her. "How does it feel?"

"Very sore."

The Eletian nodded. "I am not surprised. I shall spread some evaleoren on your wounds and that should ease some of the pain. I'd make a poultice, but Hana carried our herbs." Anything Hana had carried was gone with her. Graelalea produced a pot of the salve and spread it gently on Karigan's leg. Immediately it calmed the pain. "Only time will tell if the work of the leeches proves efficacious. I fear, however, we haven't the time to allow you the rest you require."

Karigan nodded, barely withholding a sigh. She'd like nothing more than to sleep and keep off her leg, but there could be no waiting around in Blackveil, and of course she did not wish to appear weak.

"So we are going on to Castle Argenthyne," Karigan said, feeling a strange thrill despite the circumstances, to be journeying toward a place that had, for most of her life, existed only as a fairy tale.

"The tiendan and I will resume our journey to the castle,"

Graelalea said. "Your Grant and the others have been debating whether to continue with us, or to turn back."

Grant had already acknowledged that trying to return without the Eletians to guide them was likely suicidal. Yet it did not make sense to be leading poor, blind Yates to Castle Argenthyne, or, for that matter, her with her hurt leg and unreliable visions. And they had found out the truth of what the Eletians sought in Argenthyne: the Sleepers. Had they achieved what the king asked of them, or would he want them to press on?

"We recovered your pack from your campsite," Graelalea said. "I shall pass it in to you, but first I'd like you to take a sip of this." She produced the cordial and Karigan eagerly took the flask to her lips. "One sip only," Graelalea reminded her.

Karigan reluctantly returned the flask, licking her lips to ensure she didn't miss a single drop. Graelalea crawled out of the tent, then reappeared in the opening and pushed in the pack Karigan had believed long lost.

"When you are ready," the Eletian said, "come out and see if you wish to try some food."

At the mention of food, Karigan's stomach gurgled and she realized she was famished, quite a change from when she'd felt so unwell only a day ago. Was it the effect of the cordial? The leeches? She only hoped it was not temporary.

She dug through her pack looking for a change of clothes. The contents were none the worse for wear—not even damp, which was miraculous. Maybe the Eletians possessed drying magic, and a part of her did not doubt it. She was grateful to have her own supplies and her own clothes to change into. Her old pants were shredded beyond repair. She did not think even meticulous Ty would be able to mend them.

She crawled from the tent and unsteadily rose to her feet. Placing weight on her leg sent hornets buzzing in it and she winced. She steadied herself and looked around at the campsite. Lhean fletched an arrow beside the fire and gave her what looked like a genuinely friendly smile. Grant sat hunched before the fire, pushing coals around with a stick and muttering to himself. His appearance was haggard and stubble failed to conceal the hollows beneath his cheekbones. He was much diminished, looked unwell, and appeared unaware of her.

Ard paused searching through his pack for something and gave her a hard, penetrating gaze. As if remembering himself, he schooled his expression to something softer, but for some reason he didn't look happy to see her. "Well, look who's up and about." He smiled, but his joviality rang false in her ears. Then again, she wasn't herself and maybe wasn't perceiving things right.

"Karigan?" It was Yates, also sitting by the fire, gazing in her general direction.

"Hello," she said, and limped over to him, taking his hand.

"You all right?" he asked.

"I'll live."

Ard dropped his whetting stone and swore. He bent over to retrieve it and said nothing more.

Ghosting in the background was Ealdaen, probably on watch. He spared her a glance, but it was brief and indecipherable. She did not see Solan or Telagioth, but perhaps they were in the Eletian tent, or guarding another side of the perimeter.

"Good to see you up," Lynx said, but he did not look particularly happy.

"What's wrong?" she asked.

He held up his tobacco pouch and sighed mournfully. "My leaf has gone bad. Moldy. And I'd been using it sparingly to make it last."

Karigan was just glad *she* was not the source of his misery.

"Come sit with us," he said, and he helped her over to a seat by the fire. "Would you like something to eat?"

"Yes."

He fetched her a spoon and a cup of gruel from a pot on the fire. Normally the stuff was not very palatable, but this morning—afternoon?—it tasted like a feast.

"Must be doing better if you've an appetite," Lynx observed.

She nodded and was permitted seconds. She knew enough to take it slowly, and sipped at intervals at the tea Lynx handed her. It had the tang of Blackveil, for they were down to collecting drinking water from the rain that fell through the leaves of the forest.

Her companions remained quiet. Yates tapped his toe to some unheard music. No one asked her about her adventures while separated from the group. Yates must have filled them in. Still, the tension was palpable. Grant hadn't moved one bit, transfixed by the campfire.

Graelalea emerged from her tent and stood before them, hands on her hips. Ealdaen drifted closer, and Solan and Telagioth appeared from the woods.

"The day grows old," she announced. "It is time to push on. The question is, will *you* be coming with us?" This she directed at Grant.

Finally he moved, gazing up at her with eyes shadowed by dark rings. Although it was not especially warm, sweat glided down the sides of his face.

"Ask him." He nodded in Lynx's direction. "He seems to think he's in charge."

Whoa! Karigan thought. Graelalea had mentioned there was a debate, not a coup. She could not imagine quiet, taciturn Lynx deciding to take charge. She glanced at Yates, who wore a tight smile on his face. She'd have to ask him later what had happened.

"I have assumed command of the Sacoridian contingent of this expedition," Lynx confirmed. "Second in command is Karigan G'ladheon."

Karigan almost dropped her mug of tea. Second in command? Another surprise, though it made sense. If Grant was out of favor, then certainly he wouldn't be second, and Yates could not see, and Ard was not military or in the king's service. That left her.

"What is your decision, then, Rider Lynx?" Graelalea asked.

"We will continue with you to Castle Argenthyne as our king would wish."

Graelalea nodded as if there had been nothing to it.

Karigan breathed a sigh of relief just to have a decision one way or the other.

"Suicide," Grant muttered. "You're gonna find ruins and death. You should forget those Sleepers."

"We cannot," Ealdaen said. "I cannot, and I will not. I was one of those who left them behind."

His words hung in the air, letting them all absorb what he'd said and what it meant.

"So you were there when . . ." Karigan began.

"Yes," he replied. His silvery eyes had taken on the aspect of cold pewter. "Yes, I was there when Mornhavon attacked. I led the retreat. I abandoned the Sleepers and . . . and the lady." He abruptly turned away.

Laurelyn, he'd meant. The Queen of Argenthyne.

"We must break camp and make use of what light we have left to us," Graelalea said.

Karigan wanted to help, but Lynx ordered her to rest while she could. Because Yates could offer little help, he sat with her and quietly filled her in on the so-called debate they'd had about the mission.

"The man's not himself," Yates said of Grant. "He's becoming unhinged. He was planning to march back to the wall even though he didn't know the way. He keeps going on about nythlings, too."

"*Nythlings?*"

"We have no idea," Yates said, shrugging. "Lynx says Grant's also been favoring one of his arms like it hurts him."

Karigan stole a glance at Grant wrestling with one of the tents and it was true—he was not using his right arm much.

"Anyway," Yates continued, "Lynx argued that our mission was not complete until we saw Castle Argenthyne and the grove of the Sleepers. Like he said just now, the king would want as much information as we could gather. Grant said the king could go to the five hells."

Karigan raised an eyebrow. That was not acceptable behavior for one in the service of the king and in command of a mission.

"That's when Lynx announced he was taking command," Yates said. And then he proudly added, "I seconded him. I want to go home as much as anybody, but I know my duty. Plus, I wasn't about to follow Grant, not the way he is now."

"What about Ard?"

"He preferred turning back," Yates replied. "He argued for it, but he wasn't about to go with just Grant and not the rest of us."

"I guess I didn't get a vote," Karigan said.

"I think we know which way you'd choose. But once Lynx became commander, it's his order to keep going, anyway."

So they knew which way she'd choose, did they? Her sense of duty had become predictable, but they might be surprised by how all too willing she'd be to turn around. Even if Grant was becoming, as Yates said, unhinged, his reasons for heading home were sound enough.

And yet, Lynx was right to continue, for they hadn't completed the mission. She shook her head. The mad man among them wanted to take the common sense course and return home, and the sane man wanted to take the insane route.

Such was the way of it in Blackveil, where everything was turned upside down.

⋘ HER COUSIN
UNMASKED ⋙

Estora sank into the plush chair in her parlor in the royal apartments with a cup of her bedtime tea. Her new rooms were spacious and beautiful, but impersonal. With time, she'd transform them to her own tastes, make them her home.

Time, she thought. *What time?*

How could she consider fabrics and colors and furnishings when every waking moment brought visitors offering congratulations and seeking favors? Or Cummings with interminable lists of meetings and parties and requests? Or messengers bearing news of the land and correspondence from those who were now her vassals? Or Colin to discuss the business of the castle and the realm? *Or or or!*

She sighed. The only quiet time she was able to claim were her visits with Zachary. Destarion expressed guarded optimism that there were some improvements in her husband's condition. He rested more easily, his fevers were less intense, and his wound was healing well. There had been some brief awakenings, his dark brown eyes fluttering open, but it was difficult to know how aware he was at those times. All too soon he'd slip away again. Part of the reason, Destarion said, was because of a soporific they gave him to keep him relaxed, permitting his body the time and rest to heal itself.

Besides Estora's visits with Zachary, the only other quiet time she had was when she went to bed. Usually she was so exhausted by the rigors of her day that she slept soundly and deeply. How could she not sleep well in the canopied monstrosity that had the softest down mattress on which she'd ever lain?

516

Ellen, her Weapon, entered the parlor. "Your Highness?"

"Yes?"

"Lord Spane has asked to see you."

Richmont. What did he want at this hour? She found she was displeased, but he was her cousin and had done much to help her. "I will see him."

He had not been around much of late. She imagined he'd been intriguing his way about the castle and the noble quarter in the city, securing his newly elevated position in court. He hadn't been given a formal office, but he'd taken it for granted he was her advisor and close confidant as he had been for her father. She did not favor him, but at the moment he was all she had.

"My lady," he drawled as he entered the parlor and swiftly bowed. "May we speak privately?" He cast a significant look at Ellen.

Estora nodded a dismissal and the Weapon exited to resume her vigil from outside. "What is it, Richmont? It's been a wearisome day and I'm ready for my bed."

He gave her a silky smile she did not like.

"Your readiness for bed is precisely why I'm here," he said. "There is more yet for you to attend to this night."

"Can't it wait? Early tomorrow morning ought to be soon enough. Unless it is an emergency?"

Richmont's smile deepened. "But *now* is bedtime. Should you not be going to your husband's bed as is befitting a new bride?"

She set the teacup aside and it rattled into its saucer. "He's injured—not well. You know that. He'll rest better without my presence."

"Even so, the marriage of a king and queen dictates certain traditions be followed. The witnesses have already assembled."

"You can't possibly be suggesting . . . the rite of consummation? He's *ill,* Richmont."

"All the kings and queens before you have observed the ritual, as must the lord-governors, including your mother and father, who did so unreservedly. Of course we are well-acquainted with the king's condition, so the act will be more . . . symbolic. Still, it must be done to ensure the further appeasement of the lord-governors to make your transition to regnant unimpeachable."

"Oh, gods," she murmured, shaking her head.

Estora was certain that most couples naturally desired to spend their marriage night, and subsequent nights, together doing their duty, but in front of others? She could only surmise that the whole tradition of witnesses was carried on by those who were titillated by watching their rulers perform the act.

"I could proclaim a new law revoking the rite," Estora mused, and as she thought about it, it did not seem a bad idea.

"You could," Richmont agreed, "but then the lord-governors would definitely challenge your right to reign."

She stood and paced, gown and robe flowing about her feet. Then she halted. "There is no way Zachary is able. He's not even conscious."

"Destarion says he's had moments of awareness. And you underestimate the male drive. But as I've said earlier, Zachary's condition is being taken into consideration and tonight will be symbolic. We merely ask that you sleep beside him."

"And this will satisfy your witnesses?"

"For the purposes of the rite, yes. For their personal enjoyment? Doubtful."

"Of all the maddening things. I'm supposed to be queen, but everyone else is telling me what to do. And even that which is most sacred and private must be performed before an audience."

"I suggest you accustom yourself to it. It is your life now. So, will you do this thing or must I throw you into his bed myself?"

"Richmont, I do not care for your tone. You do not have the command of me, and in fact, I am not sure I even wish you to take part in my court."

He closed in on her and grasped her wrist, wrenching it. "Think again," he hissed.

"You're hurting me," Estora protested.

He drew her close, close enough that she felt the heat of

his body. His face was twisted in an ugly way she'd never seen before.

"I have labored hard and long to bring this all to pass," he said in a harsh whisper. "You will not upset my plans."

"What are you talking about?" She tried to wrest her arm away from him but his hand was like a cuff of steel.

"You will not ruin everything I've labored for all these years, for you, your father, and myself." He released her, and shocked, she stepped away from him rubbing her wrist.

"I believe," he continued, "willing or no, I can make you comply with my wishes."

"What are you saying?"

"I am saying, my dear cousin, there are things I know about you that could irreparably harm you and your standing both in the realm and with your clan. I know about you and a Green Rider named F'ryan Coblebay."

"Zachary already knows about F'ryan and me."

Richmont smirked. "Yes, and Coblebay is dead and gone, but there are still influential persons who know nothing of Zachary's acceptance of your ... soiled virtue, and Zachary is in no condition, and may never be, to come to your defense. There are still others of more traditional leanings who'd frown upon your dalliances with a commoner. They'd be all too eager to use the information to discredit your standing across the realm. The people expect their king to be marrying a maiden pure and unbesmirched by some lowly messenger. If you do not obey my wishes, I can expand the story, add salacious details, and send it out into the world."

Estora grew cold. He was right about the traditionalists and how they'd react. Her father had been one of them so she was well acquainted with the mind-set. There were many people who'd go from celebrating her marriage to condemning her. She could be exiled, or worse. And where would that leave the realm? In the very turmoil they were trying to avoid by having moved up the wedding.

"Wouldn't that ruin all the plans you've made for yourself?" she demanded.

"I have plans for every contingency," he replied, seeming to enjoy himself immensely. "I can destroy not just your reputation, but that of your family's as well. Perhaps I could breed doubt about your parentage."

"My parentage!"

He gazed at her as if trying to discern something. "You favor your mother, but I don't see your father in you. Have you ever noticed how your sisters aren't quite the same in looks as you?"

"Richmont!"

"I seem to recall your mother having her eye on a handsome minstrel a certain number of years ago. He'd come to play and sing at the Day of Aeryon feast. Hmm, the timing is about right for—"

"How *dare* you!"

"Oh, I dare. As I question your paternity, I can call into question everything your father ever did. Or in this case, did not do." He laughed. "Or maybe it is your sisters who are the bastards. Will your sister prove strong enough to hold the reins of Coutre Province once I begin leaking my little stories? Even the hint of rumor, even innuendo, could bring her down. People will come to their own conclusions. And, once I've succeeded in tearing down your father's bloodline, they will come to me, to my line, to govern the province."

Estora clenched her hands at her sides in an effort to keep from clawing out his eyes. She seethed within. It was true that if her father's line failed, Richmont would succeed as lord-governor of Coutre Province.

"Tell me," she said, trying to master her voice, "why I should not direct my guards to arrest you for threatening the queen? I could call my Weapon in here right this instant."

"You won't because I've been busy making friends, important and powerful friends. Friends who are favorable toward me, but not necessarily toward you, and I've a trusted and loyal servant with letters in his keeping that will go to these friends of mine should anything happen to me. The letters are filled with my little stories and my friends will immediately spread them around.

"Of course," he added as if an afterthought, "theirs is not necessarily a friendship based on trust, for I know their secrets, too. A simple whisper in the right person's ear is a powerful thing, you know. It can ruin many lives, tear down entire governments.

"Just know, my dear cousin, that one misstep on your part and the whole realm will not only know of the depravities of your bloodline, but will *believe* them."

Estora refused to weep or show weakness. She wished to scream, but she had to remain calm. She lifted her chin. "My father loved you like the son he never had, and you've betrayed him."

"His feelings for me made him easier to manipulate. For instance, if not for me convincing him to hold out for the king, he'd have wed you to Alton D'Yer, or that whelp of a lord-governor from Penburn. And can you say that I've betrayed him? Truly, I am carrying out his wishes that you be queen of the realm. I will only change tactics if *you* betray him by ruining everything we've done for you. If you obey my wishes, then we both benefit. If you do not? Then I will just benefit in a different way.

"Now it is time to see your husband. You understand me, don't you?"

"I believe I understand all too well." Estora shuddered with revulsion. "You have enlightened me on many things this evening, Richmont." He in fact had allowed his mask of the good cousin to slip, and now that she saw him for who he really was, she could watch him. Eventually his self-interest would conflict with her concern for the well-being of the realm. Had he not revealed himself and his machinations this night, she'd never know what he was up to until it was too late.

He gave her a mocking bow.

"Very well," she said. "Let's have this done."

Estora led the way out into the corridor that connected her private chambers with Zachary's. Awaiting her there was Colin, Ellen, and her maid. Estora turned to the Weapon.

"Ellen," she said, "please see to it that you and the others who guard me do not permit Lord Spane into my private rooms. If he wishes to see me, he may make an appointment through Cummings like everyone else."

"Yes, Your Highness," the Weapon said.

The murderous look Richmont passed her made her tremble, but she walked down the corridor with back straight and chin held high. It was only a small act of defiance, but she had to show her cousin he did not have complete power over her. Now that she knew his true nature, she would have to find a way to protect herself, and Zachary and her family, too. But how could one shield oneself from lies that would spread faster than wildfire? He even had her doubting her own parentage. Could there be some truth to the story about the minstrel? The idea of her mother straying ... No, inconceivable. Not her conservative, conscientious mother who had loved her husband.

As Estora entered Zachary's dressing room, she had to put aside her worries for there was another task before her this night. She led the way into his bedchamber to perform her duty as his wife.

 RITUAL AND WAKENING

Naturally the five witnesses, including Rich-mont, were all men, if she judged their stature and builds correctly beneath their hoods and cloaks. They seated themselves in a row of chairs at the foot of the bed.

Zachary lay unaware of all that went on around him.

"How is he?" she asked Destarion.

"About the same, which is really more hopeful than it sounds. He has not declined, and if his wound remains clean and continues to heal, we may see more improvement before long. I think it's the poison that has held him back more than anything. It was not a large dose he received, but harmful all the same."

Estora nodded. "Thank you."

Destarion then stepped closer and lowered his voice. "My lady, your presence with him here tonight may provide him comfort. If he reacts, do not be afraid to fulfill his needs. I've not given him his soporific this evening. In fact, I've given him a slight stimulant of a sort that may make him ... more responsive. I could not say, however, when or if the stimulant will make him more wakeful." With that, Destarion bowed and excused himself from her presence.

The Weapon, Ellen, then came to her and said, "I will be posted right outside the door, my lady. If you should need anything at all, just call me."

"Thank you," Estora replied. Ellen bowed again and left her. If only, Estora thought, she could follow her out. Instead, the witnesses watched her and her maid waited expectantly. Estora squinted at one of the men in the middle whom she thought might be the priest who conducted the marriage ceremony. The moon priests were celibates, but probably took their opportunity to get an eyeful when they could.

Her maid helped her remove the robe, and then as the rite required, her sleeping gown and underclothing. She might have rushed to get beneath the blankets to conceal her nakedness as a modest young woman should, but she was angry. Angered by Richmont's threats, angered by this crass tradition. Instead of hiding, she faced them and allowed them all a slow, good look.

"This is what you're here for, isn't it?" she asked them. "To see your queen at her most vulnerable? Do you like what you see?"

"My lady, please ..." Definitely the priest. He glanced away, but not for long.

She had, she decided, nothing to be ashamed of. She knew many men coveted her body. These five must feel very privileged. Would they brag to their friends? Fellow priests? Even embellish what they saw? Let them look. F'ryan had thought her body beautiful, and it made her feel powerful to force them to stare.

It was, however, also very chilly. After she felt they had gotten enough of a look, she climbed up into the bed next to Zachary, her maid helping her arrange the blankets. "I'll be right outside if you need me, my lady."

"Thank you, Jaid."

Jaid curtsied, dimmed the bedside lamp to a low glow, and then left, bearing away Estora's clothes. Part of the rite was to prevent her access to her clothing so she could not, ostensibly, leave the bedchamber.

Richmont stood and rounded the bed, and brought to her a cup of wine. "Your marriage bed cup," he said. "Drink up."

She took it from him with a scowl. Another part of the ritual. Very often the wine was laced with an aphrodisiac or an herb to promote fertility. She supposed Zachary had gotten his ritual wine as medicine. She sighed and drank. If the wine was dosed, it was very subtle. Richmont stood over her until she drained the cup and he took it from her when she finished.

She sank into the mattress and gazed into the dark ceiling overhead. At least with the light so dim, if there was anything for the witnesses to see, they'd be able to make out few of the fine details. In time her body began to feel very relaxed, relaxed and yet aware of every texture against her skin, of how the movement of the sheets sent vibrations to her very nerve ends. Her body thrilled to the sensations and she wondered how it would respond to Zachary's touch. Yes, the wine had been dosed.

Zachary remained a warm, unmoving presence beside her. She reached out and brushed his arm with her fingertips and that simple contact sent such waves of pleasure flooding through her that she almost cried out. After that, she refrained from touching him. She would not allow herself to get overwrought for the benefit of the watchers, and so far Zachary was showing no signs of being able to reciprocate. She remained still and hoped to sleep, but the circumstances made it difficult, and the revelations about her cousin battered her mind.

Eventually she did doze off, dreaming something of her father standing at a ship rail trying to peer through a fog bank.

"Arrows," he said.

Yes, an arrow had killed him. She surfaced to wakefulness with tears burning her cheeks, at first disoriented. She was not in her old bed, nor was she in her new bed in the queen's chamber. She blinked through the darkness to where the watchers should be sitting, but she could not make out their figures in the dim light. She hadn't a clue to the hour, but they must have grown tired of watching two people sleep and left for their own beds.

"Arrows," Zachary muttered.

Startled, Estora turned to face him. It must have been he who had awakened her. His eyes were open, aware. "Zachary?" she whispered. She caressed his warm, damp cheek, each contact with his skin sending tingles through her body. Whatever they'd dosed her with had not yet worn off.

"Arrows," he said again, looking at her.

She should call to Ellen to summon Master Destarion,

but Destarion said Zachary might awaken, that it would be all right.

Instead, she said, "Yes, it was an arrow that wounded you."

The muscle in his cheek ticked. "No ... battle. The arrows ..." He gazed at her and the dim light shone in his fever-bright eyes.

"What battle, Zachary?"

"I ... I don't know. Has it happened?"

"There has been no battle."

He started to sit up, but she feared he'd try to leave the bed and stand and she thought he would be too weak to bear it. She pressed his shoulder so he would sink back into his pillows. He relaxed, but she found she could not, that she did not wish to remove her hand from his shoulder, but instead trailed it along his powerful chest, over the contours of his stomach, his muscles quivering in reaction to her touch. Each variation of texture, each hollow and rise that was the landscape of his body, quickened desire through her.

When he responded, he touched her in kind, the agony of need rolling over her like a molten wave. She could feel it taking him, too.

"Do you love me?" he breathed into her ear.

Stunned, it took her moment to respond. "Yes. I believe I do. Yes."

He levered himself above her. "Good. I've never stopped loving you."

The velvet brush of Zachary's lips against her throat made Estora think that she was the delirious one, but the touches and sensations were real, present, and she became greedy, impatient, craving more, wanting it all, and he showed her he was just as eager to provide what she required, his mouth questing across her flesh, her breasts, to secret places. She grew fierce in response, straddled him, wanton and demanding, sheathing him in her with a cry of triumph.

There was no stopping the journey they were on, and despite injury and illness, the strength was in him. He burned and drove hard. He was fire against her skin.

As their pleasure crested, however, even as she rode him into brilliance, the name upon his lips was not her own.

When they parted she lay again on her back breathing hard, staring into the dark, her body thrumming, asking for more, part of her mind, however, unnerved by the revelation of who it was Zachary truly loved.

Finally, as the dark of night dulled to the subtle gray of dawn, he lay slumped by her side deeply exhausted, his arm draped across her belly. She kissed his forehead but there was no response. She too, felt tired, but sated. Every touch no longer incited flame, and she realized whatever herb Destarion had used had worn off. It was time now for rest.

Someone applauded. Estora half sat up, heart thudding and suddenly fully awake. She held the blanket to her breast. Zachary remained insensible beside her.

"Who's there?" she demanded.

"I believe you can guess," Richmont replied, moving from the deepest corner of the chamber to stand by her side of the bed. He plucked at her blanket. "Why so modest now, my dear cousin? Your performance this night shows otherwise."

"I thought . . ."

"We were all gone? No, I alone remained as the sole witness. I was more patient than the others, and it paid off. You were my good little cousin and completed the rite. I enjoyed it very much." He cupped her chin in his hand. She slapped it away and he chuckled. "Still full of feisty energy after all that. And you exhausted the king. The parties concerned shall be pleased by tonight's results. Speaking of which . . ." He pulled something, a small vial, from a pocket. "A little pig's blood for the bed. I should not want the servants speculating as to why there was no virgin's stain upon the sheets when they go to change them, and you know how obsessive about such details members of the court can be if they catch wind of . . . irregularities." He placed the vial on her bedside table.

Estora listened to his footsteps as he crossed the room to the door. Before he opened it, he laughed once more. "Do not worry about that other female. She will be no competition."

She did not want to give him the satisfaction of her asking, but she could not help herself. "What do you mean?"

"A dead woman is no competition. Do remember all I do,

I do for you." With that he was through the door and it closed behind him.

Estora fell back into her pillow, now cold after her exertions, made colder still by the vile monster Richmont revealed himself to be. What additional danger had Richmont put Karigan in than what she already faced in Blackveil? All at once she was concerned for her friend, but a very human part of her almost hoped it was true so that Zachary would be hers, and hers alone.

She shuddered, and sheltered herself in the warmth of his body.

SHEDDING BLOOD FOR THE REALM

Later that morning, Estora paced in the cold light of the solarium. Zachary had given her the room in the fall as a place to call her own, a place of refuge from relatives and courtiers and endless wedding preparations. It felt a hundred years ago, the problems back then much more simple. It had been such a generous gesture. Zachary had known exactly what she needed, this retreat. And yet, she'd done little to make it her own. A few chairs, a table, some wall hangings, but nothing personal. She used the room rarely, instead spending time shadowing Zachary as he moved through his days, performing his duties as king. That had enlivened her more than hiding away.

The fireplace was dark and rain splattered the windows, blurring her view of the courtyard gardens. The gardens held such promise. It was too early in the season to see growth, but it was there beneath the mulch and fallen leaves of last autumn. All was barren now, but time would bear the fruits of rain and sun and warmth. Some birds had already returned from their wintering grounds and darted about the trees and shrubs, hunting for wrinkled berries, seeds, and grubs.

She pulled her shawl more tightly around her shoulders, missing the warmth of Zachary's bed, of him. He'd been strong during their coupling, but so exhausted after that he hadn't awakened. He would get well. She knew it, she believed it. He must. She'd simply wished to stay with him all morning, but there were tasks she must attend to. This first was *not* on the official list Cummings had handed her while she broke her fast.

A tapping came on the door.

Finally, she thought.

Fastion opened the door and stuck his head in. "Lieutenant Connly is here, my lady."

"Let him in."

Fastion stepped aside so the Rider could enter the solarium, then closed the door to resume his post out in the corridor.

Connly bowed, his posture hesitant, his gaze uncertain. She could not blame him.

"Your Majesty," he said, "I've come as you requested. How may I serve?"

"You told no one where you were going, whom you were seeing?"

"I spoke to no one as instructed by your message."

Estora nodded. "Good." Perhaps after Richmont's admissions she was being too mistrustful, but she preferred not taking chances. "Lieutenant, I realize this is a complicated time for all of us, but I must ask you to keep our meeting secret." *Secret.* The word echoed in her mind in Richmont's sneering voice. So many secrets. She closed her eyes for a moment.

"May I ask why, my lady?"

A bold question, she thought, when he was so uncertain of her. But the Riders were bold. She knew just how bold they could be.

"No," she replied.

He bowed his head. "I understand."

He understood that she could not trust him yet. She remembered how F'ryan used to bring her to the common room of the old barracks to play games with the Riders. They played Knights, Intrigue, even rolled dice. Connly had been there, untried and only just beginning his career in the messenger service. They'd laughed and joked and told stories. It was all different now, as though they'd never met before.

"I know you are finding it difficult to be sure of me right now," she said. At his alarmed expression she added, "Relax, please. I am not accusing you of anything."

"What of Captain Mapstone?" he asked, once again showing his daring.

Someone else, another monarch, might have punished him for impertinence. But Estora was who she was. "If it helps, I am told your captain is very comfortably settled into a suite of rooms in the diplomatic wing—the finest—and is being treated royally. And she's hating every moment of it."

She saw the flicker of a smile on his face, and then it was gone.

"When . . ." he began. "When will you release her?"

"I will not answer your question, but I did want to reassure you she is well."

"Please, may I see her?" Connly asked.

"No."

His face fell.

"Though as a favor to her, because of her long service and devotion to King Zachary, I am going to permit a visit from her friend Elgin Foxsmith. As he is no longer a Green Rider, his presence is more . . . permissible. Not a conflict of interest. I am sure you will find his assessment of the conditions of her confinement favorable."

Good. The Rider looked much relieved, and he relaxed.

"Furthermore," she continued, "based on the information you and your Riders provided us about the Eletian Sleepers and the towers, you may be pleased to know we have arranged for an extra unit of soldiers to provide support down at the wall."

His relief was now almost palpable. Relief for the added safety more soldiers could provide for his fellow Riders assigned to the towers, especially the Rider he shared his mind with, Trace Burns. From his reaction, Estora discerned they shared more than their thoughts.

By telling Connly these things, she hoped to draw him into her confidence, for she needed his help, and she believed the only ones who could truly help her were the Green Riders, and one Green Rider in particular.

"Lieutenant," she said, "I understand Beryl Spencer is due in soon."

As soon as Elgin learned he could visit Red, he wasted no time in throwing on an old patched oilskin coat and trekking from the stables where he was seeing to "the girls" and through the rain to the castle's diplomatic wing, where they'd detained his friend. Once among the fine furnishings and passing richly attired and important looking people, Elgin felt quite the pauper, quite inadequate. He'd left Sacor City after his brooch released him from the messenger service because of such feelings, and now here he was, dripping rain on a carpet worth far more than his own sorry hide, and keeping his head bowed in the presence of his betters.

The guard at Red's door looked askance at him. "What do you want, old man?"

"I am here to see Captain Mapstone."

"Go away. Only certain visitors are allowed. By the queen's orders."

"But—" Elgin began.

"Get outta here," the guard said.

A Weapon appeared seemingly from the shadows. Elgin recalled the fellow's name to be Fastion. It was not easy remembering the names of the Weapons for they all appeared the same, with their stony countenances and black attire. Elgin had a sneaking suspicion they cultivated uniformity—it allowed them to fade into the background. No single individual stood out.

"Let him in," Fastion ordered in an authoritative voice. "He is approved by the queen."

"Yes, sir," the guard said, and without hesitation he pivoted, knocked on the door, and opened it for Elgin.

"Thank you," Elgin told Fastion, and the Weapon nodded.

The chamber Elgin entered reeked of luxury, from overstuffed chairs to artwork even his undiscerning eye could tell was of the highest quality. It was a suite, really, with a sitting room, bedchamber, and a bathing room. More cavernous than anything he had ever lived in.

Within he had expected to find an agitated Rider captain pacing madly. Instead, he discovered Red lounging on a sofa with stockinged feet up, reading a book. A tray containing a pot of tea and pastries sat on a table in front of the sofa. Elgin was not sure he'd ever seen her look so relaxed.

Red glanced over her book to see who'd entered. It took a moment for her eyes to register recognition, and when they did, she dropped the book and leaped up.

"Chief!" she cried. "What a wonderful surprise." She came over and hugged him. "I have missed everyone so much." She gave him an additional hug and beckoned him over to the sofa and poured him some tea.

"You seem pleasantly situated," he observed dryly.

She grinned. "Servants looking after my every need, the finest meals from the kitchen, and this." She waved her hand to take in the suite. "Don't let it fool you, though. I'm seething inside. But comfortable. I was bored beyond tears until Destarion brought these up." She indicated a pile of dusty volumes on the table like the one she'd just been reading. Some were ledger-sized, some were much smaller, and their leather covers were very plain. Elgin opened one and found it filled with cramped handwriting.

"What are these?" he asked.

"Case histories from the menders. This is just a small pile. Destarion has apprentices looking through others."

"For what?"

"We're searching for references to Riders—or others— with true healing ability, like Ben. I'm hoping to find something that will reveal how to help him. So far nothing, but a couple references to *me*. I'm sure Destarion chose these particular records for me to look at on purpose."

"What are you talking about?"

"The menders who wrote about my cases complained *extensively* about my temper. When I was conscious, that is. One mender actually mentioned he preferred me unconscious." She frowned.

Elgin almost snorted his tea. He ended up coughing instead, shaking with suppressed laughter. He remembered what a difficult patient she could be.

She raised an eyebrow. "Are you laughing at me?"

"No, no, of course not."

"Of course not." She rolled her eyes. "In any case, Destarion did tell me this morning there were hopeful signs for both Zachary and Ben, that there'd been some awakenings for Zachary, and that Ben had a fitful night as if dreaming, which is better than lying in the deathlike state he's been in. Destarion also said his cheeks have a little pink in them. Have you heard anything?"

"No," Elgin replied. "I've been with the young ones all morning. You've heard more than me."

"It is my hope that once Zachary does awaken for good, that all of this will be cleared up. If he does not, I suppose they will have to do something with me."

"Red—"

"No, Elgin." She'd been almost buoyant before, but now she was subdued, shadows darkening her eyes. "I'm realistic. This is political and they can't allow anything to endanger Estora's new crown."

"But you wouldn't—"

"No, I probably would not interfere. The time for interference is past. But I know too much and they are not sure they can trust me, and the only true way to relieve me of duty is to exile me, or find a way to break my bond with my brooch."

The only way to break that bond, Elgin knew, was to kill her. "I won't let that happen," he growled. "They'll have to come through me first."

"Thank you, old friend," she said patting his knee. "Enough about me. Tell me about my Riders."

"After all you've done for them," Elgin muttered, not willing to change the subject so easily. "All the blood you've shed for the realm, and you practically raised the boy."

"King," she reminded him.

"What I remember is the boy who put frogs in my boots."

"Zachary did that?"

"As if you didn't know."

She gave him an innocent look, but a smile edged the corners of her mouth.

"Humph."

"Seriously, Chief," she said, "we've all shed blood for the realm, but as captain and king's advisor, I must also function in the political sphere—a role which can prove just as bloody. But I'd prefer not to dwell on it. So please, could you tell me about my Riders? Has there been any word from Blackveil?"

Elgin narrowed his eyes at her, his Red. Yes, they'd all shed blood for the realm, but one only had to see the scar that ran from her chin, down her neck, and beneath her collar, to know how close she'd come to giving her life for the realm. That scar, he knew, went much farther down her body, and was only a small part of the cost she'd paid the day she received it while serving as a Green Rider.

If there was anything in his power he could do to protect her, he would do it. He knew her Riders felt the same way, and those who had raised Estora to queenhood had not reckoned on that. He smiled.

"No word from Blackveil yet," he said. "As for your Riders, that Sophina has become quiet since that day." Since that day she'd "seen" the king struck down by arrows. "No complaints or snobbiness from her since then. Not much, anyway. She's even getting along with Merla."

He continued to chat with her for the better part of two hours, telling her about the smallest doings and accomplishments of her Riders, and she smiled as she listened, the proud captain, but behind the smile he sensed a profound sadness that no matter what he said, he could not erase.

HER PARTICULAR SKILLS

Estora was surprised to learn that only a couple of days after her meeting with Connly, Beryl Spencer had arrived on castle grounds. A secret meeting was promptly scheduled for the solarium. When Estora arrived, she was annoyed to discover a servant jabbing at cobwebs in the corners of the room with a broom. The woman hummed to herself, oblivious to Estora's presence.

The queen cleared her throat and the startled creature dropped her broom and shrieked. When she turned and saw who it was, she gave a trembling curtsy.

"Sorry, ma'am, sorry. Cleaning the cobwebs is all. Cleaning the corners." She curtsied again, a bent thing in homespun drab.

"You may be excused," Estora said calmly enough, though she wished to scream it. Beryl Spencer would not come if there were witnesses, especially gossipy castle servants, and she was due any moment.

"Aye, ma'am. Must get me broom." The woman fumbled after the broom.

"Leave it," Estora commanded. "I wish you to go *now*."

The servant unfolded and stood tall. A pair of sharp green eyes peered at Estora from beneath strands of hair hanging over her smudged face. Estora blinked rapidly at the woman's transformation from a simple servant to a personage with a commanding presence. Someone of intelligence and cunning, someone dangerous.

"Beryl Spencer," she said on an exhalation.

"At your service, Your Highness." She bowed, and there was a mocking edge to it.

"I've heard about your ability," Estora said, "but I did not expect so direct a demonstration."

"Connly emphasized discretion," Beryl replied. "If anyone saw me, they saw only a simple servant with a broom. But then most people don't really see servants. They are beneath notice."

It was true. One might be aware of servants moving about the castle as they attended to their duties, but to most who carried on their more important work as ambassadors, officers, or courtiers, servants might as well be invisible. They were undistinguished, and indistinguishable.

The role Beryl Spencer had chosen to play was clever, but in a way, disturbing. Who else could disguise themselves as a servant and gain access to the entire castle? Estora shuddered. She was being paranoid again. It was Beryl's special ability to portray a role that made her so convincing, and yet ... Estora decided she would take this as a lesson in the security, or lack thereof, in the castle.

"It appears much has happened since last I was here," Beryl said.

"Yes," Estora replied simply. She did not doubt the Green Rider had already gleaned all the fine details of the assassination attempt and the subsequent wedding and who all the players were. She had, after all, skills beyond playing roles like that of a servant attending to her cleaning. Zachary had used those skills exhaustively, and Beryl had spent years as a spy in the court of Tomas Mirwell. It was these skills Estora now intended to make use of. However, she wondered what Beryl thought of her sudden marriage to Zachary and the confinement of Captain Mapstone. Would Beryl be willing to help her?

Beryl cocked her head, but gave away nothing. Estora felt uneasy under her scrutiny. "Thank you for agreeing to see me," she said.

Beryl inclined her head. "You are the queen. I serve."

For some reason, Estora did not feel reassured by the

words. She imagined they were like the words Beryl had used with Tomas Mirwell before she betrayed him. She'd played her role in Mirwell fully, and Estora heard that many in Mirwell's court feared Beryl more than Mirwell himself. She'd served as his aide, his enforcer, his interrogator. People disappeared, never to be seen or heard from again.

What were her true loyalties? Estora wondered. But Zachary trusted her, and she was, after all, a Green Rider. Would she have been called to the messenger service if she were disloyal to Sacoridia and its king?

"What do you wish of me, my lady?" Beryl asked. "General Harborough is pressing Connly to send me north."

"Yes, I am aware of this, and you will not be sent without my say-so. General Harborough must answer to me."

There was an almost imperceptible flicker of approval on Beryl's face.

"I require your particular skills here for the time being," Estora said.

Now Beryl looked intrigued. "How may I serve?"

"Have you ever chanced to meet my cousin, Lord Richmont Spane?"

"We have not met formally, but I am aware of him, of course."

The way Beryl said "of course" indicated to Estora that the Rider knew something of his intrigues. Estora smiled. Beryl was in her way more frightening than Richmont ever would be, but Estora needed to trust her. She prayed that trust was well placed.

"I believe we've much to discuss then," Estora said.

"It would be my honor," Beryl replied.

The walking, or rather limping, proved grueling, and sweat streamed down Karigan's brow. Even with the aid of the bonewood, she could not keep up with the swift pace Graelalea set, but this time, when she straggled behind, Ard or Telagioth would call ahead telling Graelalea to wait. Karigan did the best she could, and kept focused on the path ahead. Still, dancers with masks taunted her from the shadows. Once, when she looked dead on, the dancers melted into trees, their limbs swaying with the passage of a breeze.

Another time she looked, she became so besotted with the scene of dancers strutting to some dissonance that Telagioth had to shake her out of it.

"You don't see them?" she asked him.

"See who?"

"The dancers. The masquerade."

"No, I do not. I see trees, and they wear no masks."

Karigan nodded and pushed on, resigning herself to the fact that she walked in two worlds: the one wrought by the poison of the thorns, and the other, the world as her companions saw it.

When finally they paused for a break, Karigan came up from behind to find Graelalea drawing in the mud with the tip of her dagger.

"If we can keep up our pace," she said, "we will reach Castle Argenthyne in a few days."

The drawing, Karigan saw, was a map showing where they were and how far they had yet to go. Yates looked frustrated he could not see it. They were on a squiggly path to a spot marked with an X, and they did not look far from the X.

When Graelalea finished, everyone except Yates went their separate way to sit or take a drink of water. "Karigan," he called.

She limped over to him. "I'm here."

"Good." He lifted the strap of his satchel over his shoulder and thrust it into her hands. "You need to copy whatever Graelalea's drawn," he said. "For the king."

Karigan's mouth dropped open. She wasn't much of an artist. "But—"

"You've got the neatest hand among us," Yates said. "Just do your best."

"All right," she replied uncertainly. She dragged herself to a nearby rock and sat, then removed Yates' journal and writing supplies from the satchel. As she flipped through the journal, she found pages filled with his own tidy handwriting, maps sketched out with measurements and landmarks, and other drawings that appeared to be more of a personal nature. She did not think it any of her business to pry, so she did not pause to look at the pictures, but the journal fell open to a lovely rendering of Hana. He must have done it early on in their journey, for he'd captured her with a hint of a smile on her face.

"You're an amazing artist," Karigan said. It was even more amazing she had not known this side of him.

"I take after my mother," he said proudly. "She did most of the etchings and art for my father's press."

As Karigan searched for a blank page, she caught glances of drawings of the forest, its flora and fauna, including hummingbirds. She shuddered, and hastily found a blank page. She copied Graelalea's map as best she could, jotting down notes. It was nowhere as good as Yates would have done, but passable. Thanks to her practice in keeping the Rider books, her hand was very neat.

When the ink dried, she replaced the journal and pen in the satchel, and put it into Yates' hands, but he immediately passed it back to her.

"You'd better hold onto it," he said, "in case something

else needs recording." More somberly he added, "You also have a better chance of getting this back to the king."

Karigan started to protest, but he shook his head. "I'm not giving up, just being realistic."

Another layer of gloom blanketed her. She knew he was right, but she did not have to accept it. They would get out of Blackveil. All of them. They had to.

Grant paced nearby holding his arm to himself. He was pale and perspiring. "Nythlings," he muttered. "Gotta let the nythlings come."

Graelalea came and crouched before Karigan. "I would like to take a look at your leg."

"Maybe you should look at Grant's arm."

Graelalea sighed. "I have tried, and more than once. He refuses me and becomes violent if I press him."

"I've seen it," Ard said, easing down onto a nearby rock. "He didn't show me, mind, but I saw him looking at it. Sickly in color with black lumps on it."

"I cannot aid him unless he wishes it," Graelalea murmured, and she set to tending Karigan's leg with fresh evaleoren salve. Karigan sighed as the salve absorbed the pain.

"I offered to help, too," Ard said, "and he offered to smash my face in."

Short of all of them jumping on Grant to hold him down, Karigan didn't know how else they could help him. Perhaps if he got much worse, they'd have to do just that.

When Graelalea finished with Karigan's leg and moved off, Karigan glanced at Ard who sat with his head bowed and eyes closed as he rested. The journey had been hard on him as it had been on all of them. He'd lost considerable weight. When she looked at his hands splayed on his knees, his knuckles skinned and embedded with dirt, a shining silver ring that she had not noticed before caught her attention. Had he worn it all along and she just hadn't seen it, or was it something he put on recently? If so, why?

It was not a wedding ring, though it was placed on the customary finger. Ard had stated he'd no family. It bore a sigil depicting the cormorant crest of Clan Coutre, so perhaps he was, in a way, bound to the clan in no less of an important way than a marriage. He must be held in great esteem by Clan Coutre for a simple forester to be in possession of such a ring.

Ard stirred and met her gaze. "Something on your mind?" he asked gruffly.

"I was just admiring your ring."

His hands came together and absently he twisted the ring around his finger. "A gift," he said, "from the lady."

"Lady Coutre?"

"No, my Lady Estora. When she gave a blessing upon me for my safe return from Blackveil. The ring is a gift of trust that I will carry out my duty here in the best interest of the clan, which it is my honor to do."

Ard's eyes were hooded as he regarded her and she sensed there was more to it than he said. Karigan did not have a chance to probe more deeply, however, for Graelalea announced it was time they continued their journey.

Over the days that followed, Karigan's strength gradually improved, her leg showing minute signs of mending with each application of the evaleoren salve. Her visions of dancers in the forest became less frequent as well. One or two would occasionally catch the edge of her sight but would then quickly vanish.

She still fell behind, and Ard often dropped back to walk companionably beside her, not speaking, but keeping an eye on her. On the whole, the company made little conversation. The farther along they got, the faster Graelalea led them, and the faster Graelalea went, the more Karigan fell behind. She had especial trouble on a part of the trail that was at the base of a cliff buried beneath a sloping rock fall. They had to pick their way over slick boulders and wobbly rocks. The uneven and treacherous surfaces taxed Karigan's bad leg and she fell farther and farther behind, but Ard patiently stayed with her. She was pleased by his company.

"Have you always been a forester for Clan Coutre?" Karigan asked him, her interest in his background aroused by his signet ring. Her feet almost flew out from beneath her on a slimy rock. She saved herself, heart thudding, and was once again thankful for the bonewood staff, which helped her regain her balance.

Ard, watching her from several boulders ahead, said. "Always. And my father before me. Lord Spane took him in, gave him the position to assist the head forester, looking after Lord Coutre's lands. We'd been destitute before that, but Lord Spane took care of us."

"That was very good of him," Karigan replied.

Ard stayed perched on his boulder watching her, his hand resting on the hilt of his sword. He glanced over his shoulder. The rest of the company was out of sight.

"Aye," he said. "And then the lady was born. Sweetest child ever there was."

It was difficult for Karigan to imagine Estora as a tiny child. Try as she might, she could only picture Estora as she was now, the stately, devastatingly beautiful woman.

Karigan hopped to a wobbly rock in front of Ard, her legs quivering from exertion. Ard did not move, forcing Karigan to fight once again for her balance. He did not give her a hand, but instead appeared lost in reflection.

"So kind she was," he said. "Considerate to those beneath her station when she didn't have to be. She didn't change as she grew up. Always good to me. I'm proud to serve her."

This was all fascinating, Karigan thought, but her leg was killing her as she struggled to prevent herself from falling and dashing her brains all over the rocks.

"Um," she said, hoping Ard would take the hint.

He gazed at her, his eyes chips of flint, his face set and body rigid. Karigan tensed in return. She did not understand his posture, or why he was not helping her.

"Would you mind moving on?" she said. "We're falling behind."

Ard did not move, but kept staring at her, tapping the hilt of his sword. "I'd do anything for her," he murmured.

Karigan hopped back to a more stable rock behind her, now holding the bonewood more in defense than for balance. What was wrong with him? His hand tightened on the hilt of his sword.

"Is all well back here?" It was Telagioth.

Karigan sighed in relief.

"Aye," Ard replied, and he turned toward Telagioth and strode off, leaving Karigan behind. "We were just resting is all."

Resting? Is that what he called it? Then why was she drenched in sweat and shaking?

To her further relief, Telagioth stayed with them and Ard carried on an animated conversation. All seemed as it was before. Had she only imagined he'd posed a threat to her just moments ago? She could not even guess at his change. Until now he'd been nothing but helpful to her along the journey.

Perhaps the poison of the thorns had muddled her perceptions. Even so, she intended to remain wary of Ard in case he showed his darker side again.

❧ REDBIRD ❧

"**V**ery good," Grandmother said when Lala showed her the knot of red yarn. "You have a natural knack for the art."

"Lalala goot!" cried Gubba. The old groundmite sat across the fire from them, beaming at them with a toothless grin.

In the evenings when they paused in their journey through the forest, Grandmother had taken to teaching Lala more of the craft once taught to her by her own mother and grandmother. The protection provided by the groundmites had removed some of the responsibility from Grandmother, and it was now they who guided her and her people. The groundmites also provided them with fresh meat and water, and all of them were feeling the stronger for it. Such relative ease, compared to the beginnings of their journey, allowed Grandmother the leisure to teach Lala.

If only Lala could speak. Without speech, many spells would prove inaccessible to her.

Her granddaughter's inability had always saddened her, but now it angered her. It was unfair. She wanted Lala to carry on the craft of her ancestors, to have a voice. When Grandmother finally surrendered her soul to God as all mortals must, who would carry on the art for Second Empire?

There was also that music, the flow of an almost otherworldly voice that came into her mind sometimes, its source at the wall. It mocked her with its power and made Lala's silence all the more difficult to accept. She had decided it was high time to do something about it. To lash out, as it were. So here they sat, Lala tying a very special knot.

Grandmother appraised it critically, looking for imperfections, but it was well executed, with extra knots that were Lala's personal expression. It was, after all, an art. The girl had the aptitude, and now Grandmother wished she'd done more with the girl sooner.

"You understand the next step?" she asked.

Lala nodded and picked up the knife from the blanket between them.

"Remember to pour your intent into it."

Lala closed her eyes, looking much older than her years, even beneath the dirt smudged on her face. In one swift motion, she slashed the blade across her palm. Grandmother grabbed her wrist and pushed the knotted yarn into the wound so it would absorb the blood. Lala clenched her fingers around it. They could have used a nail clipping or a lock of Lala's hair for the spell, but nothing was as potent as fresh blood.

Grandmother spoke the words of power, words as ancient as the roots of the empire itself, her voice a singsong, and a red glow seeped between Lala's fingers.

Gubba, who was accustomed to the unpredictability of Blackveil's etherea, chanted in counterpoint to buffer them from some devastating backlash.

When Grandmother finished, the glow captured in Lala's hand flickered red against her face like firelight.

"You may release the seeker," Grandmother said.

Lala carefully uncurled her fingers, the glow blooming, then coalescing into a redbird perched on her bloody palm. The remnant glow settled into its feathers as it preened.

The detail! Grandmother looked at it in awe. From its black face mask to its crest, it was every bit the real thing. The dear child had made more than a seeker—she'd taken the art to a higher level. The aesthetic alone revealed more sophistication than those so gifted showed in a lifetime. The art should not be just a tool, Grandmother thought. Too often she had used it as a means to an end, forgetting about its inherent beauty.

"Well done, child, well done."

Everyone in camp paused to admire Lala's creation. The

redbird fluttered its wings as though impatient to be off. Without further prompting, Lala tossed the bird into the air. It stretched its wings and circled above their heads once before veering north. It would fly the quickest route to seek the one who sang.

As the bird disappeared into the misty night, Gubba clapped and chortled, and Grandmother turned her attention to tending Lala's cut hand.

Despite all the groundmites provided for Grandmother and her people, the endless walking was wearying. Grandmother wished she had wings so she could fly like Lala's redbird. Alas, she was confined to the Earth with all the other ground-dwelling creatures, forced to labor to reach a destination when birds easily flew over all obstacles. At least the ruins that appeared more frequently alongside the road lent more interest to their surroundings and indicated they were nearing their destination.

Most of the ruins were entangled in vines and roots. Trees grew through roofs. Ferns and brush shrouded entrances and facades. The forest was nothing if not resilient, obscuring even the pedigree of the architecture—was it Eletian or of the empire? They did not stop to investigate the ruins, but Gubba jabbered on beside Grandmother, pointing out this and that as if they were on a pleasure outing to see the sights. Grandmother understood none of it.

Instead, she ignored Gubba and thought of the task that lay ahead, when they reached their destination. How was she supposed to awaken the Sleepers? As much as she prayed on it, the answer never came to her. It was, she guessed, a test placed before her by God. Truly, up till now she'd been more worried about just surviving long enough to reach the grove of the Sleepers. The groundmites, with their help, had lifted much of that worry from her, leaving her more time to concern herself with the how of the task before her.

She did not understand the Eletians, or how they Slept as they did. All she knew was that it was going to take some powerful art to rouse them. Would she have the ability?

She'd been so deep in her own thoughts, ignoring Gubba

and watching the road just ahead of her feet, that she was startled when she bumped into Sarat, who had stopped in the road. In fact, everyone else had stopped to gaze ahead, and she gasped when she saw why.

The forest fell away, revealing a black lake, tendrils of fog coiling just above its flat, oily surface. She thrilled to see that a statue of Mornhavon the Great stood in the center of the lake looking defiant and courageous, one hand resting on the hilt of his sword, and the other fisted as if to show whose realm this really was and by what means it was acquired. The details of his features were blurred and moss-draped. The lake level had risen at some point, and now lapped at his knees. To Grandmother he seemed to be rising from the water, not sinking. Around the edges of the lake were the roofs of drowned buildings, also attesting to the deepened water.

One of the great, black avians Grandmother had seen and heard signs of in the forest skimmed across the water, leaving ripples in its wake. The creature circled the statue, then landed on the head of Mornhavon. It loosed a screech that echoed right through her and swiveled its head around on its serpentine neck to gaze at its surroundings.

As magnificent as the statue was, it was the backdrop that she found truly arresting. Towers rose out of the forest into the sky, pale phantoms of what they must have once been, but still a powerful vision, their slender forms like graceful stems growing from the earth, their pinnacles lost to the ceiling of clouds that hung overhead. There was just enough grayness of day that the towers reflected on the lake.

"What is that place?" Min whispered in awe.

"Our destination," Grandmother replied. "Castle Argenthyne."

⋘ SPIRALS AND VOICES ⋙

Graelalea led the company mercilessly over rugged terrain until abruptly she stopped on the edge of a cliff where the forest opened up, revealing a lake below. To Karigan's eyes it seemed shaped like a beech leaf or a spearhead. Clouds obscured the far shore.

"The Pool of Avrath," Ealdaen said. "I thought never to gaze upon it again. But it is dark, defiled."

"What do you see?" Yates whispered to Karigan.

"We're looking down into a valley with a lake," she replied.

"You must remember this for the journal."

"I will." To be honest, when they stopped for the night, she was so exhausted she knew she'd probably fall fast asleep before she could get to the journal.

"What's that in the middle of the lake?" Ard asked.

Karigan could not make out the details for it was too distant, but some rock formation stood in the lake's center. Its shape looked too regular to have been made by nature.

Ealdaen, whose Eletian sight was more keen, spoke angrily in his own tongue. All the Eletians looked incensed.

"What is it?" Karigan asked.

"It is the Evil One," Lhean said. "A statue of Mornhavon."

"He thought himself a god," Ealdaen spat. "The god of all, and he would have known what it meant to our people to place a statue of himself in the pool."

"What would it mean?" Yates asked, but the Eletians were already moving on, and Lynx took Yates' arm to lead him away.

Karigan remembered sitting in the library of the Golden

Guardian in Selium. Aaron Fiori had sung of Avrath, a Shining Land. He'd believed Avrath to be a spiritual place of the Eletians. Perhaps, if Avrath were like the heavens, the Eletians believed it was reflected in the pool. Whatever the significance of the lake, a statue of Mornhavon planted in its middle clearly wounded them.

She was quickly being left behind again, and not wishing to end up alone with Ard, she made her weary body take a step forward. Then she paused. The fog on the far shore thinned just enough to reveal tall spires rising among the trees. They gleamed dully. Before the clouds layered over them again, they flashed in crystalline brilliance as perhaps they had long, long ago beneath a silver moon. Then the light died, and the towers disappeared in the fog.

Karigan blinked, gooseflesh rising along her arms. Her imagination again? The poison? As she set off after the others, she was certain of one thing: Castle Argenthyne, the legend, lay on the other side of the lake.

Their trail descended in a series of switchbacks, which meant Karigan was never really far from the others even if she lagged behind. Ard had insinuated himself into the middle of the line, making conversation with Solan. There was no sign of the strange behavior he'd exhibited in the boulder field, and she shrugged. She should be more surprised that Blackveil wasn't making them all behave in strange ways.

It was dark by the time they reached level ground, the wings of oversized bats flapping through the air above their heads.

"We shall camp here for the night," Graelalea said. "Tomorrow we shall not stop until we reach the grove."

Karigan sensed the elevated energy in Graelalea, her agitation as camp was set up. Karigan suspected the Eletian wouldn't have stopped until she reached the grove if it had been just her, but she'd taken into consideration the condition of her companions. It would not do to face whatever awaited them at the grove when totally exhausted.

"What happens when we reach the grove?" Grant demanded. He did not help to set up camp, but just stood in the middle of everything rubbing his arm.

"We shall see what we find," Graelalea replied.

Karigan knew she ought to be more worried about what the next day would bring, but she was too tired; almost too tired to eat her portion of gruel that Lynx spooned out. And when she finished, she crawled into her tent and fell instantly asleep.

The next morning the path became more level and they crossed the remains of broken roads; the ominous shapes of ruined structures protruded from moss and tangled vegetation. They were nearing the city of Argenthyne and its castle. The fog shifted above the treetops just enough to offer tantalizing views of the castle towers.

The towers remained dull, tarnished, as Karigan had first seen them the previous night. They were not made of silver moonbeams as in the songs and stories, unless silver moonbeams could die. Still, the towers were graceful and without the fog, Karigan imagined, they must have soared into the sky. Delicate arched bridges connected the towers at different levels, reminding her of interlacing tree limbs in a forest.

Argenthyne did not, in its current state, resemble what Karigan had always imagined, but she couldn't believe she was here, walking into legend. What would her mother think? Perhaps that such a thing was not so far-fetched. After all, she'd possessed a moonstone.

She knew they'd entered the city proper when more ruins appeared around them. It smelled different, too. Not just of the decayed forest, but also of the mustiness of structures long emptied of life. Paving stones had ruptured with the growth of gnarled, sickly trees. Stairs rose to nothingness. A fountain stood in the center of a square fouled by black sludge, and above everything the leaden towers loomed.

Karigan had seen this before as a vision shown to her by Prince Jametari in the waters preserved from *Indura Luin,* the Mirror of the Moon. The vision had also revealed the contrast of Argenthyne in its glory before Mornhavon's invasion, before the decay of Blackveil.

Sibilant murmurs made her shiver as though the Eletians who once lived here were just on the other side of a thin veil, as if her own time brushed against that past piece of time. Or maybe it was ghosts. Ghosts, she could handle.

"This place is haunted," Grant muttered, echoing her thoughts.

"No," Ealdaen said. "Eletians leave no shades behind. It is only your kind that is too restless in death."

If that was so, Karigan thought, then she must just be sensing air currents weaving through the towers, the moans of broken buildings. Whatever it was, Argenthyne still had a voice.

Could a whole city be a ghost? They certainly walked its corpse.

They stopped by the fountain. A beautiful figure held a cracked bowl above her head. Or, she'd once been beautiful, but the light stone she'd been carved from was stained, black tears seeming to stream down her face.

"So where is this grove of yours?" Ard asked.

"The east leaf," Graelalea replied.

"The *what*?"

"The city," Graelalea said, "is laid out in a triad of leaves, or sections. The Pool of Avrath makes up the south leaf. We now stand in the north leaf."

The castle, Karigan thought, must rise up in the middle of the leaves like a blossom, the nexus of it all.

"I have walked these streets many times," Ealdaen said, gazing at the ruins all around them. "I know every one of them, from the Great Stem to the narrowest winding. This was my home."

Silence fell upon them, though the city still sighed hollowly.

"Then you shall lead us," Graelalea told Ealdaen.

He nodded and they fell in line behind him, staying alert for danger hidden among the ruins. Claws scrabbled on stone and a rat much larger than any wharf rat Karigan had ever seen bounded across the road ahead of them, vanishing into rubble.

It was difficult for Karigan to imagine the city alive with Eletians despite the vision she'd once seen in the Mirror of the Moon. It was hard to believe there had once been so many Eletians walking the lands. Somehow Mornhavon, with his tremendous powers, had overcome them.

She studied Ealdaen as he strode ahead, shoulders set, the spines on his pauldrons catching the light. He looked from side to side, facial muscles taut. Did he remember those last moments in Argenthyne as he fled Mornhavon's armies and weapons? Of course he must. What was it like for him to see his city in ruin after so many centuries? The same way she'd feel if this were Corsa or Sacor City. Devastated. Devastated not so much by the ruins left behind, but by the loss of the civilization they represented.

When they began this journey, she'd been very unsure of Ealdaen. He'd tried to kill her once, after all, and she remained wary of him even though the bonds of the group working for mutual survival had outweighed personal motives. So far. Seeing the effect of the city on him, and having seen his reaction to the remains of Telavalieth, she no longer viewed him as quite so cold and immovable.

The cluster of towers that was the castle remained to their right, its heights fading in and out with the fog. The voice of the city came again to Karigan as she trudged along, this time as a mournful song.

Karigan soon understood what Ealdaen had meant when he said he knew every "narrow winding." There was not a single street she could discern that traveled in a straight line. The streets here put the Winding Way in her own Sacor City to shame.

They walked endless looping curves, but just when she thought they must complete a circle, they'd come to an intersection and start going around in a completely different direction. Were the Eletian road builders insane? Well, they were *Eletians,* and despite having journeyed so far and long with a few of them, Karigan could not say their ways were any less mysterious to her than when they'd begun. It was maddening that they must travel in such a roundabout manner when they'd reach their destination much more quickly if the streets were straight. It reminded her of one of those frustrating dreams where, try as she might, she could not get someplace she needed to be or complete a task.

There was no way to cut through the ruins that she could see that would shorten their way—at least none that looked safe—nor did the Eletians seem the least inclined to seek such a way. They appeared intent only on staying their course, circular as it was.

"The nythlings don't like the spiral streets," Grant muttered to himself. "No, they do not."

Besides Grant, no one showed signs of being perturbed, so Karigan shrugged and decided the Eletians knew what was best and that she'd do well not to worry about it.

She still thought the road builders must have been insane. Or maybe drunk. Did Eletians get drunk?

Such speculation amused her, held errant masked dancers at bay. It took her mind off the pain that stabbed her leg with each step and the murk that seeped low over the city—dead neighborhood after dead neighborhood.

She could not block out the city's voice. Sometimes it was a stream sluggishly murmuring unseen among the ruins, accompanied by a rhythmic dripping tapping out a secret message. Sounds like distant weeping chilled her, and sometimes she thought air currents chimed through the towers. It sucked her in till she could almost hear her name expelled on a deep exhalation.

She wondered if Yates, who must depend on his hearing more than ever, heard the city as she did. She thought about asking him, but she feared breaking the silence of the company might shatter something fragile, bring the sky down on them, or awaken a sleeping god.

Ealdaen halted and Karigan, so caught up in spirals and voices, looked up startled. They'd come to a wall that rose precipitously above them and above it yet soared one of the towers of Castle Argenthyne.

Predictably the wall was not straight or squared, but bent in a curve. They followed a street that flowed along its contours, the castle remaining at their right shoulders. On the other side of the street, the dank ruins and rubble abruptly ended, and the forest of Blackveil reared over them. It was clear to Karigan they'd departed the north leaf and were now heading for the east leaf, where the grove of the Sleepers awaited them.

When they arrived at the east leaf, there was no mistaking the grove. The conifers rose like towers themselves, their boles as wide as cottages, their limbs alone larger than most trees Karigan had ever seen. Roots snaked out of the ground like bridges. The members of the company, with the castle to their backs, craned their necks looking up toward the canopy, but like the towers, the treetops vanished into the mist.

"Could make a few houses out of these," Ard murmured.

Even as Karigan felt a thrill at seeing these living giants where Eletians rested, she could also see how Blackveil had left its mark here, for the trunks showed extensive rot. Blackened beardy lichens trailed from branches. Some of the trees had fallen and become massive corpses decaying into the earth. The canopy of the grove trapped darkness below, the air stagnant.

Graelalea started to draw out her moonstone, but Lynx touched her wrist. "Careful," he said.

"What is it?"

His brow was furrowed like he had a headache. "We are not alone here. I sense . . . the forest is aware of others."

"Can you make out who or what?"

He shook his head. "All I can tell is that they are mainly at the other end of the grove. But there are disturbances not too far off."

"Very well, be on guard," she said. Hands went to weapons in readiness, and Karigan wondered, as her companions must as well, who else in the name of the hells was in the forest with them. "I must see the grove in the light," Graelalea said. "Danger or no."

The light of her moonstone blinded Karigan at first, and seared into the darkness of the grove, plunging into relief the rot that caused the great trees to shed bark, sap oozing from the wounds like blood. The trees were so knotted and burled in places that Karigan fancied she could see faces peering back at her, just like the vision she'd seen in the looking mask at the king's masquerade ball, which now seemed so long ago. Layers of cobwebs draped between the trees and wafted in air currents. Many glittering multifaceted eyes watched the companions from the shadows.

The light shining on the faces of the Eletians revealed awe and consternation. On Ealdaen's face Karigan saw only grief.

"We must—" Graelalea began, but howls interrupted her, howls and yips and screams. Arrows sang out of the darkness. "To the castle!" she cried, but even as she turned to lead them away, an arrow penetrated the gap in her armor beneath her arm and she fell.

Faster than Karigan's eyes could follow, the Eletians responded, white arrows streaking into the shadows. Lynx thrust Yates at Karigan and lifted Graelalea into his arms.

"Groundmites!" he shouted. "We need cover!"

"This way." Ealdaen swiftly turned and ran toward the castle. Telagioth, Solan, and Lhean kept their arrows flying.

Karigan ran after Lynx, dragging Yates behind her and yelling directions at him even as groundmite arrows fell about them.

They had to clamber over the enormous trunk of a fallen tree, scrambling for finger- and toeholds. It was more like climbing the rocky face of a mountain. Bark crumbled beneath Karigan's foot and she almost fell, an arrow thudding into the wood beside her. Ard pushed Yates from below, and then they were over the top, down the other side, and running again. Mercifully the ground was relatively level, and then Karigan realized there were flagstones beneath the forest debris. They were heading toward the castle, and when Karigan looked up, she saw wide, curving steps leading up to a terrace and enormous doors framed by statues. The statues were of Eletian maidens gesturing toward the grove, though one's arm lay half-buried on the ground. They pelted up the stairs and onto the terrace. Ealdaen ordered them to take cover behind the statues.

Karigan peered around the leg of her statue, watching as Telagioth, Lhean, and Solan crouched on the fallen tree trunk, taking careful aim before loosing arrows. Groundmite arrows flew over and around them. It had to have been by sheer accident and not skill that Graelalea had been hit. She glanced at the Eletian cradled in Lynx's arms. Blood runneled from her white armor and dripped to the stone beneath their feet.

"Can't help her till we get cover," Lynx rumbled.

Graelalea's eyes fluttered open. They were a startling emerald in this dark place. "Galad ..." she began.

"Shhh," Lynx said. "You must save your strength."

"Arodroa imitre!" Ealdaen thundered, making Karigan jump.

He stood before the great doors muttering something, and if she didn't know better, she could swear he was cursing in Eletian.

"They need the moon," he said, frustration in his voice. He disregarded the arrows that skittered on the stone around him. He took out his moonstone and silvery light rippled across the doors, revealing shining, swirling designs incorporating a tree, the stars, and the moon, very similar to the moondial they'd seen in Telavalieth.

"Arodoa imitre en muna!" Ealdaen commanded.

There was a discernible *snick* of a mechanism from somewhere deep within the doors, and a groan, but they still did not open.

Ealdaen did not flinch or move when an arrow bounced off the back of his armor, and he loosed another stream of what Karigan could only guess was more colorful Eletian cursing. He actually kicked one of the doors. And it opened—just a crack—but it opened. He, Grant, and Ard threw themselves at it and pushed, opening it just wide enough to permit them to enter.

Ealdaen gestured for them to go in and Karigan hoped they were not entering something worse than what they were leaving behind. Ealdaen paused on the terrace. "Telagioth!" he shouted.

Karigan glanced back in time to see Solan, and then Lhean, leap off the tree trunk and pelt toward them. Moments later Telagioth followed. By the time Karigan had guided Yates into the castle, the three Eletians were filing in behind them and pushing the door closed.

"The groundmites have magic with them," Telagioth said. "I can feel it."

They all stood there in the castle entrance, overcome by a heavy silence—no dripping of water, no screeching of forest creatures, nothing. And it was not dark. A dull glow shone through the walls, like being inside an eggshell, and yet the castle had thick walls, didn't it? No, not an eggshell, Karigan decided, but a seashell. The walls gleamed with a pearlescent sheen, not unlike Eletian armor.

The chamber they had entered was the bottom of one of the great towers and they could look up into its seemingly infinite heights, stairs and walkways winding up along the walls, bridges crisscrossing at various levels. Doors opening to who-knew-what lined the walls. The decay of the forest did not permeate the tower. Rather, Karigan had the sense of a place long sealed off from the rest of the world, abandoned and lifeless, but still a bulwark against the dark.

Lynx had lain Graelalea on a blanket on the floor and he and Ealdaen were tending her wound.

"No," Graelalea gasped. "Need Galad . . ."

Yates nudged Karigan. "What do you see? What's happening? Where are we?"

But she did not answer him. She left him and took halting steps toward Graelalea as though some will other than her own drew her.

"Galad . . . Galadheon," Graelalea whispered.

Karigan dropped to her knees beside the Eletian. Blood stained the blanket beneath her and trickled from the corner of her mouth. Her eyes had dulled.

"I'm here," Karigan said.

"As foretold," Graelalea said, her voice scarcely a whisper. "I shall not be leaving Blackveil."

Ealdaen protested in Eletian.

"No, peace, Ealdaen," she replied. "It is a death wound. Hear me, the Galadheon ... the Galadheon must complete ..." She raised her hand and reached for her hair, and in a gesture that appeared to sap all her remaining strength, she tugged a feather loose from a braid and handed it to Karigan. "*Enmorial.* Remember. Must cross thresholds, Galadheon. Go with the moon."

Graelalea's body slackened, the life extinguished from her eyes. Ealdaen and the other Eletians took up a cry of despair that soared upward into every recess of the tower.

"Good-bye," Karigan murmured to Graelalea, and even as she watched, the Eletian's armor dimmed, darkened, as if it, too, were dying.

The Eletians settled Graelalea's body in the very center of the round chamber and covered her with her gray-green cloak. They placed her moonstone upon her chest and it gave off a dim, gentle glow, and they sat around her in silent vigil.

"This won't do," Ard muttered, pacing back and forth. "What are we gonna do? Stand around forever waiting for them?" He jerked his thumb at the Eletians.

"She was their princess and leader," Karigan said, sitting cross-legged on the floor. Her chest felt thick with sorrow, but she was unable to shed tears for the feather captivated her, diverted her thoughts. She twirled it before her eyes. It was so white it almost glowed, except for the spray of blood, crimson on pure white. It was causing something to awaken inside her.

"I don't care," Ard replied. "Telagioth said those ground-mites have magic and they might find a way in here soon."

"The nythlings don't like it here," Grant said. He sat curled up against the wall. The pale light of the castle gleamed on his sweaty face. "Almost time, but they don't like it here."

"Hey," Yates said, his voice, in contrast, excited. "I ... I think I can almost see. Just shapes, mostly gray, but ..."

Karigan was glad, but in a distracted way. Just as something was awakening in her, perhaps it was in Yates, too. The castle. The castle must be nulling the backlash effect the forest had on Yates' ability, but that did not explain what was happening to *her.*

Then suddenly she understood, for she began to remember. It came to her as a light touch on her brow, feather-light, like flurries of snow falling and flashing in the silver glow of her moonstone. She remembered standing in the snow beside her father's sleigh where a figure of light had told her she must travel to Blackveil to help the Sleepers, that if "the enemy" awakened them they would become a deadly weapon.

The figure had told Karigan she could cross thresholds and that she was "the key." Somehow all of this could aid the Sleepers.

The feather of the winter owl, given to her by Graelalea, had opened her memory, but memory did not serve her. How was she to help the Sleepers? What did it mean she was the key?

Pounding startled her. The groundmites were banging on the doors. One thing was clear: "the enemy" was without and she had to figure out how to prevent them from awakening the Sleepers.

⋙ SEEKING BLOOD ⋘

Grandmother and her groundmites had toiled their way around the black lake and through the remains of the city. The chronicles of her people had prepared her for the odd aesthetics of the Eletians and their ever spiraling streets, but the groundmites disregarded the streets, using rough trails through the ruins they must have broken and learned about over the generations. If there were obstacles or some predator in their path, they lunged forward with unbridled enthusiasm and battered down whatever was in the way.

The castle towers loomed over the craggy, dark ruins, sometimes seeming to float, depending on the whimsy of the fog. It was not absolutely clear in the chronicles if Mornhavon occupied the castle after defeating Argenthyne or left it to rot. Even if he had occupied it, the chronicles suggested he preferred his fortress in the west, on the shore of Ullem Bay. She could not blame him, for the towers here were otherworldly, disquieting, exuding the taint of Eletian power even after so much time.

They came to the grove more swiftly than she dared to hope thanks to her groundmite allies.

Gubba extended her arms wide as if to embrace the immense trees before them and proclaimed, *"Brin ban orba!"*

Grandmother, who still could not follow the groundmite's speech, assumed she'd said something very profound.

"Morrrnnhavon brin ban orba!" Gubba exclaimed, and the groundmite warriors banged the butts of their spears and bows on the ground repeating her phrase in a shout.

One thing Grandmother had gathered was that the groundmites regarded Mornhavon as a god, thought that he'd created this world for them. It was true in a sense. For all intents, the groundmites had done very well in Blackveil, a realm of Mornhavon's making. But Grandmother knew better—Mornhavon was not God. He may have been the greatest Arcosian to have lived, still loved and revered by his people, and the favored one of God, but no, he was not God. It only served to illustrate how much more sophisticated Grandmother and her people were than the groundmites.

Now that they had reached their destination, Grandmother was still unclear as to what she needed to do to awaken the Sleepers. She assumed it would require blood magic, but now that she saw the immensity of the grove for herself, and that the trees, though rotting, retained some strength in them, she realized she'd need a lot of blood. She gazed speculatively at the groundmites. She'd need several of them, and they'd likely turn on her if she tried to use even one of them.

She turned her attention to her own people. They had come all this way with her and had shown exceptional loyalty, even Sarat, who'd been so frightened of every little thing along the way. She'd grown very fond of them and hated the thought of having to sacrifice even one of them. Perhaps she could persuade someone to volunteer. It would certainly demonstrate ultimate loyalty to her and Second Empire.

She watched Lala clamber up a tree root and balance her way to the trunk to look at a nobby burl that resembled a face—a face dribbling sap. Could Grandmother sacrifice her own granddaughter?

She would if she must, for God had commanded her to awaken the Sleepers.

Lala took her eating knife and probed the burl, then jammed it into the spot of rot. The tree trembled, casting down branches and needles and scurrying creatures. Groundmites scattered out of the way.

Gubba clapped and laughed. "Lalala goot!"

The old groundmite would not be laughing had one of the truly enormous branches above dropped on her.

The wound Lala inflicted in the bark caused more sap to flow. It had an ocher tint to it.

Very interesting, Grandmother thought, and she called the child away fearing that another stab into the tree would indeed cause it to drop a limb on them.

She stood deep in thought, stewing over what to do, what had to be done. The groundmites were scattered but nearby, gabbling among themselves or picking beetles off the forest floor and popping them into their mouths. Her own people sat themselves on a tree root to rest after their arduous journey, and Lala took up a string game.

Gubba now squatted and looked up at Grandmother as if expecting some great show of the art. Grandmother in turn sighed, and then felt a twinge on the back of her neck. Something had changed. Gubba sensed it, too, and gazed in the direction of the castle.

Grandmother closed her eyes and centered herself. Quite a while ago, she had sensed the forest being distracted and God had told her to awaken the Sleepers before the "others." Now she could feel that those others were here threatening everything she'd worked for.

Gubba snuffled. *"Yelt,"* she said, her eyes wide, showing fear.

Yelt? Did she mean the Elt? Eletians were here? It certainly explained the forest's interest and God's ardent command. She concentrated more deeply and sensed the bright spirits not far from the castle.

"They must be killed," Grandmother said, but before she could plan an organized assault, Gubba shouted something and her groundmites took up their weapons. Hooting and yelling, they charged in a disorderly pack deeper into the grove.

This would not do, Grandmother fumed, but it was already done. Her men came to her side.

"What're they after this time?" Griz asked.

"They are hunting Eletians."

"Eletians! What are those unholy creatures doing here?"

"Perhaps the same as we."

Griz suddenly crumpled, the shaft of a white arrow jutting

from his chest. Another dropped one of the groundmites that had remained with Gubba.

"Take cover!" Grandmother cried.

How did the Eletian arrows find them through the trees like that? There could not be a straight line of sight. Deglin and Cole rushed her behind the bole of one of the huge trees with Min and Sarat. Lala calmly sat at their feet.

One thing was now for certain: Grandmother would have her blood.

⇻ LADY OF LIGHT ⇺

The castle beguiled Karigan, drew her to explore beyond the chamber they'd entered, so she tucked the feather into her braid as she'd seen Graelalea do and limped across the chamber, leaving behind the sound of groundmites pounding on the doors and Grant whimpering against the wall. He'd curled into himself, folded into a compact ball. She left behind Yates and Ard, and the Eletians who sat in vigil around Graelalea's shrouded body. No one stopped her or asked where she was going.

Somehow she was supposed to help the Sleepers and she needed to step away to think, to retreat from the noise, and from the emotions each one of her remaining companions projected, their confusion, sorrow, fear, and anger. She felt all those things, too, and did not need them augmented by the others. At least they were safe from the groundmites, if not from their noise. Ealdaen said they'd never be able to force their way into the castle.

She followed a winding corridor out of the chamber, her feet raising layers of dust, the bonewood tapping on marble. The curve of the corridor tantalized her—she wanted to see what was hidden around the bend—but around and around she went, and though she had a sense of spiraling inward, the curves grew no tighter, at least not in any way she could perceive. Her idea of a seashell, like one of the large conch shells her father'd collected from the Cloud Islands, remained apt, the smooth pearlescent walls scrolling inward to its core. What would she find when she reached it?

Very soon she had her answer. The corridor opened into a

vast, round chamber that soared upward like the other tower, but unlike the other, it contained no stairs winding to the top, and no bridges crossing its heights.

Upon pedestals stood four statues of winged Eletians, each perfect in form, the feathers of their wings as delicate and airy as the real thing, not at all resembling the stone they were carved from. The statues aspired to flight and the tower was high enough. Somehow Karigan knew that only the open sky would free them, and she felt the conflict of yearning to ascend with them, but of being Earthbound.

On the floor were several clumps of bones, faded fabric, and shards of steel weaponry. A spider, a normal-sized house spider, spun a web in the rib cage of a nearby skeleton. There was no other evidence of creatures living or dead, not even mouse tracks in the dust.

The dust caused the floor to appear a dull gray, but when she scraped her boot across it, the floor shone obsidian underneath. More investigation revealed some pattern inlaid in crystalline quartz too large to uncover entirely. She thought she would move on and continue her exploration, to find out what other parts of the castle would be revealed, when she heard the sound of footsteps behind her.

She turned to find Ard emerging from the corridor with bow and nocked arrow pointed directly at her.

"Ard—what?"

"My true mission," he said, "is to see that you don't survive yours. I kept hoping something else might take you so I wouldn't have to do this, but you kept surviving."

At first Karigan could only gape, but then it dawned on her. "You . . . you were there," she said, her voice barely rising above a whisper, but carrying easily across the cavernous room. "You were really there, weren't you, when I was caught in that creature's web."

Ard nodded. "I thought those monsters would finish you. No luck, so here I am. I regret this, but I've no choice."

"But why? At least tell me that. What have I ever done to you?" Karigan stepped back, her heel nudging a pile of bones that rattled. A leg bone rolled away.

"Duty to my clan," he replied. "To protect the marriage

of my lady to the king. You are a threat, and anything that threatens my lady must be destroyed."

Karigan's heart thudded. Others knew of her feelings for the king? Someone high up thought her enough of a threat to murder her? The captain had warned her that with her knighthood she'd entered the thorny world of the royal court, but this went beyond politics! Or maybe she was just being naive.

Ard tautened the bow string. "I do this for my lady, and with her blessing." He loosed the arrow, but it flew wild, hitting the wall behind her. Ard's knees folded and he crumpled to the floor, a white Eletian arrow piercing his throat. Karigan's own knees went weak.

Ealdaen appeared from the corridor with bow in hand, and he glanced briefly at Ard before stepping over the forester's body.

"I saw him follow you out," Ealdaen said. "He had an interest in you all along, but not knowing the ways of your people, I could not discern his intent. Until now."

Karigan's grip on the bonewood was clammy. It was too much betrayal to sort out all at once. Ard as murderer, with Estora's blessing. Estora, who had been her friend.

And now she was alone with Ealdaen who'd once tried to kill her. He strode toward her.

"Did you kill Ard so you could finish me off yourself?" She extended the bonewood to staff length with a shake and stood in a defensive position.

Ealdaen paused, a bemused expression on his face. "You are truly difficult to understand at times, you and your people. I am not here to kill you, Galadheon, but to aid you. The reason for hunting you in the past no longer exists. You are free of the tainted wild magic."

Karigan released a long breath and relaxed her stance.

"Omens and prophecies are not set in stone," Ealdaen continued. "A river will change course. You've a particular unpredictability, Galadheon, one that all the prophecies of the crown prince cannot pin down."

"Maybe Eletians are too set in their ways," Karigan replied, not so ready to forgive one who almost killed her based on the unreliability of prophecy.

He bowed his head accepting her words without recrimination. "It is clear that you've a purpose here, which I'm only just beginning to understand. Graelalea must have known something of it for she passed to you one of her feathers. And you are Laurelyn-touched."

He was right, she was here for a purpose, drawn by an apparition she'd seen one snowy night along the Arrowdale Road. Why she hadn't remembered that purpose before, she did not know, but it galled her to learn that yet once again other forces were directing her life. She'd work out her feelings about that later—she'd more pressing concerns now.

"I am here to help the Sleepers," she said. "I was told this."

"By whom?"

"A woman in the light." Karigan thought her words wouldn't have made sense to anyone else or under different circumstances.

"I find it interesting that you found your way to this chamber of your own accord."

"Why?"

Ealdaen produced his moonstone and strode to the center of the chamber. The shadows cast by the moonstone shifted as he walked, making the statues seem to follow him with their gazes, their wings flexing for flight. Walls of translucent light rose from the quartz in the floor.

"You saw a small version of this in Telavalieth," Ealdaen said. "You called it a moondial. This is Castle Argenthyne's moondial." He glanced at the skeleton near his feet. "I knew the defenders of this tower. They stayed to the last. Alas, the castle did fall." He gazed around the chamber some more. "The gnomon is missing. Just like in Telavalieth."

The phases of the moon shone in the light that bathed the floor, and the stars, too, transforming the floor into a celestial map. Beneath them, in the very center of the chamber, was a large round piece of quartz that had the shading and subtlety of a silvery full moon. It was, by magnitudes, larger than the moondial in Telavalieth.

"How would you awaken the Sleepers?" Karigan asked.

Ealdaen lowered his moonstone and there was that disconcerting sense of the world shifting with the light.

"We would sing to them," he replied.

"That's all?"

"There is a certain song, and a certain way of singing it. A calling it is. The Sleepers choose to heed or ignore it. But yes, that is all."

Before Karigan could question him further, another light coalesced in the chamber, a liquid column of light just like the one she had seen that night in Arrowdale. But the figure within was clearer this time: a woman with hair flowing about her shoulders and her gown touched by no earthly breeze.

Ealdaen fell immediately to his knee and bowed his head. Every song and tale of Argenthyne Karigan ever heard flowed through her mind and this time she knew immediately who stood before her—Laurelyn, Laurelyn the Moondreamer; Laurelyn, the queen of lost Argenthyne, sweet Silvermind.

Ealdaen, the woman of light said, *rise.*

Ealdaen did so, though at first hesitant; he slowly raised his face to meet her gaze. "I thought never to look upon you again, my queen."

Nor I, you, but it heartens me to see you here now for this unfolding.

They spoke at length in Eletian and although Karigan could not understand the conversation, she felt grief and anguish in their words. There was a shared history between the two, a history Ealdaen was reliving by having come home.

Excluded by their language and conversation, Karigan thought to leave them to give them privacy, but she was caught by surprise when Ealdaen spoke again in the common tongue.

"I am here to redeem myself," he said.

So be it, Laurelyn replied. She turned her gaze upon Karigan, and Karigan was arrested by the queen's eyes of midnight blue, her appearance far, far clearer than that night in Arrowdale.

Daughter of Kariny, you are here at last. My influence is stronger here, but still it wanes, and soon it will vanish en-

tirely. The powers of the forest have striven to vanquish me altogether. I still fight, and here within the castle I am a little protected.

"How do you expect me to help the Sleepers?" Karigan demanded. "Why me?"

You can cross thresholds, the liminal line, and by doing so, you will lead the Sleepers to safety. Daughter of Kariny, you can step through layers of the world.

Karigan could not remember ever being told this, and yet she knew it as if someone had explained it all to her before. Her ability to fade was really the ability to stand on that threshold, but her ability was meager, even with her brooch augmenting it. It took some additional force to push her across, like the wild magic that had once allowed her to pass through the ages to the time of the First Rider.

"I do not know what to do," Karigan said.

I will tell you, Laurelyn replied.

Just then, the other Eletians, along with Yates, Lynx, and Grant, filed into the chamber. Their eyes grew wide as they took in Ard's body and the lady of light. The Eletians dropped to their knees as Ealdaen had.

Laurelyn swept her arm up and pointed, the light sparking with anger around her. Grant cowered away, hid behind Lynx. *That one,* she declared, *brings evil into this place.*

⋙ THE POTENT SNARL ⋘

Grandmother gazed in satisfaction at the dead bodies lined up before her, eight of the loyal band of groundmites that had escorted her to Castle Argenthyne's grove, plus her own Griz. She'd plucked the white arrows from them all, the wooden shafts stinging her fingers. She'd also sensed that Eletian blood had been spilled in the grove and she believed it would only make her working stronger.

She had tied knots feverishly, using much of what was left of her yarn, holding in reserve a ball of the indigo should they survive this and need it for finding their way out of Blackveil. Lala had intently watched the tying of knots, helping and fetching as needed. Meanwhile, Grandmother had gotten Gubba to oversee the butchering of corpses, cold, still hearts placed into Min's largest pot.

Even as Grandmother worked at invoking the power of the art, she felt the darkness of the forest press in on her, the intensity of its attention. The trees of the grove had gone rigid, and she heard the sound of cracking like the winter forest, moisture freezing within the wood.

After she tied the last knot, a complex weaving of command, she slumped exhausted and gazed at the snarl of yarn in her hands. The potent snarl.

Lala nudged her shoulder and handed her a cup of tea. Her people had started a fire while she worked. She was never so grateful.

"My good girl," Grandmother said wearily. She hugged Lala's shoulders. "Now would you fetch me my special bowl?"

Lala nodded and skipped away to where their packs lay.

Gubba came over and chirped in admiration at the knots. Meanwhile, Grandmother sipped her tea, letting it warm her. Lala brought over the earthenware bowl and set it at Grandmother's feet.

Grandmother did not move, she just rested, enjoying the tea and the respite, and knowing that everything came down to this. She knew everyone watched her to see what would come next. God had not spoken to her of late, had not given her any indication of what was supposed to be done, except that she was to awaken the Sleepers.

So she'd constructed a spell the best way she knew how. The Sleepers, she assumed, were in a state akin to death, or at least as close to death as many of that immortal race would ever get. Therefore, she'd devised a spell similar to—though definitely not the same as—one that would raise the dead. This was a major undertaking considering the size of the grove, and she thought of how proud her own grandmother would be that she had used the art on a scale that had not been seen for centuries. How proud all of those along her maternal line would be; all their knowledge passed down the generations for this one moment in the service of Second Empire and God.

The spell required one more element before she could summon the awakening. She drained the last of her tea, looked mournfully at the leaves settled on the cup's bottom, and sighed. Lala took it from her and helped her rise.

"Gubba," Grandmother said, placing her hand on the old groundmite's furry shoulder. "I need another favor."

Gubba chirped a query, and Grandmother gazed into that rheumy eye. Grandmother smiled in reassurance, then slashed her knife into Gubba's throat. She sawed through the groundmite's tough flesh until she hit the vital vein.

Gubba fell with shock in her eye, arms flailing. Grandmother grabbed her bowl to catch as much of the spurting blood as possible.

The remaining groundmites, those not still fruitlessly pounding on the castle doors, did not retaliate at Gubba's sacrifice. Their eyes filled with horror, but they recognized Grandmother's strength in the art and understood Gubba had become part of a larger working. No, instead of retaliating, they fled yipping and barking into the woods and out of her ken.

The earthenware bowl looked ordinary enough, but it contained the power to preserve blood, even keeping it warm, and Gubba's blood was special, for she'd an innate ability to use the art. That made it a strong additive to the spell Grandmother was weaving.

Gubba's heart had been added to the pot with the others. Grandmother cut it out herself.

"Won't be using that pot again," Min muttered. "No, by God. Not for soup or anything."

Grandmother's knotted yarn stewed among the hearts in the pot. Not that the pot had been placed over a fire, but the words of power she invoked, drawn from the ancient language of the art, boiled among the organs making them sizzle and pop with magical heat. She paced. The grove filled not only with the scent of cooking meat, but with potential. Her people, even Lala, stood well away. She'd used some clippings of yarn to create wards to protect them, if such a meager spell could do so against the larger.

When she deemed the knots had spent enough time among the hearts, she lifted them from the pot with a spoon, which Min also declared no longer suitable for cooking, and transferred them into the bowl filled with Gubba's blood. Blood overflowed the brim, dribbling down the sides of the bowl.

Grandmother spoke softly and slowly as she swished the yarn in the blood with her fingers, making sure it absorbed as much as possible. Soon the blood started to boil.

She stepped back, her fingertips dripping crimson. The spell was not as malevolent as one for waking the dead, but she felt the shadows eating at her soul. It was, after all, blood magic. The entire forest seemed to lean in on her, eager for the spell to be loosed.

She licked her lips. "Rise!" she commanded. A sphere arose from the bowl, dull and mud colored, and hovered in the air. No blood dripped from it for it had absorbed all of it.

"Awaken the Sleepers," she said, repeating the words in the ancient tongue.

The sphere pulsed, then darted through the grove, circling the trunks of the great trees, trailing a subtle glow that settled into the bark. A keening arose among the branches as they swayed in an unnatural wind, wood splintering, shattering, cracking so loudly that Grandmother thought it was her own mind that was breaking. She covered her ears. Even the corpses nearby jerked and trembled with the force she had unleashed.

Bark exploded, peeled back. Ocher sap oozed in runnels. Enormous limbs fell around her. Trees struck the earth like thunder, shuddering the ground.

Then she saw them, the figures pushing out of the rotten hearts of the vast trees, wailing, hungry, angry, *dark*. Grandmother smiled. The light that had once been the natural essence of these Eletians had been extinguished by centuries immersed in the evil of Blackveil.

They resembled Eletians except for the dark that shone through them. They were like wraiths, thin and feral, rags that had once been the finery of Argenthyne flowing from their limbs.

She felt their hunger and their interest in her and her people. She pointed at the corpses and pot of hearts. "Feed," she commanded in the ancient tongue.

The Eletians swarmed the meat, but there would never be enough. She could not count how many she'd awakened—a hundred? Two hundred? Three?

They stripped the corpses to the bone and she knew she had to redirect them before they turned to her and her people for more nourishment.

"Go to the castle," she ordered them. "There are more you may feed on there."

They would, she knew, find the last of Gubba's band stubbornly trying to knock down the castle doors. Where the groundmites could not gain entry, the Sleepers would. Dark or not, they knew the castle and its workings. The Sleepers would take care of the problem of the others. The rest was up to God. Grandmother had accomplished what she set out to do: the Sleepers were awake.

She took in the devastation around her, the roiling fog where once great trees stood. She could not believe she had survived that, but when she reached her people, she discovered that Sarat and Deglin had not. They'd been crushed by a tree limb that narrowly missed the others.

God's work required sacrifices, she thought, and He had received them.

⋙ THE SHADOW OF LIGHT ⋘

Laurelyn's accusation reverberated up into the heights of the tower. Grant bolted, but the Eletians were quicker and grabbed him. He fought, hitting, biting, kicking, and it took Telagioth, Solan, Lhean, and Lynx to subdue him.

You must . . . Laurelyn began.

Grant howled, an inhuman blood curdling sound. Karigan clamped her hands over her ears. Grant brushed off his captors like they were nothing and staggered forward. He ripped the sleeve from the arm he'd been favoring for so long and Karigan stepped back, resisting the urge to retch.

The flesh of his arm was stark white, bloodless. Angry, bloated veins flowed into blackened pustules the size of eggs. They twitched like something writhed inside them.

"My nythlings," Grant crooned, his expression rapturous.

They all stared at him in horrified fascination.

Grant howled again, a rending cry of pain. The pustules burst and Karigan did retch. Black glistening creatures, like armored reptiles, clawed their way out of Grant's flesh, fluid sacs splattering to the floor. The creatures shook out membranous wings.

Behind Grant, Telagioth drew his sword.

"My nythlings!" Grant exulted.

The tip of Telagioth's sword emerged through Grant's chest. Grant wailed, then slid off the blade and to the floor. Telagioth stood there with blooded sword, a grim expression on his face.

"Kill the creatures!" Ealdaen sprang to and Karigan made to follow. If only they could have helped Grant before it came to this.

Wait, Laurelyn commanded her.

Karigan hesitated. A couple of the creatures dipped their sharp beaks into Grant's corpse and fed. The others stretched their wings and launched into the air, flocking around her companions.

It is time, Laurelyn said. *You must help the Sleepers.*

"But—" At that moment, Karigan felt something change, something in the atmosphere, a rending of the air; she felt the castle brace itself.

The light of Laurelyn flickered and her back arched, arms flung out. She opened her mouth in a silent scream.

No . . . Laurelyn whispered.

"What is it?" A creature darted at Karigan and she whacked it away with her staff.

Laurelyn shone again, but darkness blurred her edges.

Another power in the grove has awakened the Sleepers.

Karigan was confused. "Isn't that what you wanted?"

No, child. Laurelyn's eyes were wild. *The forest has blackened their hearts as they slept. They have awakened as dark, vile creatures that hate the light.*

"Then why did you want me to rescue them?" Karigan batted another of the nythlings with a satisfying *crack.* It hit one of the statues and fell to the floor into a crumpled heap.

Stand on the moon. Laurelyn's image fluctuated again. *Stand on the moon and I will show you. Hurry! They will soon be upon us.*

Lynx cried out as one of the nythlings dove and attacked. Lhean leaped to aid him.

"I can't abandon my friends."

If you hesitate, that which has awakened will swarm out of Blackveil and into your country, a terrible, savage enemy. Do you wish this?

"No, but . . ." She glanced at her friends hacking at the flying creatures. Telagioth cut one out of the air.

Stand on the moon, child. We haven't the time to debate!

Ealdaen ran toward Karigan, grabbed her arm and dragged her to the very center of the chamber to stand directly on the crystalline moon.

"Do as she says, Galadheon," he hissed, "or else all is lost. We will protect you as well as we can."

Sleepers poured from the corridor into the chamber like a dark wave, thin and ragged and wild, but unmistakably Eletian. Ealdaen did not pause, but pivoted and dashed back to face them. Karigan screamed when they started to tear Solan apart.

Child! cried Laurelyn. *Your moonstone.*

Karigan turned her back on the savagery to face Laurelyn's dim form. "I want to help my friends."

No. You'd be lost alongside them. You still have time to help others beyond Blackveil, and it may be, that by doing as I ask, you will change the outcome for your friends.

Karigan's heart leaped with that kernel of hope and she removed the moonstone from her pocket. Unwavering light flared up around her. The nythlings flew away from it, the Sleepers did not cross it.

I need you to stand just so, for you will be the gnomon. The moonstone will cast your shadow on the correct phase.

Karigan tried to block the cries and screams of her companions while obeying Laurelyn's instructions, stretching one arm straight out in front of her and adjusting her stance.

Use your ability, daughter of Kariny, it is the key. Use your ability to cross the threshold, the liminal line.

Karigan touched her brooch and the world changed around her, like the turning of a key. The winged statues rotated, grinding on their pedestals like the tumblers of a lock, so they all gazed down on her. The walls of the tower revolved and at its apex, it irised open to the sky. Blackveil's vapor tumbled inside.

Karigan's chest cramped and she fell to her knees gasping. The light flaring up around her turned blinding, absorbing Laurelyn so that she was barely perceptible.

The sky above had changed, cleared. A silver moon shined down on them.

"What . . . what?" Karigan didn't even know what to ask.

Laurelyn smiled. *A piece of time. You have crossed the liminal to a piece of time graced by a silver full moon, a gift of the Moonman.*

The Moonman, legend. Karigan's mind raced. It was too much.

Let us go, Laurelyn said.

"Where?"

To the grove. She extended a hand. Karigan clasped it and found it surprisingly solid, warm. She rose and Laurelyn led her from the moondial and through the wall of light.

Karigan recoiled at her double vision, the vision of the tower as she left it, with her companions clashing with the Sleepers, layered over by the vision of the tower still and peaceful, the walls brilliantly aglow, the obsidian floor free of dust, like black ice.

She felt as though a boulder pressed against her chest as she abandoned her companions, as Lynx was thrown against the wall, claw marks striating his face. Ealdaen's armor was splashed with blood as he relentlessly slashed at the horde of Sleepers, a nythling latched to his neck, wings flapping, tail lashing. Ealdaen tore it off and smashed it to the floor, along with a chunk of his own flesh. She could not see Yates.

"Oh, Yates," she murmured.

Even as she saw these things, it was as though a great distance separated them from her, layered over by the serene, silver washed chamber. Her tears fell on the dusty floor strewn with footprints and blood. She left tears on pristine obsidian.

She followed Laurelyn into the winding corridor.

It grieves me, Laurelyn said, *that your companions should suffer, but we cannot allow an army of tainted Sleepers to enter the world outside Blackveil. There would be much more suffering in your land and beyond. And as I said, this unfolding may change the fates of your friends.*

"The Sleepers are awakened," Karigan said. "I don't know what you expect me to do."

You shall see.

Laurelyn's gown trailed along the floor. More Sleepers, feral, snarling things, ran by them, through them, emanating darkness that brushed against the light of Karigan's moonstone. The layering of visions nauseated her.

"Then tell me," she said, trying to ignore her stomach, "did you give my mother this moonstone?"

Laurelyn hesitated before answering. *Yes.*

"Why?"

It contains the radiance of the moon we now walk beneath. It helped you find this piece of time.

"B-but I wasn't even born when my mother received this!"

Laurelyn kept striding along. *You know by now Eletians can sometimes see beyond the present. Ours is not always a linear existence, but seeing is different from being able to move through the layers of the world. I knew Kariny would conceive one with your ability. I visited with her in that glade, and I sang to her. I had not foreseen that your father was going to be a descendent of one of Mornhavon's folk, but there was a symmetry in it I could appreciate.*

"But you—"

I am mostly not here, Laurelyn replied. *I am here less and less as time passes and the forest assaults my strength. You see only the shadow of light.*

Karigan squinted as she gazed at Laurelyn's brightness. She could not say what she did or did not see. She'd encountered so many strange things since becoming a Rider that she shook her head and took whatever Laurelyn was as one more for the list.

"I should just go back in time to tell myself not to become a Green Rider," Karigan said.

But would you listen to yourself? Laurelyn asked with a glint of amusement in her eyes.

"Probably not. But, if I can do this, I could stop my mother from going to that fair where she caught fever. I . . . I could have a sister or brother. I—"

No. Laurelyn's voice cracked like thunder, all hint of amusement gone. *It would be disastrous, such meddling.*

"It hasn't stopped *you.*"

I have not changed the course of what is to come.

"You gave my mother a moonstone."

They stared at one another, but Laurelyn's brightness hurt Karigan's eyes and she glanced away.

They continued on, emerging into the first tower. Karigan saw it filled with Sleepers, Sleepers climbing the stairs, crossing bridges on the heights above. Miraculously they had not touched Graelalea's body or moonstone. Its light reached out to Laurelyn and her, then faded.

The Queen of Argenthyne touched the feather in Karigan's hair. *Enmorial,* she murmured. *Remember.*

Karigan paused thinking back to that snowy evening in Arrowdale, a question niggling at the back of her mind. "Why did you make me forget?" she asked. "Why did you make me forget our first meeting?"

At first Laurelyn did not answer. Then: *I feared that if you carried the memory of it, it would have left too great a burden of dread upon you, perhaps causing you to resist my plea to come here.*

"Then why bother appearing to me in the first place?"

I left my plea with you as an undercurrent, a summoning that would bolster the wishes of those who command you. Now that I see you, I know my fears were unfounded, and I am sorry I hid the truth from you.

Karigan sighed, beyond anger, at least for the moment, and she thought it true Laurelyn had spared her the burden for a time.

Above all else, I wished to see you, Kariny's daughter. Laurelyn extended her hand and caressed Karigan with light. *The one I awaited for so long, and on whom all my hopes rested. Kariny, too, was my heart friend and meeting you in the place where I so often visited her answered a yearning of my spirit.* She paused. *You are very much your mother's mirror.*

The two worlds Karigan traveled in, past and present, wavered and stormed in her vision. She closed her eyes against it, and against the tempest rising within herself.

I sang to Kariny unto her ending days, and when she was gone, I was hollow with loneliness. Do know that as brief as your mother's time in this world was, Laurelyn said, *she loved her life, and she loved you.*

"Thank you," Karigan whispered, and when she opened her eyes once again, the vision of the empty, shining tower folded over the dark one and obscured it, the tower's doors wide open to the grove awash in the light of the silver moon.

≪ A FACE IN THE FIRE ≫

So exhausted was Grandmother from cast-ing spells that she had nearly collapsed. Cole carried her away from the bodies of De-glin and Sarat, with Min trailing behind and weeping. Lala walked beside them, casting Grandmother anxious looks.

Cole halted at the edge of the grove and gently set her down. Immediately he collected wood for another fire. Min produced a blanket with which she covered Grandmother.

"I'm fine, truly I am," she insisted.

"Are we . . . are we safe here from those Sleeper crea-tures?" Min asked, fretting with the hem of her cloak.

"I do not know," Grandmother replied. "I should think, however, what is in the castle is of more interest to them than we are. At least for now. Lala will make some wards, won't you, Lala?"

The child nodded solemnly.

"Be sparing with the yarn, child. It is all we've got left."

While Lala set to work, Grandmother huddled beneath her blanket and dozed off, dreaming of sunny, drier days in her little kitchen garden in Sacor City, the birds twittering in the trees, and the smell of savory herbs and soil on her hands.

She stirred when Min gave her a cup of broth, startled to find it darker out and a campfire blazing. She closed her eyes and felt the protections Lala had placed around them—even without words, she'd given them the power to work.

"My dear child, you are a wonder! Your wards are very good." She reached out and clasped her granddaughter's hand.

How old my hand looks next to hers, Grandmother reflected. *It is good she has taken so well to the art.* Grandmother knew she would not be around to lead Second Empire forever. She hoped she'd have enough time to train Lala to take her place.

The girl beamed at her, then pulled her ratty piece of string out of her pocket with which to play games.

"What's next?" Cole asked, sipping from his own cup of broth. "Are we leaving?"

Grandmother heard the weariness in his voice. She would like nothing better than to leave Blackveil herself, though the mere idea of trekking all the way back home deepened her fatigue.

"Since we've a good fire, I would like to see what is happening in the world, and perhaps God will speak to me and provide us with instructions."

In the guise of teaching Lala knots, Grandmother sat back and rested while her granddaughter did all the work. Lala encapsulated one of Birch's fingernails into a knot and tossed the yarn into the fire.

Grandmother stared into the flames, putting her intent into seeing through Birch's eyes. How did the training with his soldiers go? What was happening on the northern border?

And then she was there, gazing through Birch's eyes only to see . . . the dark of night. She sighed. After being in the dark of Blackveil for so long, she'd gotten into the habit of thinking of the other side of the wall as perpetually sunny, but it was not. Night fell there, too.

Her sight adjusted to the dark and she realized Birch was peering into the distance where lamplight winked in windows. Someone crept up next to him. Grandmother could make out very little of the newcomer's shape in the dark.

"Report," Birch said very quietly.

"Sir, looks like thirty men or so. Just a few women. Must've sent the rest away with the children."

"Just like the last two settlements," Birch mused. "Word has gotten around about us."

"If they were smart, they'd have all left. It's just not as entertaining without them trying to defend their families."

"This is war, Corporal," Birch growled. "It's not meant to be entertaining. We're training men to fight and kill."

"Yes, sir," the corporal replied, sounding chagrined at the rebuke. "What are your orders?"

Birch glanced at the moon through the trees. It was a thin crescent like the fingernail Lala had folded into the knot. "We'll get a better lay of the land at dawn. Then we'll put the men into position. Strike at dusk."

"Thirty aren't going to be much of a challenge."

"The practice is good," Birch said. "Soon our soldiers will be facing stiffer opposition—bigger towns, trained militia. We need to take advantage of these training exercises while we may."

Grandmother withdrew from the vision. It sounded like Birch's work was going well. Perhaps she'd look into the fire tomorrow to see how his campaign fared. She began to doze, the broth warm in her belly and the heat of the fire toasty against her skin. She felt as content as a cat in a sunny window.

Curiously, she imagined a pair of eyes watching her from the fire, a pair of depthless, black eyes set in a face of flame.

She jolted to wakefulness, and the face was still there. The others did not appear to see it.

"M-my lord?" Grandmother said.

"THE SLEEPERS?"

"They are awake."

The eyes shimmered. "EXCELLENT." The face lost form for several moments, then the fire plumed and the face re-formed in a roiling fury.

"SHE HAS DEFIED ME. SHE WILL STEAL THE SLEEPERS! YOU MUST STOP HER."

He then told Grandmother what to look for as glowing embers showered down from singed trees. The Queen of Argenthyne had existed in some ethereal form all these years protecting the grove in a piece of time. It appeared she planned to awaken the Sleepers in that distant past and lead them to a safe haven.

Grandmother was not in any condition to seek a way to find the queen or figure out how to fight her across time, nor were her people, yet she must obey God's will. She did have tools. She made a knot, tossed it onto the fire, and sent a tendril of power into the dark of the grove, seeking a Sleeper. Seeking several Sleepers. One or more of them might be willing and capable of doing what she needed.

⊰ SLEEPWALKERS ⊱

Karigan saw the grove as it was meant to be seen, the trunks of the trees grand columns of silver, not mottled by rot or disease. The full moon shone through the canopy, glistening on the tips of pine needles and casting shadows of interlaced tree limbs on the forest floor. Pale flowers blossomed in the moonlight, suffusing the air with a pleasant fragrance. Crickets chirruped and the fluting song of the wood thrush rose and fell through the grove.

Karigan had not felt such tranquility since ... She did not know when. She turned to gaze at the castle and understood the legend of Laurelyn's castle of moonbeams, for the towers gleamed like the extension of moon glow.

"It's beautiful," Karigan murmured, and she realized with a start that her vision was no longer doubled, no longer overlain by the darkness wrought by Blackveil. She saw only this one shining world.

Yes, I preserved this piece of time and set it aside so it would remain unmarred, Laurelyn said. *From here I shall rouse the Sleepers. They will not be the dark beings you witnessed in your present, but Eletian Sleepers as they should be. You will lead them to safety.*

"How am I supposed to do that?"

Laurelyn gazed at the moon, her face aglow in its silver light. *I've enough strength left to create a temporary bridge. There were once other bridges out of Argenthyne, but those were destroyed long ago.*

Karigan began to grow suspicious about where such a bridge would take her.

As though Laurelyn perceived her thoughts, she said, *The bridge will take you to an island in a transitional place. I believe you have been there before?*

Her words confirmed Karigan's suspicions. The white world. She sighed, and nodded.

Good. You will know not to become distracted there. When Karigan nodded again, Laurelyn continued. *The island is small, smaller than the castle chamber you found me in. There you shall find a second bridge, a more permanent bridge. You shall lead the Sleepers across it to Eletia's grove.*

"Eletia? Truly?"

Laurelyn smiled again. *Truly. However, I must warn you, I do not know if Eletia's time will correspond to this piece of time. If you meet anyone there, it is difficult to know how they shall receive you, for they are intolerant of intruders. Once they see you've Argenthyne Sleepers with you, they should prove accepting.*

If they didn't kill her first. "Will the Sleepers follow me?"

Yes, you've the light of the silver moon on you. Some would call you Laurelyn-touched. When I rouse the Sleepers, they will not be fully awake, more akin to sleepwalkers, and they will do as I command, which will be to follow you. When they reach the grove in Eletia, some may awaken fully. Others will simply gravitate to one tree or another and continue the long sleep.

It sounded simple enough. Deceptively simple. The white world was never simple.

"Why can't you lead the Sleepers yourself?" Karigan asked.

I no longer exist beyond the grove. You, daughter of Kariny, are the one who can cross thresholds.

Karigan sighed.

You must maintain your ability the whole time, Laurelyn instructed, *or all will be lost. Once you safely reach Eletia, you may let it go and you will be propelled to your present time, but in Eletia. Or, you could hold on to it until you return here. I can maintain the bridge for a while.*

"My companions . . ." She swallowed hard. In this place, in this piece of time, she had almost forgotten about them. She closed her eyes. Surely none of them survived, but Laurelyn had said she could change outcomes . . .

Then Karigan suddenly understood. "By my doing this, there won't be any Sleepers—the tainted ones—to attack my companions in the present because I will have taken the Sleepers away in the past." It made her head spin, but there was logic to it.

Laurelyn nodded. *Be aware, however, that I've not been able to preserve the entire grove. My power has waned over these many years while I awaited you, and the fringes of the grove have slipped from my protection, so your companions will still be up against many enemies.*

"Still better odds than against all of them," Karigan murmured.

You should also know that I was unable to protect the Sleepers in Argenthyne's other groves. I fear one day they, too, shall be a threat to your people.

"Mornhavon destroyed the grove in Telavalieth," Karigan told her.

Then pray it is so for the others. Now, daughter of Kariny, we must get you on your way, because the more time that passes, the more my strength ebbs. First the bridge.

Laurelyn raised her hands to the moon and her palms filled with light. She then cast the light from her and it beamed in a glowing arc through the woods.

Moonbeams? "That . . . that's the bridge?" Karigan asked in incredulity.

Do not fear. It shall hold you, and the Sleepers, too.

Laurelyn began to sing, a melodious song without words, unearthly and unlike anything Karigan had ever heard before. She shivered. Laurelyn's voice rose and expanded through the grove, flowing between the trees and up into the canopy.

Figures emerged from behind the trees and walked toward them, as though in a dream, unaware of their surroundings. These were not the creatures that had attacked Karigan and her companions. They were beautiful as all Eletians were, and untainted by the dark. Gradually hundreds stood arrayed before her and Laurelyn's song faded. She spoke to them in Eletian, but they showed no signs of comprehension or wakefulness.

These are my people, Laurelyn told Karigan. *All that remains of them. Among them are friends, confidants, and heroes of another age. Artists, poets, smiths, and architects. Please help them reach Eletia so something of Argenthyne lives on.*

"I will," Karigan said, only now fully appreciating the responsibility she was taking on.

Then cross the bridge. They will follow.

Karigan turned to leave.

Thank you, Laurelyn said. *And remember, do not tarry in Eletia if you wish to return and aid your companions. My time is ending, and I shall not be able to hold the bridge for long.*

Karigan nodded, then trotted down the terrace steps and walked between the Sleepers to reach the bridge. The Sleepers fell in behind, following her in silence. It was eerie.

When she reached the bridge, she gazed skeptically at it, or rather through it, for the moonbeams were translucent and she could see the ground beneath, which was not at all reassuring. She shook her head and took one step onto the bridge, and then another. It supported her just as Laurelyn said it would.

She continued with more assurance. It was as steady as walking on stone, but the bridge was narrow, and being able to see through it continued to disconcert her. She picked up her pace, and as she approached the apex of the arch, the way ahead grew cloudy, indistinct. She took a breath and plunged ahead.

The scents of the grove, the gentle air and sounds, vanished. Karigan emerged into the white world blinking. She'd begun calling it the "white world" the first time she'd passed through it, for the sky and the ground were both the same milky white color. She'd learned since that it was the space between the layers of the world, a transitional place just as Laurelyn had said. The two times she'd traversed its plains, she'd been confronted with visions, some metaphorical, some positively nightmarish. Once she had even seen the aftermath of a battle, the ground strewn with the corpses of her friends . . . and the king.

At the moment she was enveloped in the white of the sky. The white world had a bleaching effect on her uniform as if color was not tolerated. And down below? She swallowed hard. Her previous passages through the white world had shown her a landscape of only featureless plains. This time she walked above a chasm so deep she could not perceive its bottom. She heard no water below, felt no updrafts or breezes, just saw the plunging depths where shades of white turned to shades of gray, and darkened beyond that.

Karigan had never feared heights, but she hastened her steps until she felt the solid white ground of the island beneath her feet. The Sleepers were right behind her, crossing the bridge in an orderly file. She thought them fortunate to be unaware of their surroundings.

It was the chasm that made the island an island; there was no milky sea or lake surrounding it. As Laurelyn had told her, the island was not even as large as the chamber that had housed the moondial. Karigan spotted the bridge on the other side that was supposed to cross into Eletia. It was a more ordinary looking bridge of stone and mortar.

She paced, waiting to ensure each and every Sleeper made it across the moonbeam bridge onto the island before she set off again. As each Eletian stepped off the bridge, she wondered if he or she were a poet or great hero. What had motivated them to take the long sleep? What were their names? What had they seen in their long lives? She cleared her throat and said hello to several of them, but none replied. They were entirely unaware of her, their eyes distant, filled with stars that did not exist here.

A gap opened on the bridge. A Sleeper hesitated on the arch, his posture different, less erect. Had he awakened while crossing? If so, he was probably startled to find himself on a translucent bridge spanning a strange chasm in the white world. Shocked was more like it. She decided she'd better help him.

She started back across the bridge. When the Sleepers started to follow her, she raised her hand and said, "No, stay." For some reason, they obeyed and remained on the island.

Her relief was short-lived, for as she approached the arch,

she realized it wasn't one of *her* Sleepers standing there, but one of the tainted ones from Blackveil.

"Oh, no," she whispered.

A second appeared through the haze behind him.

She started to back away, her staff held before her. How was she going to get her Sleepers across the second bridge to Eletia with these tainted ones behind them? It would be a massacre.

The first tainted one snarled and lunged.

MOONFIRE

Karigan did not hesitate. Her training had prepared her to act first and think later until it was instinctual. Before the tainted one reached her, she cracked him in the head with the staff's steel handle. It slowed him down, but did not stop him, and she followed up with a low sweep to his knees. He fought for balance, his arms wheeling in the air. A third blow knocked him off the bridge.

Karigan clenched her jaw at his scream as it trailed behind him. Through the bridge she saw him plummet, become smaller and smaller and smaller until he wasn't even a speck.

The second one did not charge her, perhaps learning from the other's mistake. Karigan adjusted her grip on her staff. Licked her lips. Waited. The tainted one stared at her with a malicious half-smile, his eyes like pitch.

Karigan felt time rushing away as she faced the dark Eletian. Laurelyn told her she could hold the bridge for only so long.

In a blink, the dark Eletian dove for her legs. Karigan got in only a glancing blow to his hip before he knocked her off her feet. The staff flew from her grasp and rolled down the bridge, teetering on the edge. She hit the bridge so hard that air rushed out of her lungs. The dark Eletian grabbed her legs; she thrashed and kicked, but his grip was like steel, his claws digging into her wounded leg, ripping open the old injuries and creating new ones.

She desperately glanced toward her staff, but it was out of reach. The Sleepers stood on the island as a mute audience to her struggle. She tugged on the hilt of her long knife, drew it, and gashed the creature's face. He grabbed her wrist and squeezed. Before she felt it, she heard bones snap. She screamed. Her knife clattered to the bridge and over the edge, twirling tip over hilt into the chasm.

Karigan had been trained to handle blades with either hand, but the scabbard of her saber was entangled in her legs and her position made it impossible to draw. She'd only one other weapon left to her. It was awkward getting to it. Even as the tainted one wrestled with her, she flipped her hips, thrust her good hand into her trouser pocket, and drew out her mother's moonstone. Brilliant light flared out and she blinked. The dark Eletian averted his gaze and loosened his grip. She kicked. as hard as she could.

The dark one fell back, and the moonstone's light grew in intensity and ferocity, driving him still farther back. Karigan kept kicking, landing one booted foot squarely on his jaw. This time it was not *her* bones she heard breaking. Blood rushed from his mouth. Another blow sent him flailing on the edge. He did not regain his balance and he fell.

She'd barely begun to register what happened when the dark Eletian grabbed her bad leg as he fell. She slid half off the bridge, grasping the opposite edge with her good hand. The dark Eletian dangled from her leg, his weight dragging her down. Her fingers faltered, started to slide. She kicked at the Eletian and he slipped down her leg, claws scrabbling for a hold in her flesh, but failing. And suddenly, his weight was gone.

With a grunt Karigan swung her legs back onto the deck of the bridge, breathing hard, all her hurts colliding at once. Tears pooled on the translucent bridge beneath her.

A thread of Laurelyn's voice came to her. *Karigan, you must get off the bridge now!*

Karigan looked up and understood Laurelyn's urgency. Three more dark Eletians emerged onto the arch.

Karigan crawled, taking up the moonstone that had miraculously not rolled off into the depths. She crawled, leaving smears of blood on moonbeams. The moonstone bought her time—its fierce glow flashed into the faces of the dark ones, making them hesitate. The bridge flared and seemed to be ablaze with moonfire.

She scrabbled along the bridge as fast as her battered body allowed, grabbing her staff as she went. She rolled the rest of the way, with the dark Eletians sprinting after her. When she reached the island, the bridge vanished. The three dark Eletians hung in the air for a moment before plunging into the chasm.

There are no others, came Laurelyn's distant voice, and the bridge flickered back into existence.

Karigan rolled onto her back panting, gazing into the milky sky. She wondered if she had anything left in her to get to the next bridge, much less cross it and return. She *could* stay in Eletia, perhaps get her wounds tended. Would it be so great a betrayal if she did not return to her companions in Blackveil? Surely they could find their way back to the wall as easily without her, if any of them survived . . .

No, she couldn't abandon them, especially Yates. Yates, her friend who had gotten into more than he reckoned for when he had volunteered to join the company. Thinking of him made her climb up onto her feet. No matter how her leg hurt, wrenched and torn, she knew she had to return to Blackveil to ensure Yates made it home.

She slipped the moonstone into her pocket and leaned heavily on her staff, blessing the Weapons for the foresight of their gift. With her broken wrist held close to her, she hobbled across the island, a shepherd to the Sleepers who followed her like silent specters.

The second bridge was, to Karigan's relief, shorter, spanning a narrower section of the chasm. The stones were cut in a rustic style, their earthy feel was a source of comfort to her. At the arch she stepped through a golden haze and into the sunshine of a forest glade that immediately warmed and soothed her after all the time she'd spent in the dark and wet of Blackveil. She sighed, closed her eyes, and let the sunshine wash over her. Laurelyn said her piece of time might not correspond to Eletia's. She had left Argenthyne at night, and here it appeared to be full afternoon. Karigan was glad.

When she opened her eyes again, she took in the burbling stream, the towering grove of trees that surrounded the glade, star flowers and pink lady slippers wavering against a backdrop of emerald, the warbling of songbirds. She felt alive again.

A man knelt by the stream trailing his hand in the water. Flaxen hair hung around his face. He turned to gaze at her. He reminded her, with a start, of Graelalea.

"Hui a ven?" he asked.

"I'm a Green Rider," Karigan replied, hoping that's what he wanted to know.

"Are you an apparition then?" he asked in strongly accented common tongue, his voice rich and resonant.

Karigan glanced down at herself. Because she was using her ability to cross thresholds, she was also faded out, but the sunshine of the glade prevented her from completely disappearing, leaving her appearance ghostlike. The fading usually dulled her vision, but everything here was vibrant.

"No," she told him. "I am not an apparition."

The Eletian stood, his hand dripping. He did not shake the water off, perhaps because it would have been painful to do so. His hand was blackened with the fingertips desiccated to the bone so that they resembled claws. She had never seen such a disfigurement on any Eletian—not that she'd met that many. The man himself was tall and radiated brightness.

"Did your captain send you? Speak quickly. There are arrows trained on you, apparition or no."

Karigan glanced around the grove, but saw no one else. That did not mean the Eletian archers were not there.

"Laurelyn sent me," Karigan replied.

"Laurelyn! But she was overcome. I do not believe you."

The Sleepers were jammed behind her and obscured by the mist of the arch, so she walked off the bridge, the Sleepers materializing into the sunshine and following her into the glade.

"She wishes a safe haven for these people," Karigan said. "If they stay in Blackveil—Argenthyne—they will be changed, and not for the better. Laurelyn protected them for as long as she could. Until I came to bring them to Eletia."

As the man took them in, his expression transformed from distrust to joy. "For how long did she protect them?"

"About a thousand years, I'd guess." His question made Karigan wonder *when* she was herself.

"It sounds a strange story," he replied. He took a few steps closer to Karigan, glancing at the Sleepers. They began to disperse on their own, instinctively seeking out the grand trees of the grove. "You've the fading of Lil Ambriodhe."

"I wear her brooch," Karigan replied. Had this Eletian once known the First Rider?

He glanced at the Sleepers vanishing into grove trees to resume their rest. Karigan felt her own strong impulse drawing her back to the bridge. If she released her ability, it would not pull on her. She could stay.

"I am grateful you have brought these Sleepers to us through unknown dangers," the Eletian said. "Will you not sit with me and tell me your story? About Argenthyne and Laurelyn? We've been so grieved."

"I—" The brooch pulled harder on her. She stumbled backward.

"We could tend your wounds."

Karigan thought of Yates and the others back in Blackveil and she was overcome with a sense of foreboding. "N-no, I can't stay."

He drew nearer still. There was great age and great weariness in his eyes. They were the blue of snow shadows and reflected ages past. Karigan almost lost herself in them.

His gaze grew unfocussed, far away. "Before you depart, I must warn you to be cautious of the mirror man." His voice carried the weight of prophecy. "He is a trickster who will try to ensnare you for his own amusement. Beware the choices that lie ahead, and choose wisely. You have traveled great distances for one so young. Your wits and skills have served you well so far. They will aid you in the trials ahead."

Karigan backed toward the bridge, stepped on it, and immediately the glade in Eletia began to grow more distant. The pull to return to Blackveil increased, and even the immense attraction of staying in the sunshine of Eletia and the presence of the remarkable man could not anchor her.

The man, she realized, who could only be Graelalea's father, King Santanara, the one who had defeated Mornhavon the Black at the very end of the Long War. He'd become a Sleeper himself sometime after the war, leaving his son, Prince Jametari, to lead Eletia.

The heady sensation of meeting King Santanara made her shiver even as she hastened across the bridge back into the white world.

❧ CHOOSING MASKS ❧

When Karigan limped off the bridge into the white world, an opaque mist shrouded the island.

"Uh-oh," she said. In her past experiences with the white world, the mists were usually preludes to visions she'd rather not see.

She had no choice but to wait until the mist cleared before proceeding across the island to the moonbeam bridge—she could barely see her hand in front of her and she did not want to accidentally step into the chasm.

When the mist tumbled away, she looked in dismay upon what it revealed. Arrayed before her was a masquerade ball in full swing, strains of music echoing ominously from the depths of the chasm. The colorful finery and masks of the dancers were in stark contrast to the dullness of the white world.

This is not fair, Karigan thought. *Haven't I been through enough?* She knew, however, fairness had nothing to do with it.

Making matters worse, on the opposite side of the island there wasn't only the one bridge, but a dozen that, to her eye, looked identical.

"I have no time for puzzles," she muttered, still feeling the tug on her brooch. She decided she would ignore the masquerade and she started to limp across the island.

"Rider Sir Karigan G'ladheon!" cried out a masked herald that sounded just like Neff, and who also appeared just the way he had the night of the king's masquerade ball. He most definitely was *not* Neff, however. Just a vision provided

by the strange environs of the white world. The announcement was met with scattered applause, and ladies and gentlemen curtsied and bowed to Karigan.

She might be trying to ignore the masquerade, but its participants were not ignoring her. She proceeded cautiously,
recognizing many of the masks from the king's ball, including
the king's own iridescent dragon helm. It gleamed in the dull
light as he danced ... as he danced with Mad Queen Oddacious. Jester's bells jingled from her crown, the red diamond
pattern of her skirts a garish blur against white.

No. Must not be distracted.

She started to trudge ahead, but three costumed pages
appeared before her, each bearing a mask on a satin pillow.

"You must choose one," said Neff, who strode up beside
her, "to join the masquerade."

On one pillow nestled a plain eye mask that took on the
same faded green tone as her uniform. An eye mask of midnight rested on the middle pillow. It emanated tremendous
pulsing power, but oozed a black aura of malevolence and
Karigan was immediately repelled by it. The third pillow
held the mask she remembered Estora wearing, beaded with
ocean hues that rippled in the light.

She shifted the staff to lean it against her shoulder and
reached for the third mask, the queen's mask, but stopped
short of actually touching it. Her hand hovered there for a
moment, then she snatched it back.

"I do not need a mask," she said, suddenly furious. She
would not play this game.

She turned away from the pages with their burdens and
continued her limping way across the island, but as if her
anger stoked the energies of the white world, the music
picked up to a frenzy and the dancers danced in a fury of
silk and velvet and satin; spinning and twirling around her,
knocking into her, pushing and buffeting her, kicking her injured leg. She cried out. For all that the dancers were not real,
they *felt* real, and the blows sent white-hot pain through her
and stole her breath. She was growing light-headed.

The king grabbed her broken wrist to swing her around.
She screamed and swooned to her knee. The music silenced

and the dance halted. She moaned amid a forest of legs and skirts. She would not let the white world do this to her, she would not let it defeat her. Using her staff to steady herself, she rose and found herself face to mask with the king.

"You are false," she said. She turned around. "You are all false."

Using her good hand, she threw the king's dragon helm off. It clattered to the ground raising a puff of white dust. She gasped. Beneath the mask it was not King Zachary she saw, but Lord Amberhill's smirking countenance. He raised an expectant eyebrow.

What did it mean? What was the white world telling her? If the king in this masquerade was not Zachary, then who was behind the Queen Oddacious mask? Would it be herself, or someone else?

Shuddering, but unable to resist, she pulled off the mask that concealed Queen Oddacious' face and discovered Estora gazing at her. Karigan backed away, too many questions clashing in her mind to think clearly. She just wanted out, out of the white world. Blackveil was preferable—at least it was real.

She shouldered her way through the silent, stationary dancers. A tumbler in black stepped in her way. He wore the looking mask, but it only reflected the white landscape. Santanara had warned her about the mirror man, that he was a trickster, and she found the assessment appropriate. He summoned Neff and the three pages with a gesture.

"You must choose a mask," Neff said, "if you wish to leave."

Cold sweat beaded on Karigan's forehead. What would happen if she chose one of the masks? Where was King Zachary in all this if he hadn't been wearing the dragon helm?

"I prefer not to conceal my face," Karigan said. "I will not hide, and I will not deceive."

"You must choose a mask," Neff intoned.

She contemplated striking him with her staff, but considering how real and solid the dancers had felt, it probably was not a good idea, for there might be a reprisal.

"All right," she said, thinking fast. "If I must choose, I

choose *that* one." She pointed not at one of the three offered to her on satin pillows, but at the looking mask worn by the tumbler. Her reflection pointed back at her.

Everyone vanished but the tumbler. He waggled his finger at her and slapped his thigh as if silently laughing at her. Then he backed away, making an expansive gesture toward the bridges, and then he, too, vanished.

Karigan sighed. She'd apparently passed one test and was now presented with another. She walked from bridge to bridge, tapping each one with her staff. Each felt as solid as the last. There was no telling what would happen if she crossed the wrong bridge. It might vanish beneath her feet and she'd join the tainted Sleepers at the bottom of the chasm, or the bridge might cross over into some hostile land or layer of the world from which she'd be unable to return.

"Five hells," she muttered, beyond exhausted, almost tempted to just choose one and be done with it. Then she smiled and removed the moonstone from her pocket. All of the bridges blazed with crystalline brilliance, but one was more true and continued to resonate with her moonstone long after the others faded.

She took a deep breath and stepped onto the bridge. And took another step. The others vanished. She hurried as fast as she could to reach the far side. When she stepped off the bridge into the grove of Argenthyne, it too disappeared.

She found Laurelyn on the terrace where she'd left her. The Eletian queen's form was little more than a glimmer, a mere ghost of her former radiance. Karigan glanced at the sky. Black clouds encroached on the silver moon.

Laurelyn smiled. She seemed weary beyond measure to Karigan. *You succeeded,* Laurelyn said. *The Eletians will always be in your debt.*

"I don't think they knew who I was."

Laurelyn laughed lightly. *Then they shall have a mystery, and Eletians love nothing better than a mystery to ponder and debate, and they will do so for centuries. But now my time ends. You've my thanks, Karigan, daughter of Kariny. You are as exceptional as I'd hoped you would be all those years ago when I brought your mother and father together in a forest glade. You must hurry to your companions now, and release your ability, for this piece of time is finished.*

"Good . . . good-bye," Karigan said.

Good-bye, child.

Karigan set off for the open doors of the castle, but she could not resist one last look at the true Argenthyne, and of Laurelyn reaching for the moon. She dissolved into motes of sparkling dust and then was no more. The clouds blanketed the moon, casting the grove in darkness.

Karigan hurried into the castle, her vision doubling again, and becoming even more blurred by tears of exhaustion, tears of loss. She had the feeling of some great magic passing from the world. Not the sort of magic she and her fellow Riders used, but the intangible, mysterious quality of something that was once wise and powerful and shining that would never be seen again. Laurelyn would live now only as pure legend.

Karigan shed her fading and staggered with the shifting of past and present, the profile of the first tower chamber realigning. She returned to a far dimmer, stagnant world.

The use of her ability always hurt her head and now the pounding in her skull distracted her from hurts on other parts of her body. She was cold. Passing through time made her cold.

She must seek out her companions, though she dreaded what she might find. She forced herself across the chamber and noted that Graelalea's body remained undisturbed, the moonstone at low ebb.

Karigan limped through the winding corridor trying to keep her mind aware and working. She thought about the masks. If she'd chosen one of the three masks presented to her in the white world, which one might she have picked?

Certainly not the black one—it was vile. She'd known that without even touching it. She did not lust for the power it contained. The queen's mask? No, not for her. She could not presume, especially knowing the king was absent from the mirror man's little scene.

The king, the king . . . Why had he been absent?

That left the plain green mask, which seemed to go with being a Green Rider. Why hadn't she chosen it?

"Because I don't wear masks," she answered aloud, startling herself.

She continued on, hearing the sound of fighting growing louder. When she entered the chamber of the moondial, she almost tripped over Ard's body, still in the same place where he'd fallen with Ealdaen's arrow in his throat. There was Grant's body sprawled on the floor, a pair of nythlings feeding on him. The corpses of other nythlings were strewn about the chamber.

And Solan. Poor Solan. She could not even look at what remained of him, of what the dark Sleepers had done to him.

The corpses of several dark Sleepers also lay on the floor, but more knotted around the rest of her companions who stood back-to-back in a tight circle on the full moon of the moondial, swords, and Lynx's ax, hewing up and down and side to side. About ten Sleepers assaulted them, far fewer than before, but still difficult odds.

They were all so involved that no one appeared to notice her. She weighed her options, taking into consideration her weapons and her condition. Quickly she decided to use the one weapon that had served her best so far, and limped forward to meet the enemy.

⋠ CHANGING OUTCOMES ⋠

Karigan leaned her staff against her shoulder and drew out her moonstone. The light that blazed from her hand reflected again on the inlaid quartz of the moondial, raising walls of light around her companions. Attackers and the attacked were startled alike, but only the Sleepers recoiled. Her friends sprang to the advantage, running the unarmored Sleepers through with their blades, running them through and hacking again and again till they fell. They were hard to kill.

With each step that brought Karigan closer, the light grew in intensity, forcing the Sleepers to back off. A couple bolted. The others fell and her companions finished them.

A pall of silence hung over the chamber when it was all done and the light of Karigan's moonstone settled to a comparatively low, steady glow.

"Where've you been?" Yates demanded. "We could have used your help here."

If only he knew how much she had helped! If she hadn't gone to the past and removed the Sleepers of then, Yates would not be standing here now. "How long was I gone?"

"Ten minutes at most. Felt a lot longer."

Traveling through the white world did not obey the same rules as the normal world, accounting for Yates' estimate and the much longer time period she felt she'd been away. It felt like years. In a sense it had been—centuries, actually. She swayed, light-headed and exhausted.

"Questions later," Ealdaen said. "We should see to wounds and our dead. Telagioth and Lhean, guard the entrance to the corridor so we've no more intruders."

Telagioth and Lhean trotted off across the chamber and down the corridor.

"There will not be many Sleepers," Karigan told Ealdaen.

"I know," he replied striding toward her. His armor was streaked with blood, but he appeared uninjured. Lynx and Yates followed behind. Lynx had the claw marks on his face she remembered from before, and Yates held his hand over a bleeding wound on his arm.

"You know?"

"You left with Laurelyn. But what was before is beginning to fade. Let me see your wrist."

She gingerly extended her hand to him and he examined her wrist with gentle touches. "This needs a true healing," he said, "in order for it to work properly again."

"Damn," Karigan muttered. That did not portend well for wielding her sword or anything else.

"In the meantime it must be set. How did it break?"

"A Sleeper. Crushed it with his hand."

Ealdaen nodded, unsurprised. "Lynx, could you assist?"

Lynx moved around to Karigan's side, and before she could say another word or ask another question, Ealdaen, holding her elbow, yanked on her hand and she fell screaming into unconsciousness.

When Karigan came to, she was lying on her back with one blanket rolled beneath her head and another spread over her. The winged statues filled her vision. She groaned as each individual pain flared to life; her wrist hurt worse than everything else. It felt heavy and she saw it was bound and splinted with white arrow shafts. There was something ironic about Eletian arrows being used to help heal her wrist. As much as she hurt, she was relieved to have accomplished her task. She'd helped Laurelyn's Sleepers escape to Eletia, preventing them from becoming a dark, dangerous force in her own time.

She heard a *scritch-scritch* beside her and turned her head to find Yates working in his journal, the wound in his arm neatly bound.

"What . . ." she began. She licked her dry, cracked lips. "What are you writing?"

"Drawing," he corrected. He smiled. "Since my sight is much better, I'm drawing details of this room, the moondial, that sort of thing. I did a nythling, too, after Ealdaen took care of the ones that were left."

They'd been feeding on Grant, she remembered. Yates flipped a page and then showed her the picture of the nythling, sketched in realistic detail. Too realistic.

"Ealdaen has no idea how the eggs got in Grant's arm," Yates said. "He'd never seen nythlings before. How do you feel?"

"Pretty bad."

Yates nodded. "Ealdaen said your leg was all ripped up again. He was surprised you could walk. You should really learn to take better care of yourself."

If Karigan had felt up to it, she would have swatted him.

"Ealdaen wanted me to make sure you had this when you woke up," he said, showing her Graelalea's flask, the one that had contained the cordial. "And this." He then showed her something that took her aback, for it had no context in this place.

"Is that what I think it is?" she asked.

"If you're thinking it's a Dragon Dropping, you'd be right. It's from the gift King Zachary had us give Graelalea the morning we crossed the breach."

Karigan remembered.

"Ealdaen says the chocolate is very restorative to Eletians, which is why they prize it so much. He figures it means it's restorative to non-Eletians, too, so he passed one out to everyone. Who's to say if it helps us or not? Lynx and I didn't argue the point. You should appreciate my restraint, by the way. You don't know how tempting it was to eat yours and not tell you. I mean, how would you know?"

"I'd smell it on your breath." She swiped her Dragon Dropping from him and bit into it. She rolled her eyes in pleasure, chewing slowly to savor the experience of the dark chocolate for as long as possible. After so long a diet of thin stews, gruel, hardtack, and dried meat, it did prove restorative after a fashion. And it made her dream of another favorite luxury, of a hot, languorous bubble bath. Maybe one day, if they ever made it back to Sacor City.

Yates chuckled. "I ate mine in one gulp."

When she was ready, he unstoppered the flask. "Ealdaen says that this is all that remains of Graelalea's cordial and that you are to drink all of it. The dew of Avrath, he calls it."

There were three good mouthfuls left, and Karigan savored these, too, remembering Graelalea with sorrow. She touched the feather still in her braid. The cordial dulled her hurts and made her feel strong enough to sit up. When she did so, she observed the corpses had been removed.

"Where is everyone?" she asked.

"Dealing with the bodies, I guess," Yates replied. "And keeping watch to make sure no more Sleepers get in. Ealdaen wanted to properly honor the dead."

"All of them?"

Yates nodded. "Even Ard and the Sleepers. He said Ard had been a good member of the company until he tried to murder you, and that it was no fault of the Sleepers that they became what they've become. They were once untainted Eletians."

"Poets, artists, and heroes of a distant age," Karigan murmured, recalling Laurelyn's words.

"Yes, Ealdaen said something very like that. I think he knew many of the individuals who were asleep in the grove." Yates paused, then said, "As for Ard, the others were curious as to why he'd want to kill you."

Karigan froze, heart thudding. "And?"

"Ealdaen told us what he overheard, that you were a threat to the marriage of Lady Estora and the king."

"And?"

"I think the Eletians just shrugged it off as one of those things our kind engages in. Lynx, however, gave you a long, surprised look, but said nothing."

Karigan groaned. *Must everyone know?* She thought she'd been so discreet, hiding away her feelings. "What do *you* think about it?" she asked Yates.

"I was not quite as surprised as Lynx," he replied.

Karigan wasn't sure she wanted to know, but she couldn't help asking. "Why not?"

"That last night in the forest when we were alone? You were kind of delirious. You talked."

"Oh, gods." She blushed and hid her face behind her hand.

He patted her shoulder. "Don't worry. We all have our unattainable longings."

Peeking between her fingers she saw his earnest, sad gaze, and her mouth dropped open, unable to say anything.

She was rescued by the sound of footsteps. Ealdaen, along with Lynx, Telagioth, and Lhean, entered the chamber, their expressions weary and grim.

"How are you?" Lynx asked Karigan when he reached them.

"All right, considering," she said.

He sat on the floor beside her, leaning back on his hands, his legs sprawled out before him. "Where did you go when you left us?"

"To the past and then . . . and then to Eletia."

"Eletia?"

Karigan nodded and explained how she'd gone back in time to lead Laurelyn's Sleepers to safety in Eletia. The whole reconciliation of past and present, especially trying to explain it, bent her mind in odd ways, and left Lynx and Yates scratching their heads because they recalled nothing of overwhelming numbers of tainted Sleepers attacking them. The Eletians remained unperturbed. "I think I met King Santanara," she added.

The Eletians exchanged glances among themselves.

"Did you notice anything in particular about him?" Ealdaen asked in a deceptively mild voice.

"His hand," she replied, lifting her own splinted and bandaged wrist. "It looked very bad. Blackened and crippled."

"You met King Santanara, then," Telagioth said. "His hand was thus injured when he stabbed Mornhavon with the Black Star in the last battle of the Long War. It was a wound no one, not even true healers, could fully treat. It was a source of great agony for him."

"Yes," Ealdaen agreed. "His only escape was to take the long sleep. You, Galadheon, came to him as he contemplated staying abroad to lead his people and succor them after the depredations of the Long War, or sleeping to forget the agony of his wound and the dark that clung to his spirit."

"You ... you knew I was there?" Karigan demanded. "And you didn't tell me what I was going to do?"

"No, I did not know, for you were but a blurring of the air. It was the king who told us a Green Rider brought the Sleepers. The last mortal to set foot in Eletia."

Karigan opened her mouth and closed it. This was not just bending her mind, it was twisting it into knots.

"Why does Karigan get to have all the fun?" Yates demanded.

"*Fun?*" She thrust her injured wrist into his face, then returned her gaze to Ealdaen. "If you knew the outcome for the Sleepers, why didn't you tell us?"

"We did not know. It had not happened yet. We were in a different thread of time. And as old memories vanish, different ones emerge. We had suspicions, however. There are those among us who can see across such threads. King Santanara was one, and his son, Prince Jametari, is another."

"Paradoxes," Karigan muttered. "So confusing."

"Your species is limited by its linear and mortal mold. Eletians have eternity to contemplate such complexities."

"In other words," Yates drawled to Karigan, "give up trying to make sense of it."

"If we had told you what we suspected," Ealdaen said, "it might have created a false sense of confidence leading to failure. There are thousands of possible, ever-changing threads and we could have been wrong. This was but one."

Threads or no, Karigan could not get over the feeling she'd been masterfully manipulated yet again.

⊰ REDBIRD ⊱

A shock of crimson darted through the bleakness of Blackveil, the wings of the redbird beating a steady rhythm. The redbird did not pause in its flight, was unwavering in its route, for as a creature of etherea, it required no rest or sustenance. Predators did not perceive it as prey, but as the impulse of magic, and therefore they did not hinder it. It sped bright and fleeting through the trees and murk of the forest, a spell venturing on its way to fulfillment.

Only when the redbird reached the break in the great wall did it pause, perching on a tree limb on the other side in the unfamiliar world of sunshine. It gazed upon the humans busy at work in their encampment, but the one it sought was not in this place.

And yet not far away. The redbird launched from its branch and flew eastward, the wall flowing along its wingtip. It would not be long now before the redbird's reason for existing came to fruition.

Despite the welcome spring sunshine, a gloom settled on Alton's shoulders as he left the pickets and headed across the encampment. It wasn't Estral that darkened his morning, for she brought lightness and joy to his life. He now saw the world as more lovely than he'd ever perceived it before, and the music . . . How had he gone through life without music filling his hours? Estral woke him in the mornings with song, carried him through the days with lute music, and soothed him to sleep with lullabies.

It was not just Alton who was uplifted by her presence, but it seemed the entire encampment was as well. She inspired countless campfire sing-alongs and performances by normally taciturn soldiers and laborers discovering hidden talents.

The wall continued to mend in nearly imperceptible increments, tiny cracks filling in, retreating toward the breach. The hole in the roof of Tower of the Heavens continued to shrink, all thanks to Estral and her music.

No, Alton's gloom had nothing to do with Estral, but with the horses. The anxiety of Karigan's Condor, Yates' Phoebe, and Lynx's Owl had increased steadily. The three had become restive enough that they'd had to be picketed separately from the encampment's other equines, for their mood was contagious and a worried horse or mule was prone to injure itself.

So Alton and Dale had made a concerted effort to keep a close watch on the messenger horses, and he'd gotten Leese to spare some calming herbs that he incorporated into a daily mash for the three. If Night Hawk was jealous of the attention he lavished on the others, the gelding showed no sign. Messenger horses were perceptive, seeming to understand more about the world and what was happening to their people than ordinary horses did. He would not have been surprised if the messenger horses conferred with one another in some unknown way; therefore, he kept Night Hawk and Dale's Plover picketed close to them, but out of harm's way.

Alton sought out Estral at her tent, the dining tent, by the wall, and in the tower, and could not find her. Could she have gone to the main encampment for any reason? He scratched his head, then remembered her horse had still been picketed, and she hadn't mentioned any intention to travel. On a hunch he went to *his* tent and found her sitting on a stool in front of it, her lute case open beside her. She was flexing her fingers in preparation for playing.

"There you are," he said. "Why are you over here?"

"For some reason," she replied, "people are less likely to interrupt me at your tent, *Lord* Alton."

"Oh, I see." And he did, for Estral tended to collect an audience when she played, even when she was obviously trying to concentrate on working out the mysterious measure from the book of Theanduris Silverwood. He could see how distracting that would be. Because of his own status, people tended to keep a respectful distance from his tent. "Am I interrupting?"

"Not yet," Estral replied. "I haven't started yet."

A redbird fluttered its wings in a nearby tree, its feathers bright against evergreen.

"How are the horses?" she asked.

He'd explained to her the nature of messenger horses and so she knew what it meant when they were upset.

"Still agitated," he said. "Condor the most. I can only imagine what trouble Karigan has gotten herself into."

Estral gazed at her fingernails. The nails on her chording hand were shorter than those on her picking hand, which he'd learned from direct experience when she held onto him when they were alone together. The thought made him smile, and just as quickly he replaced it with a neutral expression, recalling what they were discussing. Karigan was still a difficult topic between them.

"I often wonder what she and the others are encountering in the forest," Estral said.

"Me, too." Even though Alton had spent time in Black-veil himself, he remembered few details, and those had been awful enough. He did not share his memories with Estral, not wishing to worry her further. Such thoughts only made him gloomier so he changed the subject. "How goes work on that measure of music? Any inspirations?"

Estral sighed. "You know, I've been thinking about this even when I'm not actively working on it. I've tried so many variations, and none have been quite right. Sometimes I think I'm overthinking it, and at other times I remember what a genius Gerlrand Fiori was with music and I feel so very inadequate."

The redbird chirped as if to underscore her statement, and hopped to another branch.

"Inadequate? I hardly think so." He waggled his eyebrows

suggestively. Then more seriously he added, "If you want in-adequate, think of how I feel about the wall. *My* ancestors built it, but *I* can't fix it."

"You can't fix it because I can't figure out the music," Es-tral said. "However, I've been trying to think like Gerlrand, musically speaking, and he did not always follow logical pat-terns. The existing notes from the book ascend as if asking a question." She demonstrated for him, her voice rising in clear, ringing notes. "The assumption is that there is an an-swer. But what if there isn't an answer at all, but only another question? And what if that other question does not mirror the notes we know of, but consists of still more measures?"

Alton smiled feebly and patted her shoulder. "That's why we've an expert on the job."

"The true expert would be Gerlrand. There are just so many possible variations."

She sang the notes again, this time carrying on with a continued ascension, then drifting into minor notes, the tone eerie, before soaring once again. Alton assumed she was making it up as she went and decided Gerlrand held nothing over his Estral.

As she sang, the redbird launched from its perch and cir-cled overhead. Alton thought nothing of it until it folded its wings into a dive; it dove directly at Estral like a crimson dart, dove and slammed into her throat. It all happened so quickly, and Estral's song ended abruptly. No crumpled bird lay dazed on the ground after the collision. It had turned into a bloated serpent of red light that wrapped around her neck and slithered into her open mouth and down her throat. She gagged, gasping for breath.

"Estral!" Alton tried to grab the serpent, but it was the substance of air. Estral scratched at her throat, tried to scream, but nothing emerged. Alton did not know what to do, but then the snake faded away. Estral remained on her stool, eyes wide and tearing, hands still at her throat.

Alton knelt before her. He saw no marks on her throat except those she'd made herself. "Estral, are you all right?"

She gazed at him, forehead furrowed. She shook her head.

"What is it? What . . . what did that thing do to you?"

She started to speak, but no sound came out.

"Estral?"

She crumpled into his arms, heaving with silent sobs.

Alton carried Estral into his tent and sent for Leese. The wait was agonizing. Estral would not respond to his questions or his touch. She lay curled in a fetal position on his cot, buried her face into his pillow, and would not move.

Leese finally arrived and while she examined Estral, Alton paced outside, awaiting some sign. He heard the mender's murmured questions within, but no answers from Estral. Not a word.

Dale came and sat on a tree stump. "What happened?" she asked.

Alton explained what he'd seen. "Some sort of magical attack."

"From Blackveil?"

"Where else? She seemed all right after," Alton continued. "Frightened, but unharmed—at least outwardly. But unable to speak." He felt strains of concern from the wall guardians. They'd responded to Estral's music like nothing else, and now there was only silence and their dismay.

Leese slipped through the flaps of her tent, blinking in the sunlight.

"Well?" Alton demanded.

"I've given her a little something to help her rest," the mender replied. "She was very upset, which is not surprising."

"What's wrong with her?"

"It's beyond my experience," Leese said, "especially if what you say about magic is correct. I can identify no injury or sickness. The only thing I can find is that her voice is gone. Totally and absolutely."

Alton clenched and unclenched his hands, feeling the urge to pound on the wall—or anything hard—as he had not in quite a while.

Dale bunched her eyebrows together. "Seems like that spell was intended directly for Estral."

"She must have been getting too close to finding the right

notes," Alton said. "It was cast by someone who does not want the wall fixed."

The three fell into a heavy silence, the gloom penetrating into a deep dark within him. He would make whoever had done this pay, not just because it prevented Estral's music from fixing the wall, but because of what it had done to her, taking away an intrinsic part of her—her ability to sing.

Yes, he'd make whoever was responsible pay, even if it meant confronting Mornhavon the Black himself.

⊰ GOD AND A MIRACLE ⊰

A wave of disorientation rolled over Grandmother and she almost blacked out.

What was that? she wondered, passing her hand over her eyes. Good thing she'd been sitting. She'd felt movement, a displacement of the world, and its subsequent reordering.

The others appeared unaffected, unaware. Deglin tossed another stick of wood on the fire, and Min and Sarat discussed what to do about cooking utensils since Grandmother had "ruined" one of their pots. Cole stretched his back and shoulders, and Lala played string games.

Somehow she had the vague idea that Deglin and Sarat shouldn't be there, and that their little group had moved to the edge of the grove after awakening the Sleepers because of all the destruction, not remained where they were. It must have been a dream of the sort one exhausted to the core dreamed, a dream close to reality but not, and darker.

It was a good thing they hadn't moved to the fringes of the grove because that appeared to be where most of the destruction to the great trees was concentrated. The inner trees remained unchanged. There had not been as many Sleepers as she'd expected and she was not sure of what God's response would be. She looked into the fire, recalled that she'd seen what Birch was up to, and that God had come to her. Hadn't He? At first He was pleased, and then . . . enraged? Perhaps she remembered only the dream, and her memories of it were quickly fading.

But not the part about Birch. How strange. She shrugged. No matter, she'd done what she came here to do, and after she rested for the night, they'd begin their journey home. Maybe they'd even survive it.

"Have another cup of tea," Sarat said, pressing a mug into Grandmother's hands. "We must have you strong for our journey back."

"Thank you, my dear."

A strong gust of wind rippled the surface of her tea, bent the flames of their campfire sideways, sending sparks tumbling along the ground. The vast limbs of the grove trees groaned and carried on an angry dialog among themselves.

Grandmother set her tea aside. "Help me rise," she told Cole, and he did, resettling the blanket over her shoulders.

"What is it, Grandmother?" Sarat asked, her hands trembling.

They were pelted with pine needles and twigs, and damp, decaying cones. Leaves whirled along the forest floor in dervishes. The ground shuddered.

"Grandmother?" Sarat asked, her voice pitched higher.

"I am not sure," she replied, but the air was bloated with expectancy—the forest strainng against some imminent collision, the rising of a storm tide, something momentous, a shattering of all they'd known, and a thrill shivered through her.

The mist pushed away leaving a giant man-shaped space in the air.

"I HAVE COME."

"It is God," Grandmother whispered. The mist billowed and roiled, filling in the image of the man shape until it no longer existed.

"I AM HERE." The thunderous voice erupted this time from Deglin.

They turned as one to face him. His body was straightened in an attitude Grandmother had never seen in him before. She did not recognize his eyes—they burned as molten coals. He raked them with an imperious glare.

"Finally, our time is congruent." He laughed half hysterically, not at all like Deglin. He snapped off his laughter, looked around the grove, his face grave with disapproval. Then he speared Grandmother with his stare. "But you have failed me." His words were quiet, but Grandmother's knees turned fluid and folded. Cole caught her and helped ease her down so she did not crash to the ground and injure herself.

"My . . . my lord, I've awakened the Sleepers."

"You allowed most of them to escape through time."

Grandmother did not understand the statement, but something niggled in the back of her mind. The dream, maybe.

"Who are you?" He demanded.

"You do not know?" she asked. How could God not know?

His gaze lost focus and He appeared to look inward, then He nodded to Himself. "This one has told me all that I need to know." He must mean Deglin. He gazed at Grandmother once again, but this time His assessment was more approving. "You work against the Sacor Clans in my name to return the empire to its glory."

"Yes, my lord. It is what I live for."

"Then you shall return across the wall to continue your work. I shall see that you have safe passage through this land." Sweat streamed down the face that was Deglin's, his cheeks flushed.

"What of you, my lord?"

"The others are still here. There is one among them whose taste I know. *They* will not receive safe passage." He gave her a grim smile, Deglin's flesh turning redder as if he were burning up.

Grandmother knew her God was not a gentle God, but she had never feared Him before. She did now. Sarat had wilted to the ground sobbing, and Min and Cole kept their heads bowed, eyes averted.

Lala watched him curiously, and then like a miracle, she opened her mouth and a clear bright note came singing out of her. Everyone stared aghast at her, even God. The note rose up and up into the mist and limbs of the great trees, the voice of an angel.

God laughed again and strode over to Lala, steam rising from Deglin's body, and He placed His hand on her shoulder. "This little one has some power in her. Teach her well."

"I will, my lord," Grandmother replied, stunned by how

well the spell of the redbird had worked. Perhaps the presence of God had enhanced Lala's new, glorious voice. She concentrated for a moment, directed her thoughts toward the wall, but heard no music there; felt only consternation and grief.

"I must go now," God said.

"I love you," Lala sang out.

God patted her on the head, then Deglin's body slipped limply to the ground like a shed skin. Wind gusted once again through the grove. Grandmother crawled over to Deglin, but found no life in him, though his flesh burned so hot that she could only conclude that God's presence must have boiled him from the inside out.

Lala sang a dirge that broke them all down to weeping. They held each other, comforting one another in a strange combination of grief and joy. It was a day of loss, and a day of miracles. God had walked among them, and Lala sang with an angel's voice!

Grandmother assumed that the others God had mentioned were only going to know His wrath. She smiled through her tears, holding Lala close.

≪ THE CHOSEN MASK ≫

The companions set off through the spiraling ways of Castle Argenthyne. The Eletians, with Lynx, had sealed off the grove entrance and blocked the corridor linking to the chamber with the moondial to stop, or at least slow down, any pursuit by the remaining Sleepers. After considering their options, Ealdaen decided their best route of escape would be through the castle, traveling inward to its core, then turning outward and westward to the spiral of the castle that loomed over the lake they'd seen from the forest, the Pool of Avrath.

From there, Ealdaen explained, they could travel north and retrace their way along the trail they'd used to get here.

The Eletians maintained a severe pace. Yates and Lynx took turns supporting Karigan as she hopped and limped along, but invariably she and whoever was helping her fell behind. Now and then Telagioth or Lhean would trot back to see how they were faring.

Around and around they went, only to enter counter curves, circling in new directions. The architecture was impossible. Were they getting anywhere?

"This castle is making me dizzy," Yates muttered more than once.

They passed through numerous chambers, but never paused to look. Karigan perceived fleeting impressions of flowing sculptures, dry fountains, clusters of furniture, but it all ran together. Sometimes they skirted clumps of bone and fabric and broken weaponry on the floor. The walls retained their inner glow, though they'd grown more dusky, perhaps with the advent of night, or because Laurelyn was truly gone.

Karigan started stumbling so much that both Lynx and Yates needed to support her.

"I'm sorry," she said. Her mind felt numb, but the pain of her leg burned intensely.

"You need rest," Lynx said. "We all do, but Ealdaen fears the remaining Sleepers will regain entry to the castle either at the grove or somewhere else and come after us."

"Seems safer in here than out in the forest," Yates said.

But as they entered another chamber, they found the Eletians waiting for them, and it was a good thing for Karigan's legs gave out altogether—she could no longer make them support her weight. Lynx and Yates lowered her to the floor, and Lynx placed his pack behind her so she'd have something to lean against.

"She can't go on like this," Lynx told the Eletians.

Karigan did not hear the rest of the conversation for she fell sound asleep where she sat.

She awoke to the ghostly light of the castle. Someone had draped a blanket over her. Lynx and Yates snored nearby, but she heard the singsong murmur of the Eletians as an undertone to her sleeping companions. She lifted her head and saw the three Eletians sitting cross-legged on the floor together, carrying on a conversation in their own tongue.

The tower chamber they were in was far more vast than any of the others they'd passed through. Subtle crosscurrents breathed freshening air across her face. Three large portals, and several smaller doorways yawned around the chamber's circumference. In the chamber's center rose a giant tree carved of stone with leaves of silver that fluttered and flashed in the air currents. Roots sank into the floor, or seemed to.

"Do you like the tree?" Ealdaen asked, having broken off his conversation with Telagioth and Lhean to gaze at her.

"It's amazing," she said.

"A gift from King Santanara long before war came to us."

"What is this place?" Karigan asked.

"The core of Castle Argenthyne, its nexus, the meeting of the ways."

She peeled off the blanket and shivered in the cool air. She tried to rise, and found it difficult with both a bad leg and a bad wrist. Lhean hurried over with silent steps and helped her up.

"Should you not rest more?" he inquired. "It is the middle of the night."

"I will, but I've got to, um . . ."

"Ah. I understand. Do you require assistance?"

The idea of the Eletian helping her to relieve her bladder mortified her. "Er, no, thank you," she hastily replied.

With the aid of the bonewood, she limped for the nearest corridor and found an alcove in which to take care of her need. When she returned to the chamber, she felt herself lured to the tree. Some of the leaves had fallen from their branches and shone brightly on the floor. An elbow where root met trunk cradled an ovoid sphere of silver. Drawn to it, like a crow to a shiny object, she approached carefully. She saw her reflection in it.

"It can't be," she murmured.

"What is it?" Ealdaen asked.

She jumped, not having heard his approach from behind her, or that of Lhean and Telagioth.

"What's going on?" It was Lynx, his voice crusty with sleep. Both he and Yates were sitting up.

"Karigan has found something," Ealdaen replied.

Karigan was almost afraid to touch the thing, but she picked it up, a looking mask. She couldn't believe it. It had weight in her hand, appeared solid in every way. There was her face reflected back at her, with the Eletians gazing over her shoulders, all warped by the convex shape of the mirror.

"When I chose . . ." she began. "I didn't think . . . I don't understand." She had told them about the white world and her experiences there before they'd left the chamber of the moondial.

"King Santanara was correct when he called your tumbler a trickster," Ealdaen said. "You must have pleased him. Handle this object with care."

"I didn't want any of the masks," Karigan said, "but I had to choose." She rotated the mask in her hand and there were reflections upon reflections, a mosaic of silver leaves mirroring into infinity.

Lynx and Yates had risen, and now crossed the chamber to join them.

"Karigan always gets the good stuff," Yates said. "First the bonewood, and now this."

Karigan ignored him. "What am I supposed to do with it?"

"Whatever you decide to do with it," Ealdaen said, like an echo of King Santanara, "choose carefully."

She was curious as to what the inside of the looking mask was like. How could one see through it? She had no wish to wear it—that seemed a dangerous thing to do—but she couldn't help being curious.

When she wondered how to open the mask, a hairline seam appeared around its circumference as if in answer, the two halves subtly parting like a clam shell. She licked cracked lips and lifted the faceplate. It moved on hidden hinges.

The interior of the mask was mirrored, as well. There was no cushioning or straps to help support it on the wearer's head. It sang to her, implored her to wear it. She lifted the mask so she could gaze through the faceplate, and when she did, she almost dropped the mask. With a flick of her wrist, the faceplate swung closed with a distinct *click* and the seams vanished.

"What did you see?" Ealdaen asked.

Karigan's heart thrummed. "The universe," she whispered.

Just then a wind roared through one of the arched portals, the castle seeming to shriek, snatching leaves from the tree, the rest raging like thrusting daggers. One clipped Karigan's cheek as it flew off the tree. Warm blood flowed. The walls of the chamber dimmed, the castle stricken.

Karigan knew why, she knew what had changed. She'd borne Mornhavon the Black within her. She knew his feel. A sickening pall draped over her. Finally, their timeline had merged with his. She had not taken him far enough into the future.

She turned to Ealdaen. "It's—"

"I know," he replied.

Just as suddenly as the maelstrom had begun, it ceased. The remaining leaves on the tree clattered and chimed against one another. Those strewn across the floor looked like the shards of a shattered mirror.

Karigan peered around the chamber trying to perceive Mornhavon. He was there, but well-cloaked.

"What's wrong?" Lynx asked. "What happened?"

"Mornhavon the Black is here," Karigan replied, still unable to pinpoint him. He lacked a physical form of his own, but he could use others. She squinted at her companions, but they all gazed fearfully over their shoulders.

"Perhaps we should leave," Lhean said.

"There is no running from him," Ealdaen replied. "He is the master of the forest."

"So we just wait?"

Karigan's mind raced with possibilities. Maybe she could bear Mornhavon into the future again, let him inside her as before. She almost sobbed, remembering the violation of it. How would she move forward in time without the aid of the First Rider? Could she return to the moondial and move him to a piece of time in the future? Were the moondials able to do that, or did they only go to the past? If she could cross thresholds, surely she should be able to—

"Can I look at the mask?" Yates asked.

"What?"

"The looking mask. I was just wondering if I could have it for a moment."

"I don't think this is the time." But she felt strangely compelled to let him have it. She took one step toward him, and then another. He reached out to receive it. "No," she said, but her resistance crumbled and she took another step.

She glanced at the mask and saw Yates' reflection in it, the black, cloudy aura hovering around him. "Oh, Yates," she murmured and put her will into resisting him.

"GIVE ME THE MASK." All pretension fell away. Yates' posture changed, an inferno burned in his eyes. His cheeks flushed.

Karigan fought the compulsion, fought with herself to stand still. She heard swords drawn from sheaths.

"No," she told the others "Attacking him will not work."

"That is correct," Mornhavon said in Yates' voice, but without his inflection. There was no humor, no lightness. Only cruelty. "I will give this Green Rider back to you if you give me the mask."

"Don't do it," Lynx said. "Yates wouldn't want you to."

"It would not be wise," Ealdaen added.

"THE MASK. GIVE IT TO ME."

Karigan closed her eyes. Tears ran down her face. She recalled what she had seen when she'd looked through the faceplate of the mask—all the stars, like the lights of celestial cities. She'd seen millions of threads, as the Eletians called them, some as fleeting as the glowing tails of comets, others solid, luminous chains. They were the possibilities and variables of individuals, of entire worlds, far too much for her to take in. If she'd the control, she could tinker with the threads, change outcomes, change whole worlds, past, present, future.

It was the realm of the gods, and she could not wear the mask. Too much power, too much influence and responsibility, a path to madness.

Mornhavon must have known what the mask was the moment he saw it, and now he coveted it. She knew he'd use the mask like a puppet master, pulling strings and rearranging the workings of the universe to his own liking.

Mornhavon as a god. She shuddered.

He hadn't tried to force it from her. Perhaps it must be freely given, as it had been to her. Maybe Yates resisted him from somewhere deep inside. She opened her eyes. He stood before her. The semblance of her friend was only on the surface. Sweat poured down his face.

What remained of Yates? Her friend the jester, the pursuer of women, the skilled artist and cartographer? The Rider whose courage had not faltered even when he was blind and stumbling in Blackveil? She had seen threads when she peered through the mask.

Yates . . .

Mornhavon as a god.

Herself as a god. She held the power in her hand.

"You want this?" Karigan said, holding the mask above

her head. She knew the Eletians were poised to strike her with their swords should she try to hand the mask over to Mornhavon.

"Yes, yes. GIVE IT TO ME."

Through the mask, Karigan had seen endless possibilities for this one moment, the weaving and unweaving of infinite luminous strands. The decision was hers, and hers alone. Everything came down to what she did next.

"Here it is," she replied.

With every ounce of strength remaining to her, she slammed the mask onto the floor at Mornhavon's feet. It shattered into thousands of silver pieces. Threads snapped and unraveled, and the universe rushed out.

❧ AN AWKWARD
SITUATION ❧

Richmont was surprised by the summons borne to him by the Green Foot runner. His cousin had done what she could to keep her distance from him since the night he had witnessed the rite of consummation. It mattered not, for he was still solidifying his position among the nobles. Most were grateful to make his acquaintance, knowing he had the ear of the new queen and could grant favors or deny them.

And now the lord-governors were beginning to arrive, having learned of the sudden wedding. They demanded audiences with Estora and Zachary. Formal requests had been refused, and Richmont knew Zachary had not fully reawakened. The assassination attempt was not discussed, and no one was led to believe Zachary was in anything but good health. Mostly Colin Dovekey dealt with the lord-governors, but Richmont insinuated himself into their good graces by promising to mention their wishes personally to the king and queen.

He'd been speaking with Lord-Governor Adolind and making his promise when the runner arrived with the summons.

"You see?" Richmont said to Adolind. "I can give the queen your request straightaway."

Adolind half-bowed, deeply gratified. That was how Richmont wanted it—Sacoridia's powerful indebted and bowing to him. He strolled through the castle corridors at his ease, not hastening his steps, though he was curious to know what Estora wanted with him. He would not give her the satisfaction, however, of answering her summons like an eager dog.

When finally he reached the royal apartments he was ushered directly into Zachary's chamber. He absently took in a mender touching Zachary's forehead and a servant on her knees sweeping up ashes at the hearth.

A Weapon stood just within the door, and another on the balcony outside the glass doors looking for trouble from without. Estora stood at the foot of the bed, hands clasped in front of her, attired in a creamy gown and resembling one of the classical sculptures decorating the more important rooms in the castle, even with the mourning shawl she still wore over her shoulders. She gave the slightest nod of dismissal and the mender removed himself from the room. The Weapon stepped just outside the door.

Interesting, Richmont thought. It was to be a private meeting.

"You sent for me?" Richmont asked.

"I did."

"Is it the king? Is he failing?" Richmont could not conceal the eagerness in his voice.

"He is holding his own."

Richmont stepped closer, a smile curling his lips. "No more reenactments of the rite of consummation?"

"That is between my husband and myself."

Richmont took yet another step closer, closer than propriety permitted. "Anything," he said very quietly, but distinctly, "that pertains to you and your royal marriage shall be known to me. All the intimate details, everything, should I wish it. As you know, I can acquire anything I like whether you tell me or not."

"Because of your informants," Estora said, "because of those you've bribed or threatened."

Richmont had expected the coldness in her voice, but the rest of her remained composed, oddly relaxed. He felt a warming in his loins at her defiance, rather a surprise since he had not entertained fantasies about using her body for his pleasure since she was a child. Perhaps he was seduced by the power Estora had married into and aroused by the thought of breaking that defiant streak in her, of breaking *her.* He'd stayed away from her and her sisters to retain his good standing with Lord Coutre, but Lord Coutre was dead and gone and of no use to him now.

Swiftly he calculated the advantages and disadvantages of various possibilities.

"I asked you here," Estora said, "hoping you would recant all that you said to me that night, and that you would gracefully resign yourself from your self-ascribed position as my advisor. I wish you removed from my court."

Richmont laughed. How courageously, how naively she spoke. How he would enjoy the breaking of her, savor it. "After all I told you about what I could do to your reign, how I could bring down your sister in Coutre and ruin your father's name? After all my work you expect me to gracefully bow away without my due reward?"

He grabbed her wrist and drew her close. She did not fight him. He wished she would. "You are no more than a whore," he told her in a harsh whisper, "used to breed the new king. You shall not be rid of me. In fact, I see an even greater future for myself. For instance, if the king's condition should take a change for the worse."

"What are you saying?"

"It would be easy enough to arrange, and with whom would you replace him? Oh yes, the queen would need a suitable husband."

"Are you suggesting—"

"Suggesting? No, my dear, I'm telling you that I would be your husband. I would be king."

"I've heard enough," came a voice from the bed.

Richmont's heart thudded. He dropped Estora's wrist and stepped away. "W-what? My lord? Did you speak?"

Zachary rose up onto his elbows, his cheeks hollow, but his gaze stern. "You heard me." His voice was not at all weak.

Blood drained from Richmont's face as he thought furiously of what to say, what to do. How much had Zachary heard? How long had he been awake? Estora did not look the least bit surprised by his wakefulness. She must have known and kept his true condition a secret from him. But how was this managed? It was a trap, yes, a trap.

"This is a most wonderful surprise, Your Majesty," Richmont said. "To see you looking so well."

"An unhappy surprise for you since you were indicating you'd prefer my demise," the king said. "I heard every word, and have been told even more."

"Then you know what will happen if you do anything to me. It'll be the downfall of your reign."

"What I know," Zachary said forcefully, "is that I hereby strip you of all titles and privileges, and that shall be the least of my judgments upon you."

Rage, blinding as a stroke of lightning, surged through Richmont. He would tear Zachary down, Estora would become his slave, and all of Sacoridia his plaything. He drew a dagger from beneath his cloak. He would show them, but before he could more than imagine plunging the blade into Zachary's gut, someone grabbed his wrist and his fingers went numb. The dagger dropped to the carpet. Gray ash dust drifted from the hand that held him.

The servant? His mind reeled. He'd dismissed her existence, forgotten her presence as one always did with servants, but this one did not have the meek demeanor of a serving woman. She wrenched his arm behind his back.

"No!" Richmont roared. "You can't do this! I've plans in place that will bring you down! My valet stands ready with letters he shall distribute the moment he knows something has happened to me. The information in them will destroy you. Is that what you wish? Your reign torn down in disgrace?"

"Richmont," Estora said calmly, almost kindly, which surely meant she mocked him. "Meet Green Rider, and swordmaster initiate, Beryl Spencer. Formerly Major Spencer, aide to Lord-Governor Tomas Mirwell."

Richmont shuddered. He'd heard of her, known what she'd done to Tomas Mirwell, but the rest was all rumor. Her secrets lay even deeper than Richmont could dig. Now he identified that tone in Estora's voice—pity.

"Were these the letters you were speaking of?" Beryl Spencer asked from behind him. She shoved a bundle of letters beneath his nose.

Spane gasped, recognizing his own seal on them.

She drew him close against her and whispered in his ear, "Your valet proved most cooperative. You and I shall have much to discuss."

"I've nothing to say to you."

"How disappointing." But Beryl's tone indicated she was not disappointed at all. "I've already unraveled a good many of your schemes, picked apart your connections and networks, questioned those whom you believed loyal. I received many answers. Far fewer than you thought were truly loyal. People, it may surprise you to know, generally dislike being threatened and extorted, and most are more sympathetic to Queen Estora than, say, *you*."

Her voice was soft, lovely, almost melodic. She terrified him.

"By the time we finish our interview," Beryl added, "you will reveal everything I wish of you, and there will be a reckoning for the murder you arranged for one of my fellow Riders. Your desires, your plans, and any status you once enjoyed are perfectly meaningless while you are in my hands. And finally, when I'm done with you, the king and queen shall have you for judgment."

Richmont was handed over to the iron grip of a Weapon. Before he was led away, he cast one more glance into the chamber. Estora stood by Zachary's bedside, neither of the two paying him the least attention, but gazing at one another and talking quietly. Beryl Spencer walked beside him, smiling pleasantly.

Richmont Spane wanted to cry.

Estora sat trembling in the chair beside Zachary's bed. The scene with Richmont had rattled her more than she cared to admit. She put her face into her hands.

"My lady?" Zachary queried. "Are you well?"

"Yes," she replied firmly. And then more hesitantly, "No."

He regarded her silently for some moments before speaking. "It is never easy," he said, "to be betrayed by one who was trusted."

He spoke from experience, she knew. How could one in his position not? His own brother had tried to destroy him.

"You've also been burdened with far more than you should have while I lay here insensible all this time," he continued. "And this on the heels of your father's death. I know how responsibility to the realm prevents the time and space for proper grief and grieving. Now that Destarion has stopped dosing me so heavily, I hope I can remove some of that burden from you."

"But you are still recovering."

"And improving daily." He yawned. "Colin has told me a little of what is transpiring in the realm, and I see there are things I need to put to rights. And we must discuss this awkward situation between us, but perhaps not just now."

He was drifting off to sleep. It would be a while before he was allowed to rise and command the realm again. Today's encounter with Richmont had been too much, but he'd insisted on it, against Destarion's advice.

He had taken the news of their marriage calmly, though she suspected Destarion or Colin had broken it to him before she'd a chance to do so herself. He'd remembered the rite of consummation as a dream, he said, and an odd light had caught in his eyes. There was a sense of loss about him she could not explain, which served only to make her feel more desolate.

His chest rose and fell in easy breaths, his face peaceful. She did not know what more he wished to say about their "awkward situation." Did he wish to rescind the marriage? Punish her? Was the marriage one of the things he must "put to rights"? She would not know until he awoke again and pronounced his judgment.

⋘ KING AND QUEEN ⋙

Estora sat in state in the throne room, wearing the crown of Queen Isen that still required adjustment from the royal jeweler, and a mantle of heather and cobalt, seeded with pearls from the coast of Coutre. The colors represented the union of Hillander and Coutre. Work on the mantle had begun as soon as the betrothal was announced and was ready for her even before the assassination attempt on Zachary.

Across her lap rested the scepter, also once wielded by Queen Isen, that went with the crown. It was said that the crystal crescent moon at its tip had to be replaced more than once when the queen, during fits of impatience, had used it to smack those who displeased her.

Estora was bedecked, bejeweled, and thoroughly uncomfortable sitting in the queen's throne, now perched on the dais next to the king's. The king's chair remained vacant, and those who stood before her—five lord-governors and their aides—demanded to know exactly what was going on and what had become of the king. Mostly she let Colin handle the questions, which bordered on insolence.

"How do we know this marriage is not false?" young Lord Penburn demanded not for the first time. He'd been one of her suitors and only lately had she heard the extent of his displeasure at having been rejected.

"As I've said, my lord," Colin replied, and Estora could tell that even implacable Colin was straining to remain civil, "the marriage ceremony and consummation were properly observed and witnessed. Those witnesses will be brought before you in due time."

"There is one witness I should like to hear from," said Lord Adolind, "but he has yet to make an appearance. Just how serious was this riding accident of his?"

"Yes," Lord D'Ivary chimed in. "It has the stench of a deathbed wedding. What aren't you telling us?"

Colin was getting red in the face. "You dare insult the queen with such speculation?"

"Is she truly the queen?" Penburn asked very quietly.

Estora stood. "Enough."

The five and their aides silenced immediately and craned their necks to look up at her.

"Colin has explained the situation plainly," she said. "The king is attending to urgent matters of state with his military advisors." It was partly true, anyway. He'd had briefings from most of his military chiefs over the last couple days. "He will come before you when he is ready." Which, she hoped, would be soon. He was improving each day. They had been unable, however, to complete the conversation begun after they'd given Richmont into Beryl's hands. Zachary was either sleeping, or too busy catching up on the news of the realm, and constantly surrounded by others. She slept alone in her own chamber.

"While I should like to see the king and hear it all from him myself," said an unchastened Lord Penburn, a sly glint in his eye, "I'd also like to know where Captain Mapstone is. There have been some rather strange rumors circulating."

Estora could only imagine. She knew Lord Penburn took especial interest in Captain Mapstone because she was from Penburn Province, and her closeness to the king exalted her status with the lord-governor as one of his own people who had influence with the king. Estora had suggested the captain's release from house arrest. Colin and Harborough demurred, preferring to move slowly, probably so they could prop up their own positions in the advent of Zachary's royal fury.

Zachary had also asked for the captain, and had been put off, told that she was ill, but recovering rapidly. Estora did not think prolonging the charade and lying to Zachary was going to help their causes any, and she decided if they wished to hang themselves, that was their business. She then *ordered* that the captain be released, but it appeared someone had delayed that order, something she would rectify just as soon as she finished here.

"The captain is—" Colin began, but he did not have a chance to finish his statement. The side entrance to the throne room creaked open and in walked two Weapons, Master Destarion, and Zachary's secretary, Cummings, followed by—much to Estora's surprise—Zachary himself.

The lord-governors immediately dropped to their knees and bowed their heads. Zachary ignored them. Dressed simply in black, he walked over to the dais, his gait a little slow, and his face pale, but it was really him. He mounted the steps. Estora saw what the effort cost him, the exhaustion, but he did it all without help. When he reached the top, he gave her a long indecipherable look, and they both sat.

"What Counselor Dovekey was about to tell you," Zachary said, his voice strong and sure, "is that Captain Mapstone is in the mending wing."

Colin blanched, and Estora gave Zachary a sideways look. There was an upturn to the edge of his mouth, a cant to his eyebrow.

Lord Penburn appeared alarmed. "Is she well, Your Highness?"

"I am to understand she is very well."

The lord-governors glanced at one another. Where once they'd been unafraid to voice their questions, they no longer seemed to know what to say.

"It is good to see you, Majesty," Lord L'Petrie finally said. "We'd wondered about your welfare. There'd been all manner of stories, and then the marriage."

"You see me before you now," Zachary said, "and I am no ghost. After my riding accident, it seemed prudent to move the ceremony up in case something more serious happened before I had the chance to take the lady as my queen."

Estora exhaled a breath she hadn't realized she'd been holding. He was sticking with their story. He all but proclaimed the marriage valid.

"I assume," Zachary continued, "you're all just disappointed to have missed the feasting and festivities." The lord-governors chuckled. "Not to worry, we shall feast on the original wedding date, for we do wish to celebrate with our family and friends. Do we not, my dearest?"

Estora jumped when he addressed her. He'd never addressed her as other than "my lady" before. Was he mocking her? But his expression was serious. She swallowed. "Of course."

"It is a great relief all is well," Lord Adolind said. "And I congratulate you and your bride on your union. It will only strengthen the realm."

"Hear, hear," said the others.

"I know you have many questions," Zachary said, "and much needs to be discussed about what is happening with Second Empire and Blackveil. For now, however, I must confer in private with my wife and advisors."

Dismissed, the lord-governors bowed their way out of the throne room. When they were gone and the doors shut, Zachary slumped in his chair.

"Your Highness!" Colin cried. "You've exerted yourself far too much."

"I am not finished exerting myself by far," he said, giving Colin a dark look. "Cummings!"

"Sire?"

"Send for General Harborough, Castellan Sperren, and Captain Mapstone. I don't care what they are doing or how inconvenienced they are."

Cummings bowed and left by the side entrance. The time that ensued was interminable. Zachary sat in his chair with eyes closed, resting, perhaps collecting his thoughts. If any of them tried to speak, he silenced them with a curt gesture.

Estora had seen Zachary angry before, but this was deeper, colder.

Laren wasn't sure what was going on, only that Destarion had sent one of his journeymen to inform her she ought to see Ben. At first she'd been alarmed until the journeyman smiled and told her it was good news. A lightness spread over her, and she outpaced both the mender and her guard as she raced to the mending wing.

She found him sitting up in bed sipping broth. He was pallid and thin, but very alive.

"Captain!"

She collected herself, but could not help grinning. "It's about time you woke up, Rider."

"I know. I'm starving, but all they'll give me is broth."

Laren stepped all the way into the room and pulled a chair over to his bedside. "Perhaps you'll remember what it's like to be a patient when you're well again and treating others."

He glowered. "If my patients want steak, I shall give it to them."

They laughed, then Laren asked, "Does Destarion know what changed, what allowed you to awaken? We were digging through the old case histories to see if we could find some way to help you, but found nothing."

"I did not awaken all at once, or so I'm told," Ben said. "And I've no idea how much was dream, and how much was real, but my connection to the king weakened until . . . until I was no longer needed."

"Connection? You were connected to the king all this time?"

Ben nodded. "I was . . . I was trapped. His body fed off me, off my healing ability. I remember darkness mostly, but sometimes I was aware of a thread of light leaving me. And then sometimes I could hear someone reading to me—or to him, rather. I could hear other voices, conversations. And then—"

He blushed furiously. "Was Karigan back by any chance, er, visiting with the king?"

"No," Laren replied. "She's been in Blackveil. We've heard nothing from her."

Ben seemed perplexed. "A dream then, I guess. Sure seemed . . ." He cleared his throat, still blushing. "Him, not me. Dreaming."

Laren crooked an eyebrow. *That* kind of dream, she thought. As amusing and a little alarming as it was, she was more concerned about what it meant for Zachary if Ben was no longer providing him with healing energy. No one had told her anything. She'd not seen even Destarion for days now and wondered if they'd forgotten about her. She was about to ask Ben what he knew about it when a Green Foot runner appeared in the doorway.

"Your presence is requested in the throne room, Captain," the girl said.

Laren rose, wondering if she'd find out Zachary's fate, and, finally, her own.

⋐≫ JUDGMENT ≪⋑

Laren's guard sputtered and cursed as he tried to keep up with her. He was not the youngest of soldiers and limped with a bad knee. Too bad, she thought. Confined to a room too long, no matter how spacious and comfortable, it felt good to be on the move, uncaged and stretching her legs to full stride, the blood pumping through her veins, even if she feared what may lie at the end.

She halted before the throne room doors to catch her breath and straighten her shortcoat, her guard stumbling up behind her. She recognized the Sergeant of Doors standing before her, with his vast ring of keys hanging from his belt. She nodded to him, and he nodded in return. To her guard he ordered, "Dismissed." Then he and an underling opened the throne room doors for her to enter. She did so without looking back.

She strode down the runner as fast as decorum permitted, passing through columns of sunlight slanting through the tall windows that alternated with shadow. The light, the dark; the warm, the cool. She saw others there waiting for her, Castellan Sperren leaning on his staff of office, General Harborough whose blocky form was unmistakable, Master Destarion with his mender's satchel slouched at his feet, and Colin Dovekey, whose black garb made him sink into shadow.

Estora sat upon her throne chair very still, seemingly turned to stone, her expression blank. Laren could not help but feel for her, placed as she was in so complicated a position.

Laren had taken in the assembled in mere moments as she walked, but her attention fell mainly on *him.* Zachary slumped in his chair next to Estora, his head bowed into his hand. Joy quickened her stride. He was awake! Out of bed even! It took great restraint for her not to run to him and hug him, but protocol did not allow it. Right now he was the king, and she his servant.

Her joy was also tempered by concern for the way his shoulders sagged, his thinness and pallor. He'd always been robust and strong and it was difficult to see him looking, to her eye, almost fragile.

When she reached the dais, she dropped to her knee with head bowed. "Your Highness . . . es." She bit her lip at almost forgetting there were two now.

"Rise, Captain Mapstone," Zachary said, his voice as she remembered, though the tone somehow quieter. "Rise and stand beside me as you are accustomed."

When she stood and looked upon him, he smiled warmly at her and her eyes blurred with emotion. When she moved to his side of the dais, he added, "You are looking well. I had been told," and now his tone was acerbic, "you'd been indisposed."

"I am well now that I see you up and about, my lord. I had not heard . . ." She swallowed and thought she had better stop. It was not her time to speak, and she was not sure she could manage it without loosing a torrent of tears. All of her fear for his life—what could have been—was so raw and near the surface.

"Yes," the king mused, stroking his beard. "One hears and does not hear many interesting things. I've assembled you all, my closest, my most *trustworthy* advisors, because of these things I've heard, and judgment must be rendered."

The tiredness came out in his voice with these words, but his countenance was fierce as he looked down on the others. They, in turn, cast their gazes to the floor, their expressions sober, even strained.

"Castellan Sperren."

The old man stepped forward. Laren thought he might crumble to dust right in front of them. "Your Highness?"

"I understand you did not initiate or conspire anything while I recovered from my so-called riding accident. You were laid up yourself. However, it is my understanding you did not voice opposition to the proceedings, either, which is personally distressing, but not a crime. You have been dutiful in your service to the realm since the days of my grandfather, and you gladly came out of retirement to be my castellan when the one that had been serving me turned out to be a traitor. It seems to me I have asked too much of you by keeping you here much longer than we originally agreed upon, and so I now commend you to your retirement, to which you may return with honor intact. Find ease and pleasure, old friend."

Sperren trembled visibly, a sheen of tears on his wrinkled cheeks. He bowed and backed away. To Laren's mind, it was very much past time. Sperren slept through more meetings than he was awake for, and his sharp mind had dulled considerably in recent years. He'd once been indispensible in his wisdom and advice, but no longer, and with all the challenges Sacoridia faced, Zachary needed the ablest, sharpest minds around him he could muster.

"I have been made aware of what went on around me while I lay unconscious," Zachary said. "It saddens me that my own advisors, who knew me best, save one, had no confidence in my judgment, did not wish to take a chance in what I had or had not placed in the Royal Trust as far as a successor is concerned. I thought they knew me better than that. I had planned, in the event of my premature death, that a transition would occur as smoothly as possible. However, my advisors would not wait for the opening of the Royal Trust as law decrees must be done. Instead, they took matters into their own hands and moved up my wedding. A wedding I was not even conscious of.

"Meanwhile, my one advisor who did exhibit trust in me was dosed and bundled away under house arrest so she could not interfere with the plans of you gentlemen. Yes, I have heard all the reasons why you chose the course you did, listened to each of you by turn, but it all comes down to trust. I cannot have people around me who disrespect my wishes, disregard royal law, and who do not trust me. Master Mender Destarion."

The mender stepped forward and swallowed hard. "Your Majesty."

"You, like Sperren, have a long history of good service to the realm. In all but this you have attended me faithfully. As you know, such actions as you took should provoke the severest of penalties. Disabling one of my officers, my own messenger, in the course of her duties is enough for the ultimate punishment."

"Yes, my lord," Destarion whispered. "I am aware."

"Yet I hesitate," Zachary continued, "to condemn to death a learned man who has done more good in his service than bad. Therefore, I shall strip you of your status as chief of the menders, and reassign you to the River Unit, where they've an outpost in the far north by the headwaters of the Terrygood. They've been long without a proper mender, and I expect the settlers and lumbermen in the region will find your skills useful."

Destarion looked humbled by the king's mercy, but frightened as well. He was not a young man and he'd find conditions far more rugged up north than he did in the castle's civilized, and warm, mending wing.

"General Harborough."

The general clicked his heels together and bowed.

"You thought to support the conspiracy with the backing of the military. You, one of my best strategists." Zachary shook his head. "That is a crime that requires the death penalty. However, I shall leave your fate in the hands of a military tribunal. In the meantime, you are stripped of all command, office, and insignia, and shall remain in prison until the tribunal comes to me with its recommendations."

Zachary gestured and a pair of guards came to escort the former general away. He hung his head like a whipped dog as he left the throne room.

"Colin Dovekey."

Colin stepped before the dais looking older than ever, his movements stiff.

"If there is something that makes me more angry than the conspiracy you organized, it's being forced to sit here and pass judgment on good men. You led them into it."

Colin fell to both knees. "I beg of you, Your Majesty, to condemn me to Saverill's fate."

"I will not be so merciful," Zachary replied.

Merciful? The histories spoke of a traitor among the Weapons named Saverill who'd undergone weeks of torture for his crimes, only to be chained to the castle roof for the vultures to feed on. He'd still been alive.

"You are stripped of your authority over the Weapons, and I'm sending you to Breaker Island. You will never leave that island again, and your peers will decide what to do with you. Perhaps they will choose Saverill's fate for you, or perhaps not, but they will ensure you never have a voice in the affairs of the realm again."

A pair of Weapons led Colin from the throne room, followed by a dismissed Sperren and Destarion.

Laren could not believe they were let off so easily.

"Speak, Captain," Zachary said. "You look . . . concerned."

"They all could have received the death penalty. Easily. But you did not choose that for them."

"It may be that I have. Destarion will find the north perilous, and I expect those judging Harborough and Colin to be very harsh. Condemning them to death all at once—men who were known to be very close to me—would raise questions I'd rather avoid regarding my close call with death and the validity of my marriage, among other things. I also took into consideration that they're essentially good men who thought they were doing what was best for the realm, and depending on how things go for them, I may yet call on them. You can not simply replace all those years of experience, and I believe we've a trying time ahead of us.

"Now, to my Lady Estora . . ."

Estora stiffened, her knuckles whitening as she gripped the armrests of her chair. "I understand," she said, "if you wish to invalidate the marriage contract."

He gazed hard at her. "That could be easily done under the circumstances. My lady, you were placed in an untenable position, and it was your cousin who set these events in motion. You were made a victim in this. However, I find it grievous you saw fit to relieve Captain Mapstone of duty and place her under house arrest."

"My lord," Laren said.

He ignored her. "Laren Mapstone is closer to me than any blood relation has ever been. She practically raised me."

"Zachary," Laren tried again.

"Furthermore, she is apparently the only one who trusts my judgment."

"*Moonling!*" That caught his attention. "Queen Estora placed me under house arrest for my protection."

"Say again?"

"She knew my opposition to the conspiracy placed me in danger from Lord Spane and the others, so she placed me out of reach. It certainly made *them* happy I was not out there contradicting them and turning the whole messenger service against them. You know what a disaster that would have been."

He nodded slowly. Messengers on the loose carrying the truth to all corners of the realm—it would have caused problems on a grand scale for the conspirators.

"She also," Laren continued, "wished to protect me from you."

"What?"

"I offered her my fealty, to help her, but she believed I'd be better off away from the turmoil because we all knew you'd be angry if—when—you recovered, and she did not want you finding fault with my conduct."

"I would know better," he reflected, "or at least I hope I would."

"You do have a temper," Laren said. "Though you don't show it often."

He raised an eyebrow at her, then turned back to Estora, gazing at her with new respect. "I thank you then, for looking out for Laren, who supports me even if I apparently have a temper."

Laren smiled.

"I know how much you value her," Estora replied. "And I thought perhaps I should need her in the coming years, as well."

He nodded gravely. "Though this has not been an auspicious start to our marriage, I am not inclined to invalidate the contract. I can't imagine the havoc that would produce, and we've enough to worry about between Blackveil and Second Empire without adding to it.

"Also, between confessing to me and updating me on the realm's affairs, Colin told me you came up with a clever strategy to trap Birch and his forces. With the loss of some very able advisors, it looks like I'll be making use of your keen thinking."

"Karigan is the clever one," Estora said, gazing at her knees. Laren sensed a subtle intensification in Zachary's regard. "I just used her example."

Laren learned that Estora had been inspired by Karigan's actions in the fall when the Rider had rescued her from kidnappers. Karigan had disguised herself as Estora, then created a diversion that led the kidnappers away on a merry chase, allowing the real Estora to escape without harm. It had been a dangerous plan on Karigan's part, but it had worked.

Estora modified the plan to fit the situation in the north. Birch used trained soldiers to raid small, underprotected civilian settlements. She ordered the settlers of a few villages to evacuate and replaced them with Sacoridian troops—well trained and well armed—but had the soldiers disguise themselves as civilians in such a way that they appeared to be yet another underprotected settlement ripe for the plucking. Their watchers would alert them to Birch's movements so they wouldn't be taken by surprise, and they were instructed to carry on like settlers so all would appear normal to Birch's scouts.

A trap meant that Sacoridia's troops didn't have to chase Birch's all over the north, although there was a troop that continued to do so to maintain the illusion so Birch would not suspect anything. Estora was apprehensive, but anticipated positive results.

While Estora explained the plan, Zachary, who had already heard the details, nodded off where he sat. Laren called over Fastion and Willis to assist the king to his apartments.

"I will walk on my own," Zachary protested when they lifted him from his chair. When they set him down, he did leave under his own power, pausing only to kiss Laren's cheek. She hugged him fiercely, but carefully so as not to hurt his healing wound.

When he was gone, Laren turned to Estora. "My lady, I wish to thank you for your protection, though I did not know ultimately what might have become of me had things gone poorly for Zachary."

Estora smiled. "I know what it is to be a game piece on an Intrigue board, Captain. One has to move carefully. I would not have allowed you to come to any harm."

Laren bowed her head. "That is what I hoped, but I could not be sure."

"You've my full confidence, Captain."

"Thank you, and you've mine."

Estora sighed. "I fear your Riders may not think much of me, however."

"If that is the case," Laren replied, "it shall be remedied."

Estora nodded her acknowledgment. "There is one Rider I inadvertently placed in additional danger."

Laren then heard about the loyal Coutre forester Lord Spane had insisted join the company Zachary sent into Blackveil.

"I gave him my blessing," Estora said, "not knowing what his true purpose was in going."

Laren vaguely remembered the man. Very ordinary, rather humble. "Which Rider was his target?" she asked, already knowing the answer.

"Karigan. Richmont wanted nothing to threaten the marriage contract. If Ard kept Karigan from returning home, it eliminated one of those threats."

"You know about . . ."

"Zachary's feelings for Karigan? I do. It explains much."

Laren nodded, not sure what to say. "I tried to keep them apart."

"I do not believe it worked." Estora said it without irony, but with acceptance. Often state marriages were just that—a legal union to produce heirs and solidify alliances, not unions of love. Estora would know this. "For a moment, I . . . I wished Karigan would not come back. Only for a tiny moment," she added hastily, and she cast her gaze down at her feet.

"You love him," Laren said.

Estora nodded. "But Karigan is my friend, and I allowed an assassin to follow her into Blackveil."

"You did not know," Laren replied quietly. "And though she is beyond our help, she is resourceful, and the other two Riders in the company will watch out for her."

"I pray it is so," Estora said, and Laren believed her.

Laren hesitated, then recalling something Ben had said earlier, she asked, "My lady, did you, by any chance read to Zachary while he lay unconscious?"

"I did. *Tales of the Sea Kings.* It allowed me, in a way, to speak to him, give him comfort, while taking more dire matters off my mind."

It pleased Laren that Estora had cared for Zachary in such an intimate way. "May I make a recommendation?"

Estora looked curious. "You may."

"Go to him. Go to Zachary and spend time with him. You are his wife. He may claim to be busy, but he is always busy, and always will be. You must insinuate yourself into his private world. I think reading to him is a very fine idea."

"But he is tired . . ."

"A perfect time to read to him, when he is too exhausted to do anything else but sleep or listen to your voice."

Estora nodded, taking in the advice. "Yes, I shall do this. I shall go to him now."

Laren smiled, much pleased. "He is very partial to the poetry of Tervalt. It's full of manly deeds of slaying dragons, hunting the highlands of Hillander, admiring fair maidens, and going to sea."

"Excellent. I shall have Tervalt's poems brought to me from the library." Then Estora returned her smile. "Though I myself prefer the nature poetry of Annaliese of Greywood." Her smile deepened. "I can see, Captain, that you have already become my essential counselor."

Laren took her leave of the queen. She would do what she could to encourage a strong union between Zachary and Estora, to bring them closer together. The fate of the realm did not require the two get along, just that they produce heirs.

Laren, however, loved Zachary too much to not wish for his happiness and promote it in anyway she could.

Now that her interview with the queen was over, Laren was confronted with the fact she would no longer be kept under guard and confined to her luxurious prison. The first thing she would do was seek out Connly and Elgin and get updated on the doings of her Riders, then she'd visit her beloved Bluebird.

However, when she stepped through the throne room doors, she found herself faced with two columns of green clad messengers standing at attention in the corridor. Elgin stood to the side with a grin on his face. Overcome, she could not find her voice at first. Word that she was released had reached them fast.

"At ease, Riders," she said finally.

They broke out in cheers and clapping, and Laren's cheeks practically hurt from smiling so hard.

Connly came to her and shook her hand. "Captain, I've never been so glad to see you. I gladly relinquish all responsibilities back into your keeping."

"Not so fast, Lieutenant," she said. "Some while ago I received an invitation to visit a friend in Corsa. Do you know it's been years since last I took leave?"

Connly's expression fell. He looked absolutely horrified. "But . . . but, all those meetings, those brain-deadening meetings . . ."

Laren smiled at him, and left him so she could greet each of her Riders individually. Yes, some leave time would be marvelous and she did not think Zachary would deny her.

Her smile faltered, however, when she realized that when she reached Corsa, she'd have to explain to her friend, who happened to be a certain merchant, why his daughter had been sent into Blackveil. He would not, she thought, ever forgive her for that, especially if Karigan did not return.

◈ THE DRAGONS ◈

Amberhill stood in the crow's nest, exulting in the wind that streamed through his hair and filled the sails into billowing clouds beneath his feet. He felt he walked in the sky. The horizon tilted around him as the *Ice Lady* plowed through the waves of the Northern Sea, the green cluster of islands that was his goal discernible in the distance.

In Midhaven, he and Yap had disembarked from *Ullem Queen* to take passage on *Ice Lady*, a sealing vessel headed for the arctic ice, a course that took them near the archipelago. They'd not lingered on land for long before they found *Ice Lady,* but Amberhill had taken what little time they had to climb the Seamount Lady Estora had once so lovingly described, and he found the vistas not wanting. It seemed years, and worlds away, that day he'd sat with her and Zachary talking of Coutre Province and his plans to take a voyage.

His initial seasickness after leaving Corsa Harbor, too, was a dim memory, for he'd flourished at sea, his cheeks burnished bronze with the sun, and he felt alive in the salt air as he'd only felt when inviting danger as the Raven Mask. He'd taken to climbing to the crow's nest and along the yardarms to maintain his trim and challenge his balance. His training as the Raven Mask made him as nimble as any sailor, if not more so. Captain Irvine had invited him to join the crew of *Ullem Queen,* and he'd only been half-jesting.

Amberhill also exercised with his rapier, repeating lessons once drilled into him by Morry. Yap was pulled into these sessions as an awkward sparring mate, using a practice sword carved for the purpose by the ship's carpenter, and a lid of a pot as a buckler. The crew was much amused.

As for Yap, he was permitted to assist the crew, but Amberhill made sure he did not revert to his pirate ways, ordering him to maintain daily ablutions and to launder his clothes as frequently as he did Amberhill's. The sealing vessel was far from luxurious, but Amberhill had personal standards that must be maintained.

When gray-blue clouds intruded on the horizon and the sails slapped fitfully against line and timber, Amberhill climbed down from his perch and sought out Captain Malvern on the bridge. She gazed through her spyglass to the north, then turned east toward the building clouds. The captain was a small woman, but no less imposing for it. She kept her dark hair, peppered with gray, shorn short, and she looked at him with eyes that seemed creased in a perpetual squint from too many years of sun. She was another of those uncanny women, like Beryl Spencer, or the G'ladheon woman, that made him uneasy. Like the others of this ilk, she did not fall for his charms. Not that he'd tried to charm her, but he was well-aware of his own natural attributes, which were, he thought with a smile, enough to attract women like ants to spilled sugar.

"We've a storm bearing down on us," she said. "Can see it, smell it, and my aching bones confirm it."

"Will you take shelter then? The archipelago is ahead."

"Nah. That'd be a trap. The currents around the islands would tear up the *Lady*. We'll ride it out at sea, but it means we go now."

"*Now?*"

"Aye. Ready yourself and Mister Yap, or prepare for a season of seal hunting with the *Ice Lady*."

Amberhill did not doubt the captain's weather sense— she'd not been wrong once since leaving Midhaven, but the plan had been to leave him and Yap closer to the islands. She had refused to take him into the archipelago itself, citing the perilous currents and the more superstitious claptrap about witches and bad luck. Now he'd have to rely on Yap's experience as a seaman to get them there. Amberhill had picked up a thing or two along their voyage, but little in the way of practical knowledge. He had left the sailing to the sailors.

"Mister Yap!" he cried. "Prepare the gig!"

"Aye, sir!"

When Amberhill had sought passage from Midhaven to the archipelago, it had proven clear that no captain desired to venture among the islands, not even for a large purse, claiming them too far off course, or the currents too hazardous, but underlying all these excuses, like those of Captain Malvern's, was superstition.

So Amberhill took matters into his own hands, purchasing a sloop that had been the gig of a merchanteer captain. The small vessel, Yap said, would sail well around the reefs and currents of the islands. Captain Malvern had not argued about hoisting the gig up alongside *Ice Lady* when Amberhill paid extra. Her voyage was proving profitable even before she reached the sealing grounds.

Odd, Amberhill thought as he watched Yap and crew secure their supplies in the gig, that others should be so repelled by the very islands that lured him. He was drawn to them like he was coming home. His true home. His ring sent a pulse of warmth through him.

Captain Malvern joined him at the rail. "Remember to steer clear of the Dragons—that's where the currents are the worst—and we'll look for you on our return from the ice. Otherwise, Spring Harbor is your closest port in Arey."

Amberhill nodded. He'd pored over charts with Yap. Now that it was coming to it, he felt a little apprehensive, a little queasy, like his seasickness was coming back, but thankfully it was fleeting.

"Ready, Mister Yap?" the mate called.

"Ready!" Yap clambered back over the rail from the gig to the ship, and it was lowered to the waves below. It looked small down there, tossing like a piece of driftwood.

"Luck," Captain Malvern said as Amberhill followed Yap over the side of *Ice Lady* onto the rope ladder.

"And to you," he replied before scrambling down along the barnacle-studded hull. When he reached the bottom of the ladder, he stepped carefully into the gig. It bucked like a wild horse and only Amberhill's excellent balance prevented him from falling into the water.

Yap cast off the lines holding the gig to *Ice Lady* and scrambled from the bow to hoist the mainsail, and then lunged for the stern to take command of the tiller. The gig heeled away in the gusting winds. Amberhill was impressed by how quickly the distance grew between them and *Ice Lady*, and he felt at once free and anxious. Thunder rumbled in the distance.

The storm rushed upon them as they made for the islands, slamming them with rain, waves washing over the rail. The gig strained, groaned, complained at the forces that battered it. Lightning slashed through the sky accompanied by deafening thunder. Yap fought with the tiller and Amberhill clung to the mast and sent up a prayer to the gods. The *Ice Lady* was completely gone from sight, vanished behind walls of waves and curtains of rain.

Both fresh and salt water assaulted them, burning Amberhill's eyes. All he saw was water above, water below, turbulent darks and darker, visibility cut off by downpour and foamy crest. Yap was yelling, but the roar of wind slapped the words back at him. He pointed.

Amberhill peered over the plunging bow. Was there something ahead? When the bow reared back up and the gig climbed another wave, he saw only the gush of rain. The bow surged over the crest and this time, as they slid into the trough, he made out a pair of shapes darker than waves or rain or clouds, green and white froth dashing against them. They looked like monsters of the sea.

The Dragon Rocks!

The bow reared again. Monsters indeed—the currents around them would crush the gig. He glanced at Yap. The expression on the pirate's face was one of terror.

"Steer clear!" Amberhill shouted. "Those are the Dragons ahead!"

Yap jiggled the tiller. It moved too easily. Amberhill did not hear the word, but read Yap's lips: "Broken."

Like the stick of driftwood Amberhill had imagined earlier, the gig was tossed around by the ocean, and when they neared the chaotic, churning currents near the pair of sea stacks called the Dragon Rocks, an enormous wave curled over them and Amberhill found himself wishing he'd taken an unexpected interest in seal hunting.

She walked among the wrack and blue mussel shells and the foam at the ocean's edge. Bare of foot, she stepped surely, as though her toes knew every contour of every stone of the beach, every cobble and pebble. A hermit crab scuttled out of her way.

She liked to stroll the shore after storms, for the ocean tossed up so many interesting things. Sometimes they were secrets long hidden in darkling depths; often they were the flotsam and jetsam of far passing ships. Today, as gulls argued over a crab and an osprey tested its wings in air currents still restless from the storm, she found a bottle shining in the foam. She picked it up and discovered the cork still sealed, the wine safe within. That was a rare gift. Continuing on she found tangled fishing gear, some battered boards.

Soon she came upon more debris: wood planking, a barrel bobbing in the shallows. Perhaps she would be gifted with an entire cask of wine. She smiled.

A sheet of white undulating in the waves caught her eye, a sail, and it was snagged. It was snagged around a man. The gods were being very generous to her this day—if he still lived. She lengthened her strides to reach him. He lay half out of the water, his head resting on his outstretched arm, kelp trailing from his wrist. The sun sheened on wet black hair that straggled across a well-formed face. Much more handsome than the sailors she usually received.

He still breathed. A wave stirred his hand in an eddy. The red of a ruby on his finger flared in her eyes. She dropped to her knees and grabbed his hand to see the ring close up. She knew it, had known the ring before and the hand that had worn it, the hand that had caressed her so tenderly, so lovingly, so long ago. She stroked the man's hair away from his face.

"Are you he?" Yolandhe, sea witch out of legend, asked. "Have you come back to me, my love?"

⊰ RETREAT AND RESOLVE ⊱

Something had gone terribly wrong. Grandmother had felt it like the snap of a bone in the small hours as they passed the night in the grove. She'd heard a horrible wailing in her sleep like some enormous beast receiving grievous injury, and upon awakening, she found the limbs of trees quivering above, and that the forest had grown uneasy. God said he'd ensure their safe passage home, but as they hurriedly packed and sought their way out of the grove, the forest was as hostile as ever, unseen eyes glaring at them, unnamed creatures lusting for their blood, and now they didn't even have their groundmite companions to protect them anymore.

Grandmother had had to create a salamander compass to help them navigate the curling roads of Argenthyne until once again they found the main road around the lake. Even the lake was disturbed, its surface curdled and waves slapping the shore. When she glanced back toward the castle towers, they had grown darker as if decayed, dying, and then wet clouds swallowed them. Acrid raindrops began to pelt her face.

With two of her men gone—three if she counted Regin, who had been lost so early on in their journey—setting up camp for the night proved despairingly difficult in the rain, as if they'd never done it before. With a little help from Grandmother's art, Cole did manage to get a fire burning.

Though Lala now had a voice, she said little. Occasionally she broke out in small snatches of song.

"Mum," the girl said, cuddling up to Grandmother before the fire.

Grandmother's cares and aches and chills melted away to hear Lala call her that, and she wrapped her arm around her little girl.

"I will teach you some songs one of these days," Grandmother said.

"I think I know some," Lala replied. "They came with my voice." And she sang the chorus of a ridiculous drinking song.

"No, no," Grandmother said as gently as she could. "I need to teach you some songs of Arcosia that have been passed down, and others that will help you with the art."

"Oh."

Grandmother was too tired for teaching this night so they sat in silence for a time as rain hissed and steamed in their campfire. It looked like their journey home was going to be no easier than their journey in, especially since it appeared God had rescinded his promise of protection. Grandmother sighed, not looking forward to the perilous walk. She brightened when she thought to look in on Birch. She had wanted to see how his campaign fared, and maybe God would come to her and she could plead for His protection.

So she knotted some of her precious dwindling yarn, and with a nail clipping of Birch's wound within, she tossed it onto the fire.

And saw dusk. The evenings there were less dark, and it was not raining. She heard the clash of steel, and she gazed through Birch's eyes. The dead surrounded him where they'd fallen in the woods. They appeared to be— No! Not their own!

"Retreat!" Birch bellowed, waving his sword.

A glance over his shoulder revealed men coming after him with pikes and swords, whose mail glinted beneath homespun clothes. Snatches of black and silver uniforms showed from beneath plain coats and cloaks.

From Birch's mind she gleaned he'd allowed his men to walk into a trap. He'd gotten overconfident and his band of warriors had been overwhelmed—there had been more than the thirty of the enemy his scout had reported. They were slaughtered by the Sacoridians.

"Retreat!" he cried again to those of his men who survived.

Grandmother withdrew from the connection and placed her face in her hands. She had to get home now. She could not permit Second Empire to fail.

⤜ THEIR SEPARATE WAYS ⤛

The wind hissed across the tips of dead grasses, but the scent of new, green growth crushed beneath Lynx's body filled his nostrils. He gazed up at the sky—it was dull, brooding, but it was not Blackveil. The alien voices of the forest were gone, replaced by the ordinary minds of somnolent wolves awaiting the evening hunt and ground squirrels busy in their burrows.

He sat up to the endless, undulating plains before him, and discovered stony ruins behind him, two partial walls, the rest crumbled to the ground. How had he gotten here? What happened? Silver glass glinted on his legs, torso, and arms, slivers he pulled out of his flesh with sharp little pains and tossed aside. They winked with light as they fell among the grasses.

They'd been in Castle Argenthyne, the chamber with the tree, but that's as far as he got. Someone moaned nearby.

Another moan and he found Yates likewise speckled with silver glass, but worse, with shards deeply embedded like daggers, his flesh pale.

Lynx knelt beside him. "Yates!"

"The beast burned me out," Yates whispered. "She wounded him good, but . . ."

And then Lynx remembered—Mornhavon the Black had occupied Yates' body.

"I am ashes," Yates said.

"No, I'll take care of you," Lynx replied, but with each moment, Yates slipped farther and farther away.

"Tell her . . ." Yates' whisper was ever so faint. "Not her fault."

"I will," Lynx promised.

Yates did not respond. A stillness blanketed him; his eyes, his face, lost all animation. Lynx clenched his hands and growled as if to threaten away the looming grief. This was why he stayed solitary, why he remained aloof from the others. Forming attachments only meant being speared with unbearable pain when there was loss. His growl grew into a howl. He howled as the wolves do.

And when his voice faded over the plains, he gently closed Yates' eyes.

Telagioth and Ealdaen found him carrying rocks from the ruins to raise a cairn over Yates. The wind had taken on a mournful note as it rushed through the ruins, and Lynx had felt restless souls among them.

"Friend Lynx," Ealdaen said, "let us aid you. We are sorry for Yates, for his spirit held much joy."

As they labored with the rocks, they came to an agreement that they were somewhere on the Wanda Plains.

"I will know more when I see the stars," Ealdaen said.

Neither Lhean nor Karigan appeared, and after raising the cairn, they spread out and searched, but without success. Either of the two could be lying in the deep grasses and they could be missed at even a few feet away.

At night they took shelter near the ruins and built a large bonfire from old timbers they found in the collapsed structure, and dried thatches of grass. If Lhean or Karigan were out there, perhaps they would see not only the fire, but the light of Eletian moonstones.

"I judge we are in the north-central plains," Ealdaen said, gazing into the sky at the stars that shone through the clouds. Telagioth agreed with him.

"I have quite a walk home then," Lynx said, missing his Owl intensely.

"As do we," Telagioth replied.

"What happened? How did we end up here all the way from Castle Argenthyne?"

"We believe it was the Galadheon," Ealdaen said, "and that mask. That mask was nothing to trifle with."

"The looking mask," Lynx murmured, and he remembered. Karigan had smashed it on the floor at Yates' feet and then . . .

And then he'd awakened among the grasses.

"It caused a rupture in the wall of the world." Ealdaen sounded uncertain of himself. "I believe so, anyway. And with the Galadheon's ability to cross thresholds, it may be that she is elsewhere."

"And perhaps Lhean with her," Telagioth added.

"Elsewhere?" Lynx asked.

"If what I surmise is correct," Ealdaen said, "she could be almost anywhere, anywhen. But I think it is no mistake the trickster allowed *her* to handle the mask. Whether he expected her to destroy it in such a fashion?" He shrugged.

"Yates said Karigan wounded Mornhavon."

"We believe it is so," Telagioth replied. "We heard the Dark One's lingering cry of pain even as we found ourselves here."

"The rupture was a terrible, powerful force," Ealdaen added. "And it was directed at Mornhavon."

During the night, neither of their missing friends appeared at their fireside, so in the morning Lynx and the Eletians went their separate ways, the Eletians bearing south toward Eletia, and Lynx, after paying final respects at Yates' cairn, began his long trek eastward. He'd come to the grasslands without his supplies, only what he'd had on him when he awoke in the chamber of the tree: his clothes, a cloak, and his knife. Telagioth gave him his longbow and what remained of his quiver of arrows, as well as his water skin. Both Eletians shared out some food. With these items and his knowledge of the wild, Lynx believed he would have no trouble making it to civilization.

Over his shoulder he carried Yates' satchel with his journal inside, as well as his winged horse brooch. Yates' brooch would return home into Captain Mapstone's hands to wait until some new Rider was called into the messenger service and claimed it. It had always been this way.

Lynx carried inside himself Yates' loss, a terrible, yawning pit opening up before him. He shook his head and kept
walking.

She tumbled through an abyss of no dimension, of no
known depth; falling, falling through the unending midnight
well of the universe. Light streaked by her in searing hairline strands, and in great beams humming with energy that
punched through the blackness, driving relentlessly forward,
but doing nothing to illuminate the void.

They were the threads of lives and worlds, of time and
place as she'd seen through the faceplate of the looking
mask, but now she was among them, as if she'd fallen *into* the
mask, insignificant, nothing more than a grain of sand in the
desert. Much less than even that.

Some threads intersected, wove into a grid, weft and warp
drawn tightly into luminous tapestries, while others came
glancing close but bypassed one another, destined never to
meet.

Stars and celestial bodies shone around her, and shards of
silver glass glimmering with their far-off light trailed in her
wake like the tail of a comet.

Realm of the gods. Her own inner voice came to her from
a far off vestige of consciousness.

Consciousness? Was she even alive? Or was she an incorporeal spirit traversing the heavens?

But even as her plummet increased in velocity, she felt
mortal fear, a fear that in this infinite dive, all that she was, all
that she had been, and all that she might become, would slip
away until she was nothing but dust, dust mingling with the
shards of silver glass, falling forever.

Nothing, nothing ...

Her mind ripping; her inner voice screaming.

Then great wings filled her awareness, their beating the
rhythm of a heart. They matched the speed of her fall and
the arms of no earthly being reached out and caught her. He
drew her to his chest, a giant's chest of alabaster. He hurtled

downward with her, his vast wings gradually slowing their descent.

She looked upon the visage of a raptor, stars shining in eyes that reflected the heavens, and there was no mistaking Westrion, the god of death.

The Birdman has come for me. I must be dead.

All grew still and black, and became nothing.

All was still and black. When Karigan opened her eyes, she could tell no difference.

Do you have eyes in the afterlife? she wondered. Artists depicted the souls of the dead with eyes, but how did they know?

Other sensations came to her: she lay on smooth, cool stone. The space felt close, the air thin and poor. Her body hurt, in some places worse than others.

Not dead, she thought with rising hope. *Just a bad dream.* She had only imagined Westrion's wings, of being borne in the death god's arms.

She patted herself to make sure and felt flesh and warmth and more pain. She sliced her palm on a shard of glass jutting from her thigh. She yanked it out with a cry. *Definitely not dead.*

She tried to sit up but bumped her head on stone. She explored around herself with her hands. Smooth, cold stone all around her. She was enclosed in a rectangular box.

Seized by panic she screamed, kicking and hitting the sides of her prison despite her broken wrist. Warm blood trickled down her forearms from shredded knuckles. No one responded to her cries for help. She tried to force herself to calm down, her breathing ragged.

She would suffocate, expire in some unknown tomb. No one would ever know what happened to her, or where to look. Was she still in Blackveil? Elsewhere? What had the shattering of the looking mask done with her?

Taking another shuddering breath, she realized she probably would never find out.

Kristen Britain is the author of the bestselling Green Rider series. She contemplates life and fantasy from her tiny log cabin in the woods of Maine, which she shares with her canine companion, Gryphon. She can be found online at www.kristenbritain.com.